I0562715

The Girl Who Wrangled Asteroids

Daniel Basil Lyle

LylePublishing

Sulphur, Oklahoma

The Girl Who Wrangled Asteroids

ISBN 978-0-9985937-0-8

Published by LylePublishing
505 W. 12th Street, Sulphur, OK 73086
(www.LylePublishing.com)

Printed by CreateSpace, an Amazon.com company. Available from
Amazon.com and other retail outlets. Also available as an ebook on
Kindle and other devices.

LCED08062019

DISCLAIMER and FORWARD

Although this book draws heavily from some of the author's own experiences, all characters in this book are fictitious. Any resemblance to real persons, living or dead, is purely coincidental. Although a simulation of Mahatma Gandhi is depicted in this book, his words and behavior are fictionalized. This book is a sequel to "*The Girl Who Chased Spaceships*," beginning where that book left off.

Chapter 1

LAUNCH

Gravity is a bitch

Clutching you to her breast

Though you try to escape

She drags you into her orbit

And draws you back yet again

As you furiously circle in fear

Knowing the fire that awaits

Your fall back to the surface

When you give up your hopes

Fold your wings against your body

And plunge helplessly to your death!

Or against all odds to SOAR

Do you have a choice?

The Minstrel's Lark, 1:24-27

IMPACT MINUS SIX MONTHS, *CAPE CANAVERAL*...

Susan King was afraid she was about to die, quite spectacularly! And her fiery death would seal the fate of the entire planet. There just wasn't enough time for the nations of Earth to launch a replacement mission.

"Oh, sweet Jesus," she whispered to herself.

Catching a glimpse of her helmeted head reflected back in her computer screen she saw a very worried young lady. Her green eyes were pinched nearly shut. Her normally full lips were pressed together in a straight line. Even her usually fluffy blond bangs looked straggly and wilted, poking out to each side of her head behind the round-

1

ed edge of her hard helmet, visible through her closed transparent faceplate.

"Nervous, King? I thought you liked firecrackers!"

The young man seated beside her grinned widely. He was clad identically to her: in an orange flight suit, gloved, also a closed helmet on his head. Through his transparent faceplate Susan saw his seemingly jovial brown-skinned face. He was speaking in suit-to-suit physical contact communication mode, with a gloved hand laid lightly on her arm.

The attempt at private communication shocked her. She knew Ben understood she didn't like to be touched, even if only through the fabric of a flight suit. So he was violating her personal space deliberately, trying to jerk her out of her sudden funk.

She liked Ben.

The flight suits would hold pressure, staving off instant death in the case of catastrophic cabin depressurization. The suits weren't designed for spacewalks but worked fine inside the cramped Orion capsule. But if the rocket stack exploded on launch, the relatively thin flight suits would be scant protection.

"No," she lied to him. "I'm fine, Ben. No joking around, please!"

She irritably jerked her arm to the side, breaking the contact. But he'd brought up good memories. They'd had a fun time last 4th of July. She'd gone with him and other Houston astronauts to a big fireworks display in the city center. It was so overwhelming she even allowed Ben to give her a brief hug. That wasn't inappropriate since they were the only two single astronauts at the event. Susan knew he was "sweet" on her, but romance out of the question. She was much too driven and busy to be distracted by trivial "relationships"—at least until after this emergency mission was accomplished, one way or the other.

Besides being a flirt, Ben was also a notorious prankster. He was a lot of fun in off-work hours. But when it came to the job, he was dead serious. He was the crew's physician. He'd already been on two previous ISS missions. Launching into orbit was old hat to him. However, it was her first time. She knew he was just trying to ease the tension by the unwanted contact.

But she shouldn't need his help!

Damn it, she was a certified astronaut in her own right, just never yet launched!

So she moodily reclined in her flight chair next to him, seated along with four other of their crewmates atop a giant *bomb*, hoping it wouldn't explode and kill them all. Ideally it would just blast them up into orbit around Earth. She knew she should feel elated. All her NASA training and simulations had led to this moment. Finally she was poised there at the top of a 426 foot-tall, 8.5 million-pound rocket stack! But, instead of being joyful, she found herself sinking ever deeper into an unexpectedly black mood.

"Priyanka hitting on you?" the man positioned above her good-naturedly laughed over crew-wide communications. He was peering to his side and downward to see her.

That was George Wilson, the flight engineer. He was a very dependable, solid sort. He was married to a lovely lady fellow engineer, with three small kids. Though not much older than her, he was always there to give her fatherly advice and support. Through his faceplate, looking upward, Susan could see his square face and short, blond crewcut hair.

"No more than usual," she grinned back, feeling momentarily cheered up as he turned back to his own computer screen. Clearly, he was concerned for her. He'd flown previously, on a lunar transit mission. She was the only "newbie" in the crew. But she felt well-supported by her more-experienced crewmates.

It helped to lighten her dark mood, a bit...

"*Solid boosters armed—at T-minus five minutes,*" a mechanical-sounding voice from Mission Control came over her helmet speaker, interrupting her musings.

Susan glanced out of the thick porthole nearest to her. It was one of three that were set at equal distance around the perimeter of the cramped cabin. The protective shell covers were still open. She glimpsed outside a bright blue sky and a couple wispy clouds floating past. If everything proceeded according to schedule, in five minutes she would ride a *column of fire* up into that blue sky, piercing it to enter an empty black void. It was her dream come true, the culmination of years of intensive efforts.

Susan thought back on her tortuous struggles leading up to this point: earning a Ph.D. in astrophysics, completing an applied post-doctoral research program in near-asteroid modeling, getting accepted into the highly competitive NASA astronaut training program, and then rigorously preparing for the fifth Mars expedition. Yes, finally making it into space was a dream come true. But the present mission was also—literally—her very worst nightmare!

Since she was a child, she often awoke in the middle of the night drenched in feverish sweat. It was her recurrent dream: drifting in space facing a *hurtling mass* of thousands of asteroid fragments *smashing* into her and her little brother Billy!

She involuntarily shuddered as sweat sprang onto her brow. She knew her recurrent nightmare wasn't true. It was only a fantasy. It had never happened in real life. But still it drove her mercilessly. Space beckoned to her, both beautifully and cruelly!

"It's ok, Susan," she heard Ben's soothing voice again as he reached over to touch her suit for personal communication. This time he definitely wasn't joking around. His gloved hand on her suited arm was firm. His voice was calming, serious. "We'll be up in orbit before you know it. Just relax! Hey, hum a happy song to yourself. That always calms me!"

"You know I can't sing," she whispered back.

"That's not true. You have a lovely voice. I've heard you humming to yourself. I'll just step out and get my *sitar* to strum with you and we can..."

She mentally "tuned out" his chatter. So, he was back to joking around again, bringing up his Hindu heritage. But she was a "big girl" now. She didn't need his jokes!

"I'm fine, Ben!" she cut him off, frowning. She had to concentrate on her readouts monitoring the flow of the spaceship's coolants, gases, and lubricants. Even a slight falter in the rates might herald a serious problem. It wasn't her main expertise on the mission, but it was important. Once they got up into orbit she'd be the astrodynamics expert, plotting complex stellar intersections and analyzing asteroid compositions. During the launch she was mainly just dead weight, doing routine monitoring duties.

"Keep it together..." she grimly muttered to herself.

She again caught a glimpse of her face reflected from her own computer screen. Within the faceplate of her helmet she saw the comforting image of a lean, green-eyed, blond-haired, resolute, competent *astronaut*. Yes! Though she still kept her hair in bangs down her forehead and long to each side instead of the buzz cut favored by other astronauts, she wasn't a frightened kid anymore. No, she certainly *wasn't* floating in space with her dorky brother, about to be crushed to death by hurtling asteroid fragments!

No nightmares. Concentrate on your immediate duties. Monitor the fluidity charts and graphs. Sure, you're just replicating what's going on in Mission Control. But the Commander needs your immediate confirmation—Susan focused herself, pushing away any pesky nightmares.

That recurrent, nightly horror had plagued her sleep ever since she was a kid. But that childish fear wasn't real!

This was real—sitting reclined with her crewmates inside the cramped Orion-3f crew module atop an SLS-8Z heavy launch array. It was the largest rocket configuration ever assembled at the Kennedy Space Center, sporting not just two but four solid rocket boosters positioned around the central main fuel tank. Its task was to loft an unprecedented 200 tons beyond low-Earth orbit, breaking the Saturn-V record of 140 tons by a whopping 60 tons!

This was a very ambitious mission, assembled at breakneck speed to accomplish a desperate, civilization-saving goal.

"Susan—OIPs?" Commander Torey Kunle asked over the crew-wide channel.

Kunle was positioned out of sight on the other side of the Orion capsule. Susan couldn't see her normally dour, black-skinned face. Torey Kunle was a naturalized African American who had been born in Nigeria. She had lived in Africa until her parents immigrated when she was just ten years old. As a small child she'd directly experienced the religious wars raging on that continent, the awful destruction and chaos. Rampant unchecked population growth, largely encouraged by short-sighted religious doctrines, had turned that lush "garden of Eden" into a deforested hellhole. Having escaped with her parents at an early age, she thrived inside the relative order and secular tolerance of the USA, taking full advantage of her educational opportunities.

After earning an engineering degree in college, Kunle enlisted in the Navy, becoming a test pilot. Then she joined NASA and excelled in the astronaut ranks. She was a no-nonsense, by-the-book, middle-aged technocrat who as mission commander was totally respected, if not loved, by her crew. That was fortunate as they were about to spend six months together in close quarters.

Indeed, they were even now jammed in like sardines into the cramped crew compartment. The Orion capsule was intended as a short-duration vehicle, mainly for delivering astronauts to more "roomy" habitats. Next to Orion, the International Space Station (ISS) or their present destination, *Hermes*, the International Transit Vehicle (ITV), were space resorts! Orion was larger than the tight Apollo Capsules which took astronauts to the moon in the 20th Century, but not by much.

"Nominal," Susan replied into her helmet-mounted microphone, as Ben leaned back away from her, concentrating now on his own duties.

She'd been mentally "tuning out" most of the crew comments as the others methodically went down their various checklists, plus Mission Control's responses and updates.

In addition to her fluidics graphs, she was intensely following 3D graphs overlaid upon each other on the mounted screen up in front of her face. The colored lines showed the positions, velocities, and extrapolated flight paths of three key objects: *first* the projected vector of their Space Launch System (SLS) away from Earth after their hopefully successful launch; *second* the incoming arc of the Mars Transfer Vehicle (MTV), Hermes, as it prepared to slingshot around the Earth; and *third* the still-distant descending position of *Asteroid PHA-15384.*

Damn that awful thing!

"Susan, what's the time constraint now for optimal *Orbital Insertion Parameters?*" Commander Kunle repeated, distinctly stating each word of the "OIP" acronym. She sounded irritated at Susan's previous curt reply.

"Twenty seven minutes, fourteen seconds," Susan hastened to reply, carefully keeping her voice neutral. "Without any further holds or problems, we're good," she added.

Due to the particular orbital mechanics of the three objects relative to the Sun, Earth, and Mars—there was only a very narrow launch window for accomplishing their emergency mission. Their immediate task was a risky rendezvous with the incoming Hermes vehicle, returning from its last Mars transit. The usual protocol was for Hermes to settle into earth orbit to be reconditioned and refurbished before going back to Mars. Now it was plummeting in for a "sling shot" around Earth to leap up above the planetary disc of the solar system to put it on a higher path roughly parallel to Earth's orbit. If they could precisely join up, they'd crew the Mars Transfer Vehicle for an encounter with PHA-15384.

In this stepwise manner they intended to match the incredible speed of the Asteroid fast-descending from above the planetary plane. Arriving at the Asteroid in three months, they would begin to study it in detail. They'd have a further three months to figure out how to prevent it from *catastrophically striking Earth* and *killing off* all higher life forms, including humanity!

But to accomplish their planned asteroid-divergence mission (ADM), they must absolutely rendezvous with the hurtling, giant rock no later than three months out from its projected Earth-impact. Any less time and they might not be able to alter its path. And it likely wasn't just a matter of pushing it aside or blowing it into powder. No, they must conduct a thorough on-site investigation of its composition before taking any precipitous action.

The "Potentially Hazardous Asteroid," or PHA, was massive, a full ten kilometers in length. Susan translated that to an over *six-mile long rock* coming in from a high orbit relative to the planetary plane. It had been detected only a scant three months earlier by an amateur asteroid hunter using a new method which relied on star obscuration rather than reflected light.

At first no one believed the report. It was widely assumed that the larger asteroids had long ago all been detected. They were wrong. The lack of prior detection of the potentially planet-killing Asteroid was chalked up to its low albedo. It was completely black, barely reflecting any sunlight. Plus it apparently had a very long orbit, taking some 100,000 earth-years to circle the sun just once.

Earth's governments and scientific organizations were thrown into widespread panic by the shocking discovery. The standard view of such a deadly scenario was that there'd be decades of lead time to plan a response against any threatening PHA. Now they had only weeks to do what normally took years! NASA, along with other cooperating space agencies, considered their best chance at deflecting the massive Asteroid was to launch a crewed mission. The only feasible fast way to do that was by piggybacking onto the existing MTV, which fortuitously was returning to Earth.

But configuring the emergency mission for launch up to Hermes had taken mankind right to the edge of planetary disaster. Not only did they have to lug up gear to deal with the Asteroid, they had to fully restock the depleted MTV. There was no margin for error or further problems. They only had *one shot* at saving Earth!

"We'll do it," Susan whispered to herself, again trying to shake the terrible funk she'd fallen into.

She'd been happily training for an upcoming Mars mission—only the fifth such in human history—as a Science Officer. She was slated to be one of a crew of three to descend to the surface of Phobos, Mar's largest moon. They'd be the first to attempt such a feat. But since she had a Ph.D. in Astrophysics, plus postdoc in asteroid composition, she was bumped up from the Mars Mission to the Asteroid Deflection Mission: the so-called "ADM." She was uniquely qualified to help confront the looming planetary threat.

With its low albedo, they had scant data on what they might encounter at PHA-15384. Even the aging successor to the James Webb Space Telescope, JWST-2, only revealed a ten kilometer-long black blob outlined against a missing sprinkle of blocked-out stars. If necessary, the ADM team was prepared to blow the Asteroid into pieces using atomic *hydrogen bombs*, a key part of their heavy payload. But any surviving large asteroid fragments could each still be deadly to Earth!

The possible permutations of various-sized fragment projectiles slamming into the planet were endless. But Suzy was ready—using her expertise in asteroid characteristics, composition, and orbital mechanics. If anyone could determine how to either push aside or safely blow up the giant Asteroid without pieces raining catastrophically onto Earth, it was her.

But *deflection* was still a better and safer use of their hydrogen bombs—if they could somehow figure out a way to make it work! That's why they needed the full three months at the Asteroid, to make sure that whatever course they decided on had a high chance to succeed. They wouldn't get a second shot.

No wonder she still had her recurring nightmare of asteroid chunks zooming at her in space!

"Closing and locking all visors," Commander Kunle reported to mission control, "at T-minus two minutes and counting."

Susan's transparent faceplate was already closed and locked into place. Some of the other crew still had theirs opened, but quickly snapped them shut as well. In case of a catastrophic failure of the launch vehicle, Susan was confident she wouldn't die from immediate asphyxiation. Of course with the massive volume of liquid and solid fuel positioned beneath her butt—not to mention *three* hydrogen bombs in the payload compartment—dying from lack of oxygen would be her least concern. More likely she'd just be instantly incinerated! She likely wouldn't feel a thing...

It wasn't a comforting thought.

She considered whispering a prayer but thought better of it. Though she'd grown up going regularly to Sunday church service and Bible study, once she'd gotten away from her small hometown of Sulphur, Oklahoma she gladly left behind all that "church stuff." She was still perplexed and intrigued by serious spiritual enquiry, but no longer felt it must be part of a formal religious structure. She just didn't feel the need for ritualistic prayer to "communicate" with whatever Higher Intelligence might exist beyond the physical universe.

Still, how could it hurt?

So she closed her eyes and mentally, grudgingly, reached out.

Dear God, if there is a God, please help us—she reluctantly articulated in her mind. *I know that we humans are a sorry lot. We do lots of bad things. But we're trying to be better! At least we're not cooking our planet as badly as we were from Global Warming. The out-of-control population growth rate is lessening. That counts for something, right? We're trying! We don't deserve to be wiped out by a giant space rock. Please give us another chance, won't you?*

Somewhat ashamed of her muttered prayer—attributing it to her inexplicably foul mood—she opened her eyes and looked around sheepishly. But the other five crew members weren't paying her any attention, including Ben. They were each intently focused on their own tasks, even though they were all tightly strapped next to each other inside the Orion crew capsule.

She wished she could "whistle a happy tune" to relieve the tension, as Ben had suggested. But she'd long ago given up her musical aspirations. As a kid she'd thought that she wanted to be a new-folk/rock star, but that fantasy quickly faded. After an accident riding bikes in the Park with her brother Billy, other priorities had swamped her nascent artistic leanings.

The accident in the Park was a near-death experience. Instead of bump on her noggin she could just as easily have snapped her neck! It focused her like a laser beam on her science classes. And she still retained that "focused" attitude. It was an ability that had served her well: pushing away nightmares by asking the simple question "what's next?"

But the graphs on the screen in front of her were blurring as *sick jokes* sprang into her mind, trying to divert her.

*We're just sardines in a can...*she almost laughed aloud. *We're set to be opened up and tossed into the gumbo of the Universe—hah! What a tasty stew we'd make!*

The countdown suddenly reverberated loudly in her helmet. She had accidentally kicked up the volume. Hastily, she dialed it back down.

Christ, where did the last five minutes go?

It was happening.

"Ten...nine...eight..."

Susan felt the deep vibration of the main engine's hydrogen burn-off flaring up.

"...three...two...one..."

She clutched her armrests tightly with her gloved hands as the main engine lit and she felt a deceptively gentle *pressure* pushing down on her chest.

Then a huge, bone-shattering RUMBLE *vibration/noise* swept through her body.

"Liftoff of 'ADM-1' in defense of all humanity!" Mission Control yelled in her helmet, not needing any volume increase. *"Go with God! The hopes of mankind are with you!"*

Suzy heard happy cheers in her helmet from the Mission Control personnel as the pressure on her chest kept increasing and increasing.

Glancing outside the nearest porthole Susan saw a *bright orange glow!*

"Sure, right," she snorted bitterly to herself, being shaken and smashed worse than any of her training ever did!

Susan was suddenly convinced that she would *never* again walk the green surface of Earth. This was a one-way mission. She wasn't coming back!

But if her sacrifice resulted in saving Earth, she was ok with this being a *suicide mission.*

The ROAR of the engines was overpowering. Susan had expected the shaking, modeled in her flight simulations. But this was different. Something was wrong! *Violent vibrations* erupted, threatening to tear her out of her constraints and fling her around the small cabin!

"We're e-experiencing heavy t-turbulence," Commander Kunle reported back to Mission Control, barely able to get the words out. "Auxiliary Booster Three is s-shaking in its c-clamps."

Oh hell—Susan grimaced, briefly shutting her eyes. *The vehicle's coming apart!*

Yep...maybe adding two extra solid rocket boosters hadn't been such a good idea. The original SLS design was for two boosters attached to the main tank, not four. Susan saw on her bouncing computer screen that their steadily lengthening trajectory was off course. The boosters were still lofting the heavy payload up into orbit, but not along the planned flight-path.

Indeed, the entire vehicle was *wobbling* as it shot through the upper atmosphere.

And if the aerodynamic strains got too great, the ship and everyone inside indeed would be ripped to pieces!

Cold *fear* plunged into her heart. This was definitely not "nominal" performance!

"I should have stuck to writing science fiction books," she weakly muttered to herself, closing her eyes, focusing on breathing while a bouncing *piano* pressed down on her chest!

She had never enjoyed the astronaut human centrifuge training, even though it usually didn't get beyond three G's. Her crew members laughed at her discomfort, considering the giant centrifuge a great "roller-coaster" ride. To her it was just a royal pain.

Well, they certainly were on "a hell" of a ride now!

—all of which began when she was just *ten years old...*

Ten-year-old Suzy King ran breathlessly into the living room of her parents' home, panting heavily.

She was covered with dirt from when she'd fallen off her bike. Her whole body was bruised and her wrist itched. Her Turtle Tattoo was enflamed. Damn Turtle Tattoo! Why'd she snuck away and gotten that thing etched on her wrist in the first place? Usually she was very obedient and proper. Getting that tattoo was uncharacteristically rebellious of her.

Right behind her staggered her younger kid brother, Billy, complaining loudly...

"You *left* me behind!" he yelled at her.

She glanced back at her little six-year-old brother. His crewcut smaller head bobbed up and down. The black fuzz of his hair was hardly visible on his skin, making him seem even younger and more infantile. His smooth-skinned face was scrunched up in frustration. He was panting loudly. And, she was startled to see he was sobbing!

What was wrong with him? Usually he was a pest going a million miles a minute on his own trajectory. She remembered having to rein him in a zillion times. How'd he changed into a whimpering scaredy cat?

But she didn't have time to worry about him. Her news was too important!

"Mom! Mom!" Suzy called out, racing around the back of the living room couch to confront her seated mother...

But it *wasn't* her mother. Suzy stood frozen in place, shocked.

"Hey, Suze—did you have a nice ride in the Park? Oh my, how did you get so dirty? You could use a shower, honey."

Frozen in shock, Suzy looked at a woman who was twice as heavy as her mother should be. The mother she remembered, Sally King, was trim and fit. This woman must weigh over two hundred pounds! She was staring at a wide-screen T.V. hung on the wall, upon which a Saturday evening cartoon show was playing. She was munching happily from a large bag of Oreo cookies.

The Sally King that Suzy recalled from breakfast that morning was a super-fit athlete who could hike for days up steep mountain trails. Whenever Suzy's family went on frequent wilderness adventures their mother led the way. Suzy's mother habitually wore hiking shorts around the house and didn't have an extra ounce of fat anywhere on her body. *This* woman wore a wide house robe and looked like she'd have a hard time making it from the couch to the kitchen. And instead of the well-kept long red-brown hair she should have, this woman's hair was short, stringy, and greying!

But the *face*...

Horrified, Suzy recognized the *bright green eyes* submerged in that pudgy face, now listless and drab—plus the *Turtle Tattoo* which Suzy had gotten copied onto her own wrist, now stretched out and distorted on the other woman's wide, fleshy left wrist.

"M-Mom?"

"After you get showered, Suze, get the T.V. dinners that I set out to thaw in the kitchen. Pop them in the microwave for you and your brother. Or just get yourself some ice cream out of the freezer, if you'd like. In fact, bring me a bowl! Dr. Chill's up next. He's really funny. Hah! He's gonna reveal who Rowana's baby's father is from the paternity test. Get cleaned up and come watch it with me. I thin he's the father, but he doesn't."

Billy ran on into his room, sobbing about having been "abandoned" in the Park. Suzy just continued standing there, staring at this strange aberration claiming to be her mother. She vaguely noticed Billy now pulling on a clean shirt as he slunk back into the kitchen.

"Something wrong, Suze?" Sally asked, popping another handful of Oreos into her mouth and chewing lustily.

Crumbs fell across her double chins.

Suzy gulped, backing off a step.

"Uh...where's Dad?"

"Where do think? He's off in his shed, doin' his stuff. He keeps callin' for Billy to come help him. I yelled to him you two had gone riding out in the Park on your bikes. But he's got some sorta new project of his that needs fourteen hands to do and..."

"Ok, then," Suzy gulped, finally backing off. "I'll just...I guess...go see him...and, where is this 'shed' place again?"

Sally's glazed eyes now focused on her daughter, jerking away from the T.V. set. She heavily rose from the couch, taking Suzy's head in her fat fingers.

"What's this?" she said, gently fingering the raised lump on the side of Suzy's head.

"It's nothing," Suzy said, backing off.

"She fell off her bike," Billy said, no longer sobbing. He was walking back into the living room slurping noisily at a bowl of melting ice cream. "I put this chocolate in the microwave to melt. It's really good. I'll make some more and take it out to Dad and..."

"Are you hurt?" Sally said, swaying in front of Suzy as if having trouble keeping her bulk erect. "We'd better get you to the emergency room to get checked out so that..."

"No, I'm fine! It was just a little accident," Suzy said, turning and darting away. "I've got to go talk to Dad!"

She ran out the back door of the house, headed toward the garage.

But the garage she remembered was gone!

In its place was a ramshackle collection of several overlapped structures. They looked haphazardly built upon each other. They clearly weren't up to code. To Suzy's astonished gaze the roofs looked improvised, with tiles overlapping at odd angles. The exterior walls were painted different colors. Some of the walls were just bare plywood. There were no windows, just one big steel door with a large metal lock, hanging open to the side.

She walked up to the skewed front door and cautiously entered.

"Dad?"

The interior was crowded with various large pieces of esoteric-looking equipment. The instruments were ancient. Instead of electronic readouts she saw rusted dials and gauges. Myriads of knobs and levers sprouted like junkyard rejects. Spools of coiled printout paper sat above ancient typewriter machines. It was a movie set from a bad "B" science fiction movie straight from the 1950's!

It certainly wasn't what Suzy remembered: a well-ordered large garage holding their family's black van and ORV Ranger.

What the hell is happening here? This is crazy!

"Hey, Suzy—I hear you out there, kiddo! Come look!"

She hurried on into the dark interior, hearing strange "clicks" and "whirs" as the looming equipment did strange tasks. There was the faint smell of something scorching. Lights glittered here and there in rusty equipment racks—from *vacuum* tubes! This was truly ancient equipment, pre-transistor.

And there—illuminated in the glow of a single hanging lightbulb—was an older man sitting on a wooden bench. He had long, greasy grey hair hanging to his shoulders. He was excitedly scanning folded papers accumulated in an out-tray. Suzy saw on the faded sheets the intersecting lines of a continuous graph. But a slight bump on one of the lines fascinated the thin old man.

"I think I've got something, Suzy! The core temperature jumped a half a degree! Now if we can just get an excess of neutrons..."

He kept mumbling to himself as he frantically searched through the readouts, twitching a few knobs off to the side from time to time.

Suzy sat down at his side, patiently waiting.

"Ah...well," he finally sighed, setting the printouts to the side. "I guess it's nothing, Suzy. I increased the density of the copper interfaces of the matrix. I thought that might enhance the deuterium flow, but..."

"Dad, do you think other dimensions could exist?"

"Eh?"

"I mean, like other timelines...other worlds?"

"Why do you ask? Oh—and did you see Billy? I need him to change some spools where it's hard for me to reach and..."

This old man with an obvious short attention span certainly *wasn't* her father. The Father that she distinctly remembered—David King—was a tough, athletic, middle-aged man! She helped him from time to time keep their Ranger in good running shape, handing him tools as he expertly optimized the engine parts. This doddering old fellow didn't look capable of lifting out a car battery!

She was getting very confused.

"So what happened to the Ranger?" she gulped, changing the subject.

"Something happened to one of the Park Rangers? Do you mean Losa? We can ask him at church tomorrow. He's leading the song service, I think. Hah, you know someone at the men's business meeting last week wanted to bring in a *piano* to the services? Wow, that really caused a reaction, though everyone was kind to him. He was a new convert who didn't realize the Bible says we can only sing acapella, without man-made instruments that..."

She shook her head in disbelief as he rambled on about a supposed "human voices only" doctrine that was, actually, nowhere to be found in the actual scriptures. She'd have loved for there to be pianos and guitars at the service, like some of her friends had with their folks at their churches. In fact, she had an old guitar in the back of the closet in her room. She'd always yearned to take it out and start writing songs. But she knew that was a waste of time. She had to fight her way through school, get top grades in hardcore science courses! And now after nearly knocking her skull to pieces in the Park, she was doubly determined to do so! Life was too short to waste it writing silly songs no one would ever hear. At least getting "A's" in science classes pleased her science-teaching parents...or...her *previous* parents?

Everything was changing. She felt dizzy.

"I was out in the Park with Billy, Dad," she interrupted his disjointed ramblings, "and something happened."

"Really! Sounds exciting, kiddo! You just tell me all about it. I need to take a break from my failed experiments. Hah! Nothing surprising about that—it's just 'par for the course.' So where is Billy, anyway? I've missed my little helper today."

"He's still inside eating ice cream with Mom," she sighed. "Maybe I shouldn't bother you with..."

"—nonsense, kiddo," he stopped her. "You just tell me everything. I'm all ears!"

He cupped his two hands around his ears to exaggerate their size, grinning widely.

Where'd he get this playful sense of humor? He was usually very serious!

"You really want to know?"

"Of course I do!"

He stood up from the workbench and went over to an old folding chair, happily flopping into it. Taking a deep breath she decided she'd do exactly what he said. She'd tell him *everything*: about discovering the little dinosaur, falling with Billy into the hidden compartment buried in the wilderness area of the Park, being transported to a Cretaceous-era dinosaur swamp, finding a Native American village following a herd of buffalo on the plains, being taken up by a rocket ship to the moon, escaping an evil "sister" of her mother's, traveling into the distant past in the spaceship, being hijacked by a team of intelligent velociraptor dinosaurs from another dimension, blowing up the Asteroid that was about to crash into Earth, being killed by a swarm of asteroid fragments, resurrected into an "afterlife" where she was reunited with him, his Mom, and an android "brother," battling and defeating a "Spider" monster from another universe, then being left behind when the others "moved on," and finally being sent by someone that might be God Himself back in time to the present—where everything was *different* from what she remembered!

It took her a full hour for her to finish her detailed account. During part of her intense story Billy walked in, chocolate ice cream smeared on his chin, took one look at Suzy excitedly telling her story, then turned around and left. She only vaguely noticed him, marveling in the back of her mind that he didn't just walk up and interrupt her. She'd never known him to be so polite...or docile?

David King sat in complete silence up until the end—then stood up and began loudly *clapping* his hands.

"Marvelous! It's a wonderful story! Suzy, you've got to write it all down. You've come up with some very entertaining fantasies before, but nothing this detailed or imaginative! I don't know if anyone will ever buy it or read it, but you've got to get it onto paper. It's great! But I'm starving, aren't you? Let's go get some dinner. I haven't eaten all day. Did you say there was ice cream waiting for us? Sounds yummy!"

"But Dad," she weakly protested as he stood up, took her by the hand, and started leading her out of the maze of looming equipment, "I think it all really happened."

He stopped and frowned down at her.

His well-wrinkled face looked especially old, definitely not the vibrant, youthful father she remembered.

"So...you're saying...?"

"What if what I did millions of years ago in the other dimension somehow affected this one also? What if that explains why you and Mom are...different? That might mean your experiments can work! You told me when we were around the campfire that the Ranger was powered by a *Dark Energy generator* based on your cold fusion experiments."

He bent and gave her a warm hug before releasing her.

"Hey—thanks for the encouragement there, kiddo! I sure need it, don't I? I guess I do spend too much of my free time out here with Billy obsessing on my crazy experiments. And who knows what might have happened if I'd had some financial grants or decent equipment with which to work. But when I met your Mother I realized this was just a fun hobby. So when we got married and moved to your grandmother's old house here in Sulphur when she passed away, I realized I had much more fun things to do than spend my free time on useless physics experiments. But then I fell back into my old habits, don't know why! Well, I'll soon be able to retire from the High School and then spend all my time puttering away out here with my surplus research equipment. Hah! Well, I sure won't miss grading Physics 101 papers by kids who hate being in my class. And then there are all the administrative headaches and..."

"How did you meet Mom?" Suzy asked, refocusing his meandering train of thought.

"I've told you this a hundred times, Suzy."

"Again, please!"

"Well," he sighed, sitting back down, "the short version is that when I took *my* Mom—your grandmother—to a cancer treatment center in Ada, I happened to meet your Mom's mother, got introduced to her daughter, and that was it! We both decided to put aside my scientific obsessions and raise a family. So I got a job teaching at the high school here and she began working in a Sulphur restaurant. Then we proceeded to have you and Billy. And it's been great. I wouldn't change a thing."

"But...you and Mom don't seem...?"

"I'm telling you the truth, Suzy," he firmly stated. "I'd rather have our life here than anything you described in your amazing story. Really! There's nothing for you to feel guilty about. I know I still spend too much time on my hobby out here. I do, on occasion, forget to eat such that I'm a bit scrawny, not the strong dynamic fellow you described. But who needs a bunch of useless muscles, anyway? My real life is here with you, Billy, your Mom, church, and teaching physics to the kids at school—the normal things. Don't you worry your cute little head about other 'timelines' or 'parallel dimensions' or 'subspace spiders.' And, yes, I know I've promised you and Billy we'd take some camping trips. We'll do that, maybe during the school summer break. How'd that be?"

"Dad...please—I have to know. Could we go together and check out the Park? I know just where the Obelisk was buried. And you—I mean the *other* you—told me where the *second* Obelisk crashed in the Park that..."

"No problem, kiddo!" he laughed, grabbing her hand again and firmly leading her out of the maze of bizarrely oversized equipment. "Tomorrow after church we'll go check out your 'Park Science-Fiction Adventures.' But it's a very sneaky way to get me to go biking with you. I don't even know if I can still ride my mountain bike it's been so long now. I'm not getting any younger, you know. But I understand. You had to beg Billy for a week to get him out of my lab and go biking with you. He takes after me, maybe too much, so..."

"Thanks, Dad," she said, squeezing his hand and stopping his rambling. "It's probably just some nightmare I had when I conked myself on the head and..."

"You hit your head?" he said, sounding suddenly serious and worried.

"I'm fine, I'm fine!" she hastened to reassure him.

"But if there's subdural bleeding then...?"

"If I feel woozy I'll let you know."

"I think we should go to the hospital and..."

"I'd rather go out to the Park, *tomorrow*...ok?"

"Sure, we can do that, but...?"

"I have to make sure. I can't get stuck in a hospital for some little bump on my head. If the weird things are really out there, then we've got to go find evidence before it all disappears!"

"Alright, then," he shrugged, smiling wanly. Her "old" Dad would have grabbed her hand and dragged her to the hospital, despite her denials. Suzy found this new version of her Dad surprisingly easy to manipulate.

"Turkey or meatloaf?" he grinned at her.

"Uh, what?"

"Your T.V. dinner! Come on, kiddo. You remember that I don't know how to cook—and your Mother's too tired after her workday at the restaurant to do so. Our favorite Star Trek movie—'Captains Across Time'—is on T.V. tonight. Did you forget? I'll bet that's what's got you imagining these other wonderful dimensions and timelines. Anyway, we've got to get our meals cooking in the microwave or we'll miss the good parts of the movie!"

She laughed, walking happily along beside him back to the house. This certainly wasn't the crisp, dynamic father she remembered—but then again, this mellower, seemingly older version wasn't so bad either?

Maybe it was better that everything she remembered was wrong. She had her family back and a fresh, new future. And best of all, she was no longer *history's most infamous killer!* Jesus, what a nightmare... At worst she had a great story to turn into a real science fiction book. But still, she had to check, to make sure...

—tomorrow, after church! For now there were T.V.-dinners, bags of Oreos, buckets of chocolate ice cream, and a great movie to watch for the hundredth time.

Who could ask for more?

But her head still hurt, she felt illogically wracked by a horrific guilt, the world was turned upside down, and she was consumed by a nameless fear. And yet, for the moment, she was content.

Impulsively she grabbed her Dad's liver-spotted hand.

"Thanks, Dad."

"For what?"

"For being you."

Chapter 2

ORBITAL MECHANICS

A dance of gravity and velocity

Two bodies trapped in intimate embrace

Balancing escape versus approach

Fearful of losing each other forever

Or smashing into each other catastrophically

Ruled by inviolable NATURE'S LAWS

A simple matter of cold equations

—or is it?

The Minstrel's Lark, 2:56-59

IMPACT MINUS SIX MONTHS, *LOW EARTH ORBIT...*

"Can we still make it to Hermes, King—or do we *abort?*"

Susan groggily opened her eyes. They hurt. Her eyelids felt like they'd been nailed shut with spikes struck by a very heavy hammer. The unanticipated extra G-forces had knocked her out!

Glancing at the nearest porthole she saw the *deep black* of outer space. Did they survive the launch? Did they make it up into orbit?

"Come on! Snap out of it, Susan! *Wake up!*"

Something was wrong. Something was *very* wrong!

"What happened?" Susan mumbled, turning her head to the side to assess the condition of the crew cabin.

The flight chair she was strapped into was twisted at an odd angle. The flight chair that should have been to her right was missing. The crew cabin was dark, lit only by flickering light from a couple still-functioning computer screens. At least three other computer screens were dark. One of them hung weightless just an arm's length away. It was slowly spinning in the air. Its torn-out connections grotesquely sprawled like robotic guts.

21

Oh bloody hell...the capsule was designed to withstand every sort of violence...something terrible must have happened!

"We survived the launch, for the moment," the irritating voice buzzed in her ear.

Either her helmet's speaker was loose or her ears were damaged. Indeed, her ears felt moist—as if fresh blood was trickling from them.

Likewise helmeted, Commander Kunle floated above Susan in her orange flight suit. Normally Susan could read Torey Kunle's mood by minor variations in her relentlessly stern, dark-skinned face. But Kunle's faceplate was fogged up. That was unusual. It bespoke a temperature differential. Indeed, Susan felt unusually cold. A glance at a monitor on her screen reported that the air pressure in the crew cabin was dangerously low. If her faceplate hadn't been down with her suit's limited automatic reserve air supply kicking in she would have asphyxiated!

"Susan, please focus," Kunle's harsh voice admonished her. Her tone was cold and crisp, as if she were just reporting a minor problem. "Booster-3 tore loose from the main tank before its scheduled detachment."

Oh, Jesus! That's no minor problem. That's a catastrophe!

"Then—we're either dead or descending with the LAS, right?"

"No," the Commander curtly replied in Susan's helmet. "For whatever reasons, the *Launch Abort System* failed. Lucky for us booster-3 didn't completely tear loose until we reached forty kilometers. So we didn't burn up falling back into the atmosphere. We achieved low earth orbit but lost the booster's last five kilometers worth of thrust."

"Ok..."

"Plus we warped God knows what out there in the main stack," Kunle continued. "We're still bolted to the core tank which should have separated and fallen away. So we're alive but in bad shape. Right now I have to know if we've *still got a shot at reaching Hermes* and accomplishing our mission—or do we attempt a manual abort back to Earth? Got it?"

Susan blinked her eyes several times to read the curiously flickering graphs on her still-attached screen.

"Ok...I'm on it," she gulped, blinking her eyes to focus better on the data. "Give me a minute—but Mission Control's probably got it already calculated, so..."

"We lost touch with them," Ben's voice abruptly cut-in on her speaker, interrupted her. "Our hull got smacked really hard—probably from booster-3 or resultant shear forces—which damaged our communicator array. I'm trying to restore contact with the ground through backups. But that may take a while."

Kunle leaned in close, touching helmet-to-helmet.

"What I need from you right now, Susan," she spoke clearly over the private channel, "is the 'take-home' message: 'go' or 'no go'! Got it?"

"Yes, Ma'am," Susan nodded in her helmet, finally getting her wits back around her.

She griped her wireless "mouse" that she still clutched tightly in her gloved hand and began clicking in coordinates to the graphs, based on the last set of readings of their vehicle's trajectory and speed.

Hermes was arriving at a high angle relative to their orbit around Earth. But the MTV wasn't due to slow down for a normal orbital insertion. No, it was purposed to whip around the Earth at near 36,000 mph, accelerating as it went, in order to give them a shot at matching the speed of the incoming Asteroid. As a scientist, Susan knew she should be thinking in terms of kilometers, liters, and centimeters—but her mind stubbornly hung onto the American notation of miles, gallons, and inches. For her, PHA-15384 was traveling at near 60,000 miles per hour. Achieving orbit, the SLS-Orion stack was up to around 17,000 mph. The mission plan was for their Upper Stage J-2X engine to accelerate them the last leg of the journey to join Hermes right before it went into its "slingshot" maneuver. Of course getting to Hermes in time assumed J-2X and Orion separated properly from the empty main fuel tank below it. Attached to the depleted first stage they couldn't do anything.

Now they were far from their optimal launch conditions! In a much lower orbit at a lower initial velocity, with the fuel tank still stuck stubbornly onto J-2X, they might only be able to "wave" as Hermes zipped past—*unless*...?

"They'll have to slow Hermes by approximately 10,000 mph before it goes into the gravity-assist maneuver in order for us to reach it," Susan reported to the still-hovering Commander. "It'll be close, but that's within the MTV's design specs. They've got enough hydrogen and oxygen stores left for the high thrust engine on Hermes to accomplish the abrupt slow-down, but just barely."

"Will we still be able to rendezvous with the Asteroid?"

"Wait...calculating..."

"*Well?*"

Blocking out the hovering commander, Susan concentrated on the graphs in front of her. She made intricate assumptions in her mind, adjusting uncertain probabilities into a new target window.

"The slower nuclear-thermal rocket on Hermes will have to recapture the lost velocity and then continue to accelerate as planned, but along a longer elliptic."

"So?" Kunle impatiently insisted. "Can we do it?"

"Yes—yes we can—but we'll catch up to the Asteroid just a week before it impacts Earth instead of the planned three months."

There was a brief moment of total silence in the cabin.

"*Damn!*" Kunle swore. "That close to Earth, how can we...?"

"It can't be helped, Commander," Susan insisted. "It's just orbital mechanics and..."

"—which will severely limit our options..."

"—assuming we can even get there intact!"

In the continuing silence, a limp flight suit floated past.

The outer insignia on it read "George Wilson." The faceplate was severely cracked. The face inside the helmet was grotesquely bloated. George's eyes were white and sightless. He was dead.

"Oh...George!" Susan gasped.

"It happened too fast to save him," Kunle flatly stated. "The edge of a ripped-loose console struck him square on his faceplate. We didn't know it happened until after we got the air leaks in the pressure vessel sealed. By then it was too late. You were unconscious, King, from the extreme G-forces we experienced during the stack's tumbling."

"His family..." Susan whispered, the awful consequences of their disaster hitting her.

"Get a grip," Kunle ordered her. "Our first priority now is to save ourselves and get to Hermes. When we have time, we'll properly mourn our friend. But since he's dead I need you to take his place in one of our two EMU's. I'll be in the other. If I remember correctly from your dossier, you used to work on cars with your father, right?"

"That was a long time ago. I just handed him tools."

"Good enough. You can assist me."

"Commander, surely one of the others would..."

"The other three are up to their asses in other crucial tasks. It's up to you and me to free our upper stage from the core. Let's get to it! We got no time to waste. We've a narrow window for firing the J-2X, right?"

"I'm sure...but I'd have to calculate..."

"Every second counts. Let's get to it!"

Each of the crewmembers was cross-trained in the different duties of flying a spaceship. Susan had spent several hours inside an Extravehicular Mobility Unit (EMU) in the Neutral Buoyancy Training Pool at the Johnson Space Center in Houston, Texas. That was fun. But she'd never expected to actually have to step out into space within an EMU. That was the job of others on the crew who'd had far more intensive training and experience, particularly their now-deceased engineer, George. She was just the "computer nerd" stuck in the ship doing calculations and lab analyses while others went on spacewalks and excursions. But now she had to step up to the task...or out! And Commander Kunle was correct: time was short. In round numbers she knew that if they didn't start their final burn within 24 hours it wouldn't matter how fast they could accelerate— Hermes would be long gone, out of reach. To accomplish major repair in low earth orbit in a severely damaged spacecraft would take at least take hours, assuming it were even possible!

And with the Asteroid rendezvous now drastically delayed, their main payload was even more critical to saving Earth. No matter what, the *three hydrogen bombs* secured below in their payload bay must get to that damn Asteroid! Sure, desperate nations of Earth could still try firing missiles directly at the approaching Asteroid, but that was likely to have little effect on its massive momentum so close to the planet. For nuclear intervention at such a late stage to be effective, it likely would have to be exquisitely directed and focused by the Hermes crew.

"So how do we exit once we're suited up?" Susan asked. "We're still docked to the cargo fairing, right?"

"After we free up our two EMU's from storage and get into them, we'll open the auxiliary docking port on the side of the cargo module. A bit of 'luck,' the protective panel on that side of the stack was ripped away. We'll have direct access to space."

It was yet another task they never expected to have to do. The auxiliary docking port was for connecting to an extended-out tunnel leading directly into Hermes or into the ISS (International Space Station). But the very act of space-travel—floating through the vast void alone—was by definition an exercise in "working the problem." This concept had been drilled into her at every step of her astronaut training. Don't panic or give up, just focus on the problem and possible solutions. And what a *hell* of a problem they now faced!

"Right," Susan answered. She resolutely grit her teeth and loosened the restraints holding her into her tottering flight chair.

She floated in zero-G after Torey, drifting through the crowded wreckage. They managed to dig down to the hatch that led from the Orion capsule into the storage compartment below them. She tried not to look at the bloated face of her friend George as his helmeted corpse again floated past. She couldn't help thinking of his three cute little kids. He and his wife Janette had kindly invited Susan over to dinner several times. Now Jan was widowed, his children fatherless. They probably wouldn't even get his body back to Earth. The kids would only have memories of their Dad.

—just like her...

Suzy and her Dad rolled out of their cyclone wire-fenced yard onto Ardmore Street, beside her house. She had a feeling of dark foreboding, as if something terrible was about to happen to her and her Dad. She wanted more than anything to abandon this expedition and return home, ignoring what might be lurking out in the Park. But regardless of the danger she had to *know*...

She peddled her girl-sized blue mountain bike. David King confidently sat astride his big black-and-orange Cannondale.

They both wore biking helmets, his resting easily on his thin grey hair. Hers was fighting a mob of bushy blond hair! God, she hated wearing the thing. But she knew her Dad would insist if she pulled it off. He was a stickler for safety.

But he looked frail and feeble, unsteady on his mountain bike. He was wryly complaining he hadn't been out on it for years. And yet Susan had vivid memories of a lean, trim version of him riding with her on that bike just a month earlier. What was happening?

It was hard to believe her memories, which seemed to be rapidly fading...?

"Ready, kiddo?"

She was jerked back to the immediate reality.

"Ready, Dad!"

They headed to the main road, West 12th, right in front of their house, which led directly south to the Park entrance.

They'd changed out of their nice church clothes into hiking gear. Suzy was glad church was over. It, like everything else, was different from what she remembered. She vividly recalled a modern rock group leading the congregation in rapturous celebration followed by a relevant, stirring sermon. Instead, this "new" service was incredibly boring, not just to her but to the other members judging by their expressions. The sermon was a standard, accepted explanation of a particular Bible passage. She got the feeling a "rock band" would be considered blasphemous, although she actually did enjoy the "a-cappella" singing where her sweet soprano enhanced the totally verbal music. She still wished she could play her guitar in accompaniment, but that was forbidden by the group's fundamentalist doctrines.

In fact, it'd been a long time since she'd even picked up her guitar. It was gathering dust at the back of a closet, waiting for her to someday take advanced lessons on it. But today at church the a-cappella singing sounded particularly flat. Their song leader, Mr. Yanash, seemed listless, leading well-worn old hymns everyone knew by heart. There was little inspiration, nothing Suzy and the other dutiful members hadn't heard many times before.

But now she was returning to the Park—to her and Billy's incredible adventure! At least that's what she remembered, assuming it was more than just a noggin-banged dream. Regardless, this was Nature, God's true magnificence. To Suzy, the best "church" of all was the Park: a *Cathedral of Creation* right in their backyard that Suzy always enjoyed.

To her the Park—or, more formally, the nearly 10,000 acre "Chickasaw National Recreation Area"—represented a *cosmic construct* stretching forward billions of years while solidly set upon rocks dating back many millions of years to the time of the dinosaurs!

And if that little dinosaur is out there in the woods I'm determined to find it!

She remembered it distinctly: a man-sized lizard standing on its powerful hind legs. But could she trust her memory?

They both had on bright orange-fluorescent riding vests, with well-packed saddle bags draped over the rear of each of their bikes. It was Sunday afternoon, 2:00 p.m. It was cool for springtime, with a gentle wind blowing. The sun was high, pleasantly warming the skin of Suzy's face. It was a perfect day to go biking for a couple hours out in the Park.

"Too bad Billy couldn't come with us," Suzy said to her Dad as they coasted along the gentle downward slope of 12th Street toward the main Park entrance.

"You know he's not as organized or adventurous as you, kiddo," her Dad good-naturedly replied. "Leaving his homework until Sunday afternoon means he's got to get it done before evening. He knows that perfectly well. In fact, he probably planned it that way so he didn't have to venture out of the house."

"Yes, that's true," she sadly nodded, lightly touching the hand-brakes to not accelerate too rapidly along the downward slope of the street. After falling off her bike yesterday she sure didn't want a repeat! Her head still ached around the prominent lump she'd sustained.

But she was sad that her Dad was making an excuse for Billy, further confirming things were radically different than she remembered. Normally Billy dragged *her* to go biking in the Park with him and not do *her* homework! Now when she asked him if he wanted to go with her and their Dad he just frowned, mumbling something about needing to do calculations for a new program he was writing for the "lab."

He was smart for a six year old. But how had he suddenly transformed into such a computer nerd? She was sad that now she didn't
have the slightest idea what was going on in his fuzzy little head. She
only remembered him as a pesky kid zooming around making mis-
chief!

"So where are we going, Suzy?"

Ah, yes, their present goal. It brought Suzy's thoughts back to
what she liked most: the immediate task.

"We're going through Rock Creek Campground to the gravel road
that's right before you reach Veterans Lake."

"We could just bypass the campground, staying on the main
paved road. It'd be faster."

"The main road's too steep for me, Dad, even walking the bike up
the slope. Besides, I like going through the campground. It's like
we're off camping somewhere in the woods."

"Yes...I know I keep promising to take you guys off to other wonderful adventure-areas of the nation—but my experiments...?"

"It's ok, Dad," she hastened to reassure him. "I'm just glad we've
got this time, right now. This is great. I hardly ever get you to myself,
except when you're working on the car."

"And you're a great assistant! I couldn't keep our creaky old
Cavalier running without you. Since we're not rich enough to have
several cars, you help keep our family chugging along."

"Ah...thanks, Dad."

It's true they didn't have any extra cash. Suzy didn't think about
it much, but High Schools and restaurants didn't pay that much. And
their family income had to support the four of them. She didn't feel
deprived, though, just aware that they couldn't afford extra stuff.

But she did feel rich in the things that matter the most: the gentle
wind rustling her clothes as they zipped along, the warm sunlight on
her face, and her Dad grinning like a little kid there beside her.

His bright smile briefly eclipsed his scraggly gray beard and
white-gray longish hair—making him briefly look much younger.

"Well, it's been a long time since I've been out here," he continued, "too long, in fact. Your Mother and I used to ride our mountain
bikes all the time. That was before you and Billy came along, of

course. We were more athletic back then. But I got older and your Mom got chubbier. Hah! Just more of her to love," he chuckled.

No cars were on the road. It seemed they had the whole large *Chickasaw National Recreation Area*, to themselves. It was peaceful. A forest of medium-sized green-leafed trees loomed in front of Suzy. It was inconceivable that the greenery hid an *extinct dinosaur*, a buried *trans-dimensional travel device*, a radioactive *Martian Obelisk*, and a *ravenous monster* from beyond normal space-time bent on consuming the world!

Surely they were just fantasies conjured up by her noggin-rattled brain when she got conked-out the previous day. But what if they weren't?

Well, they were about to find out.

"So why did Mom get so fat?" Suzy said as they slowly drifted along on their bikes, side-by-side, past the large brown Park-entrance sign.

Sally King was definitely *not* the vibrant, fit mother that Suzy remembered. Yes, she was warm and loving—just overly absorbed in her T.V. shows and junk food when not working at the local restaurant.

"That's not nice to say," he gently chided her. "You shouldn't call people who are overweight 'fat'."

"Plump."

He grinned, wryly looking down at his somewhat shriveled, skinny body.

"Well, it didn't happen overnight," he shrugged. "It's just how many women react physiologically to having and raising babies. It's a big stress on their metabolism."

"There are other ladies I know at church who had babies and aren't...chubby."

"Well, that's true, I guess," he sighed. "But your Mom has delicious, greasy food around her at her work. She's always nibbling on stuff, tasting it, making sure it's ok for the customers. Plus she bakes the goodies at the restaurant herself. You know how addictive her cakes and pies are, right?"

"Are you sure she works at a restaurant?"

David King looked at her with concern on his face.

They briefly paused before rolling through the stop sign at the empty intersection, going to the right toward Rock Creek Campground. The two-lane road inside the Park was sloped to cross a low bridge over Rock Creek.

They picked up speed, steadying their bikes to zoom across the bridge.

"Sure, kiddo, you know perfectly well. That's her job—at the 'Cowboy Country Café' on Sulphur's main drag, Broadway Street. She's been working there for years. You love their steamed lobsters. Say...did you get hit worse on your head than you admitted?" he asked, frowning at her.

"Uh..." Suzy squinted in confusion. She didn't even like to eat *fish*, let alone *shell*fish! "But mom also teaches calculus at the high school, right?"

Suzy concentrated on the exhilarating "swoosh" and rattle of her bike zipping over the Rock Creek Bridge. Then they turned onto the right branch of the road that led straight into the camping ground. The upward slope slowed their bikes to a comfortable peddling pace.

"Suzy, you know perfectly well that your mother never went to college," her Dad replied. "She's always worked in restaurants. She waited on tables until she got promoted to being the Chef. That's where I first met her, waiting on my table at 'Georgia's Happy Home Kitchen' in Ada."

"She never did math?"

They slowed further as the bikes hit the rougher single-lane graveled road inside the campground. A panoply of arched tree branches curled over them, drawing them in.

"Not that she ever told me," he shrugged.

"So why did you marry her, Dad? You're a scientist. Shouldn't you have found a lady scientist who could help you with your research?"

"Let's take a rest at that park bench up there," he puffed, breathing heavily as he drifted up alongside her. "I'm not used to this exertion!"

"Sure, Dad."

They stopped. Suzy hopped off her bike and leaned it up against a nearby tree. Her Dad rolled to a stop and carefully stepped off, leaning his bike against the back of the park bench.

It was very peaceful and quiet. It was still early in springtime, too early for the yearly rush of summer campers. The sites were empty. Suzy and her Dad had the entire campground to themselves.

She sat next to her Dad, looking at him expectantly.

"Kiddo, guys and gals are attracted to each other for many reasons."

"You mean like sex-appeal?"

"Right," he nodded. "There's a 'magnetism' of females and males that draws them together. With enough kissing and hugging even total opposites can get 'hot and bothered' for each other. That's why you have to be careful once you're older so you don't get tied to someone who you later discover isn't a good companion or friend for you."

"So you don't love Mom?"

"No, no! She's great, Suzy. Honest to God! I'm totally happy I found her and we made you two kids. But..."

"But?"

"Well, I did think she'd be more interested in my research. When we first met, she seemed fascinated by what I was trying to do. But..."

"But?" she repeated, determined to figure out this totally unexpected aspect of her parents' life.

"Well, she had a 'hippy' type of boyfriend before me, who superficially suited her better. But when he was tragically killed, I guess she was on the rebound—and found me to be...maybe exotic? Anyway, that was fine with me! Sure, I wasn't a long-haired, dropped-out, tattoo-covered, drug-snorting, tobacco-addicted youngster like her previous boyfriend. I was a totally obsessed, regular church-going, bachelor scientist puttering around on discredited experiments in my garage in Edmond, Oklahoma. But she was into deep computer things in her free time, particularly gaming. She could have had a bright future in computer coding if she'd gone on and gotten a higher degree. As I recall, she was fascinated by computer pseudo-intelligences, but...."

He shrugged, smiling at her, leaning back and looking up silently at the sunlit green leaves glowing above them, set against a bright blue sky.

"What happened to him?"

"Who?"

"The boyfriend that was killed."

"Ah, right. A stupid terrorist drove a pickup into the restaurant where your Mom and her boyfriend worked. The terrorist wanted to kill everyone, apparently. A couple police were there eating breakfast and shot the terrorist, but not before he fatally wounded her boyfriend. It was tragic. It was on all the national news networks."

"Wow."

"Yep, 'stuff happens'—that's the way of the world."

"Stuff happens..." Suzy repeated, struggling with this new concept. At church the preacher regularly talked about God having a grand Plan for humanity plus little plans for each and every person. Your duty was to discover God's plan for your life and align your actions with it. Stuff just randomly happening wasn't supposed to be the way God dealt with humans.

"But doesn't God...?" she tentatively began...

"Yes, the Church has a lot of doctrines, Suzy," he cut her off, apparently knowing what she was going to say. "But those are teachings that have come down through many centuries. If you go back to the actual teachings of Jesus and what the Bible says, you often get a different take on things than the 'party line' of any particular church group."

"Like what?"

"Well, there's a verse that says 'the rain falls on the good person as well as the bad person' or something to that effect."

"Uh, ok. So that means...?"

"—you just have to accept the bad with the good and keep on rolling."

"But what about God's plans?"

"Well, God lets Mother Nature have a lot of freedom. Also, God lets us humans have 'free will' so we do lots of strange things that unexpectedly effect each other. And then again, there's just being in the wrong place at the wrong time. Stuff happens!"

"You mean like Mom's prior boyfriend getting killed by a terrorist and you being there to help her. So can 'stuff' be bad and good at the same time?"

"Something like that," he shrugged, "But what do I know? I'm not a preacher. I'm just a puttering scientist who teaches high school courses. By most academic and scientific standards your Old Man is a failure."

"*I* don't think you're a failure!"

He smiled, putting an arm over her shoulders.

"Yes, *you* make me a success, kiddo," he sighed, looking again up at the sky. "Sometimes we get dragged down...but other times we bounce back up, even higher than we were before! So that's what happened to your Mom and me. We got slapped down, but because of it we found each other—and that's why you and Billy are here. *You're* my biggest achievement."

He hugged her on the park bench before briskly standing up.

"Good story, Dad."

"Right! Well, I've got my breath back. You ready to get biking again? I want to find your 'dinosaur' plus your other imagined, marvelous anomalies!"

"Sure, Dad."

And so they kept on rolling through the empty campgrounds, deeper and deeper into the forest. Then Suzy carefully led her Dad around a chain that blocked the road where a hanging sign proclaimed: "This section closed." Laboriously peddling the bike up a slope she ascended along her familiar route to the very back of the campgrounds and then onto a cement sidewalk. It opened up onto a gravel road. Across the road was the wide, blue expanse of *Veterans Lake*. But to the right, the gravel road descended back toward a secluded section of Rock Creek.

"You have your Geiger counter, Dad?" she asked him as they paused, their feet planted to each side of their bikes.

"I sure do, Suzy. It's ancient surplus equipment, but still works!"

He reached back and unstrapped a large pouch hanging to the side of his mountain bike's backpack. He extracted an old, black rectangular device. He held it by its handle, switching it on. Suzy heard a lazy series of "clicks" coming from it.

"That's the background, normal radiation—cosmic rays and such," he nodded in satisfaction. "Let's make sure it's working ok for higher readings," he said, pulling out a small lead-lined vial. Unscrewing its lid he held it close beneath the device. The slow "clicks" changed into a torrent of "*brrrrrrrppppsss*"! Yep, it was working just fine.

Carefully resealing and putting the source container back in the pouch, he secured the counter so it dangled from his handlebars.

"If we get close to anything radioactive, we'll get a good warning signal," he said. "I've put it on maximum sensitivity. Of course it's just detecting hard radiation, like gamma rays. But that's what your mysterious 'Obelisk' is supposed to exude, right?"

"Well, in my...dream...that's what happened—at least that's what *you* told me at the campfire on Mars," she weakly concluded, feeling more and more foolish taking her dad on this wild-goose chase.

"Hey, I hope we find it, kiddo. It sounds fascinating!"

"Not what's inside of it."

"Oh right, a giant spider—from another dimension?" he grinned, clearly enjoying her fantasy.

"I think it's supposed to be from 'sub-space'?"

"That's even better! Let's go find it!"

"I just wish we had our rifles," she mused, rolling along beside him.

"Suzy! You know we don't keep guns. They're much too dangerous for us town folks to have around. If we lived on a farm that might be another matter, but we don't."

Yes, yet another marked difference from her "fantasies" and the present condition of the world. In that other "reality" she'd imagined that both she and Billy were well-schooled in the use of rifles, from adventure trips into the wilds of the U.S.A. with her athletic folks. In fact, they'd used those rifles to help stop the giant subspace Spider.

But now without the guns, if they *did* find something dangerous— how could they kill it?

Suddenly Suzy was *very* scared.

Before, it'd been just a compulsion to find out if any of her nightmares were true. But now that they were—maybe—about to encounter the real thing, it was terrifying! And they were biking down an isolated gravel road in the Park where few ventured, even when the Park was filled with visitors. No one knew where they'd gone. By the time her Mom missed them and rescuers were sent they could be long vanished, *eaten* by the *Black Spider* from *Subspace*!

Wow. That *would* make a nice science fiction story or movie!

Suzy listened with growing apprehension to the slow "clicking" of the dangling Geiger counter on her Dad's bike handles. Was the pace of the clicks accelerating? She suddenly realized that they had no protective gear of any kind. If the counter erupted into a ROAR then they'd be totally exposed to lethal radiation!

And—according to what her Dad said in that supposed other 'timeline'—the *crashed Obelisk* was right up around the bend in the road!

"Oh, boy," she whispered.

It was too late to turn back. As her Dad had told her, she just had to "keep on rolling" either up or *down...*

—and she knew too well from her outer space nightmare that gravity *was* a bitch!

Chapter 3

GRAVITY

A mutual weak attraction

Unless one party is very large

Warping Space-Time somehow

Einstein watching the stone roll

Way down into that big, black bowl

With dour satisfaction at Theory

Turned from abstract equations

Into flaming debris and wreckage

Atmospheric friction exploding

The loftiest dreams brought low

Sucked in, smashed, and crushed

Might as well cherish the hug?

The Minstrel's Lark, 3:31-34

IMPACT MINUS SIX MONTHS, *DEGRADING ORBIT...*

"Ready?"

"All set, Commander," Susan replied into her helmet microphone. She was poised at the other end of the locking bar.

They were positioned upside-down to each other.

They were each inside their EMU's, floating within the tight constraints of the storage module. Around them, sealed containers were fitted together as white-bricked, curved walls. It'd taken them a full hour to reposition the cargo boxes, free up the packed EMU's, get into them, and do a minimal series of safety checks. That was breakneck speed. The full procedure would have taken much longer. But they didn't have time to do everything "according to the book."

The *Extravehicular Mobility Units* (EMUs) were much advanced from the original Space Shuttle design. These fit around their orange flight suits and connected to the same helmets. Thus there was no problem in being exposed to the thin atmosphere inside the cargo module. Plus the life support backpacks of the EMU's contained small built-in thruster nozzles driven by compact liquid-nitrogen tanks. They weren't as mobile or powerful as in a *Manned Maneuvering Unit* (MMU), which was a self-contained, small one-person spaceship, but still were better than nothing. If either Susan or Kunle lost their tethers they'd have a shot at getting back to the vehicle, rather than helplessly floating away into space!

"On three, King—one...two...*three!*"

The locking bar was designed to be hard to open. They'd had to extract three tightly screwed-in pins to free the bar for movement. Once they managed to rotate the bar 90°, wall ratchets would be withdrawn and the entire attached panel would open outward on hinges. Normally the cargo containers were unloaded through the top hatch when the cargo module was docked with the Hermes or International Space Station. But for extra-large items, such as were below in the main payload, this was a necessary method of exit.

"It's...stuck!" Susan groaned, straining as hard as she could to pull her end upward with her feet planted firmly on the flooring beneath her.

Kunle, upside-down on the other side of the bar with her spacesuit boots planted on the ceiling above, was having the same trouble getting her end of the bar to move.

"Hold on..." the Commander panted, resting her arms.

"Maybe if we each pushed instead of pulled?"

"Alright then, get repositioned."

Susan crouched and placed the palms of her gloves up onto the bottom of her end of the bar. Now she was set to use her much stronger leg muscles rather than just pull with her arms. Opposite and upside-down, Kunle did the same.

"On three, again—one...two...*three!*"

This time the bar slowly rotated.

"Hold up!"

The panel had lurched outward but then stopped, jammed at an angle against something outside.

"I thought the outer shell was ripped off?"

"Apparently not completely," Kunle replied, peering around the edge of the partially opened exit panel.

Through the gap Susan saw a mangled, blackened barrier. It was the inside surface of one of the three outer protective panels that encircled both the payload compartment and the attached J-2X engines, right below the Orion capsule. It should have smoothly ejected after the main RS-25 engines cut out. But it hadn't. Clearly, it was part of the problem of them not being able to release the core stage. If they couldn't get the upper stage free, then their J-2X secondary engine couldn't fire. They'd either fall back into the atmosphere and be incinerated, or have to find a way to repair and use the *Launch Abort System* (ALS) that was still affixed atop the Orion capsule. Either way their world-saving mission was terminated.

"What do we do, Commander?"

"Push harder!"

Kunle floated around to position her feet against the partially opened exit panel, bent-double holding the edge with her gloved hands. Susan did the same at the other side opposite to the hinges.

"Again, on three...one, two, *three!*"

They thrust their feet into the hard material. Nothing...

"Again!"

Susan coordinated her thrust with the Commander's, straining as hard as she could. Still nothing...

"*Again!*" Kunle yelled as together they *slammed* their boots into the panel—which suddenly *flipped outward* from beneath her feet!

Susan was left dangling by her hands, her legs and torso floating free in space. Now drenched in sweat inside her EMU, she eased herself back into the storage compartment. Kunle did the same.

The ventilation automatically kicked to a higher gear in her suit, helping to clear the sudden fog that sprang up on the inside of her helmet.

"Looks like we should have tethered ourselves first, huh?" the Commander said, her normally calm voice breaking. "We almost went for an unscheduled spacewalk without a safety line!"

"Yes, Ma'am," Susan agreed, trembling from relief. "I'll get us secured."

She floated back away from the now opened portal, grabbing two tether coils. She secured one end's hook to an inner ring then the other end to her suit. She did the same for Kunle while the Commander freed up a large rectangular box. It was a full three feet across. Then, together, they carefully climbed out of the storage compartment, still clinging to the edge of the opened portal.

Susan switched on her electrically magnetized boots, standing upright. Fortunately the latest construction methods for the ship's outer hull included ferromagnetic materials as well as the lighter-weight aluminum and exotic polymers.

"Oh, my!" Susan gasped.

Rotating from her left to her right—while simultaneously flipping up over her head—was the *wide, blue-white expanse* of Earth. Kunle crouched beside her, lifting out the big black box from the cargo hold. They were in the full glare of sunlight, Kunle's faceplate now automatically darkening so Susan couldn't see her face. Kunle's EMU was momentarily a dazzling white against the utter blackness of space before being thrown into darkness in the shadow of the rocket, then back in bright sunlight!

"We're tumbling. Don't look up, King," the Commander ordered. "We can't correct our spins until we get the Upper Stage freed. Just keep your gaze fixed on the hull at your boots."

Susan felt an overwhelming urge to vomit. She had reacted ok to her first space-experience of zero-G in the cabin. But this was completely different. In the cabin, most everything was fixed in place, even the drifting debris. Here, the entire Earth was spinning and bouncing around above her head! But Susan knew this was the Commander's fourth trip into space, which included seven different spacewalks. Kunle certainly knew the best strategy to stay focused, effective, and not dead.

"Alright. I'll try."

Susan fought back the rising bile in her throat. If she threw up in her helmet, the result could be deadly. Uncontrollably aspirating floating vomit could clog her lungs and kill her!

"Christ, it's a mess," Kunle said, also slowly standing upright, planted by her own magnetic boots on the partially metallic hull.

"Booster-3 must have impacted the upper sections when it prematurely broke free..."

Susan looked up at the top end of the spacecraft. The slender, pointed Launch Abort System was still in place. But its white side was deeply indented. Apparently that damage happened simultaneous with the inner crew capsule being breached, disrupting their control systems.

"—and the stresses did a number on the other adaptor rings as well."

Now Susan looked down the length of the rocket. It was gigantic. She was used to seeing it from a distance neatly assembled upon a launching pad at the Kennedy Space Center. This was completely different. She and Kunle stood on a big cylinder which was as long as a football field. The curved hull was nearly thirty feet across. A glance upward showed the panel they'd knocked loose lazily spiraling away into space, twisted and blackened.

In front of Susan was a large, exposed section of the main payload fairing. Its white paint was scorched and burnt. Beyond that was the section containing two hidden J-2X engines. Further on was a black/white-checkered Inter-stage section. Finally there was the long, orange-painted Core, housing the empty main fuel tank. But where the stack should have been perfectly straight, it was now *crooked*. The side boosters were long gone. But the unbalanced ripping-away of booster-3 had caused frightful damage.

The base of the Inter-stage against the lower Core was buckled, scrunched-up to one side. But that shouldn't have affected the next interlocking section where the Upper Stage needed to slide out, should it?

Apparently it did, though the damage wasn't obvious.

"What do you think caused this disaster?" Susan said as she resolutely kept her eyes fixed on the lower, buckled section instead of the tumbling Earth.

"The combined stresses may have been too much. They'd never stacked an array so high before or used four boosters instead of two. But still, it should have worked!"

Yes, where large payloads were involved—such as the Mars mission components—separate SLS launches were normally used. But due to the tight time constraints of meeting the newly discovered, hurtling Asteroid, everything was piled up onto this one available launch. Instead of just two boosters they'd gone to an unprecedented four. And instead of launching a crewed capsule separate from the heavy payload, they'd put them both together. So between the Orion crew capsule and the Upper Stage engines was sandwiched the large payload section: the cargo module.

It was just too many new things slapped together at once without benefit of NASA's usual piece-by-piece methodical testing.

"I guess it doesn't matter at the moment what's the primary cause," Susan stated, her mind now focused on the immediate problem. "Our immediate need is to get loose from the Inter-stage, right? The coupling looks skewed, preventing release. Isn't that what we've got to fix?"

"Well, King—let's just go take a look!" Kunle brightly answered. She started to carefully "clomp" her magnetic boots forward. The big black box floated "obediently" along behind on its own short tether, connected securely to her white EMU suit.

Susan wished that the low side rails of the Core Stage extended up this high. But they didn't. If they slipped off the big cylinder, only their thin tether lines stretching to the cargo hatch would save them from drifting helplessly away into space!

Take it slow—she sternly ordered herself. *One step at a time.*

They inched down the side of the long curved surface to the Inter-stage coupling. Yes, the joint there was mashed on one side, jamming the two sections together. At the base of the Inter-stage the damage was much worse. The metal there was warped and torn. There was not much they could do for that mangled mess. But at the higher joint with the Upper Stage where the edges were just mashed together, perhaps...?

"This damage needs to be repaired at the Michoud Assembly Facility," Susan observed, keeping her eyes studiously away from the tumbling Earth swooping around above her. "This is major warping, Commander."

"Then we're lucky we're not going to attempt to repair it," Kunle curtly replied, pulling the black box down and pressing it onto the still-smooth section right behind the strained steel. "We're going to cut it free."

"*Commander, we've got contact with Mission Control,*" an urgent, deeper voice sounded from Susan's helmet speaker. "*It's intermittent, but audible. Our antennae array is still badly damaged by the loose booster, so the contact may not last long. They want an update on your spacewalk.*"

"Good. Tell them we're assessing the external damage," Kunle replied. Then, to Susan: "It's up to you to keep the box parallel and pressed up against the curved surface. I'll be guiding the laser beam right next to the metal. The beam applies a thrust so you'll have to *muscle* the box to keep it steady."

"But Torey, it's..."

"Yes, I know. We've got around 95 feet of steel to cut through. That's a hell of a lot. But our laser unit here runs at 30,000 watts right next to the source. It should slice through the hull. And if we make it around the circumference, part of the Inter-stage may still be attached in the ring that's left on our side, but the J-2X engine should still have plenty of room to fire through the gap."

"There's enough juice in the laser rig?"

"That's what we brought it for, remember? It's a TRUMPF-adapter industrial laser for reconfiguring our nukes onto whatever containment structure we may have to build when we reach the Asteroid. There we'll have a cable running from Hermes' nuclear reactor to power it. But, lucky for us, close to Earth we can still use one your brother's internal 'miracle' batteries, huh?"

Yes, Bill King was her billionaire brother, whose *High Temperature Super-Conducting (HTSC) battery* was transforming the world. A single unit had an almost unlimited storage capacity. Where massive amounts of liquid fossil fuels had been required to do most mechanical jobs, now small batteries could store huge amounts of clean energy for virtually any task. Only a few special applications—such as space vehicle launches—still required liquid or solid fossil-based fuels. Even there, battery-powered launch vehicles were being designed. But space vehicles such as the Mars Transit Vehicle *Hermes*, for the foreseeable future, required conventional liquid fuels. The super-batteries drew their vast energy from previously loaded individual subspace "sinks" locked-into the Moon-Earth gravity-well. Too far distant from Earth and the "super-batteries" just petered out.

"The laser unit's got a kick and the hull's thick in places," Kunle continued. "It's going to take every bit of our concentration and control to cut away the lower stages: you from the top and me from the bottom."

"I'm ready."

"Alright. I'm switching it on...*now!*"

A *bright blue glow* flared up from beneath the square black box. Susan felt an uneven pressure trying to wrest the box from out of her hands. Momentarily, one of her magnetic boots lifted off the hull.

Struggling to get the squirming box under control, she grasped it firmly in both of her spacesuited arms, following the directions of the Commander.

It seemed to take an eternity, but it was only two hours until they had advanced inch-by-inch around most of the circumference of the big cylinder. By that time Susan was shaking inside her suit, utterly exhausted. But they were almost finished. Only three more feet of the hull remained to be cut!

"Uh oh..." Kunle muttered.

"What?" Susan barked back, tensing...

—when suddenly the rotational forces of the still-spinning stack *ripped* the lower section outward, *twisting* it...

"Commander!" Susan yelled, staggering backward trying to keep her magnetic boots on the steel hull—as the lower section completely *tore free* and went *tumbling* off to the side!

Still clutching the industrial laser on the retreating, cut cylinder, Commander Kunle rose unsteadily to her feet. She grabbed with one hand at her tether line—which went taut and *yanked* her white spacesuited form *straight into* the black box!

The line snapped but it was too late.

Kunle slumped limp and unresponsive. She was still glued by her boots to the tumbling giant cylinder. But the entire thing was fast retreating into space.

"*We read the Upper Stage as free,*" a voice sounded in Susan's helmet. "*Come on back inside!*"

"We've got a problem..." Susan quickly replied as she slipped off the closed hook from her suit belt and *leapt* after Torey!

"King...go back! *Go back!*" Susan heard a slurred voice in her helmet. "I'm...hurt...leave me."

Ignoring the order from Kunle, Susan mentally integrated the tumble of the Core Stage, the different spins of the Upper Stage from which she'd jumped, and the rapidly diverging resultant vectors.

She fingered the controls at her belt, firing off brief bursts of nitrogen gas through the small thrusters in her backpack. Luckily it hadn't required many hours of simulation for her to develop the skills necessary to make the minor but crucial course alterations. It was second nature to her, a gift from her mother's mathematical-genius genetics.

Susan neatly landed on the sliced-open end of the Core structure, grabbed Torey's arm, and jumped back toward the fast-receding Upper Stage. Behind them trailed the still-attached and glowing laser-box.

"You...shouldn't have come...damn it—I gave you an *order!*"

"You can put me on report later, Commander," Susan calmly replied as they floated along in the void. She concentrated on calculating the odds of making it back to the Upper Stage. "But right now you are essential to this mission!"

"Losing both of us is much worse than..."

"I'm not losing either of us," Susan insisted, firing the remainder of her small nitrogen canister in one long burst.

"We...won't make it back. We're too far away. There's not enough thrust in our small suit-packs for..."

"You are correct, Commander," Susan interrupted her. "But I've got a plan."

She squirmed around to latch herself onto the front of Torey's spacesuit, wrapping her legs around the woman's waist. Quickly keying in coordinates to the Commander's control panel on the front of her suit, Susan fired off Torey's suit's nitrogen reserves.

Now the Upper Stage wasn't receding. But it wasn't nearing either.

"And for the last stage of this untethered spacewalk," Susan calmly stated as she pulled in the black box trailing behind them, "we'll need just a bit more thrust."

With her legs still firmly wrapped around the Commander's waist Susan maneuvered the laser box up against the Commander's back.

Feeling at the controls on the top of the box, Susan widened the still-firing laser beam and jacked it up to maximum output.

Gently pushed by the powerful, outgoing laser beam, they drifted right up to the looming gap on the side of the storage module and floated inside.

Susan grabbed the edge of the opened portal and pulled the hinged panel over. She jerked her gloved fingers out of the way as it slammed shut. Then she tightly cranked-over the locking bar.

Susan collapsed into herself, totally exhausted and trembling.

"I was right," Torey's voice whispered from the speaker in Susan's helmet.

"About what?"

"You *do* make a great mechanic's assistant."

Suzy rolled to a stop beside the thickly forested, high bank of Rock Creek. They were in a wide, graveled parking area. In the tourist season, it was a popular place for fishermen to come and park their cars.

Now it was completely empty. Indeed, it felt totally isolated, away from everything else, spooky.

No one at all was there except for Suzy and her Dad, standing with their legs to each side of their straddled mountain bikes.

Dave King had on a pair of old jeans and a long flannelled shirt. Suzy had on her hiking shorts and a short-sleeved shirt. The green *Turtle Tattoo* glared up from her wrist as if accusing her of subterfuge. But that was silly. It happened! Her story was true! Wasn't it?

"So, is this where the 'Martian Obelisk' crashed?" Dave King grinned at his daughter.

She wasn't amused. It wasn't a joke. She was dead serious about finding proof of her incredible story.

But there wasn't any uptick in the steady, slow clicks coming from the dangling Geiger counter.

"You told me in my...dream...that it was right out there in the creek, mostly buried into the mud. The radiation was killing off the fish. They were floating on the surface, dead."

"Ok. Let's go have a look."

They carefully laid their bikes flat on their sides on the gravel and walked to the edge of the forest, peering carefully through the thick foliage down at the creek which meandered along twenty feet below them.

It was a widening section of the creek. The water was placid, a green-brown color. Suzy could see neither a giant Obelisk nor any dead, floating fish.

"Ah, not there," Dave shrugged, "sorry, Suzy. Are you satisfied?"

"Let's go to the fishing spot," she insisted. "I've still got a feeling that something's not right."

"Hey, you're the boss on this expedition, *boss!*" the gray-bearded man smartly nodded, walking back to his bike and straddling it. "Let's roll!"

Not too far along, in the direction back toward the camping grounds from which they'd come was a small, open descent. The narrow opening led through the thick foliage down right next to Rock Creek. This was where people liked to fish. Suzy knew it well because it was so peaceful. She liked to go there when no one else was around. There she felt one with Nature, nothing artificial within sight. There she was no longer an interloper but a participant.

They dismounted. Suzy watched her lean, orange-vested Dad go down the slippery descent. He held onto large tree roots to each side to not fall. Then he reached back with a strong hand to help Suzy carefully climb down behind him.

Shortly they were down to the actual creek bed, surrounded by tall, rough-barked trees. Thick vines grew on the tree trunks, making the site look ancient. Extensive ground shrubbery was on both sides of the wide creek at the water's edge, isolating the spot from the rest of the world. Off to Suzy's right was a small series of rocky drops where the water ran in white cascades.

Fluffy cattails pushed up through the shrubs, swaying gently in the cool breeze. A couple of flat mud-turtles sat placidly on a half-submerged tree trunk poking out from the opposite bank. The turtles were happily sunning themselves.

"So, here we are, kiddo," Dave grinned, sitting heavily upon a fallen log. "No giant alien spiders that I can see—just this nice wide pond. Too bad we didn't bring our fishing poles with us, huh? There might be some tasty catfish out there just waiting for us to catch, take with us back home, and cook up for dinner!"

Suzy sighed in resignation, sitting down next to him on the log.

"Thanks, Dad."

"For what?"

"For humoring me, I guess—it just all seemed so real. My memories of the Obelisk and the Spider are getting blurred now, but yesterday they were as clear as everything around us. When Billy and I came back it was like everything in the world changed. But now...?"

He suddenly stiffened, his relaxed expression vanished.

"What?" Suzy asked, peering around in concern.

The hair on the back of her neck stood up. She felt static electricity crawling over her skin. And a *cold lump of fear* was rising into her throat!

"*Shhhh!*" he said, holding a finger to his lips.

She heard it.

Across the creek there was a rustling of the bushes, a "scuttling" sound!

"Something's over there," Suzy whispered, wide-eyed.

She saw the thick greenery and higher branches *jerking* as something ran through the forest, headed away from them to their left.

"Wow," Dave gulped, visibly shaken. "That was *big!*"

"Was it just a deer?" Suzy asked, now not so eager to meet a ravenous, giant alien spider.

"Deer *glide* through the forest, Suzy—not *charge* through it! I think we best get back to a ranger station and report what we saw."

"But what *did* we see?"

He paused, standing up slowly. He scratched his head with one hand, frowning. He looked across the pond where some of the higher tree branches were still swaying.

"Just branches moving, I guess," he shrugged. "Maybe it was the wind?"

"There's no wind, Dad."

"Then a passing breeze?"

"Those were *big* branches moving around. Something was *pushing* them!"

"Whatever it was, it had to be big and strong."

"Yep. I didn't see what caused it either," she gulped. "How about a loose horse or something?"

"Or something."

"They'd never believe we saw something strange since we actually didn't see anything except branches moving," Suzy mused, standing up as well, following her Dad as they climbed back up the short ascent to the higher creek bank.

"Don't slip now," he warned her. "Keep hold of the roots to the sides."

"I know, Dad," she called back up to him.

And then they were at the top, hastily climbing back onto their faithfully waiting bikes.

"We better head on back," Dave said.

"No!"

"What?"

"We can't leave it like this, Dad! Now I'll never know for sure. *Something* was out there in the woods! What if the Obelisk took off before we got here, leaving its passenger behind?"

"Suzy, the creek bed wasn't disturbed. The mud turtles on the log were fine. There wasn't any radioactivity beyond a few normal background 'clicks.' And we didn't see any monster out there, just rustling branches."

"I know, Dad! But there's another place we can check before we head back to the house. It's not too far from here!"

"But, whatever that was out in the woods...?"

"It wasn't attacking us! We were totally exposed there on the bank, helpless. But it just ran away from us! Whatever it was, I don't think it was a threat."

"Well, that's probably true."

"Please, Dad? It won't take too long! Please?"

"I don't know—I'm still your father, remember. If there's a bear or something out there I'm not going to put you in danger just to..."

"There aren't any bears around here!"

He sighed. She knew she was winning the argument.

"*Please?*" She said, looking up at him with her deliberately wide-eyed "little girl" face.

He sighed in resignation.

"Will this settle the matter in your mind, once and for all?"

"I'm just about 100% certain...maybe...yes, I *am* sure! If what I remember really happened and wasn't just a hallucination or dream, then there should be a *big long empty pit* in the ground not twenty minutes away from here!"

"And just what was inside that trench?"

"Well..."

"Suzy?"

"I don't know for sure. Maybe it was a second Obelisk. But it was a big box that transported Billy and me to another, parallel dimension where there were a *whole bunch* of *real dinosaurs!*"

"Fascinating," he mused, grinning. Suzy could see she was engaging both his physics and reptilian interests. "I'd sure love to see real live dinosaurs!"

"Well, I doubt the box is still there to take us to the other dimension—but the trench should be!"

"Ok, then—we'll go. But we head back in an hour whether we've found anything or not. Agreed?"

"Agreed!" she happily replied. Then she hopped back up onto her bike.

"So where to?" David King cheerfully asked his daughter.

"Back to the bend in this gravel road, then out onto the hiking paths behind Veterans Lake."

"It's rough-going out there, if I remember correctly."

"Yep. We'll have to walk our bikes most of the way. But it won't take too long, I promise!"

Her Dad looked up at the bright blue sky above them. The sun was still high in the sky. It now seemed impossible to Suzy that any real danger was lingering out in the woods on such a wonderful spring day.

He mounted his bike and they peddled away, side by side. He reached down to the dangling Geiger counter to switch it off, preserving its battery.

The slow sequence of "clicks" stopped.

"That was kind of scary," he grinned at her. "I could almost imagine a T-rex was out in the woods, shaking those trees. I'd sure love to see that!"

Suzy suddenly had a vivid memory of her and Billy dashing through the woods as a *whole pack* of towering T-rex-like dinosaurs *stomped* along behind them in hot pursuit!

She shakily replied: "No, Dad, you wouldn't."

He laughed, having regained his regular good humor: "I do love reptiles—especially the extinct kind."

They got off their bikes at the bend in the gravel road, walking them forward into the woods across rough, rocky terrain.

"Mom told me once that before you and she got married you had a whole house filled up with reptiles."

That was a strange statement. She did indeed have that memory. But it competed in her brain with her "fantasy" memory of her Dad actually having a "reptile room" in their own house. Which was true? It was like her lifelong memories were being superseded and overwritten by newly acquire neuronal pathways.

Wow. What a strange and disturbing idea...

"True enough, Suzy. I had cages and habitats throughout my house in Edmond. But I was an aging, totally selfish bachelor just doing whatever I wanted. I liked reptiles, so I had a bunch of them as pets. You can do stuff like that when you're a happy-go-lucky bachelor! But the first thing a new bride says is: 'either those snakes go or I go!' Hah."

"Did Mom say that?"

"Well, no, but I got the message. When we moved here I gave away my remaining critters to zoos and such."

"What kind did you have?"

"Oh, nothing dangerous, Suzy...just pet-store types of reptiles: various tortoises, lizards, and harmless snakes."

That caused her to grimace.

"Harmless? Can't snakes bite you?"

"Sure, but they don't."

"Why not?"

"They're not too smart, but they're definitely not dumb. They quickly learn that you are their friend, bringing them food, being nice to them. They grab food with their teeth, of course. But if you're not a rat, bird, or mouse then you've nothing to fear from a tame, non-poisonous snake. Of course you have to know how to handle them on their terms, like any animal."

"You can tame any animal?"

"Most."

"Even alien ones from outer space?"

"Hah...who knows?"

"So why don't you have any now, reptiles I mean?"

"Well..." he shrugged, pushing the bike around protruding boulders. "It's just a practical consideration. Your Mom takes up space. You kids take up space. All your stuff takes up space. And there are only so many rooms in the house. As families normally expand, some things have to be stored away or left behind. It's no big deal. I suppose I could have cages out in my sheds, but the gigantic surplus-WWII research equipment takes more room than I can manage as it is."

"Are you sorry you have me instead of snakes?"

The grey-bearded man beside Suzy laughed, plodding along pushing his bike up the rough hiking trail.

"Not at all, kiddo. You're worth more to me than a hundred snakes."

"Only a hundred?"

He paused, as if thinking the matter over.

"Well, come think of it, maybe a *thousand* snakes."

"Are you sure?"

"Well, that is a whole of snakes..."

"*Dad!*"

"Ok, ok! I wouldn't trade you for a thousand snakes, satisfied?"

She snickered contentedly, pushing her smaller bike along beside him.

If this was really a different timeline from the one in which she'd originally grown up, it definitely had its advantages. Things were slower and mellower here than what she remembered of her supposedly previous, fast-paced family. They'd always been traveling somewhere. Plus both her Dad and Mom taught at the high school and were often swamped with grading homework and tests. In addition, her previous "Dad" coached the school tennis team, taking them to competitions on the weekends.

Although he made time now and then for her, the "fantasy" Dad hardly ever went out biking with her in the woods on a Sunday afternoon. She almost told him to forget about the possible mysterious trench waiting out there...that they should just turn around and go home.

Almost—but not quite. Regardless of the consequences, she *had* to know!

Chapter 4

SLINGSHOT

It's not hitting the mark

It's riding the wave

Not a jarring impact

But smooth acceleration

At the end of a long whip

Slung out into space

Hurtling to a distant spot

Riding a wild boomerang

After such a long journey

Returned again to the beginning

Where you try to contemplate:

"Why did I leave in the first place?"

The Minstrel's Lark, 4:29-33

IMPACT MINUS SIX MONTHS, *HIGH EARTH ORBIT*...

They stored George in the payload compartment.

It was sad to leave him that way, still in his flight suit, strapped against a wall of boxed supplies. But it did give them more room in the crowded, disrupted Orion capsule.

Officially they put him there to preserve his body for eventual return to his family on Earth. Once the temperature fell back to freezing in the compartment, his body would be preserved indefinitely. Unspoken, they knew that their provisions were meager at best to last them their long journey to the Asteroid. If worse came to worse—they'd eat him.

It would never go onto an official report, of course. But if a pile of dry bones was returned, his family and NASA would know he'd helped the expedition in more ways than just the initial launch.

"Burn in thirty seconds..."

They were about to try and reach Hermes.

Hermes was hurtling in toward Earth from Mars. Normally it would have settled into a high elliptical orbit, awaiting resupply and refurbishing before eventually being sent back to Mars. Going into orbit required weeks of constant reverse-firing of its weak nuclear thermal reactor thrusters aimed forward, as it approached Earth. But now it needed to garner speed from Earth's gravity, not settle into orbit. Braking maneuvers using liquid fuel stores aligned it for the ADM crew's rendezvous. Thus Hermes was now positioned to "sling-shot" around Earth in order to leap up high above the planetary plane to match the path of the descending, deadly Asteroid.

Hermes' present crew of six had already been in space for two-and-a-half years. It'd taken six months to reach Mars, a year and a half exploring on the surface of the planet, then six months for the return journey. They were exhausted and physically frail from their long space mission. Even if the Mars crew wanted to stay on Hermes to proceed onward to the Asteroid, they weren't physically capable of handling the additional physical stresses.

Also, the Hermes resupply and crew-return flights had been co-opted by the vital Asteroid Deflection Mission. So as Susan and her crewmates attempted to reach Hermes, the existing Hermes crew was simultaneously departing via their own Orion capsule. Hermes' course adjustments and rendezvous with Susan's craft would be managed distally by Mission Control at the Johnson Space Center in Houston, Texas.

"Fuel flow is optimal," Susan reported back. "Our J-2X engine doesn't appear damaged, at least so far."

Susan was back in her flight chair, which had been somewhat straightened up from its bent position. Her computer console was working, as were two others. At least they'd stabilized the orientation of the Orion/supply-module/J-2X short-stack using steering jets. Commander Kunle recovered quickly from her near-death experience in cutting the lower stage free. She was back in her flight chair, monitoring readouts. Adriana Johansson, their pilot, was readying the craft. Although a few wires and conduits still dangled, much of the damage in the crew capsule was repaired.

Air density and temperature were back to normal. But the large gaps they'd had to seal in the crumpled hull were "iffy." They'd used all their available tar-like exterior sealant plugging the leaks. But the seals might blow out unexpectedly at any moment. Consequently Susan and her crewmates were still in their flight suits, their helmets locked shut.

"Ten...nine...eight..."

Susan was even tenser than she'd been for the initial launch. Back then—just a few hours before—they were flying an exquisitely configured and 100% functional rocket. Now they sat atop a badly damaged, jury-rigged small stack with no assurance it would even light-up, let alone fly straight.

"...three...two...one...*ignition!*"

Susan felt pressure on her chest as their craft leapt forward. The J-2X engine was firing ok, despite the ragged ring of cut-off Interstage which was still attached. And Susan saw on her screen that their trajectory out of low-earth orbit looked good.

"Flight path is nominal...uh, oh..." she paused.

"What's wrong?" Kunle asked from the helmet speaker.

"The two nozzles must not be correctly aligned. We're off course."

"How bad?"

"I'm having trouble compensating!" Adriana added.

The onboard computer was trying to correct for the misalignment, but it could only do so much. Without the two nozzles being perfectly in sync they could not achieve their desired vector.

"We're going to miss Hermes by ten miles," Susan grimly reported, looking at the diverging lines on her graph.

"That's not acceptable," Kunle growled.

"Matching its incoming velocity without it settling into orbit was already difficult for us," Adriana added.

Now Susan felt a disturbing, erratic vibration as they continued to accelerate. If the engine shook apart they might not have to worry about missing their appointment with Hermes. They'd just blow up!

"Mission Control can redirect Hermes to..."

"Commander, we've lost contact again with Mission Control!" Ben Priyanka excitedly reported. "The broken antenna array must have shaken loose again."

"Damn!" Kunle cursed. "Can you fix it?"

"When we stabilize...*if* we stabilize...and it'll probably require another spacewalk..."

Susan was having trouble focusing on her screen. They were pulling heavy G-forces trying to ramp-up to Hermes' velocity.

"They'll...see our altered trajectory," Susan ventured as she was roughly jostled in her seat.

"If they can react in time—if they can alter Hermes' path. It's a big vehicle and they've already used most of its liquid fuel reserves drastically slowing it so we could reach it before it slingshots around Earth," Ben grimly offered.

"We've no other choice but to ride it out," Kunle concluded.

"Yes, we do!" Susan gulped, fighting through her blurring vision. She was rapidly "clicking" in instructions with her distal mouse to the overhead computer.

"Susan?" Kunle barked at her.

"Wait...ok...I bypassed the programming that shut down the LAS when the booster impacted it. And I think I've got it reconfigured now to compensate for..."

The slender escape rocket perched on top of their Orion capsule was officially termed the "Launch Abort System." Due to the tumble and impact of booster-3 it had malfunctioned. That was fortunate, because if it had worked properly it would have snatched them away, terminating the mission. As it was, the entire unit was still attached and, now that she'd reactivated it, programmable.

"You can't do that!" Vladimir Yegorov, their payload specialist, yelled harshly out of Susan's helmet speaker. "It's an automatic sequence that..."

"I've already reconfigured it," Susan gulped, fighting to stay conscious in the heavy G's they were drawing. "I've reprogrammed in a differential between its nozzles that should correct the problem with the J-2X. But it's not going to be a prolonged firing. It'll produce a lot of G forces!"

"But we need the LAS to get us safely back to Earth," Vladimir protested.

What was wrong with the man? He was talking nonsense. The entire unit should already be gone with the ejected lower panels!

They certainly did *not* need the LAS to reenter the atmosphere. They needed to reach Hermes!

"Do it!" Kunle ordered.

Susan fired the LAS while simultaneously inactivating its mechanism for snatching Orion off the attached stack. The resultant spectacle must have been startling to Mission Control back on Earth. While the J-2X main engines fired askew below, smaller and briefer pulses above added to the confusion!

"Prepare for up to eleven more G's!" Susan yelled out as she was brutally SLAMMED back in her seat and felt her body being *crushed...*

"If we make it...to Hermes...I'm putting you in for a medal...of some sort...or maybe just not put you on report...for saving me."

"Thanks...Commander," Susan whispered as she slid reluctantly toward a black pit of unconsciousness.

If they didn't make it to Hermes, nothing else mattered. The Asteroid would continue unimpeded, slam into Earth, and kill everyone. It'd be much easier to just not wake up.

Suzy and her Dad were in the seldom-visited back territory of the Park. There were no roads or structures in sight. It felt like they'd gone back in time to before humans inhabited the region.

Even the supposed "hiking paths" were mere poorly delineated trails amongst boulders and trees, marked by occasional hoof prints. It was too rugged to ride their bikes. So they walked, pushing their mountain bikes alongside.

Around them were rolling hills dotted by clumps of low trees. Shrubbery, bushes, and scraggly grass covered the rest of the ground. The sun was sinking toward the horizon. They weren't yet in danger of getting caught out in the dark, but they'd have to head back soon.

"Are we there yet?" Dave King smiled down at his ten-year-old daughter. "I'm not as young as I once was!"

Suzy knew he wasn't just joking. He put up a brave front. But it was clear to her that he was tiring. He wasn't a young man anymore.

Truth to tell, she was getting tuckered out as well.

"It's not far," she insisted, determined to get there soon. They were nearly an hour into their back-country hike. But she knew her

Dad wouldn't insist on their turning back even if they did come up against the time limit. He wanted to put her fantasy to bed as much as she did—or make an amazing discovery! Either way, he was backing her up 100%.

He was a great Dad.

"I think it's just over that low hill," she pointed with one hand, holding her bike up with the other.

She tried to sound confident. But she was getting confused. Everything looked different. She thought this was the trail that she and Billy took following the "dinosaur" out to where it was digging in the dirt, but wasn't sure. Her memories of the event were getting fuzzier and fuzzier. And after the little dinosaur pushed them into that box and they reemerged, they were in a completely different place—where the paved roads, Veterans Lake, and even the entire town of Sulphur, Oklahoma had all vanished!

So trying to orient the position of the pit that'd contained the box was proving much more difficult than she'd thought.

And the whole thing seemed more and more fantastical every time she reimagined it.

It could well be just a crazy hallucination.

"Ok, kiddo," David King nodded in determination, sweat streaming down his forehead. "I'm right beside you, Suzy. But if we don't find something soon, we'll have to turn back. Don't worry, though. If we need to return for more exploring—such as next weekend—we'll do it. This is actually fun for me. We should get out like this more often!"

Yep. He wasn't just a great Dad...he was a *super* Dad!

But she shouldn't push his endurance too far.

"There it is!" she laughed, running ahead with her bike bouncing along beside her. "I recognize that clump of trees. It's located right over beside them!"

Breathing hard she put her bike down on its side and scampered forward to see...nothing!

It was just hard packed dirt, with various weeds growing up. It clearly hadn't been disturbed or dug into. The ground was exactly the same as everywhere else.

Well. Ok. Then her wild adventures were just a hallucination from conking her head. Too bad, though—it was so amazing!

"Suzy! Over here!"

She saw her Dad standing looking down at his feet, ten yards away.

"What is it?"

She lifted her bike to stand back up on its wheels, and rolled it over to stand beside her Dad.

Together they looked down into a long, partially collapsed *trench!* It looked twenty feet deep, twenty feet wide, and a hundred feet long.

"Wow," Suzy gasped, astonished. "You found it!"

Yes, it was really there.

"Something was buried in it but recently removed," Dave said, kicking at fresh clods that'd come from the long hole.

"Are we too close, Dad?" Suzy asked, suddenly fearful.

"Ah, yes...the 'Obelisk'," he nodded, backing off. "You better come over here also. I'll break out the Geiger counter."

From a dozen feet distant from the lip, he switched on the box and held it toward the trench. To Suzy the slow pace of the "clicks" seemed just the normal rate of "background" that Suzy had heard earlier.

"Ok..." Dave said, looking down at the readout dial. "That's just normal background radiation. But maybe if I move closer..."

He took a couple steps nearer. The number of clicks *increased.* Then up at the lip of the trench the slow progression of clicks increased *again*, both in rate and in volume!

Or maybe it was just Suzy's overactive imagination. Was she hearing things that weren't there?

"Can I help you folks?"

Suzy whirled around. Walking nonchalantly up to them was a medium-sized, uniformed man. He wore dark green pants, a blue short-sleeved shirt, a flat straw hat, and carried a backpack slung over his shoulder. Out of the backpack stuck a walkie-talkie's long antennae. Holstered at his waist was a handgun. And on his shirt was the gold badge of an official *National Park Service Ranger.*

"Hi, Losa!" Suzy grinned at him. "What are you doing out here?"

It was *Losa Yanash*, a long-time Park Ranger and friend of theirs. He was a full-blood Chickasaw Native American who'd worked as a Ranger in the Chickasaw National Recreation Area for many years. In addition, he and his family attended the same local church as did Dave and Sally.

In fact, he'd led song service that very morning!

"Hi Suzy. Hi Dave. I work here! I saw you guys hiking out here and came over to say 'hey'."

Suzy was embarrassed she'd questioned him, an authoritative adult. It was just that she remembered from her dream that her imagined Dad said Losa had gotten "infected" by the Giant Spider, becoming a zombie!

But he looked completely normal now...

"You hiked all the way out here?" Dave said, lowering his Geiger counter and backing away from the trench.

"Not all the way, guys. My patrol car is parked a short distance from here. It's too rough to get closer. I'm not out here because of you, but to check to see if some work by a contractor's been completed."

"Contract work?"

Losa's wide, sunburned face lit up in a friendly smile. The deep crinkles at the corners of his eyes were endearing. His thick lips were parted in a smile, revealing somewhat broken, uneven teeth. His longish black-grey hair hung proudly straight to each side of his head. He was overweight but not grossly so. He was the very picture of a competent, friendly, huggable park ranger. But his piercing black eyes were narrowed, *questioning*.

"Yep," he casually replied. "There was an old cattle watering trough in that trench there, from way back in the days before the Park was established. It was buried but then partially excavated by natural erosion. It was a hazard to our visitors—particularly horse riders that come through here fairly often—so we eventually got a grant to have it removed and the site restored to its original condition. It looks like the construction tracks are gone, the ground restored to its previous condition. But they haven't yet filled in the pit. That's a problem for them. They won't receive their final payment until they complete their work."

"A watering trough?" Suzy dumbly repeated, "Twenty feet deep and a hundred feet long? Isn't that kind of large?"

"For today, sure," Losa agreed. "But back in the 'olden' days water in the wilderness areas came from collecting rain water. The tank was for storage, in addition to being a watering trough. That's why we needed to get it out of here, since it's so large. A person falling through the covering layer of dirt and weeds could be hurt—even drown if it filled up with rain water."

Yes, that did make sense. Had she heard about it—a story in the local newspaper maybe—and added it into her imagined "amazing adventure"?

"Well, I think we actually have an excess of ionizing radiation here," Dave said, handing the still-clicking Geiger counter over to Losa. "How do we account for that?"

The Park Ranger closely examined the readout dial.

"Yes, it's maybe a bit over background, Dave. But how well is this unit calibrated? It looks rather ancient."

"That's an understatement, Losa. It's vintage WWII equipment. I use it in my high school physics laboratory experiments."

"Why'd you bring it out here?"

"Oh, Suzy here thought there might be 'radioactive monsters' wandering around in the Park. She's writing a science fiction book so I'm helping her do legwork researching it. She's thinking of setting the story in Sulphur, right here in the Park!"

Wow, quick thinking! Suzy was proud of her Dad for coming up with such a good cover story.

Losa nodded thoughtfully. "It sounds fun, Dave. I'm sure it'll be a great book, Suzy. But I still wouldn't trust this old machine of yours. Come to think of it, though, there was a concrete trench holding the steel shell of the tank. I've heard that older concrete sometimes had uranium ore mixed in. If your counts are accurate, that might account for getting a reading that's slightly above background."

What now? Did the original builder of this "watering trough" have concrete and steel? But she put the thought aside for something more urgent.

"We saw something out by Rock Creek—in the woods! It was *big!*" Suzy blurted out, seeing her fantasy adventure receding further and further away from her.

"Huh? An animal, maybe?" Losa said, frowning.

"There was definitely something stomping around out there, Losa," Dave answered. "I don't know if it was the radioactive monster that Suzy imagined, but it sure wasn't a deer. It was brushing against high branches, making them sway."

"Good! You found it! I'll call it in!" Losa excitedly answered, pulling out his walkie-talkie unit.

Suzy was puzzled. Losa knew about it? There really *was* a radioactive monster?

"Call what in?" Dave asked.

"The Arbuckle Wilderness Park reported that several of their exotic animals from their free-roaming safari area escaped out a broken section of the high fence that normally keeps them in. Most were quickly rounded up. But a few are still on the loose."

"You mean like..."

"Three of their big ostriches are still on the run. It's not that many miles from here to there. So we've been keeping an eye out for them since we've not yet got too many visitors this season. The Park is a wide-open place that they'd naturally migrate to and take up residence within."

"Ostriches?" Suzy gulped, her fading memories showing her a long-necked, tall, blurry creature prancing around on three-toed feet. Sure, it was the general size of a grown ostrich—but it was leathery, with sharp teeth, and a long flexible tail!

"Yes. They're full-grown ones, Suzy," Losa smiled at her. "They're powerful so don't try to approach any that you see. They could kick the dickens out of you. But now that we've got at least one of them located, the zoo personnel will come and round them up. You won't luck upon one of them rustling the bushes much longer."

"An ostrich," she laughed weakly. "Well—I guess that's better than having a dinosaur out there scaring people."

"Dinosaur?"

"For her science fiction story she's thinking of having an extinct T-rex or maybe Velociraptor running around in the park. You know, like in the 'Jurassic Park' movies," Dave smiled at Losa.

"Ah! Now *that* would be amazing!" Losa heartily laughed. "I'd love to meet one of those in the flesh."

"Me too!" Dave laughed along with him, taking back the ancient Geiger counter.

"But I guess we're much too late for that," Losa good-naturedly shrugged. "Didn't the Velociraptors die out 65 million years ago?"

"So I hear!" Dave jovially acknowledged. "It was mainly due to a *giant asteroid* slamming into the Earth, right?"

"That's what we tell our Park visitors, Dave. In fact, at the Nature Center we have some actual fossils from the Jurassic dinosaur *Saurophaganax maximus*—found right here in the Park."

"I haven't seen that yet," Dave smiled. "I'm going to have to come by there more often."

"It is a new acquisition," Losa excitedly gestured, holding his hands wide. "We've got one of its large femurs. The animal itself was big, though not as large as a T-rex. It looked similar to a T-rex but was smaller, only three tons, around forty feet long. Plus it lived much earlier than T-rex, 150 million years ago if I recall correctly."

"Isn't that the official Oklahoma state fossil?" Suzy added. "I think I heard about it in my Oklahoma State history class at school."

"You are correct, Suzy. *Saurophagus maximus* fossils were first dug up right here in Oklahoma, back in the 1930's."

"So you're a dinosaur enthusiast, like my son Billy?" her Dad asked the Park Ranger.

"Ah, Dave. My ancestors recognized the extinct reptile-like animals many years ago. In fact, Native Americans ground up fossil bones into a powder. They called it 'ghost creature bone.' It was used as a medicine to treat infections and wounds—very powerful magic!"

"Powerful, indeed," Dave nodded. "Well, we'll be getting on back home now. Thanks for checking on us, Losa. And thanks for the extinct-dinosaur lecture."

"It is my pleasure, Dave. If Suzy needs any other information on the Park for her science fiction book or school assignments, please ask me. We see each other at church each week, so I can readily bring her booklets and such."

"Thank you, Mr. Yanash. I will," Suzy answered. "I hope you catch those ostriches. They scared us!"

"We'll get them, don't you worry."

Suzy waved goodbye to him as she pushed her bike after her Dad's, backtracking the way they'd come.

As they hiked over a low hill and out of sight of the trench excavation, Suzy glanced back over her shoulder.

"Yikes!" she gasped.

For a moment, against the setting sun, she saw the silhouette of a *long-faced, toothy Velociraptor* staring after them—standing on two powerful legs, sporting a whipping, reptilian tail!

But when she blinked, it was only the somewhat chunky Park Ranger standing with his hands on his hips, apparently making sure that they safely departed the isolated wilderness territory.

*Well, that was interesting...*Suzy thought. *My dreams were just that, dreams. I'm where I belong, with my loving family. I'm safe. There are no intelligent "raptor-sapiens" or other, different timelines. I didn't cause the whole human race of another Earth to wink out of existence. I'm not the greatest murderer of all time. Now I can just live my life in peace.*

"You ok, Suzy?" Dave asked. "I'm sorry we didn't find any weird stuff out here."

"It's fine, Dad. It was fun! Thanks for humoring me."

"My pleasure, kiddo, any time!"

But she knew that wasn't true. His heart was in the right place, but he was obsessed by his determination to get his thoroughly discredited cold fusion research to work. He'd soon be lost again out in his ramshackle sheds, buried in his war-surplus machines, reading crumbling paper roll-out charts. He'd keep on fruitlessly searching for excess neutron emission signatures that would always be just "one experiment" out of reach.

Indeed, she felt that same burning compulsion herself—yet was mature enough to *not* dismiss it. On one hand it was a curse that isolated her from the common pleasures of life and family. It caused her to put aside compelling things she'd love to explore, like music. On the other hand, though, that inner compulsion was a *relentless drive* that might someday take her to the stars.

Only time would tell.

It was a long ways to the stars.

Chapter 5

<u>HERMES</u>

Greek god of transitions

Darting across boundaries

Quick, cunning, and divine

The Messenger of the gods

Carrying souls to the afterlife

A protector of all gypsies

A herald of Creativity

But with wicked humor

Tricking those he saves

Thinking they can relax

He wraps them up in snakes...

The Minstrel's Lark, 5:67-70

IMPACT MINUS SIX MONTHS, *APPROACHING HERMES...*

"We've jettisoned the ALS, Susan. We're close but still short of the goal. Got any other brilliant ideas?"

Susan groggily opened her eyes. Kunle hovered over her again. At least this time the Commander's faceplate wasn't fogged up. Susan was "treated" to Kunle's undiluted scowl! Susan had blacked out again due to the high G-forces. How long had she been unconscious?

"Just how...close are we?" she gasped, trying to get oriented.

"We're only a few thousand feet away, but the gap is steadily growing. We've shot our wad, but it wasn't sufficient."

"Christ!" Susan swore. "So close?"

"Take a look for yourself."

Sunlight was streaming in the ports on one side of the crew capsule. Outside, Susan saw the star-sprinkled black void. Since the ajar

ALS outer protective wall had been jettisoned, the crew could now easily see where they were going.

Susan loosened her straps and floated up out of her seat, pushing herself weakly over to the nearest porthole.

She stuck her helmet up to the window to take in the full view.

There, seemingly just out of reach less than a mile away, hung *Hermes*. It was a spectacular sight. Hermes was longer than a football field: a series of linked cylinders, floating weightless in the blackness of outer space. To Susan it was the most magnificent thing she'd ever seen!

"Fantastic," she sighed.

To the left of the view she could see the leading end of Hermes: the *dual nozzles* of its nuclear thermal engine. After that came a *shield* beyond which was attached an encircling, external *strut-array*. The strut tracks supported two robotic arms, one on each side of the vehicle. Securely contained within the overlapping struts were *three large tanks*, one following the other. Above the struts and tanks were fitted rectangular boxes, *storage containers* readily accessible by either robotic arm. The three large tanks contained water, a precious commodity for many purposes, particularly in providing additional radiation shielding from the powerful nuclear reactor.

After the three linear tanks came yet another metallic *shield* that connected directly to the central *Service Node*. A rounded *Observation Deck* with large *circular windows* sat atop the Node. Susan noted four *docking ports*: one on each side, one on the bottom of the Service Node, and one at the top of the Observation Deck. Attached to both sides of the Service Node were two docked, rectangular *Transit Vehicles*. The bottom dock was empty, awaiting the arrival of Susan's Orion capsule. The Orion capsule which had been there had already departed, carrying the returning Mars crew safely back to Earth.

Continuing to the right of the central Service Node, Susan noted the three large, linked *Habitat Modules*. They were puffed-out inflatables. The new Hermes crew would spend most of their time onboard there. Work stations, housing, and bio-regenerative environments (farming) were contained within the "Habs." If Susan and her comrades could just make it to Hermes they'd have everything they needed to survive their projected six month journey. But to thrive inside the Habs they first had to reach them!

"Surely Mission Control can shift its position so that..."

"They used up the accumulated hydrogen and oxygen stores slowing it down enough so that we could catch up," Kunle glumly replied. "And there's not time for Hermes' electrolysis system to generate more hydrogen and oxygen from their remaining stored water. Likewise there's not time to prep and deploy its remaining transit vehicles. We're too far away for its steering jets to make any difference. We might have been able to send a couple of us over in our EMU's, but when we cut away the lower stage we depleted their nitrogen canisters, remember? But even then, there's no way we could transfer all our supplies and equipment in time."

Susan was briefly annoyed. It was as if Kunle was blaming *her* for saving the two of them with the suit jets! But no, the Commander was just stating a fact. Bottom line: they were damn close, but "no cigar."

If only they had more time!

"Remember, King, we *must* get our hydrogen bombs onboard, plus our additional supplies. Hermes' supplies were depleted during its long Mars transit," the Commander added. "We've got to get our *entire remaining stack* to Hermes, not just our warm bodies!"

"Yes, of course."

"And with the projected late arrival date it's doubtful we're going to be able to shove the Asteroid to the side as it is," Kunle coldly stated. "We're dealing with a giant rock zooming down to slam into Earth! At the late date we could now reach it, it's not going to alter its course just because a few humans in their puny spaceship joined it. Maybe a few decades ago in its orbit around the sun a circling gravitational load might have altered its path enough to miss hitting Earth, but not now. We'll have to blow it up with our hydrogen bombs!"

Susan was the astrodynamics expert. Especially since Mission Control was out of communication, she knew it was up to her to figure out the impossible. There *had* to be some way to make it the last mile to Hermes—before it sped on, completely out of reach!

"Can we link into the Hermes controls from here? We could at least try using the steering jets to..."

"We've been trying to get our communication array online while you were snoozing, King," Kunle sighed. "You've got to increase your G-tolerance!"

Huh. She was certified to the regular G-forces. It was superhuman extra G's she couldn't handle!

"Anyway," Kunle continued, "we're running totally silent, dead in the water. Ben says maybe he'll get ship-to-ship communication working in a few hours. But by then it'll be much too late. Like us, Hermes used its last dreg of reserves to slow enough for us to catch up to it from our suboptimal orbit. It's waiting for our supplies, Susan. It's a classic 'catch-22,' where we need them but they first need us!"

"What about our own maneuvering jets? Surely they can...?"

"We used our last reserves to make the inflight course corrections to match Hermes' deflected vector," Kunle interrupted her. "We're tapped out. We intended to replenish our own canisters at Hermes. And Vladimir says it'll take a full day to reroute our remaining air supply into the steering jets."

"Alright then, Commander," Susan grimly nodded, a desperate plan taking form in her mind. "I get the picture. Our conventional options for dealing with this crisis are moot. I think...we have to go EMU again."

"You know full well that we used up the suits' nitrogen canisters."

"Yes, but I spent time in an *Indian village* in my childhood. I helped *wrangle* horses and buffalo!"

Actually, that didn't really happen. She'd long ago concluded it was just a vivid hallucination from being conked on her head falling off her mountain bike, keying off her limited knowledge of the local Chickasaw tribe. But it seemed real enough at the time. And it did leave her with a lasting impression.

"Buffalo?"

"I'll explain as we go, Commander. It's a last resort. But we're desperate, right? We can't waste a second!"

"Ok, then," Kunle agreed, sounding unsure but willing to follow Susan's lead.

Yes, Hermes was out of reach, retreating rapidly. But the plains Indians required buffalo to survive and horses to catch them. Neither the Buffalo nor the horses "wanted" to be used or caught. So the hunters resorted to whatever tactics worked no matter how limited or primitive.

And Susan King could do the same.

Yes, she was a "wrangler" at heart. Ride 'em cowgirl!

"Are you ok, Suzy?"

She stood at the gravesite beside the closed casket, still not believing it. Everything seemed unreal, just another horrible nightmare.

"Sure...yes...I don't know..."

Her brother, Bill King, put a comforting arm around her shoulders. His long, stringy hair hung to his shoulders. His black beard was likewise long and greasy-looking. He had on a faded black shirt and pants. He wasn't dressed properly for a funeral, but he never did pay much attention to his appearance regardless of the occasion.

He actually looked like a bum that'd just walked off the street, not a grieving family member. But Suzy wasn't repelled by his rumpled appearance. He was her brother!

She loved him just as he was: a cleverly befuddled "hippy."

They'd been a strange family: the chubby cook, the mad scientist, the eager assistant, and the "black sheep" student who escaped to college. And now they were just three.

"At least he didn't suffer at the end. It was quick," Bill softly added.

She laid a hand on the polished, curved top of the casket. It was warm to the touch. The grain of the wood was luxuriant. Bright sunlight suffused the rich brown color, becoming part of it—making it a living entity unto itself.

"I'm sorry I wasn't here," she choked, struggling to speak.

"Hey, he was real proud of you," Bill stated in a louder voice. "He was happy you were in graduate school. He knew you couldn't be coming home every weekend."

"Thanks, Billy."

"Sure..."

They'd grown apart after she'd gone away to college. She didn't mean for it to happen. It was as much a natural separation due to different interests and distance as anything else. As kids in grade school they'd been as thick as thieves, at least up until the "incident" in the Park. After that, Susan rarely returned to the Park. Billy didn't either. He sank deeper into his own isolation, preferring to spend his free time out with their Dad puttering in their ramshackle "laboratory."

Actually, he was now an amazing programmer. He was mostly self-taught, having apparently inherited a gift for mathematical concepts from their mother. She claimed to love computers as a kid but rarely touched one now.

So Suzy knew this must be hitting him hard, much harder than he let on.

While he stayed at home, she'd gotten a partial scholarship to The University of Oklahoma (OU), based on her science achievements in high school. She enrolled in their Astrophysics Bachelor of Science program. It was a rigorous science curriculum that included various courses on astronomy, physics, wave optics, electronics, and quantum mechanics. Since it was an hour and a half away from Sulphur she lived on campus in a dormitory while working part-time at a local grocery store. The college effort devoured her time. Her folks were great, helping where they could, but they didn't have the money to pay her way through college. After a couple years, though, she won a paid stipend as an RA (research assistant) in a campus laboratory. But this took even more time than working at a grocery store, though it was much more enjoyable.

So she got by. But her having to work part-time while going to school fulltime—taking a demanding load of tough classes—left her little time for family matters. So she saw Billy and her parents less and less, going home only for holidays and major events.

Then, immediately after earning her Bachelor of Science degree, she was accepted directly into OU's Ph.D. program in Astrophysics. If she thought she was swamped previously with work and school, she was inundated now. In addition to work and classes, she had the option to start her own research program under any one of a dozen possible Professors. There were many incredible directions to pursue in the graduate program which included cosmology, extragalactic astronomy, quantum optics, supersymmetry, nanostructures, and other fascinating areas. It was exhilarating but incredibly time-intensive!

So there were many choices for her to pursue in her own research, but she was still most interested in the so-called "mundane" rocks of the solar system. Those were commonly found in the "asteroid belt" located between Mars and Jupiter. Presumably they were the remnants of an unformed planet. They were loose material from the early circumstellar disc that failed to coalesce sufficiently to become a planet, leaving instead a ring of rocks and pebbles.

Of course she couldn't just do anything she wanted in regards to research. She had to find a Professor with an existing program that paralleled her own interests.

So Susan chose a doctoral dissertation research program studying extrasolar planets forming in young circumstellar disks. It combined her obsession with asteroids with the orbital mechanics and interactions of various primordial materials. Not only did it "hook" her into a "hot" academic field of trying to study planets circling other stars, but also tied into potentially commercial "asteroid mining."

Various authors and scientists had long speculated on the riches awaiting mankind just out of reach in the asteroid belt: mainly water and precious metals, including platinum—all necessary to building space-manufacturing facilities, as well as replacing diminishing resources on Earth. So her growing expertise in that field attracted commercial "suitors" eager to sign her on as a resident scientist once she obtained her Ph.D., or to award her a coveted postdoc position in one of their labs.

Meanwhile, Billy continued living at home. He grew his hair out into the prevailing "hippy" style. And then he stopped shaving. He liked to wear flowery shirts, baggy pants, and sandals. He indeed did look very much like one of those 1960's "hippies." But he didn't take drugs or smoke. He just became his own person.

And instead of going to college for a formal education he took online courses in business and higher mathematics. Far from being contemptuous of his different path, though, Susan was proud of her brother. It took discipline to "self-educate" sufficiently to acquire an advanced degree apart from a formal college structure. Indeed, he was about to achieve an online Bachelor degree. Following that he intended to earn an online "MBA," a Master's Degree in Business.

Staying at home allowed Billy to continue working closely with Susan's Dad in the backyard "laboratory" shacks. Bill—as he wanted others to call him though Suzy had a hard time seeing him as other than her little snotty brother "Billy"—enthusiastically shared their Dad's obsession with discredited cold fusion research using their ancient, surplus WWII equipment. But despite their best efforts they only found tantalizing hints at excess heat, neutrons, or gamma ray generation. However, they found enough rare anomalous results to keep them working late into the night on the "next experiment."

Yep, the "next one" would work!

But it never did.

And via text messages and e-mail, Billy assured Susan that he and their dad were close to making a breakthrough. Susan wished it were so. She wanted only the best for Billy and her father. But her formal physics background insisted that Bill and Dave were on a hopeless quest.

For significant, sustained nuclear fusion to occur, it required a starting temperature of around *14 million degrees—not* room temperature! In essence, Earth-based fusion needed to replicate the *heart of the sun*! Susan was well aware that was what hydrogen bombs were: using *fission* bombs (splitting atoms) to boost the temperature high enough so that the even-greater energy of *fusion* (combining atoms) could be released by forcing hydrogen atoms together to form helium.

So she didn't pay much attention to a phone message from her mother saying that Dad was feeling ill. Dave King had both Susan's mother and Billy to look after him and take him to a doctor or hospital if necessary. But if she'd taken the e-mail more serious and hurried home, she might have gotten there in time to talk to her Dad one last time. As it was, he had a heart attack on the way to the local hospital, couldn't be revived, and died.

Now there was just the closed casket, sitting on its wheeled cart awaiting internment, as the mourners filed away. Susan was struck by the futility. This was the sum total of her Dad's life, his obsessions. They came to *nothing*—just a dead corpse, *dust-to-dust...*

"I'm so sorry for your loss, Suzy," a kind, quavering voice interrupted her thoughts.

It was a man with a leathery, wrinkled old face. Falling to each side of his head was long, snow-white hair. He was holding out a withered hand to her.

She absently took his hand, trying to recall who he was amongst the many mourners.

Ah. It was Losa Yanash! He was now elderly. He was the full-blood Chickasaw Native American Park Ranger who'd helped them that fateful day long ago in the Park. In addition, he was a long-time fellow church member at the local small congregation which her parents attended. How could she possibly forget him, even momentarily? Perhaps it was his appearance. He'd aged considerably in the intervening years. It highlighted the long path she'd traveled away from her small home town. So much had happened in between...

"Thank you," she muttered as he briefly squeezed her hand.

"He was a very fine man," Losa continued, his gravelly voice quavering. "We will miss him greatly. But I know that both you and Billy will carry on his work. He was very proud of the both of you—and I know that you each will do him great honor in your future pursuits."

"Uhm...ok...thanks again," Sally gulped, nonplussed by his unexpected praise.

Then he was gone, merging into the departing crowd.

"So we'll see you at the restaurant?" her mother asked, reaching up from her wheelchair to grab hold onto Susan's hand.

"Oh...sure," Susan nodded.

Her mother was now retired on social security, her "chef" days at the local "home-style cooking" restaurant finished. But she still had lots of friends from her many years working there. Close family and friends, remaining for a couple hours after the funeral and graveside service, were gathering there for a meal. They would renew old acquaintances, reaffirm their mutual connections, and reflect on David King's personal influence upon each of them.

Many of his prior high school students and colleagues attended the public funeral. Several hundred people had gathered at the local church where the funeral was held. But now that the peripheral acquaintances had departed, only a dozen people remained.

So it was in Susan's life.

She was acutely aware that she had many people she could count as "friends," plus a number of folks she could legitimately label as "good" friends, yet only two "true" friends remained: Billy and her Mom. *True* friends were those who would cry upon hearing you'd been killed, for whom your departure would leave a hole in their lives that would never be completely filled. True friends were interested in you not just for that which resonated with their own selfish sensibilities, but because you were a part of them. That was a very rare connection. That was precious. In her whole life she'd had only three true friends—one of whom was now gone.

Susan didn't want to face the others at the restaurant. She realized that she barely knew them. And she was ashamed that she'd grown apart from Billy and her parents. Sure, she could list a number of compelling excuses, all valid and reasonable. But in the end what did those other things matter if she left behind her own family?

"Then we'll see both of you there," Sally King said, letting loose of Susan's hand. "They've got a special lobster buffet laid out for us. It's going to be nice."

With the help of the local minister who'd preached the funeral Suzy's mother heavily rolled away in her wheelchair. She went down the neatly mowed, gentle slope away from the grave.

Sally King was now overtly diabetic, surviving on daily insulin injections. She was grossly overweight. Though she was only five foot six inches tall, she weighed in at over three hundred pounds. She could no longer walk unaided. She had diabetic ulcers on both feet which stubbornly refused to heal. It was clear to all that she was rapidly following David King to the grave.

"You ready to go?" Bill asked, patiently standing at Susan's side.

He looked thin and small, more like the younger kid brother she remembered. His long black hair blew around his head in a warm breeze. His scraggly beard seemed an afterthought, like it was pasted onto his face.

She didn't want to go. But she didn't want to stay. So she just sighed deeply, looking down at the green grass under her shoes.

"We can stay longer if you want," he gently stated.

She looked around one last time.

They were in the Oaklawn Cemetery just outside the small town of Sulphur, Oklahoma. It was peaceful. Gravestones protruded regularly along a neatly mowed, sloping lawn. Here and there, small trees spread their branches. It was early springtime, much like when she and her Dad had gone hunting for the "monsters" in the Park years ago. The sky was blue, seeming to stretch above them forever. A gentle breeze fanned her face, telling her she was just "dust in the wind"—although the wind itself continued onward.

Very "Zen"—very Buddhist...too bad she didn't think much of any formal religion.

Her mind was still a zillion miles away cataloguing newly forming exoplanets circling distant stars. But her feet were planted firmly on the soil of Mother Earth.

"Just one more thing, Billy, and I'll be ready to go," she said, reaching into her shoulder bag and drawing out a slim, leather-bound volume.

"Is that...?"

"Yes, it's that old book we found that day in the Park."

"You've kept it?"

"Kept it and read it."

"Why?"

"I don't know, Billy. No one else I know has ever heard of it. But every now and then—when I'm...discouraged or 'down'—I read it and it gets me out of my funk."

"That's cool. Whatever works for you is fine. I know you're always under pressure, Suzy."

"You seem to be taking this well."

"Nope—not at all. I'm just hanging on by my fingernails."

"So then what's keeping *you* going?" she asked.

"Well..." Bill paused. "I've got Dad's work to continue. The life insurance policies he left will keep me working full time in the lab for at least a couple years. Plus I've got Mom to look after. I've got *duties*, Suzy. I may look like a miserable failure to you—with all your big achievements—but I'm firmly grounded right where I am."

She was impressed. She'd always respected him, but in a casual way. She was discovering that there was more to him than she'd ever suspected. He wasn't just a withdrawn introvert lost in his mathematics texts and computer programs. His head was on straight, maybe even more than she?

Now if Billy could just learn to be more assertive—she thought to herself. She'd been saddened to see how that after high school he became even more withdrawn, letting anyone push him around. It wasn't that he couldn't fight back. He just didn't care enough to make the effort.

"Billy..." she started to respond.

"—and maybe none of Dad's experiments will ever amount to anything," Billy soberly admitted, "but like Mr. Yanash said, I am helping Dad's legacy by continuing his exotic-ceramics electro-physics experiments. In fact, Losa's son—Scott—is interested in my work. He just came home from Caltech with a degree in physics. We're going to start looking at his ideas in our lab. Just like with me, none of the established agencies will fund him. He's kinda crazy, just like Dad. But the sheds of surplus science equipment I inherited from Dad can do more than just cold fusion experiments. They're a real resource for us "crazy" scientists!"

"Well...that's great, Billy," she smiled at him, humoring him. She was disturbed about his continuing obsession trying to do real research with junk facilities and equipment. He was glad he'd found a friend to take her Dad's place. But she knew it was a total waste of his time.

"I *am* going to accomplish great things! And it'll be part of Dad's legacy," he insisted, as if he'd read her mind.

She was somewhat taken aback by his intensity.

"I'm happy for you," she lied. "You have a new friend who shares your passion. I know you work hard it at. Even if it never fully succeeds, your effort is impressive. I've always been proud of you and Dad!" she truthfully admitted.

He shrugged.

"Aw—I suppose it's just a fancy hobby, a waste of time," he now ruefully grinned. "But who knows? Maybe someday an experiment will work and I'll be a billionaire entrepreneur! I've got the business degrees now to take a new invention to the next level, even if the degrees are just from online courses."

"Sure, I believe it," Susan now sincerely encouraged him. "When you're a billionaire you can give me a grant to buy my own giant telescope. I can search for asteroids from our backyard!"

"Yep—happy to do so, Suzy," he laughed, "But what were you going to do with that old book?"

"Oh, right..."

She opened it to a well-worn, ear-marked page.

"I guess I should have done this at the funeral itself with everyone there, but I just...couldn't..."

She paused for a second to regain her composure before resolutely continuing.

Turning to face the coffin she quietly said: "Dad, I'm sorry I wasn't here for your departure from this world. I'm glad Billy was here with you at the end. But I wasn't absent because I didn't respect your work. In fact, I always admired you and Billy for keeping on doing your experiments whether or not anyone ever approved or supported them. That was very brave and noble of the both of you. In fact the scientific world should have awarded you a Nobel Prize, if not for your results then for your heroic efforts. But they didn't and you still deserve the recognition that you never got. For what it's worth, I'm proud of you. I'm proud to be your daughter."

She saw tears trickling from Billy's eyes, running into his scraggly, black beard.

"And right then...in tribute to you, I want to read something from *The Minstrel's Lark*, chapter 6, verses 1-4."

Billy snuffled but stood silently, respectfully, as she began to read in a sing-song, poetic manner:

"BEYOND POLITICS:
Societies are configured to fail
Conglomerations of competing interests
Each seeking their own advantage
With clashing and even opposing agendas
Trying to strike a dynamic balance
It's a miracle that any of them persist
A collective pursuit of security and safety
Cemented by the probability of the 'next time'

When, yes, one's preferred Leader will prevail
And Power will devolve into the hands of the few
Who (obviously) know best for everyone else
Those (undeniably) stupid idiots or fools
And finally have the means to insist
That the "dunces" dance to their tune
Sticking it to them with a grin..."

She sighed, closing the book and putting it back into her shoulder bag.

"That was beautiful, Suzy," he sniffed, wiping his eyes. "What does it mean?"

"Hell if I know, Billy," she replied. "Most of the book's like that. It just says stuff that sounds important, but doesn't get to the point. But for us who fight against the 'status quo'—who keep on doing our little thing despite society giving us little or no support or encouragement—I think that section tells us to just 'keep on keeping on.'"

"Ah. I see. It lets *you* figure out the 'point' instead of the author just assuming he's smarter than us. He's trying to *intrigue* us rather than just lecture us."

"That's right, Billy," she congratulated him. He'd never paid much attention to the "softer" pursuits like literature. He was continuing to surprise her! "It's more of a 'Socratic method'—asking nagging questions rather than insisting on the final answers."

"It's tough to read, though, huh?"

"That's true. It's not 'commercial.' Hardly anyone wants to read poetry, especially weird stuff that doesn't go anywhere. I'm surprised the author ever got this book published in the first place."

"Who *is* the author?"

"Don't know. The author-copyright pages are missing, torn out. So I don't even know when it was published. It could be hundreds of years old."

"I'll bet it's recent. It's probably self-published," he astutely observed. "A lot of people will pay good money to get a few copies of their very own book, whether anyone else ever reads it or not."

"That's likely. I figured the same."

"But it's *good!*" he continued, laying a hand on the coffin as if knowing their Dad would also approve. "It's different from a normal book. Could I borrow it and read some?"

"You wish!" she snorted at him as they both turned away from the gravesite. "Remember when you threw it away in the trash can, out in the Park when we were kids? If I hadn't rescued it, it'd be rotting in a landfill somewhere!"

"Right..." he grinned, wiping away lingering tears from his cheeks as they walked down the grassy slope. "You keep it, Suzy. You need it more than me."

She grinned back at him. "It's short, Billy. I'll scan the pages and send you a *pdf* file—how about that?"

"Deal!" he laughed, taking her arm. "So shall we go face our admiring fans, the *millions* of people out there cheering us on?"

She knew he'd likely run away in terror if he ever had to face "millions" of people. But it was nice to hear him trying to be upbeat.

"Hah. Very funny! Mom's the only one who's behind us."

"Yep, she's our one true supporter. But we gotta go and thank the others also, even if they don't love us quite that much. I can put up with them for an hour, for Dad's sake."

"Yes, Dad would like that," she nodded, glancing back at the receding gravesite, then away. "He was always gracious. I guess that's why everyone liked him so much."

"So true," Billy agreed, looking back as well.

This time Susan didn't look back. It would probably be the last time she'd ever visit the place. Her Dad wasn't there, just his decaying remains. But like the rescued old book, she had a sudden conviction that he still existed...somewhere!

And she had a chilling premonition that she would soon join him.

Chapter 6

AEROBRAKING

That which you cannot see

Invisible to routine usage

Can slow you considerably

Or even doom you to fail

Consumed in raging flames

You scream: "WHY? WHY? WHY?"

Such an unexpected termination

Flying high above restrictions!

Then to hit an unseen brick wall

A bug splattered on a windshield

One moment fluttering along happily

And the next just an ugly smear

Caught on a speeding barrier

An Angel skirting the Earth

Flying just a bit too low...

The Minstrel's Lark, 6:22-26

IMPACT MINUS SIX MONTHS, *DECAYING ORBIT...*

Susan and Torey were back in their EMU suits in record time, floating in the cramped storage module. Once suited up they closed the access hatch above to the Orion capsule, depressurized the compartment completely, and opened the exit port directly into space.

"Hermes is even further away," Commander Kunle grimly observed. Her voice coming from Susan's helmet speakers sounded uncharacteristically *scared*.

But Susan was also shocked by what she saw out the portal. Hermes looked only half as large as it had earlier. It must be more than a mile away by now. Even more ominous, though, was the green-blue globe rushing up beneath them. Hermes was about to plunge into its outer atmosphere, attempting to use Earth's gravity to slingshot up above the planetary plane.

"Steady the bar," Susan directed Kunle.

Together they stood on the outer casing of the storage module, their magnetized boots precariously anchoring them in place. The hinged exit panel was beside them. They both had a firm grasp on the crossbar.

Susan was breathing steadily inside her helmet, trying not to fog up the inner surface. She knew she had to see clearly in order to pin-point her target, with every detail exquisitely clear and sharp.

"Now let's get it off," Susan said.

Removing the thick bar from the door should have been difficult and time consuming. But Vladimir had found the schematics for Susan. With a precision wrench which she removed from her workbelt, it was straightforward to loosen a set of large bolts. It was similar to changing a tire on a car. Susan could do that in her sleep. Her aging Pontiac Fiero back on Earth gave her lots of practice at changing flats, since she tried to make her tires last as long as possible. Fortunately, everything on or in their craft was designed for removal and multi-tasking.

"You've got the coil?" Susan asked as she lifted the long metal bar away from the now freely swinging door.

"The coil inside is loose," Kunle said as she pulled out its almost-invisible end. "I removed the spring withdrawal mechanism. It should flow out with virtually no resistance."

"Thanks, Commander. Hold the bar steady for me, please."

Susan took one end of the slender thread and passed it through the bolt-holes in the thick metal bar. It was tough to do so with her thick space-suited fingers. Susan had to go slow. The entire bar was five feet long. It was meant to ensure that the ratchets of the exit port remained physically locked in place. It was titanium alloy, virtually indestructible. Without the bar, any electronic malfunction might "blow" the ratchets and explosively decompress the storage chamber. But the bar wasn't necessary to the actual functioning of the hinged port.

"So just what are you doing?" Kunle asked Susan.

Susan was methodically passing the end of the slender thread through each of the now-empty, central bolt holes then re-looping it back multiple times.

"This nano-tube thread isn't just the strongest cable ever manufactured, it's also the slickest. If the knot on the bar pulls loose, then this will be for nothing."

"Of course, take your time—but not too much time."

Susan worked methodically, carefully handling the slender thread. Not only was it immensely strong, it was very sharp. Pulling it the wrong way might wrap it around one of her fingers, slicing off a digit!

"This is the strongest knot known to man, Commander. Climbers and hardcore sailors use it. Their lives depend on it. It's called an *8-follow-through*."

"Yes, I know. Where'd you learn it?"

"I don't remember, some prior life maybe."

"Still, we're asking it to do a lot."

"No doubt about that," Susan nodded in her helmet, sweat starting to wet her forehead as she squinted at the tiny thread. "But as the force gets higher it should latch tighter, not pull loose."

She blinked rapidly to keep the sweat drops out. She couldn't wipe her eyes, unreachable as they were inside her helmet. But if she could just maintain her focus a few seconds longer...

"Got it!" she triumphantly said, lifting up the bar with its now-trailing, almost invisible thread.

The tiny line caught some sunlight. It looked like something a spider might spin. That was apt, actually. The original nano-fibers upon which the thread was based were patterned after super-strong spider's silk. What was now attached to the bar, however, was not just a thread but an interwoven complex of carbon nano-*tubes*. The tubes were incredibly small, but individually very strong. They were grown in furnaces by vaporizing carbon particles with a powerful laser. When woven together, a single thread became the equivalent of the massive cables which held up long suspension bridges back on Earth.

At least that was the theory. Nanotube cables had never been used for this purpose in space before, especially for something as extreme as linking together two massive, diverging spaceships! But now the slender thread was going to be put to the test. They'd brought a large spool of it which stretched a total *ten miles* in length. It was intended—if required—to bind parts of the Asteroid together or secure structures to the Asteroid's surface. Now it was their last hope of reaching Hermes.

"I think we're ready to attempt a toss, Commander," Susan said, hefting the long bar in her space-gloved hand like a spear. "Can you secure the spool?"

"Give me a minute."

Kunle climbed back inside with the spool. She wrapped the distal end of the thread—which stuck out the spool's end—several times around a central horizontal beam. The structural support was made of the same nearly indestructible alloy as the door bar. Then Kunle deftly moved the entire spool in and out of the floating thread pile to synch it into a tight knot, taking care not to impede the outflow spigot.

"What knot did you tie?" Susan asked, looking down into the opened hold.

"It's a modified bowline, similar to what you tied at your end. Again, the greater the stress the tighter the knot gets. It's not coming off the support beam unless we use our atomic diamond cutter to snip the line."

"So you know your knots also?"

"I was raised on a farm, King. I'll put my horses against your sailboats any day."

"I guess we'll find out."

The two ends of the nanotube cable were secure. Now it was just a matter of getting the bar to Hermes.

"Commander, could you please give me additional stabilization?"

"This is low-tech insane," Commander Kunle ruefully sighed as she lifted her torso out of the hatch, locked her legs around protruding handles inside, and wrapped her arms around Susan's legs. "You're sure you've done this before?"

"I've *seen* similar done—spears used to bring down galloping bison in churning herds. It was back in the Native American encampment I mentioned before. And I've completed the calculations in my head. Now it's just a simple matter of applying the right thrust along the right vector..."

"—as is any sport," Kunle snorted. "It took me just weeks to understand the mechanics of tennis and *years* to become a top player!"

"I didn't know you played tennis," Susan said, carefully aligning her right arm behind her helmeted head, her upright gloved hand holding the bar.

She was in a javelin or spear-tossing position.

Her space-suited left arm was thrust out before her. Weightless, it wasn't a matter of gravity but reciprocal balance allowing precise control. Her throw had to be perfect.

"In my youth I was good at tennis," Kunle's voice calmly replied inside Susan's helmet. "If we make it back to Earth I'll play you a set. I'll beat your pants off!"

"Not in space, Commander. Now please shut up. I've got to concentrate."

In outer space there was no gravity and no air resistance. Yes, there was still gravity reaching up to them from the Earth and from the Moon, plus a tiny amount of air molecules. But effectively, a thrown object would continue to travel forever in a straight line. If Susan could accomplish a hard toss, releasing at the exact correct instant, theoretically she could hit Hermes. Yes, the two spacecraft were distinct objects with their own rotations and different velocities. It was certainly difficult to hit Hermes from this distance. But even that wouldn't be enough. She had to strike Hermes in the forward-leading struts where pulling the bar back with the super-thread might cause the long bar to catch onto something.

"Bows and arrows and spears," Susan muttered to herself, narrowing her eyes. She focused on the distant, running-away "herd of buffalo." They were lined up for her. It was now or never...

Throwing her right hand forward while whipping her left arm back to her chest, she released her grip and saw the bar sail away into the black void, straight at Hermes.

"Nice throw," Kunle complimented her from below.

Indeed, there wasn't any wobble. The bar was flying like a spear, straight ahead. It dwindled, dwindled, and then became a tiny dot.

Susan held her breath, staring at the little pinpoint glittering amongst the unblinking stars...

—when the smoothly spooling-out thread suddenly coiled in front of her face!

"You hit Hermes. Pull it back!" Kunle yelled.

"Alright, Commander—you keep me steady!"

Susan slowly pulled back on the suddenly slack line, hoping it would catch on something.

It did! Incredible! Susan was elated! But then the thin thread was loose again...

"Damn it!" Susan groaned. "It's pulled loose!"

Indeed, the distant glittering dot was now *retreating* away from Hermes!

"Do we have time for another throw?"

"I doubt it, Torey," Susan grimaced, feeling utterly defeated. "By the time we reel it back in...."

"Wait, what's that?"

A tiny, space-suited figure floated away from the distant Observation Deck of the Central Node on Hermes. It was jetting to the loose bar! Susan could see tiny puffs of white gas pushing it along. And then the figure had the bar in its spacesuited hands and was carrying it back to the struts surrounding the large water tanks. Susan saw the distant figure moving the bar and out of the external struts, securing it in place.

"How is there someone there?" Susan gasped. "I thought the Mars crew already departed for Earth?"

"Apparently someone stayed behind," Kunle crisply observed. "Get back in here King. Let's get the loading panel closed!"

"But we've got to pull ourselves to Hermes!"

"Negative on that!" *Adriana Johansson's* smooth tones urgently sounded in Susan's ear. "The Commander's right. We've got about three minutes until we hit the atmosphere. Seal the door and hope we hang together with Hermes!"

"The nano-cable won't snap in the door's seal," *Vladimir's* deep voice chimed in. "But the tight seal there just add a margin of support to prevent us from pulling loose at our end."

"Copy that..."

They were just yanking the exit panel shut as *tongues of fire* began appearing around the edges of the spacecraft. Earth filled their view. It seemed close enough to reach out and touch!

As air flooded back into the sealed compartment, Susan snapped up her helmet's locks and shakily lifted the entire thing off her head. Kunle did the same. Susan saw that they were both drenched in sweat, their hair hanging in wet, ungainly globs.

"Why the hell did they program the slingshot to graze the atmosphere?" Susan groaned. "If we slow Hermes too much we'll both burn up!"

"You know all our changes cut everything to the razor edge. To build up enough speed we have to dip in close to Earth."

"Oh, right...sorry..."

"We're all on edge, King. None of this was supposed to happen. If the worst happens, though, it's been an honor to serve with you. For a 'newbie' you've performed admirably."

Susan grinned, embarrassed.

"I'm just doing my job. But I have to admit you're not as intimidating as I originally figured. It's been *my* honor to serve with you."

"Yes, I know I'm too intense at times, sorry."

"You've got a heavy load to be mission commander, Torey. I couldn't do it."

"You're made of sterner stuff than you may realize."

"Thanks..."

"Well, we've done all we can do. That was a great idea of yours to use the nano-cable. Hopefully we'll all shortly be on Hermes with room to move, breathe, and work."

"I *could* use a shower," Susan laughed.

"I'd prefer a Perm—though it's not too smart for either of us to be helmetless," Kunle frowned, looping an arm through a handle-support behind her.

"If we're going to burn up zipping through the atmosphere, I guess it won't matter if our heads are in fish bowls or not," Susan shrugged, gingerly rubbing at her salty eyes with the tip of a space-gloved finger while she held tightly to the cross-beam behind her.

"You think the nano-cable will hold?"

"I have no idea," Susan replied, closing her eyes wearily. "We're asking it to do something for which it never was never intended—nor even imagined!"

"We'll know soon enough," Kunle grimly observed.

Outside, the going was getting rough. Susan felt the spaceship being battered, knocked violently back and forth!

"We're deep into the outer atmosphere," Susan gasped as she was jerked around brutally.

"How fast are we traveling?" Torey asked.

"Somewhere around 26,000 mph... If we dip too low into the atmosphere during the slingshot maneuver then we're toast."

"Us and Hermes both," Torey stated.

"I just hope we're not dragging Hermes down."

They clung to their supports and watched the interior wall of the storage compartment turn pink, then *red*. Without its protective panels, the storage module was exposed to forces it wasn't designed to withstand.

Indeed, the fate of the entire planet literally hung by a thread.

Susan was just starting up the stone steps leading to the arched white entrance of Nielsen Hall when her cellphone buzzed.

"Oh, hell," she grimaced.

She considered not answering, but the "ring-through" numbers she had programmed into it were from only family and close friends. So she paused at the bottom of the staircase and pulled it from her shoulder bag, looking at the display.

It was from Billy. He was probably calling to wish her luck.

Inside, in just a few minutes, she was going to face the toughest grilling of her life: her *oral qualifying exams* for her Ph.D. Candidacy! It was a terrifying ordeal that she'd dreaded for two years now, ever since she'd begun the Ph.D. program, and for which she'd extensively studied. She'd already endured two practice sessions: first with fellow graduate students and then with a panel of friendly professors.

This, however, was the real thing—only minutes away.

Her entire future career hung in the balance. A panel of five Professors expert in her field was going to grill her for a full three hours— asking her anything they wanted! Not only was the entire scope of astrophysics fair game, anything else could be brought up. So that meant she had to have a command of all physics, biology, mathematics—anything applicable!

If she passed the grilling she'd be approved to continue on into the Ph.D. program. That meant she could spend most of her time attempting original research under her graduate Professor. If not, she was kicked out of the program, a failure!

She'd crammed into her head all the many courses she'd taken in her life. Her brain was loaded with every science subject imaginable, in addition to hardcore astrophysics. The night before she was tossing and turning, unable to sleep. Her mind was spinning. She felt weak, sick. She wouldn't be surprised if she just collapsed right there at the foot of the stairs and crumbled into dust!

And now Billy was calling her. Well, maybe his encouragement wouldn't hurt.

"Hey, Billy," she spoke into the receiver.

"Suzy! You've got to come here to Sulphur! Come today! You've got to see it!" his voice crackled from the small speaker with an electric excitement.

She frowned, wavering there on the sidewalk in the pleasant sunshine in front of the high brick building. She was on the main campus of Oklahoma University, in the city of Norman, Oklahoma. It was a beautiful day. Since it was early Fall the many high trees surrounding the building were adorned with orange, yellow, and red leaves. The spacious lawns of the campus were still green, not yet given over to the browns of winter. The elegant, bricked buildings of the campus grandly soared up around her. It was a great day to be alive, maybe back riding her mountain bike with Billy in the Park in Sulphur—not facing the *worst ordeal* of her entire life!

"Billy! I'm going into my Orals! I'll have to call you back."

"Oh, that's today? Oops, sorry to bother you, Suzy. But I'm dead serious. The *minute* your test is over, you've got to call me back! Promise?"

"Billy, I..."

"*Promise* me!"

"Ok, ok! Now—wish me luck, won't you?"

"You don't need any luck," he snorted. "You're the smartest girl I ever met. You'll blow them away!"

Her irritation at his "trivial" phone call melted away. That was the exact encouragement she needed. She felt a lift in her steps. Maybe she wouldn't instantly be awarded a Nobel Prize for her performance, but she was as prepared as she could be. Even if her mind went blank, or if she vomited or ran screaming out of the examination room—she'd know that she at least *tried!* Susan knew there was no dishonor in failing when you've tried your best.

"Thanks, Billy. So how's Mom doing?"

"She's about the same, maybe doing a little better. She's flashing me a 'thumbs-up' sign to send to you. We're with you!"

"Alright, then. Gotta go."

"Call me back!"

She silenced her cellphone, slipping it back away in her shoulder bag. Resolutely squaring her shoulders she strode up the staircase to the wooden doors, determined to give it her best shot.

Four hours later she was back in the laboratory of her graduate Professor, celebrating with her and Susan's fellow graduate students and lab techs. They had cookies, a "well-done"-labelled cake, and lemonade. Despite her worst fears she had passed the three hour grilling with flying colors. Though they'd stumped her once or twice she remembered from her preparatory sessions to give the proper answer: "I don't know. But the way I'd go about getting the answer would be..." Looking back it hadn't been all that bad. A lot of it was procedural, how she'd attack various problems if they should crop up while attempting her written research plan.

The examining Professors weren't just looking for factual knowledge, but also how she dealt with difficult questions, her manner, her thinking, and her strategies in approaching cosmic Questions. Yes, they probed her tentative, written plan for her doctoral research. But that plan had been worked out with her advisor, Professor Diana Jeworski. It was a good plan for which Susan had high confidence and the necessary expertise.

It was a novel method of combining x-ray diffraction data with the visible spectra for detecting nascent forming planets within nearby circumstellar disks. No one had ever done it before. There were no guarantees it would work. But Professor Jeworski had dedicated space to make the attempt on the coronagraph at the Subaru 8.2 meter telescope on Mauna Kea. Susan planned to correlate that data with simultaneous observations from the IXO-3 x-ray astronomy satellite.

So it was a solid plan of action with defined resources.

Since the forming planetary discs were intimately associated with the central new star, she and her graduate Professor theorized that she could use developing suns as internal x-ray machines to reveal never-before seen details of forming planets. If it worked she might, along with Dr. Jeworski, be launched to instant fame in the astronomy community. If it failed she'd be out on her ass, lucky to get a high school physics teaching appointment like her Dad! But, also like her Dad, it wouldn't be for failing to set a high personal bar. And now that she'd *passed* her Orals with flying colors—she indeed *did* have the chance to attempt her ambitious experiments!

"Hey, Susan—I hope you're going to take the evening off and get some rest. You look totally frazzled," her Professor grinned at her.

The party was breaking up. Susan did indeed feel drained. The rigid lab instruments around her seemed to be melting, twisting into strange shapes. The adrenalin surge caused by the three hour test was fast departing, leaving her limp. And Diana, though as driven as the rest of them, was a good mentor. She knew from her own experience what Susan had just endured.

Jeworski was one of the "good" Professors. She was spoken highly of by her students, postdocs, and staff. She was genuinely concerned for her people. Maybe it had to do with her being relatively young herself, an "Assistant" Professor newly hired. She put in the long hours just as did her people, teaching classes and doing department duties in the day while toiling away in the lab in the evenings. Susan often said good night to her at midnight as the brown haired sender lady sat toiling away on grants and journal paper drafts at her desk.

"Thanks, Diana. I guess I am wrung out. It'll be real nice to go back to my dorm room and just crash! I didn't get any sleep at all last night."

"Well, good night, then!" the Professor firmly concluded, pushing Susan toward the door, "And again, congratulations! From everything I've heard you did a great job in there."

"Thanks," Susan smiled back as she departed the lab. "I'm happy finally to be able to work full time in the lab."

But that was *not* today...

Oh, yes! Back to her dorm room and *crash!* She wanted to sleep for a *week!* She might not even come in the next day. Well, maybe not arriving at her usual 8:00 AM starting time...

"Oh, hell!" she groaned, grabbing her phone out of her shoulder bag. "I completely forgot!"

Billy wanted her to call him.

It could probably wait until she recovered from her ordeal. He tended to get overexcited about things. But she'd promised!

"Ok...I'll call you up," she sighed, sitting down on the steps to the building.

She dialed him up. But there was no answer. She let it keep on ringing. What was going on? Her Mom was there in the house near the landline. If Billy wasn't there, Sally King should pick up. If neither of them was present, the answering machine should kick in. But it didn't!

And then the ringing stopped entirely. When she tried dialing it back she didn't even get a busy signal. The landline was completely dead! And neither Billy nor her Mom bothered to have and use cellphones.

"Something's not right," she said, walking away from Nielsen Hall into the early evening.

Weak with exhaustion, not thinking straight, Susan knew she needed to be in her dorm room, sleeping. But she also knew that she *wasn't* going to her bed in the dorm. Instead, she went straight to the parking lot and climbed into her vintage Pontiac Fiero. It was a classic that she'd rebuilt from the ground up. It was a fiery-red, sleek, two-seater sports car. It was ancient, from the last year they'd made them, 1988. But completely restored it was a beauty, fine for tooling around the campus and town. Now, though, it was going for a race, as high over the speed limit she dared without being pulled over, down I-35 from Norman to Sulphur. The engine tended to overheat and skip if kept too long at high speeds. Well, that was just too bad...

Now that her "critical-duties" were stabilized, at least for a while—it was time to turn her attention back to her family. Billy had said that Mom was fine. But something else was so urgent he'd completely forgotten it was her "Big Day." Whatever it was he'd called about, he needed her.

"Hang on, Billy," she whispered as she whipped the Fiero out onto the city street, forcing herself to concentrate on the thick traffic all around her. "I'm on my way."

Chapter 7

<u>DEPARTING EARTH</u>

Such a lonely, scary thing
Leaving behind not just Family
Or one's Home, Tribe, or Country
But departing the entire Planet
Jumping upward into blackness
Almost like an ethereal Space Angel
Flapping heavenward on golden wings
Which, sadly, flutter and flounder
Broken, twisted, and stunted
You fight to continue upward
As if you were evilly poisoned
Strength drained by your Enemy
That deadly foe you've fought so long
Laughing as you drift into the Void
Earth dwindling to a little spot
Unable to turn around or go back
Your single, pitiful hope
To just "soldier on"!

The Minstrel's Lark, 7:39-45

IMPACT MINUS SIX MONTHS, *ABOVE THE PLANETARY DISC...*

"Helmets!" Kunle yelled, *slapping* her helmet back on her head and *snapping* closed the faceplate.

Startled as she sat on the floor beside the Commander, Susan did the same—without pausing to think or wonder why it was necessary. It was clearly a desperate, panicked *order*, not a request!

And then Susan saw why...

The taunt, translucent thread extending from the central horizontal beam was *moving* through the red hot wall of the exit panel...

—suddenly *slicing* across it!

The entire compartment *jerked* violently beneath them as the tiny, taunt thread moved like a knife cutting through hot butter!

"Get back!" Kunle shouted, pushing Susan to the side as the plunging line *cut straight through* the Commander's legs! Kunle screamed as she lost hold of the horizontal beam behind her. Then the thread plummeted into the floor beneath them...

—the exit panel *blowing outward* along with everything not secured within the storage compartment, revealing the blackness of space! Simultaneously, the writhing upper body of Kunle was also sucked out.

Susan watched helplessly, clutching desperately at the beam behind her, as Kunle's white-suited body spun away. Trails of flash-frozen red blood droplets spiraled from her leg-stumps like sad confetti.

Her lower feet and legs floated beside Susan.

"Goodbye, Torey," Susan gasped in horror. "I wish I'd known you better."

Then the spinning of the spacecraft on the taunt, super-sharp nano-cable *sheered a hunk* out of the compartment below. Dazed, Susan looked down to see a cloud of cut storage containers flying away, following Kunle.

Then a huge spray of *white "snow"* erupted out around them into space—their big tank of water that was meant to replenish Hermes' stores!

"Oh, Jesus," Susan whispered in disbelief. "We needed all that stuff!"

Again, the whole spacecraft *lurched* violently—and Susan saw through the gap beneath her the *entire lower stage* of the spacecraft, containing their main rocket engine, *break away* and float off into space!

But the line held taunt.

The waves of fire outside were diminishing. The violent jerks were subsiding. They were moving out of Earth's upper atmosphere, flung "slingshot"-fashion upward. Now they were headed into deep space above the solar system's planetary disc. They were still attached to Hermes! They still had a chance to complete the mission...maybe.

Had they lost the hydrogen bombs? Did they lose too many of their critical supplies? Was it even possible to make it to Asteroid PHA-15384 alive?

"King! Are you still there?" the deep voice of Vladimir yelled in her ear.

Susan shook her head sharply inside her helmet, trying to get her wits back together.

"I'm alive. Kunle's gone. We're still attached to Hermes. I'll see if we can get closer."

"Oh, thank God you're there," Ben's softer voice replied. "We thought both of you were dead. But Kunle...?"

"She saved me. She sacrificed herself. But we can't dwell on that. We've still got to get to Hermes or this will all be for nothing. Can you get me hard numbers on how far away we are?"

"You need to get back into the Orion capsule. Your air supply is running low," Ben's anxious voice sounded in her helmet.

She glanced at the readouts projected on the inside of her helmet. She still had forty five minutes of air left in the EMU.

"You'd have to depressurize the entire capsule," she argued. "I'm open to space here. It'd be better if we can dock with Hermes before I come inside. That's safer for you."

"We'll be fine," Ben insisted. "Our pressurized flight suits will keep us safe, Susan. It's too dangerous for you outside the capsule. Come on back in and we'll figure out..."

"No, she's right," Vladimir cut him off. "King, you've got to find a way to get us all the way to Hermes. That's our immediate objective. Everything else is secondary."

"Susan, we're 1,931 meters from Hermes—1.2 miles," Adriana broke in. "That's a precise reading, from our laser distance finder. Are we still attached?"

"I'm checking," Susan said, carefully moving over the ragged edge of the cut-away floor to the intact half of the exit panel.

Hanging on tightly to the panel she looked out, careful to stay out of range of the taunt, translucent thread. It plunged through space straight and true to the distant Hermes. Susan was shocked. Looking "down" she saw dangling cables and jagged edges from where the line had sliced through the storage module while incredible stresses broke off huge chunks.

Hermes wasn't in much better shape. They'd both taken a severe beating yanking on each other during the slingshot maneuver around Earth. One of the two distant Surface Access Vehicles was askew, ripped partially from the side of the Central Node. The struts on the line of storage tanks where the nano-cable attached were pulled outward at an odd angle. Susan saw that the mechanical arm on that side of Hermes was twisted and loose. Even worse, the nuclear thermal rocket at Hermes' end was ajar, dangling at an angle when it should have been perfectly straight. Though they were already traveling incredibly fast, they needed its additional thrust to speed up even more to match the Asteroid's velocity!

"Yes, we're still attached," Susan reported. "But I don't know how to reel Hermes in. The spool at our end isn't connected to its wheel mechanism. Even if it were, the thread is knotted onto the central beam. If I tried to pull on the line with my gloves, I'd just get my hands sliced off. Anyone have any ideas?"

Silence...

They were literally just hanging by a thread. After the awful damage to the Orion stack, the nano-cable might pull loose at any moment. Then the disasters they'd endured would be for nothing. Hermes would move on and they'd be left behind, adrift.

"Wait—something's happening at Hermes!" Susan said, squinting against a sudden glare of sunlight bouncing off the distant ship.

The tiny, spacesuited figure was re-emerging from the top port of the Observation Deck. It was climbing along the struts, headed toward the hanging-ajar nuclear rocket.

"We see him. What's he doing?" Adriana gasped.

"He is going toward the nuclear reactor," Vladimir soberly replied. "He must be trying to fix something."

"What?" Susan gasped, transfixed by the far-off sight of the tiny person pulling him or herself along the twisted outer struts, hand over hand.

"He's not on a tether. He must know this has to be done quickly or we may pull loose," Ben added. "He has no time for established safety procedures. It is very courageous of him."

And then he was there, reattaching dangling hoses before retreating. He lowered himself back into the EVA airlock of the Observation Deck.

"What did he do?" Susan asked, bewildered.

"Well, if the nuclear reactor was still online, he probably just killed himself," Vladimir replied. "Other than that 'minor' detail, he obviously fixed something that was broken."

"Killed himself?"

"That near a cracked containment vessel, he may have exposed himself to a lethal dose of radiation," Ben quietly explained. "That's why the crew quarters are located at the other end of the stack, remember? There's lots of metal and stored water as shielding between the two. But maybe..."

"Wait, something else is happening!" Susan said, transfixed.

Indeed, she saw a few spurts of fire come out of the rocket jets on the end!

Then the spurts abruptly stopped.

"They must have managed to split some oxygen and hydrogen out of water during the slingshot," Adriana excitedly observed. "That was the auxiliary liquid fuel rockets trying to fire through cantered nozzles. But still, there's no way they've got enough fuel to push Hermes over to us..."

"Maybe not," Susan smiled, seeing what was happening and hoping the thread would hold. "But he's gotten Hermes *spinning!*"

Sure enough, Susan saw the distant, long line of lumpy cylinders beginning to *rotate* around its long axis! The nodular Observation Deck on top was dipping away, hidden behind the central Service Node, appeared below, and then rotated back on top again.

And as Hermes continued to rotate, the secured nano-cable was getting wrapped around the titanium-alloy outer struts! The spacesuited figure over there was using the entire vehicle of Hermes as a spool! It was brilliant!

"If we don't pull loose at this end, they'll draw us up alongside them," Ben laughed.

"How long tell we get there?" Susan asked, speaking breathlessly into her helmet's microphone.

"At the rate of spin we're seeing, I'd say less than thirty minutes," Adriana's soft voice answered from Susan's helmet-speaker. "Once we're there, you'd best go directly into their EVA airlock. Your air supply will be almost depleted. Once you're inside you can help whoever's over there get us docked using the undamaged robotic arm. You can put Orion into the empty re-entry vehicle position on the bottom of the Central Node. Then once we're safely inside we can use the arm to start unloading whatever is left of our cargo."

"And we can see to fixing their nuclear thermal engine," Vladimir growled. "It looks severely damaged. That will be my main immediate job..."

"And we're glad to have you here to do it, Yegorov," Ben sincerely broke in. "Maybe we've still got a shot at getting to the Asteroid!"

"—and *you* will assist me," Vladimir concluded. "So be mentally prepared, Priyanka."

"I...d-don't think...I'm best s-suited for..." Ben stammered, obviously startled.

"You are the most expendable of us, Priyanka. It is an executive decision. Do not question my orders."

"Orders?"

"With Kunle gone I am now ranking crew member. I am taking command of this mission. I'm sure that Mission Control—once we've re-established contact—will concur."

This was an international mission. Most of the world had pulled together to make it possible, even though strong divisions and rivalries still existed on Earth. The Russian Federation was not happy that Kunle had been put in command, even though her background wasn't pure USA. But now that Kunle was dead, the Russians would surely insist that Yegorov take command.

Whether that was good or bad, Susan didn't know.

She only knew that she already missed Torey. Kunle was tough and gruff—but Susan knew she always put her people first, even before the success of the mission. She had a good heart. Vladimir was another question entirely. Susan didn't know much about him. He came from Roscosmos, the Russian space agency. She hadn't even met him until just a few weeks ago.

Susan looked around from her perch on the ripped-apart panel to try and spot the Commander's spinning-away body.

But there was nothing to see.

Commander Kunle's body was forever lost in the vastness of space. And unless they could get Hermes repaired and fully functional, they would soon follow her.

As Susan drove rapidly down I-35, weaving in and out of the heavy traffic, her elation at having passed her Ph.D.-qualifying Oral Exam was rapidly fading.

Simultaneously, the sky darkened. The gloom wasn't just due to the late hour, though it was now early evening. Susan realized that she was driving into a storm!

"It figures," she sighed, clutching the wheel tightly as *spatters* of heavy rain fell loudly onto her windshield.

She switched on her wiper blades that "swooshed" back and forth. She flipped on her headlights. She would have turned on the radio to keep her alert, but it'd stopped working ages ago. She still didn't have the money or time to get it replaced, so she usually just enjoyed the quiet driving around Norman in her car.

But now she was barely able to keep her eyes open. She hadn't slept well for weeks. And last night she'd crammed until early morning.

"Better slow down," she muttered, watching the road under her wheels getting wet and slick. Now she was "only" going 75 mph, still above the speed limit of 70 but not as insanely fast as before.

She'd been so involved preparing for her Orals that she'd not checked the weather reports for over a week. She was driving into a squall. The sky in front of her was pitch black. Sheets of yellow lightning flickered in the distance.

By the time she left I-35 at exit 55, driving through the small town of Davis toward Sulphur, the rain was pouring down in sheets. She could barely see the road in front of her. She was now driving considerably *under* the speed limit. That was good as the ancient engine in the Fiero was laboring. It'd been strained by the high speeds she'd been traveling the last hour. She'd be lucky to make it to Sulphur without her car breaking down.

She was totally exhausted, so tired that her hands on the wheel were trembling, wanting nothing more than to get back to her parent's house and collapse upon her comfortable bed in her old room. Her folks had kept it for her so that she could "pop" home from Norman whenever she wanted. It was good to go home, even if infrequently.

Finally rolling into Sulphur, Susan saw that the traffic light at 12th Street was out. A 4-way stop-sign sat in the middle of the intersection, almost obscured by the pouring rain. She carefully inched forward into the intersection, turning south down 12th street, headed toward the Park.

So that's the trouble, she thought to herself. *I should have just checked the weather channel while I was still in Norman. The power's out, probably from a lightning strike hitting a transformer. Or maybe a tree branch fell in the storm, dragging down an electrical power line, maybe taking out the phone lines as well. Nothing to worry about after all!*

She was relieved to have a logical explanation for not being able to get in touch with Bill and her Mom.

And it was good to be home.

She certainly deserved a rest away from the pressures of the University and her graduate laboratory. She just might take a couple days in Sulphur to recover from the brutal psychological and physical trauma of the last few months. Maybe once the storm passed, she could break out her dusty old mountain bike and go for a leisurely, peaceful ride out in the Park and...

"Holy crap!" she yelled, shocked.

Usually she didn't use crude language, thinking it was beneath her. But this time nothing else fit the situation.

Appearing out of the continuing sheets of rain, on her left, was her parent's house—a *smoldering, blackened* ruin!

Several fire engines, police cars, and ambulances were parked close by, their red lights flashing through the pounding rain. Officials in ponchos hurried from one place to another. The side street beside the destroyed house was blocked off by a police barrier.

She slammed on the brakes, grabbed her shoulder bag, jumped out of the Fiero, and ran up to the nearest official.

"*What* happened here?" she yelled at him through icy gusts and continuing sheets of pounding rain.

"Suzy? Is that you?"

"Who else would I be? I was trying to call Billy and only got a busy signal—until the phone cut out on me! So I came down from Norman! What the hell happened here?"

She recognized the man. It was Leroy McGurk, the Chief of Police. She'd known him since she was a young girl. He was a kindly, portly man. Now he stood in the pouring rain in his black uniform, his thin hair slicked across his balding head.

"It was multiple lightning strikes, Suzy," he loudly replied through the pouring rain. "Both the house and the other structures on your lot were burned to the ground and..."

"—in this rain?" she interrupted, holding out her arms as her blouse was plastered onto her skin.

"Yes, it's distressing!" he yelled back through the increasingly thudding rain. "But the neighbors report the same thing—huge rolling thunder with blinding sheets of lightning! Your house and sheds literally *exploded!* There wasn't anything we could do when we arrived but watch what was left burn to the ground, despite the rainstorm!"

"Oh, Christ...Mom and Billy?" she asked, getting thoroughly drenched standing there but not caring.

"They're ok!" he yelled back over "booms" of nearby lightning. "They got out in time! Bill went with your mother to the hospital, just to make sure she's not hurt. She got drenched and chilled in the rainstorm, but that's all. So an ambulance loaded her up. Scott's still here, though. You can talk to him!"

"Scott?" she said, following McGurk as he led her over to a black van that was sitting off to the side of the road. "What's he got to do with this?"

"He was conducting experiments with your brother!" McGurk shouted back at her, banging a fist on the side door of the van. "At first we thought the fire was related to their experiments, but the neighbors confirm it was just an act of God."

"*God* burned down my home?"

McGurk wiped streams of still-pounding rain water from his face before answering.

"You should know that Mother Nature can be completely unpredictable," he shrugged in the pouring rain. "Don't you study stars collapsing then exploding onto their planets, destroying whole worlds? We're proud of what you're doing at OU, Suzy. The odds are long, sure—but any of us can get hit by a falling meteor! Your house was just in the wrong place during this freak hurricane!" he yelled again through another rumble of thunder.

The side of the van slid open and Susan ducked inside, dropping her shoulder bag beside her on a seat.

"Sorry about your house," Officer McGurk said, poking his head inside before withdrawing, hastily slamming shut the door behind her.

Sinking gratefully into one of the seats in the dark rear of the van, Susan grimaced from the icy soaking she'd just endured. She felt a big towel put over her shoulders and gratefully wiped her head and face with it.

"Here, Suzy. Have some hot tea," a kindly, quavering voice urged her.

Bizarrely, a big mug hung in front of her nose. Steam curled lazily up out of its top.

"Don't worry about your house," a younger voice added from the shadows inside the dark van. "Whatever your insurance doesn't cover we'll make up. We'll have it built back better than ever, before you know it."

Slipping the towel around her soaked body, shivering, she gratefully took the cup of tea, holding it tightly in her trembling hands. Then she looked up into the kindly brown eyes of *Losa Yanash*. He sat there in a comfortable-looking brown jacket, his long white hair braided and resting lightly on his shrunken shoulders.

"Sugar?" he smiled at her, holding up a teaspoon heaped with white crystals.

"Why not?" she replied.

He dumped the spoonful into the cup, giving her the spoon to stir with. She gratefully sipped at the hot, sweet tea. It tasted strange, though. With all that sugar should it still be bitter? Maybe it needed yet more sugar? What kind of tea was this, anyway?

"It's a bad night out there. But it's also a momentous evening. We need to talk, our *doctoral-candidate* Susan King. First, though, please accept my congratulations on passing your oral exams today. Well done!"

The polite words came from an athletic-looking young man sitting next to Losa. Now that Susan's eyes adjusted to the dim interior, she recognized his son, *Scott* Yanash. A chauffeur was dimly visible in the front driver's seat.

Susan mainly knew Scott from church, years ago. He was the same age as Billy. If he'd been her age or older she might have had a crush on him as a teenager. But she'd been so busy in school and writing her fanciful science fiction stories, then consumed by the struggles of college and graduate school... Well, she'd said hello to him a couple times since he'd come back from college at Yale with his degree in Physics, collaborating out in the sheds with Billy on their impossible-science hobbies. But that was the extent of their prior interactions.

In recent years she'd forgotten about him. But now he was here. And just *why* was he in a van alongside her destroyed family home?

"You said 'make up the difference.' What did you mean?" she suspiciously asked him. Something wasn't right here...

She took another sip of the hot, bitter tea. Though it tasted strange she gulped it, grateful for its warmth and caffeine. Setting the empty mug to the side she gave her complete attention to the two men.

"We're backing Scott and Bill's work," Losa replied, his voice quavering. "The Chickasaw Nation has considerable resources. Now that there is definitive proof, the Nation is happy to invest fully. We will be Scott and Bill's major backer."

"Proof? Backer?"

"Ah...Bill hasn't talked to you about our recent results?" Scott innocently asked.

"I had a phone call from him today. He wanted to show me something. He said it was urgent. I came as soon as I could."

"Yes, but it was fortunate you didn't arrive sooner," Losa nodded, his voice a dry rattle. "You might have been caught in the conflagration, Suzy. Scott and Bill just made it out before the main explosion destroyed their research huts. Then they just barely got your mother out of the main house before it went up as well. But don't worry. She's fine now."

Somehow, his casual words *enraged* her!

"*Fine?* My mother is dying of *diabetes* if you hadn't noticed! And what with the trauma of her house getting burned down around her and...?"

"—your mother can stay at the *Artesian Nursing Home* until her house is rebuilt," Losa calmly interrupted her. "As you certainly know, that's only a few blocks from here, right next to the Park. We'll pay for any fees not covered by her medical insurance. At the nursing home she can get round-the-clock medical care for her advanced diabetes. If she's able, she can return to the rebuilt house. But she will likely need continued assisted care even there, as Bill is likely to be rather busy, doing a lot of traveling. We'd be happy to pay for in-house medical care for your mother. Bill will have many additional duties now as both CEO and Founder."

Susan shook her head in confusion, her limp, soaked hair flopping over her eyes. *Inverted, withdrawn, computer-geek* Billy was going to be a CEO of a corporation? That didn't make any sense! How could he suddenly, overnight, become a raging extrovert? And yet he did have those online degrees in business management.

She was feeling very woozy and confused.

"Look, guys—I've had a very stressful day and my mind is not clicking along too well at the moment. I'm not following what you're saying. I arrive back here in Sulphur to find the home I was raised in burned to the ground, despite a pouring rainstorm! My most precious physical possessions from my childhood, inside my old room, are incinerated. My mother's in the hospital. Billy's not here. And you're implying it wasn't just a freak lightning strike that caused this destruction. Start from the beginning and tell me *everything!*"

Susan felt a strong, warm hand taking her own. Looking down she saw it was Scott's.

She looked up, directly into his big brown eyes. Though she'd always considered him just a kid, a friend of Billy's, she suddenly realized he was now full-grown and handsome. Versus the stereotypic modern Native American who was commonly depicted as overweight, sunburned, and slow—he was the exact opposite! He exemplified the ideal of the pre-European American Native: *lean and trim* with chiseled features, *strong gaze*, smooth *copper skin*, plus *braided rich black hair* falling past his neck. His *high cheek bones, angular nose,* and *thin lips* made him every bit the image of a noble warrior Indian "brave"—inspiring both confidence and strength!

Wow. He was *dreamy.*

Stick a few feathers in his hair, bows and arrows in a quiver on his back, and a rawhide shield on his arm—and he'd be the spitting image of the life-sized bronze statue standing proudly at the entrance to the Chickasaw Cultural Center just a few miles away.

He sure wasn't a kid anymore!

And his dark, unblinking eyes *drilled* into hers.

As the rain continued pounding on the roof of the van he spoke gently to her, his voice resonant and rich: "We'll put you up in a suite at the Artesian Hotel, Susan. You'll get a good night's sleep. Then tomorrow you, I, and Billy will meet for lunch in the main dining room. I promise you that all your questions will be answered. Believe it or not, Suzy, we have big plans for you!"

"Oh?" she laughed, put-off yet somewhat flattered, "—big plans, you say? For me?"

Her head was spinning. It was hard to concentrate her thoughts.

Wow. She'd just had a big dose of caffeine and now she could barely keep her eyes open? What the hell was going on here?

She tried to concentrate on Scott's incredible claim. She found his words offensive. She had "big plans" of her *own* for herself! She didn't need or want anyone else deciding her future. Scott's words were a massive insult!

Yes, after finishing her Ph.D. she might then be open to considering various future employment options. But that wouldn't be for at least two more years.

Auuuuggghh!—she mentally groaned to herself. *I'm vulnerable! I've used up all my "moxie" today! After the incredible highs of this afternoon I'm sinking so low a mouse could throw me for a loop, let alone a suddenly appeared, gorgeous, young Indian warrior!*

Her mind was floating away into a fluffy white void. This was just too much to take in!

She felt like jumping out of the van in disgust at Scott's arrogance and unwanted advances, but she was too exhausted to even try. Her eyelids weighed a ton. And he was so...hypnotic! His deep brown eyes seemed to peer deep into her very soul.

"Ok, then," she weakly answered, trying to get up and open the van's sliding side door. "I'll go get my Fiero."

"Please don't bother, Suzy," Scott said, gently pulling her back with a strong arm. "We'll have your car driven to the Artesian. It'll be there in the covered parking structure, waiting for you whenever you want it. You'll catch your death of cold trying to go back out into the storm. We'll drive our van straight to the Artesian. You just lean back and rest. Everything's taken care of!"

"Everything will be fine, Suzy," Losa added. "You'll be very comfortable at the Artesian."

She preferred "Susan" but he'd known her since she was a baby. It was ok for him to call her by her little-kid name.

The Artesian was the small town's feature luxury hotel, extensive spa, and premier gambling casino. It was built and owned by the Chickasaw Nation. Along with their other gambling casinos it was one of the main sources of revenue for their fortunes. She'd heard it joked that the casinos were the revenge of the Native Americans upon the invading Europeans—taking not the "white man's" scalps but their wallets!

She'd actually never been to the Artesian. The locals considered it mostly a money-pit for out-of-town high rollers. Also, she'd never had enough cash to risk losing what little she had to "the house" so she had no need to be one of the "scalped" white victims. But she'd heard from others who'd gone there that the hotel was impressive.

And now Losa wanted to put her up there?

Ah well, why the hell not? Where else was she going to go? There was a "Super 8" motel on the outskirts of town, but compared to the Artesian it was just a hole-in-the-wall. She might as well let them spend their casino-derived money on *her!*

"We'll let Bill know you're here and..." the voice trailed off into the distance as she yawned widely, closed her eyes, and slumped back in the seat.

Her last thought before losing consciousness was not to face "the" nightmare again. She hoped that maybe this time she'd be so deeply asleep it couldn't reach her.

But that was asking a lot. She knew that the swarm of *giant asteroid fragments* zooming straight at her was poised and ready. She'd be *crushed* to death again, for the zillionth time!

And there was nothing she could do about it, at least not yet.

Chapter 8

<u>ABOVE THE PLANETARY DISC</u>

It's lonely up above the sun
Out of the solar accretion disc
Beyond the reach of Mercury,
Venus, Earth, and Mars all distant
Jupiter, Saturn, Uranus, and Neptune gone
Pluto dwindled into a dwarf amongst midgets
The asteroid belt just a hazy afterthought
But swarming unheralded in odd, slanted circles
A dispersed sphere of odd objects eternally swirling
Rocks and comets hurtling from all directions
One in particular plunging down from on high
Destined to slam into the third planet
Incinerating its fragile atmosphere
And ending the tyranny of Man
A fist-thump between neighbors
"Making friends" in an unsettling way
Sad alignment of ancient orbits...
The Minstrel's Lark, 8:45-48

IMPACT MINUS SIX MONTHS, *HERMES*...

"I'm jumping over!" Susan breathlessly reported into her helmet's microphone.

She'd been seeing the moment coming closer for a while now, dreading it. But she knew it was her last hope. She was rapidly running out of air in her spacesuit, her breathing becoming more and more labored.

Here goes nothing—she groaned to herself.

Susan gathered her legs under her then leapt out into space toward the floating spacesuited figure from Hermes. The figure was not tethered. Instead, it now wore a "Manned Maneuvering Unit." During the approach—as Hermes slowly spun, steadily reeling-in the Orion stack—the person had climbed back to and into the Observation Deck airlock, emerging in only a few minutes contained within a full MMU.

The *Manned Maneuvering Unit* was a bulky, white spacesuit with armrest controls that extended from a large rectangular backpack in which the person "sat." In essence it was a one-person spacecraft powered by jets from hefty nitrogen canisters. It was the "full-sized" version of the emergency, depleted units inside Susan's more-limber Extravehicular Mobility Unit (EMU).

Susan still couldn't see who was inside the suit. The visor of the white helmet was darkened against the glare of the undiluted sunlight.

"You've one minute to impact," she reported back to her crewmembers as she sailed along between the two craft. "The spin isn't slowing over there. Apparently they've got no fuel left to correct the rotation. Our two linked vehicles are going to collide!"

The Orion crew still didn't have ship-to-ship communication with Hermes. Hermes had experienced substantial damage throughout their stack, particularly to their own communication array. And it had taken longer for the rotating Orion to "reel" in Orion and its sliced-open lower stage than anticipated. Luckily the other person over there realized Susan's desperate situation and came out to rescue her. Susan only had five minutes left of oxygen in her suit. If she didn't make it into Hermes quickly she'd asphyxiate. That would not be pleasant.

"It's pretty out here," she observed mostly to herself. "If we weren't so damaged this would be fun!"

"Concentrate on your destination," Vladimir's deep voice ordered her, hearing her musings. "We need you not to be bouncing away!"

"Copy that," she said, focusing on the approaching spacesuited person. On the side of the large backpack unit was written in large red letters "NASA." On the person's white shoulder was a red, blue,

and white American flag. Red "racing stripes" circled the bulky upper
legs. A thick white glove reached out for Susan...

—as she *slammed* into the other person, despite Vladimir's warning almost bouncing off! But the extended hand had a firm grip on
her workbelt, causing them to do a slow, mutual *twirl* in space.

They were weightlessly dancing!

"Hey, thanks for the assist," Susan said, able to speak suit-to-suit
now that their spacesuits were in physical contact.

"My pleasure, Dr. King," a higher-pitched, *female* voice replied
from Susan's helmet speaker.

Ah, Susan's rescuer was a fellow woman astronaut.

"This is a royal mess, huh?"

"Indeed it is. But please hang on tight. We've got to make a rapid
maneuver or we'll be squashed."

They suddenly shot upward as nozzles in the back of the MMU
fired, spurting out a steady stream of white haze.

Susan, holding tight to the other woman, saw right below her the
slow-motion impact of the two massive space vehicles. The leading
Orion capsule took the blunt of the blow. The already damaged cargo
compartment hit Hermes slightly after the crew compartment. If
they'd been in an atmosphere capable of transmitting sound, Susan
would have heard a horrendous "crash" and "crunch." Instead there
was dead silence—except for an ominous "hissing" now coming from
her helmet's speakers.

"Some of our emergency seals have broken loose!" Ben frantically
reported. "We've got nothing more to patch them with. We're rapidly
losing cabin pressure!"

As Susan clung to the other person's MMU she saw the Orion configuration rebound from Hermes, caught by the nano-cable, then
bounce to the other side of Hermes, just missing Susan and her rescuer as they serenely floated above it.

The impact and rebound bent the outer truss structure of Hermes
even further outward, but the nano-cable remained secured.

Wow—that was a great "thread"! Its designers and manufacturers
should be proud.

Rapidly retreating away below the two spacecraft was the small
blue-white pearl of Earth. Beside it was the much smaller white

sphere of the moon. Susan and her fellow travelers could no longer count on any direct help from their home planet. If they were to survive this disaster they'd have to do it on their own!

Goodbye, precious Earth—she thought to herself. *But don't be too sad. We're not actually leaving you behind. We're still following your orbital path as we leap up high above you, catching the Asteroid on its way down, and eventually arcing back down to rejoin you six months from now. Don't get too scared. We'll be back to save you!*

That is, if the two spacecraft didn't smash each other into pieces in the meanwhile...

But the collision was spent. The two vehicles now bumped alongside each other, stably tethered by the reeled-in nano-cable. Orion and its gutted, attached cargo compartment were dwarfed by the much longer, larger Hermes. Now they just had to get the Orion crew to safety!

"Get into the airlock and to the robotic arm controls," the female voice from the MMU directed Susan. "Meanwhile, I'll locate the external leaks to your crew cabin. I have a patching kit with me."

She indicated a flat package attached to her workbelt.

"That's great, but...?"

"I thought we might have this problem," she continued. "Your capsule looked pretty banged up already even before crashing into Hermes. Only one of the two robotic arms is working. But that should be enough to position the Orion capsule for docking at the bottom port underneath the Service Node. That's our best immediate option for saving your crew. Got it?"

"Copy that... Orion, do you read?"

"Loud and clear, Susan," Adriana answered. "Your suit's boost is letting us hear our kind rescuer. I can help you with the robotic arm's control interface once you're inside. Switch to visual mode and I'll be able to see the layout along with you."

"Will do," Susan replied. The MMU moved closer with brief spurts of its jets to the opened EVA airlock.

Then they were there. Susan grabbed onto the ring and pulled herself inside as the woman in the MMU floated away toward the white oblong Orion capsule.

Susan locked shut the port, repressurized the small chamber, and then opened the inner port.

"I'm inside," she reported as she floated through and into a larger chamber.

She unlocked and removed her helmet, with relief breathing in "fresh" air. She hadn't realized how stifling her suit air had become. But the air inside Hermes wasn't what she'd expected, either. Instead of the canned, faintly ammonia-smelling air she'd heard was inside ISS, this air was *rich*, even musky! It smelled like being in a meadow, or in an active barnyard. It was startling but not unpleasant, as if she wasn't on a sterile spacecraft anymore, but in a heavenly "ark" filled with life.

But she mustn't allow herself to be distracted, rather attend to urgent business.

"Alright, then—so where are the Arm's controls?"

Around her were large, circular observation windows. Through them she saw the undamaged side of the water tanks and cargo holds where the still-intact robotic arm lay folded. She'd done a few simulations on its control mechanisms, as had everyone else, but had no expertise using them. Trying to get the floundering Orion up to the docking ring below was going to be difficult.

For a moment she panicked, not recalling details of her brief robotic arm orientation during her astronaut training.

But then she recalled with relief that Adriana was there by proxy. Johansson was their Orion pilot, well-experienced in controlling robotic arms. The primary arm controller in their crew was supposed to be George, the flight engineer. But he wasn't available. His dead body still hung securely suspended within the remaining husk of the cargo compartment.

"Can you see this, Adriana?" Susan asked.

Susan slapped the helmet back on her head so Adriana could see through its small camera out of the opened faceplate in addition to communicating by the helmet speaker.

"To your right and downward," Adriana urged her.

Yes, there they were: various sliders, push-buttons, and a small joy-stick underneath a protective clear cap. Flipping the cap off, Susan activated the proper sequence of buttons and watched the robotic arm outside start slowly extending itself. It was designed to be mobile, moving along the truss-structure. It was fully fifty feet in length, fifteen inches in diameter, with six degrees of freedom coming from six joints. It was strong and flexible—if controlled properly.

That was the trick. It was extremely delicate and difficult to control.

Susan flipped on three sets of attached cameras, giving her extraordinary views along the length of the arm plus its working end where various clamps were situated.

"We're on our flight suit air reserves, King," Vladimir's deep tones vibrated in her helmet. "Won't last for long..."

"I see that our friend is moving up to the cracks on the outside of the capsule," Susan reported, glancing out of the side windows. "And I've got the Arm up and running. Fortunately it was folded up to my side of the thread spool, so it's free and fully functional. Hang in there...Commander."

It sounded strange to call the Russian that, but she'd better get used to it. Not only was he now in command of Orion, he was in charge of the entire Hermes mission.

It didn't take long until their space-mobile friend located the worst leaks and patched them with special tiles and a tar-like substance. With Adriana's help, Susan got the Arm working, latched it onto Orion, and gently guided the ripped-up stack into place.

Below her, Susan heard a *"clunk"* of solid connection. Then the outer hatch of the airlock to the bottom docking port opened. Shortly the Orion's crew would be safely aboard Hermes.

After detaching the Arm from Orion and guiding it back to its locked, folded position along the outside of the truss-structure closest to the Service Node, Susan finally took her helmet off for good.

They'd made it. They were on Hermes.

And now the truly difficult parts of the mission could begin. They had to fix Hermes' nuclear reactor and rocket, if possible. They had to patch up the damage the slingshot around Earth did to both of their vehicles. They had to get back in touch with Mission Control. And then they had to accelerate the combined vessel faster than any human had ever traveled before. And those achievements depended on their having retained enough supplies for them to stay alive for the next six months.

"And then we finally catch up to and rendezvous with the Asteroid," Susan sighed to herself, "and find out if we can stop the damn thing from crashing into Earth!"

She'd seen it before in her nightmares, many times.

It was an old "acquaintance" out there, just waiting to get reconnected. But it wasn't her friend. It wasn't someone she'd invite to join her Facebook page. Instead, it was an *evil monster*, eager to *devour* her and everyone else!

She shuddered. But then she caught herself, relentlessly *focusing down* on the next immediate task.

She went to the inner hatch and awaited the signal from the other side to open it up and help her friends onboard. This little outpost of humanity, floating up above and away from Earth, was now their home.

And she would defend it to her last, dying breath—against whatever evil monsters lurked outside in the black void!

Susan awoke dazed but completely relaxed. Wow. What was in that cup of tea she drank? Then she sat upright, panicked!

Where the hell am I?

Ah...right...the fire that destroyed her parents' home—sitting in the backseat of the van in the rainstorm...trying to keep her eyes open but failing.

Had they put something in her tea? Did they *drug* her? And if so, *why* on earth would they do such a thing?

She started remembering more.

Had they said something about bringing her to the Artesian Hotel? Yes—and then didn't Scott say to meet him and Billy at lunch?

So, that was the explanation. They couldn't have drugged her. That made no sense. They were just being nice to her. She was totally exhausted after not having enough sleep for many days, coming home to *not* find her welcoming bed...

But this one was also nice!

"Wow—so *soft*," she said, pushing aside lush blankets and swinging her legs slowly out over the edge of the king-sized, hotel bed.

But this was no mere hotel room.

The décor of the bedroom was creamy off-white, with subtle plant-flower patterns painted into the wallpaper. The floor-length drapes were a deep, rich brown. The floors and lower walls were gorgeous, paneled wood. The bed, however, sat upon its own thick carpet, so that her feet hit a warm surface first rather than cool wood.

This was a far cry from her cramped dorm room at the University which she shared with an undergraduate female roommate. And it was a far sight more luxurious than her small childhood room as well!

"Where's the bathroom?" she whispered, peering around intently. First things first!

She was dimly seeing around the room only by a small slant of warm sunlight falling through a crack of the curtains that covered a large window. On a side table was an elegant, crystal lamp. She leaned over and flipped on a switch, bathing the room in white light. Beside the lamp, a phone sat with a red message light flashing. She should listen to it. But she desperately needed the bathroom first! She'd deal with the message later.

She stood up beside the bed.

"What's this?" she said, feeling tentatively at her legs and sides.

She realized that she was clothed in a pair of soft, blue pajamas. She hadn't worn pajamas since she was a kid. In her dorm she usually just collapsed down onto rumpled bed covers fully dressed, exhausted late at night. Here, someone had undressed her—removing her rain-soaked clothes to put her into bedclothes! Outraged at the invasion to her privacy, her mind went back to that funny-tasting tea.

Was I molested?

But she didn't feel any different, other than her full bladder urgently demanding a toilet. She resolutely shoved that perversely alluring vision of the handsome Indian "taking her" out of her head—though fantasy visions of Scott lifting her up in his strong arms kept springing into her head! *Auugggghhh!* She didn't need the baggage of "relationships": unavoidable complications plus heavy mutual responsibilities!

She still had a mountain of work ahead of her to complete her rigorous astrophysics Ph.D. program! She couldn't afford the time that any serious romantic alliances required. Getting an innovative research program to work, acquiring extensive defendable data, writing a massive amount of data up into publishable papers, and getting a dissertation completed then approved would take every bit of her time and concentration over at least the next two years. Since her first year in college she'd already made the conscious decision to postpone romantic entanglements until completing as much as she could of her formal educational goals.

Sure, she was tempted now and then. She was only human. Mother Nature was constantly urging her to find a willing sperm donor to fertilize her eggs—cleverly masquerading that reproductive mandate as "falling in love." But she was determined to delay mating and resultant babies until a time and place of her own choosing, not driven by blind genetics.

Similarly determined to control her own biology, she temporarily put off the urgent need to empty her extended bladder—walking over to the window and sliding the long curtain to the side.

"I'm way up high," she marveled. "I must be on the top floor."

Indeed, the Artesian was an old-style multi-winged, four storied, brick building. It was a simple but also elegant design. And through the top-story window Susan looked out over the whole town of Sulphur, with the Park a green forested canopy extending to her left. The vista was welcoming and warm, with the sun hanging low on the horizon. But Susan felt a chill run through her as if something very scary was lurking out there hidden in the forest!

"Ah, nuts," she shrugged, feeling the Nightmare again trying to grab hold of her mind. That damned exploding Asteroid just wouldn't let her alone!

But...she *didn't* have the nightmare last night! Why not? She felt she'd missed an appointment with an old friend—not a horrible pseudo-memory permanently branded into her psyche!

They did *drug me last night*—she thought to herself, now convinced it was true. *That's the only thing that explains my not having my perpetual nightmare. Whatever those Indians are up to, it's no good. I best be on my guard!*

A loud "knock" sounded on an outer door.

"Miss?" Susan heard an outside voice muffled by an intervening wall. "It is room-keeping services. Would you like us to clean up for you? I have your pressed clothes. After we got you out of them last night we sent them to laundering."

Ah. The maids! Ah, yes. Susan now had a fuzzy memory of nice ladies helping her change when she was groggily out-of-her-mind. They probably thought she was drunk! Maybe she was over-reacting with her "drugging" accusation. But then again, it never hurt to be cautious.

"Just leave them by the door!" she called back. "I just got up. Please come back later! Thank you!"

"As you wish, Miss," the voice came back.

Bathroom—Susan's bladder also called-out to her, now very urgently, even louder than had the maid!

"Alright, alright!" she answered herself, clutching her aching lower belly as she stumbled out of the door of her bedroom into what she expected to be a small, motel bathroom.

Instead, it was another complete room even larger than the bedroom! In the corner stood a five-sided bathtub the size of a small Jacuzzi. A long, marble-topped counter sporting two large sinks filled the other side of the room. A wall-sized mirror behind the sinks made the bathroom look even larger. A separate shower stall sat to the side. The floor was completely composed of marble slabs. The toilet was in a small off-set room to itself. And behind it all, yet another wall-sized window looked out over Sulphur and the Park.

"Christ, the bathroom's a palace!" she laughed, rushing to satisfy her physical needs. They said they were going to put her up in a "suite"—and apparently they weren't joking!

Later—after retrieving her neatly folded clothes from the hallway, taking a long shower, and getting dressed in her professional, freshly cleaned Orals-taking pantsuit—she was ready to face the world. As a protest against the formal attire, though, she rolled up the sleeves on her arms, revealing the little green *Turtle Tattoo* on her left wrist.

"Now you behave yourself!" she laughed, pointing an accusatory finger of her right hand at it.

She should get the damn thing lasered off. But she'd had it since she was a rebellious kid. It was part of her. And it looked back at her with its cheery little green smile, a comforting friend in an unfamiliar place.

A separate "living room" of the suite was just as comfortable and spacious as the other rooms. It adjoined onto a kitchen that sported a full-sized refrigerator, microwave, and oven. She found the suite incredibly calming. The wooden floors gave it a very non-hotel feeling, more like a luxurious condo. Throw-carpets strategically placed made the place downright "homey." The fixtures and furniture were clean, soft, and functional. Even the large, 70-inch flat-screen T.V. on the wall felt comfortable, as if she'd watched its theater-quality projections forever.

She could get used to this!

"Ok...messages," she muttered, hitting the red button on the living room phone extension.

"Hey, Suzy—it's Billy!" a cheerful voice came from the speaker. "Looks like you're not up yet for lunch. That's ok! You just take as long as you need to recover. Scott said you were dead-on-your-feet when he and Losa got you to the hotel last night. Thanks for coming back to Sulphur after your tests were finished yesterday. Sorry everything was such a disaster when you arrived. We had no idea things were going to get so dramatic. Mom's fine. We moved her from the hospital to the nursing home this morning. I'm making a reservation for 7:00 this evening in the main dining hall. I assume you'll be hungry by then! Hah! Seriously, there's snacks if you wish in the 'frig in your room. Anyway, talk to you then!"

The message stopped. She saw that her shoulder bag with her cellphone in it was sitting on a long couch. She could call Billy on it if he carried a cellphone, but he didn't. So she just had to wait until the dinner appointment. But that was somewhat of a relief. She didn't feel like getting back into the "crunch" just yet. By a large, old-fashioned bronze clock on a wall she saw it was already 5:00 pm. Wow, she'd slept all day! Well, she could just relax for a couple more hours, though she was indeed starving.

"So what's these 'snacks' in the 'frig?" she cheerfully asked, going into the kitchen.

Everything...

It was fully stocked with anything she'd ever even thought of snacking on in her dorm room. There were sandwich fixings, various packaged slices of pies and pastries, custards and yogurts, frozen T.V. dinners and pizza, on and on.

I could hole up in this room forever!

Taking a couple cartoons of fancy, exotically branded raspberry yogurt plus a spoon from a drawer she went over to a recliner, leisurely rocked back in it, and picked up a hotel brochure.

As she ate the exquisitely sweet, fruity desert she leafed through the beautifully illustrated booklet.

"Ah...spa services!"

There was everything available here at the hotel that a rich gambler (or spouse thereof) might want to relax with after a "fun" day of losing millions in the attached casino: a large indoor swimming pool with a swim-tunnel out to a sunlit outside pool, invigorating massages, luxury facials and detox services, steam rooms, saunas, soaking tubs, a spacious fitness center, three restaurants, and even live entertainment in the evenings.

Tonight it was the "New Orleans Jazz Quartet" playing in the main ballroom. Super! Susan had always enjoyed the various genres of music though she had little time to even listen to it what with her incredibly demanding academic pursuits. Maybe it was time for...

—what the bloody hell am I doing?

Horrified, she threw the slick brochure onto the floor, dropped the half-eaten carton of fancy yogurt in a trash container, grabbed up her shoulder bag, and strode straight to the door leading out into the hallway.

She slammed the door shut, not looking back. This was part of the Indians' plan, to *seduce* her into abandoning her own path to fit theirs!

Yes, she knew there was no proof. It was just a feeling deep in her bones. So far, Scott and his dad had been nothing but considerate and kind. But she knew something nefarious and *evil* was coming at her!

"You can't have me," she muttered angrily, stalking down the hallway. "You're not buying me off!"

She wasn't going to give in to them. She wasn't going to allow Billy to get seduce by them either. She was going to find out what they were up to and put a stop to it. Then she'd drive straight back to her cramped, smelly dorm in Norman. Maybe she wasn't going to be a rich executive until many years in the future, if ever. But her impoverished student life was the life she'd chosen. She was on a Mission of which she alone knew its true dimensions—and she was *not* going to be diverted!

Now just where was that "main dining hall" anyway? Maybe she shouldn't have tossed away that brochure—but she wasn't going back into that seductive suite!

"Someone will know where it is," she resolutely muttered again to herself as an older, well-to-do-looking couple walked past, looking at her curiously.

She just smiled benignly at them, walking straight to the elevator.

The sooner she was out of the Indians' honey-trap, the better.

Chapter 9

<u>NUCLEAR REACTOR TROUBLE</u>

Once heralded as the scientific salvation of mankind

Devolved into a lingering, radioactive hellhole

Its immense power deemed uncontrollable

Nuclear Power Plants were demonized

When as with any tool, they can be helpful

Providing reliable power for many years

Yes, presenting both Positives and Negatives

As with anything, a mixed bag of tricks

Pull out a Prize and amaze people

Or yank out a snake and antagonize

Keep it under tight constraints and it hisses

Yet with its poison contained and utilized

Neither to hurt nor destroy, but heal

Amazing properties contained therein

Exotic enzymes and compounds

If it doesn't first kill you...

Take us away, hot destiny!

The Minstrel's Lark, 9:28-32

IMPACT MINUS 5.9 MONTHS, *PRE-BURN...*

Being inside Hermes was like being in the stomach of a living creature.

"Bunk with me, King?" Ben cheerfully smiled at her.

Yep, he was one of the "tapeworms" lurking in the Creature's guts—looking to suck the life out of her!

No, not really. Ben was a good friend, just amusingly vulgar at times.

"Find your own bunk," she laughed back, floating in the middle of the Hab.

She was arranging her "hammock"—a loose net that extended from one extended hook on the side of the Hab to another. A large, flat mat of woven vines was folded to the side. It was rooted and alive, ready to be pulled out around her hammock to give her a degree of privacy.

"Mind if I cuddle up close beside you?" he grinned.

"As long as you're outside my nook you can get as close as you want," she shrugged, no longer so amused by him.

Around them, a lush jungle of twisted vines hung. Branches, leaves, and clusters of fruit floated thick and rich in the zero gravity. Susan and Ben were in the third and last "TransHab" Module of Hermes. It was the main combined "farming" module plus sleeping quarters plus exercise module. During the "tumbling pigeon" maneuver for providing artificial gravity, which they'd hopefully initiate soon, that module—there at the end of the centripetal-force arm—would have the highest "gravity" of half a "G."

"Hungry?" Ben asked, plucking a large red berry from a cluster and holding it out to her.

A complex reprocessing and recycling system returned their feces as nutritive soil for the extensive network of genetically engineered vines. The crew's urine was completely recycled as farming or drinking water. From the vines came a variety of edibles: potato-like tubers, bananas, and various fruits. The sunlight-lamps bathing the plants were abundantly powered by electricity generated by the large nuclear reactor located at the other end of the spaceship. The farming component of Hermes was a largely self-sufficient system capable of maintaining a crew of six in space for up to a year at a time.

"Thanks, Ben," Susan smiled, taking the big red berry from him and popping it into her mouth. It was sweet and juicy. "But we'd best not be snacking unscheduled. Remember we lost half of our rations in the wreckage."

She was being cautious, but was still elated. It was good to be out of the cramped Orion capsule into the much roomier Hermes modules. She particularly appreciated the three linked "Habs." They were large cargo containers originally launched on SLS missions that were then inflated to four times their original volume. Hardened foam filled the outer, originally flexible skin, making them rigid. External portholes and three stories of usable space within each Hab made them relatively roomy.

"Hey, loosen up Susan. We made it here. We're alive. We've got a shot at getting to the Asteroid. We deserve a treat!"

"Yes, I suppose you're right."

"Enough chit-chat! Six hours of sleep! That's an order!" Commander Yegorov barked as he drifted down from the higher, working module. "We must be fresh to tackle the reactor tomorrow. That will be a big job!"

"Yes, Sir!" Ben replied, now dead serious. "I will do my duty."

"Of course you will, Priyanka," Vladimir answered, starting to set up his own hammock. "Dr. Yamamoto kindly volunteered to keep watch. She will awaken us if there's a need."

It was a pleasant surprise to Susan to find out who remained behind of the Hermes Mars crew. Dr. Kame Yamamoto held duel Ph.D.'s in the seemingly disparate fields of engineering and microbiology. She was both the main horticulturalist taking care of the thriving "jungle" and Hermes' chief flight engineer. Having been informed by Mission Control that George Wilson was killed during the launch mishap, she'd at the last minute decided against joining the returning Mars crew as it evacuated back to Earth. She stayed behind to replace George and provide continuity in operating the complex space vehicle, particularly the delicate farming system. And then she'd saved them all, helping the Orion-stack make it to Hermes.

Now, Yamamoto was continuing to help them. Susan knew full well the extent of the sacrifice Kame was making. Not only was she prolonging a long absence from her relatives back on Earth, but the cumulative effects of radiation exposure and low or zero-G travel were ravaging her body. Returned to Earth she'd now be a semi-invalid: fragile, weak, and barely able to move in a full one-G gravitational pull. But on Hermes in zero-G she was still quite vigorous.

It was a true blessing to have her there.

Susan tried not to think of poor George. His flight-suited and helmeted body was still tied up, frozen solid, in the open-to-space broken cargo module now securely docked beneath the central Service Node. Hopefully in six months they'd return his body to Earth for a proper burial. As it was, his frozen presence served as a constant reminder of the deadly peril they faced.

"I will talk more to you both in six hours," Vladimir stated, closing his eyes as he settled into his hammock. He didn't bother pulling one of the living mats around his nook. Susan preferred having privacy, so dragged a thick mat around her body.

"Don't let the bed bugs bite!" Ben softly called from the side of her, beyond her concealing mat.

"Shut up Ben," Susan snorted, closing her eyes. She was exhausted. But Ben's flippant tone wasn't just a joke. The flowering, genetically engineered vines still needed insects for pollination and cleaning. *Big black beetles* crept through the undergrowth just inches away from Susan's face. Fortunately, they were codependent on the vines and rarely left the woody surface. But it was disconcerting to have them as roommates!

So...two guys and three gals on a spaceship loaded with bugs hurtling up above the sun—fun stuff!

But Susan knew that wasn't true either. They might joke around to relieve the tension, but at their core she and her fellow astronauts were consummate professionals. She didn't know Yamamoto's family situation. Vladimir, though, had a wife and kids back in Russia. Adriana was single, like Susan, but with married sisters and brothers. Lots of relatives were worried about the astronaut pilot back on Earth. Ben was single and flirted playfully, but was not a womanizer. He was as focused and driven as Susan. There'd be little or no "hanky-panky" on this mission. Their goal was much too serious: saving humanity from immediate extinction.

But then again, they *were* only human, susceptible to all human compulsions. In six months relationships that went beyond duty might develop. Who knew? But their immediate problem was not jostling romantic alignments. It was fixing the Nuclear Thermal Rocket. That was critical if they were going to complete their mission. But Susan was still worried about the long-term problem, something even more volatile and dangerous than thermonuclear reactor: the *unpredictable* and *selfish* nature of the human animal.

Now that was a disturbing thought!

Why was she fixating on playful human emotions? Maybe it was exhaustion scrambling her thoughts—or just the low-level turmoil of a human mind entering the fantasy stage of dreaming.

Whatever! She had to shut off or suppress all those turbulent thoughts. She needed to be as rested as possible for what awaited them the next day.

If they couldn't get the NTR fixed, they wouldn't make it to the Asteroid. In fact, they'd never return to Earth. They'd be lost in space, forever!

Susan sighed deeply to herself, enjoying floating weightlessly as she drifted off to sleep.

Let tomorrow take care of itself—she sighed to herself, para-phrasing a verse in the Bible. *For now be grateful and rest.*

Scott showed up exactly at 7:00 pm. Billy, as usual, was late.

"How was your room?" Scott Yanash said as he slid into the booth opposite to her.

A wide smile graced his bronzed, strong face. Susan felt suddenly defenseless, at his mercy. He was just so dreamily handsome!

Off at a short distance the soothing sounds of the live band *The New Orleans Jazz Quartet* were wafting into the main dining hall. Susan had been sitting in her booth for a full hour sipping at a big mug of hot chocolate, thinking. It wasn't wasted time. It was a nice reprieve. It was the first time in months, maybe years, that she had a chance to consider her life without being "under the gun" from im-mediate work assignments, ongoing research experiments, and a mountain of material to study for her Orals. Sitting there alone in the peaceful high-end restaurant she'd come to a firm decision: she was *headed for the stars!*

In the dazzling fountain of Human Creativity—so wonderfully il-lustrated by the intricate harmonies from the traditional jazz quar-tet—she was determined to rise beyond the narrow constraints of Earth!

This was more than just finding a suitable astrophysical job if she ever managed to graduate from the University with an earned Ph.D.

This was a Quest!

At her first opportunity she was going to apply to NASA to be an astronaut.

"It was fine, thanks Scott," she politely replied. "And please thank your Dad for putting me up here after my parent's house burned down last night."

She put her arms up on the lacquered wooden tabletop, folding her fingers together. She meant to portray a professional, business-like demeanor. Instead, her Turtle Tattoo grinned from her wrist. She'd forgotten to roll her sleeves down to cover it.

"Cute little fellow," Scott remarked, looking at her wrist.

"I got it when I was a kid."

The sweet combined harmony of flute, mellow trumpet, "clang-ing" banjo, and thumping upright bass made her want to get up and dance. Even more, she felt a burning urge to go and grab a micro-phone and start singing the lead part of the tune they were presently playing. Wow, her head was totally screwed up! Despite her revela-tion of where she wanted her life to go, she was falling back into her childhood fantasies of being a *rock star*. Hah! That would have been a total waste of her life. And trying to sing now with the jazz quartet would be a total disaster!

She felt a pang of regret having again to push music out of her top priorities, but resolutely centered her thoughts back on her yet unfin-ished academic career. Passing her Orals though a big achievement to be proud of was merely one further step of a long journey.

NASA wasn't going to accept her as a graduate school dropout. Competition for the few open slots in astronaut training was fierce. To even be considered, she knew she must first complete her Ph.D.

So the laboratory beckoned to her. She realized she *was* wasting her time sitting in the luxurious dining room. She needed to get back immediately to OU. Her top priority now that she knew her relatives were safe should be to hop in her faithful Fiero and drive straight back to her cramped dorm room.

But she forced herself to sit still, staring with a sober, unblinking expression at the handsome young man. He was dressed in an expensive-looking velvety blue turtleneck sweater. His long black hair was held back by a golden clip in a ponytail that hung at the back of his head.

And his deep brown eyes *glittered* with an alluring depth.

Was he trying to *hypnotize* her into abandon her lifegoals, just to use her as a corporate "suit"? Well, if so, it wouldn't work!

"I'm sure your brother will be along shortly," he half-smiled at her. "He was on a conference call with additional potential investors. The Chickasaw Nation is all-in, but we can only bring millions to the venture. We're going to need hundreds of millions. So what Bill is doing is absolutely critical. But the conference call was running longer than anticipated. There's considerable excitement about our present achievements, which he'll tell you more about once he arrives. But we can go ahead and order now, if you'd like?"

She had many questions but deliberately didn't interrupt him. She didn't want to seem eager or even interested in their venture. Though she appreciated their efforts to help Billy and her Mom, plus their accommodation of her the past night, she was going to turn them down flat. Any delving into the details of his proposal was just a waste of her time.

But she was starving! She hadn't had anything to eat since yesterday afternoon except for that half cup of expensive yogurt. But she didn't want to give the impression that she was in any way compliant.

"I prefer to wait for Billy."

The high, rich fabric of the booth was at her back. The dark wood of the table was shining under her arms. Round marbled pillars rose around her. Suspended yellow-red lights glowed, giving the dining room with its high ceilings a sense of both isolation and expansiveness.

It was intimidating. It was dominating. It was frightening! Starving or not, she had to *get out* of there!

"Sure, that's fine," he immediately replied, sounding somewhat miffed. His eyes briefly narrowed, almost too fast for her to notice. In that instant they had a *predatory* gleam that shocked her!

Yes, she knew she was being entirely irrational. She should just wait and listen to whatever they were proposing before making any final judgment. But the whole situation was putting her off. At best it was a diversion from her public and private life-objectives. At its worse it was a cop-out, an excuse to not give her best effort at achieving her toughest goals. It would be easy to fall into their crazy scheme, whatever it was—to "sell out" rather than continue on through the grueling Ph.D. program and possible rigorous NASA training. But she was determined not to be "bought off" by whatever they were offering!

She started to stand up to leave...

"Look, Susan, I..." he sighed, waving her back down in her seat. It seemed he was about to apologize.

"Hey, guys! Sorry I'm late!"

Bill slid into the booth next to Scott, facing Susan. She was shocked. She hardly recognized him. He wore a neatly pressed *suit* complete with a corporate, blue tie. Plus his black hair was cut short, carefully combed. Even more disturbing, he was *clean shaven*.

She barely recognized her brother. They'd co-opted him!

This was not at all the disdainfully independent "hippy" brother, mad-scientist she was used to and loved.

"Hey, Bill," Scott greeted him, playfully thumping him on the shoulder with a balled-up fist.

Susan noticed that Bill winced but nodded agreeably. "Hi Scott, you been talking with Suzy?"

"Billy...what the hell?" she frowned, reaching over an arm to touch the fabric of his expensive suit.

"Hey, I'm finally putting my business classes to good use, Suzy. Dad's research produced a major breakthrough and I'm going to do everything necessary to make sure it pays off for us, even if that means presenting a more appropriate image."

She shook her head in disbelief.

"Dad's *cold fusion* research? You got it to work? Really?" she grimaced, not believing him.

This was even crazier than she'd expected. Cold fusion was a fantasy. The feeble "results" gotten to-date by the scientific world were mostly explainable by methodological errors. True fusion power required huge temperatures. It simply could not be accomplished at room temperature!

She was more certain than ever that someone was pulling a huge scam on someone...but not her!

"Take a look for yourself!" he grinned.

He slid a laptop-sized metallic rectangle onto the table in front of Suzy. She hesitantly picked it up. It was cool to the touch but was *vibrating!* At each of its ends a thick copper electrode protruded. And on an inset computer screen a 3D graph showed a *molten-lava wave* flowing repeatedly against a solid-black shore.

"What the hell is this, Billy?" she frowned.

"Hi, my name is Akocha," a big-boned man in a white uniform smiled down at them. "I'll be your waiter tonight. Can I bring you drinks?"

Susan pointedly took a sip of her now-cooled hot cocoa. She shook her head in the negative.

"I'll take a rum and coke, please," Scott politely nodded.

"Just water for me," Bill answered.

"What is this thing?" Susan repeated as the waiter walked away.

Bill leaned forward across the table and spoke softly. "We've not gone public yet, Suzy. But the tragic events of last night proved it works. It's Dad's matrix plus novel modifications from Scott. It's our prototype, which will change the world! We're going to..."

Bill stopped short as the polite waiter returned.

"A rum and coke for the gentleman...plus water for the other gentleman—and would you like to order now? Or would you like me to bring some horderves first?"

"What's your special tonight?" Scott asked.

"The filet mignon is especially good. It is served wrapped in bacon, with butter-fried mushrooms and almond rice. Also, the spinach is..."

Susan laughed sharply, cutting off the waiter. She disdainfully pushed the laptop-sized device back to Billy. Then she slid over and out of the booth, wobbly standing erect.

Geez...I'm weaker than I thought. I should have eaten something substantial from that free frig in my room!

She knew a good scam when she saw one, physical "evidence" or not. No spiffy graphics video was going to seduce her into giving it more than a glance. Sure...secret modifications making "cold fusion" work, all in a vibrating modified laptop! And if you believed that, then Susan would be happy to sell you a bridge in Brooklyn...

But she didn't want to needlessly discourage Billy. She'd never seen him so excited or motivated. Let him have his fun with Scott, thinking they'd made some huge scientific breakthrough. She knew enough *real* science to be certain his little "invention" would come crashing down around him. No legitimate investor would ever want anything to do with it.

Without a word she strode resolutely and swiftly away, headed for the closest exit.

"Suzy! Where are you going?" Bill asked as he rushed to catch up to her, placing a hand on her shoulder.

She turned around and *slapped* him hard on his freshly clean-shaven cheek!

"What did you do that for?" he asked, shocked.

Alright, he wanted a confrontation. Then he was going to get a confrontation!

"That damned 'research' took our Dad away from us for most of our childhood years—and now *you're* off on a hair-brained scheme to commercialize it? It's always been and always will be just a colossal *waste of time*, Billy! I don't care what you think happened during the lightning storm last night, but usable power from sustained cold nuclear fusion *isn't possible!* I don't have to hold a finalized astrophysical Ph.D. to know that! As long as it was just a hobby that you and Dad had fun with puttering around in the sheds, I could overlook it. But if you're trying to rope-in investors for your impossible goose chase, you've gone too far. I want nothing to do with it!"

"That's not true. Scott and I..."

"Scott's too slick to be anything but a con-man, Billy," she interrupted him. "If the Indians are so sure it 'works' then why do they need additional investors? They're rich enough raking-in the white man's casino losses! I'll be they could come up with a hundred million bucks if they really wanted to do so. Whatever you're into with Scott can't be any good!"

"You've got me all wrong," Scott said as he calmly walked up, sipping amber liquid from a crystal goblet. Ice cubes "clanked" against the sides, sloshing a green slice of lime back and forth.

He slid an arm around the shoulders of Bill as if to reassure him. To Susan it was a controlling gesture, making sure that her brother was suitably contained.

"I thought you Indians couldn't drink alcohol?" she sneered at him.

"I take my pleasures seriously—but never to excess. I'm proud of my heritage and am certainly no stereotype. Please just hear us out. I know you're a rightfully skeptical scientist and respect your achievements. Give us a chance!"

"Suzy, what's got into you?" Bill asked, sounding aghast at her behavior. "Scott's our friend. He's been nothing but helpful!"

"She's just stressed out," the copper-skinned young man answered for her. "I'd be too after surviving Ph.D. Qualifying Exams only to rush home and find my familial home burned to the ground. She's just not thinking straight. Isn't that right, Susan? Maybe if we went back to your room where it's more private we could order-in and then..."

She grabbed the goblet out of his hand and flung its contents into his face!

"You're not getting me that easy!" she hissed in his ear.

Gasping, he took a step backward. The waiter rushed over, a heavy-set security guard right behind him. Scott accepted a napkin before waving both of the men away. He delicately dabbed at the fluid dripping from his face and hair.

"I'm sorry," he shrugged nonchalantly, grinning slyly. "I didn't mean anything untoward by my invitation to..."

"You *stay away* from me!" she snarled again at him, turning and striding for the exit.

But a restraining hand held her back.

Spinning, she looked straight into Bill's worried eyes.

"Please, Suzy. Don't go. Let me at least have a chance to prove to you that I'm not on a wild goose chase. I know that fantastic claims require extra-powerful proof. I promise you that you'll be impressed. We just finished setting up a demonstration chamber at the Chickasaw Cultural Center. Let's go there and we'll show you what we have. After that—if you wish—you can head straight back to the University.

But I don't think you'll want to go after you see what this little box here can do!"

She looked uncertainly down. In his other hand he held the laptop-sized rectangle. She noticed that the two innocent-looking electrodes, one at each end, were *glowing!*

If this was a trick, it was exquisitely crafted.

"What's it going to do?" she suspiciously asked.

Around her, curious diners were looking at them.

"Not here," Bill said, keeping his voice low and taking her by her arm. He led her toward the wide exit doorway. "We're not ready to make it public."

"You mean, no public spectacles allowed?" she giddily laughed. She already regretted her outbursts. But she'd said what she had to say. To hell with the consequences!

"A bit late for that," Scott sighed from behind them.

"Alright—but you're driving with me in my Fiero," she insisted to Bill, not wanting him in Scott's clutches.

"I wouldn't have it any other way, Suzy," he gently answered, cradling his "laptop."

"And it better be something amazing."

"Oh, it is! It's a *miracle.*"

In her irrational rage, Suzy had forgotten she was starving. Now her empty stomach hit her hard. She stumbled from weakness but steeled her resolve.

Ok, so she was going to miss a nice steak dinner. But maybe she was at last going to put a stop to Billy's nonsense. Since Dad was gone, it was time that he got serious. Instead of throwing away his small inheritance paying for more pointless amateur experiments, maybe he could use it to earn a solid degree at a real college.

In fact, it might be a good thing that Dad's ancient crumbling equipment and "research" sheds were burned to the ground. Now Billy wouldn't have an excuse to waste his life. That is, unless Scott's new "wrinkle" wasn't put to rest as the blatant scam it likely was!

Sustained "cold fusion" was not possible.

"Ok, then. Let's go see your 'miracle'!" she exclaimed, heading resolutely toward an exit sign that read "parking garage."

It was time to leave behind alluring fantasies and face the realities of the Universe. Billy's *Obsession* and her own *Nightmare* were both of the same kin: distractions from their real goals. And by debunking her Dad's experiments once and for all she was finally going to put to rest her own demons.

At least that was her angry, improvised plan. She refused to be an enabler. It was time for "tough love."

"Where there are prophecies, they shall fail!" she angrily quoted as they walked down a steep stairwell. Perhaps she could reach Billy through their shared religious upbringing. *"Where there are languages, they shall stop. Where there is knowledge, it shall vanish away. Only Love endures."*

"First Corinthians, chapter thirteen?" Bill asked, seemingly bemused. "I thought you didn't believe in that stuff anymore, Suzy?"

"Just because I don't waste my time going to church anymore to hear boring sermons doesn't mean I don't recognize wisdom in the Bible. You should do the same, Billy: learn to set your priorities properly!"

"Ah..." Scott spoke softly from behind them both. "I also gave up going to Church. But I still remember the key elements of Christianity, particularly that lovely verse!"

She defiantly and loudly continued quoting the passage: *"But when the Perfect is come, the partial will be done away! When I was a child, I spoke as a child, thought as a child, and reasoned as a child. But when I became a man I did away with those childish things!"*

"That is so true, Susan," the handsome young Native American agreed. "But you should take a lesson from your own words."

"Don't try to turn my words back on me!" she snapped at him.

"Ah, but do you remember the *rest* of that quote from I Corinthians 13:10-12?"

"What's the rest of it?" Bill asked. "I forget..."

"For now we see in a mirror, dimly," Scott softly continued. His rich, sincere tones were more disturbing to Suzy than any unctuous preacher she'd ever heard, *"but then, face to face, we will see sharply! Now I know in part. But then I will know fully—just as also I have become fully known to you!"*

A shiver went down her spine.

She wasn't sure she wanted to know the "truth." She didn't want to be drawn deeper into what was seducing Billy. But it was too late to turn back. Whatever poison Scott was trying to feed her, she would just throw it back in his face!

That is, unless it was so powerful that it stopped *her* dead in her tracks?

She laughed to herself, shaking her head ruefully. He was handsome, she'd give him that. But he wasn't near as smart as he apparently thought he was.

Their little "demonstration" would fail.

Chapter 10

RADIATION POISONING

Too fast and your cells dissolve

Subtly-slow your cells turn to cancer

It can't be avoided, only lessened

Even if you live underground

Ionizing radiation fracturing DNA

The stuff of life being punctured

Yet also fueling evolution

Without a constant error-rate

New genes, structures, pathways absent

A few fortuitous errors helping us adapt

Across eons and countless replications

Changing-environments accommodated

Finding new capacities, ways to fit in

Where the human race develops

Only if individual humans die

Indebted to cosmic gamma rays!

The Minstrel's Lark, 10:57-61

IMPACT MINUS 5.9 MONTHS, *DEEP SPACE...*

Susan wished she hadn't insisted she go with Vladimir and Ben. But it was too late to turn back.

They were all three suited up, each loaded with bulky tools.

"Airlock depressurizing," came the voice of Yamamoto over Susan's helmet speaker.

"Copy that," Vladimir curtly replied.

They were gathered in the Observation Deck, departing one-by-one through the overhead EVA Airlock.

Vladimir, their payload specialist as well as mission Commander, was already in the airlock, exiting first. He would attempt the main repairs to the Nuclear Thermal Rocket. Kame had previously reattached critical conduits to the hydrogen and oxygen tanks that'd pulled loose during the violent slingshot maneuver around Earth. That allowed the short burn from the auxiliary liquid fuel engine to occur, which spun-up Hermes and reeled in the trailing Orion vessel via the intervening nano-cable. But the entire aft rocket module was hanging ajar. It wasn't stable enough to accomplish the prolonged hydrogen nuclear thermal thrust required to accelerate them to match the descending Asteroid's blistering 60,000 mph.

"Depressurization is complete. Port is opening."

"Exiting—I see the laser unit. I'll retrieve it as King and Priyanka follow along behind me."

They were carefully describing their operation, recording what they did for Mission Control back on Earth. Hermes was now much too far away for any immediate direction from Earth. Except for consultation on specific problems—assuming the malfunctioning communication array could be repaired—the crew was largely left to its own expertise and resources. But the fragile link to Earth might still be helpful for post-operation analysis.

The black rectangle with its intensely powerful focused laser beam hung at the end of the robotic arm. Susan could easily see it through her helmet out of one of the Observation Deck's large windows. Adriana was controlling the arm though it couldn't reach to the aft Nuclear Rocket module. A large part of the intervening truss structure was still wrapped in the gossamer web of the nano-cable, preventing the arm from traveling much more aft. It would be Susan's job to cut it free, using a specially designed diamond cutter to separate the carbon chains at the molecular level.

The right side of the truss structure was still bent outward, but there wasn't much they could do about it. The robotic arm on that side of the stack was useless. Fortunately the entire truss-structure still held the three contained large tanks in a straight line. The cargo containers on top and bottom of the tanks were out of alignment but not badly. If they could get the webbing cut away then they'd have a shot at getting the Orion's remaining cargo stored away. Also, they'd be able to use the Nuclear Thermal Reactor to accelerate sufficiently to catch the Asteroid.

Unlike her previous, perilous experience, this should be a straightforward spacewalk. But Susan couldn't help feeling nervous. And it must have shown on her face...

"We shouldn't receive too high a radiation dose," Ben reassured Susan, placing a gloved hand on her spacesuited shoulder for suit-to-suit communication. "We've still got the aft shield protecting us. Also, the nuclear reactor was powered down before Hermes went into the slingshot maneuver. So it's not cranking out its maximum ionizing radiation."

"I'm not worried about that, Ben," she replied over their private line. "It's Yamamoto."

"What?"

Ben looked back to the side through his helmet at where the red-haired Swede, Adriana, and the black-haired oriental woman, Kame, were working side-by-side at the control panel.

"We're leaving Adriana alone with Kame," Susan cryptically stated.

Susan and Ben were standing shoulder-to-shoulder in their full suits, awaiting repressurization of the airlock for the next of them to enter. Commander Yegorov was clad in the MMU that Yamamoto had worn when she rescued Orion. The Manned Maneuvering Unit had full independent vectoring capabilities. Also, the fabric in Hermes' MMU contained an additional layer of lead that was specifically designed for protection when having to approach the nuclear reactor. The shielding in the special suit couldn't stop all the radiation, particularly if the reactor were running at full capacity, but it helped a lot. Ben was in Hermes' backup MMU, which had been packed away but survived the slicing-open of the cargo module. It was the same as the Commander's but lacking the extra lead lining, making it less bulky and more maneuverable. Susan herself wore just a standard EMU which required her to be tethered in order to conduct a safe spacewalk.

The operation was well planned and straightforward. But Susan noticed an air of suppressed but intense disapproval from Yamamoto when Yegorov casually appropriated Hermes' MMU. Maybe it was just Susan's imagination, but Kame did not seem happy turning over command of Hermes to the Russian. Plus she looked...unstable. Of course she'd just endured over two and a half years in space on the Mars mission. She was entitled to be out-of-sorts. But to Susan it was more than just the normal friction of a crew's altered command structure. Kame seemed *fragile* to Susan, possibly mentally unhinged by the stress of extended spaceflight.

Ben nodded in his helmet, as if understanding her vague fears.

"Should we warn Adriana to keep an eye on her?" he asked.

"Johansson's a smart cookie, Ben. That 'eye-candy' exterior of hers hides a tough interior. I know the lady well. If Kame falters I'm sure Adriana will step up. I'm probably worrying about nothing, though. We're all professionals here."

"Huh, don't I know it! We won't even sleep together!"

It was her turn to "snort" at him, mildly amused. "What, Ben—have you tried to hit on her and been rejected?"

"I know better than that here on the ship—I tried it back in training, a couple years ago. I slipped my arm around her for some friendly 'necking' and she almost dislocated both my neck and my arm! Still hurts, in fact...not my bones, but my ego!"

"Ah, poor Ben...time for you to go."

The light above the airlock entrance flashed "green."

"Ok, then. See you on the other side, Susan. Stay frosty!" he said as he unbarred the port and swung it opened above him.

"When it's *minus 450°* Fahrenheit outside, I'd prefer to be *toasty.*"

"Ok, then—stay toasty!" he grinned back at her.

She laughed at him as they separated and he floated upward into the hatch. Their private suit-to-suit communication stopped, so she couldn't continue their intimate exchange. Actually, both Ben and Adri were the closest people to true friends she had amongst the astronaut corp. Sure, Susan was friendly with everyone. But Ben reminded her of her little brother—at least before Billy became a haughty mega-millionaire tycoon of industry! And despite Ben's playful advances she knew without a doubt that he respected his colleagues, particularly the females.

But Yamamoto was another matter entirely. Susan was ready to greet the seasoned Mars explorer as a hero, immensely grateful to Kame for saving the Orion crew, willing to overlook any minor frictions or questions. But Dr. Yamamoto stayed decidedly restrained and aloof. When they first got out of their suits Susan tried to give Yamamoto a grateful hug but Kame backed away. Yamamoto was rigidly polite and agreeable, but apparently not a "huggable" type of person. Yet there was something darker and deeper behind those liquid black slanted eyes than a formal bent. It not only puzzled Susan, it felt *ominous*.

"You can enter the airlock," Yamamoto's voice spoke in Susan's helmet, startling her.

She'd been floating there musing, losing track of time. Ben had already passed through the airlock. The light had again cycled to green.

"Right," Susan quickly replied. "I'm entering now."

And in a few more minutes she was outside yet again, floating in the vastness of space beside the long Hermes stack. She carefully hooked the end of her tether spool to a ring set into the side of the Observation Deck. It would extend out a hundred feet, allowing her to reach most of the storage boxes, water tanks, and outer struts. On command it could detach so that—if necessary—she could pull it in and hook it into a further distant ring.

"Looks like I've got quite a job here," she spoke into the helmet microphone. "The nano-cable is snarled and tangled."

"Just cut it loose segment by segment," Yegorov ordered her from farther ahead. "Then discard the cut-up sections into space."

"Yes, Sir—that's the plan," Susan replied as she went hand-by-handhold toward the middle tank.

Yegorov was slowly jetting along the side of Hermes toward the Nuclear Module at the far end of the stack, careful to stay well away from the glittering "web" that encased most of the middle tank. On the other side of Hermes, Ben was doing the same.

The faster Susan could get the web chopped up and discarded, the sooner Adriana could start transferring what remained within the cargo module of Orion's manifest to the more-secure storage boxes saddling the water tanks. They still weren't sure how much of their supplies and nuclear weapons remained in the sliced-open cargo module. Fortunately what remained of it was still firmly attached below the docked Orion capsule. Since it couldn't be pressurized, they'd not yet tried to reenter it—figuring the safest approach would be to reach in with the surviving robotic arm through the open gap. But they had to have a place to transfer the contents to sort them out before bringing into Hermes the most critical packages. The web was both a barrier and a danger. Its super-sharp strands could easily slice through both the packages and the fabric of their spacesuits! Fortunately for the surrounded water tank, the outer titanium struts had borne the pull of the Orion stack.

"Approaching the web," she reported.

Susan floated up to the tangle and decided the safest approach was to slice straight through it along a line at the top of the vehicle. It was going to take time. The diamond cutter dangling at her workbelt had been meant for making a few cuts, not hundreds or thousands. And it was hard to see the "web"—easy for it to drift up around her and then slice her to ribbons!

And up close she saw that the outer struts were twisted on the left where they'd thought it was ok. Even when she got the webbing off, the remaining arm still wouldn't be able to reach back to the nuclear reactor.

It was even worse than she'd feared.

"It's not as bad as we thought," she heard Ben, as if reading her mind and arguing against her.

Startled, she looked up to see his suit lit by stark sunlight, glaring whitely at the far end of Hermes, poised above the large, circular aft radiation shield.

Ah, he was talking about the terminal reactor module, not the nearer tanks, containers, and struts.

And behind him Susan saw a small blue dot, Earth. Before the stored hydrogen and oxygen gave out, Adriana had managed to flip the Hermes stack over such that the NTR was behind them rather than leading. They were fast departing their home planet, hurtling up above the planetary disc. The Asteroid zooming down at them from much higher was not visible. It was still much too far away. But it was out there—a *bullet* fired at the heart of the human race. And to catch a bullet you needed to become an even faster bullet yourself!

Without a well-functioning NTR they had no chance of catching the Asteroid.

"Three of the main bolts that hold the NTR to the shield pulled loose," Yegorov reported, hovering out of Susan's sight behind the radiation shield, floating right above the nuclear reactor. "The intervening lines are intact, though stretched out of position. You got them back together nicely, Yamamoto. Good work reattaching them. The radiator wings are still locked flat. We lucked out there."

Susan knew that the radiator wings were critical for when the nuclear reactor was generating electricity to power Hermes' systems. That required the reactor to run at maximum. The opened-out wings allowed the hot reactor to vent vast amounts of excess heat. But now they were folded back since the reactor was only minimally functioning in its shutdown mode. The minimal level was enough to supply electricity to the most-essential of Hermes' systems, particularly life support, but not for its more intensive functions.

They had batteries of course, but even at a full charge they couldn't run Hermes' complex systems for more than a few days. And since they had a large nuclear reactor, solar panels weren't even part of Hermes' design.

"Thank you, Commander. Glad the conduits held up," Yamamoto replied.

Kame sounded pleased. Susan was also pleasantly surprised to find that the Russian could be encouraging to his crewmembers. Most of the time, he was predictably dour and brisk, likely needing a round of vodka to loosen up. But they had no alcohol on this journey and Susan wasn't looking forward to a perpetually grim Commander.

"Fortunately the bolts don't appear broken," Vladimir continued, his harsh voice crackling in Susan's helmet speaker as he moved further behind the heavy shielding. "Most of the nuts on the other side broke off. But a few just ripped out...stripping their threads...if I can swing the main unit back into alignment, Ben...you can weld the protruding ends of the remaining bolts into place behind the shield. Are the holes on your side still open, Ben?"

"Yes they are. I can do that—as long as the laser welder works as anticipated," Ben answered as he drifted with the black laser unit behind the last cargo box. White spurts erupted from his MMU's steering jets. Then he was out of Susan's sight, between the last aft tank and the conical radiation shield.

They were getting far enough away from Earth's gravity-well that the "super-battery" in the laser box was losing its connection to the subspace depot containing its energy pool. Prior experiments aboard Hermes showed that farther than three lunar distances the batteries became unreliable. At ten lunar distances they stopped working entirely.

Susan turned her attention to her immediate task. She began carefully snipping at the barely visible strands in front of her. The otherwise incredibly strong strands parted easily enough. A built in, tiny laser beam was exquisitely tuned to the exact excitability of the carbon bonds. That sufficiently weakened the nano-tubes such that the diamond tips of her device could then successfully separate the intertwined strands. Fortunately its tiny laser was powered by conventional batteries and didn't lose its "zap" with distance from Earth.

It took all of her concentration as she inched forward, holding on by one hand to rings set into the outer surfaces of the tanks and on the "saddleback" storage boxes while working the pincer-like device with her other hand. She strained to see the loosely floating strands, gently trying to herd them into loose clumps to more quickly sheer through them.

"Radiation readings, Vladimir and Ben?" Susan heard Yamamoto asking.

"Nominal," Ben reported back. "I'm shielded well enough, at least at the moment."

"Elevated...but not dangerously so," Yegorov's rough voice crackled in Susan's speaker.

"Our data stream from your suit is breaking up," Kame stated, sounding concerned. "Wait! The reactor...!"

"I'm at the nozzles...grabbing...moving it...I..." Yegorov grunted.

"I see the end of the bolts," Ben answered. "They're through! I'm welding the first bolt into place."

Susan saw *spurts of bright light* from behind the curve of the last aft water tank.

"I don't have readings from the NTR's systems! Did you clip some lines, Priyanka?" Adriana's worried voice suddenly reverberated in Susan's helmet.

Susan looked up from her "clicking" of the strands, trying to get a glimpse of Ben around the side of the large water tank she sat astride.

"I don't think so," Ben retorted. "Wait! The central bundle coming through the main central port in the shield is being pinched, there...how's that?"

"Ok. I've got the data stream back again."

"Good. The first bolt is set and cooling. I'm working on the second..."

"The reactor's *coming on line!*" Adriana suddenly shouted. "Get out of there, Vladimir! Abort! *Abort!*"

"Not yet...holding it in place...Ben, how's it...?"

"Oh, gods, it broke loose!" Ben yelled. "Susan, get up here, *now!*"

The entire Hermes stack visibly *jerked* as violent vibrations ran through the tank beneath Susan.

"What?" she gasped, pulling back her clipper and reattaching it to her workbelt. "What happened?"

"The bolt snapped off at the weld point! It and the other ends have pulled back out of their holes!"

"Difficult...stabilizing..." the Commander's voice crackled, "My steering jets are on full...I need help!"

"I've got to go on the other side and help Vladimir get the NTR module back in realignment!" Ben urgently yelled. "Susan, you'll have to do the welding on this side of the shield! *Get up here!*"

"I'm coming," she gasped, starting to move forward.

She brushed away the haze of webs—then froze!

Her arm was caught. She saw a *slice* in the outer fabric of her suit! If it got any deeper she'd instantly depressurize and die. She had to find the offending thread and clip it before she could move. Keeping her right arm rigidly still she fumbled for the diamond cutter with her opposite hand.

"Kame...shut the damned reactor *off!*" Yegorov shouted. "It's powering up...without the hydrogen coolant flowing through...the closed radiators...turning *red!*"

"Data stream is off again. I don't know what's..." Adriana's urgent voice reported.

"Susan, where are you?" Ben called out to her.

"I got tangled! But I'm cutting myself free," she said as she sliced at the offending thread. "Hang on, Ben!"

It seemed to take forever, though it was likely only a few moments.

Then her arm was loose of the web.

She snapped the diamond cutter back on her belt and drifted upward—held back! What now? It was her tether! It was extended out as far as it could reach. So she pulled the small lever that commanded it to release at the other end. She felt the vibration of the spool at her waist as it tried to reel in the loose tether. But it was just yanking her backward! The tether didn't detach at the other end!

"Damn!" she swore, frantic to go forward and help Ben. Something was either wrong with the clip at its end, the command sequences for it to let loose, or the attachment point.

There was no time to figure out the cause of the problem. Susan released the entire spool and let it spiral away behind her.

Freed of the tether, she kicked herself forward, floating just barely above the deadly haze of still-wrapped nano-cable web. Then she stretched her arm out as far as she could and just barely caught a protruding ring on the other side of the tangle of threads. A few inches higher and she'd have sailed on past Hermes, headed back toward Earth!

"I'm here, Ben," She breathlessly said as she pulled herself forward and down by small hand rings set into the curved side of the tank. Then she was right next to the large, circular radiation shield, beside Ben.

He was struggling with the black laser box while simultaneously trying to straighten a mass of wadded conduits and cables that extended through a central opening.

"I've got the laser unit," she said, grabbing it as she simultaneously locked her legs around one of the end struts to the side.

An *ominous red glow* was now shining around the thick cables protruding from the central hole, coming from the other side.

The shield was visibly *trembling* from vibrations on its other side.

"Good!" Ben nodded at her. She saw through his helmet that sweat covered his forehead. He was rapidly blinking, trying to maintain his vision. "Be ready to start welding whichever bolt comes through first. There's still a stub left from the one I was working on. Apparently I heated it too rapidly, allowing too large of a temperature differential between the melt and the space-frozen part, where it sheared off. You'll have to go slower. Dial it down to where it's just melting the metal. Try to get the other intact bolts secured first. Then fix the one I snapped off as best you can."

"How's the laser doing? Is the charge holding?"

"Nope...we're losing the charge from the super-battery, too far away from its subspace depot back on Earth. I think that's the core reason why my initial weld failed. The narrow beam is sputtering badly, putting out blasts that are too hot. I've now got it on half-strength. Decrease the strength to keep the beam steady if you must. It'll mean we have to hold the nuclear reactor module in place longer. But you've got to get good welds or the reactor won't be stable on the stack! And without it firmly in place, we're dead in the water!"

She nodded inside her helmet.

"Ok, I've got it, Ben. But the radioactivity...?"

"There's no time to worry about that, Susan. See if you can help Adriana get control of the reactor. Data lines may still be blocked. I didn't have time to straighten everything in the central bundle!"

"Ok, then..." she gulped, overwhelmed by the urgent tasks facing her.

He fired the jets in his backpack and slipped out of sight to Susan's side, headed past the shield.

Oh, Jesus—he didn't have any lead lining in his suit! He was going to get *fried!*

"Ben!" she cried-out, but it was too late. He was out of sight and beyond reliable communications.

As the ominous *red glow* grew brighter around the edges of the shield, the crackling in her speakers got louder. The nuclear reactor wasn't just putting out ionizing and infrared radiation. This close it was throwing up strong electromagnetic radio interference!

"Fiber-optics line...!" Susan barely heard Adriana shouting over the crackling in her helmet.

Looking down she saw a bundle of hard-plastic looking lines snaking out of the hole in front of her, wrapped about each other as a single hardened bundle. And, yes, they were "smushed" to the side by other harder, larger tubes that transported water, oxygen, and hydrogen back and forth from the nuclear reactor to segments of the tanks behind her. She freed up the squashed fiber-optic lines. Then she pulled with all her strength.

Slowly, they straightened.

"...that's better...damper rods now inserting back into the reactor..." Susan heard Adriana.

"...aligned?" Susan heard Ben shouting over the crackling in her helmet.

With a "thunk" she felt rather than heard, gleaming metal bolts were suddenly pocking through the smaller surrounding holes around the central conduit.

"Hold it there! I'm welding!" she shouted over the interference.

Susan suddenly heard *agonized screaming* over her helmet. Despite the heat she felt coming through the shield, penetrating her suit, those awful sounds chilled her to her bones! She couldn't imagine what it was like on the other side of the thick radiation shield! Ben and Vladimir were getting cooked! She expected the bolts to pull back at any second as the two astronauts were forced by the heat and radiation to retreat, releasing their combined jet-pressure that was keeping the reactor module in place. But the bolts stubbornly stayed in place, their ends still thrust through the holes!

Susan pushed her black box such that the laser end was next to a bolt, briefly sending out short bursts. She had the power at only a quarter of maximum. The laser beam came in ragged but potent bursts.

The hard metal studs were melting...

Susan ignored the *continuing screams* to focus on her job...

The bolt Susan was working on sizzled at its edges, fusing with the metal of the curved wall in front of her. But it took forever, far slower than when Kunle had previously freed up the core tank. But even though her intense laser beam continued to flicker badly, she got the bolt melted into place. Then she lightly attached each of the other two. Finally she went back over each one in turn, "bubbling" their tops to coat the lower melted and now solidified regions.

The laser sputtered off and stopped. It was "out of juice."

The welds she'd done weren't the large, fixed nuts which should have been there. But maybe her repairs would be enough to hold the aft nuclear reactor module in place.

"I've got it!" she yelled, shaking from the strain. "Is it holding on your side?"

"...solid...we're coming back..." came the gurgled reply.

She saw Ben float into view on her left, white vapor bursts shooting from his backpack, his arms reaching for the side of the water tank. His helmet was steamed up so she couldn't see his face. But his suit was charred black! The jets abruptly cut off as he drifted forward, no longer moving.

He hit the side of the tank and bounced off...

"*Ben!*"

There was no reply. He was either dead or unconscious.

Susan grabbed onto rings and clambered toward him, desperate to reach out and grab him before he floated too far away from the ship. She needed to set a tether in order to jump away from Hermes to reach him!

Oh, hell! I left the jammed tether behind!—she gasped to herself. In a panic, she saw the distance between her and Ben lengthening.

Now a *haze* was in front of her. What was it?

Ah! It was part of the "spider web" she'd already sliced through, drifting away. She lightly grabbed onto the filmy mass, lodging its closest end through a handhold. Then gathering it in, she gingerly stuck her boot into its further end.

"Please don't slice my foot off...please don't slice my foot off," she muttered as she let loose of the tank and pushed off toward Ben.

She just managed to grab the heel of his boot with her grasping gloved hand, feeling the web tug on her own boot.

Moving very slowly, not putting any more pressure than necessary on her caught foot, she gently reached down and lightly pulled with her other hand at the web—just enough to send her and Ben floating back toward the curved white side of the tank.

Breathing heavily, she grabbed a ring, pulling Ben securely next to her, and then reaching down to free her foot.

The nano-cable threads had dug into the tough fabric of her boot. Any deeper and her suit would have breached. Both she and Ben would have been lost in space.

"Whew!" she sighed, closing her eyes briefly to get her trembling body back under control.

Opening them she watched in fascinated horror as the burnt and ruptured MMU of Yegorov drifted past, dwindling steadily as it spun away into space. His helmet had fractured and exploded outward. His dead, frozen eyes stared sightlessly at her from a distance as he dwindled to a dot then disappeared into the void.

"Unnggghhhh," Ben groaned.

He wasn't dead!

"Ben, can you move on your own?" she urgently asked, thinking that if his jets could work they might yet retrieve Yegorov's body and his mobility suit.

"Don't think so...air not moving...the suit's damaged," he weakly gurgled.

"Don't worry, buddy," she said, grabbing the blackened spool at his waist and attaching the end to a rung. "I'll get us back inside Hermes in a jiffy."

She worked her way up the tank clutching Ben's bulky MMU. As she slowly and carefully maneuvered them both along she had time to sort out her scrambled thoughts.

What the hell had happened?

Something had gone terribly wrong! The powered-down nuclear reactor should not have reactivated on its own. It required a specific series of deliberate commands to bring it back up!

And the only one in a position to do that inside the ship...was Yamamoto!

No, it couldn't be. That wasn't possible.

There had to be another explanation than *sabotage!*

"Ben, can you hear me?" she asked, suddenly very afraid for him.

But there was no answer. She couldn't see into his fogged-up helmet. She had to get him back into Hermes soonest. He likely needed immediate medical care!

He'd been directly exposed to the reactivated nuclear reactor, without lead lining in his suit. She glanced at the radiation monitor on her own chest. It showed an elevated reading—and she'd been behind the large fixed shield the whole time. In addition to the fierce heat of the closed-down reactor trying to function at maximum power, poor Ben must have been exposed to a massive dose of radiation!

She emerged above the storage box on top of the aft tank, pulling Ben along behind her, again seeing the remaining haze of uncut web swimming loosely in front of her against the backdrop of space.

How would they get across? There wasn't time to snip her way through!

She commanded the end of Ben's suit-spool to detach from below. It, at least, worked! Then she reattached the end hook onto a ring next to her.

She deliberately breathed in deeply, getting her racing emotions back under control. Then she jumped out into space, slanted forward. As the tether snapped straight, her momentum forced her and Ben downward across the lethal webbing. They SLAMMED onto the opposite side of the webbing onto the distant tank next to the Central Node.

Fortunately she'd spied the exact handhold she needed to grab onto with a death grip!

Quickly she got back to the airlock, shoving Ben inside.

"Take care of him!" she radioed to Adriana who waited on the other side. Once the airlock filled up and could be opened from within, Ben could be treated.

"You're not coming in?"

"I've got more cutting to do," Susan spoke distinctly into her microphone. "I'll be back inside in maybe an hour."

"You've taken too much radiation," Adriana insisted. "You've got to come back inside now!"

"I'm already outside," Susan responded. "My dosage isn't in the red yet. I'll be ok, Adriana. We have to get the webbing off Hermes or we can't stabilize the cargo we brought with us. If we don't get it properly stored we could lose part or all of it at any time out of the sliced-open end of the cargo module."

"Do what you have to, King," Yamamoto's voice calmly agreed in Susan's helmet. "But don't take any longer than necessary. Is the laser unit intact? If it is we can stow it later with the Arm."

Huh. Who died and put Yamamoto back in charge of Hermes?

Oh, *Jesus*...Vladimir was dead. Yamamoto *was* back in charge. Too much was happening too fast!

"I don't know...I had to get Ben here...I think it's still wedged in between the water tank and the aft shield."

She wasn't thinking straight. Her thoughts were scrambled. Time was fragmenting around her!

Oh, hell!—Susan groaned to herself. *Things are going from bad to worse. This whole rescue mission is cursed! What new disaster is going to happen next?*

Susan, Bill, and Scott were at the *Chickasaw Cultural Center*. It was located just outside of town on a one hundred acre campus.

The Cultural Center contained art, historical, and traditional displays nested within elegant architectural blends which joined the past to the present. It was a fitting counterweight—located at the opposite end of the small town of Sulphur, Oklahoma—to the overtly commercial Native American casino and hotel situated at the other end.

But now it was late in the evening, long past public viewing hours. Most of the lights were off, the buildings shut down. No one beside herself, Scott, and Bill were out walking along the concrete path in a simulated village display. The guards had let them in without hesitation, calling Scott "Sir." Now she had a strange feeling that she was descending into the past, yet where she'd been before!

It was that damn hallucination again, the one she'd had in the Park so long before—when she and Billy were just kids. They'd been trapped within a strange, Martian Obelisk that seemingly carried them back in time. In a series of bizarre adventures, they'd lived for a while in an actual Native American encampment. In her delusional fantasy she and Billy were accepted, trained, and skilled at hunting and living off vast buffalo herds.

But this sterile, simulated "village" was nothing of the sort.

"You couldn't follow a buffalo herd living like this!" she snorted, seeing around her in the darkness high thatched roofs of both rectangular and circular houses. In her fantasy they'd lived in large, portable teepees.

"Of course not," Scott mildly answered from just ahead of her as he led them along. "The Chickasaw were not plains Indians. They originated from the Southeastern Woodlands, from what now are called Mississippi, Alabama, and Tennessee. They only came here when the U.S. government stole their lands and banished them on the 'trail of tears' in the 1830's."

"They didn't follow the buffalo herds?"

"This is just a silly story she made up when we were kids," Bill laughed in a good-natured way. "She actually wrote a science fiction book about it when she was a teenager. The book never got published, of course, but it was fun for our family to read to ourselves. In it, she and I were out riding our bikes in the Park and ended up being captured by *talking dinosaurs* from another dimension! What an incredible imagination my sister Suzy has! And that was after first getting lost then taken in by Chickasaw Indians and living for weeks in one of their tribes following a buffalo herd. But what really happened is she just fell off her bike, got conked on her head, and had some sort of hallucination."

"Fascinating," Scott laughed as they walked on past the shadowy, empty buildings. "Talking dinosaurs you say—from another dimension? You must be quite a good writer, Susan. I'm sure it's just another sign of your marvelous scientific intelligence being expressed in whatever medium is immediately available."

She was somewhat flattered but also embarrassed. Not many people knew about her little attempt at writing a science fiction book. But it wasn't just a fanciful story she made up—it *flowed* out of her, the words appearing on her computer screen as fast as she could type them, as if it was something she had actually experienced!

"Ah, it was just a fun kid thing," she shrugged. "And they were intelligent *raptors*, from a dimension where the asteroid that destroyed the dinosaurs fragmented instead of hitting Earth square-on. So the destruction to Earth's surface was spread out. The larger dinosaurs like T-rex died as predicted, while the smaller dinosaur predators thrived and evolved. The little pre-mammals, though, all got eaten up so us humans never developed in their dimension."

"Well, I'm sure it was a great science fiction story, Susan," Scott softly continued. "But you certainly got the Chickasaw history wrong. My ancestors lived in developed towns just like you're seeing here. They farmed the land, had laws and their own religion, and were renown traders plying the rivers."

Suzy was confused. It just didn't sound correct. She'd seen it with her own eyes, hadn't she? But no, of course not—it was just a fantasy of hers. But...wasn't there something else, something her father in her dream had explained to her? Her "story" wasn't really in the past, but the *distant future!* And her mother had been there also—but not the grossly overweight, diabetes-riddled sad figure she was now!

"I...I..." she stammered, suddenly very confused.

She was exhausted and low on blood glucose.

"It's ok, Suzy," Bill said, grabbing hold of her elbow to steady her as she wavered, stopped dead now on the sidewalk. "You should have eaten something before we came here. Your glucose is probably low and you're not thinking straight."

Huh. He sure knew her well.

"That past stuff when we were kids isn't important," he continued. "I know how you can get excited with your own research projects and go all day long without eating. I do the same thing when I'm experimenting. Maybe we should go back to the hotel and..."

"No! Let's get this over with!" she firmly said, steadily herself as she shook off his hand. "Show me whatever it is you think you've got. Then I'll stop by McDonalds before I leave town and get a salad or whatever."

"Alright, then," Scott said. "We're almost there."

They continued on past the sidewalks and onto a dirt path. Off at the back of the compound, surrounded by low green trees, was what looked like a large, metal-sided, airplane hangar!

"That's new, isn't it?" she said, apprehensive at entering the large structure.

"Sure is, Suzy," Bill answered as Scott punched numbers into a keypad to the side of a locked door. "We just finished building it last week. It's only the start, though. It's mainly for testing and demon-stration. The manufacturing facility will be behind it, though still safely located on Chickasaw property. So we'll have excellent security and ready access to transportation, materials, whatever we need!"

She walked through the open door into a gloomy, large steel building. Lights hanging a hundred feet up at the ceiling flickered on. The entire hanger—which could have held several large airplanes—was empty...except for *two high metal spikes* in the center of the space, twenty feet apart, each sporting circular heads. Plus there was an array of surrounding equipment banks.

"So that's it?" Suzy asked as she walked forward. "You brought me here to show me two 'mad-scientist' *Tesla Coils?*"

"Yep," Bill nodded, seemingly delighted at her surprise if not her sarcasm.

Scott was likewise smiling beside him, clearly proud of the display in the otherwise-empty huge hangar.

"No, really?" she snorted, turning to Scott. "What are you trying to pull here, Scott? And what sort of name for a full-blood Chickasaw Indian is 'Scott' anyway? Shouldn't it be 'pulls-wool-over-face' or 'forked-tongue *snake*'?"

Bill looked shocked at her wicked sarcasm.

Scott's previously pleasant smile faded as his eyes narrowed. She again saw that disturbing, predatory gleam. "My given name, Susan, is 'Choola'—The *Fox*! It denotes great cunning, dexterity, and speed. In English, my parents used the somewhat rhyming word of 'Scott.' So it's no great mystery, huh? In the white world, Choola Yanash is a distracting name. Scott is much easier for others to grasp. In fact, I'm thinking of legally shortening my name to 'Scott Nash'—would that suit you better?"

Bill looked from her to Scott, seemingly confused by her belliger-ence and Scott's icy response. She saw again the Billy that she recog-nized, uncertain and withdrawn, looking for a place to go and hide.

She was doubly certain that Scott's scheme wasn't anything her little brother should be mixed up in.

"Come on, guys," Bill softly responded. "Let's not fight, huh? For this to succeed we've got to work together, right?"

"For *what* to succeed?" Susan sighed, getting very tired, feeling very weak, and just wanting it to be over.

That McDonald's chicken salad was sounding better and better.

"This! This! This!" Bill said, holding up the rectangular "laptop" above his head.

"*That! That! That!*" Susan mocked him, pointing her finger derisively at it.

His expression fell. He looked devastated.

Scott stalked forward, snatched the "laptop" out of Billy's hands, and walked toward the scientific gear in the center of the large hangar.

"Sorry, Billy," Susan sighed, putting a hand to her forehead. "I don't mean to fall back on being the 'older sister' mocking her little brother. That was stupid of me. I'm only so concerned because, well, I love you. So, please explain. What is it you think you've invented here?"

He looked relieved by her confession.

"It's a battery!"

"A...battery?"

"A *rechargeable* battery!"

"Oh, ok," she shrugged, "a rechargeable battery—like we've already got zillions of in the world already?"

"No, it's nothing like them!"

"You're not making any sense, Billy," she sighed, very tired of whatever game he and Scott were playing.

"Just look! *Look* at what happens!"

"Alright, then—I'm looking! But I'm not seeing anything!"

Scott was hooking two long, thick cables to the laptop-sized "battery." Thick clips now held each cable onto one of the two electrodes on the opposite sides of the "laptop." The two cables ran to the towering "Tesla Coil"-type towers.

"Hooked up, Bill," Scott said as he backed away.

"I'm turning it on," Bill said as he pulled out a cellphone from an inner pocket, flicked up an app, and his fingers danced over the small keyboard.

Clearly the cellphone was communicating with the "laptop" by Bluetooth or whatever.

A faint "humming" filled the air.

Despite her skepticism, Susan was intrigued. She saw a *glow* suddenly appear around each of the two towering heads of the metal spikes. Then the glows became *spheres* of dancing electricity—which grew until they suddenly *arched out* toward each other into a *sputtering, crackling* CLOUD OF LIGHTNING BOLTS which filled the air between the two spikes with a sizzling howl!

Susan was almost blinded by the immense spectacle.

"Powering back down," Billy said as he flicked settings into his cellphone app.

The *blazing mass of electrical arcs* slowly dwindled then faded away.

The air was filled with the smell of scorched metal. As her vision returned Susan saw that the towering spikes were slumped to each side, *melted!*

It took a minute for Susan to gather her wits.

"That was just not possible," she gasped. "You must have had those electrodes hooked up to power lines! You probably blew out all the transformers in Sulphur to pull off a stunt like that!"

"You can go inspect the remains," Scott calmly observed. "You'll find that the only power source was the prototype that I hooked the Tesla Coils onto."

Yes, the "laptop" was still lying there on the concrete floor, although the cables where they'd connected from it to the towering metal columns were now shredded and black.

"And that was on setting number 'two' out of a potential 'ten,' Suzy," Bill excitedly told her. "And the settings are not linear—but each factors of ten! If we had the proper replacement equipment, we could repeat that demonstration many times over using the same power source!"

Scott walked over, unhooked the flat rectangle, and brought it back to Suzy, placing it in her hands.

It was cool to the touch.

"So how's that for a battery, Suzy?" Bill grinned.

"What *the hell* is this thing?"

"It's Dad's matrix plus key, secret modifications from Scott," Bill grinned at her. "Dad suspected his matrix could weaken the normally inviolable interface between normal space-time and what he called 'subspace'!"

"*Jesus*, Billy," she said, shakily handing the rectangular metal object back to him. What he was telling her couldn't be true! There had to another explanation for what she'd seen. Two would-be scientists without real credentials working with ancient equipment in a garage couldn't find a way to crack open space-time! If that were even possible, it would take gigantic linear colliders. "You mock me for writing science fiction and now you're spouting it back to me!"

"No, Susan, it's true," Scott said, coughing lightly from the black smoke now hanging thick in the air. "I recognized Dave and Bill's research potential, which correlated with theories I was working on in college. I lucked upon a way to cause your Dad's matrix to allow concentrated energy to seep through into a 'bubble' of subspace—in other words, *virtually infinite* storage capacity!"

"And what sort of research was this?"

"It's something you'd laugh at as much as your Dad's 'impossible' research—*high temperature* superconductivity!"

"Yes, superconductivity is a real thing, but not at *room* temperatures where...?"

"Yes, Susan," he interrupted her, "it's yet another 'impossible' goal for achieving and harnessing vast amounts of energy. But as you just saw..."

"It works, Suzy!" Bill happily exclaimed, interrupting Scott. "We've the means to collect *all sorts of energy sources* and use them to power not just small things but cars, trucks—everything! Instead of struggling to go a couple hundred miles on one charge, this one small box could power an average car or truck or train for an entire *year!* 'Clean' energy can be easily harvested from many sources, stored, concentrated, and readily dispensed. It will revolutionize the entire world!"

"So...you're saying...that what's in that 'collector' is...?" she gasped, still not believing what he was claiming.

"Yes! It's lightning from the storm last night! We put up high lightning rods. The results definitely went too far, burning down our buildings, but also super-charging our *'super-battery'*! You see, not only does the matrix allow us to make a bubble in subspace for collecting energy, it *attracts* energy sources! The 'sink' it creates *draws in* whatever weak or strong energy is nearby within the local gravity-well!"

"I d-don't know about...?" she stammered, amazed.

"Susan, just consider the phenomenon of lightning," Scott calmly noted. "It's been estimated that if you had capacitors able to save the power from one year of lightning strikes it could power the entire world for *five* years."

"The amount of power in just one average lightning storm is equivalent to that of an *atomic bomb!*" Billy chortled. "It's staggering! And that's just the beginning! There's also..."

Susan tuned him out, her thoughts churning. She wasn't so sure of that 'atomic bomb' statistic, but the implications were still staggering. If true, Billy's claimed effect could be valid. If this wasn't an elaborate hoax, it would revolutionize the world—allowing diffuse or transitory energy sources to supply immense energy needs while virtually eliminating polluting wastes!

"—and we want you to be part of it," Bill soberly concluded. "Scott's known you since you were a kid, just like me. We're on the ground floor here of something *huge!* Scott's Dad, Losa, is working with the Chickasaw to set up a corporate governing board. As we both know, the Chickasaw Nation is highly qualified in running big businesses of various sorts. But we've got to start with a core of trusted executives. We can't patent the matrix, of course. It'll have to remain a trade secret and..."

"But can't someone just analyze and reverse-engineer it?" she interrupted him.

"Not at all," Scott stated. "Any attempt to analyze or mess with it causes it to break down into molecular goop. We thought it was a 'deal-breaking' problem when our matrix kept dissolving on us—but it turned out to be a blessing. Our final version is tamper-proof, meaning we've got a lock on it. It's all ours, Susan."

"Jesus Christ," she gasped. "You're talking billions..."

"No, not billions of dollars, Suzy—*trillions!*" Bill triumphantly proclaimed.

He was dancing-about with excitement, even though the black smoke was making him also cough and sputter.

"Our new corporation will control the world's energy source and distributon," Scott concluded.

"And I'm the Chairman, Founder, and CEO," Bill giddily continued. "Scott's the COO and CFO, handling operations and finances. And we want you to be the chief scientist, *Vice President* in charge of Research and Development! Don't worry about not knowing everything already. We'll hire experts to fill in the gaps: lawyers, scientists, engineers, managers, whoever we need. So what do you say, Suzy?"

She was also starting to cough from the smoke that was filling up the high hangar...turning back to the exit...walking through and out into the cool night air...keeping on stumbling along—headed back to the parking lot and her patiently waiting, ancient Pontiac Fiero.

"Suzy?" Billy called out from behind her.

She whirled around and pointed an accusing finger at him.

"*You* brought the massive lightning sheets that destroyed our house! That damn machine *attracted* them! You almost killed Mom!"

"We didn't know it would be that bad! We certainly didn't intend..."

"Have your fun, Billy. I wish you all the best. Maybe you do have something that's going to revolutionize the world. But I want *no* part of this!"

She started to walk away again as Bill ran up and stood directly in front of her, blocking her path.

"Ah, come on, Suzy..."

"I have my own work to do!"

"What—to look at stars a zillion miles away? Suzy, this is making a zillion little stars all over our *own* planet! You'll have more money than you can count! You can go and buy a whole institute of astrophysical Ph.D.'s to work for *you!*"

"It's not just about getting a 'Ph.D.' after my name."

"Sure, you want to change the world, right? Isn't that why you're doing all the graduate school stuff? I *need* you, Suzy! We're going to do this *together!*"

She glanced behind him at the emerging, long-haired Indian.

"Please, Suzy," he begged her now, looking at her with tears running from his eyes. "I get...flustered...when too much happens or too many people come at me. I need your help! You've always been the one who could deal with people!"

"I think you've got all the help you need, little brother," she now gently replied. "Isn't Scott ready at your elbow to tell you exactly what to do?"

"Well, sure, but..."

"I thought we were driven by the same thing, Billy—the same as Dad!" she now dejectedly sighed. "But I was wrong. You're just like all the rest. You've become a clone of 'foxy-Scotty' and his casino-building friends who..."

"You're *wrong!*"

She shook her head sadly, stepping around him.

"I hope you get what you want."

She ran away, back through the eerie darkness of the silent, fake Indian village. Guards stepped aside at the entrance to let her past. But in the parking lot Scott appeared beside her, his long strides easily catching up to her staggering steps.

"And what drives *you*, Susan?" he asked.

"The 'two C's'!"

"That's amusing," he laughed as he abruptly turned back, leaving her utterly alone.

His scorn was palpable.

No it *wasn't* amusing! It was deadly serious and incredibly exciting. For her it was the ultimate "Church," the most profound motivation, the very best Worship to the Real God: exercising her God-given human *Curiosity and Creativity!* She considered herself to be the one and only member of the *Church of Godly Creativity!*

And for her that wasn't just making mountains of money off a better battery, but exploring the wonders of the Universe!

"Matthew 6:24," she muttered angrily to herself as she walked up to her Fiero and jerked open the driver side door. She'd probably break speed limits careening down the road to McDonalds. But she was so mad she didn't care. Maybe she'd even treat herself to not just a dry salad but a cheese burger and a milkshake! "...'*no one can serve two masters,*" she quoted to herself. "*Either you will hate the one and love the other, or be loyal to the one and betray the other. You cannot serve both God and money'!*"

She was certainly finding a lot of timely wisdom in her childhood Sunday-School studies...

As illogical as it might seem, Susan feared her brother had sold his soul to the devil.

Chapter 11

TAKING INVENTORY

It is necessary to periodically "take stock":
Do you really have what you think you have?
We take so much for granted, assuming
Thinking that it is just part of the landscape
An inalterable feature that will always remain
Even though time, weather, and the hand of man
Can alter mountains, lakes, rivers, or planets
Putting a dent in the very Nature of Reality
A "constant" we choose blithely to ignore...
That, still, "the sun will come up tomorrow"
As the Flower Drum Song *Musical explains:*
"Somehow or other it will, it will..."
SOMEHOW OR OTHER IT WILL!
—until, shockingly, it doesn't.
The Minstrel's Lark, 11:19-22

IMPACT MINUS 5.8 MONTHS, *SUSTAINED BURN...*
The mood in Hermes was grim.

A sputtering message from Mission Control attributed the spontaneous reactivation of the nuclear reactor to a glitch caused by the slingshot stresses. Well, *duh!* Supposedly the initial shutdown was premature, due to the unplanned maneuver zipping close to Earth. The reactor turned off prematurely because safety limitations were breached. Then, when the crimped fiber-optic lines were straightened by Ben, the reactor automatically rebooted itself. Susan did not buy the story. To her it seemed implausible. But it was the official reason given for the disaster that exposed the spacewalkers hovering just above the reactor to high levels of ionizing radiation plus fierce temperatures.

Susan was still suspicious of Yamamoto, who seemed strangely unaffected by the terrible consequences of the spacewalk. They had no way to retrieve Vladimir. His body was lost in space. He died a hero, using his suit's power-pack and jets—along with Ben's assistance—to steady the reactor module at the far end of Hermes long enough for Susan to weld it back into place.

Ben survived, but badly injured.

Having been behind the aft shield plus having floated above the reactor for a shorter time than Vladimir, Ben received a debilitating but not lethal radiation dosage. This was despite his having no lead shielding in the fabric of his suit. Vladimir's body and suit had partially shielded hm. So he was, perversely, "lucky." Priyanka suffered severe radiation sickness and extensive burns across his body, but was expected to recover.

This, however, restricted Ben to his hammock, too weak and in too much pain to help in any of the ongoing tasks. Transferring the remaining cargo from the Orion stack to Hermes sat squarely on the shoulders of Susan, Adriana, and Kame. They worked around the clock with the robotic arm and frequent spacewalks to stow the surviving packages and equipment. Much of it was put into the external cargo containers atop and below the three big water tanks. Smaller packages were ferried in either through the Orion capsule, using it as an airlock, or through the Observation Deck's top EVA airlock. After completing their inventory, it turned out that when the Orion stack got sliced open they'd lost half of their supplies, all the water they'd brought to replenish Hermes' tanks, and one of their three hydrogen bombs.

On the plus side, they had barely enough provisions to supplement their on-board "farm" for the duration of the trip. So if they were very careful, they just might have enough to eat on their journey. The genetically engineered jungle—mainly located in the farming Hab and to a lesser extent dispersed throughout the other modules— supplied half the crew's daily calories. In addition, the jungle sucked in CO_2, produced oxygen, and recycled their solid wastes. But making it to the Asteroid would still be tight. The crew wasn't yet on restricted rations, but if anything bad happened to the jungle they'd soon be starving.

Having only two of their three hydrogen bombs was a concern. But two should still be enough to accomplish whatever they needed to do at the Asteroid—either to provide thrust to knock it out of its orbit or to blast it into pieces. The third bomb had been an extra margin of safety. As it was, they possessed a total of two megatons of combined yield. Strategically placed on the Asteroid, that would hopefully be sufficient to save Earth. Deployed inappropriately, though, it might make the resultant holocaust even worse.

But that was a worry for the future. Rendezvous with the Asteroid was still over five months away. The immediate concern after retrieving and stabilizing Orion's remaining cargo was to accelerate Hermes up to the speed of the Asteroid.

Adriana with Kame's help got the nuclear reactor-powered electrolysis unit up and running, splitting hydrogen and oxygen out of the remaining water in the large storage tanks. Small liquid fuel thrusters, using the accumulated hydrogen and oxygen stores, aligned the unwieldy craft on the proper vector toward their encounter with the Asteroid. Now they were set to begin a prolonged burn using the main Nuclear Thermal Rocket, in which hydrogen heated to 2,500° was spewed out to generate thrust. The NTR used much less fuel volume to generate the same thrust as the smaller liquid fuel jets.

Unfortunately, this required using up most of the remaining water in the tanks. The Hermes crew thus not only had to watch their calorie intact but their water usage. Even though they had near-100% recycling in the Habs, the planned replenishment from the Orion resupply, which should have topped off the water tanks, was lost. Thus they'd be slowly but steadily losing water from Hermes' stores.

On the plus side, they would have a measure of "gravity" from the constant thrust supplied by the NTR. As such, the entire living quarters needed conversion to having "floors" pointed aft. The pseudogravity wouldn't be much—since the NTR was a long-acceleration, low-thrust mechanism—but it would feel like 5-10% G. Fortunately, the contents of Hermes' working, sleeping, exercise, and farming modules were configured to swing into three orientations: nondirectional for zero G (when not under thrust), with floors positioned aft (when under thrust from the NTR), and floors forward (when using centripetal force in the "pigeon-tumbling" mode; after the NTR acceleration finished and they set the entire stack spinning on its long axis).

As Kame and Adriana made the final preparations up in the Observation Deck for firing up the NTR thrusters, Susan's job was to secure everything in the living compartments.

"How are you feeling today, Ben?" she asked as she adjusted his hammock to the aft-horizontal position. It was just a matter of unclipping the ends from one set of rings and onto another. But she wanted to do it gently, maneuvering the floating hammock carefully so not to jar him needlessly.

He grinned at her wanly. He looked terrible. His normally dark skin was sallow. Half the skin of his face was burned off, exposing raw flesh. His eyes were bloodshot. His previously cheerful, rounded face was hollowed out. His full head of hair was now thin and ragged. He looked like a cancer patient undergoing aggressive chemo and radiation-therapy.

"I'm getting better," he whispered, breathing shallowly. "Maybe a little water...?"

"Of course, Ben," she answered, finishing the reorientation of the hammock that swaddled him.

The green leaves and gleaming fruits of the jungle vines cradled his hammock, seemingly actively protecting him. The big black beetles clung to branches over his head as if worried about him. The air was rich with oxygen and musky, earthy smells.

She likewise reoriented the personal storage bag secured below his hammock. Extracting a squirt bottle filled with water she held the nozzle up to his lips, extruding round spheres of water that floated up to his mouth.

He gulped the drifting spheres like a fish out of water, sighing.

"I don't know if I'm...going to like gravity...no matter how little...it's going to hurt."

"I know, Ben. I'm so sorry. But if we don't accelerate we'll never make it to the Asteroid in time to save Earth."

She put a hand gently on his forehead. His skin was simultaneously clammy and hot. He was feverish. An infection was setting in.

Though the intense radiation dose hadn't killed him, it had decimated his immune system. Despite his brave words, he was worse than he admitted.

Susan saw in his eyes that he fully understood his own condition. Yes he was hurting, but also was determined to recover.

"You need to increase...antibiotics in my i.v. drip," he gasped, closing his eyes.

"How much?"

"...can tolerate...double..."

"Do we need to change to a different antibiotic?"

"No...broad-spectrum already...should be ok until my WBCs rebound...a week or so...if I can make it..."

"Ok," she comforted him. "I'll ask Adriana to prepare the solution after we start the sustained burn."

Besides being their main pilot, Johansson was their onboard nurse. Fortunately her knowledge wasn't just superficial. She had solid training and experience as a nurse, having put herself through engineering school by working at a local hospital. That was fortuitous for the crew because their assigned medical doctor, Ben, was the patient needing treatment!

"How soon...until it starts?"

"Oh, an hour or so I guess. It'll be gradual. It shouldn't shake you around. You just go to sleep, ok?"

Susan turned away, about to push off and drift up out of the farming-sleeping-exercise Hab.

"Susan..."

He reached out with a clawed hand, holding her back.

"What, Ben? Is there something else I can do for you?"

"What about...Yamamoto?"

She froze in place, narrowing her eyes. After the nuclear reactor repair disaster, she hadn't mentioned again her suspicions concerning Kame. Indeed, on further reflection she'd felt ashamed of herself. Kame not only stayed behind when she could have safely returned to Earth, but risked her life in her extravehicular excursions saving Orion. Other than her somewhat cool manner, she'd done nothing overt to merit Susan's continued suspicion.

"She seems...fine, Ben. You just rest now."

"Do you...know her background?" Ben gasped, seemingly eager to continue the discussion though it was clearly difficult for him to talk.

She floated closer to him, putting her head near his so he could whisper to her. He was drifting in and out of consciousness, his eyes rolling back in his head. She needed to be close to hear him. But she also wanted to make sure the others couldn't hear them talking. There were microphones throughout the ship to allow easy communication—or spying!

God, she was back into her conspiracy mode. This wasn't healthy. She needed to get a grip on herself, get back to her duties.

But she was fascinated that Ben knew something she didn't about Yamamoto.

"Her mother...was *Sanako* Yamamoto."

"Who?"

"Not many people...aware of the disgrace."

"Disgrace?"

"Dr. Sanako...was a renowned virologist...at the Ehime University in Japan."

"Virologist?"

Aware that she was stupidly just repeating his words, Susan nevertheless was trying to keep him focused on the subject. Sweat was popping out from his forehead. Patches of previously thick but now brittle black hair slid out of his scalp. He was falling to pieces before her eyes!

She suddenly realized that he was dying. He wasn't going to survive. He would soon join Vladimir and George as yet another heroic victim of this whole desperate mission.

I need to know what he has on Kame!

"...banned retroviral research—inserting animal genes into the human germ line...allowing the embryos to develop in the lab..." he gasped weakly.

"But why?"

"Supposedly...to determine the variables...which distinguish us from other animals—why we're humans...genetic alterations in the differentiation of tissue layers—folding of the developing brain in different orientations in the embryos that..."

"I never heard anything about this, Ben. Are you sure that..."

"It's *true!*" he unexpectedly yelled at her, surging up out of the hammock only to collapse back into it. "As the Mission's physician, I have to go over...the medical records...of the crew...even related psychiatric information...on the relatives...just in case of any problems."

"Ben, we'll talk about this later. You need to rest and..."

"No," he gasped, grimacing. "Not...time to delay...Kame's mother, Sanako, was investigated, disgraced—her Ph.D. was revoked, research banned...and then she did the 'honorable' Japanese thing."

"What are you saying?"

"Sanako...split her own guts open with a knife—ritual '*seppuku*' in the middle of her university laboratory, by herself late at night. They found her next morning in a pool of her own blood, face down on the floor."

Susan was shocked. She of course knew of the ancient Japanese tradition of ritualistic suicide, but didn't know it was still done in today's world—and by Kame's own mother! No wonder she looked perpetually traumatized.

"That's tragic, Ben!" she gasped. "The University must have covered it up. I never heard anything about it in the news or professional literature. But if the Professor had a daughter, how could she justify suicide? I've heard that the Japanese hold their family duties even higher than..."

"Kame was...illegitimate."

"What?"

"Yes...an affair with a married Professor...given up at birth. It was only later...that Kame learned the truth of her ancestry...disgraced to be illegitimate...then tainted by the shameful behavior of her mother...both in the laboratory and in her final behavior."

"But if she'd been adopted by another family..."

"She embraced her heritage...both the positive and negative...even officially changing her last name back to her mother's."

"I can see how she'd be ashamed, but not to take the last name..."

"She's...not ashamed. That's just it, don't you see?"

"What?"

"She sees...the *ignoring* of society's norms...even the ritual suicide at the end...as *commendable*."

"How do you know this?"

"I saw...confidential psychiatric files...suggesting the same flaws of her mother's mental make-up...in addition to the genius...had come down to her."

His voice was so faint she could hardly hear it.

"Ben, that can't be right," she whispered back. "Yamamoto never would have been accepted into astronaut training at JAXA, the Japanese Space Agency—let alone gone on an international Mars mission—if there was the slightest question about her mental stability. It sounds to me like her mother got into outlawed research and just got carried away. That happens, particularly when you're brilliant. Even my own father and brother have..."

But Ben had lapsed into silence, his mouth hanging open like he wanted to say something but couldn't get the words out.

"Ben?"

"You're right," he struggled to reply, "...can't happen...but it did!"

"So you're suggesting...a conspiracy?"

"Yes."

She was silent. She was growing more and more suspicious of Ben's thinking process. His neuronal synapses were likely scrambled by the intense radiation he'd endured. His paranoia was probably just a product of his desperate physical condition.

"But there's...even more," he whispered, his words barely audible.

"More?"

"Kame...brought a *knife* onboard with her, Susan—I saw it when I was vomiting and she was cleaning up the mess with a cloth from her kit."

"We've all brought a few personal possessions, Ben."

"Not...like this."

"I've got an old poetry book I brought that..."

"It's got...a wooden handle," he continued as if he didn't hear her. "It's sheathed inside a curved wooden holder—a ritual *seppuku* knife. I studied this when I completed a minor in WWII history, in my pre-graduate work."

"Ok, but still, that could just be..."

He grabbed her arm, pulling himself closer to whisper directly into her ear: "Susan, her mother dishonored her University. The officials there forced Sanako to do what she did! And now her daughter is out to *avenge* her mother—on everyone!"

"Everyone?"

"You...me...everyone on Earth...I don't know...that's my professional evaluation."

He coughed weakly, sagging back into the hammock. His eyes closed. He was barely breathing.

For a moment, Susan thought he was dead.

"How is he?"

Susan jerked back, floundering for a moment in the zero-G.

It was Kame, at the connection leading up to the next higher Hab, looking downward. Her short black hair stuck out in all directions in the zero gravity. Her subtly slanted, intense black eyes seemed to drill directly into Susan's brain!

"He's delirious," Susan hastily replied. "I think he needs a blood transfusion. His WBC count is way down. I'm not a perfect tissue match, but I'm the closest of us three. As soon as we get Hermes' burn going I think Adriana should take a few pints from me and infuse him. Otherwise..."

"That's why I came down—to make sure we could do everything possible for Ben, both immediately and long term. Also, I'm certifying for the record that each Hab is prepared for sustained thrust. From what I've seen you've done a good job, King, putting everything in order. Now I need you to come up and survey the external cargo boxes via their internal cameras. Their load distribution will be critical when we fire up the NTR. The forces won't be as extreme as when we eventually attempt the Tumble. But I still want everything precisely load-balanced as best as we're able."

"I'll be there in just a minute," Susan forced herself to smile back. "I've got to finish getting Ben tied down. He's thrashing around."

"Good. Do it."

Then Kame was gone. Had she heard what Ben was saying? Did she see the suspicion in Susan's eyes? But no, it wasn't possible. They'd been talking too low—mostly.

Susan made sure Ben was strapped in securely to his hammock then readied to push herself upward with her legs.

She paused, launching herself instead over to Kame's screened private cubicle. It was set-into the waving vines of the surrounding jungle foliage opposite to Ben's. She fumbled underneath into Kame's bag and felt something long and hard. Pulling it out Susan held in her hands a flat wooden case. Yanking it open she saw a sharp, curved knife. And flecked here and there along its short blade were *faint red* smears!

Yes, it was dried blood.

Is this the very knife with which Kame's mother committed seppuku?

"Ok then, we've got a possible motive," Susan muttered to herself as she hastily slid the knife back into its case, replacing it where she'd found it. She was appalled yet relieved to discover there was a tangible basis to her prior suspicions. "But we've got to be fair," she cautioned herself. "There may be nothing to this. We can't convict her without evidence. And we need Kame's skills. There's none to replace her. We're stuck with her!"

She half expected Ben to answer from his hammock, but he was barely breathing, unconscious.

"Hang in there," she affectionately said to him as she floated upward and out of the jungle Hab. "I need you Ben. If it comes to a fight, I need you healthy and strong."

It may have been her imagination, but she thought she saw a fleeting grin on his sweat-drenched, burned face as she floated up out of sight.

At least she wasn't in this alone. Adriana was a great friend, but not given to conspiracy theories. It seemed that only Ben shared her "warped" train of thought. Who'd have thunk it?

It was the critical day of her *Dissertation Defense*. Susan had a premonition that something very bad was going to happen—harking back to that day three long years ago when Ben had called her on her cellphone right before her similarly critical Orals examination.

Much had happened since that fateful day.

"The PowerPoint and videos are loaded up and ready to go, Susan. The 3D matrix is active."

"Thanks, Leroy."

They were in the main lecture amphitheater of Nielsen Hall. Leroy was a fellow graduate student who'd volunteered to run the audio-visual equipment. The auditorium could hold up to five hundred people. Susan and Leroy were at the back and top of the amphitheater, looking down over a number of rows of descending chairs toward the stage. A lower, large stage was already set up there, plus a podium off to the side. She would stand at the podium as her slides and videos played upon the screen. She'd timed the entire presentation to thirty minutes on the dot. After that there'd be a period of questions from the audience that could last as long as necessary. The main questioners would be her research review board professors. But after their questions anyone else could stand up and ask a question. Right now the amphitheater was empty. But in a few minutes it would start to fill up. She was scheduled to begin her Ph.D. Dissertation Defense talk in one short hour.

Though it was comfortably warm in the large room, she involuntarily shivered.

Outside, it was icy cold. It was December, right before the Christmas holidays. Uncharacteristically, heavy snow had fallen the night before, coating the lawns and the stately buildings of the University of Oklahoma, Norman campus in a blanket of frosty white. Oklahoma usually had mild winters. But rampant global warming was increasingly screwing with the weather, producing large local swings.

Though Bill and Scott's breakthrough invention promised to revolutionize energy collection, the elevated CO_2 levels from two centuries of industrial burning of fossil fuels remained. Humanity had a long way to go to dig the planet out from under run-away global warming. There'd likely be many more screwy winters before Bill and Scott's miracle device helped turn the tide. She hoped they'd succeed, but still had deep reservations.

But that wasn't her immediate concern.

"You ready, Susan?"

It was her research advisor, Professor Diana Jeworski, who'd just walked into the amphitheater. She was leaner and older-looking than she'd been three years ago. But Diana was still the same kind-hearted, careful researcher who'd shepherded Susan past her intense

Qualifying Exams. Her careful direction was why Susan was still there, ready to present and defend a successful run of original research...

—which was despite everything *not* going smoothly. Indeed, there'd been many bumps along the way, huge problems, even blind alleys that led nowhere. But Professor Jeworski helped Susan steer a course through the terrible setbacks to a successful conclusion. Susan had been tempted on several occasions to just give up and quit! But having one of the better graduate professors guiding her onward was what made the difference. Instead of quitting or getting kicked out, Susan just kept plodding forward, even when she had to make "progress" going backward or sideways!

Now, at last, the end was in sight.

Susan looked at the older woman fondly. Diana's trim brown hair was shorter now, with hints of gray showing in her roots, but she still had the cheerful enthusiasm of a kid. She was well-liked among her department colleagues and staff. In fact, she'd helped Susan to acquire not just astronomical technical knowledge but the managerial, social, and political skills necessary to running a big research program. Susan was immensely grateful to her graduate professor.

"I'm totally pumped!" Susan happily replied. "It's going to be fun!"

Actually, she didn't feel that positive, though she knew how to put on a brave face. She knew that even at this late stage there might be questions that could throw her conclusions into doubt or even necessitate further supportive research before she could be granted her doctoral degree. But that was unlikely. Susan had presented the various parts of her research several times already, at seminars, conventions, and in peer-reviewed papers. Yet this was the first time she'd put it together as a coherent visual package, with the entire department, her doctoral review board, and visitors sitting in judgment.

That prospect didn't worry her. After three years of intense effort she was undoubtedly the expert in the subject matter being presented.

But the *reporters* were another matter entirely...

"Just keep to the subject and you'll be fine," Diana encouraged her, giving Susan a friendly pat on her shoulder before turning away. "And smile for the cameras!"

Yep. There was a line of cameras already set up at the top rim of the room. Normally, reporters cared little or nothing about a graduate student's Dissertation Defense presentation. But this was a "twofer" for them. First, Susan had found evidence of extrasolar life on a nearby planet that was only 16.1 light-years away. Second, she was the sister of Bill King—who was half of the billionaire duo of "King and Nash." In just three short years they'd revolutionized the energy-storage industry, allowing whole fleets of trucks to switch from fossil fuels to clean energy sources. Bill was an industrial "rock star"—and she was his glamorous, photogenic, and brilliant-yet-controversial sister!

"Well, I'm going to have a last look over my notes."

"Don't obsess, Susan. You'll do fine. Remember you know your material far better than anyone here other than me. And I'm 100% on your side!"

Yes, that helped her feel better. Susan gave a grateful smile to both Diana and Leroy.

"Thanks for coming by early and helping me set up. You guys can take a break if you want. I'm just going to go down to the podium and flip through the slides one last time before people start arriving."

"See you in a bit!" Diana waved at her as she and Leroy walked away, going back to their lab.

Susan descended the steps to the bottom of the amphitheater. Then she looked up at the banks of yet-inactive cameras glaring down at her. She grimaced.

"Gonna be a circus," she muttered to herself.

She wished that the reporters were present just to document her part in discovering a possible hint of chlorophyll at Gliese 832C. The groundbreaking discovery was a large-team effort, facilitated by the recent launch and activation of the James Webb successor: the *High Definition Space Telescope* (HDST). Versus Hubble's 2.4-meter-wide single mirror and James Webb's 6.5-meter-wide segmented mirror, HDST had a whopping 11.7-meter-wide segmented array. As such, plus recent innovations in starlight-exclusion, it had achieved the herculean task of imaging the incredibly faint and distant super-Earth planet of Gliese 832C. The image revealed what looked like clouds and oceans. But any chlorophyll signature was still too low for detection—that is until Susan discovered a way to use her X-ray planetary disc probing to amplify the signal.

That was a bad memory, a time of intense frustrations.

She'd spent over a year fruitlessly trying to use x-rays emanating from new suns to help locate and analyze forming planets within coalescing planetary discs. It was a great idea that didn't work, no matter how she tried to tweak the data or methods. On the verge of giving up her research and slinking away to work for Scott and Bill, Diana had helped redirect her effort onto the HDST search. Her expertise on the IXO-3 x-ray astronomy satellite proved to be the key to detecting the faint chlorophyll signature.

But that wasn't the main reason the reporters would be eagerly filming her presentation and (when their turn came) plying her with questions. She was an outspoken critic of the new "super-battery" that her brother had helped invent. Everybody else were fawning over the duo, talking about them likely winning a Nobel Prize for "saving the world." But when asked about it, she raised reasonable doubts concerning its reliability. She publically challenged her brother and his partners to reveal their "super-battery" fundamental principles and design, which they steadfastly refused to do. She pointed out that storing vast amounts of energy in such small devices violated several laws of physics, regardless of the company scientists repeatedly invoking a theoretical "subspace."

She wasn't antagonistic, though. She was merely and properly remaining scientifically skeptical. Yet since she was both an intimate observer of her father's research—plus being a qualified physicist—the media gave weight to her objections. Thus her brother—always flanked by the devious Scott—now rarely spoke to her, accusing her publically of "betraying" him out of jealousy! Hah, as if she could be jealous of his bumbling with their Dad in the sheds behind their house! He hadn't discovered anything. He just stumbled by blind luck upon some strange and scary new physics principle!

But as he and his company grew ever richer and influential, her interests turned increasingly in an opposite direction. While Scott and Billy focused on the mechanics of Earth her eyes turned outward. She became more and more fascinated with the prospect of extrasolar life. As Earth's scientific community turned inward to meet the needs of the planet's huge, still-increasing human population, she dreamed of going to the stars.

She, along with a cadre of other exploratory scientists, viewed their precious "blue marble" as just one amongst millions or billions of other planets hosting sentient life in the cosmos—making Earth not the unique platform envisioned by the average human. So she became disconnected from the seemingly "trivial" problems of a planet being relentlessly cooked, drowned in its own garbage, depleted of natural resources, and irretrievably losing most of its marvelous animal species. For Susan, looking outward at the near-infinite Cosmos was definitely preferable to being smothered by a dominant species that was at war with itself, broken into bitter political factions, and obsessed with day-to-day survival.

So she was one of the few voices left with enough clout and expertise to be credible on the subject of planetary survival. Using her celebrity platform she delivered cutting critiques to the increasingly cut-throat energy-industry. She was happy being one of the few scientists speaking out against "crazy" research, such as Scott's adaptation of her Dad's failed cold-fusion obsession. Sure, it worked, but for how long? What terrible problems were hidden behind their "proprietary" secrets? She was convinced it *could not* be as good as they claimed!

So she was surprised when she felt her cellphone vibrate in her shirt pocket, pulled it out, and saw from the caller i.d. that it was Bill.

A stab of fear went through her.

She almost didn't answer it. She doubted he was calling to wish her luck at her Dissertation Defense. So it must be the bad news she had been dreading for some time. But she couldn't ignore the call. Whatever the problem, she'd learned facing it head-on was the best approach.

"Hey, Billy—what's up?"

"It's mother."

Her heart sank.

Oh, God...she'd been expecting this call for over a year now. Her mother, Sally King, took a turn for the worse a couple years back, almost dying. Intensive therapy brought her back. But her condition steadily deteriorated. And for the past five weeks she'd been in a diabetic coma, kept alive on machines. The doctors felt that there was still hope that Sally King might emerge from her coma. So they were watchful while cautioning the immediate family to expect the worse.

Susan, ever in the throes of her research—swamped by her dissertation write-up and unexpected "mop-up" research demanded by her advisors—couldn't fault her brother in the least for calling her now, as he'd taken on the brunt of looking after their mother. Sally hadn't even been to Sulphur for months. Plus Bill paid for the best possible medical care for Sally King. The one role that Susan had studiously maintained for her mother was to not allow Bill to move Sally away from the Artesian Nursing Home which her Mother had grown to love.

Susan's mother, in her prior lucid moments, readily agreed that her medical needs were too extensive for her to continue living at her nicely rebuilt house on 12th street. To her credit, Sally didn't want to be a burden to anyone, particularly her son and daughter. But Susan knew her mother didn't want to die in a sterile hospital ward. At the nursing home Sally was cared for by loving, familiar staff. Plus she was surrounded by friendly fellow patients in a comfortable rest-home environment.

And, most importantly, Sally was right beside her beloved Park. When she was healthier, the staff often rolled her out in her wheelchair through the fence gate and across a narrow two-lane road. There she'd sit surrounded by tall trees in a grassy meadow. It was her one passion. She could no longer go running or biking as she had when she was young. If nothing else, her massive weight—now over four hundred pounds—prevented her from such. But at least Sally could often—for whatever brief periods—breathe clean air and feel fresh breezes on her skin.

And after just a half hour sitting in the Park she cheerfully allowed her attendants to wheel her back inside to watch her beloved soap operas and game shows on T.V.—happily living out her final years.

So it had finally happened, had it?

Yes, Susan had been expecting the news. But it was still a shock. Losing your father or mother is always a devastating blow to one's sense of continuity and stability. *But why did it have to happen now?*—Susan angrily yelled in her head. *God, I'm just about to go on-stage for the biggest presentation of my entire life! I don't need this right now! Couldn't you have held off until tomorrow?*

Susan was immediately ashamed at her selfish mental outburst. She sighed deeply and spoke into the cellphone: "So she's dead?"

"We don't know."

"Say what?"

"She's missing, Suzy. When the nurses did their morning rounds, Mother was...gone."

"Gone?"

"Well, her tubes were pulled out and hanging. The machines were turned off, which is why the alarms didn't bring people running. And her wheelchair is missing."

For a moment, Susan was dumbfounded.

"So...you're saying...?"

"I don't know what happened, Suze. Her doctors are baffled. But it looks like she just woke up, unhooked herself, managed to climb unaided into her wheelchair, and took off into the Park."

That could not happen. Maybe she might come out of the coma. But she certainly couldn't jump up and go rolling into the Park!

But, whatever, Sulphur was a small town located right beside the wide-open Park. If Sally King was out there in the Park it should be an easy task to locate her.

"Well then *find* her!" Susan snapped.

"We're trying, Suzy. Park Ranger search parties are out scouring the main areas. Losa's got a bunch of his Indian friends combing the less accessible surrounding forest. She couldn't have gotten far. But so far, there's no sign of..."

"Could it be a kidnapping?" Susan interrupted him, starting to think clearer.

Scott, Bill, and the Chickasaw Indian coalition that were funding and manufacturing the "super-batteries" had rapidly accrued a long list of enemies. Perhaps if they'd kept their long list of original secondary backers they'd have allies instead of sworn enemies. But as soon as they could they'd cast aside their other backers. The Chicka-saw Nation was now synonymous with "Nashoba Energy." Many powerful vested interests were arrayed against the revolutionary de-vice. Scott and Bill regularly got death threats, even from trivial com-plainers such as "classic energy" drivers. They only trusted "God-given" gasoline in their tanks. Industrial enemies, though, were far more subtle and dangerous.

Consequently, the security apparatus at Nashoba Energy—as Bill and Scott named their new company—was extensive. "Nashoba" in-voked the Chickasaw legend of the loyal *Big White Dog* that helped lead the tribe along the "trail of tears" to their ultimate new homeland in Oklahoma. Also, it incorporated the main part of Scott's original last name: Yanash. And it made the company seem all his, from his changed last name: Nash! But despite Scott's deviousness, the Chick-asaw were a very prudent and careful people, well-schooled to be se-curity-minded by their long history of resisting well-funded govern-mental organizations.

"It's possible, Suzy—but there's no sign of a struggle or penetra-tion of our multi-layered defenses. Beside our police and Park forces, you know that I pay for round-the-clock, state-of-the-art security at the nursing home."

He sounded petulant, defending himself.

"I'm not blaming you, Billy," she hastened to add. "But if your en-emies have gotten hold of Mother then they have a big stick to hold over you!"

"I know that perfectly well, Suzy," he said, his voice carefully con-trolled. "But mother is..."

"She's a *weak link!*" Susan yelled at him through the phone. "It's bad enough I'm your sister always having to look over my shoulder if a crazy is coming after me because of your spooky invention. But Mother shouldn't have to be in danger!"

"Your 'danger' is easily solved, Suzy. You could have all the body-guards you wanted!" he snapped back at her.

"Do we have to fight over this again?" she growled.

"Just come and work with us, Suzy!" he pleaded. "Come on! You've played around long enough with your little star-searching stuff! After today everyone's signing off on your Ph.D., right? So come and join us! Do something that's *really* important, that's helping people on *this* planet! And you'll be helping *me*, your brother. I'm getting worn out by all this, Suze. I can't sleep anymore. I'm always on edge. If it wasn't for Scott I'd..."

"*Focus*, Billy! This is about *Mother*, not you! Didn't your security cameras at the nursing home show what happened to her?"

There was a moment of silence.

"Billy?"

"They were being upgraded," he reluctantly admitted. "We were switching our cloud supplier to one we thought was more reliable. We thought the feeds were being backed up appropriately. It turns out that..."

"Oh, *Jesus*, Billy! How could you screw up like that?"

"That's why I need you here, Suzy! I'm not a practical person. I'm a *dreamer*, just like Dad! You're the one who figures out every little tiny detail, just like Mom always did when she was healthy. I'm no good at managing people! I've got the financial and technical details organized in my mind, that's no problem. But these *people* keep nagging at me! You're the good 'people person.' That's why you've excelled at being in college for years and years and years! Why can't you see that we're a team, better together than apart?"

She didn't need this argument, particularly with her Presentation looming just minutes away.

"Billy, let's not fight. Just find Mom, ok?"

"Can't you come and help?" he begged her.

"Well I've got...a 'little' something here to take care of first," she just managed not to yell at him, controlling her pent-up rage. "After it's finished, I promise you I'll hop into my Fiero and drive right down—just like three years ago when you turned my world upside down!"

"How many times do I have to say I'm sorry about what happened to our home and your bedroom and your childhood stuff and..."

"Oh, just forget it! I have to go! I'll get there as soon as possible."

Jesus Christ! She just committed to speeding to Sulphur on I-35 in her Fiero, just like before! It was happening to her again! It was a continuing nightmare...

"I wish you'd let me buy you another car—powered by one of our wonderful, new, compact Super-Batteries," he complained.

"I don't need anything from you!" she snapped at him. Then, more gently, she added: "I'm sorry, Billy. I meant I don't need anything from you and your corporate friends. Maybe I am just a 'stargazer' who is 'wasting' my time exploring a Universe we can never hope actually to reach—but I do still love you, little brother. I don't act like it much, but it's true. Just do what you have to in order to find Mom!"

"Well...I love you too," he quietly replied. "And we'll find her. There's an army out looking for her. And if it's an enemy, well Nashoba has offensive capacities as well as defensive."

She had no idea what that meant, but didn't like it. What had Billy gotten his self into? He sounded sincere about having a nervous breakdown. He'd always been a shy introvert with no talent at dealing with hordes of new people. She'd tried to shield him, protect him. But it was his decision to get in bed with Scott! She'd escaped Scott and his seductive appeals. And now he was drawing her back in!

"Oh, Christ," she gasped, trembling with anger. She closed her eyes, struggling to regain her composure.

"Are you alright?"

It was the University President, standing right in front of her. She forced a smile onto her face, nodding to him pleasantly. "Just a family matter, I'm fine! Please take a seat up front."

People were starting to file in. She hadn't had a chance to go over her slides for a last time. But that was ok. She had her notes in front of her on the podium. And she'd already practiced her talk dozens of times. She was as prepared as she'd ever be.

"See you shortly," she spoke softly into her cellphone. "Take care of yourself, Billy."

Not waiting for a reply, she stuck the phone back into her pocket as she took up her place behind the podium.

From the controls located on the top she lowered the auditorium's lights and triggered the holographic display. It wasn't a 3D moving video, but it was great at displaying static life-like objects without the need for 3D glasses.

There in the middle of the room, hanging above everyone, sprang up a *large sphere*.

It was an actual holographic image of Gliese 832C, assembled from multiple viewings from the HDST. It was a huge planet, several times the size of Earth. Its atmosphere was barely visible as a faint blue haze. Vast blurry white clouds covered deep blurry blue oceans. And here and there was just the vaguest hint of brown—continents!

It was magnificent!

Yes, it'd already been on countless news and scientific channels and publications. It was nothing new to the attendees. But it certainly set the stage for her recounting her small part in the extensive team's efforts to unlock its distant secrets, for tweaking out the chlorophyll signal.

It was so faint she'd had to jump through statistical hoops to make her case for its presence. But she was convinced it was real and had made the case persuasively in her dissertation.

There were likely plants up there.

And who knew if chomping on the plants might be a civilization of *aliens?*

She'd probably never know for sure. She would certainly never travel to that planet. But someday in the distant future she was sure that humanity—if it survived its present self-generated problems—would encounter beings from another star.

Billy was wrong. She wasn't just a nerdy bean-counter at a lab bench. She was *also* a Dreamer!

And, yes, she was reasonably good with people. She didn't find them scary. Despite her "alien" interests, Susan found the human species endlessly fascinating!

Chapter 12

COSMIC BOREDOM

Floating amongst the stars

Even at the blistering speed of light

Oh, Jesus, such a long, sweet ride

Immense distances even between planets

And stars so far apart you'd never survive

In your lifetime not even coming close

To travel from one to the other

The closest extrasolar suns

Effectively isolated and unreachable

Our own little lives but a brief twinkle

Until we "wink out" in the night

Drifting along like a leaf on a river

Floating alone in the night

Suddenly disappearing

Pulled beneath the waves

Snorkels are optional.

The Minstrel's Lark, 12:40-44

IMPACT MINUS FIVE MONTHS, *ACCELERATING...*

Ben survived his bout with acute radiation sickness. But he wasn't the same.

Before the fateful spacewalk, he was a vibrant, dark haired, smooth faced young man. Now, he looked to be in his 70's—with splotched skin, gray-white hair, plagued by perpetual exhaustion.

He spent most of his time lying in his hammock, his eyes closed, immersed in the surrounding greenery. The black beetles that normally kept to the branches of the intertwined vines even started crawling out upon him. They sat on his forehead and scraggly hairs as if he were merely another branch.

Hermes was under constant, slow-but-steady acceleration, relentlessly pushed faster by its nuclear thermal rocket. Gradually they were approaching the speed necessary to rendezvous with the rapidly descending Asteroid: near 60,000 mph. They were traveling faster than any humans had before in the entire history of mankind. And yet they had only an apparent 0.1 G within the ship, barely enough to provide a "down" orientation in the direction of the aft, constantly firing nuclear engine.

"And how are you feeling today, Ben?" Susan asked, settling into her own hammock next to him. Her living-mat screen was pushed to the side. She reached into her bag to pull out her moldy old leather-bound poetry book. Then she reached up, pulled out an extendable lamp, and turned on a reading light.

He opened his eyes, staring off into the canopy of leaves above him. A couple big black beetles crawled slowly on one of his arms.

"You off duty?" he said in his creaky "old person" voice, ignoring her polite but pointless question.

He wasn't doing well. This was obvious to anyone.

"Yes, for a few hours. There's trouble with the water recycling system. We're steadily losing volume, but don't know why. I inspected the seals in the connecting lines, but can't see any leakage. So I thought I'd take a break, let my subconscious chew on the problem for a while."

"Sorry I'm not...keeping up...my fair share."

"Hey, don't worry, Ben. We girls are doing just fine. We don't need you 'boys' getting in our way!"

That brought out a feeble grin on his splotched face. Yes, just the three "girls"—Susan, Adriana, and Kame—were running a ship normally requiring a crew of six. The three of them kept very busy trying to keep the complex ship's systems operating. Hermes had been due for a refit and complete refurbishment after its last Mars transit, which was missed due to the Asteroid emergency. Even more problematic was Hermes' close swing around Earth, brushing the atmosphere, which did even more damage than they'd first thought.

They were just barely keeping the ship together.

"I don't...have any energy," Ben now quietly sobbed.

"You rest up, Ben," she reassured him from her hammock, hoping he'd quiet so she could read. "Once we get to the Asteroid there'll be more than enough work for you."

"Like what?" he now snorted.

Sighing to herself, she lay the old book open on her chest and reached out her hand to lightly touch his arm. Clearly, he needed encouragement more than she needed some "alone" time.

"The only way we're going to figure out how to deflect or destroy the Asteroid safely will be by consulting experts back on Earth once we've directly analyzed the situation. You're our communications expert. You'll have to talk us through it."

"You'll do fine without me."

"Ben, don't despair! Your body is recuperating. Just give it more time. We've got several months still before we join the Asteroid. You'll be fine by then, back to your old self. You'll see!"

He weakly laughed, closing his eyes tightly. Tears trickled off to each side of his eyes. She sadly withdrew her hand from his arm. He knew she was humoring him, trying to keep his spirits up. He wasn't going to get any better. But it was a nice fiction to maintain, much better than speaking frankly of his grim situation.

"How's Kame doing?" he asked. His tone was neutral.

After that first conversation concerning Kame's background, they hadn't mentioned or discussed the knife she had hidden away in her bag. Yamamoto was as inscrutable and detached as always. But she'd done nothing to provoke any further suspicion. Furthermore, as the new Commander of the mission, she'd been both fair and reasonable.

"We're pulling together, Ben. The immediate concern is the water leakage. Hermes' tanks were already low when it got back to Earth from Mars. We used most of what little was left generating the hydrogen and oxygen we needed for our liquid fuel. Losing the water we were bringing with us in the SLS was a big blow. At the end of our present acceleration burn we'll only have half a tank left where we should have had three. That's why the recycling problem is so important. We may have to start rationing water. Thank God the jungle is doing well. Otherwise we'd also have to start rationing our calories."

"And...the radiation level?"

She paused before answering.

"You know full well as our ship physician that being in space for a prolonged period means we all get an elevated dose of radiation, versus being back on Earth under its protective atmosphere. And, yes, we're also constantly exposed to additional radiation from the nuclear reactor. Without the full three tanks of water between us and it, we'll be in the danger zone before we return to Earth."

He nodded thoughtfully. "Tell Johansson...to double the vitamin C dosage in our daily rations."

"Sorry, Ben—it won't work," she interrupted him. She didn't want to be short with him. But they'd already had this discussion several times. His memory was starting to fail him.

"But...it's an antioxidant that will help...mopping up radiation-generated free radicals in our cells that...?"

"The renewal supply of vitamin C was part of what we lost when the nano-cable sliced through the lower part of our Orion stack," Susan gently reminded him. She was trying not to get upset at continually having to repeat what he already knew. "We only have what remained in the stocks here on Hermes. We have enough vitamin C to prevent scurvy from setting if—God forbid—we should lose our fresh jungle fruits. But that's all we've got, just a minimal dosage. There's no increase possible."

"Then..."

"There's just nothing we can do about the radiation, Ben. We'll all be impaired by the time we make it to the Asteroid. Hopefully it'll not be acute, as it was in your case. But none of us are getting out of this mission intact. At a minimum each of us will have sharply elevated cancer risk. At worse our bodies will be failing."

"I guess that's...only fitting," he sighed.

"And why's that, Ben?" she said, now getting irritated with his fatalism, no matter how ill he was. "This 'act of God' is threatening the entire planet. We're a symbol of human defiance! But..." she sighed in resignation, "I guess we're not in some heroic disaster movie. We're not superheroes. We're just tiny bags of flesh and blood daring to confront a giant space rock!"

Ben snorted weakly, agreeing.

"So you're a Christian, right?"

They hadn't talked about religion before. This was something new. Ben was apparently confronting not just the possible extinction of mankind, but his own personal mortality as well. He was getting "sage" in his radiation-induced old age.

"I was raised that way," she soberly replied. "I still believe in Jesus' teachings. But I'm not a church-goer. I came to the conclusion that the *concept* of 'God' is way too big to fit within any of the established religions' traditions. At least that's how I feel."

"And...I...was raised as a Hindu," he mused. "As you did, I also gave up formal rituals as mostly a waste of time. But I too...accept many of its basic teachings."

"So how do you reconcile what's happening to our planet with a greater spiritual reality?" she asked, truly curious for his perspective. She didn't know much about the Hindu religion. "Do you even believe in God? I thought that you Hindus have many deities—worshipping many idols?"

"We do believe in...one Supreme Being—but not as a discrete entity. This *Absolute* is...dispersed...into many forms and characters."

"That's confusing, isn't it? I thought that the great religions all recognized one single God: being '*monotheistic*' in their beliefs?"

He laughed then coughed for a while before regaining control of his voice.

"But you...Christians...split 'God' into three parts—do you not?"

Susan sighed deeply, not wanting a doctrinal debate, but happy to engage Ben, keeping him from falling deeper into his crippling depression.

"Well, Ben—you won't hear that from any Christian preacher. But I guess you're right: '*God the Father, God the Son, and God the Holy Spirit*'...the '*Holy Trinity*'—yep, God in three parts!"

"And yet you preach that God is one, not three—a contradiction," he weakly stated.

"Yes, it's confusing...but I think that all the religions have internal contradictions that the members just ignore or explain away."

"That's true."

"And for many people, religion is just a way to have a comfortable framework against Nature's cruel realities," she shrugged in her bunk, looking up at the surrounding plant life. "We're all temporary, struggling to survive for a few moments more, fighting to get enough to eat. Religion gives many people a sense of safety in unpredictable chaos, rather than a means of searching for the Infinite. I've heard that at the heart of all religions is an *unknowable* Mystery. That's what I find most fascinating, not the many rituals and clashing doctrines. That's the 'god' that I perceive, as seen vaguely in the Laws of Nature."

"That's the best 'religious' viewpoint," he softly stated, his voice strengthening. "And it certainly underlines the limits of our feeble human understanding. What you personally believe sounds much like the Hindu concept of one Absolute with many manifestations. Yet our Hindu view of the Universe is definitely different from yours, much more expansive."

Ben was indeed sounding stronger. He wasn't hesitating as much. This discussion was good for him.

"But I definitely do perceive the Unknowable Mystery in Nature, Ben. Are you speaking of something else?" she asked.

"Did not Jesus teach a linear life, both for individuals and the world?"

"A 'linear' life? Uhm...I guess so. You live, you die, and then you go to heaven or hell. And finally the world will be destroyed by God— with mankind standing in Judgment before Him. That's the main doctrine of Christianity, I guess."

"So...are you alluding to something like the Big Rock coming at us?"

"*Jesus*, Ben—that's exactly right! Jesus talked of the world being destroyed in fire. That fits with what we're trying to prevent. If the Asteroid hits Earth then there'll be a fireball like none other. It'll be the equivalent of thousands of nuclear bombs going off at once. The experts think it'll cause a global firestorm that will kill everything that's not buried underground or deeply submerged. That's pretty much what happened when an asteroid ended the reign of the dinosaurs, 65 million years ago, according to the latest core readings from the impact site. So, yes, I suppose Christianity does teach a *linear* destiny."

"But Hinduism sees beyond that."

"What?"

"We see the Universe in terms of endless *cycles*."

"Cycles?"

"Yes, Susan, a looped *creation* then *preservation* and then *dissolution*—which endlessly repeats!" he barked the words to emphasize them. "We see the Cycle as being under control of our three major Deities: *Brahma* the Creator, *Vishnu* the Preserver, and *Shiva* the Destroyer. These three deities each play equal roles in regulating that which we call 'reality.'"

This was a completely new idea to Susan. She'd heard those names before, but never associated them with the problems and disasters of day-to-day life. It *did* put things into a completely different perspective.

"It kind of boggles one's mind," she mused. "So you view the Asteroid threat not as divine punishment, but a natural part of the cycling of both our lives and the Universe?"

"Yes, I do. But we're back again to our feeble little human brains. We barely see beyond our own individual deaths, let alone to the end and rebirth of this Universe."

It was interesting but very disquieting. A "linear" Universe was far easier to comprehend than what Ben was proposing.

"But if everything is in flux, with no linear goal to work toward such as heaven, then how does anything we do *matter?* It's all destined to be undone then redone, over and over!"

"Oh, quite the contrary, Susan—what you and I personally do *does* greatly matter. You've heard of 'karma' right?"

"Yes, personal responsibility...cause and effect...right?"

"Right, Susan. From the Hindu perspective, each one of us creates our own destiny—by our own individual thoughts, words, and deeds."

"But destiny for what?"

"The ultimate goal is to finally and completely *merge* with God!"

Wow. That was a new concept for Susan—an *inspiring* one!

"That's interesting, Ben. So we're back to what is 'God'?"

"Yes, we are, Susan. It's a marvelous destiny that we may never achieve, or only do so after countless cycles of creation, preservation, and destruction. But along the way our individual thoughts, words, and actions carry great weight. And that includes *truth, honesty, peacefulness, sexual discipline, cleanliness, contentment, meditation, self-control, perseverance, accountability,* and *community.* Those are the key focus-points for Hindus struggling to live their everyday lives."

"That's heavy responsibility for each single individual to..."

"Yes, it is, Susan," he interrupted her. "And have you also heard of 'Reincarnation,' where each person's karma is gradually resolved and refined over many lifetimes, expressed from within many lifeforms?"

"Of course, but there's not much evidence for..."

"This is more than mere rational evidence, Susan!" he urgently insisted, now sitting up in his hammock. "Again it comes back to our feeble 'ant' brains! Our 'facts' are what our tiny little minds can perceive! What we can't perceive doesn't exist, right? It's not even part of the conversation, not even acknowledged as a possibility, no matter how remote!"

This was a strange turn of the conversation. Why were they taking about the inconceivable? Was he trying to get her to think beyond the normal limitations?

"But what other basis is there for making decisions than our own rational thoughts?"

This was getting to be a deep discussion. She enjoyed this rare span of lucidity from Ben. It distracted her from the immediate, escalating problems—and the giant deadly rock hurtling down at Earth!

"Oh, I'm not going mystical on you, Susan," he sighed, lying wearily back down in his hammock. "Don't worry about me going crazy. I am too good of a physician and scientist to get lost in self-delusional dead ends. I'm simply pointing out to you yet another belief of Hinduism—that there are *unseen worlds* that *extend beyond* this one, where *other, strange beings* which we often call 'gods' reside. From the Hindu perspective the true extent of 'reality' is far greater than we acknowledge or can even conceive! We think that the microscopic rock upon which we live in our solar system is the center of everything. But it's actually not even a tiny, tiny fraction of the whole. I'm sure you intellectually recognize that our sun is but one of billions in our galaxy the Milky Way, which in turn is but one galaxy amongst trillions! In the 'whole' of just our presently conceived reality we barely register as even being present!"

Susan was silent for a moment, thinking. Clearly Ben was a much deeper thinker than she'd previously recognized. In their training for this mission she saw him as a smart, nice, friendly young man. Now— maybe due to his physical transformation into a feeble old man—she saw he was more than just a friendly contemporary.

But what did that mean?

"You know, Ben, I have a book here which I brought with me that you might also find interesting. It says the same things you just related to me but in strangely different and even troubling ways."

"Ah—so you *do* have a strong spiritual side to you, despite your having given up on formal religion. Where was it that you got this book?"

That statement revived troubled memories that linked-into her still-continuing Nightmare.

It *scared* her.

"You know, that's the funny thing, Ben. It wasn't something I looked for—it was an accident. I found the book abandoned in a Park near my home. Apparently someone had thrown it away. In fact, I rescued it out of a trash can where my little brother tossed it."

He laughed.

"So, what one person considers 'trash'..."

"—another person discovers is a *treasure!*" she excitedly completed the sentence. "Who said that? Was it a famous philosopher or an actor in a movie?"

He laughed again, weakly.

"That notion has been around for a long time, Susan. An oft-quoted proverb from the 17th century was: '*One man's meat is another man's poison.*' It's a 'tasty' concept, huh? Accepting that other people can see contradictory qualities to what one's own mind perceives, well that's the root of collective advancement. It's the foundation upon which the scientific method rests."

"That is both profoundly disturbing and intriguing! I wish during my many school years that I'd had time for discussions like this. But I was swamped by my 'factual' science courses and research efforts."

"Yes, that's so typical of Western schools—prioritizing that which leads to tangible results or jobs, while discounting or rejecting mentally creative pursuits."

"But we do have strong artistic programs."

"True, but largely unrewarded—where only a tiny fraction of the participants benefit financially," he casually observed.

Though mentally stimulated, Susan felt her body giving-in to the low-G delights of the gently swaying hammock. She was finding it hard to stay awake.

She yawned widely, settling back.

She reached up and turned off her reading lamp, figuring she'd already had sufficient "mentally creative" stimulation. She cradled the book in her arms. It was comforting.

"I've got to get some sleep so I can be fresh for my next shift, Ben. You try to rest also, ok? We're going to have lots of time to talk more about all of this when..."

"Don't let the bedbugs bite!" he laughed as she drifted off.

That was funny. The beetles were an integral part of the jungle ecosystem. They didn't bite. They were friendly!

But then a chill went through her as she heard Ben's puzzled next shout: "The damn bugs on my head just *died!*"

Ah well, he was back to his hallucinations. Poor Ben...she had enjoyed his brief period of lucid discussion. Now he was back to his babblings. This world-rescuing space mission was just getting weirder and weirder.

Again, Susan was exhausted. But she found the hour-and-a-half ride from Norman Oklahoma to Sulphur strangely exhilarating.

Versus the last time she'd done this hectic dash, she now didn't face several more years of uncertain struggle in graduate school. Her major professors on her dissertation board had officially signed off on her presentation. She'd passed her Dissertation Defense with flying colors. She now possessed a Ph.D. in Astrophysics. It wouldn't be finalized until she received her official diploma in the mail, but her marathon college education was over.

Now what?

Sure, she could toss everything she'd done to the side and go work for Bill and Scott. They still wanted her as their Vice President for Research and Development. Having a Ph.D. in a legitimate field of physics, she'd be accepted by the business community as a legitimate VP for Research. Plus she'd be paid a nice, fat salary. Nashoba Energy certainly didn't require her expertise in astrophysics as they were already doing quite well—manufacturing millions of units per year. But it would be a coup for the corporation to get the "doubting Thomas" onboard, especially with her high profile in the mass media. She could overnight go from being a struggling graduate student to a rich, comfortable corporate executive!

Uggghhh...not attractive, no matter how much money was involved.

"*Mom's* the priority now," she muttered to herself as she zipped along the crowded I-35 freeway. "After putting off my responsibility for years, she has to come first."

Yes, despite the murkiness of everything else, *that* was very clear to Susan. She could still be there for her mother while *not* taking the VP offer. There were other interesting offers on the table. Her prospects weren't limited to "giving-in" to Billy and his conniving friend Scott! Already some small colleges had offered her lecturing positions, though they didn't have any attached research money. She'd have to fight for grant money on her own. A couple of intriguing "post-doc" positions were dangled out there, ready for her to apply. True, she'd be working for near slave-wages as a post-doc. But she'd be on the cutting edge of astrophysics at some world-class laboratory. Also, she'd heard that NASA was recruiting for a new class of astronauts to crew an upcoming Mars mission. She'd never forgotten her nagging compulsion to become an astronaut. And of course she was welcome to continue her present line of research in Diana's lab at the University of Oklahoma.

It would be several months until the funding for her present research appointment in Diana's lab ran out, so she had time to consider her options.

"Where are you, Mom?" Susan grimaced, pushing the intriguing thoughts of her future prospects out of her head. "I want you there with me. I don't want you either lost or dead. Please be ok!"

Turning off at exit 55 she left I-35 and drove rapidly east through the small town of Davis. In ten minutes she was at the outskirts of Sulphur. At the second stoplight she turned south on 12th and soon was at the Park entrance. Instead of entering the Park she turned to her right and approached the nursing home. Her heart sank at seeing the road blocked by police cars. All along the ride down she'd hoped that Bill was exaggerating or had already found Mom rolling around in her wheelchair. But a lot of officials were present. The major news channels were there also, their vans crowding the parking lot, their cameras taking in everything.

She pulled over onto a side street, parked, and walked the remaining distance.

"Ms. King! Ms. King! Any news of your mother?" several reporters shouted at her as they saw her approaching.

"We'll have a statement later!" she heard a shrill voice. "Let her through!"

"Is it true that aliens abducted your mother?"

"That's ridiculous..."

"Have kidnappers submitted a ransom demand?" another reporter shouted. "How is it that your security was breached?"

"Please get out of my way!" a male voice insisted

Bill King, surrounded by security guards, pushed through the crowd, enveloped Susan, and swept her on into the building.

Despite her anger with Bill, she was concerned to see he was trembling. The encounter—brief as it was—with the reporters outside had drained him. His face was ashen, his skin pulled taunt. He looked worse than she'd ever seen him. Clearly he was proof that being a rich Nashoba executive had its negatives!

Charitably, though, she pushed that thought aside. Shy Billy was always traumatized by unexpected situations and crowds of people. It wasn't Nashoba Energy's fault that he was a strong introvert pushed into an extravert role.

"We found her wheelchair," he breathlessly said to her, grabbing her arm and pulling her along.

"So where's Mom? What's happening? Why are the reporters here?"

"Please come with us and we'll tell you what we know," a policeman said, moving between her and Billy.

He was a beefy, jowly man with a buzz cut. He was one of the local Sulphur police, competent in the normal small-town environment but unused to such turmoil. He was clearly nervous, out of his depth. Following him into a conference room, Susan was startled to see FBI and state police there. They stopped talking as she entered with Bill.

"So she's either kidnapped or murdered?" Susan abruptly accused the roomful of law-enforcement officers. "Which is it?"

Nothing else could explain the presence of such an extensive task force.

"We've located your mother's wheelchair below the pier on Veterans Lake where..." a uniformed, older woman began to explain.

Not waiting to hear more, Susan turned and dashed out of the room, running through the crowd of startled reporters, sprinting for her parked Pontiac Fiero. She slid in behind the seat, cranked-on the engine, and gunned the car. She skidded up to the entrance to the Park, turned right at the stop sign, and shot up the road toward Veterans Lake. The speed limit was 25 mph. She was doing upwards of 45 mph. At the Veterans Lake entrance she took a hard right and skidded up the narrow street to the small pier that jutted out onto the lake.

The area was roped off. But she ignored the protests of the officers on duty and drove right through the security tape. Then she stopped, jumped out, and dashed through a throng of detectives gathered at the end of the wooden pier.

There, just visible beneath the surface of the water, Susan saw the round metal wheels of her mother's self-powered wheelchair.

"So..." Susan gasped. "It's not a corporate kidnapping or murder—but...*suicide?* No...this can't be! It's impossible!"

"We've got divers coming to look for the body," a female police detective kindly told her. She took hold of Susan's arm and attempted to steer her away from the site.

"No. I can't believe it!" Susan said, shaking off the hand and moving back to the edge of the pier. "She wouldn't have killed herself. No matter how sick or confused she was, she never thought of suicide. She wouldn't even authorize denial of end-of-life care should she be incurable and comatose! She refused to sign any 'do not resuscitate' order! She wanted to fight to the absolute end!"

The muddy water below the pier churned as if in denial.

"A lot of things change when you're in pain or find yourself in a hopeless situation," the female detective sadly shrugged. "I've seen situations where..."

Suddenly *the ground shook*, sending large waves rippling out across the blue surface of the lake!

"Uh oh," the detective said, backing off from the edge of the trembling pier and pulling Susan with her. "It's an earthquake."

Again the ground dropped away beneath their feet, only to *totter a couple feet to one side* then to the other! It was a *large* earthquake, possible a 7.0 or greater!

"What's that?" Susan said, shakily pointing as she struggled to stand upright.

Out in the center of the lake, a *whirlpool* was forming! White cascades of water were now *swirling* around an expanding, downward funnel.

The others on the pier were retreating as well, but Susan stood her ground, staring out across the previously placid surface of the lake.

Steam arose from the center of the whirlpool spinning there in the middle of the lake!

"I thought there weren't volcanos in this region?" the detective gasped.

"There aren't!" Susan said as she *dropped* to her hands and knees, still staring out over the swirling water.

"The earthquake must have opened up a vent to deep lava tubes," the officer said, also staring at the rising column of hot steam. "Aren't there Sulphur Springs here, which are somewhat famous?"

"You're not from around here, are you?" Susan observed, afraid to stand up due to continuing aftershocks.

"I just moved here recently, from Colorado."

"Sulphur's famous healing springs are *artesian*, coming from underground *cold* springs. There's zero risk here of volcanic activity!"

"But that water is going somewhere—and it's *hot!*"

The gathering white steam indeed was hot, now obscuring the entire lake. It stung Susan's face. She flinched, turning to crawl back toward her Fiero. Maybe it would protect her...

—when another huge EARTHQUAKE *flung* her red Fiero sports car up into the air to *crash* over upon its top!

"Jesus Christ!" Susan gasped, turning to grab onto the arm of the lady behind her.

They clung together as the violent shaking increased then gradually subsided.

Susan cautiously stood up, peering around.

Trees were toppled in all directions. It looked like a tornado or nuclear bomb had flattened the entire area. She walked out onto the wobbly, collapsing boards of the pier, careful not to tumble into the lake. But that wasn't a worry. The shallow lake was now *empty*, just a muddy bowl with nothing in it but a few flopping, dying fish! And running down its middle was a *deep vent* that plunged out of sight into the heart of the earth.

Sally King's body was nowhere to be seen.

Chapter 13

TUMBLNG PIGEONS

Topsy-turvy, flopping forward

Spinning about in mid-flight

What is that, a freak show?

Or a survival tactic of quick art

Dodging the diving hawk or eagle

Just the tiny edge to continued life

Letting death drop past to the side

Or keeping firm on the ground

Even when you're a thousand feet up

Walking on fluffy clouds

Rather than dropping through

Remodeling gravity like clay

Defying the Laws of Nature

A "slight of feet" and slick surfaces

Where up is down

And down is sideways

And sideways is up

Oh, yes, sweet unpredictability

Jazz in full flight!

The Minstrel's Lark, 13:67-71

IMPACT MINUS FOUR MONTHS, *DRIFTING...*

They were gathered on the observation deck. Surrounding them were large portholes through which they could see the linked, linear structures of Hermes set against the utter black of star-sprinkled space.

They sat silently, just staring out the portholes.

They were each in their orange flight-suits, now no longer crisp and clean. Rumpled, smeared, and dirty the clothes reflected their own mood of haggard exhaustion. Kame looked the worst, her head hanging, short black hair sticking out in disarray. Adriana looked almost as bad, her eyes squeezed shut. Her normally neat brown-orange hair drifted limply to each side of her head. Susan had tied her blond bangs back in a ponytail, but the rubber band was loose. Consequently her longish hair stuck out in tangled clumps.

Susan wearily stared out an OD porthole at the three lined-up, curved white water tanks. Each had its "saddleback" square storage box sitting astride. At the end of the line was the circular radiation shield, behind which lurked the nuclear reactor module. The brightly gleaming, titanium-alloy truss structure girded it all together. Turning her head to the opposite porthole she saw out of the opposite port the three linked Hab units, bulging outward in a straight line. And glimpsed between the tanks and the Habs, jutting out to each side below the level of the OD, were the two docked surface access vehicles. Below the upper level of the observation deck was the cylindrical, central Service Node. And unseen underneath the SN was the Orion capsule linked to the sliced-open, now emptied cargo module.

But Susan knew the cargo module wasn't completely empty.

Hanging frozen stiff in the module was the motionless, suited body of George Wilson. They yet hoped to return him to Earth to his relatives for a suitable burial. For the moment, though, he was out of the way while perfectly preserved, frozen solid in the near absolute-zero of space.

At the moment the various units of the Hermes-stack were relatively secure and steady.

God only knew what would happen if they tried to *spin* it all up.

"Well, this is fun!" Adriana tried to lighten the grim mood of the crew.

No one laughed.

A table was pulled out from a wall, around which they "sat." Actually, they were floating in place, belted into plastic chairs fixed upon clips set into the inner hull of the module.

The day before they'd finally completed the prolonged hydrogen burn from their nuclear thermal engine. Since the constant thrust was now gone, so was the perceived, weak 0.1 G. After the burn stopped, they'd quickly reconfigured the interior of Hermes to accommodate zero-G floating, such that no one direction was "up" or "down."

"So we've a hard decision to make," Yamamoto wearily stated, refocusing their wandering attention. "Do we remain in zero-G or attempt *tumbling?*"

Susan sat opposite to Kame. The Mission Commander looked pale. Her rounded face was drawn, with newly acquired faint wrinkles around her slanted eyes. Her usually jet-black straight hair looked frazzled, with a hint of white now showing at their roots. She looked like she'd aged a decade in the two months they'd been together on Hermes.

That wasn't surprising. Susan often forgot that Kame had already served an entire Mars mission in space. The surprising thing was that Kame was as fit and cogent as she was.

"I don't know if our bodies can accommodate to the higher gravity," Adriana weakly replied, her higher pitched voice resigned. "As the mission's nurse I agree 0.5 G definitely could help us maintain bone density and muscle tone—but at what cost to our overall, dwindling strength? The higher radiation levels are sapping us, constantly degrading our tissues. We might be healthier just staying in zero-G."

The meeting was being recorded for transmission to Mission Control on Earth. Hermes was now too distant to get any immediate feedback from Earth. The crew was essentially on its own. But Susan knew NASA's official position on long-voyage centripetal "gravity." They maintained that "tumbling" was a critical component for long-duration space missions, regardless of possible negatives. Without pseudo-gravity to help keep their bodies strong the astronauts might not be able to accomplish the necessary tasks once they arrived at their destination, such as Mars.

But the present situation was entirely different from that of a Mars mission. They were headed to a celestial rock which would only have a tiny gravitational field. In essence their work at the Asteroid would be a glorified spacewalk. They might not need strong muscles or bones to complete their mission.

"Adriana...is correct...the bigger problem...is the radiation..." Ben ventured, changing the topic. He sat scrunched up in one of the chairs. His voice was barely audible. His dried-up, cracked lips hardly moved. "Four more months of this radiation...I'll probably be dead...and you ladies will be severely compromised."

Ben looked terrible.

He was now completely bald. Open sores dotted his nose and cheeks. Despite ointments and bandages, the sores wouldn't heal, so he'd stopped trying to treat them. His partially recovered immune system was again failing. His eyes were bloodshot, listless. Several of his teeth wobbled loosely in his mouth, barely hanging in their sockets.

Though he'd regained most of his mental functions, he looked like a living corpse.

"We need more water," Susan added more for the official transcript than to inform the others. "We've just barely enough water left—just a fifth of one of the three tanks—to keep both us and the plants alive. We burned off most of our water stores for electrolysis-generated hydrogen, which the nuclear thermal rocket needed in order to get us up to full speed. We still have enough hydrogen and oxygen left in the smaller internal storage tanks to do our course corrections, but just barely."

"That was my point as well," Adriana nodded. "We have to consider the unanticipated constant stress that our bodies are undergoing. We've lost the main barrier that was protecting us from the nuclear reactor: the filled-up water tanks. Despite the two metal shields and other structural components of Hermes, we're being irradiated daily at a dangerous level—and not just in regards to a hypothetical future cancer risk, but degrading our immediate, mission-ready performance."

"And we can't power down the nuclear reactor because we depend on it to generate electricity to run the ship's complex systems," Susan added for the record.

"We need someplace to go and hide...get away from Hermes," Ben mumbled. "But...we're stuck here...aren't we?"

He giggled as if he'd said something funny. His mind was clearly drifting. His question was so ridiculous it needed no answer. They couldn't abort to Earth. Neither could they divert to some other safe haven. They had nowhere to go but forward.

That is, if they could last that long.

With a few more mid-flight course corrections, they were set to rendezvous with Asteroid PHA-15384 in less than three months, just one week before it was due to slam into Earth. They were now traveling at better than 60,000 mph. If they'd had more ejection volume for their nuclear thermal engine, they might have been able to rendezvous with the Asteroid earlier in its descent downward toward the planetary disc. But due to the catastrophes they'd endured, that was impossible. And since they'd lost even the partial replenishment tank in their ascent to Hermes, they were now dangerously low on water mass. They had no choice but somehow try to survive the increased radiation level, reach the Asteroid, then divert or destroy it in one mere short week—regardless of their physical condition.

"More...water...mass?" Adriana mused, stroking her longish red hair.

Susan was horrified to see small clumps of Adriana's hair pulling out and clinging to Johansson's brittle, broken fingernails. It was a consequence of both the continued radiation and having to ration their water. Not just Ben, but all the crew members were withering away. Long before Hermes reached the Asteroid, they'd be dried-up husks!

"What are you thinking, Adri?" Susan asked, frowning.

Despite the official recording being made for transfer to Earth, Susan couldn't help but refer to Adriana by her shortened nickname. They'd grown closer over the last two month, "kindred spirits" as it were. Except for lately, poor Ben was only rarely coherent, mumbling fearfully of unseen demons. Kame was, as always, cool and distant—withdrawing into an isolated "Zen"-like state as the situation on

Hermes became increasing desperate. That left Adriana as Susan's only real confidant.

"What about a *comet?*" Adriana suddenly blurted out. Her blue eyes squinted, concentrating. "They're mostly made of water left over from the formation of the solar system. Could we perhaps make a 'pit-stop' along the way?"

They were all silent for a moment, digesting the outrageous notion.

Startling the group, Ben *laughed* into the silence. Then he hung his head down.

Kame glared at him but said nothing.

"No, seriously," Adriana continued. "Is there a chance?"

"The odds of encountering a comet on our trajectory to PHA-15384 are slim to none," Kame shrugged. "We don't need to fantasize on improbable 'movie' rescue scenarios. We need to concentrate on what's achievable."

That closed off the improbable topic.

"The immediate question is whether or not to maintain zero-G for the next four months—or try to initiate Tumbling!" Kame relentlessly got the back on topic. "Mission Control's S.O.P. is clear on this point. Despite the problems with the Hermes-stack, they want us to spin up. But they're not here with us on Hermes. So they've rightly left the choice to us. Let's make a decision!"

If they could replenish their water stores, though, many of their problems would be solved. Although Susan agreed it was an incredibly improbable long shot, they were desperate! She was determined to explore every possibility, no matter how remote.

"Could we maybe spend a little time looking into Adriana's comet idea—just in case?" Susan politely ventured. "After all, the Oort cloud that surrounds the solar system has many billions of comets, which sometimes do get knocked into the inner system and..."

"Why not?" Kame snapped sourly at them both. "We 'only' have to keep Hermes running for the next four months on less than half its regular crew complement, *plus* we're becoming increasingly ill, *plus* our life-support system is failing and needs continual troubleshooting! Sure, Susan, go off and spend your time hunting for a nonexistent miracle—why not? In this vast volume of outer space we might just stumble over a stray comet!"

Kame's sarcasm was thick.

"So...that's a 'yes'?" Susan hesitantly replied.

"In your 'spare time'—after completing your other duties—sure, King, go ahead and knock yourself out!"

Susan nodded gratefully. Maybe she was just grasping at straws. But at least Adri's idea was something hopeful. They *needed* hope, no matter how tiny.

Kame looked away, out of the aft porthole, back in the direction of the no longer visible Earth, before proceeding.

"So...back to the immediate concern—spinning up Hermes or not? It's my decision as the Mission Commander, but I want each of your considered opinions: do we *drift* or *tumble*, King?"

Susan pushed thoughts of deliciously cool frozen comets out of her head, focusing on the tumbling question.

"Well...Scott Kelly and his Russian counterpart first showed us way back in 2016 that astronauts on the International Space Station could still function in zero-G after a year of floating. It was tough on him when he returned to the full 1.0 G of Earth, but that's a secondary concern to us. We just have to make it to the Asteroid. So I think the risk of further stresses on the ship and our bodies of spinning up Hermes are too great. I think we should *not* attempt Tumbling. For whatever it is worth, I vote 'no'."

"Priyanka?'"

Ben slowly lifted his head. He stared straight ahead, hardly acknowledging the question. His sunken, red eyes looked utterly defeated.

"The beetles—I miss them."

Apparently due to the increased radiation, the black beetles of their "jungle" had all simultaneously dropped dead. That was totally unexpected. It was generally believed that if a nuclear apocalypse occurred on Earth, the few land-dwellers that might survive would be insects. But the beetles on Hermes were genetically engineered to groom and pollinate the hybrid vines, plants, and fruits. Unfortunately, that unexpectedly made them super-sensitive to irradiation above the standard Hermes environmental level. They were, in essence, the "canaries in the mine" to warn miners of subtle hazards such as increased CO2. Well, the "canaries" had croaked. God help the miners.

"*Ben*, should we drift or tumble?" Kame sharply repeated her question. "You're still our ship's physician. Please concentrate! How do we best arrive at PHA-15384 in the least-compromised physical shape?"

He gathered himself together. He squinted. His garishly bald, scarred head made him look like a pumpkin sliced up for Halloween.

"Ah, yes...weakened by the radiation...counter-effects of zero-G...but *counter*-countered by the debilitating effects of larger loads on our already feeble bodies...a puzzlement...a pretty pickle..."

His voice trailed off as he continued staring dully ahead.

"Well?" Kame snapped at him, clearly exasperated.

"Oh why not—*spin us up!*" Ben again burst out laughing. "We're *fighters!* We *fight!* We've got to keep on fighting or we'll drop out or 'take a dive'—and go stark raving *mad!* Hah!"

He stopped laughing and put his bald head into his arms.

He began quietly crying. His tears floated away to the sides of his face in the zero-G, a circle of tiny spheres.

"Johansson?" Kame barked at her, turning away in distain from the sobbing physician. "You're the pilot. You'll be responsible for spinning us up. Do you think Hermes can take the strain?"

Yes, that was a real concern. Even under the best conditions—with full water tanks, an undamaged truss structure, intact modules, and optimally responsive water-distribution to balance personnel movement—it would be a strain on Hermes. Now, with emptied tanks and an altered center of gravity, the truss on one side pulled out while severely damaged on the other, with water recirculation "iffy" at best...spinning up the ship was a big risk. They could fly to pieces.

It would be nice if we had science-fiction type "artificial gravity"—Susan mused to herself. *But the closest we can get is creating the illusion of gravity by spinning the ship along its longest axis, using centripetal force to simulate gravity.*

"Let me think a second. Perhaps we should define our terms for the record?"

"For the record," Kame snidely explained, speaking slowly and distinctly, "what we're now discussing is termed 'tumbling.' The maneuver is named after what some pigeons do during flight: called 'pigeon tumbling.' We'll be flipping forward around our long-axis center of mass-distribution. At five revolutions per minute, the centripetal force generated will throw objects outward in a manner that will seem like gravity. We'll be pushed down as the deck in turn pushes up against our feet. In this way, we will generate a simulated 0.5 'G' at the ends of Hermes' stack. It doesn't fully simulate Earth's gravity, but it is fine for preparing for Mar's 0.38 G. The body still deteriorates. But it definitely would be better for our physical functionality at our mission's end than just floating weightless the entire trip."

"We're just beetles...poor dead little bugs," Ben continued to sob, his head still buried in his arms.

"So, what do you say, Adriana?" Kame continued, ignoring Ben. "Have you had enough 'thinking' time?"

Adriana sighed deeply, nodding her head.

"If we can balance the loads, I think we can achieve a stable rotation," she reluctantly admitted. "We can ramp up gradually. If we encounter problems, we'll back off. I think the risk is manageable. If it doesn't work then we just counter the thrusts and return to zero-G."

"So you can do it?"

"I think so."

"Then that's my decision," Kame stated firmly for the record. "As backed-up by two-out-of-three of the rest of the crew, we tumble. We don't know what urgent, strenuous tasks we'll face at the Asteroid. We can't just hope that we'll be fit or strong enough to accomplish what's necessary. We've got to do everything we can to be as physically ready as possible. We're ramping up to full-Tumble! Have you got any problem with that order, King?"

Susan shook her head wearily in denial. It was a judgment call one way or the other. But now that a decision had been made by Yamamoto, at least they were no longer debating. It gave Susan a renewed sense of direction.

"I'll do my part," Susan firmly agreed for the record.

"Johansson, begin the calculations and programming. King, start securing the compartments for tumble-mode. Priyanka, can you check out the water circulation system? If we can't use it to balance our own movements throughout the ship, then the controlled rotation will degenerate, causing unacceptable strains."

"But the beetles...?" he sobbed as he lifted up his bald, sore-ridden head.

"The damn beetles are *not* critical!" Yamamoto shouted at him, loosening her belt and floating up out of her seat. "The jungle can continue without them, at least for the duration. But Ben, can we count on you?   Can you check out the load-balancing water-circulation? It ties back into your precious 'jungle.' Can you do this thing for us?"

"Damn it, Jim!" he suddenly snapped at her, pointing an accusing finger at her. "I'm a *physician—not* an engineer!"

Kame sighed deeply, shaking her head in disbelief at his reaction. She loosened her seat straps then kicked over toward the conduit leading to the central Service Node.

"Yes—and you're not 'Bones' and this is not the original Star Trek TV series!" she angrily retorted, pausing at the exit. But then she caught herself, replying less forcefully: "Forget it Priyanka, I'll do it myself. You just go back to your hammock and rest. We'll take care of it. King, Johansson—let's get to work!"

Susan hated that Ben was being cavalierly dismissed. But she had total faith in Adriana's abilities. They'd been friends since Susan began astronaut training. Petite Adriana might look like a cute bubble-head to the casual male in a bar, but those good looks hid an iron will and fierce competence.

Susan observed that Kame's words to Ben were tightly controlled but utterly disdainful. Clearly, the Japanese woman did not tolerate anyone failing to do their duty, no matter what valid excuse they might have.

"Ok," Ben gratefully sighed, wearily lowering his bald head back into his arms.

He seemed relieved to be dismissed back to his bed in the third, outer Hab.

So it was official. The crew complement that should have been six was now only three. Ben was no longer an active participant, just a

dead weight. He was the same as George, except for taking up precious oxygen and calories. For the first time, Susan resented him.

Then she immediately caught herself, forcing those negative
thoughts away. Susan was sad for Ben, but sympathetic. Sure he was
in bad shape, but he was still their crewmate. She wasn't giving up on
him. With proper care he might yet recover sufficiently to help with
the mission. After all, their task was not to cull humanity, but to save
it. And she knew that despite Kame's contempt it was ok to cry—even
for dead beetles.

They never found Sally King's body. The original "girl with the turtle
tattoo" was gone.

This was a continuing source of pain for Susan. Her mother
would never be buried alongside her husband in the Oaklawn Cemetery. She would never "rest in peace" inside a casket there outside the
small town of Sulphur, Oklahoma. Instead, her body had apparently
been dragged down to the bowels of hell.

As best as the geologists could figure, a deep volcanic vent had
opened up under Veterans Lake. It didn't spew out superheated water. Instead, it sucked the lake dry, the water boiling as it plunged
into the depths, sending back clouds of steam. Presumably Sally
King's body was sucked down along with the large volume of water. It
was an unprecedented disaster to the town.

Although Oklahoma was known to be crisscrossed with fault lines
dating back to before the time of the dinosaurs, most were inactive
and shallow, reaching only down about four miles into the earth's
crust. The fault that cracked open under Veterans Lake, however, was
much deeper. It allowed magma to surge upward as the simultaneously triggered earthquake knocked down many structures and trees.
The incident had a prominent place in national news reports for several days. But since it didn't reoccur, it quickly became just a strange,
forgotten anomaly.

But Susan could not put it behind her. She often woke up sweating and moaning from a vivid nightmare in which she experienced the
horror over and over. Perversely, though, she welcomed it alternating
with her other still-continuing nightmare: that of a mass of asteroid
fragments hurtling at her and Billy as they both floated in their space-

suits helplessly in space, about to be crushed to death. *Damn aster-oids!*—she shouted soundlessly in her mind. *Damn earthquakes! Damn Mother Nature laughing at me like a malignant Demon!*

"Ah, hell," Susan sighed out loud, shaking her head to clear her frightening visions. "I've got work to do."

She put wireless headset earbuds into her ears, keying up an ancient "Beatles" album. It was their 1970 famous last album "Let It Be." She heard the soothing sounds reverberating in her skull, providing a wall of sound unheard by those around her, insulating her from the voices of the other people in the laboratory complex. The "cocoon of silence *noise*" allowed her to concentrate on her specific work without external distractions.

She focused her eyes on the computer screen in front of her. There she saw an overlapping set of graphs. Red, blue, and green lines traced the actual observed movements plus extrapolate orbits of a newly detected cluster of potentially hazardous asteroids. The data was just arriving from the *Sentinel Space Telescope Successor* (SSTS), which orbited the sun near Venus. In that orbit it could peer outward at the Universe with the sun's overwhelming glare at its back. It continuously watched and analyzed the night sky, utilizing an infrared telescope to detect slightly warmer space rocks set against the icy cold of outer space.

She felt a tap on her shoulder. Lifting out her earbuds she heard: "Anything interesting?"

A tanned, weathered hand appeared to the side of her keyboard, laid flat on the desk surface, as someone leaned in from behind her to look over her shoulder at the screen.

It was her postdoctoral advisor, Professor Theloneus Cafferty. A few old friends called him "Theo" but all others—including the post-docs—were careful to call him "Professor" or "Doctor Cafferty." He was a distinguished older scientist, with a mane of snowy white hair and a perpetually hungry look in his darting eyes. He was a world expert in asteroid analysis: including their orbits, spin states, 3D shapes, and composition. That was his consuming passion. But his secondary passion was stalking vulnerable young female postdocs.

Never having married, he relished a life of "freedom" chasing after whomever he wished, having brief "relationships" with a parade of young women. Though he was careful to never cross any legal or ethical lines—always claiming "mutual consent of mature adults" whenever questioned on his sexual escapades—he was perpetually on the prowl for his next conquest.

He was a throwback to an earlier age of astronomy, where young females were often sexually harassed and victimized by powerful male Professors. Now, thankfully, there were exacting work rules in place against such practices. But in over a lifetime of "playing the game" Cafferty had learned how to evade or "skirt" the rules. His private life was kept carefully separated from the work environment, under tight control...mostly.

Susan had been ecstatic to be accepted by him to a "postdoc" position in the *Postdoctoral Scholars Program* at the *Jet Propulsion Laboratory* (JPL) in Pasadena, California. He held joint appointments at several local Universities. In addition, he was the Branch Chief of JPL's *Asteroids, Comets, and Satellites Group*—just where she wanted to be! Unfortunately, she'd not thought to check out his reputation with his former or present students. Having been under the wing of the exemplary Professor Diana Jeworski at the University of Oklahoma for the past five years, she'd gotten used to having a protector for a boss.

So it was a shock to realize her immediate superior was a cunning sexual predator.

When first coming into contact with his "friendly" hands attempting to pat her shoulder on their first meeting, she'd politely informed him she was a private sort who preferred not to be touched. Also she was in excellent physical shape, working out regularly at the JPL gym, and could easily overpower him if he ever tried anything overt. She didn't have a black belt, but regularly did serious kickboxing as part of her exercise routine. He knew that and politely kept his distance— most of the time. But he loved going right up to the line without crossing, as he did now. His other hand lightly brushed her blond hair as if by accident, leaning further in over her shoulder.

She deliberately turned her head and stared into his kindly appearing blue ones. He didn't look like a wily, hungry predator!

But she knew from experience that those kindly eyes were a mask he'd perfected over many years of predation. Many young females had fallen under their sway. Susan knew it was the beguiling gaze of a *hunting panther*. He should have been dressed in velvety black to denote his villain status. Instead, he had on pristine white pants and a silky yellow shirt. He looked to be the perfect "surfer"-type California older, but still-handsome man. He wasn't dangerous to Susan, though, just an annoyance. She knew how to deal with him.

She just kept her gaze locked on his, refusing to blink.

As with most bullies, he gave up first. He reluctantly backed off a step, but wet his lips with the tip of his tongue. Yes, he was a horny old bastard. But scientifically, he was still an excellent mentor and boss.

"Hi Professor," she said, giving him a polite nod. "These just came in. From the spectral shifts and projected orbits they look like a cluster of dead comets passing through the belt. Also, they appear to be slowly circling each other. They may be fragments from a larger single object which suffered a past mishap."

Dead comets were ice-bearing bodies that had swung in too close to the sun too many times, shedding most of their water ice into their characteristically long, streaming tails. The rocky cores remained. Asteroids, which tended to stay in the "asteroid belt" between Mars and Jupiter, might or might not have ice. So the definition of a "dead comet" hinged on their orbits, whether the heavenly rocks remained in the asteroid belt or swung in closer to the sun.

"Ah...yes...worth a follow up. Good work, Susan. Can you schedule them with Arecibo?" he politely asked.

The world's two primary facilities for radar astronomy were located in Puerto Rico and California. The *National Astronomy and Ionosphere Center's Arecibo Observatory* in Puerto Rico had a wider view of the sky but was less steerable than the *Goldstone Solar System Radar* located in California. This cluster that Susan had just discovered was deep in the asteroid belt, but still within easy range of Arecibo. The newly arrived SSTS data was based on infrared detection, which derived from the sun's incident radiation or the object's internal heat. Arecibo and Goldstone, however, detected the reflection of human-controlled wavelengths deliberately bounced off the asteroids, allowing the generation of detailed models.

"I'll see if they can fit them into our allotted time slots, Professor. But we may have to bump something else of ours. Is that ok?"

"Do so if necessary," he said. "You're sure those objects show some ice?"

"I'll bring up the absorption band at 2.9-3.6 micrometers...there. I estimate that 2-5% of the mass of this cluster is water ice."

A graph appeared on the screen, translucently imposed above the orbital tracks.

He grunted happily. "Dead comet fragments for sure. Give it priority for a deeper scan, Susan. We should get particularly good data on them as they move closer to the sun out of the asteroid belt. Good work!" he repeated, moving away.

She was relieved the man was leaving. He had a brilliant mind which she totally appreciated, despite his roving hands. However— she grudgingly admitted to herself—if she'd been less driven and more gullible she might have found the older, still-handsome man attractive. As it was, her small apartment near the JPL campus was rarely used even for sleep, let alone for sordid "affairs." She often worked through the entire day, taking cat naps at her desk when she could no longer stay awake.

But there was plenty of opportunity for appropriate romance if she'd wanted it.

Truth-to-tell, though—other than her somewhat outdated morality imposed by her church upbringing—she was just plain too selfish to let a man possess her body other than in a full-contract, legal, loving marriage. And even doing that sounded to her like too much work and commitment. Regardless, it might be old fashioned of her, but temporary "relationships" just didn't float her boat. Plus she'd deliberately and consciously postponed such considerations until after having gone as far as she could with her academic accreditations. And now having finally earned her Ph.D. she found she liked being single—in full possession of her space, her body, and her life without the complications and responsibilities of a romantic partner.

In addition, she still had more heights to attempt to climb before eventually plateauing. She might still find a mate, get married, and have kids—the whole nine yards. But it had to wait. She'd just submitted an application for the latest round of NASA astronaut trainees.

The competition for the few available slots was fierce. The last thing she needed right now was a live-in boyfriend holding her back or, God forbid, impregnating her. There was plenty of time for all that later.

Yes, there was a bright future, but what of the past? Determined to not bury her main concern she instead mentally articulated it: *How the hell did my dying mother get her grossly obese body into the wheelchair? And how had she driven the self-propelled chair so far out on the road to Veterans Lake? If she wanted to commit suicide why drown? With the powerful medical drugs floating around the nursing home, why not just grab a bottle and chug it?*

No answers...

But however it happened Susan's frustrated mind could not forgive Bill his part in it. Eager to make millions, to be a big-shot executive, a world-famous inventor, he'd neglected his own mother! Oh, he vehemently denied doing so. He pointed to the expensive security he'd paid for to protect her at the nursing home. He insisted he'd gotten her the very best medical care possible. Susan knew she herself bore some of the blame. But with her demanding academic track it had fallen to him to look after their ageing mother—and he'd dropped the ball!

Consequently, she hadn't talked to him now for over a year. Let him go be the "big shot." She was content to be a lowly postdoc doing fascinating research working for slave wages, just scraping by. Though she still got handwritten notes in the mail from Scott begging her to go to work for Nashoba at an unbelievable salary, she just balled them up and tossed them in the trash.

Still, it was sad to leave behind her brother, her only close relative. They shared a strange history.

A group of young staff and fellow postdocs came by her desk, interrupting her musings. They were laughing and cheering.

"What's up?" she grinned at them, happy for the distraction.

"We're goin' to Smitty's—wanna join?" said a tall, thin, dark-skinned young man.

He had an easy smile and beguilingly curled black hair topping his clean-shaven face. It was Pete Collins, a local college tennis champ as well as "comet-ice-organic-matter" fellow postdoc expert.

He liked to say his title in a rush as one word. He was a very nice young man with a good sense of humor. Susan liked him.

If she'd been less driven, she might have dated him.

Smitty's Grill was one of the local Pasadena watering holes frequented by JPL personnel. It wasn't so much a bar as a classy restaurant suitable for celebrations, formal or informal. And if people wished, they could get great "regular" food like barbeque ribs plus big mugs of cold beer. Everyone loved the lobsters, big giant ones. Susan hated the ugly things, usually settling for a simple salad.

Let the others have their giant sea-cockroaches!

"What's the occasion?"

"Haven't you heard?" he laughed, seemingly beside himself with excitement.

"Sorry, I've been finishing a paper the last few days. I haven't watched the news. I've been buried in my computer, Pete. So what's the celebration?"

Indeed, she'd pulled an all-nighter last evening, trying to finish the first draft of a paper for submission to *The Astrophysical Journal*: "Dust Dynamics in Planetary Disc Formation Mirrored in the Asteroid Belt: Insights from UV, IR, and Emission Lines." It wasn't groundbreaking work. But it documented her first step from doctoral thesis to her own peer-reviewed postdoctoral research results.

She wasn't the first author on it, so it wasn't that big of a deal. Her boss had insisted his name go first with her name second, with the names of other collaborators following. That was unusual since it was composed mostly of her original work. Postdoc Advisors usually took the "lab director" last-name-slot place of honor on a publication. But he was the boss and deserved first place authorship if he so wished. The initial part of the paper was his team's results before she'd arrived. So she didn't make a fuss over it. He had also written large parts of the report himself, particularly the first of the critical "discussions" section. She was certain that as she subsequently proved her worth, accumulating a pile of her own data, and doing most or all of the writing herself she'd have her name listed first on subsequent papers.

Now, though, she was dead tired—just wanting to finish up the latest data that had come in, get the further radar interrogation of the dead comets scheduled, and then go back to her apartment, take a shower and crash. The last thing she needed was an unplanned social event!

But then again, she hardly ever went out with the other young staff of their branch at JPL. Maybe she did need some fun. Why not?

"Mars-3 has found life on Mars!" Pete blurted out.

"What? *Really?*"

The others were headed out of the door to the street, Pete hanging back to get her answer to going celebrating with them.

"Yes!" he excitedly continued. "They dug down twenty feet—below the irradiated dead top surface layers—and found *DNA residue* in a buried fossilized mudflow! They used our JPL sequencer-array to discover it."

"Really? DNA? Is it similar to that of earth organisms?"

He paused, visibly curbing his enthusiasm.

"Well, we don't know. Actually, it's just nitrogen bases—adenine and cytosine. But it's very suggestive!"

Huh—hardly DNA at all, just a couple of the key components that went into making the stuff. Discovering trace amounts of adenine and cytosine didn't mean there was now or had ever been life on Mars. Those fairly simple compounds could form from natural processes not requiring living cells. In fact, the tremendous pressures and heat of *comets* crashing into a planet—as frequently happened during the early formation periods of Mars or Earth—had already been shown in the laboratory capable of changing comet-derived formamide into three of the four nucleobases that make up DNA: adenine, guanine, and cytosine. So the astronauts on the Mars-3 mission may have just found ancient remnants of a comet impact.

As far as anyone knew to-date, Mars was a dead rock containing hardly any surface water and even less atmosphere. Billions of years ago it might have supported developing, primitive lifeforms in a watery soup of organic molecules. But that was long before the planet lost its protective magnetic field due to its metallic core cooling. That resulted in virtually the entire atmosphere being stripped away because solar radiation streaming at the planet wasn't diverted by a planetary magnetic field. Even if there were rudimentary organisms billions of years ago, there was no chance DNA could have survived to the present date. However, just finding components of DNA was still amazing!

Far be it for her to rain on their parade.

"Come on, Susan. You work too hard! It's like pulling teeth to get you to play just an hour of tennis with me now and then. Take a break!"

He made a "pouty" face at her.

"*Please?*" he mock-begged her, opening his eyes wide.

When was the last time she'd played tennis with him? She'd been so busy in the lab she couldn't even remember. Well, whenever it happened he'd blown her off the court! He was a really good tennis player, lean and tall. But his point was valid. He was as a good a friend as she had at JPL.

She'd even shared with him her irritation with the subtle harassment she'd gotten from Professor Cafferty. Pete was sympathetic but nonchalant. He told her that she was, after all, a "cutie" that any guy worth his salt would want to hit on! In fact, he eagerly replied that he was willing to go punch Cafferty in his smug face if anything went beyond a "little" flirting. She assured him that she didn't need his fists. If anything like that were to actually happened, she told him she'd punch Cafferty's face to pieces herself!

But she definitely appreciated Pete's macho chivalry, even if she didn't need it. And so she felt guilty. He deserved a bit of her attention, from time-to-time.

"Oh, alright!" she laughed, giving in. "I'll meet you guys at Smitty's. I've got a few quick things to finish up."

"Don't be too long!" he called back as he hurried after the group. "We're getting there before the dinner crowd so we get the pick of the ribs-and-seafood buffet. You don't want to be left with just lobster claws. You know what 'astronomical' appetites our crowd has!"

"Right," she snickered at his lame joke. "See you there!" she called after him, waving goodbye.

Ok—back to her computer. Get the incoming data properly displayed, e-mail the charts to the various members of the team, post it up on Professor Cafferty's website on the JPL Intranet, sandwich in the follow-up radar interrogation at Arecibo, then lock-down her worksite.

Ah hell!

The lights in the room blinked off. It was a power outage! That happened sometimes in the summer as electrical power usage spiked upward what with air conditioners turning on all across Pasadena. Bill and Scott's super-batteries hadn't yet been integrated completely into the local power grid. Nashoba Energy promised that overloaded grids would soon be a thing of the past. But though JPL hadn't yet gone over to the expensive super-batteries, she anticipated the power coming back on in a few minutes. Then the computers could get re-booted.

But that would be a long delay. There was no sense in her waiting around—she couldn't undo the hard shutdown and would arrive too late at Smitty's.

"Well, I didn't lose anything important," she mumbled to herself as she grabbed her shoulder bag and walked through the dark hallways to the front exit.

On to the restaurant!

Momentarily she thought of dropping by her apartment to change into something more formal. She was only dressed in a pair of old blue jeans and a faded blue shirt. But this wasn't going to be a formal celebration, just a bunch of her lab friends getting together. She was fine.

Slipping her sports head-buds in her ears and dialing up the volume on "Let It Be" on her MP3 player, she strolled out of the lab building onto a sidewalk leading to the back parking lot. She swung her old leather tote bag happily back and forth beneath her right hand. Around her were big green trees and neatly mowed lawns. The sun shone brightly. There wasn't a cloud in the sky. The air was warm and dry. It was a beautiful afternoon in early summer—perfect for driving an hour to the beach or going out with friends to a classy restaurant!

JPL was a very friendly, inviting place to work.

The campus was a small city. More than 6,000 people worked there—complete with various stores, offices, laboratories, cafeterias, spacecraft assembly buildings, testing facilities, and everything else! Civilians freely mixed with military personnel, other government workers, students, and staff in a dynamic and productive atmosphere.

Atmosphere...

"It's so nice and cool out here," Susan sighed to herself as she leisurely walked toward her little red Fiero.

That was the main difference she'd felt from the moment she'd gotten out of her car in California. Located at the edge of the LA basin, JPL was part of an inhabited desert. Used to being around medium-to-heavy humidity, Susan found it a real pleasure to be in a dry environment. Even when the temperature was in the 90's it still felt cool. What a delight!

Susan glanced at the low rocky hills surrounding the campus which were dotted with scrubby trees. Elegant, large office or laboratory buildings towered up around her, interspersed with lower, older buildings. The JPL campus was built starting from the 1930s—successively administered by *Caltech's School of Aeronautics*, then by the U.S. Army, and now by NASA. In the past it developed military hardware and missiles. Now it was a hotbed of making and testing sophisticated space equipment, with many related sidelines manned by lots of eager, young postdocs. It was a marvelous place to work on astrophysical problems. Plus—due to the sensitive military and industrial work they still did—it was safe. The large campus was fenced in, gated, and well patrolled by security guards. Any people entering the facility were required to show JPL badges or be accompanied by official personnel.

So Susan was startled when a *strong hand* suddenly *grabbed her arm* and *pulled her backward*, swiping the earbuds off her head!

"Stop!" a raspy voice ordered her.

She pulled free and was about to launch a spinning back-kick when she realized it wasn't some totally unexpected mugger.

Rather, it was *Professor Cafferty*. What?

He was slumped onto his knees, feebly grasping at her. His clean white pants and yellow shirt were splattered with blood. Indeed, he was *bleeding profusely* from his eyes, his ears, his nostrils, and his mouth.

"Professor!" she gasped, immediately grabbing him by his armpits and lowering him over onto his side on the nearby grass. She reached into her shoulder bag, withdrew her cellphone, and punched out "911."

"What is the nature of your emergency?" a voice sounded from the cellphone.

"One of our scientists is hurt, bleeding profusely. I need an ambulance, right now—to the parking lot behind building 122!"

"Closest intersection?"

"Pioneer and Sergeant Roads."

"How was the person injured?"

"Just get here! Hurry!"

"An ambulance and police are on their way."

"Susan," Cafferty whispered, reaching up to pull her head down next to his.

She looked into eyes that were so filled with blood they looked like the red eyes of a demon.

"What happened?" she gasped. "Did you get mugged? Was there a lab accident? Did you get hit by a car?"

"The...the *lizards*...they want you...to stay here...but I tried...."

His voice was barely audible. She looked around frantically for any guards, the local police, or the ambulance. In the distance, she heard the "wail" of approaching sirens. They were close!

"Don't try to talk, Professor. Help is almost here!"

Suddenly he *grabbed her throat* with both his hands, *throttling* her!

She gagged, not able to breathe! Everything was blurring around her as she struggled to break free. In desperation she *flailed out* with her fists, *hitting him* in his face time and again, trying to make him loosen his death-grip! She felt warm, sticky blood splashing onto her face, her hands, and her clothes!

Then she fell backward, freed from his grasp. Coughing and rolling onto her side on the grass she was vaguely aware of a policeman running up to her, with two medical personnel close behind carrying a stretcher between them.

"I...I..." Susan gasped, squinting against the sun that now shone directly into her eyes, blinding her.

"*She* did this! She *attacked* me!" Susan heard Cafferty scream beside her as he twisted from side-to-side on the blood-smeared lawn. "She's a maniac! She tried to kill me! Save me! Save me..."

And then his screams abruptly cut-off.

"He's nonresponsive," one of the EMTs said, kneeling beside the now-motionless body of Cafferty, feeling at his neck for a pulse. "Get the defibrillator. We'll try to bring him back."

Dazed, still trying to get air into her lungs, not believing she'd heard Cafferty say those incomprehensible words—Susan rolled over onto her stomach to get away from the glaring sun. She felt her hands roughly jerked behind her. She felt a knee jammed painfully into the small of her back.

Then she felt cold steel encircling her hands, cuffing them together.

"You have the right to remain silent," the policeman began reciting behind her. "Anything you say can and will be used against you in a court of law. You have the right to an attorney..."

What the bloody hell?

This didn't make any sense! But if she wasn't having another of her vivid nightmares, it could mark the end of everything she'd worked so hard to achieve.

For whatever perverse reason, Cafferty had succeeded in "nailing" her! Figuratively and in reality, she was now *royally screwed*.

Chapter 14

<u>CHAOS THEORY</u>

The flutter of a butterfly's wings
Changing the course of a hurricane
Or a random mutation giving advantage
Elephants arising to challenge tigers
Pendulums so predictably swinging
Screwed together sketch out unique art
Where fierce storms, typhoons, and tornadoes
Seem but random acts of cruelty and destruction
Within the whirling vertices and layers hidden
The same patterns reoccur higher and lower
"Fractals" of fractured repeating splits
Pulling Fate to one side or the other
Determining if you live or I die
Or humanity itself survives...
How positively fascinating!

The Minstrel's Lark, 14:28-33

IMPACT MINUS FOUR MONTHS, *TUMBLING...*
"Ready to initiate burn," Adriana reported.
"Proceed," Yamamoto curtly replied.
They were strapped into reclining chairs that they'd secured firmly to the "floor" of the Observation Deck. Even Ben was there, despite his protests to remain in his hammock down in the jungle Hab. They were in Hermes' white flight suits, helmets on with faceplates shut—inconvenient, cumbersome, and unnecessary since they were safely contained within the ship. But Kame had ordered a full suit-up. They

were speaking to each other over internal speakers located inside their helmets.

The main reason they were sealed in the Hermes flight suits was to ensure internal air recycling. In case cabin pressure was lost, their suits would allow each of them to breathe for several hours before needing a recharge from air canisters placed strategically around the interior of Hermes. Of course that wouldn't occur unless serious structural damage resulted from their spin-up for Tumbling.

Kame confidently reassured the rest of the crew that the water-rebalancing and recycling system she'd extensively checked out would quickly smooth out any load problems as they spun-up the ship. But Susan was fearful. What with the existing damage to the outer struts, the severe loss of water mass, and the split-open cargo module still attached to the Orion capsule, she suspected there could be big problems in the spin-up.

So despite the discomfort, Susan was happy to be in her pressure suit. It was much better to be uncomfortable and safe than comfortable and dead!

Of course they'd already closed and sealed the connecting hatches between Hermes' various modules. Should they God-forbid have any leaks or breaches, the damage would be limited to only that particular module. The hatches leading to airlocks or external to space were physically screwed down and latched with bars, requiring sheer muscle power to open. The internal hatches in the Hermes stack, however, could be opened or closed by computer commands. But she and Kame had checked each by hand, making sure each was firmly closed, not relying only on computer monitoring.

Positioned as it was at the top of the middle of the stack, the Observation Deck was particularly sensitive to ship stresses, so they'd made doubly sure that everything was locked tight. They were as prepared for things going south as humanly possible.

"*Ignition*—5% thrust achieved."

Susan felt a small *lurch* beneath her, escalating into a continuing *vibration*—as she heard through the structure of Hermes the *rumble* of the aft liquid fuel jets firing up. The jets, located beside the main nuclear thermal rocket, were gimballed to provide an angled thrust that wouldn't accelerate the vehicle but rather send it tumbling forward as it continued speeding upward above the planetary disc to meet the descending Asteroid.

"I see the stars starting to shift outside," Susan reported. "We're starting to spin."

Indeed, the brilliant pinpoints set against the utter blackness of space were moving backward along arcs that centered on the Observation Deck.

"Our center of mass is beneath the OD," Kame verbally added to the record for clarification. "The center should have been back on the first water tank. But with the loss of water mass it's shifted forward."

"That's actually not bad," Adriana noted, again for the record. "It gives us easy docking and departure of our two transit vehicles, plus a place of zero simulated gravity that we can always easily access."

Although Susan knew this, as did the others, they were all "speaking for the record." The entire procedure was being recorded for eventual transmission and analysis at Mission Control on Earth. But that canned transmission would have to wait. Long-range communication along a narrow beam was difficult if the sending platform wasn't stable. In order to lock-into Mission Control once they achieved full "tumble" they'd have to deploy a small communication array to travel alongside Hermes without tumbling.

"Our tilt forward is stable so far," Susan reported. "The rate of star drift is steady. I think we can accelerate the spin whenever you're ready, Commander."

Screens set into the walls between the portholes provided key data and interactivity to each person. Adriana was piloting the craft, via a 3D-"mouse" held in her gloved hand, which communicated distally with the command functions displayed on her screen. Yamamoto was monitoring the load strains on her display, ready to adjust water containment nodes if needed. Susan was directly observing the entire Hermes stack through aft and port windows. Ben, though, had no assigned duties. He sat morosely in a corner, muttering incoherently to himself.

Suddenly Ben gave out a loud "*whoop*" that startled Susan and the others!

"Beetle wings! Beetle wings! Beetle wings!" he chanted happily, reaching to the sides of his chair to flap his arms up-and-down like a bird. "Open to the sky—free to fly! Hah!"

"Ben, please be quiet. You are distracting us," Kame sternly chastised him.

He snorted derisively but complied, withdrawing his pressure-suited arms.

Beetle wings? What in the world was wrong with Ben now? Susan knew that some beetles on Earth did have wings, but Hermes' dead jungle beetles had been deliberately selected to *not* have any. They were intended to groom and pollinate the jungle plants, but could not be allowed to flitter around gumming up the air filtration systems. So they'd been bred to have excellent grasping legs in order to stay firmly attached to the branches, vines, and leaves of the plants upon which they obediently crawled.

Did Ben feel the vibration and think the entire vehicle had turned into a beetle, which was now flying with its own set of wings?

The poor guy was getting sicker and sicker. He was sinking deeper into his own fevered imagination.

"Take us up to 50% tumbling thrust, Johansson," Kame ordered.

"10%...15%...we're now up to 20%—*uh oh!*"

Suddenly the steady vibration under Susan's chair changed in character. Instead of the pleasant feeling of sitting on a therapeutic lounge chair, she felt a random "buzzing" at her butt. Simultaneously, the stars began jerking back-and-forth outside the portholes.

"We're out of balance!" Kame grunted. "Stop adding thrust, Johansson."

"Holding."

Susan saw the lurching reflected on Kame's screen as *random violent spurts* occurring outside the control lines of an oscilloscope-like graph. It looked serious, potentially a disaster if they continue their slow initial tumbling!

"I'm trying to compensate with the water balance," Kame grunted, intent on her display. "It should be working, but it isn't! The main problem is the water load in the last tank—sloshing around unpredictably rather than settling smoothly toward the back of the tank.

The interior surface must be damaged, interjecting a small inconsistent variable that..."

"*Beetle wings!*" Ben happily shouted before lapsing back into silence.

Susan tried to focus on the erratic star movements, trying to discern repeating patterns she could advise Kame on counteracting.

"Should we bring up the secondary jets along the stack?" Adriana interjected. "They'll burn more of our fuel reserves, but if we can use them to stabilize us then...?"

"Prime them," Kame said, intently watching the load balances displayed as various colors glowed along a line-drawing of Hermes. The colors changed as she made small adjustments in the water flow and content of each reserve tank located within the three Habs connecting back to the first water tank. "Ok, then...I think I've got it. How's it look outside, Susan?"

Susan was surprised by Kame's use of her first name. Usually she was very formal, especially in recorded conversations. But they were under severe stress. Spinning-up Hermes could be a boon to their health or an unmitigated disaster!

"The jerks in the star movement are smoothing out," Susan breathlessly reported.

Indeed, Susan saw that the steady, slow progression of the outside stars along arcs moving backward was returning.

"Good, good," Kame's head nodded behind her transparent faceplate. "Ok, then. Adriana, please continue taking us to 50% tumbling thrust—but slowly!"

The vibration increased. The "roar" of the liquid fuel jets burning behind them got louder. The stars started to move faster. But the lurching did not return. They were holding steady!

"We're at 50% thrust, Commander."

Susan held her breath. The tension was palpable. The stars were now rapidly moving around the Observation Deck at 2.5 revolutions per minute—that was a full revolution every 24 seconds. Susan began to feel dizzy. She knew it was the "Coriolis effect" kicking in at higher than 2.0 rpm. She was becoming disoriented due to the effects of the rotating vehicle acting upon the fluids in her inner ear canals. From her astronaut training she knew that the disorientation should subside as her body adapted to the tumbling. But the Coriolis Effect might get downright debilitating before adaptation kicked in, especially for their radiation-weakened bodies!

But it would be worth the temporary nausea if the jungle Hab—furthest from the rotational center, out at the edge of the swinging vehicle—was able to achieve 0.5 G. Then their bodies wouldn't waste away from floating continually in zero-G despite their rigorous exercise schedule. They might still be relatively fit and strong when they arrived at the Asteroid.

"Take us up to full Tumble, Adriana—slow and steady."

"Yes, Commander...0.6 thrust...0.7....0.8..."

"Gandharvas! Gandharvas! Gandharvas!" Ben suddenly shouted, jerking and struggling to get out of the straps that held him in his chair.

He now appeared to be *terrified*.

"What's he saying, Susan? You know him best."

"I don't know, Commander—maybe it's some Hindu god?"

"Priyanka!" Kame sharply spoke his name. "We're ok! There's nothing to be..."

Suddenly the entire ship *jerked to the side* then began *lurching* unpredictably!

"Adri, what's happening?" Kame yelled.

"It should be balanced!" Adriana yelled back. "Something's not working right! Either the steering jets are misaligned or the computer signals are scrambled!"

The forward jerky tumbling accelerated.

Susan heard ominous metallic "groans" and "snaps" as various parts of the vehicle *broke* under the sudden, uneven stresses!

A blast of air moved Susan's arms to the side. Even through the thick fabric of her pressure suit she felt a sudden icy chill. They'd lost cabin pressure! They were rapidly spilling air out into space!

The Observation Deck must be breached! But looking around fearfully, Susan didn't see any obvious cracks or gaps. What was going on?

"Oh, Christ," Adriana gasped. "The jets didn't kick off automatically! We're up to 8.9 rpm!"

Susan saw the stars zipping around the portholes, randomly seeming to pause then slip to the side—as the ship lurched uncontrollably, not in the predicted steady Tumble! Now she felt so dizzy and nauseous she could hardly focus her eyes. If this continued for much longer they'd be helpless.

"Shut off the damn gimbal jet!" Kame shouted.

"It's not responding! We've lost control! The fiber-optic cable must be kinked again, or broken! Or the computer's damaged!"

Susan struggled to stay conscious, not black out.

"Then cut off the fuel that's flowing through the main line!" Kame shouted.

"Alright...yes...got it."

The increasing acceleration stopped—but they were still flopping forward and around, *much* too fast!

"You're the pilot, Adriana!" Kame snapped. "You must get control of Hermes! You still have manual control, right? So use the secondary steering jets along the length of the stack. Forget about what should be happening. Just judge by the results of your inputted commands. You've got to compensate for the altered vectors or we'll be torn to pieces!"

Ben began chanting what could only be a Hindu prayer, seemingly invoking the gods to help the crew. Some of his words were in Hindi and some in English. Susan made out references to *trees*, *bark*, *sap*, and *blossoms*. Strange rhyming schemes transformed the mad chant into a compelling piece of wild music. Susan felt a sudden desire to join in, but stopped herself. She'd given up music long ago, channeling those creative urges into her science studies. Now she felt deficient to aid Ben in his appeal to Higher Powers.

But it was oddly fitting.

Yep—Susan thought giddily to herself. *We're singing a hymn as the Titanic sinks!*

"Diverting fuel stores to the secondary lines," Adriana tensely stated.

Susan realized she was on the verge of blacking out as the stars whipped unpredictably around outside the portholes. The crewmembers were still at or near the center of mass of the long vehicle, so the

G-forces on her body weren't intolerable. But her brain was getting scrambled by the wild thrashing!

Stay awake! Stay alert!—she ordered herself, resolutely focusing her gaze on the jerking computer screen in front of her.

"I'm...firing by the...seat of my spacesuit pants, Commander...as ordered," Adriana gasped out, rigid in her still-secured reclining chair.

Susan felt *jerks* and *jabs* as the steering jets along the length of Hermes alternately blasted then quieted.

And gradually the wild swings subsided, the vehicle steadied, until finally they were tumbling straight forward as planned. But it was still much too fast! The ship couldn't stand the strain. Hermes wasn't designed to tumble at 10 rpm. Neither was the human body. The negative effects on both Hermes and their brains would be far greater than any benefits from the simulated higher G forces. Susan was already struggling not to vomit into her helmet.

"Can you slow us...back to 5.0 rpm?" Kame asked, tightly clutching each side of her chair with her gloved hands.

"If the primary gimbal jet still works, we can fire opposite to the previous setting. That should slow us. I'll restart the fuel flowing to the main jet."

"Do so."

Ben had quieted, his head now lolling to the side. Through his helmet he looked asleep, his eyes tightly closed.

"Damage assessment, Susan?"

Susan was silent a moment, straining to peer out each of the portholes, not trusting her instrument readings.

Looking forward Susan could see the furthest Hab *twisted to the side* instead of being in a straight line with the rest of the stack. A *white stream of vapor* was spurting out of its linkage to the next closer Hab. In the opposite direction, looking aft, Susan saw *one of the struts flopping free* instead of fixed to the others. More ominously, the main circular radiation shield directly behind the Service Node, protecting the forward crew sections, was *badly askew*. A whole section of the shield was slid to the side, directly exposing part of the SN. That would make the chronic radiation bathing the crew even worse.

"Structural damage, Commander—it looks severe. But I think we can repair it, given enough time. Our worst immediate problem is air pressure loss. It's not caused by something here in the OD—but in the jungle Hab. The hatches between here and there must be open!"

"But we closed those hatches. We double checked them. Opening them back up requires a set of deliberate computer commands."

"I know, Kame. But it happened! Maybe they malfunctioned?"

"What, four hatches between us and the jungle Hab? That's impossible!"

"But it must have happened. We've lost air here while the breach is at the farthest hatch. With your permission, I need to go there immediately and try to seal the leak!"

"Alright, then, we'll figure out how it happened later—after we recover."

"So can I leave?"

"Hold in place, King," Kame ordered, back to her more formal manner of communication. "Going down that long tunnel with all the hatches open, at greater than one G, will be dangerous. It'd be like falling down a well. Johansson, how long will it take for us to reduce the rotation to 5.0 rpm?"

Susan felt new trembles and distant "roars" through the metal as the rear jets kicked in opposite to their prior orientation. The stars zipping around the OD were slowing.

"Not long, Commander, but there's more bad news."

"Speak!"

"We burned a lot of our fuel reserves getting the thrashings under control. But we're still unstable. With the further damage to the stack, there's no way we can keep the Tumble smooth without constantly compensating with our steering jets. If we maintain Tumble we'll quickly burn through all our remaining fuel!"

Kame was silent for a moment, considering.

Annoyingly, Ben was now loudly *snoring* into his helmet microphone...

He was totally oblivious to their incredible danger!

"Then bring us back to zero-G, Johansson. We're low on our oxygen-and-hydrogen fuel, with very little water-mass available to generate more. We'll just have to do without simulated gravity."

Kame didn't say what they were all thinking. Their attempt to generate a simulated "gravity" had been a complete failure! Even worse, the integrity of the ship had been compromised. It was yet another disaster! If they ever made it back to Earth, Yamamoto was likely looking at dismissal from the Japanese astronaut core for her decision-making. According to rumor, JAXA did not take any failure by its astronauts lightly.

Plus the breaches—in spite of multiple containment protocols— would have killed them all if they hadn't been in their pressure suits.

How the hell did this happen?

"Do you think you can get to the farming Hab safely now, King? The centripetal forces should be tapering off shortly."

"I can do it."

"Then please proceed. I see on our internal sensors that we've lost most of our internal atmosphere. We've got to seal that breach before attempting to repressurize the ship!"

"Right away!" Susan gulped, still struggling not to vomit into her helmet, her head still spinning. She started unlatching the straps holding her in her flight chair.

"And take *him* with you!" Kame snapped, pointing at the irritatingly snoring Ben.

Trying to ignore the still-moving stars outside, Susan drifted up into the cabin's interior and over to Ben's chair. She began unstrapping him...

"Eh? Going back home?" he sputtered happily, widely opening his red, bloodshot eyes. "We're still alive?"

"Yes, Ben," Susan gently answered, taking him by an arm and guiding his now-floating body toward the exit hatch. "We're alive and we're going home."

That was a comforting thought.

But she had a terrible feeling that what they'd find in the jungle Hab would be *ghastly*.

Susan sat with glazed eyes in a small jail cell, staring at nothing in particular. She was on the lower bunk of a two-decker iron bed, glumly contemplating her dreadful situation.

Above her snored "Shelly," exhausted from a recent episode of violent convulsions. Shelly was Susan's cellmate, a heavy-set, middle-aged woman arrested for drug dealing. Apparently heroin was still the drug of choice for Pasadena users: highly refined, highly addictive, and very profitable for elicit providers.

Shelly told Susan that her troubles started out as a broken leg on a tennis court. Huh, imagine that! Tennis was touted as a "safe" sport—and Shelly here managed to jump for a ball, trip, and slam her knee into the hard court surface. From a successful upper class family, Shelly became addicted to prescription painkillers for the excruciating pain from her shattered knee and leg. When the doctors cut off her supply of the drug following successful surgery, she graduated to heroine and never looked back.

To fund her heroin habit Shelly began pushing the stuff herself. That was after a humiliating stint as a prostitute in the seedier LA slum areas. By that time she'd lost her family—an optometrist husband and two young kids—"living in hell to get a taste of heaven," as she starkly put it. She was arrested just three days ago. Now she was suffering intense withdrawal symptoms in the top bunk, moaning and shaking. It was sad. But Susan had her own problems. She was in for attempted *murder one*.

She wasn't yet convicted of the crime. But Susan was incarcerated until her upcoming trial. Due to the "heinous nature" of the crime, she'd not been granted bail. So at least until the trial she was a "resident" of the Pasadena Police Department's local jail.

At least the cell was clean and reasonably comfortable. Everything was painted in an antiseptic white. Other than the bars, she might have been inside a hospital ward.

Even her jail uniform was like a hospital gown, freshly laundered and white—except for large red letters that proclaimed: *"Jail Inmate."* Pasadena, an upper class community, had nice jails. That was some consolation, but not much.

However, being in jail wasn't the worst thing. Susan was a mild introvert who could readily sink into her own mind on a moment's notice, with everything around her blurring. It was the *incredible boredom* that was hammering her! There'd been security concerns lately, so they'd taken away even the jail TVs. Now all there was to engage Susan's super-active mind were the howls and curses of fellow inmates echoing in the outside corridor.

"King, your lawyer's here. You want to take the meeting?"

It was Cecilia, one of the beefy female officers. She was of Mexican heritage, one of the friendlier guards. Susan knew that she didn't have a choice to talk or not talk with her court-appointed lawyer, but it was nice of Cecilia to ask.

"Sure, why not?"

She waited patiently as Cecilia loudly unlocked her door with a large, old-fashioned, metal, "clanking" key. Then Susan endured the indignantly of having her hands handcuffed in front of her and ankle chains linked onto both her legs. As an accused murderer, she was subject to the strictest security procedures. She meekly shuffled along beside the guard to the visitation room, sitting down at a round plastic table in a cheerfully yellow plastic armchair.

Cecilia went back to stand nearby against a wall. She looked relaxed, but Susan knew that the watchful guard would pounce if necessary.

Upon being arrested Susan discovered that she didn't have near enough money to hire a decent LA lawyer. They cost much too much to pay for one on a lowly postdoc's salary. God, the lawyers typically charged hundreds of dollars per hour! Susan was just barely paying the high rent for her small apartment, let alone enough to hire a lawyer. So she had to take what the state offered, a court-appointed Public Defender.

She'd half expected her brother to ride to her rescue with "King and Nash" billions of dollars, surrounding her with a team of high-priced super-lawyers. But she heard nothing from him. Apparently politics got in the way. She'd read how that Nashoba Energy was negotiating with several world agencies for trans-global rights to transform energy storage systems. A widely reported scandal such as hers could taint the "world savior" image of Nashoba, who was supposedly allowing "clean" energy sources to catch up to and surpass fossil fuels. The company was still fighting many powerful interests who saw their industries crumbling if virtually infinite energy could be stored and released at will from compact devices. And of course there was her own previous stubbornness in cutting off her brother.

So she was left to "swing high," all by her lonesome.

"Hi, Susan," a professional-sounding female voice greeted her. Susan saw papers being laid out neatly on the table top from an opened briefcase. "Sorry it's been a while since I saw you last. I've got nearly a hundred clients at the moment. You're at the top of my list but I've got to service my entire caseload or I'll be fired. And I've only twenty minutes for you, sorry again. I have to be in court shortly. So we've got to stay focused and brief. How are you doing?"

Susan looked up into the kind but weary eyes of *Gale Landers*. Gale was a round-faced young woman not much older than Susan. She wore a standard dark, professional pantsuit with a white shirt unbuttoned at her throat. Her hair was short and bright orange. She had freckles on her pudgy cheeks. She was a natural "redhead." Also, she seemed to Susan very inexperienced and over-worked. This was Landers' first year at being a Public Defender, newly graduated from law school.

And this was only the second time in four weeks that Susan had talked to her. The first time was a full two weeks ago, at her initial, disturbingly brief court arraignment.

"Well, Gale..." Susan sighed deeply before proceeding. "If you're not just being polite, I'm officially reporting to you that I'm really, really *bored!* Can you get them to give me access to a laptop or computer terminal? If I could just get into the JPL website then maybe I could still get some of my research work done and..."

"I'm sorry. That's just not possible."

"Ok, I understand, but..."

"Yes?"

"Look, there's a small book I had in my shoulder bag when I got arrested. It's just a book of poetry. It's called '*The Minstrel's Lark.*' I always have it with me because whenever I get bored it's got layers on layers of interesting depths to occupy my mind. Can you get them to give it to me? *Please?*"

"Well, I can try."

"Thanks—so is anything new happening with my case? Is that why you're here?"

"Well, there is a *little* bit of good news that..."

"What? Tell me!" Susan interrupted her.

"Professor Cafferty's going to survive. He's no longer in the Intensive Care Unit at the UCLA trauma center. He's still in a coma, though, on a ventilator. But the brain swelling is going down."

"So I'm no longer accused of murder?"

"—just felony assault with intent to kill..."

"Ouch!" Susan spat before grinding her teeth together, trying to get her swirling emotions under control.

She wanted to scream! But Cecilia would just yank her back to her cell. Also, she didn't want to offend the young lawyer. Gale was her only link to the outside. Susan knew she had to suck up her outrage and try to stay rational.

The clock was ticking.

"Gale, you know I didn't do it. I was defending myself against him. He went crazy or something!"

"Susan, I believe you. But the evidence says different. That's what the Court examines. That's what a jury will evaluate: the evidence."

"*What* evidence?" Susan snapped back at her.

"You know perfectly well. You were covered in Professor Cafferty's blood. The approaching EMTs and officer saw you on top of him, pummeling him. Your knuckle-prints were all across his face. And before he lapsed into unconsciousness he directly accused you of attacking and trying to kill him! Unfortunately, the evidence superficially seems to prove you attacked him."

"Well...yes, there's *that*...but..."

"Plus your friend at work—Pete, I think—reluctantly testified that you threatened just minutes before the incident to 'punch Cafferty's face to pieces' with your own fists! That's pretty damning."

"Yes...well, I did say that—but it was a hypothetical if the bastard ever tried to force himself upon me sexually!"

"Ok, then. We'll continue to claim self-defense. That's a time-honored counter against accusation of assault, battery or homicide. But in your case—sorry—it's not likely to fly. In addition to your previous threat, there's the *other* evidence."

"*What* other evidence?"

Susan saw Cecilia looking at her large, black wristwatch. Inmates were only allowed thirty minutes with their attorneys. And Gale said she had to leave within twenty minutes. Time was running out!

"There's the matter of your *underwear* that was found by detectives in a drawer in Professor Cafferty's apartment."

Susan was stunned.

"But...that can't be! I've never even been to his apartment. I don't even know the address! Somehow he must have stolen it from me. I had an 'apartment warming' party when I first got here. Everyone from my branch was there, including him!"

"So...you think he *stole* your underwear," she repeated. "And did he also steal your toothbrush?"

"Toothbrush?"

"The detectives found your toothbrush above the sink in his bathroom. It was a big flat one, quite distinctive, which matched other ones in your apartment. And it had your DNA on it."

"I...I...I..." Susan stammered in disbelief. But...if the man had sunk so low as to sneak around her apartment and steal her panties, he could have taken anything, including a loose toothbrush!

"Still, that's all circumstantial," Gale conceded. "So you apparently had an affair with your postdoctoral advisor. I'm told that this is not uncommon in postdoctoral programs between consenting adults. Plus this particular advisor had a known history of seducing his female charges into consensual affairs. That alone doesn't prove you tried to kill him."

"Of course not—and I *didn't*—and I *wasn't*...!"

"But the 'nail in your coffin' is the matter of the research paper you just co-authored."

Susan squinted her eyes closed, trying to make sense of Gale's words. She just wanted out of the horrible jail cell, to go back to her life! How could the research paper she'd been working on be a "nail in her coffin"?

"Well, yes...I just finished the first draft the night before. But there wasn't any problem!"

"I'm told it's highly unusual for the advisor to insist on his name coming first on a postdoc's research publication. The Prosecutor claims that was your main motivation for attacking Cafferty in the parking lot. So that professional insult when added to being sexually rebuffed was..."

"*What?* I *wasn't* 'sexually rebuffed' by him! I didn't want anything to do with his crude sexual advances! What the hell are you talking about?"

"Pete's testimony is strong evidence that you *were* upset concerning sexual matters with Cafferty," the lawyer relentlessly continued. "The physical evidence in Professor Cafferty's apartment is damning, indicating that the situation went beyond the mild 'flirtation' you admitted to in your conversation with Pete. Plus there's the Termination Notice that..."

"Oh, God, what now?" Susan interrupted the woman. "You've got to be kidding me! I never got any Termination Notice!"

"You didn't know? Well, your one-year probationary period was almost up, right? That very morning Cafferty sent an e-mail to Personnel telling them he *wasn't* going to renew your contract."

Susan was stunned. Her mouth hung open in disbelief. She had no words. If Cafferty had turned in a "nonrenewal notice" even *she* would convict herself if she was on her own jury! The evidence was overwhelming that she'd flown into a rage and attacked the man!

"But...wait!" Susan gasped, trying to think clearly. "When he came up behind me he was *already* busted up! Most of his injuries occurred *before* he grabbed my arm. He must have been dripping blood all down that sidewalk!"

"There wasn't a trace of blood except at the fight scene."

"That can't be true!"

"Susan, you know I want to help you, but..."

Susan jerked up out of her chair, her cuffed hands flat on the tabletop, glaring down at the woman. To the side, she saw Cecilia starting forward...

"I just defended myself! Maybe the blood didn't drip off of him right away. I don't know! But he snuck up behind me and grabbed my arm! When I turned around he was *already* injured. Then he unexpectedly tried to choke me to death—and I had to fight him off. That's what *really* happened! Honest!"

Before Celilia could grab her, Susan slumped back into her chair and starting sobbing.

Gale looked down at her watch, starting to stand up from her chair...

"I'm sorry, Susan. The evidence just doesn't support that story," Gale said, gathering up her papers and slipping them back into her briefcase as she stood. "We can change your plea of not guilty to a temporary-insanity defense if you wish, but that'll just land you in the looney bin even if it somehow succeeded, which is unlikely. I think it's better to consider emphasizing extenuating circumstances. Maybe we can get the sentence reduced from life in prison to..."

"The security cameras!" Susan shouted, jumping up again and reaching out with her cuffed hands to grab Gale's arm, holding her back. "They're all over JPL! They'll show Cafferty bloodied up before reaching me—then *him* trying to kill *me!* Just subpoena the camera discs! Jesus, Gale, I could be out of here tomorrow if..."

The Public Defender held up her free hand to stop Cecilia from pulling Susan away. Gently, Gale loosened Susan's clawed hand from her own arm.

Chagrinned, Susan sagged back into her seat.

"The power blackout..." Susan nodded morosely. Tears of frustration were dripping down both her cheeks. She angrily wiped them away.

"That's the first thing the investigating officers did, Susan. But, yes, you're correct. The cameras weren't working due to the power failure. And the bodycam of the responding officer showed exactly what he and the EMTs say they saw. True, the bodycam didn't see what happened before the fight, but the outcome was crystal clear— and when added to what Cafferty himself yelled out before he collapsed, well..."

"But what about my 911 call? I made it *before* he grabbed me and I fought back. Surely...?"

"That's your story, Susan. Just as plausible is you attacked him, tried to cover it by phoning 911, then he fought back just as the first responders arrived."

Susan groaned. She was amazed at how everything seemed to fit tightly together against her.

"So I'm royally screwed," Susan whispered. "What's your best guess as to my probable sentence?"

Gale looked at her sadly.

"Oh, with good behavior, claiming an aggravated act of rage—probably twenty years. That's the best case scenario, what with the publicity surrounding your case. Any lesser sentence would be very difficult for the Judge to justify. After all, you nearly killed the man. And there's still no guaranteed he'll ever come out of his coma."

Susan shook her head ruefully.

"Guess I'm not going to make it into space," she weakly laughed.

"Space?"

"Forget it," Susan sighed, standing up and shuffling over to Cecilia who'd retreated back against the wall. Her ankle chains "clanked" on the hard floor. "I'm ready to go back to my cell. Maybe I can help Shelly hang in there, huh? That's something good to do with all my 'free time'!"

"You're one of the nice ones, Susan," the guard softly replied, gently taking Susan by an arm. "Sorry you got yourself into such a mess, girl. But stuff happens. You just gotta make the best of things and..."

"Dr. King!" Gale called after her. "I can submit a change in your plea if you..."

"Just cut the best deal you can," Susan cut her off, her head hanging, not looking away from her own chained feet. "If I need to sign something, I'll do it. I've got a whole new life to adjust myself to...if you call it living."

Twenty years, at a minimum. That was a long time. But then again she'd only be in her late forties when she got out. Maybe there'd be a mission to Pluto by then?

—but certainly not for middle-aged ex-cons.

The few applicants of the thousands who applied, who made it through the extensive competition into the NASA trainee ranks, were typically squeaky-clean.

Her dream of becoming an astronaut was dead.

Chapter 15

<u>COMETS</u>

Flying too close to the sun

You gain world-wide fame

Snapping up Gold Medals

Flaring to many times your size

Your beautiful golden tail fills the sky

A heavenly tadpole metamorphosing

You swim against the fiery tide

Hoping the price will not be too high

A Satanic Bargain gone awry

You either spill your guts

Leaving behind a rocky husk

Or plunge into the glowing corona

And ingloriously get snuffed out...

Or swing back into the eternal dark

A "has-been," largely forgotten

But what a long Olympic dive!

The Minstrel's Lark, 15:48-52

IMPACT MINUS FOUR MONTHS, *STARVING...*

The jungle was dead.

The loss of atmosphere plus plunging temperature in the outermost Hab doomed the plants. When Susan climbed down into the habitat, pulling the babbling Ben along behind her, she was horrified to seen them frozen solid. The waving green vines, clusters of multicolored fruits, and wide leaves were icily rigid, coated with a thin white crust of frost.

"Noooooooo!" Ben howled in drawn-out denial. He floundered in the fast-fading weak gravity, his flight-suited arms breaking off rigid green stalks that clustered about him in the air. "The *Gandharvas* are mad at us! They will *devour* us for killing their plants! We're doomed!"

Still devastated by the awful disaster of the failed attempt to ramp-up the "tumble" Susan did not need Priyanka's crazed antics.

"What are 'Gandharvas', Ben?" Susan said, trying to distract him with intellectual engagement as she surveyed the awful scene.

"They're spirit singers and dancers," he gibbered fearfully. "But they're also part animals. They're messengers from the gods to the humans, *inhabiting* plants and flowers so that…"

"They sound nice, Ben," she said, gently pushing him toward his hammock. Its fabrics hung bizarrely frozen in place.

"—not when they herald the eminence of *painful death* and fiery rebirth!" he screamed, thrashing wildly.

"Please get into your hammock, Ben!" Susan cajoled him, concerned the knocked-off debris was filling the air around her. "I'll tie you in nice and securely. You can go back to sleep. Things will be better when you wake up, I promise. The Gandharvas will calm once we get them air and warmth. Then the jungle will recover. You'll see!"

"No! We've got to escape. Open up the doorway, Susan. We must flee this place. We've got to get out of this *deathtrap!*"

He tried to squirm away from her, to raise his helmet, to embrace the thicket of frozen white plants around him.

"I'm sorry, Ben," she said as she plunged a hypodermic needle through the fabric of his suit and deep into his leg muscle.

He "squeaked" in dismay at the pain from the needle, looking down in bewilderment at the syringe protruding from his leg, his arms flailing in the air.

But then he quieted, slumping. The sedative syringe that Susan kept in a nook at the exit node had proved handy. Ben was knocked out for at least a couple hours, long enough for her to complete her tasks without having to babysit him.

She withdrew the syringe and immediately slapped a thick adhesive bandage in place, sealing the small pinprick hole in his suit. He wouldn't depressurize.

She kicked through the now zero-G to float the still deliriously muttering Ben to his hammock and tie him securely in by its sleeping straps. He'd be safe there and out of her way. His suit would keep him from freezing while the Hab regained air and warmth.

Then she surveyed the interior of the jungle Hab. Surprisingly, everything looked relatively undisturbed. The exercise equipment at the bottom of the Hab was still securely fixed in place, just as before. Also, luxurious growth still surrounded everything, filling up most of the Hab interior. The sleeping sections were undisturbed. But the place indeed had an *ominous* feel, as if it had been turned into a *tomb* rather than a welcoming sanctuary.

And it was definitely icy.

Susan shivered, knowing her suit insulation wouldn't keep her from freezing for much longer if she didn't plug the leak in the Hab. Frantically she searched for the breach. The enclosure was no longer in the straight alignment it should have been. Drifting down from the upper Hab she'd had to turn at a slight angle. The breach had to be somewhere nearby the connector adaptor.

"Yes, there you are!" she said in satisfaction, looking at a long crack right at the entrance. It was substantial, with further fractures splintering outward inside the main crack.

Grabbing a prepositioned emergency sealant tube she squeezed it hard, liberally squirting the contents directly into the crack along its entire length. But it wasn't enough. She kicked up to the higher Hab, grabbing its emergency sealant tube. Back at the crack she squirted it in also...ah...just enough. She smeared the upper layer of the goo outside the crack along its edges to make sure she had a good seal.

"And yet another mystery solved," she nodded in satisfaction.

As the sealant hardened, she realized she knew where the mysterious water leakage came from that had plagued them since leaving Earth orbit. It was from the subsurface spider-web of fractures she'd seen inside the crack. They must be radiating out beneath the inner surface into the hardened foam of the Hab's wall. Since the near-Earth swing—when the hidden fractures likely originated—the unseen breaches had been quietly "siphoning" off the jungle's dispersed humidity into space.

The hardened foam that should have been insulating the Habs was instead functioning as a microscopic sponge, sucking out their moisture!

Fortunately, active molecular feedback mechanisms machined into the hardened foam had prevented the air from likewise siphoning off. That was a small blessing. But the microscopic fracturing had somehow subverted the mechanisms preventing the "wicking" of H_2O molecules.

"Commander?" she spoke into her helmet microphone, nudging it with her tongue into ship-communication mode. Previously it was on short-range output, only audible to Ben and her.

"Yes, King? How's it going?"

"The breach is sealed. If that's the only one reaching through the Hab's skin out into space I think we're good. But we'll know better when you start pressurizing the ship. There's small debris floating in here that'll get pulled to the site of any additional leaks."

"Alright then, I'll start with the jungle Hab first. Are the other hatches locked?"

"I closed them as I passed through each. I'm closing the hatch now to the second Hab."

"Ready?"

Susan swung the hatch closed and cinched it down.

"We're secure, start the air."

The vines brightened up as Susan felt air rushing back into the enclosure. But the sudden "resurrection" of the jungle was just frost melting due to the sudden warmth. The plants themselves immediately wilted. The various fruits shrunk inward. Even the packed "soil" at the roots of the plants was affected, flaking out in big brown chunks.

The air was now filled with a mixture of dirt, dead plant matter, and rotted fruit.

"There's no movement of the floating debris," Susan reported into her helmet microphone. "The breach is sealed, at least for now. I don't know about realigning the entire jungle Hab, though. It may have to just hang ajar. Pushing it back into alignment may be beyond our capabilities."

"We'll worry about that later, King. Work yourself back up to the OD, module by module, as we restore pressure. Make sure there aren't any other further leaks before we open up the hatches for un-fettered passage."

"Ok...but..."

"Yes?"

"From what I've seen here, the farm is dead. It'll take months for us to grow up new crops. By that time we'll be at the Asteroid. Rations will be tight, Commander. You might want to start thinking of the best strategy for surviving the rest of our trip."

There was a short silence. Susan heard Kame sigh deeply.

"Well—we'll make do, somehow. Thanks for the 'heads-up', Susan."

"We may have to think the unthinkable," Susan pointedly added.

"We'll consider every possibility. The Mission comes first."

That was for the recorded transcript. It was a "heads-up" not just to the crew but to Mission Control back on Earth. With the farm dead, half of their expected calories were instantly gone. The crew's bodily solid wastes would no longer be "magically" transmuted into tasty bananas, mangos, soy beans, tomatoes, or potatoes. Instead, the crew was immediately on half-rations. That meant that when they arrived at the Asteroid they'd be starved skeletons. Not only would they not benefit from 0.5 G to stay strong, they'd have hardly any muscle mass left on their weakened bones!

And the water crisis was even worse. Tearing opening the fractures in the jungle Hab's foam during the aborted Tumble had rapidly sucked a large volume of water out into space, in addition to the out-rushing air. The water loss was what Susan had observed as a *white plume* spouting out into space when she first saw the problem through the porthole in the OD. The water vapor was solidifying into a snowy plume. If they'd lost too much water they might not even make it to the Asteroid. The human body could go for a month without eating, digesting its own substance for its energy needs. But most people would be dead after a week without water.

Susan had a sinking feeling that without a *miracle* their mission was doomed—and with it, the entire Earth.

Still with her helmet sealed, she licked her lips. They felt dry, flaky.

Well, that was only the start. She might as well get used to the unpleasant sensation. Without fresh water to deplete their meager reserves they were all going to get very thirsty.

Susan lay on her prison bunk, her head on a small hard pillow, engrossed in studying her one, single book.

She hadn't seen Gale Landers since their last meeting, but at least the lawyer did one thing for her, getting the jailors to give her the old poetry book from her shoulder bag. She was reading from Chapter 15 on "Giggles":

> *"Presumably only for children*
> *Little babies struggling to articulate*
> *A little glee belched out in a burst*
> *It's too precious to restrict*
> *Only for immature children*
> *But rather should erupt*
> *From anyone caught in fun*
> *Unexpectedly finding a hint*
> *Not of horror or pain or drudgery*
> *But spontaneous humor cutting*
> *Lancing the cyst, releasing the puss*
> *And relieving the nagging ache*
> *If only for just a moment..."*

Wow. That was heavy. What wisdom! Susan saw that the author was encouraging her to find the humor buried in any situation, no matter how horrible—and use it to laugh, releasing tension! But it wasn't just a polite "hah, hah" but rather the spontaneous, totally authentic *giggle* of a delighted small child!

"You're free, Susan. You can leave."

Startled, Susan looked to the side to see Cecilia standing outside the jail cell, using her large key to open the barred door.

"*Tee, hee!*" Susan exaggerated a giggle, choosing to appreciate the very bad joke from her jailor rather than snorting in anger.

Wait a minute...Cecilia had never before showed any sign of having a sense of humor. What was happening?

"No, I'm serious, girl," the beefy woman replied. "All charges against you have been dropped. I just got the order to bring you to Processing to retrieve your belongings and sign you out."

Susan lowered the poetry book, frowning. She knew this had to be a dream from which she'd sadly awake in a minute or two. This was the very miracle she'd prayed for—knowing it would never arrive! She was resigned to spending at least the next couple decades of her life as a prisoner of the State, for a crime she never did. She'd accepted that terrible fate, patiently awaiting her trial. Her drug dealer friend had recovered enough to move on out of the city jail to a long-term facility. Now Susan was by herself in the small cell, teaching herself a Buddhist-type meditation. But she was no good at it. She was an "action" person who preferred to be working at defined tasks rather than musing over abstractions. In an actual prison there'd be work programs. That would keep her occupied. But here in limbo, in the local jail awaiting her trial, she was mostly restricted to her cell and her own dark imagination.

"Stop kidding me, Cecee," Susan snorted, wearily settling back into her uncomfortable but familiar bunk. She'd gotten to know her jailor on a first name basis. She closed her eyes and laid the still-opened book across her chest. "You know my lawyer would come tell me in person if that was true."

"She's out at Processing, waiting for you."

Holy crap! Is it really true? Is my nightmare finally over?

Susan's eyes snapped open. She abruptly sat up on the edge of her bunk.

"Really?"

"Grab your stuff, girl. You're going home."

Susan didn't have much in the cell with her—just her bathroom toiletries, the prison clothes on her back, her book of weird poems, and a small cardboard picture drawn by Shelly. It turns out that the heroine drug addict/dealer was a talented artist. Using just crayons, the woman had drawn a spectacular picture of a female blond-haired angel with large, feathery wings.

In the picture, the elegant angel was sitting covered by her purple-hued wings on the edge of a green pond. Off in the distance, pink flamencos stood on stilted legs, spearing fish. The pond merged seamlessly up into a leafy forest half-hiding a rocky, ancient bridge stretched above a mysterious river. It was a haunting picture of a fantastical Nature where humans could leap up into the sky and fly away. In the increasingly dreary days alone in her cell, the mystical picture had sustained Susan.

Shelly gave it to Susan out of gratitude for comforting and encouraging her through her acute withdrawal symptoms. Shelly's last words on being transferred out of the cell were: "I deserve to be here because of my stupid choices. You deserve better, Suzy. But you won't be trapped here like me. You'll fly free. You'll see. Hang in there, girlfriend!"

And now, amazingly, Shelly's kind prediction was apparently coming true!

But no, it had to be some sort of trick...

Susan tucked Shelly's small picture along with the poetry book into the wide pocket of her prison uniform, grabbed her toothbrush and other toiletries, and got up to walk with Cecilia down the long corridor to Processing. It felt strange to not be shackled at her wrists and ankles. Around her in the female ward other lost souls sulked behind bars, pacing back and forth, or lay on their bunks—banging their heads on the walls, or shouting out curses. This was a place of despair and grief, of punishment and pain, of loss and failure. And yet the fallen women here had great talents, largely unrealized—exemplified by crayons smeared across discarded cardboard, producing a piece of art worthy of hanging in a museum!

"Here we are," Cecilia smiled at Susan. Her wide, brown face radiated happiness at escorting Susan to freedom. "You be good, girl!"

Susan paused before proceeding.

"Thanks Cecee... I still don't know if this is real or not. I'm expecting to wake up any second. But if this is truly happening, maybe I needed this whole experience. I've flown high and fast for a long time and I think I forgot what it's like to walk on the ground with everyone else. I was lucky to have you for my jailor. You were kind to me. Thanks!"

"Just doin' my job, Suzy. I never believed those news stories about you. And I do like to look up at the stars at night—those millions and millions of pinpoints. It's nice to know you're out there bringing them down to earth for us!"

Susan smiled gratefully at the departing woman who gave her a friendly wave, turning away.

"Susan!"

She turned and found herself looking into the excited, youthful face of Gale Landers. The lawyer's blue eyes were sparkling, the freckles on her cheeks almost popping off her smiling face!

She was carrying a large shopping bag.

They were in a large room containing a number of desks at which personnel worked. The officers were standing up to greet Susan. When they saw her they broke into a loud applause!

"We never thought that you did it," an older, uniformed man said. He held out a hand which she took, hesitantly shaking it. The man's hand was firm and steady. He was the local Chief of Police, Officer "Zeke" Zackary. Chief Zackary was a strict "law and order" official who had been elected repeatedly over the years to oversee the police force in Pasadena. She remembered him personally questioning her after the incident. At the time he was formal and matter-of-fact, while appearing genuinely puzzled by her strange story.

It was nice to meet him again under this new situation—her processing *out* rather than in!

"May I speak with my client in private, please?" Gale said. "Also, I'd appreciate access to a computer."

"Sure, take my office," he grandly gestured to an ordinary-looking office over to the side of the open area. "The computer's on, visitor access mode. Just stick your thumbdrive in whenever you want. I assume you want to play the video for Ms. King?"

"Yes, Sir!"

"I'll have the paperwork ready for her to sign whenever she's ready. Her possessions she was arrested with—her wallet and handbag contents—are ready to be returned to her, minus the evidential items, of course. They're still at the FBI office where they were being analyzed. They'll be returned to her in due course."

Susan, bewildered, followed directions, sitting down at the Chief's wide desk in front of a computer screen. Gale stood at her shoulder, inserting the thumbdrive. A video window booted up. The picture in the window was grainy but discernible. It was of a wide green lawn through which ran a glaringly white sidewalk. The picture flickered regularly, as if the camera were being shot with a telescopic lens from a great distance, but quickly regained focus after each blip. The perspective was at a slight angle looking almost straight down from above. Susan could see off to the side the familiar lines of the side of her laboratory building.

"It's the sidewalk leading to the parking lot," Susan excitedly nodded. "I thought you told me before that the security cameras were off during the power blackout. How did you get this?"

"Just watch it, Susan."

"Ok..."

Coming into view was a person walking along the sidewalk. Susan could see blond hair with something bobbing back and forth below. It was *her* swinging her shoulder bag in time to the song playing in her earbuds. The view centered on her, flickering in and out. Up ahead were cars, one of them fiery red—her classic Fiero.

And then behind her came another person, walking quickly toward her on the sidewalk.

"That's Cafferty!" Susan exclaimed. "See his white hair...we're looking down on him! And he...*doesn't* appear to be hurt. What's...?"

"Keep watching, Susan."

But this scenario was exactly what the Prosecutor claimed! How could this exonerate her? It contradicted her vivid memories. They said he wasn't injured until she began fighting him. Was what they claimed really true? Did she just imagine that he grabbed her by the neck, forcing her to defend herself? Or did she fantasize the attack to use as an unconscious excuse to smashing his arrogant face in, releasing pent-up frustrations against him?

If that were true, then why was she being released?

But then the flicker obscured the scene just as he walked up behind her—when she saw on the computer screen him standing there *beating on his own face* with his own fists!

The visible top of his head was turning red from soaked-up, splattered blood.

What the hell? He beat *himself* up?

But why hadn't she heard the beating? Ah, yes, she had her earbuds in playing loud music!

Then his arm reached out and grabbed the person in front of him, yanking her backward, with her earbuds spinning off to the side.

"See there, Susan," Gale said, pointing to the screen.

After calling 911 the blond-haired person was lowering the slumped white-haired person onto the green grass. As his head lolled to the side his face was revealed to the overhead camera. It was a mass of fresh bruises and blood. Then his arms came up, grabbing the blond-haired person by the throat. A full thirty seconds went by as the person on top tried to pull free.

"For whatever reason, he attacked you," Gale said from behind Susan. "There's no doubt what happened. He made it look like he was injured, pummeling himself just before getting to you. You likely didn't hear the blows because you were listening to music on earbuds, just like you said. Then he throttled you as you tried to help him."

Finally, the person on top started thrashing out with her fists, punching the lower person in his already-bloodied face.

Stumbling free, the person on top—clearly revealed as Susan—fell backward to the green grass, staring upward at the sky, spattered with red blood.

From the right of the view a black-uniformed policeman and two white-clad EMTS came rushing up.

"The rest of the recording shows what was already known from the testimony of the first-responders."

"Where did this video come from?"

"No one knows. It was submitted anonymously to CNN. The experts think it was taken by a fortuitously passing military spy satellite."

"A *satellite* from orbit took this? But the detail is..."

"Yes, it's amazing. But remember this was on a sunny day with no clouds in the sky. Still, it does flicker in-and-out, just as you'd expect from atmospheric turbulence."

Ah...maybe Billy and Scott did something for her after all, behind the scenes. Perhaps they used their considerable and growing influence to get the spy agencies to search their recordings for that particular day. And since neither they nor the agencies could admit to their involvement or advanced technology, that recording had been "leaked" to the press.

Whatever had happened, the video proved her story was right!

But...why?

Why did Cafferty beat himself up and try to frame her for attempted murder?

"It came out this morning. It's been playing on all the major news feeds. I immediately went to court and sought an injunction on your behalf. After the Judge saw the video he granted your release with no reservations or restrictions. The Prosecutor Office agreed. They hypothesized that maybe Cafferty thought you were going to rat him out concerning your affair with him after you learned that your appointment was being terminated. Apparently his scheme went too far and he ended up in a coma instead of just bloodied-up. So you're completely free, with all charges dropped."

Susan stood up, turned around, and embraced the red-headed woman tightly.

"Thanks," Susan sobbed. "But...honestly...I *didn't* have any affair with him. It still doesn't make any sense," she said as she pulled back, wiping her eyes.

"Whatever, Susan, it doesn't matter now. It's over."

"How can I ever thank you?"

"I'm just glad I could help," Gale replied. "Unfortunately with my case load and indigent clientele I don't win many cases. It's nice to chalk one up for the good guys for once. That's enough reward for me."

Susan felt like a huge weight had been lifted off her shoulders. She yanked the thumbdrive out of the computer's slot.

"Can I keep this? I'd like to examine it in greater detail."

"Sure. It's actually a copy of the original. I got it straight from CNN, which they sent to the court as evidence. So it contains all the original pixels—not just a copy of the video feeds."

"That's great...but my clothes...?"

"The clothes you were wearing were splattered with blood. As the Chief said, they're still at the FBI. I brought you some of mine to wear out of jail. You're so fit and slender they'll be baggy on you. But better than nothing?"

She handed Susan the large shopping bag.

"Oh, that's really nice of you, Gale. Where can I change?"

"They've got a 'fitting' room a couple doors from here. After that I'll help you with the exit paperwork. And then we'll have to face the reporters outside. But don't worry. I'll be right there with you. Thanks to you, Susan, I'm *also* famous! I'll be able to write my own ticket to any big legal firm I want."

"Reporters?"

"Susan, this is international news. Your case became a worldwide fascination, with everyone speculating as to why an already-famous, super-smart celebrity like you would do such a stupid thing. Every gossip rag, blog, and legitimate news source had you tagged as a demon, a whore, a Satanist, a crazed mental case—and everything else imaginable!"

"Wow—can I ever get back to being just a lowly astrophysicist hunting asteroids?"

"I'm afraid not, Susan. But maybe you can find a way to leverage this additional attention to your advantage."

"I just want to put it *behind* me."

"Well, you can try."

The rest of the day was a swirl of activity. After leaving the jail, Susan was subjected to endless interviews. She stoically persisted through each of them, wanting to put an exclamation point on her innocence. She steadfastly denied any "affair" with the older Professor, or pent-up resentment at his stingy treatment of her on the first publication of their joint research. She maintained her story: she had no idea why he attacked her. Maybe he'd just gone crazy! But she didn't mention his wild claim that "lizards" made him do it. She hadn't even told the police about that, sure that such a wild claim would make her behavior look even more suspicious. As it was, it took a week before the news cycles moved onward and she was relegated to "old news."

Finally she was able to get back to work. Another senior scientist had taken over for Cafferty. She could continue her asteroid-belt research, but now with a new emphasis on water content. Indeed, she was now working alongside Pete in his long-distance organics-content research. He profusely apologized for having to tell the cops her final words to him that morning. But she told him not to worry—he was obligated to tell them everything. She didn't hold it against him. In fact, the next time a group went to Smitty's she was right there with them—not hanging back to be assaulted and sent to jail this time!

But there was always a cautious space between her and the others. She knew the group didn't believe her claim of *not* having an affair with Cafferty. They wouldn't admit to it, but she suspected they thought Cafferty may have had a valid reason to attack her. So she was accepted back to JPL, just not completely. There was always a space between the others and her.

However—besides having been obviously black-balled at NASA, hearing nothing from her now long-submitted application—things gradually got back to "normal."

About a year later she finally had occasion to meet up with Billy. It was bitter-sweet, but informative.

The chance meeting occurred at the well-attended *Lunar and Planetary Science Conference* held in San Francisco, hosted by the Planetary Society. Nashoba Energy had a large, expensive display booth advertising usage of their super-batteries on near-earth orbital platforms. Unfortunately, the new devices didn't work if they were taken too far away from their initial subspace energy depots. It had something to do with Einsteinian "gravity wells." Scientists were still debating the cause. But the effect was that they weren't useful out of earth orbit, such as on the Mars Transit Vehicle, Hermes. But there were many other near-Earth industrial, scientific, and military applications sponsored by NASA and other space organizations for the new super-batteries.

"*Suzy*, is that you?"

She considered just walking away. But curious eyes were on her, including some reporters she'd spied. She didn't need to make a scene. Things were finally getting back to normal in her life and she didn't want to appear on a gossip site dissing her brother.

"Hi, Billy," she reluctantly acknowledged his presence.

He was standing behind the display case, proudly showed off gleaming, silvery tiny batteries that claimed access to enormous power reserves. Flanking him she saw attentive lackeys ready to step in if he got flustered or tongue tied. He was dressed in a slick, expensive suede suit. He had gold cufflinks and a large gold wristwatch. His hair was professionally styled, swept to one side. He looked enormously successful, but tired. She felt a pang of sympathy at wrinkles at the corners of his eyes, which hadn't been there before. He was rapidly aging in his corporate job.

Also, she was afraid of how he'd react to her. Did he hate her for withdrawing from him after the disaster at Veterans Lake?

But his wide smile of greeting was genuine and warm.

He grabbed her up in a bear hug.

"I didn't know you were coming!"

"I've a holo-display in the scientific 'posters'—a real-time, flowing model of the asteroid belt. We've quantified the total distribution of water within the matrix of other components. Also, we have a handle on the organics that..."

"Let me look at you!" he said, holding her off at arm's length.

Now feeling uncomfortable—others were looking at them and snapping pictures with their cellphones—Susan gently disengaged his hands and backed off a step.

Now was a good a time as any to make amends, to try to set things right. She hadn't planned on it, but why not?

"Is there somewhere we can go to talk?" she said.

He glanced around, realized they were the center of attention of the milling Conference attendees, and led her away to a private meeting room behind the display. They sat down at a cluttered table.

"You look tired, Billy—older."

He shrugged. "Of course I am, Susan. It's been *two years* since I saw you last. You look older also—but it looks good on you!" he hastened to add: "You look more...well, mature. You're not the pouty kid I once knew. Hah!"

"Huh," she snorted in return, pleased with the "backhanded" compliment. "But I'm always going to be older than you!"

"Just four years!"

"I'll always the 'big' sister and you just my *dorky* little brother!"

"Am not!" he laughed back at her. "I'm a big rich tycoon and you're just a wannabe lab tech who..."

He broke off, sighing deeply, seeing that his offhand remark had cut her deeply. Here she'd sacrificed so much to stick to her scientific goals...and not only was she *not* a NASA astronaut, her scientific discoveries were minimal at best, hardly world-shaking. It was a hell of a lot of effort to wind up with so little.

"Sorry, Suzy—I didn't mean..."

"Forget it!" she snapped at him, now recalling why she'd distanced herself from him and his buddy Scott. "I just want to thank you in person for getting me out of that jail mess a year ago. If it hadn't been for that video, I'd have..."

"We didn't have anything to do with that," he quietly admitted, looking down at the floor.

"What?"

His gaze hardened, the wrinkles at the corners of his eyes standing out sharply.

"Look, Suzy—I'm not a saint, but fooling around with your old Postdoc Advisor was..."

"I did *no* such thing! The tabloid blogs made that up!"

He looked away. "I read that the police found your undergarments and toiletries in his apartment that..."

"—which were planted or stolen! I was never in his apartment. To this day I don't even know where it's located!"

He shrugged, as if dismissing the topic.

"Whatever, Suzy...the fact is that both the Board of Directors and our major funders—particularly the Chickasaw Nation—insisted we couldn't go near your scandal even with a ten-foot pole. Scott and I had to promise to not even communicate with you, let alone actively participate in your defense."

"But surely...under the table, didn't you get the military to...?"

"—*God*, no, Suzy! I don't know where that video came from that saved you, but we had nothing to do with it. We couldn't risk..."

"Then—someone in the government...?"

"Not in our government, that's for sure. I'm wired-in now for U.S.-associated classified spy satellite stuff. They're using our new batteries for prolonged, safe power. Besides, none of them would risk revealing their surveillance capability to enemy nations. The resolution on that video, from orbit, was cutting edge stuff!"

"But if it wasn't us, then...?"

They were both silent for a moment.

"I shouldn't tell you this, but..."

"Yes?"

He lowered his voice so only she could hear him.

"For you, Suzy—I've a contact. Don't let anyone know I've given you this information, particularly Scott or the Company. It's strictly confidential. He's one of the foremost covert U.S. experts in orbital surveillance technology. Just talk to him 'off the record' and don't pass on whatever he tells you. I'll give you his private cellphone number. He lives right here in San Francisco. You might be able to talk to him before returning to Pasadena."

"I...thanks, Billy."

"Sure, Suzy, no problem. And, listen—I'm really sorry I couldn't reach out to you when you were in jail, but..."

"I understand," she held up a hand palm-out to stop him from going further. "I've got my own job-mandated limitations. I'm not at the 'top secret' level, but I handle classified information at JPL. There are things I can and cannot do, regardless of personal connections or priorities. So next time *you're* in jail on a murder charge..."

"—*you'll* come to save me!" he laughingly broke in.

One of his numerous personal assistants was at the door, motioning frantically for him. Obviously an urgent matter needed his attention.

"It's so good to see you again, Suzy," he continued, hurriedly writing on a notepad and handing her a slip of paper. "Let's make the next time sooner and longer, ok?"

"I'd...like that," she wanly smiled back.

"Love you, 'big' sister."

"Love you too, 'little' brother."

And he was gone.

Later in the day after giving a short talk on her poster in one of a small breakout sessions, she sat on a lounge chair and dialed the number Billy gave her.

After several rings someone picked up.

"Speak."

"Hi. My brother Bill King gave me your name and number. I'm his sister, Susan King. Maybe you know me from recent news reports. I'm rather...infamous, unfortunately. Is this Mr. Yishai Hovah?"

"That's me."

"I wonder if I might impose on you to take you out to a restaurant for dinner, perhaps this evening? I've a confidential question for you regarding the latest satellite technology. You see, I'm in town at the Planetary Science Conference and..."

"Sorry. I'm too busy to give you an evening of my time."

"Oh, well, then maybe...?"

"Tea, in one hour—can you be there?"

"Uhm, I'm free for the rest of the day. Sure, if it's not too far from the Conference Center. Where should we meet?"

He gave her an address of a restaurant in downtown San Francisco.

"Ok, then. I'll see you there. Thanks!"

He hung up.

So, not too communicative over the phone—but Billy said he was a communications expert, right? Short and sweet! Right to the point! She liked that, very focused and precise.

He sounded like an interesting character.

Outside the Conference Center, she flagged down a cab and departed. Her faithful leather shoulder bag—cleaned of the blood from her fateful encounter a year before—hung from her shoulder. In it was a small laptop plus the thumb drive holding the copy of the original video file which had saved her from an attempted murder conviction. Also, she had her faithful small volume, *"The Minstrel's Lark."* She had a strange feeling it might be important to her investigation.

"Where to, Miss?" the cabby—a bald-headed, middle-aged Asian-looking man—grinned at her as she slid in beside him in the front seat.

Susan told him the address. "Can we be there within an hour?"

"No problem, long as the traffic cooperates."

They zoomed up the crowded 101 freeway toward downtown San Francisco from the Conference Center that was located near the International Airport. Susan enjoyed the ride, for once letting a chauffeur drive her along rather than nursing her ancient Fiero. Off to her right was the sweeping blue expanse of the San Francisco Bay. Large transport ships and small sailboats shared the water. In centuries past, tall ships and pirates sailed those very same waves. Now it was a busy channel for commercial, military, and leisure vessels.

The sun was out. The temperature was cool. It was a great ride for Susan. It was different from the dry, hot desert environment of Pasadena in Southern California. Susan found the humid, salty air from the Atlantic Ocean refreshing.

"You visiting?" the cabby asked, noting her fascination with the ocean view.

"Here for a conference," she replied, "just going into the city to meet a friend."

"Where you from?"

"I work in Pasadena...lived in Oklahoma before that..."

"It's different here in San Francisco, huh?"

"Very different—I like it!"

They were now into downtown San Francisco proper, swinging onto highway 80. Ahead of her loomed clusters of high skyscrapers. They were headed for the *"Franciscan Crab Restaurant"* on Fisherman's Wharf. The cabbie now swung out onto the city streets, expertly threading through thick traffic up and down rolling city hills.

Susan looked around in fascination. She wasn't used to big cities. It was unpleasantly crowded yet enticingly vibrant. Everywhere she looked there were people walking, storefronts and signs, odd shops. It was a place not to just visit, but explore!

But she didn't have the time. Her flight back to Southern California was the next morning. And she had to find out what Billy's acquaintance could tell her about the video. She felt it was crucial. Certainly knowing where it came from wouldn't change the result. The accusations were long since dismissed. She could put it behind her. But still its mysterious origin nagged at her.

"We're here, Miss," the cabby interrupted her musings. "That'll be fifty three bucks."

She handed him three twenties.

"Keep the change."

"Thanks—and good luck to you!" he said as he pulled away.

Susan looked at her watch. She was eleven minutes early. So she strolled along the sidewalk for nine minutes, looking into the surrounding store windows. She saw lots of fish stuff, curios, and collectables. Fun stuff! Then she returned, entering the restaurant.

Inside, the *maître d'* politely greeted her.

"I've got a reservation with a Mister Hovah?"

"Right this way."

She was escorted to a table where a chubby, bearded man in a dirty brown fisherman's vest sat alone, staring out of floor-to-ceiling windows at the deep blue ocean. He might be retired. He had that easy, "I'm in no rush" air about him. And his grey hair was turning white. It was like he was in disguise. No one would mistake this "old fisherman" for a military satellite expert.

"Hi, I'm Susan King!"

He casually motioned for her to sit opposite to him. He glanced at his wristwatch.

"Ah, Dr. King, right on time—excellent," he nodded. "I admire punctuality."

"As do I," she smiled back at him, extending her hand across the tabletop. "Thanks for meeting with me, Mr. Hovah."

"Please, call me Jessie," he kindly replied.

"Ok...Jessie—and please call me Susan."

He took her hand, squeezing it lightly before releasing. Susan noticed that he had hard calluses on his palm. So he wasn't just a desk jockey like her. He did "real" work!

"I do recognize you from the news reports," he said. His voice, though low and gravelly, sounded sympathetic. "A sad business, that. But you don't look like an 'easy lay' if I might be so bold. Possibly the tabloids got you wrong, eh?"

"Very wrong indeed!"

"Glad to hear it, young lady. This town was built on the so-called Four Deadly Sins: *gambling, whisky, guns,* and *prostitution!* I'm not a fan of any of them. I prefer a good glass of hot tea on a cool day, the special kind you get in Chinatown or the better older restaurants. It's good for *savoring* not just guzzling. A little caffeine buzz is all I need."

"I'm a teetotaler myself," she agreed. She was getting to like the older gentleman.

"Good. That was just subterfuge, however, limiting your visit to just a glass of tea. If you turned out to be a reporter sniffing for classified information, I could make a quick exit. But you look legit. Care to join me for dinner? I relish my pleasures, particularly the consumables of this little world."

That was a peculiar way to say he liked seafood.

"I'd be delighted," she laughed, shrugging off her brief unease at his somewhat strange wording. She picked up a menu. "What's the specialty here?"

"Specialty?"

"I enjoy experiencing new things, not just the same old stuff that anyone can make."

"Ah...then I'd recommend the *crab enchiladas*. They're to die for. Crabs are the specialty here—as their sign outside proclaims—and when mixed with the Mexican cuisine..." he smacked his lips loudly together. "I'll order for both of us if you'd like?"

Ugh. She didn't care for shellfish. But then, again, she wanted to get on the man's good side, not antagonize him. At least it wasn't *lobster* Mexican food! That she couldn't tolerate no matter how much it offended someone. Eating giant sea cockroaches? No way!

"Please!" she smiled in her best, most-friendly manner—though inside she was cringing. A nice, plain salad with chewy fresh bread would be so much nicer!

"—or perhaps would you prefer a nice cob Salad?" he quickly added. "Their blue cheese is another of their local specialties. It's unique, very tangy though sweet!"

She was startled by his perceptiveness. Well, it certainly proved he could "read" people by their subtle expressions. Was he a CIA spy?

It wouldn't surprise her. He certainly wasn't an ordinary fisherman lounging there after a big day out on the sea catching lobsters.

"Uhm—that would be even nicer, Jessie. I'm not hungry for a full meal anyway..."

"Nor am I—a nice salad would be just fine with me as well."

Having gotten their orders in, hot cups of rich tea steaming before them both, Susan got down to business.

"I need to know where something came from," she said. "Billy told me you're an expert in the subject: spy satellite formats."

"I may know something of the subject," he cautiously replied. "Distance surveillance is one of my specialties. But first tell me *why* you want to know this information?"

"I need to know if I can *giggle* at it."

"Say what?"

She shrugged, taking a sip at the hot tea before continuing.

"Sorry, it's from a poem I recently read...in *'The Minstrel's Lark.'*"

He fingered his gray beard with a hand, his eyes flickering around the restaurant. No one was near, at least within easy-listening distance.

"I've heard of that book. It's very rare. Only select people are allowed to find a copy."

That was another curious way to phrase things. This "Mr. Hovah" was definitely an interesting fellow!

"Well, I do have a copy here with me."

"Really?" he eagerly replied. "Could I please see it?"

She slipped the old, thin book out of her shoulder bag and passed it to him.

Seemingly reverently, he opened it. His stained fingers lightly flipped the faded pages.

Then he read a passage, his gravelly voice playful: "*Into the Wild...*

> *What fun to 'get back to Nature,'*
> *When you've got camping gear and supplies*
> *And powerful guns to shoot deer and beer cans*
> *All the weapons and benefits of modern science*
> *Bending the harsh realities of cruel existence*

Into a happy stroll along peaceful streams
But when you're alone, lost, and defenseless
It's actually not the fantasized mild dream
But a terrible nightmare of starvation
Sickness, injury, and even death
But hey, it teaches lessons
If you can survive!"

He paused, closing his eyes for a moment as if savoring the words. Then he slid the slim volume back to her.

"I added in the word 'cans' to show that 'beers' wasn't a misspelling of 'bears'...editing is a compulsion of mine," he slyly admitted. "Improvements can be made in anything."

"Your minor change fits well," she smiled, "almost as if you were the primary author. Do you write books?"

He laughed good-naturedly, shrugging off the compliment.

"I do write a bit of poetry from time to time. But few people appreciate good poetry without attaching it to a melody, making it into a song. Anyway, what does that passage say to *you?*" he asked.

His tone was now dead-serious.

"You picked one of my favorite passages," she thoughtfully replied. "I'm fascinated with all aspects of Creation, particularly the rocks which formed the planets that provide the platform for the development of life. But 'Beauty' always goes hand-in-claw with the 'Beast'—which to me says that in order to appreciate the 'Grandeur' I can't be afraid to grab the 'Guts.' Hah! It's funny, in a macabre sort of way."

He nodded knowingly.

"I like how you speak some of your words in *Capitals*," he said, slyly emphasizing the last word to harmonize with his phrasing. "Not many people are capable of appreciating such a divine book. Perhaps that's why you were chosen, do you think?"

"Chosen?"

"You're not religious?"

This was a curious turn of the conversation.

"Not in a traditional sense. But I do see a higher Order beyond that of superficial religious Doctrines. To that greater, eminently *un-*

knowable Mystery I gladly give my Allegiance. I am, after all, a certified scientist."

He grinned widely, displaying a mouthful of yellowed, broken teeth. Clearly he knew she was gently teasing him. This was a form of "verbal banter" common to powerful males. She knew that he'd take it not as an attack or disrespect, but as the invigorating jabs she intended.

"I do appreciate your 'capital' *jags, Dr.* King," he grinned again, seemingly reading her mind, while also subtly twisting her words. "But that's sufficient testing of your intellect and intentions. I'm satisfied. Please, how may I help you?"

She slid the thumb drive to him across the wooden tabletop.

"Ah—right," he nodded. He squinted at it closely as if mentally reading the contained files. "Can I take it with me?"

"I'd prefer you view its contents here on my laptop."

At a nearby booth a family with three kids arrived. They were laughing and talking. It was a nice cover having them close, just in case she and Hovah were being surveilled—two spies meeting out in the open!

Susan was thrilled to be sitting across a table from a spy satellite expert, finally getting some answers.

"Well, I can't do a detailed analysis here in a restaurant, but I'm happy to give you my tentative impressions. So let's take a look!" he cheerfully agreed as she pulled out her laptop, turned it on, slid the thumbdrive into its slot, and turned the screen toward him.

He watched the short video with a blank expression.

"At first I thought the camera view was from a U.S. military spy satellite, but then Billy told me..." she started to describe her impressions.

He held up a single finger at her, silencing her.

After the video concluded he dropped the top of the laptop and slid it with the attached thumbdrive back over to her.

"Well?" she asked.

He paused before replying. "I saw this of course on the news casts when it first came out. I had my suspicions then, but didn't have the real artifact upon which to get confirmation. I see this is a copy of the original, not just a screencast. Mind if I slow it down and look at it frame-by-frame?"

"Whatever you need and can do here is fine with me."

He did a few keystrokes and watched it again. He paused it here and there...fingering parts of the screen.

"Well, I'd have to run detailed analysis in my lab before being certain, but I'm 95% convinced of its origin."

"Great! So where did it come from?"

He lowered his voice, leaning forward toward her.

"It was taken by a recently launched spy satellite, state-of-the-art—but not from the U.S. military."

"Who then?"

"I believe that the particular satellite which caught your sidewalk encounter was in a payload launched a year-and-a-half ago on an H-6B rocket from the *Tanegashima Space Center* in the Pacific."

It took a moment for that to register.

"So you're saying it's *Japanese?*"

"It has the proper designators, pixel density, and other attributes, yes. It's intriguing. By allowing this video to go public, they risked revealing to the entire surveillance community their latest technology. They'd only do that if they were facing something of the highest possible priority."

"You're saying I'm a priority to Japan?"

He shrugged.

"But why would they want to get *me* out of prison?"

"Look in your poetry book."

"Say what?"

"Many Answers are there lightly hidden as Questions, right? Did I place the capital letters in the right places?" he grinned again at her.

She nodded, struggling to understand.

"Well, then, Dr. King—please take a look in your book at *Chapter 2, verses 32-34!*"

Frowning, she took out the slim volume again, simultaneously sliding the laptop back into her shoulder bag.

Flipping to those verses she looked down at the book, concentrating on the words, and softly read out loud: "*A Waking Dream...*

Sometimes dreams turn into nightmares
While other times sleep is soothing
But be it horrible or wonderful
Letting the mind run loose is strange
For who knows what will pop up
When the Rules no longer apply
And all your thoughts are dangerous
When anything you can conceive
Can suddenly come to life?
Beware rampant imaginations..."

She shook her head in confusion, staring down at the cryptic words. She'd read them a number of times before, of course, but never applied to this particular type of situation. What did that passage have to do with a Japanese spy satellite helping her evade a long prison sentence?

"But what does...?"

She looked around in confusion. He was gone! Had he slipped off to the restroom? But...?

The waiter was returning with their food. Yet he had only a single large salad!

"Did you see where my friend went?" she asked.

"He paid for your meal, Ma'am. He said he had to run—unexpected business apparently—and sent his apologies. But he did leave this for you."

He held out his hand. In it was a Fisherman's Wharf-labelled souvenir—an emerald-looking, exquisitely carved baby turtle!

He nodded politely to her: "Enjoy."

He turned and walked away.

She slid back her left sleeve and compared the delicate figurine to the childhood green tattoo on her wrist.

They were identical.

Chapter 16

FOOD

So would you eat a pile of worms

Or thick leaves yanked from a tree

Or "mud pie" made from real mud

Or the rotting corpse of a "road kill"

"NEVER," you say, "never, my friend!"

Unless, of course, you were starving

No longer feeling Disgust or Delight

Merely a week of an empty belly

The mind casting off all niceties

Not requiring cooking nor taste

Anything edible is acceptable

A whole banquet from trash

You greedily gobble-down

Like a wild hyena scavenger

Gulping raw protein and fat

Hanging from gnawed bones

Leftover from the lions' feast

It's a lot better than nothing.

The Minstrel's Lark, 16:31-35

IMPACT MINUS THREE MONTHS, *STARVING*...

"I don't believe what I'm seeing," Susan gasped.

"Oh, it is true...it is *very* true!" Ben replied, grinning from ear to ear like the proverbial "Cheshire Cat."

Susan was perpetually hungry. Being on half rations was debilitating to the entire crew. In the four weeks from the spin-up disaster they'd each lost at least twenty pounds. At this rate they'd be wasted away and helpless even if they survived the next three months to reach the Asteroid.

In addition, Susan was perpetually thirsty.

They'd lost most of their meager water stores through the plume out into space when Hab-3 fractured. The jungle was dead, both from being frozen and from lack of water. The still-rotting plant remnants that hung throughout the ship permeated the wet atmosphere with a sweet stink.

It was miserable.

But Susan no longer noticed the rotting plant smell. Foul ammonia fumes emanated from their half-processed feces, which no longer were suffused by a vital network of living roots. Instead of being constantly worked into the soil of the ship's plants, the wastes were pooling and festering.

Hermes was now a closed sewer cesspool.

Even worse, without a rich agriculture sucking in CO_2 and generating oxygen, the crew was forced to leach oxygen from their electrolysis-generated liquid fuel reserves, further depleting their meager water stores. The emergency CO_2 scrubbers were almost depleted. Susan's thinking was sluggish. Once the CO_2 level got too high, they wouldn't just be mentally impaired, they'd be dead!

To make things even worse in the ship, the air in the ship was uncomfortably muggy, due to the malfunctioning water line network. Instead of the air being regularly wrung out, with purified water returned to a storage tank, it was "backing up" in the ship's atmosphere. There was plenty of foul, contaminated water dripping off of everything—but precious little pure water to drink! That meant moisture was seeping into everything, including the sensitive electronics throughout Hermes. Crucial systems were "glitching" or crashing. It took constant maintenance by the three women to keep Hermes barely functioning.

And the temperature controls were also erratic. One day they'd be freezing and the next sweltering. But the average of the wild swings was increasingly *hot!* It was now *steaming* inside—as if they were in a true jungle!

So Susan was starving, thirsty, panting, and hot. She was perpetually drenched in salty sweat.

But she still hoped for a miracle...maybe from Earth.

Communication with Earth, though, was spotty at best. Hermes was now far above the planetary disc, the equivalent distance from Earth of a Mars transit. Complex data was arriving from Earth only in spurts. In addition to their glitching computers, their already battered external antennae array had been further damaged by the aborted Tumble. Someone needed to go outside on a spacewalk and attempt to repair the damage. But that was a low priority versus battling the terrible living conditions inside Hermes. They needed their oxygen stores to replenish the air, with none left over for extensive spacewalks. So the antennae reception remained poor at best.

They could have tried their deployable communications platform intended for autonomous parallel flight when Hermes was tumbling. But, mysteriously, it was inoperable. Its key electronic components were fried. In one of his lucid moments Ben suggested a power surge during the aborted Tumble had cooked it. Susan didn't see how that could happen since it was not turned on when they were attempting to ramp-up the Tumble. But, regardless, the backup auxiliary platform was useless.

Susan had sent various data requests in jerky transmissions, particularly to colleagues at the Arecibo Observatory for a series of dedicated deep-space scans. She didn't even know if her request had been received, let alone acted upon. If they had, the data would have had to be sent in self-verifying packets to be combined piece-by-piece inside Hermes' malfunctioning computers. Even with everything working optimally, the complex data set she'd requested would have taken several days of transmission to be received and assembled at Hermes.

So Susan didn't expect much.

With only three months to "doomsday," Earth had its own problems. From the brief news reports that got through, Hermes' crew saw that panic was spreading across the globe. National boundaries were collapsing as vast floods of people attempted to move to "safer" areas of the globe, particularly the pole regions. Constituencies were demanding that politicians "fix" the hurtling, heavenly problem or be thrown from office. Since there was no magical "fix," governments were crumbling. And every religion on the planet was cashing-in on the impending doom, bringing in thousands of new members to virtually any congregation that promised miraculous "salvation" for its flock. Worse of all, fanatics of all stripes saw this as a chance to advance their own agendas. Society was breaking down into warring factions, each struggling to provide a "safe haven" to the detriment of everyone else.

The only positive on Hermes was the nuclear reactor. In spite of continuing to irradiate the crew—because of the lack of an effective water barrier—the reactor steadily supplied continuous electricity. If they could somehow replenish their water stores, they'd have plenty of electrolysis-generated liquid oxygen and hydrogen. Thus they'd be able to replenish their air and do the extensive spacewalks needed to repair Hermes. The "grow-lights" were still operating at full capacity, capable of fueling a new crop if only there were time and properly prepared soil. The grow-lights continually poured artificial sunlight into the Jungle Hab, though Ben dimmed them to a more comfortable "twilight" level. Fresh water could allow a new crop to sprout up not just there but throughout the ship. However, hope of finding a water depot in the vast emptiness of outer space was slim to none. Without additional water, their continuing strong source of internal energy was of little use.

"Susan!"—a loud shout came from off at a distance. Susan recognized the now-shrill voice of Kame, calling down through the modules from the Observation Deck. The internal communication speakers were on the blitz again. They'd had to resort to yelling through the modules in order to be heard. "There's a priority communication for you up here! We need you to decode the information! It's scrambled!"

"I'll be there as soon as I can!" Susan yelled back. "Something's up in the jungle Hab! Give me a minute!"

Normally, Susan spent most of her scarce "free" time up in the OD, looking through the portholes at the magnificent array of stars. She'd even taken to sleeping there, transferring her hammock out of the rotting jungle Hab. Above the planetary disc, with the sun beneath them, the distant suns and galaxies were grandly displayed. It comforted Susan to be cradled in their magnificence. Also, she could no longer tolerate being down in the stinking Habs. She went there only to nurse critical failing systems. The prevailing stench amongst the blackened, rotted plants and festering "soil" was so thick she could hardly breathe. And the backed up humidity down there—which was lower somewhat in the metal-only OD—made it seem she was drowning in the ocean: "water, water everywhere but not a drop to drink." So she hadn't even been to the Jungle for over a week now. The other two women had likewise abandoned the farming module, allowing Ben to lurk down there all by himself.

Ben was now...bizarre!

He'd recovered from his initial acute radiation sickness, but continued to deteriorate in other ways. His brown eyes were huge in his shrunken, burn-scarred face. He wore only a loin cloth. His arms and legs were sticks. He was covered in sticky mud and crumbling roots. The other two women thought that he'd transformed himself into an old, starving caricature of Mahatma Gandhi. He looked just like the iconic figure following one of the holy man's lengthy fasts. But to Susan, Ben was one of his oft-invoked plant-spirit "Gandharvas." He'd become a creature of the dead jungle, integrated into its fetid mass. He "chittered" amongst the jungle's rotted entrails, as if he were a demented zombie monkey. But he did have occasional periods of lucidity, as when he'd just loudly summoned Susan to come visit him.

Reluctantly, she went to him, expecting further horrors.

But drifting down into the jungle Hab, Susan was *stunned* by what she saw there!

"Mushrooms?" she gasped.

The Hab was *filled* with them, sprouting out of the blackened, moisture-drenched rotted soil and twisted organic tangle. They surrounded Susan, making a strange "forest" that descended down all three stories in height to the base of the Hab. There were pure-white button mushrooms, golden brown larger ones, and spreading flat ones. The stalks pushed out from all corners of the Hab, the white knobs or flattened heads seeming to pulse with vitality. Many were small, sprouting—but others were as a large as a person! In addition, poking out here and there, were bright yellow ones which looked like flowers.

It was a cornucopia of gilled fungi!

"How is this possible?" she marveled.

Ben grinned at her from within the thicket of gently bobbing growths. "Genetically engineered plants, don't you know? The jungle vines had the capacity to grow up a variety of foodstuffs. Some of the genetic programs were cryptic, waiting for the right conditions. And so we get this! Hee, hee!"

He was grinning widely, his big sunken eyes glimmering with excitement.

She blinked rapidly, slowly spinning in the zero-G taking it all in. She realized that the high humidity, low illumination, higher CO_2, and abundant rotting soil were perfect for mushrooms.

"But...to grow up so quickly? The last time I was here there wasn't..."

"Mushrooms can grow fast! Hee, hee!" he chortled gleefully. "They suck up moisture! They 'pop up like a mushroom,' right? This erupted out of the soil over the last few days! I waited until I was sure they were going to 'take'—then called you. Are you pleased?"

He giggled like a little girl, bashfully holding out a flat, brown "cap" to her. The head of the mushroom already had a large bite mark on one side. Ben was happily chewing, presumably on a chunk of the leathery looking object.

"Eat!" he ordered her, launching it through the air at her.

It floated up at her, hanging in the air, spinning seductively—as if begging her to take a bite out of it!

She felt like Alice going down the rabbit hole, offered strange mushrooms to nibble on.

But this wasn't some fantasy. It was real, spinning right in front of her face. She grabbed it out of the air. It felt warm, spongy.

"But...what if it's poisonous? A lot of mushrooms are..."

"You think that the geneticists would program the jungle to grow poisonous plants? No guarantee, but I think not! It's good, Susan. I tried it already. Don't you believe me?"

He grabbed another hanging mushroom and tore the head off, scattering the dangling grey gills into the air. Without restraint, he stuffed it into his mouth, chewing noisily.

"See?"

Hesitantly, she took a nibble at the edge of the round cap...

It was chewy, juicy, and meaty—delicious!

"Oh, Christ, Ben, that's so good!"

She devoured the rest of it in only a few bites, reaching out for another...

"No!" he yelled, popping out of the jungle to hover in the air between her and the crop.

"But...?"

"*Mine!* They're all mine! I protect them! You come ask me—and I will give you nice ripe ones. You and the other girls must come to me! I give you whatever you need. But only me! If you try to take them they will all die. They only give their bounty to *me*, their friend and protector!"

"Uh...ok, Ben, whatever you say. Can I take some up to Kame and Adriana? They're also very hungry!"

He hunched his skinny back, squatting down—looking about furtively as if thinking someone was coming to steal his precious "stash."

"Yes...you must all eat," he admitted, reluctantly receding into the thicket of white-brown fleshy growths.

Then he was back with an armful of the mushrooms. These were the golden brown ones. His thin arms held both the wide, flat heads and white, sturdy stalks.

They looked great for cooking!

"Thank you, Ben. You've done great here...growing this crop. Good work! Now if you'd just bring us a nice, fresh stream to drink from then..."

He grinned slyly, looking about furtively as if to make sure they weren't overheard.

He crocked a finger at her, beckoning her closer.

Still clutching the precious armful of rubbery mushrooms, she drifted in the air up to him.

He leaned his head close to hers.

"Kame knows!" he whispered.

"She knows what?"

"Where to get the water...but she won't let you go!"

"Uhm, I don't think that's right, Ben. Yes, we were suspicious of her before, but she's proven herself capable as the Mission Commander and..."

"You'll see!" he shouted as he swam back through the air into the waving stalks filling the zero-G Hab-3. "Come back when you need *enlightenment!* It's sure not coming from anywhere else! *Hee, hee!*"

Cackling wildly he was swallowed up by the mushroom forest.

She couldn't see him anymore in the gloom of the Hab. But other things seemed to be moving in there with him. She thought she glimpsed *large reptilian, slant-pupiled eyes* staring back at her from inside the wild growth! But it was surely only her imagination.

"Uh, ok then," she said as she turned and kicked back upward. "I'll return, then, when we need to harvest more of your delicious mushrooms. Thanks, Ben!"

But there was no answer, just the rustling of the stalks.

So the crew had food. Now if only they could find some *cool, clear* water. But that was highly unlikely. They'd just have to make do with what little they still had.

Susan returned from the San Francisco Conference to JPL jubilant with her new information, only to encounter even more trouble. People who'd been friendly to her before were now distant. And those who'd been cool to her before were openly hostile.

What had happened?

A fresh, insidious rumor was circulating. The video that freed her was *faked!* At least, that was the anonymous claim. It could be no coincidence that the scandal/mystery resurfaced right after her meeting with Yishai Hovah in San Francisco. Experts were interviewed on TV news who pointed to this or that inconsistency in the video "proving" it was a fake. No one in authority doubted the visual evidence, but many others who'd followed it on the news feeds were happy to have their initial condemnation of her supposedly confirmed.

It apparently didn't matter that a video of such detail, with its impossibly overhead orientation, and confirming events (such as the exact same policeman and EMT personnel at the end, seen from on high) were irrefutable. The *conspiracy theorists* were particularly impressed. The scandal sheets and underground bloggers happily embraced the "fake video" theory, attributing it to Susan's "unparalleled" space technology genius! And if it were actually a real orbital view, then *she* must have somehow jiggered the contents to save herself.

Hah. If she was such a genius to pull that off locked in her jail cell, then how'd she get caught in the first place?

But logic and reason don't matter to most conspiracy theorists.

And it didn't help matters that Cafferty finally woke up from his coma. He claimed to remember nothing after leaving work that day. His lawyers argued that since there was no sound track on the video, or clear view of people's mouths, Susan could have been taunting him as he approached from behind, goading him into a crazy rage. So the County Prosecutor perversely ruled there wasn't enough evidence to independently charge him with assault, further fueling the scandal-sheet stories. Susan, not wanting any further association with the terrible incident, declined to press charges. Consequently the whole, sorry affair was back in the news.

As if in retribution—"certainly" not overt discrimination after the charges having been dropped, but clearly *covert* retribution by JPL—Susan was assigned a new postdoctoral director. He was an administrator with little actual research experience. So Susan was left to her own devices, with no hope of renewing the grant that supported her work. Accepting the new restrictions, she focused on just trying to complete the research she'd signed on to accomplish in her three year postdoc, knowing she'd have to move on once her time ran out.

Likely she'd end up at a small college giving lectures on introductory physics, with no further active research possibilities. She was labelled as "bad seed" throughout the astronomy community. Her research career was dead!

But she didn't blame the JPL hierarchy.

Unwanted negative scrutiny had fallen on JPL because of her incarceration and continued scandal. Although JPL likely had no more or less sexual harassment than did any other institution, a past history of females being subjugated, particularly in the field of astronomy, fueled rampant speculation by the media. Every program was consequently put under the microscope by management. Although it took months for the new controls to be instituted, harsher sexual harassment norms and requirements were now coming on-line. They included biyearly mandatory training, an explicit duty to report any suspicious circumstance to an independent authority, strict complainant protections, and zero tolerance. The heavy oversight put a damper on things previously thought to be just innocent, fun behavior. And everyone knew that the new restrictions, requirements, and headaches were all because of Susan!

Even those who sympathized with her now shunned her. She had caused too much trouble for everyone.

There was less than a year to go in her postdoc. She was desperately searching for her next job. So she didn't obsess on being excluded by her present peers. She was on her way out. But she heard absolutely nothing back from her applications to various low level professorial positions, industry space technology positions, or research posts! True to form, a couple small colleges were interested in her despite her notoriety—maybe because of it. They'd use her "fame" to give their otherwise invisible profiles a boost.

But giving up her research and dreams to teach introductory physics was an awful prospect to Susan. She'd struggled so hard to climb so high, her fall from grace was devastating. Well, there was a bright side. At least she wouldn't be like her jail mate Shelly had been, on skid row, turning tricks to get her next meal. She'd have a bill-paying job. But she was still determined not to accept Scott's continuing entreaties to join Nashoba Energy as a top executive. Sure, his e-mails (that she refused to answer) were tempting—particularly compared to her other dismal possibilities. But she still knew in her gut that their "super-battery" was just too good to be true. If she had nothing else left in her life, she still had her integrity! She wasn't going to be a shill to push something she didn't believe in!

But it was getting definitely painful to go to work each day at JPL. She was looking forward to moving on.

No, she wasn't overtly punished. That would clearly violate the new sexual harassment reporting rules. But she was subtly excluded, made to feel unwelcome. She was now excluded from group social gatherings, someone always "forgetting" to inform her of them until they were past.

Even Pete was cool toward her. He interacted with her on a professional level when he had to do so, but avoided her otherwise. Susan knew he wanted to advance his own career, not slow it down by being associated with a "loser" like her.

The media still had an eye on her, reporters and investigators appearing unexpectedly whenever she tried to go "off campus." The gossip-sheets and rumor-blogs still accused her of having started the whole uproar. They cavalierly assumed she was lying when she stubbornly denied having any sort of affair with Professor Cafferty. But her panties in his apartment plus her toothbrush in his bathroom were all the proof that the general public needed. In their eyes she somehow initiated the whole train of events, even though she continued to claim that he must have stolen her personal items.

It made for a lonely existence—ostracized at work, harassed at home, with her active research career crashing and burning. But she stubbornly persisted, refusing to either take extended sick leave or resign. They weren't going to bring her down. After all, she was a moderate introvert who didn't need much outside stimulation. She could happily sink into her work for weeks at a time. But even she needed to raise her head now and then, acquiring external stimulation occasionally. She was a "herd animal" like any other human.

So she was startled one day to look up and see *Professor Cafferty* himself walking hesitantly into the laboratory! She'd heard he was out of his coma, but bedridden. Clearly he was much improved. But he was thinner than she remembered, drawn and old. He was walking unsteadily, his hands half-out in front of him. He looked dazed, fumbling with his keys to open his long-shuttered office. She saw through the large windows that he sank into the dusty chair behind his desk and dropped his head into his arms.

Making a sudden decision, she got up from her computer, walked to his office, knocked, and then briskly walked in.

She sat down in the visitor chair across from him.

"Trying to start up where you left off?" she coldly accused him.

He raised his head and looked at her with haunted, deep-sunken eyes.

"Ah...Dr. King...I didn't want to bother you or anyone else...just coming to get my stuff...I'm retiring, effective immediately...don't want any further trouble..."

She caught his furtive gaze and locked her eyes onto his, refusing to even blink.

"Why'd you do it? Why did you attack me and make it look like I attacked you? What did I ever do to you that was so bad? I didn't sleep with you, true—but you had plenty of other women, so I hear. You ruined my career! I know you say you can't remember. But I don't believe you. You know something—and I want you to answer me, right now!"

To her eyes he was physically shrinking as each moment passed. He was no longer the charismatic older professor. Now he was just a scared old man, plunging toward his own death, looking for a way out.

"Please, Susan," he begged her. "Just let me get my stuff and leave."

"Tell me what I want to know!" she shouted at him as he cringed back in his chair. "What did you mean when you said *the lizards* didn't want me to go?"

Outside, Susan could see that someone had called the campus police. Several officers were dashing into the laboratory building, heading toward the side offices.

"You wouldn't believe me," he whispered, tears dripping from his sunken eyes. "It was just...just..."

"Dr. King! Please exit Dr. Cafferty's office!" a uniformed guard barked at her, standing panting in the doorway.

"*Tell* me!" she yelled at the cowering Professor, ignoring the advancing guard. She was now leaning far forward over the desk so her face was inches from his.

"It's...on the other side...of the door..." he croaked back at her, stark terror in his drawn face.

"But do you...?"

A firm hand grabbed her shoulder, pulling her backward and around. Another officer entered, grabbing her other arm.

"Do we have to arrest you, Dr. King? We'd rather not. It would be terrible publicity, on top of everything else that's happened."

"No, I'll be good," she sniffed, pushing their hands away as she turned her back on the whimpering Cafferty. "I'm finished here."

A crowd of personnel and fellow postdocs outside were standing silently, watching her as she walked briskly back to her desk and started yanking opening the drawers. The onlookers were busily snapping photos and videos with their smartphones. Undoubtedly many were already posting their videos on the Internet. In another hour she'd be on the newsfeeds, yet *again!* She knew that JPL couldn't allow her to continue as an employee after this new publicity.

Well, she'd save them the minor headache of firing her.

There wasn't much she needed to take with her: backup thumb-drives of her files that she could use to finish writing up her research results elsewhere, personal items, and small desk-figurines. One was the emerald turtle she'd been given in San Francisco. It was comforting. It was always soothingly warm to the touch. She'd kept it on her desk sitting happily beside her computer mouse. Now she'd take it with her.

She took pride in cleaning up her own messes. Cafferty was retiring in disgrace. And now she was leaving JPL. That wonderful, dynamic organization could finally get back to its normal routine.

Without a word of goodbye she stalked out of the laboratory building. Pete ran up behind her and called out but she didn't pause. She didn't look back. She'd phone in her resignation. And maybe she'd finally give Scott a call.

It was time to swallow the last vestige of her pride.

If her active research career was truly finished and she was cut-off from going into space with NASA, then she might as well have money. After all, "scruples" don't pay the bills.

Chapter 17

<u>PURE WATER</u>

"Keep on a-movin', Dan
Don't you listen to him Dan
He's the devil, not a man
He spreads the burning sand
With water...cool, clear, water,"
A powerful song for the ages
Penned in 1936 by Bob Nolan
About a man and his mule, Dan
Contemplating a beguiling mirage
Struggling to survive in the desert
Cooked by a relentless, blazing sun
Extolling the Virtues of "Cool Water"
An Elixir which many take for granted
The very stuff of continued life or death
When present just an unremarkable fact
When absent, the essence of existence...
Are you thirsty yet? I am!
The Minstrel's Lark, 17:12-16

IMPACT MINUS TWO MONTHS, *DYING*...

Yes, because of the unexpected mushroom forest they now had enough food. But they were down to their last few gallons of water. The main water tanks were empty.

Unbeknownst to the crew, the fractures running throughout the Hab outer foam structures had been relentlessly spreading, molecularly "wicking" the moisture from the overlying packed soil. Too late to fix it, the crew realized that microscopic cracks in the outer skins were allowing the moisture leached from the hard-packed crop soil to escape out into space.

But there wasn't a solution available, even if they'd had the fuel to make the extended spacewalks. The cracks in the outer skin were too pervasive. They didn't have enough sealant to plug the tiny cracks, even if they could somehow locate all of them. And their wastes-reprocessing system was tied into the farm network. Even their urine was gradually vanishing away instead of being recycled.

Fortunately, though, their supply of compressed oxygen was enough to replenish the loss of air that occurred when Hermes had depressurized. The oxygen-rejecting molecular characteristics of the insulating hardened foam still worked. They were back to having a full atmosphere throughout the living spaces. They'd die of thirst before they died of hunger or suffocation.

But their miraculous mushroom forest needed water also. It was drying up. The crew was drying out. The ship seemed to be consequently *shriveling*.

Susan hadn't had a good long drink of water for over a week. She even missed the oppressive humidity. At least then she could lick drops of water off her skin. The crew only had one cup of water per day per person. That ration was far below what a human required. The normal intake of a single person was *eight glasses* per day!

"Do you...have that data...yet?"

Susan looked up into the glazed black eyes of Kame. Susan was belted into her terminal in the Observation Deck. She was still trying to assemble the jumbled data they'd received four weeks ago from Mission Control's last transmission to get through. Either Hermes' receiving equipment was beyond repair, or their computer programs were irrevocably damaged, or Earth societies were too far gone into chaos to transmit. In any case, they'd heard nothing more from Mission Control after the last massive download. It turned out that the received files were in response to Susan's request to the Arecibo Radar Telescope facility. But they weren't readable. The files were fragmented and jumbled. Maybe the maze of fragments was nothing of importance, but it kept Susan occupied. Working on trying to unscramble and reassemble the data was better than giving-in to her searing thirst by sinking her teeth into one of her crewmates and draining their blood!

Oh my...where did that terrible thought come from? Was she becoming a *vampire* on top of everything else?

She weakly laughed.

"I'm on the last pieces, Kame—once I've got them unpacked and expanded I think they'll all 'snap' together. It's like a big board-puzzle where all the individual pieces got caught in a fan and shredded. So instead of one ordered puzzle it's now thousands of smaller puzzles. Or, if you'd like, it's similar to analyzing millions of fragments of DNA which have overlapping regions—then laying them on top of each other to come up with an intact genome. Then using that information to try and build a 3D model of the chromosomes."

"Impressive, Susan...let me know when you're finished."

"Sure."

Kame drifted away, floating down the connecting node to do whatever. Adriana was strapped into her hammock in the corner of the OD, faintly moaning. She sounded bad. Susan stopped her work. She unbelted, kicked over to the woman, and examined her. Adriana's lips were cracked and dry, her swollen tongue protruding through purple lips. Her eyes were clenched tightly shut. Susan put a hand on Adriana's forehead and felt heat. The woman had a fever. That was scary.

Kicking herself over to the bottle holding the last of their daily allotment of water, Susan drew out a full glass-equivalent into a bulb, kicked back over to Adriana, and stuck the straw past the swollen tongue. Gently, she squirted the water bit by bit into Adriana's mouth.

The moaning eased and Adriana fell peacefully asleep, breathing shallowly.

Susan floated back to her terminal and painfully belted herself back into the seat. Her whole body hurt. She wanted to go curl up in her own hammock. But there was work to do.

"You should ask me before exceeding the ration," Kame said, drifting back up out of the connecting node.

She'd startled Susan.

"I'm sorry...she was fading fast."

"We're all fading fast, Susan," Kame gasped, kicking over to Susan's terminal. "Is there anything I can do to help with the process? I'm afraid that without some new variable thrown into the stew, we'll not last long enough to make it to the Asteroid. Mission Control put out a huge effort to get this information to us before they went silent. It *must* be important!"

Susan settled back into her seat in front of the terminal. "Well, Commander, you're great with mechanics, being the flight engineer and all. But how are you at computer coding?"

"Bad—but you mentioned DNA sequencing?"

"Yes?"

"For my Ph.D. in microbiology, I did some of that."

"Is that so?"

"Yes—I sequenced and assembled the entire genome of an anaerobic thermophile isolated from within a volcano. That research helped me get into NASA. It was the same expertise necessary to analyze possible similar prototypic bacteria which might still exist on Mars."

"Did you find any on Mars?"

"Ours was a Polar landing at a site where surface ice still existed, hoping to find proteobacteria. But the temperatures were incredibly cold, down to -238° Fahrenheit. We dug as deep as we could, attempting to find frozen microfossils."

"Any luck?"

"Oh, trace nucleobases, as have been already found at other sites on the planet. There was nothing exciting, unfortunately. But, regardless, my point is I've had experience in assembling overlapping DNA sets."

"Isn't that mostly done by computer programs?"

"Of course, but the final 'fixes' are still done by hand—there's nothing as clever as the human brain for pattern recognition."

Susan was impressed. She didn't realize Kame had such a rich background.

"Well, Kame—I've a dozen 'pieces' here that don't fit anywhere. Could you maybe see if you recognize any coding overlaps or paired adjacencies? The Mission Control transmission is in a new, condensed format that has multiple layers. Assembling the fragments is a three-dimensional chess game, where the levels themselves keep changing. It's baffling. Just when I think I've got it figured, everything shifts!"

"I'll try. A second pair of eyes can't hurt."

"Sending them to your terminal now..."

"I've got them. Let me scan through the data—God, Susan, it's huge!"

"Yes, there are several gigabytes per layer. And the transmission got broken up and restarted several times. So we have incomplete and scrambled fragments. It's not just choosing what to fit back together but also what to discard as too corrupted to be useful."

"Ok. I understand. And do you have your 'big picture' file somewhere?"

"I'm sending that now—the general 'overlay' I've discerned to-date."

"Got it."

They both worked silently for a while. Susan was very tired, barely able to keep her eyes open. She wanted to take a long break. She desperately needed to go over and crawl into her hammock, close her eyes, and drift off to sleep—not caring if she ever woke up or not. At this point she wouldn't even mind ending up like *Captain Robert Scott*'s ill-fatted 1904 expedition to the South Pole. He and his team made it there, but on the way back died from exhaustion, starvation, and the extreme cold. In a raging blizzard they pitched their tent for the last time, crawled into their sleeping bags, and never woke up. It was a heroic way to die, for which he and his team nailed their place in history.

Now the Hermes team seemed fated to do the same—attempting a noble feat only to die short of finishing their expedition. It was a sobering thought, particularly since there'd likely be no humanity left to remember the ill-fated ADM-1.

"We *have* to make it to the Asteroid!" Kame muttered at her terminal, working feverishly. Susan knew that the Commander was as exhausted and frail as she, yet kept herself going through sheer willpower.

"You know," Susan sighed around her parched lips, her normal careful thinking muddled by extreme exhaustion and dehydration,

"Ben and I were suspicious of you at first, thinking that maybe you wanted to sabotage the mission by..."

"What?" Kame frowned at Susan.

"Well, we did happen to find your knife in your personal baggage and..."

For a moment Kame looked startled, like she was about to yell in anger at Susan, but then seemed to consciously relax.

"Oh...that."

"But—just in case we don't find any solution in this mountain of data—I wanted to tell you I'm sorry for suspecting you. You've done a great job, Kame, keeping Hermes and us together for as long as possible. I now see that you want this mission to succeed more than anything."

Susan vaguely thought that Kame was taking the revelation well— but maybe it was just inattention...

"Yes...and...I think I've got it!"

"Huh?"

"We often encounter this in DNA sequencing—reversal of long stretches of nucleotides. I think it's an artifact of the new compression algorithms. When I correct for the inversions...take a look, Susan!"

Susan blinked her bleary eyes to focus on her screen, watching the layers of coded colors scrambling then reemerging...

"That's it! You did it, Kame! Now I think I see how to put everything together!"

Kame drifted up out of her seat and floated over to Susan's terminal, watching over Susan's shoulder as the representative blocks of the underlying data merged together. They fit like a film of an exploding building played in reverse. Translated into an optical program, a *picture* was emerging!

"What is it?"

Susan grinned for the first time in days. She knew exactly what she was looking at.

"It's a three dimensional scan of the Oort Cloud, Kame. It's incredible!"

"But that's far away from the planets. It's a 0.8 lightyear-wide shell that surrounds the sun and the planets. Sure, it's estimated there's 100 trillion comets out there—more water than we'd need in *millions* of trips. But they're all incredibly far beyond our reach."

"That's true...but this is only an overall image. I think Arecibo was looking for specific movements within the Oort cloud components, exposing particular vectors for more-detailed scans."

"Like?"

"The narrative is missing from the transmission. It must have gotten hopelessly scrambled. So we're left to figure it out for ourselves. They were doing a 'hail Mary' search for me, to see if any stray comets are actually within our reach."

Kame shrugged her thin shoulders, clearly disappointed.

"No, it's all incredibly far beyond our reach, Susan," Kame bitterly repeated, turning away. "We already knew they were far distant from us. They didn't need to do a new scan to tell us that! The closest source of comets, the *Asteroid Belt*, is between Mars and Jupiter, also far distant from us. Then way beyond Neptune is the *Kuiper Belt*, which also has comets. And the Oort Cloud is far beyond even them! This is all just a waste of time, Susan. We might as well quit."

Susan sighed deeply, licking her parched lips with her swollen tongue. Yes, Kame was correct. Still, though...

"But Kame, where did *our* world-ending Asteroid come from?"

"No one knows, except it's zooming down from above the planetary disc where..."

"Right! What if it originated out in the Oort Cloud and in its passage toward us *knocked* or *dragged* a few comets out of place?"

"That's a very long shot, Susan."

"I know! But I specifically asked for a scan along the track of our doomsday *Asteroid PHA-15384*. And look at what they found!"

Susan "zoomed-in" on a red-marked elliptic track that extrapolated backward into the Oort cloud then forward to a fatal encounter with Earth.

"See?" Susan said. Her eyes were stretched wide. She was hardly able to breathe from excitement.

There along the red curve was a scatter of smaller dots!

"Can you zoom in more?" Kame asked, now floating right behind Susan's shoulder, looking on intently.

"Normally we couldn't. Other observatories couldn't resolve all that volume of space. But Arecibo's given us sufficient data! So let's just look along our path which Hermes still must travel in order to join up with the Asteroid and..."

A cluster of small, rocky objects appeared. There were several dozen, too small to appear on general scans of the sky. But each one was sporting a *tail*. They were *comets!* And they were travelling down at the planetary disc on paths roughly parallel to PHA-15384!

"That's...amazing!" Kame exclaimed. "But our killer Asteroid is much too small to divert clusters like that. It doesn't have near enough gravity to...?"

"Sure, I agree," Susan breathlessly broke-in, plotting the exact courses of the scatter of small dots. "But somehow, Kame, it *did!* Maybe it just knocked them away—or whatever knocked the Asteroid out of the Oort cloud did the same to them. We can worry about writing up a journal paper on the astrophysical implications later. The fact is that they are sitting *right out there* within possible reach!"

"So can we divert Hermes to intersect with them before arriving at the Asteroid?"

Susan quickly did complex calculations.

She sagged back in her seat, dejected—but still not ready to give up.

"We might be able to divert Hermes, but then we couldn't reach the Asteroid in time before it hits Earth."

"But what about...?"

"—the *Surface Access Vehicles!*" Susan gasped, anticipating Kame's words. "We have two of the SAVs, fully fueled! But we were saving them for when we arrive at the Asteroid to...?"

"They won't be of much use to us if we're dead," Kame grimly noted, interrupting Susan. "Can they reach that cluster of comets and return to Hermes in time?"

Susan again ran the calculations.

"Yes, the SAVs can do it. It'll be tight. But if we use all our liquid fuel reserves then it's feasible. With both vehicles and two pilots we might have a chance at *grabbing* one of those comets and *bringing it back* to mine its frozen water! We still have the remaining coil of nano-cable, the length that was left over after getting Orion to Hermes. We could theoretically build a loose net between the two vehicles to snag an appropriate comet. We'd be two cowgirls *wrangling cattle* out of an icy herd!"

Kame frowned, scratching her head with one hand. Clumps of her black hair floated into the air. That was unsettling to Susan. Though she put up a brave front, Kame was also in very bad health.

"What about Hermes' critical course corrections?"

Yes, Kame was absolutely right. They still had two major course corrections to accomplish in order to align Hermes with the rapidly descending Asteroid. If those corrections couldn't be made due to lack of sufficient liquid fuel, then—once again—their efforts would be for nothing.

"Yes, that's a consideration."

"How soon do we have to decide?"

Even though her head was spinning, Susan forced herself to concentrate. The overlain vectors of the various objects were on her screen: the cluster of comets, Asteroid PHA-15384, Hermes, and Earth. It was just a matter of doing complex orbital mechanics in her head.

"If we launch the SAVs...within ten hours...then we've got a shot."

"Any later?"

"Then it's impossible."

"Good work, Susan. You got this giant scrambled puzzle reassembled just in time. Do whatever you can to get Adriana functional, even if you have to give her the last of the water reserves. Give her stim shots, whatever! We've got to put all our heads together."

"What about Ben?"

She paused, grimacing.

"He's useless to us, Susan," Kame sighed. "He hasn't been coherent for weeks now. He played his part getting the mushroom forest up and maintaining it. But without additional water it's lost to us. It's already starting to wither away."

"He's our physician. Maybe I can..."

"*Forget* about him!" Kame yelled. Susan was startled. Clearly the extreme stress was getting to Kame as well. Then Kame caught herself, speaking more softly. "Adriana's our pilot. We don't know what to expect at the cluster. You're our asteroid/comet expert. I'm the ship engineer. Together we've got all the knowledge necessary to give this a shot, assuming it's our best option for completing our mission."

"What other options do we have?"

"Nothing good, Susan—but there *are* other options. We have to be realistic, *deadly* realistic. The fate of Earth hangs in the balance! We must be willing to make *any* necessary sacrifices."

"Well, yes...of course."

"Fine—then get Adriana up. One way or another we're going to take drastic action within the next few hours."

"Ok..."

What "other" options were there? What did Kame have in mind? Susan no longer doubted Kame's motivation to get to the Asteroid and save Earth. But was her intense devotion affecting her good judgment?

But, then again, she *was* getting both Susan and Adriana's input into the final decision, right? That sounded very open-minded.

But then why was Ben being pointedly excluded? And hadn't Ben in his last lucid period warned him again about her?

Perhaps after tending to Adriana, Susan might go and check on him. She'd always communicated well with him, even after he went completely insane. Maybe she could do it again. Yes, that was a good idea. She would ignore Kame's order to have nothing further to do with him. Ben saved them before. Might he do so yet one more time?

Susan was driving overland in her red Fiero, returning in disgrace to her hometown of Sulphur, Oklahoma—when she got a call on her cellphone.

She was despondent, now driving through downtown Phoenix, Arizona. What little possessions she had were sitting in a garbage bag on the passenger seat. That was all she had to show for her three year postdoctoral research appointment at JPL: a couple changes of clothes! None of her submitted research papers had been accepted by the journals. Anonymous reviewers cited a long list of problems with her data, the analysis thereof, and the write-ups. No, it "certainly" wasn't overt discrimination due to her pariah status. But it was clear-ly a slap in her face, meant to keep her out of respectable journals. Most of the problems cited were minor, easily solved if she'd had more time to work on them with her collaborators. But now she was out of time, barred from returning to JPL.

She was at the lowest point of her entire life.

And it wasn't just due to her tanked research career. When she got back to Sulphur she had an appointment to meet with Scott Nash. It was scheduled to occur at the new corporate headquarters building of Nashoba Energy, located on tribal ground. It was a brand new, twenty-story corporate edifice of gleaming reflective windows and aluminum struts. From the videos which Susan had seen of it, it was an architectural marvel, integrating the surrounding landscape into its structure. The entrance was living parkland complete with a central waterfall. But despite its "ecological" trappings, Susan knew it was a cold-hearted, money-making machine now overseeing multiple manufacturing sites located across the world.

Nashoba Energy's proprietary super-battery design was still top secret. Although there'd been many attempts to crack its secrets—by scientists in the U.S. and elsewhere—all failed. The batteries just melted into slag whenever anyone tried to tamper with them. Whenever those covert attempts surfaced, the institutions or governments trying to duplicate the technology were cut off. Without access to the new technology, the offenders were thrown far behind the developmental curve. Others quickly learned not to put the knife to the "golden goose" that laid the precious eggs—to just be content with the golden nuggets themselves, while paying through the nose for the privilege.

Normally, Susan would find the stark landscape around her interesting and exotic. She'd opted not to travel along the major highways, but take a more scenic route. Now beyond the skyscrapers and highways of Phoenix, the surrounding red rock hills were soothing—standing above fields of prickly cactus and scrubby brush. The air was dry, the temperature hot. The sun blazed. It was similar to Pasadena but more so—much further from the ocean. Susan had the random thought it might be a nice place to settle and make a new life. There were certainly academic institutions where she could apply for a job, even if it was only at the high school level. She'd heard that public grade schools always needed good science teachers.

Scott would be pissed off when she didn't show up for her appointment, but maybe that was to the good!

"What the hell?" she swore. She again heard the irritating buzz of her smartphone. She'd put it on "sleep," only allowing persistent callers to get through.

She took one of her hands off the steering wheel and pulled the cellphone out of her shoulder bag and glanced at the number. She didn't recognize it. It originated from Houston, Texas. Who did she know there? She couldn't remember any friends or acquaintances in Houston. It wasn't that far from Sulphur, Oklahoma—only four hundred miles—but she'd rarely had occasion to travel south to Texas.

She saw a voice message had been left for her. Curious, she tapped on the icon to play it as she continued driving along the two-lane country road.

"Hello? This message is for Dr. Susan King. My name is John Ploudy. I'm with NASA. I'm one of the administrators for our applicant program. I'm pleased to inform you that of over 18,000 applicants you are one of the finalists. The next step is a personal interview before our selection board at the Johnson Space Center. I'd be pleased to set up that appointment if you're still interested. Please get back to me within 24 hours and we'll make the arrangements. This, of course, doesn't guarantee you a final selection spot—we only have ten slots available—but we're impressed with your application. I've seen review copies of your postdoctoral asteroid and comet work, impressive stuff. We're looking to put a crew onto one of Mars' moons, for which your expertise would be ideal. Ok, then. I hope to hear from you soon. Goodbye!"

She barely avoided crashing the speeding Fiero as she slammed on the brakes and pulled over onto a sandy shoulder.

Grabbing the phone with both hands she dialed back, her fingers shaking.

Someone picked up.

"Hi, this is Susan King, returning a call from John Ploudy?"

"Ah, Dr. King! Yes, this is John. Good to hear from you. I called to see if you're still interested in becoming a NASA astronaut?"

Her heart almost stopped. Taking a deep breath she forced her voice to stay steady.

"Indeed I am. I'd sort of given up hope hearing back from you guys. It's been two years since I submitted my application."

"Yes, I'm sorry about the long delay. The wheels of governmental agencies sometimes move agonizingly slow. But then things can suddenly pick up and zoom along at light speed! It has to do with chronic funding problems, congressional priorities, shifting agency needs and resources—all of that and more."

"Well, whatever happened, I'm very happy to hear from you, Sir."

"Please call me John."

"Sure, John—and please call me Susan."

Oh, Christ, this was going well!

"So, Susan, when can you be here for your interview?"

"I'm actually traveling across country in my car, headed in your direction. It'll take me two days to get there."

"That would be perfect! My secretary will call you back in a few minutes and you can hash out the details. How's that sound to you?"

"Wow—that'd be great, but...?"

"Yes?"

She knew she shouldn't say more, but couldn't resist it.

"I really didn't expect this, what with my recent legal problems."

He hesitated as if being very careful in his reply.

"Yes, such...things...would normally disqualify applicants. But in your case we made an exception. As I mentioned in my voice message, you are superbly and uniquely qualified for a particular mission we're planning."

"That...can't be all there is to it," she gently probed.

She suddenly had a burning need to know more. She'd already been badly burned embarking on a "life crusade." Now that she was finally free of commitments she was unexpectedly wary of getting into another all-consuming "Quest" that might only turn out to be a huge disappointment. She wasn't rejecting a guaranteed, high-paying (but boring) corporate job just to be, yet again, squashed!

"Well...I can't go into details over the phone—but let's just say you have friends in high places."

"High places?"

"*Very* high places."

"Well, that's nice, I guess..."

"So I'll see you in two or three days?" he briskly continued.

"Sure!"

"Then you'll get a call from my secretary within an hour. Her name is Beverly Styles."

"I'll be looking for it. Thanks again, John!"

She set her cellphone onto the dashboard, amazed at the unexpected turn of events. Outside the car, the air was shimmering with desert heat. Since she'd turned off the engine, the unstirred air inside the small two-seater was rapidly warming up as well.

But she hardly noticed it, transported in those few moments to a new, amazing place!

—a "friend in high places"? That must be Scott or Ben! Somehow they were ok with her going into space and had put in a good word for her, maybe twisted a few arms at NASA. Or did Nashoba Energy see her as a good advertisement for their company? But...that didn't make any sense. Or did the phone call tie to her meeting with the mysterious Yishai Hovah? And—come to think of it—how had NASA gotten hold of her submitted journal papers? They were supposed to be confidential until published.

But...

"It doesn't matter!" she shouted. She opened the side door, slid out of her seat, and hopped up and down in the sand, doing a little "war dance" around her car!

A startled rattlesnake slid out from beneath a log and slithered off into the scrub undergrowth.

"*Wahoo!*" she yelled giddily. "I'm going into space!"

Well, she wasn't actually going to space—just to a "finalist" interview that might or might not pan out. But it was a hell of a lot better than slinking back to Sulphur Oklahoma with her tail tucked between her legs!

She hopped back around to the driver's side and slipped behind the wheel.

She absently noted that her hands gripping the driving wheel were visibly *trembling*.

She wasn't driving home anymore. She was driving straight to Houston, Texas!

It seemed too good to be true, a desert illusion of desperately-desired distant blue water...

But real or not, she was going for it!

Chapter 18

MIRAGE

We tend to see what we want
A trick of frustrated expectations
Where a distant plume of smoke
Becomes a welcoming shower
Instead of a roaring forest fire
But hopeful delusions aside
What if we're selecting from options
Painted beneath our comfortable view
Where dependable, set-reality wavers
And other possibilities are skewed
Not so much as fevered dreams
But as an endless variation
Some promising salvation
But others dragging us down
Into the putrid stomach
Of the cackling Demon
Promising eternal Joy
While delivering daily Pain
Can we believe what we see?
Obviously, intriguingly not...

The Minstrel's Lark, 18:59-63

IMPACT MINUS TWO MONTHS, *DESPERATE*...
Susan floated down out of the Observation Deck hatch into the Service Node.

Most of the volume there was crammed full of the many instruments and equipment required to keep Hermes running. While the OD was the command center, the SN was the operational heart of the complex vehicle. And, in addition, it was their portal to other worlds.

Below her she saw the closed airlock that led to the Orion capsule and its attached, sliced-open cargo module. Those vehicles hung beneath Hermes. If the crew ever made it back to Earth, Orion was their ticket home. And to each side Susan saw the opened airlocks leading into the two *Surface Access Vehicles* which protruded out to each side of Hermes. Fortunately, standard protocol was to keep the two SAVs fully fueled and ready for use. In just a few hours, Susan expected to be piloting one of them to the nearby swarm of stray comets which the Arecibo Telescope discovered. Those vehicles were the crew's ticket to possible salvation.

Sadly, Susan was beginning to *hate* Hermes.

She was eager to "get about it," to do something proactive instead of dying slowly of radiation poisoning while also starving and dehydrating. The giant Hermes stack of modules—which had been so welcoming when the SLS struggled to gain orbit—was now a nightmarish *hell hole!* Susan was convinced there was no way they'd last the remaining eight weeks to rendezvous with the Asteroid if nothing changed. Whatever "alternate" plans Kame was considering were doomed to fail.

The comet swarm was their one and only desperate hope for completing their mission.

"Going to see Ben?"

Susan turned her head around to see Adriana floating in the air behind her. She looked better. Susan had fed her another glassful of water containing several dissolved pills: a stimulant, pain killers, and antipyretics to lower her fever. She was now functional. But she still looked awful, cheeks drawn and eyes sunken.

"I'm going to try to talk to him about..."

"Don't bother!" Kame ordered, unexpectedly floating out of the open hatch of one of the SAVs. "We don't have time. Come on back to the OD, Susan. I think I've got our options figured out. I was checking out the fuel leads in the access vehicles and I think what I've got in mind might actually work!"

"Uh...but I wanted to..."

"You'll think differently afterward. We have to talk—*now!*"

Well, the Commander certainly wasn't in a good mood anymore. In fact, she sounded downright nasty!

Susan considered ignoring Kame and going to talk to Ben. But this was still a military-type operation. Commander Sanako was still their leader. It wasn't...yet...a time for mutiny.

Pensively, Susan pushed off fixed cables and drifted back up into the OD. Actually, she was somewhat relieved not to have to immediately encounter Ben. What with the rubbery mushroom forest below dying, the putrid *smell* was again overpowering. It was the rancid odor of a waterlogged house that'd been caught in a flood: rotted out, filled with mold, the floors covered with a thick layer of filth, with dead animals festering in the walls.

Poor Ben was one of those festering corpses: yet horrifically still alive and twitching!

Susan shuddered, floating over to her computer terminal and belting herself into her chair. She swiveled to face the other two similarly secured women.

"Well?" Susan asked.

"I've done the calculations," Kame snapped at them. "I'm sending the numbers to you and Adriana. There's nothing out of the ordinary in them. It's straightforward. And be aware I've started the formal log going again. Everything we're saying in this meeting will be recorded for eventual transmission to Earth."

"Ok...?"

Susan suddenly didn't want to look at the calculations. She was distracted by the surrounding portholes revealing the grandeur of the Universe—deep black pierced by millions of glaringly white pinpoints, against which the forward and back-linked modules of Hermes was an incongruous intrusion. It was as if Eternity were beckoning, besmirched by the crew's mundane creature concerns.

But she forced herself to look away from the portholes and concentrate on her computer screen.

"So what do you see, Susan?"

Susan tried to concentrate on the numbers neatly arrayed in columns of different colors.

"Well, these are the minimal caloric, water, and air requirements of an average crewmember," Susan shrugged, struggling to make sense of the matrix of numbers on her computer screen. "You must have taken them straight out of one of our training manuals. I don't see what..."

"You can't be serious, Kame!" Adriana suddenly gasped.

"What?" Susan added, not seeing what had disturbed Adriana.

But then she saw it—putting those irrefutable minimal requirements up against their "total ship resources" for the remaining nine weeks left before they, hopefully, would land back on Earth...the numbers said that they *could* make it to the Asteroid! But how was that possible?

"You see, don't you?" Kame insisted. "It's quite clear. When we add up *all* of Hermes' potential caloric, fuel, and water resources for completing the mission we *don't* have to go on a desperate, mission-jeopardizing side-search for any theoretical new water source."

"But if we *had* a fresh source of water, then..."

"Sure, it'd be great! The nuclear reactor could split the fresh water we brought back to restock our liquid fuel tanks, providing plenty of oxygen and hydrogen. Excellent! We'd have lots of water to drink. Super! We might even be able to restart the dried-up mushroom forest, allowing it to scrub CO_2 out of the air and produce fresh oxygen—plus converting our festering feces into tasty mushroom meat. Great! It'd solve our problems—*but...*"

"But?"

"But we have *no* guarantee that the comets are actually reachable, that we could capture a suitable one, or that we could subsequently extract any usable water. All of those are big giant 'ifs'! And yet such an expedition *would* absolutely use a big chunk of our remaining fuel stores—thus making it impossible to do Hermes' necessary course corrections. That is, unless water was found, extracted, and electrolyzed in time. In other words, if the side trip didn't succeed, our larger mission would be doomed. All our efforts would be for nothing! That is a *last resort* command decision: *after* all other possibilities are exhausted. Isn't that correct?"

"I don't think these numbers are valid," Susan frowned, staring at the matrix on her computer screen.

She was confused. Her head was spinning. Her lips were so deeply cracked they were dribbling drops of thick blood onto her chin. She knew she should have drunk some of the water she'd given to Adriana. But the woman was already in such bad shape Susan had given up her own daily small ration to revive the woman.

What she wouldn't give for one small glass of *cool, clear*, water!

"So here's the *viable alternative*," Kame grimly continued. "We'll ramp up our existing closed loop environmental equipment."

"I thought we were already running them at maximum—yet still failing to staunch the gaps?" Adriana cautiously ventured.

Kame gave her a dirty look. "We've been depending on the extensive plant growth inside Hermes—first the farm and then the fortuitously sprouted mushroom forest—to produce oxygen, scrub out CO_2, and provide us with complex organic food. Hermes uses its extensive farming system to support *long-term* crew viability. But in the *short term* our closed loop equipment *can* keep us alive."

"But that's only for two or three weeks, and the Asteroid is..."

"Correct, Adri. But everything's in place. We've nothing new to invent or jury-rig. The nuclear reactor is still functioning optimally, so we've plenty of electricity, at least for the moment. Of course with its necessary coolant running low we'll eventually have to shut even it down, leaving us dead in space. But before that happens we have sufficient electrical power."

"But you're saying...?"

"We'll use our remaining hydrogen fuel to combine with the CO_2 that's already been scrubbed out and stored by our *Carbon Dioxide Removal Assembly*. In that way, we'll produce water and methane via the Sabatier Reaction. It's standard procedure."

"Sure—one CO_2 molecule plus four H_2 produces CH_4 plus two H_2O molecules plus recovered energy—a rudimentary astronaut-training formula. We all know it, whether we're chemists or not. But that'll deplete our hydrogen. And what will we do with the excess methane, just dump it into space?" Adriana asked.

"No. The methane we'll store as an alternate liquid fuel. But the point is this: I calculate that we can produce 20.3 gallons of water in this fashion from our hydrogen fuel tanks. That will be enough to compensate Hermes for the continuing slow leaching of our water out into space. Aggressively recycling the water from our urine and the cabin air through our *Oxygen Generator System*, powered by the nuclear reactor's electricity, will give us sufficient fresh oxygen to breathe plus recycled water."

"But we need the liquid fuel in those hydrogen tanks for the course corrections!" Adriana strongly insisted.

"That's where the fuel already stored in the two STVs comes in. They're our 'ace in the hole.' We'll simply divert their fuel to Hermes' main pivotal rocket. Doing so will use up the STV fuel, but allow the remaining course corrections for reaching the Asteroid."

"So then we get there alive—but have to descend to its surface in just our spacesuits?" Susan asked, not convinced. "We might do that, of course, but the mobile suits require their own fuel. And for heavy-duty work which requires an STV we can't...?"

"We'll reconfigure the STVs to use the *methane* fuel which we'll be generating and storing. It's a compressed liquid-combustible, like hydrogen."

"But the STVs don't accept methane as a fuel for..."

"Then we'll figure out the necessary modifications," Kame cut off Adriana.

"You said we wouldn't need to jury-rig..."

"—for the environmental recycling! Fuel burns are another matter entirely. That's rocket engineering, *my* specialty! I know what needs to be modified in the STV engines. It is doable. *I* can do it!"

Susan was looking at the matrix of numbers with a growing sense of horror.

"But...that still doesn't address the question of the calories our human bodies need to survive for the next eight weeks in space. We can't get to the Asteroid dead—or helplessly weak and starved! We must have sufficient strength to do God-knows-what at the Asteroid."

"Yes, that's correct, Susan. That's the limiting factor isn't it? We can't put ourselves into a science fiction-like 'stasis.' Even a resting body must burn calories to stay alive. There's a minimum intake of food we can't do without. And we're *already* weak and sick as it is. Cutting our rations further just isn't possible."

"Then without enough water to grow more plants, how do we...?"

"We have to put the mission first, above everything else—including our veneer of civilization, our scruples, and even our basic morality. Remember, Susan, you agreed to this. You said you were willing to do *anything* to complete this mission!"

"But...there just aren't enough calories onboard to...?"

"We will have to *eat* George—and *Ben!* Their bodies will make up the caloric deficit when Ben is no longer on the consuming but contributing side of the equation. Because of their sacrifices, the three of us will make it to the Asteroid fit enough to do what's necessary."

Susan was stunned.

"*Eat*...George and Ben?" Adriana whispered, obviously also horrified.

"George is dead," Kame answered. "We'll simply thaw out his frozen corpse and process the flesh. It'll be a challenge to our sensibilities. But we can do it. He'd want us to use his body in this fashion to save not just us, but his family back on Earth—not to mention saving mankind from the Asteroid!"

"But Ben *isn't* dead," Susan flatly stated.

"Essentially he's just an animal now," Kame replied, narrowing her eyes to slits. "We don't have the onboard calories needed to maintain a useless animal, especially when *its* meat would enable the rest of us to survive. We will thus be able to subtract the huge amount of calories he'd consume otherwise, plus add his flesh to the total. There's no other option. This must be done."

Jesus Christ! Kame was calmly advocating not just cannibalism but *murder!*

"We *can't* kill Ben," Susan angrily insisted. "He may be sick beyond recovery, but he's a fellow human being. If he dies of natural causes, then that's another matter entirely. But no one here is murdering Ben. I *won't* allow it!"

Kame looked at her with real sympathy.

"Look Susan, if there were any other rational predictable way to reach the Asteroid still capable of doing what's needed, I'd say go for it. I know he's our crewmember. I know he's been particularly friendly to you. But he's not coherent any longer. The radiation damage to his brain is irreversible. We *must* humanely euthanize him and process his body along with George's! This isn't just another option amongst many. It's our only option. This is a sad necessity."

"No!" Susan insisted, now scowling at Kame. "I might go along with eating George's corpse, as horrible as that sounds. But we can't kill Ben!"

"By the time he dies of natural causes it'll likely be too late to help the mission," Kame coldly stated. "Look at the numbers! If there's another more-reasonable alternative, please tell me. I've added up the remaining calories in our meager supply of preformed food packets. The mushroom forest helped but now it's gone, rotted-out and useless. *Ben's flesh* is the difference between our barely surviving to encounter the Asteroid—or Earth perishing in a cataclysmic fireball!"

"Then you should kill *me* instead," Susan insisted. Yes, to save the Mission, she'd do it. But she wouldn't let them commit murder on a person who no longer could agree to that extreme action. If nothing else, Susan still had her honor and her morality! What did it matter if to save mankind they lost their shared humanity?

Adriana sucked in her breath in horror.

"Well, that's noble of you," Kame shrugged. "But your skills and training are critical once we reach the Asteroid. You can't be spared. Adriana is our only expert pilot. She can't be spared either, should she also 'nobly' volunteer to be eaten. And if I die then there's no engineer. Face it, Susan. Even if Ben were healthy, in his right mind, he'd still be the logical choice."

Susan shook her head defiantly in the negative. She couldn't let them do it! But—the logic, the numbers, were inescapable.

Desperate for an alternative, she hit on the only compromise possible.

"But *he* might agree to it," she softly spoke, "even volunteer to do it. That would still be awful but ethical. But to just *murder* him is..."

"—*necessary!* He's not rational any longer, Susan. Like I said before, he's devolved into just an animal. His brain isn't functioning on a human level any longer. The decision is out of his hands!"

Adriana put her head into her own hands, sobbing weakly.

"I have to agree...with *Susan*, Kame," Adriana softly stated, struggling to get her emotions under control. She was visibly trembling.

"Despite the cold rationale you present, Kame—murder is unthinkable!"

The three women stared at each other as they sat bathed in starlight from the portholes. Kame's gaze was steady, unblinking. Adriana looked upward with tears dripping from her sunken eyes. And Susan was *furious!*

But her anger gradually faded.

She was too weak and sick to maintain a strong emotion.

No matter how much she raked her brain, she didn't see any alternative.

As much as she disagreed with Kame's conclusion, the numbers didn't lie. Ben's sacrifice and flesh were the difference between the crew making it to the Asteroid alive and reasonably functional—or not.

Ben had to die.

"The numbers don't lie, Adri. As awful as it seems, Kame's right."

"What?"

"I'll do it," Susan she dully stated. "I'm his closest friend in the crew. It should be me to euthanize him. I'll need something to inject him with that'll act quickly but not be toxic when we consume his flesh."

Adriana gulped, lowering her head back into her hands. She looked completely horrified, but likewise defeated by the naked logic or their awful predicament.

"There's a toxin in one of the research kits that might work," she muttered. "There's only a tiny amount of it, but injected all at once it's probably sufficient to paralyze and kill a human."

"Why would we have something that toxic aboard?" Susan asked, grateful but puzzled by its presence.

"It is one of a series of membrane-active signaling reagents," Adriana tearfully answered. "They're meant to use in weak dilutions to interrogate the ability of specific cell types to respond to appropriate stimuli. It triggers a specific receptor found at the junction of nerve-to-muscle cells. It's a neurotoxin."

"I didn't know you were planning on doing cell culture work," Kame asked suspiciously. "How did you know of this?"

"Well—since I got so sick," Adriana hesitantly admitted. "I was...thinking of using it on myself. I didn't want to be a burden to the crew if I knew I was sick beyond hope of recovery."

"Is it soluble? Can it dissolve in saline to go into a syringe?" Susan asked, focusing on the immediate need.

"Yes."

"But will it remain toxic in the meat?" Kame coldly asked.

"The toxin must be injected. It's harmless by mouth. Hunters in the bush use it on darts to immobilize their prey, which they later consume."

"Large animals?" Kame asked.

"Even big monkeys, baboons...darting them from a distance up in high trees," Adriana answered. Her voice was so low Susan could barely hear her. "So it works on primates like us. It's a synthetic derivative of *curare*, which for centuries was smeared on poisonous arrows by South American natives. It causes paralysis, or in sufficient dosage...death."

So, they had a "humane" means of killing Ben.

"Alright then, go get it," Susan said, unbuckling from her chair and floating up into the cabin air.

"We don't have to do it right now," Kame frowned. "Beside, we'd need time to prepare for..."

"We'll flash-freeze his body next to George's," Susan matter-of-factly replied. "When we're ready we can process both of the corpses together. If we're committed to this course instead of trying to capture a wayward comet, I say we get it over with."

"So you both agree?" Kame tentatively asked.

"—sparing you a 'command decision' to be condemned by future historians or subjecting you to a possible criminal trial? Yes, I formally agree that this is our best option. The 'comet capture' plan has too many unknowns. That's obvious. Adriana, do you also agree? For the record are the three of us unanimous?"

"Yes."

"Then go prepare the syringe."

Susan was ecstatic to be at the *Lyndon B. Johnson Space Center* in Houston, Texas. It was even more magnificent than she'd ever imagined.

It was a large complex of over a hundred buildings constructed on 1,620 acres outside of Houston, Texas. It dated from 1963, from the start of the post-WWII Space Race. It hosted over 3,000 civil employees plus many other contractors. It was a small city unto itself.

She wasn't too happy with the climate. Houston was right on the Gulf of Mexico, on the southern edge of the U.S.A. Consequently, as Susan walked along the sidewalk in early summer the weather was simultaneously miserably humid and broiling.

She'd arrived the night before, gotten a motel room, cleaned up, and dressed this morning in her professional blue pantsuit. Though it was late when she got in, the motel staff kindly did an "emergency" dry-clean and press of her "presentation" clothes.

But she needn't have bothered.

Her previously neat clothes were already rumpled and sweat-stained, just from her walking from her car to the designated Visitor's Center.

But that didn't matter because she was *finally* here at "Mission Control"! JSC directed U.S. manned space flights from the time they lifted off until they landed. In addition, it was where most of the hundred or so NASA astronauts lived and trained: an elite group that Susan was thrilled to finally, hopefully, be joining.

—that is, *if* she made it through the last round of interviews!

"First time here, Dr. King?"

Susan wasn't hiding her excitement, looking around in all directions as she walked with her guide up to the entrance to the high Museum building. Her guide was a first-year astronaut trainee herself, a petite red-haired woman. Her name was Adriana Johansson, one of the international candidates for the Mars missions. She was from Sweden. She was of slight build, barely five feet high, but with a regal bearing. Unlike the stereotypical Swedish woman, she wasn't blond like Susan but redheaded. She admitted to having some Irish blood in her background. Her hairstyle fit her prior occupation. She was an experienced military jet pilot in Sweden's small but modern Air Force.

She'd been assigned to show Susan around during her day-long visit to the Space Center.

Susan found Johansson nice, intelligent, and helpful. NASA was certainly rolling out the "red carpet" giving Susan the "royal treatment." She'd expected a just few hours of intense interviews in air conditioned office buildings. Instead, she was being given the grand tour, including walking between the buildings out in the heat.

"Yes, Adriana. And please call me 'Susan.' I grew up not far from here—in Sulphur, Oklahoma. That's 400 miles away."

"Oh, that is certainly much closer than where I grew up, in Sweden. And do please call me *Adri*, everyone does. But you say you never visited here?"

"I'd have liked to do so. But without a specific reason to come, I just never got around to making the trip. Now, however, I'm thrilled at being interviewed for, possibly even joining your esteemed ranks! Can you tell me about the interview process?"

"Sure, whatever you want to know."

They were now in the Museum, surrounded by magnificent artifacts of the Space Age. In addition to the welcomed air conditioning, Susan was awed by a *Faith 7* capsule flown by Gordon Cooper in 1963. It was a conical tin can barely large enough to contain a grown man. Not far from it was the much larger modern *Orion capsule*, used to ferry groups of astronauts in relative comfort up to the *International Space Station* or to the *International Transit Vehicle*, Hermes. Susan hoped one day to be strapped into a seat of an Orion capsule rocketing up from Earth into outer space!

"Just relax, Susan. Be yourself. That's the best strategy. I'm sure you have a wealth of expertise to offer them on whatever specific questions they have concerning your background."

"I did bone up last night on the Martian moons. The person who called me thought that I might be considered for landing on one of them. That would be something, huh? Wouldn't it be great to be one of the first humans to land on Phobos or Deimos?"

"That *would* be great! Maybe I could pilot you down?"

Susan snickered, feeling at home for the first time in her life—talking to someone who shared her aspirations!

"I'd be honored. Of course that's assuming I'm even accepted."

"That's true, Susan. Remember that you're competing with maybe a hundred other finalists who have equally impressive resumes. But in my experience the biggest thing that the reviewers are looking for is your ability to be genuine and steady under pressure, to interface well with your colleagues."

"Uhm, well—I'm definitely a moderate introvert. I guess that's no secret..."

"Most of us 'tech' types are also."

"—but I work together well with others, at least from my own perspective. Others may or may not agree, though. I suppose you've heard of my recent troubles?"

"I'm sorry, Dr. King...I mean, Susan...the training here is pretty all-consuming. I don't keep up as well as I should with current events."

"So you don't know of my 'notoriety'?"

Adriana laughed.

"You don't look particularly villainous! Whatever happened to you can't be that bad or you wouldn't be here, right?"

Susan furtively glanced around, making sure she wouldn't be overheard. She saw Adriana's puzzled but inquisitive look. They were walking past a *Curiosity Mars Rover* exhibit. "Curiosity" was indeed an appropriate emotion. The car-sized vehicle sat upon red sands, poised with its various mechanical arms extended. The Mars Rover exhibit was very realistic, a whole other world brought "to life" in front of Susan. Other strolling visitors were likewise entranced, not paying any attention to Susan or Adriana.

"Well, I didn't kill anyone—but I was accused of trying to do so, a couple times actually."

"Really? You don't look a murderer!"

"Well, thank you for that," Susan wryly laughed. "But I suppose we all have a 'dark side' within us—just waiting for the 'right' conditions to be expressed."

Next to the Curiosity display was a likewise compelling exhibit of a *Lunar Rover* set not upon red sand but harsh, black boulders.

"That's a profound observation, Susan," Adriana replied. "I've always thought that it was silly when people say 'that person could never have done that crime!' In my experience, *anyone* is capable of doing *anything* under the 'right' conditions—as you stated. Instead of denying our 'dark' side we should recognize and control it: even utilize its energy to accomplish productive goals. After all, on our extreme Missions into deep space we might be called to do the unthinkable at any time."

Huh. That was interesting.

But Susan couldn't think of any possible scenario where she'd have to murder someone in space...

"So you *don't* think my 'dark side' disqualifies me from being an astronaut?"

Susan knew she shouldn't be saying that to her guide. Adriana could be one of the people evaluating her qualifications. But the small, red-haired Swede inspired a confidence in Susan unlike any other she'd met previously. She felt like a 'sister-in-arms' to the woman, as if they'd been in battle together.

"I'm not yet a fully qualified, experienced astronaut, so I don't know everything about NASA," the petite lady carefully replied. "But our training instills in each of us specific knowledge for every contingency imaginable—while *also* equipping us on facing completely unknown scenarios. When we're out there in space with only what we've brought with us, we may have to take initiative and do whatever is necessary in unimaginable situations. So when we learn specific systems we are also encouraged to think *beyond* the predictable. Problem-solving skills are just as important as known trouble-shooting methods. We're not just glorified technicians, Susan. At NASA we're trained to be Explorers!"

Susan nodded thoughtfully. They were passing actual moon rocks. One of them was exposed so visitors could touch it, a rock from another world! A line of people stood waiting expectantly.

She remembered the first moon landing where Neil Armstrong had to extend his flight across the surface of the moon to find a spot clear of boulders to set down upon. The whole world held its breath! They were seconds away from running out of fuel and crashing. But Armstrong took the initiative and saved the mission from having to abort and return prematurely to Earth. That was the "command mentality" that astronauts must possess.

Maybe it wasn't so bad, then, that she'd done what was required to survive the unexpected attack by her trusted advisor at JPL. Success in extreme occupations *wasn't* just being a good technician, but as Adriana said: "being explorers."

Susan felt comforted, much better prepared mentally to face the upcoming round of interviews.

"We have time to get lunch before you start your meetings," Adriana smiled. "We can go to the cafeteria or to a little dive where we trainees hang out. Both places are right here on-campus. The cafeteria has good, healthy food. The 'Greasy Spoon,' however, serves the goodies we're not supposed to eat: salt, sugar, fat, and alcohol. What's your 'poison,' Susan?"

"Well, I was raised as a good church-goer and never got into the habit of drinking alcoholic beverages. I'm not offended when others do so in moderation, of course—but I'll pass on that. Right now, though, a good blast of sugar and fat sounds great!"

"Ok—how about this: *double-chocolate cake* with several scoops of *strawberry ice cream* on top, plus a side dish of a *vanilla milkshake?*"

"Oh, my goodness—that sounds heavenly!"

"We have a rigorous exercise and healthy-eating low-fat and low-cholesterol program here designed to keep us strong and fit for our missions. So what I'm describing is a rare treat for me as well. I think we should celebrate this day, the two of us. I have a feeling we're going to be friends—maybe even go on a mission together!"

Susan felt warmed by Johansson's easy, humorous friendship. It brought her to tears, which she blinked away. It'd been years since she felt such a response to another human being—back to when she and Billy were little kids out in the Park riding their bikes together in the secluded forest.

Her fears vanished. Suddenly she had no doubts. She would do fine in her subsequent interviews. She'd be accepted to the latest class of trainees. She'd move to Houston. And she would go into space.

It was her destiny.

Chapter 19

<u>VACUUM</u>

In deep space
Near absolute zero
Nothing but a few atoms
Float in an empty void
Yet that lonely volume
Is hardly a vacant parking lot
But is filled with ghostly particles
Winking in and out of existence
Annihilating each other instantly
A bubbling soup of Quantum Foam
Where everything and anything happens
Then vanishes before it solidifies
As if it never was and is
A place of perpetual death
And hidden life...

The Minstrel's Lark, 19:59-63

IMPACT MINUS TWO MONTHS, *SACRIFICING...*

Susan floated in the air at the top level of the first Hab, reluctantly accepting the loaded 1-ml syringe from Adriana.

"You have to be quick, Susan. Don't hesitate."

Susan couldn't believe it'd come to this. Since they'd launched from Cape Canaveral it had been one disaster after the other. They barely made it to Hermes, but without the full resupply stocks required for the subsequent lengthy voyage to the Asteroid. Then the slingshot around Earth damaged the stack. Then the nuclear engine fired up unexpectedly, irradiating them. Then the "tumbling" attempt at generating simulated gravity failed miserably, further damaging Hermes. Then their vital farming component failed. And now the grim reality of dwindling calories necessitated their decreasing demand and/or increasing supply, or both.

Those disasters culminated in an inescapable conclusion: one of the remaining four crew members had to die—and that was Ben.

"But...he's not going to wait while I find a vein in his arm...?"

"Yes, it would be best if you can inject it into a vein—but just jam into whatever large muscle group is closest," Adriana said, refusing to meet Susan's gaze. "The drug is deadly. Within a few seconds he'll be unconscious. After five minutes, at the outside...he won't be breathing."

To Susan the sheathed needle was a deadly *knife* poised to plunge into poor Ben's heart.

"Don't poke yourself with it once you have the needle exposed," Adriana glumly warned her. "Even if the entire volume isn't injected into your body, just a bit of the diluted toxin would likely paralyze you. This toxin is thought to be the origin of zombie legends. You don't want to become a living corpse."

Susan nodded, carefully placing the syringe into the side pocket of her white jumpsuit.

"I'll remember," she replied. "Thanks. I'll be back shortly...with Ben's body."

Susan saw Kame floating in the port leading up to the Service Node. She looked very strange since she had on her spacesuit, faceplate down, fully pressurized and ready to exit the central airlock into the Orion capsule. From there she'd void the capsule's air and pass directly into the long-vented cargo hold.

"*I'm ready to freeze the body as quickly as possible,*" Kame spoke over a small external speaker on her suit. "*We want to keep the meat fresh.*"

It chilled Susan to hear those words. Despite having gone crazy, Ben was her friend. He wasn't just a slab of meat!

"Yes," Susan gulped, now not so sure of her resolve. It was a dreadful course of action.

"I'll follow you down to the last Hab in case you need help," Adriana volunteered.

"Thanks."

Susan oriented herself "down" and kicked off a wall of instruments. Even in the first Hab the rotted smell of the dying mushroom forest was overpowering. About a fourth of the space between the close-packed instruments and storage containers was filled with wilted, drooped-over, dried-up mushroom stalks. The next Hab's volume was half filled with farming nodules. And the last Hab where Ben lurked was mostly interwoven, thick plants which occupied a full four-fifths of its total volume.

Each Hab was the equivalent of a three-story apartment. A lot of equipment, living space, exercise apparatus, ongoing experiments, and plant life were packed into the nine different Hab levels. Normally the Habs made a lush, green, beautiful mix of artificial nature and electronics. Now it was an increasingly horrible descent into a stinking *hell!*

As Susan floated down through Hab-2 the stink was revolting, almost forcing her to turn around.

But she persisted, drifting onward through the final, opened port into a packed maze of large, dried stalks. They were so thick she couldn't see through them. Somewhere deeper inside them, hidden, was her fellow crewmember—a friend she was going to kill.

"Ben!" she called out. Her voice was strangely muffled, as if the dried stalks were absorbing the sounds. "Hey, how are you doing, buddy? I'm here to visit you. It's me, Susan. Come on out, Ben!"

For a moment there was no sound except for the dry rustling of the desiccated stalks and crinkly caps, brushing across each other in the circulating air streams. Then Susan heard a strange "snuffling" deeper in the packed stalks.

"Ben?"

She floated further into the dried-up forest, cautiously pushing the packed stalks to the side as she squirmed deeper. Then she was surrounded by them. They pressed upon her from all sides. They were *suffocating* her!

More than anything she wanted to turn back and escape their wilted grasp!

"I know...why you're here," she heard a feeble whisper.

"Ben, you're lucid! Please come to me. We have to talk."

She reached into her side pocket with her right hand and pulled out the syringe, carefully pulling off the sheath and exposing the metallic needle. She held the syringe tightly in her right hand like a knife, ready to plunge it into her victim.

"No need...I monitored your conversation in the SN. I agree there's not enough food for us all. I voluntarily remove myself...from the consumption side of the equation. I'm leaving Hermes."

She could barely hear him. His words were rasping gasps.

"Leaving? Ben, please come to me. Let's talk!"

She heard him laugh, a dry "wheeze" like a sick monkey huddled far overhead in a tall tree.

"It is time...to end this cycle...and begin another."

"Ben, what are you saying?"

"I am returning...to where I began."

Susan had a horrifying realization of what he was threatening. She pressed deeper into the crackling tangle of dried man-sized mushrooms, trying to reach him.

"Ben, we need you! If not for your expertise, then...for your calories! Will you deny us the means to saving Earth? It's not just the consumption side of the equation that must be balanced. We must increase the supply side also!"

"That is *not*...what you truly need."

"Please, Ben! Come to me!"

She was fighting down to the lowest level of Hab-3. Ben had nowhere else to go. He was cornered. He was somewhere right in front of her in the tangle of dead growth, pushed to the end of the Hermes stack. He couldn't escape deeper. She was poised to plunge her needle deep into his wasted body.

"I commend you...into the hands of *Brahma, Vishnu, and Shiva*," the whispered reply came now like the whistle of a hot wind across a dry desert.

"Ok, Ben, I get it! We're in the hands of the Creator, the Preserver, and the Destroyer. That's truly the *Holy Trinity* of Hindu Divinity. But we *don't* have to surrender to the Destroyer! We can still fight back. *Please...*"

She heard the unmistakable sound of a fixed-in-place *airlock bar* being moved, hard metal scraping upon hard metal.

"No!" she yelled, struggling to flounder forward through the last tangle of dry stalks.

"I am...your true friend, Susan...'*He who delivers another from danger, who removes terror from the mind, is the greatest of friends*'..." he quoted Hindu scripture.

"Stop, Ben! Don't do it!" she shouted as the packed, dead plants prevented her from moving forward.

"Oh, one last thing..."

"What, Ben?" she sobbed in defeat, her trembling fingers slipping the sheath back over the needle and placing the syringe back into her pocket.

Her whole body was shaking from the effort she'd put out struggling to the lowest level of the Hab.

"Kame was never a saboteur," he whispered, just inches from her but still well outside her grasp.

"I know, Ben. We were wrong. She's not..."

"It was me."

"What?"

"I'm sorry, Susan...for everything," he sighed, his words barely audible. "It's time I made my 'last confession'—too bad you're not a Catholic Priest, huh? You could absolve me of my sins."

"It's not too late to..." she whispered back.

"My bad karma is mine to carry," he grunted. "It was me that managed to slip a small explosive pellet into the Booster-3 latches during launch-assembly inspection. I was trying to keep us from getting up into orbit. The launch abort tower was supposed to snatch us away, but it also failed, though without my help."

What was he saying? Could this really be true? It seemed impossible!

"I can't believe that you..."

"It was difficult to manage," he quietly laughed, somewhat hysterically. "But who would suspect one of the inspecting crewmembers of sabotaging his own launch vehicle?"

"But—why?"

He ignored her question, continuing... "But since you so cleverly and miraculously got us up to Hermes, I had to insert a cryptic program in Hermes' computer to get the nuclear reactor to come online just as we were out trying to repair it. Both Vladimir and I were sup-posed to die, crippling the mission. But once again you saved me. Then I corrupted the steering jet command sequence so that when we 'tumbled' we did so uncontrollably. I ordered the internal hatches open so we'd decompress. But you still kept us going, Susan. You are persistent! I admire that in you, even though it caused me great prob-lems. Then I damaged the antennae array links and the auxiliary communication platform such that we increasingly lost connection to Mission Control. But yet again you managed to foil me, piecing to-gether their last transmission. You've stopped me at each turn, but no longer."

Susan—still trying to push her way forward through the last few feet of packed dead vegetation to reach Ben—was both horrified and stunned.

"You did all that to us? But if you really wanted to stop us why didn't you just depressurize the ship when we were out of our suits?"

She heard a "scrunch" as the hatch of the airlock was swung open far enough to let a person squirm inside.

"I had no choice," she heard him sob. "I'm so sorry, Susan. I was forced to do just the minimum required to slow or stop us. It had to be subtle! Any more and I'd have been *prevented!* Now, though, without my flesh to eat, you won't make it to the Asteroid. You'll starve. So I've finally fulfilled my duties. I state this as my last con-fession and report. Goodbye, Susan. Perhaps we'll meet in another life."

"No, Ben—don't!"

"Remember this, Susan," he cryptically stated: "'*The heart of an excellent person is like a coconut—which though hard without, con-tains within refreshing water and delicious food.*' It's not much, but I leave you this as a gift: not meat, but even better. It's all I can do. Good Karma to you, my dear friend."

"No, Ben, *no!*"

She began kicking out with her hands and feet, desperately bash-ing the thicket of dried plants to the sides.

Then she was at the now-closed terminal airlock door. It was not meant to be opened. It was there to link up with another module should anything more be added at the far end of the Hermes stack.

On the other side of the airlock was just the *cold vacuum* of outer space.

"Oh no," she gasped as she saw the light above the airlock turn red.

She felt rather than heard the "thump" of outrushing air which *shot* Ben's body out into space!

Then the light turned yellow as the outer door automatically swung shut and the airlock began to repressurize.

"Why would you betray us, Ben, *why?*" she sobbed, banging her fists on the closed inner hatch.

No...he hadn't betrayed them. He couldn't do it. She knew him too well. This so-called deathbed "confession" had to be the last spurt of his radiation-fried mind trying to make sense of their catastrophe. He'd just gone crazy, nobly attempting to take responsibility for all the disasters they'd faced.

"I forgive you, my dear friend," she whispered. "You didn't know what you were saying."

Slumping, she was again enveloped by the fragile, dead plant life. The deep "soil" at her feet felt like a depleted sponge, yielding to her body. She spasmodically reached out with her hands, hitting and bashing at anything within reach.

Suddenly she felt something round and hard.

Startled, she looked down to see in her hand a *bright red mushroom*—which looked like a little round watermelon!

"What's this?" she gasped, holding it up to her eyes.

Whatever it was, there were a *lot* more of them.

Looking around in the gloom beneath the dried remains of the dead mushroom forest she saw cluster after cluster of sprouting red mushrooms.

"It's hard but mushy!" she hysterically exclaimed, cradling the rounded mushroom in both her hands.

Indeed, its tough shell was rubbery and swollen. Was it perhaps similar to little red cactus plants adapted to survive in a dry desert, storing up and hording precious water?

Well, there was only one way to find out for sure.

She sank her teeth into it, piercing the skin—then greedily sucked in a rush of sweet, satisfying liquid!

"Oh, Jesus Christ!" she grinned, holding the growth back out in front of her face, closely examining it. Yes, beads of moisture were flowing from the gash she'd just made! Then she sank her teeth back into its tough surface, devouring it completely.

Yes, it was filled with a semi-liquid "meat" much like that of a watermelon. It was the most delicious thing her parched lips had ever tasted. If there were enough of them, Ben had saved them!

But why would he do this—*how* did he do this—if he was trying at the last to stop the mission from succeeding? Didn't he space himself to keep them from eating his body? But hadn't he also said something about being "forced" to do the "minimum" to stop the mission? And what about his final "report" verbally articulated? Did he think he was talking to someone? Did he think he was audibly confirming their end while leaving them a cryptic "gift" as he said? Clearly, he was a reluctant saboteur, even in his final delusional state.

She remembered an Indian saying Ben had been found of quoting: "*Let the traveler fainting on his journey take rest under a tree which contains both fruit and shade.*" After piously proclaiming his religious "excuse" he'd plop down to rest from whatever rugged astronaut physical training they were enduring. It was his "religious" excuse to take a break, being very "holy" while grinning beguilingly. It was a great memory.

But now he was gone.

"Poor Ben," she whispered, closing her eyes.

Whatever his fantasized crimes he'd paid the ultimate penalty.

Now, his frozen-stiff body was shooting away from Hermes, following poor Vladimir to oblivion. The radiation had indeed ended up killing both of them, Vladimir directly and Ben indirectly: causing Ben to go insane!

But Ben had given the remaining crewmembers both "shade"—the mushroom forest—and now "fruit." Susan decided that she wouldn't tell Kame or Adriana of his whispered bizarre claims as to sabotaging their mission. Clearly the radiation plus the subsequent deprivation had driven him completely mad. If the *red mushrooms* persisted, however, they were undeniably real: providing the crew of Hermes with both calories and precious fluids!

Though his body was now lost to outer space, in Susan's mind Ben was nothing less than a hero.

"Susan! Are you ok? What's happening?"

Susan recognized Adriana's high-pitched voice, shouting into the growth-clogged terminal Hab.

"I'm ok—but Ben's gone! He went out the airlock to free up his rations for us to eat. I couldn't get to him in time to stop him. But I've got something equally valuable as his dead body! I'm climbing back up!" she shouted.

Pushing through the thick stalks around her, Susan groped into the dried-out soil. Buried everywhere were more clusters of the base-ball-sized red mushrooms. She gathered up an armful of them. Then she started pushing upward through the rotted stalks toward the far-off Adriana.

But she wasn't making any forward progress...?

"Susan! Do you need help? Should I come down?"

"No, Adri! Stay there! I'm just momentarily caught on some-thing! There's no need for you to get entangled also! I'll be free in a minute! I'm alright!"

But she wasn't "alright." Indeed, her head was spinning. Some-thing was wrong. She felt—*drugged?*

The stalks surrounding her were melting away, dissolving, re-placed by *swirling rainbows!*

"Oh, hell," she muttered to herself, barely hanging onto her arm-ful of precious fruit. "Something was in that red mushroom I ate...but I thought the crop's cryptic genetic matrix didn't have any poisonous genes?"

But then again, the plants had been continuously irradiated for weeks now—resulting in who knew how many mutations?

And *her legs* hurt where something was *tightening* upon them?

"Let go of me!" she shouted. Twisting and trying to jerk herself free, she involuntarily clutched tightly down on her load of fruit— which *exploded* around her torso like lethal red hand grenades!

A *red haze* of the squashed fruit enveloped her. And from the spinning fragments spurted out *white fogs* of explosively freed *spores!*

Coughing and gasping, she managed to reach down with her now-freed hands, trying to push away the grasping plants...

Plants?

Looking at her feet Susan was horrified!

Peering back up at her were *two beady black eyespots* of what looked like a *dog-sized red lobster!* Its powerful pincers were clamped onto one of her boots. Its smaller hind legs were scrambling frantically at the surrounding stalks, dragging her downward. Its tail was flipping inward, further "swimming" her backward in the zero-G.

"Oh, come on!" she deliriously laughed. "That's ridiculous!"

But there were more of them.

A *whole swarm* of the giant red lobsters suddenly emerged from the kaleidoscopically spinning dead stalks—clamping onto her legs, dragging her ever deeper!

"Oh, no...no, no, *no!*"

She suddenly realized they were pulling her back to the *airlock*.

Apparently Ben hadn't been so generous after all.

Susan was totally helpless. The "lobsters" were all over her, easily gliding her body through the brittle stalks. And then her head *banged* into hard metal!

"Ouch! Watch it!" she angrily complained.

But she was in no shape to tell the lobsters what to do. They were in complete control. And the airlock door was painfully pushing her head to the side as it opened up, revealing a cramped interior barely large enough to accommodate one person.

"I'm not going in there," she firmly stated.

But she was helpless to resist the many shoving lobster claws. Her mind had no control of her listless, poisoned body. She felt detached from her body. She could only watch what was happening as she was nudged into the airlock and the door swung firmly shut behind her.

She heard the air being sucked from the chamber, felt the rasp of her strangled last breaths, and saw the light inside the chamber turning from green to yellow to *red*.

"I'm coming, Ben," she whispered as the outer door *popped* outward and she was *flung* into the endless black vacuum of outer space!

Bill King stood in a crowd of likewise-standing people looking across the blue water of a causeway at the distant *Kennedy Space Center*'s main launching pad. The countdown was in its final minute.

His eyes were riveted on the distant slender white rocket that was surrounded by metallic-gray launch towers.

His sister was part of a crew of six sitting in an Orion capsule on top of the heaviest rocket stack ever launched up into space. It was a desperate mission thrown together hastily, in response to an existential threat to the entire planet: *Asteroid PHA-15384*—on course to slam into Earth in six months!

"You didn't have to sneak away, Bill," a deep voice sounded at his shoulder.

Startled, he looked away from the launch site to see *Scott* casually standing at his left. A loudspeaker gave an update on the launch: "THIRTY SECONDS AND COUNTING."

Scott Nash had on a brown windbreaker. His stylishly long black hair was braided in the back, falling past his wide shoulders. Incongruously, he wore a white baseball cap that shaded his brown eyes. His high cheek bones, angular nose, and thin lips made him stand out from the crowd as if he were athletic nobility. But his eyes were narrowed, peering at Bill with a quiet cunning.

"Hi, Scott," Bill carefully replied. "I didn't think you'd be here. I just wanted to see my Sister off and..."

Scott frowned—then *punched* Bill hard on his left arm!

"Ow!" Bill grimaced, clutching at his left arm with his right hand. "That hurt," he whimpered as he cringed away.

But Scott moved even closer, glowering at Bill.

"I thought we agreed to withhold both public and private support for Susan's misdirected adventure here with NASA?" Scott grated through clenched teeth.

"I've not done any of that!" Bill protested. The pain in his arm was still intense. "I'm here strictly as a private citizen, 'incognito.' No one knows that Nashoba Energy has any connection to the official NASA/international expedition to the Asteroid. I have zero presence for the so-called ADM or Asteroid Deflection Mission. So why, then, are *you* here?"

"I saw your travel agenda, Bill, *not* to the conference you were supposed to attend—and I'm actually here to support *you!* Despite our company's disagreement with the present international allocation of resources confronting the threat to our precious planet, Susan is my friend also."

"TEN, NINE, EIGHT..."

The Crowd around them was poised and tense, cameras and cell-phones pointed across the wide channel at the distant launch site.

Steam was starting to rise on the other side of the causeway at the base of the massive rocket.

"Well, even Susan doesn't know *I'm* here. So I don't know if your support of *me* matters much. But—I am glad you're here, Scott," he meekly assented, looking down at his feet. "It's spectacular, isn't it?"

"Sadly, yes."

"What do you mean?"

"THREE, TWO...WE HAVE IGNTION OF THE RS-74 ENGINE..."

Blasts of flames spread out as a cushion beneath the distant, towering spacecraft.

Then a *pillar of red fire* extended itself at the launch pad, pushing the rocket upward.

"AND WE HAVE *LIFTOFF* OF ADM-1 IN DEFENSE OF HU-MANITY—GO WITH GOD! THE HOPES OF ALL THE PEOPLE OF EARTH ARE WITH YOU."

A bone-jarring vibration and deafening *RUMBLE* blasted into Bill, causing him to gasp in awe!

The white spear ascended slowly into the sky on a straight column of thick white vapor.

"It's dangerous, isn't it? Anything could go wrong with such primitive technology—riding a 'fire-stick' up into the sky?" Scott spoke directly into Bill's ear.

Scott's deep voice was almost lost in the ROAR of the ascending spacecraft as it sped into high fluffy white clouds dotting the deep blue sky.

Bill turned to him and grabbed the man by his shoulders, staring straight into Scott's implacable brown eyes.

Normally he readily gave-in to Scott's overly aggressive behavior, not wanting to make a fuss. But it was Bill's *sister* who was riding that giant torch up into space!

"What the hell are you saying?"

"She should have stayed with us, Bill. She could have gotten rich being a top-level executive, earning herself a good life right here on Earth. There was no need for her to turn her back on the Company."

"She's going up there to save the world, for Christ's sake!"

"Our alternative plan is much better. Instead of foolishly trying to chase down the comet, *our* plan will use our own Earth-based super-battery technology to confront that big rock directly, as it approaches Earth. When the official NASA/international mission fails—as it, sadly, is fated to do—then they'll return to our initial plan. Susan's brave but foolish sacrifice will have been for nothing!"

"'Sacrifice'? *What* have you done?"

"The Company has a certain amount of leverage..."

"TWENTY SECONDS INTO THE FLIGHT...GOOD ENGINE CONTROL IN THE FIRST STAGE."

The *rumble* of the ascending spaceship was still deafening, giving Bill and Scott a "cocoon of noise" within which they could talk "privately."

"You've sabotaged the mission?" Bill gasped, horrified, "My God! I knew you hated Susan for not coming in with us. I knew that the Board was keeping things from me. But I never dreamed...?"

"Oh, don't be so melodramatic," Scott interrupted. "We didn't want this to happen, Bill. But I have it on very good authority that...anomalies...are likely to occur. This mission was configured too hastily. For instance, this is the first time they've ever attached four boosters onto the SLS instead of its normal two boosters. To make that one addition would normally require several years of careful tests before being implemented. For this mission, though, they just cobbled it together. I have inside information that there's a high probability of failure during the initial launch—right now!"

"You *knew* this?" Bill said, angrier than he'd ever before been.

"Of course I knew it. Everyone knew it. But don't worry about Susan, she's..."

"NOW PASSING THIRTY SECONDS, 3.8 NAUTICAL MILES DOWNRANGE DISTANCE."

"She was *right!*" Bill growled back. "Our Company's come too far too fast! Your small Native-American group wasn't capable of handling an operation generating billions of dollars yearly. I should have gotten out when..."

Scott gripped him by his shoulder, *tightly*. Bill winced again from the pain inflicted on him by Scott.

"Without us you'd be nowhere, Bill," Scott snarled back at him. "If it wasn't for what I myself contributed to the research design—the high-temperature superconductivity component—you'd still be puttering around in your sheds using your pitiful surplus-WWII instruments! And we have additional, advanced help you don't know about—giving us the capability to go far beyond just being a top-100 company. Soon, we'll dominate the entire world. Nation-States will be just the means to accomplishing our ends!"

The rocket was now downrange, its bone-jarring RUMBLE fast fading away.

"What?" Bill gasped, not following Scott's logic. "But...we're facing extinction! It's the same as 65 million years ago! A giant Asteroid is poised to end advanced life on the planet as we know it! And you're cheering for NASA's mission to *fail?* God, that's like a T-rex greedily knocking back its competitors in order to gorge on a brontosaurus as a *fireball* spreads across the horizon!"

Bill shook his head in disbelief while Scott just calmly smiled.

"We know exactly what we are doing."

"TRAJECTORY IS ALTERED BUT NOT CATASTROPHICALLY."

"Altered?" Bill gasped, peering nervously up at the sky. It was just as Scott predicted! Suddenly he was very afraid for his sister. "*How* did you know this was going to happen?"

Scott shrugged as he disdainfully pulled loose from Bill's grasp.

"It was inevitable. As I said, anyone could have predicted it. Actually, I'm sorry Bill."

"Get the hell away from me!" Bill moaned, turning away, stumbling into the crowd.

"Get your act together!" Scott shouted after him, "We're moving forward! You've got to do your part regardless of your fragile emotions!"

Tears now streaming down his face, Bill fled into the crowd away from Scott, then pulled up short and looked back up at the sky.

Everyone else was still staring at the long vapor stream that stretched into the sky and downrange. Even from a distance, it was obvious something was terribly *wrong*. The previously steady stream was now *jerky*—as if the rocket were being *thrown* back and forth!

"Don't die, Suzy—don't die!" Bill sobbed.

"THERE'S BEEN A MALFUNCTION IN BOOSTER-3...IT HAS PREMATURELY SEPARATED FROM THE VEHICLE."

Bill looked up at the distant vapor stream expecting any moment a catastrophic explosion. If Susan wasn't already dead she'd certainly be so in the next few seconds! But, wait...wouldn't the *launch abort system* on top of the Orion capsule yank the crew away for a safe return to Earth? Maybe that was what Scott was talking about?

And just where *was* Scott anyway?

Bill looked around, half expecting Scott to pop up out of the crowd and start playfully hitting him again. The crowd around Bill on the shoreline was subdued, looking up hopefully but fearfully. Scanning the crowd, Bill didn't see Scott anywhere.

He was conflicted. He knew Scott was right in his arrogant claim—Bill would be nowhere without Scott and Nashoba Energy. Scott was truly the brains behind the operation. Bill knew that he himself was just a computer nerd, a happy programmer with his nose stuck in his software. Without Scott to guide him he'd be lost in the corporate world.

But still...

"THREE MINUTES THIRTY SECONDS IN AND..."

A *brilliant flash* occurred high in the sky far downrange.

Bill felt a horrible sinking feeling in the pit of his stomach. The crowd around him collectively "gasped." Little kids looked up at the clouds with tears in their eyes as their parents tried to comfort them.

"WE HAVE SEPARATION OF THE REMAINING THREE AUXILLARY BOOSTERS...THE VEHICLE IS STILL INTACT, THOUGH ON A LESS THAN OPTIMAL TRAJECTORY."

A hopeful, partial *cheer* went up from the crowd!

"FOUR MINUTES, TEN SECONDS INTO THE FLIGHT...THE CORE BOOSTER IS RAMPING UP TO FULL POWER."

Bill held his breath. Apparently the main central tank was still intact and firing!

"GOOD CHAMBER PRESSURE IN THE CORE BOOSTER."

Go, go, go!—he mentally urged her. *Come on, Susan, you can do it! You can't die! Sure, something went wrong. But it doesn't have to stop you! Make it up into orbit!*

He was frozen in place, staring up at the sky.

"FIVE MINUTES INTO THE FLIGHT. STANDING BY TO GO TO PARTIAL THRUST COMMAND."

Bill had always been very interested in space flight. If he could, he'd have been up there with Susan. So he knew the generalities of what had to occur during a launch to put a manned craft or an unmanned satellite into a stable orbit. If the last booster, the central tank, could just complete its burn and separate from the upper stage, then the mission might yet succeed!

"THE MAIN ENGINE HAS CUT OFF...STANDING BY FOR STAGE SEPARATION."

The crowd again cheered.

There was a long pause from Mission Control.

"THE MAIN FUEL TANK HAS NOT SEPARATED AS EXPECTED. THE VEHICLE IS STILL INTACT, BUT IN A LOWER, DEGRADING ORBIT. PLEASE STAND BY FOR FURTHER UPDATES."

Oh, Christ! They didn't make it into a stable orbit! The whole mission was in jeopardy!

But there was nothing Bill or those around him could do. Dejected, they started to disperse. Many were shaking their heads and commiserating with each other. Knowing the gigantic stakes of the mission—the survival of the entire planet hanging in the balance—they looked not just concerned but scared.

And crowds afraid of existential threats with no way out are capable of anything...

Bill was deeply troubled, afraid of what could still happen to Susan and the mission. But *he* could do something about it! He was going to get to the bottom of what Scott had revealed.

There was no doubt now in Bill's mind that a *conspiracy* was in play, one that reached beyond the Company to who knew where?

Bill was determined to find out. He wasn't in the technology business just for the fame, the money, or the power. In the end he was his sister's brother—both of them driven by the twin curses of Curiosity and Creativity.

He was *so* unlike the charismatic bully, Scott, who he'd hooked up with to further his Dad's invention.

Beyond rational thought or genetic motivations both he and Susan shared a *Godly Compulsion!*

And it would not be denied.

Chapter 20

<u>REPTILIAN DAZE</u>

Oh, the cold heart of a snake

The lizard's flicking tongue

The dinosaur's killing claws

A T-rex hunting its next meal

Hard, tough, focused, and brutal

Slashing teeth ripping out flesh

What purpose could such evoke?

In Theistic Evolution a mere joke

Or a Top Predator doing its job

Loosening the lower levels to evolve

MAYBE NOT THE WHOLE STORY

Perhaps a thing of amazing beauty

Yes, bounded by its own limitations

But with clear Purpose rising above

Within its own complex genome

An incredibly warm Creature

So much naked Potential...

Eager to be fully revealed

—whether we like it or not!

The Minstrel's Lark, 20:103-107

IMPACT MINUS TWO MONTHS, *CAPTURED*...

Dazed, Susan lay on her back looking up at a high, blue sky. Wispy white clouds floated past as something *heavy* was constantly pushing across her entire body—*squashing* her onto what felt like hard concrete at her back!

Oh, right...that "something" was called *gravity*.

But how was this possible?

Just moments before, she'd been floating in zero-G inside the cramped airlock being ejected out into empty space!

And now...?

She was lying on a flat, hard surface. It was moderately warm on her back but noticeably cooling. And around her was a rapidly fading *blue haze*.

And her arm hurt, as if she'd just had an *injection*.

"Are you ready to get up, Reverend Mother?"

It was a raspy voice. Each single word was precisely articulated. It was as if the speaker were with great difficultly speaking a foreign language.

She looked to the side.

Standing beside her hard "bed" was what appeared to be a *human-sized lizard!* It had a long, angular head with parted jaws. Revealed inside its elongated mouth were many long, pointed teeth. A big yellow eye with a long black vertical slit was staring at her from the side of the head that was turned toward her. Its long, powerful tail whipped back and forth. Its body was covered with thick, overlapping green scales. And its three-fingered hands flexed in the air, grasping at her!

"Don't touch me!"

She cringed back, nearly falling off the other side of the hard slab upon which she lay. Floundering, she managed to slide off and land on her feet.

She just stood there, her hands flat on a white marble surface before her, steadying herself. She stared at the talking lizard which was undeniably there on the other side of the slab!

"Do not be alarmed, Reverend Mother," it said, cocking its big, oblong head to the side. "We saved you from certain death. We counteracted the poison in your body. We will not harm you."

"Just *where* am I?" Susan demanded, shakily looking around.

Her legs felt very weak as she struggled to keep standing erect. After four months in zero-G, despite daily exercises, her entire body ached! Plus, she was half-starved and sick, making her muscles even weaker.

"Why, you are on Earth, of course!" the talking lizard gestured grandly around him. He held a scepter in one of his clawed hands which looked to be made of pure gold. It sported a giant diamond on its end that caught the sunlight, breaking it up into a blazing rainbow!

Susan noticed that the talking lizard had on a royal-purple gown that flowed down its long neck, across its arms, and onto to its upper tail and lower legs. The robe was exquisitely tailored, perfectly fitting the curves of its powerful reptilian body.

"You...you're a...?"

"Yes, I am similar in form to the equivalent of my ancient ancestors upon your planet, the Velociraptors."

"You mean—you're a *dinosaur?*"

"If it helps, you are welcome to refer to us as 'dinosapiens.' I am the *High Priest of the Ascension.* My name is unpronounceable by your voice box, so please call me 'Fred.' Does that help you, Reverend Mother?"

In response to her incredulous stare, "Fred" assumed a lecturing pose and continued: "As you evolved over millions of years from ancient upright tree-dwelling mammals, so did my species derive from what you know as dinosaurs. In your world a huge asteroid killed off most of the dinosaurs, giving evolutionary room for mammals to evolve. In this dimension, however, the asteroid broke into many fragments—'softening' the overall blow to the planet. While the largest dinosaurs still died, the smaller top predator dinosaurs survived the impact, primarily Velociraptors. We retain many of their features. But our brains are far larger and more convoluted than our dinosaur ancestors. Additional cognitive structures evolved—much as did your brain as compared to your ancient simian ancestors."

"You said...*my* planet? Is this 'earth' *different* from my Earth?"

"Yes, *our* Earth is far different from this planet, Susan—yet topologically the same," a different, softer voice said from behind her. "Continental drift, apparently, doesn't notice what species evolve upon the surface of the dry land."

Turning, she saw *Ben* walking hesitantly up to her. He was leaning heavily on a wooden cane. His face was drawn and thin. But he was broadly smiling, his eyes glowing with vitality! Clearly he was no longer on the verge of death, nor floating frozen in outer space.

"Ben, is it really you?" Susan gasped. "Is this a dream or hallucination? I ate one of those red mushrooms and..."

He grinned at her, revealing gleaming white teeth.

Her voice trailed off as she studied him.

He now looked very similar to the venerated early twentieth century leader of Indian independence, *Mahatma Gandhi!* He had on a white robe. He wore wooden sandals. His hair was cut to a faint haze on the top of his head. Across his upper lip he now sported a small mustache. And on his dark-brown face he wore small round gold glasses.

"I am quite real," he nodded, patting her gently on her cheek with his free hand. "Look around you! Can you deny the glory of this place?"

Since regaining consciousness she'd been too startled to broaden her gaze. Now she looked past the patiently waiting dinosapien "Fred," to see a line of high, craggy peaks stretching out to the far horizon. The black rock of the sheer mountains was adorned with vast snow drifts. Glaciers flowed in icy streams here and there down steep mountain slopes, ending at emerald lakes far below.

She was on the top of one of those peaks! And beside her, spiraling up into the thin air around her was a complex mechanical construction of interwoven antennae. It looked to be a communication array or observatory, reminding Susan of the Arecibo Observatory in Puerto Rico. But the construction was clearly alien, having sprung from minds different from humans. It soared up into the sky from a series of white-domed structures, out of which more purple-clad lizards were happily running, their long tails wagging excitedly behind them!

They were swarming toward the elevated marble slab upon which Susan had found herself, as if to pay homage to her—or eat her!

They were chanting in unison in a foreign "clicky" language, composed of loud whistles and grunts.

"But...what is...?"

"We're high up in the Alps, Susan. Can you walk? If you can come over to the railing with me, I want to show you something that's magical."

"More magical than this stuff?"

"See for yourself."

Hesitantly at first and then with more confidence she placed one foot after the other, slowly walking beside Ben over to an iron railing that looked out over a deep valley. The foggy cleft below was nestled between the high mountain upon which Susan stood and another even higher one to the side.

Pushing up through the clouds *below* them was a *fairytale castle!* It had high white towers topped by pointed grey turrets. It sprang up from a circular battlement, perched on its own minor peak. Off in the distance where the lower clouds thinned Susan could see the luxuriant green of mountain meadows on a wide valley floor. Great swaths of distant red and yellow flowers painted the slopes between green groves of pine trees.

"It's...magical indeed, Ben," Susan sighed. She was stunned to be back on Earth, outside of the false "tin can" reality she'd been dying within. "But...how are we here? *What's going on, Ben?*" she shouted at him, suddenly deathly afraid!

She pulled away, looking around frantically, seeing the dinosapiens running at her with their jaws spread wide!

"No! Please calm yourself, Susan! They could have easily killed us—solving, for them, a terrible existential problem. But instead they saved us. When we exited Hermes we voluntarily put ourselves beyond the normal causality of our species. Thus they were 'permitted' to scoop us up! The only thing that our human history will record—if such continues upon our Earth—is that we died on Hermes, exiting or being blown out one of the airlocks into space without our spacesuits. So they've altered nothing of human history by their actions."

She suddenly lurched against him, grabbing the front of his loose white robe in her fists and knotting it up tightly at his neck.

"*Tell* me!" she demanded.

His startled face was turning white, his air and blood circulation cut off by her furious grip!

Suddenly ashamed of her anger, she loosened her grasp. The crowd of dinosapiens paused, making a half circle around them, respectfully maintaining their distance.

Then, as one, they all bowed down to her.

"You're...their *Creator!*" he gulped, vainly trying to push her choking hands away. "They revere you! They've waited eons...for you to be born and pursue your destiny. They've watched it unfold! But they don't want it to proceed...to its full conclusion. They're trying to *interrupt* the cycle. They want to *stop* you—us—from reaching the Asteroid!"

Stunned, Susan completely let loose of Ben's robe. Gasping, he fell back a couple steps.

The prone half-circle of dinosapiens didn't even look up, just stayed still and silent.

"This is much too fantastic, Ben. I can't believe a word of what you're saying. I must be in a bad science fiction movie. And I certainly didn't 'create' this world. That's utter nonsense!"

He weakly laughed, rubbing at his throat with one hand.

Around them, the dinosapiens stood up on powerful hind legs, bobbing their heads up and down.

"Is it such a stretch, Susan? I'm here aren't I? I'm alive! It's been *six months* since they brought me here—time apparently moves in random spurts across dimensions. They've fed me, cared for me, and healed me of all the results from my severe radiation poisoning. Look at my face! The scars are gone! And they rescued you the same as me. You tried to get me out of the airlock and ended up getting ejected yourself, right? But you're not dead, correct? Also, they immediately treated you with an antidote to the mushroom toxin. You just now regained consciousness and..."

"That's not how it happened, Ben. The genetic diversity of Hermes' farm was far greater than..."

"*Whatever*, Susan!" he stopped her. "Both of us are now in one of their preeminent scientific communities. It's a hybrid between a cloistered religious order and an academic university. Their headquarters is located below in the valley. Up here—as far away as possible from any electromagnetic interference—is their main transdimensional observatory, which is focused upon *our* Earth. And because they've managed to tap into the virtually inexhaustible heat at the core of the planet, they can break the Dimensional Divide and transport individuals from here to there then back again!"

Susan laughed, shaking her head in abject denial. She refused to look at the semi-circle of purple-robed dinosaurs. Instead she resolutely kept her eyes focused on the high mountains and glaciers below.

"Intelligent dinosaurs spying on us from another dimension— *really?*" she snorted. "And they're grabbing people to come appear on a slab? Even if that were possible, why would they care?"

He looked at her kindly, apparently amused at her ignorance.

"My family has a secret history with them that extends back thousands of years," he gently continued. "I'm one of a long lineage that has been tasked with preventing *our* discovery and exploitation of *their* particular world. They've been intelligent and industrious far longer than *Homo sapiens* have even existed!"

Right...it sounded like one of her crazy sci-fi imaginings.

"I can't believe any of this, Ben. This has to be a nightmare or drug-induced hallucination. You're saying that these screwy lizards have been meddling in human affairs for centuries? That's ridiculous!"

"Cafferty!"

"What?"

"If you want proof, you've already got it. The terrible things that happened with you and your post-Doc Professor, which almost derailed your NASA application—they were orchestrated by these intelligent creatures."

"I...well..."

Indeed, it had been mysterious. Cafferty's behavior was beyond strange. Hadn't he invoked "lizards" somehow directing him to do what he did? This could indeed explain what he meant, unless it was just her overactive unconscious mind inventing it?

"But they're not devious by nature, Susan. These are sentient creatures who, for the most part, only want to continue peacefully coexisting in our crowded slice of space-time."

Oh, Jesus...back to "multiple dimensions"? Really?

"So there are other Earths?"

"There are many others, Susan. But this world is the closest one to us. We touch each other. We affect each other—and have done so for many cycles. And *your* actions brought their reality into existence! You indeed *are* their Creator! Surely you must remember?"

Her actions—wait, that day long ago in the Park, when she as a child regained consciousness after falling from her bike? Did she really fall from her bike? Or did she...?

Other memories came flooding back to her! She was in space, in the past, in another Dimension!

—and hurtling at her and Billy was a *swarm of giant fragments* of a blown-apart colossal *asteroid!* And it was *her* spaceship impacting with the zooming rock that fragmented the asteroid instead of letting it smash intact into the Earth!

Yes, it was her reoccurring nightmare—which prompted and nagged her into becoming an astrophysicist and then an astronaut!

"You're saying...my nightmare was *real?*" she gasped.

"Yes!"

"So...this is a 'Reptilian Utopia'? But how is our stopping the Asteroid about to obliterate *our* Earth any threat to them? Why do they want to stop us from saving ourselves?"

"Well, it has to do with..."

Suddenly an EXPLOSION knocked her and Ben to the floor. Looking up, she saw one of the giant metallic spiral-arrays swaying back and forth—*toppling* down toward them!

The surrounding crowd of dinosapiens scattered, *squealing* in fear!

And ZOOMING over and above them was a squadron of strange-looking jet aircraft, *THUNDERING* as they passed mere yards over the top of the peak!

Everything is so loud, so abrupt, so crisp and crackling around me! Can this be just a hallucination? I've never heard, felt, or seen anything so believable!

"There are factions that don't want you alive, Susan!" Ben said, throwing his cane to the side and tottering unsteadily to his feet. "They think the best way to solve the existential 'problem' is just to kill you! On the other side they were prevented from directly attacking you. But now you're here! That's a military space brigade from the Warrior Caste.   They're trying to destroy the whole complex. There'll be hell to pay for them attacking a Sanctuary of the High Priesthood, but apparently they're willing to risk it!"

Susan lurched to her feet and watched in horror as the squadron of weirdly shaped jets swung in an arc over the high Alpine mountain peaks, circling back for another run at them!

Absently, she was amused that they reminded her of the shapes of flying dinosaur pterodactyls—quite appropriate to a reptilian culture!

Susan observed that they weren't thrust along by a rear plume of fire as with a typical jet plane, rather "coasted" on a swarming yellow glow.   They were certainly unlike any "jets" she'd ever seen, powered on a completely new principle!

It was intriguing, fascinating.

But then her attention snapped back to their present imminent destruction.

"What do we do?"

"Come back to the Transport Pad!" Fred was frantically gesturing at her. "We'll send you back!"

"That's the only solution," Ben agreed, grabbing her arm and pulling her back toward the marble slab. "If you stay, you'll certainly be killed now or executed later.   Back on the other side you're protected. You've got to go!"

"But...?"

"Hurry!" the lizard yelled, its big oblong head bobbing up and down upon his long neck.

The distant attack jets were now tightly grouped together, rocketing back toward the peak...

"Alright, then—do it!" Susan said, still dazed and confused but beyond trying to deny whatever was happening.

She scampered over and flopped upon the top of the marble platform.

And as a shuddering series of more EXPLOSIONS began rocking the peak she felt a warm glow surrounding her.   The blue haze was reforming....

Then another tall spiral array above crashed over and *through* her!

Amazingly she was unharmed, ghost-like, as she felt herself *fading away...*

The last thing she saw was Ben's serenely confident, saint-like "Gandhi" face smiling gently at her as yet another explosion *swept* him from the peak!

"Goodbye, Ben," she whispered, closing her eyes. "You were a true friend, both in space and on the dinosaur planet. I guess...if any of this is real!"

For all she knew, the improbable fantasy was just the last squirt of adrenalin blasting her brain as she froze to death spinning out into space.

Bill King stood nervously in the Oval Office. He was stiffly standing beside Scott Nash.

Of course, Scott stood slanted forward at his waist, pushing Bill subtly into the background even though they were side-by-side. Bill resented Scott's positioning but knew it was pointless to protest. Scott was the "alpha" dog and he was just a member of Scott's pack. That was a reality to which Bill was resigned.

They were both dressed in politically correct conservative yet exquisitely tailored expensive suits. No casual sweat shirts or jeans were appropriate when you were publically initiating a series of multi-trillion dollar collaborations between industry, the scientific and military arms of multiple governments, and the leading academic institutions of the world.

Yes, the world was finally united in a last-ditch effort to save the planet.

His and Scott's present task was easy: to stand supportively behind the *President of the United States* along with other heads of various key agencies and institutions, as she tried to calm the rising tide of world-wide panic!

"*One minute*, President Swartz."

Casandra Swartz sat confidently behind the wide, warmly brown "Resolute Desk." Its wooden panels bespoke history, solidity, and determination. It was a gift from Queen Victoria to President Hayes in 1880. It had been crafted from lumber salvaged from the British vessel HMS Resolute, which had become trapped in ice attempting to explore the Arctic. Abandoned, it was subsequently found adrift by an American whaler, refitted by the United States government, and returned to Queen Victoria as a gesture of friendship. As such, it represented mutual support between governments for perilous expeditions of worldwide significance. When eventually decommissioned its parts were used for various purposes, including providing the wood for several commemorative desks. Never was there a more fitting symbol of a speech by a U.S. President on a global crisis and worldwide collaboration than the presidential Resolute Desk.

Indeed, President Swartz looked particular "resolute," sitting staring grimly into the camera lens. Her normally handsome face was sagging. Her usually sparkling blue eyes were watery and red. Her impeccably blond-dyed hair was showing its gray roots. In the last few months she'd visibly aged a decade.

She was looking more and more like her famous mother, Julia Schwartz, a past President of the United States of America. Her mother had gone into politics from science. So did her daughter. Casandra held a Ph.D. in economics, had taught at Harvard, was elected as comptroller of her state, and from there was elected governor. Then she'd gained her party's nomination and was elected President.

It was a long, arduous path. But she'd always managed to look fresh and young.

Now, she just looked old and tired.

There were two dozen other people lined up in addition to Bill and Scott, standing nervously behind and to each side of the desk. The camera was set at a wide angle to show all of them, before narrowing to the speaking President.

Bill recognized most of his fellow standing "affirmations" of the President's gigantic new project: captains of industry in smart suits, military leaders in dress uniform, religious leaders in full garb, Nobel Prize winners, and ambassadors from key allies. Bill was particularly impressed with General Cheryl S. Harclave, the present Chairman of the Joint Chiefs of Staff. She was a stone-faced woman with short-cut gray hair. She was a five-star general, an Army ranger who saw action in the African wars, who held a master's degree in international law.

She was directly overseeing *Star-Shield*, the massive project that the President was announcing—a trillion dollar collaboration mainly between Nashoba Energy and the U.S. military. Bill and the Board of Directors had teleconferenced with her on several occasions. Bill was impressed with her clear thinking and ability to focus to key factors inhibiting or blocking set goals. She was idealistic but ruthlessly practical. If anyone could ramrod this immensely powerful new weapon into outer space deployment, it was her.

"Thirty seconds."

Scott whispered to Bill: "Don't look so glum, buddy. This is a great day for us. Smile!"

Bill ignored his friend. Sure, they were getting a gigantic contract to supply the most compact and powerful weapon ever developed by mankind—but that incredible success was built upon the *corpse* of his dead sister, Susan.

He tried to push his grief to the side and concentrate on the occasion.

A lot had happened in the last four months. Despite heroically making it up to Hermes, the doomed Orion crew encountered escalating problems. Indeed, living up to Scott's predictions, the Hermes expedition to the Asteroid was fatally flawed. Communication with the crew was sporadic, finally ceasing altogether. Despite increasingly desperate attempts to contact them, Earth had heard nothing from them for several weeks. And now Earth's sophisticated off-world space-monitoring program was crumbling. Across the globe essential systems had fallen prey to the breakdown in societal order, implementation of martial law across the globe, and failure of fragile infrastructure. Mission Control no longer had the means to track the trajectory of Hermes. The last reliable reading was that Hermes was still on course to the Asteroid, but would rendezvous with it only a mere week before the massive rock smashed into Earth.

And what with the last reports from Hermes being of lethal radiation exposure, massive onboard system failures, and food and water shortages—it was doubtful anyone would be alive on the craft when it silently slipped past the Asteroid a week out from Earth.

So Bill had backed off from his covert investigation of Nashoba Energy. It didn't seem worth the effort. Even if there had been a conspiracy to stop Susan and the Hermes expedition, the company was now focused on a new plan to which everyone agreed.

Their goal was to *incinerate* the six-mile-long hurtling rock with a devastating explosive force ripped from the very heart of the sun!

At least that was the plan.

"...*two...one*...you're live!"

"My fellow Americans and citizens of the world," Schwartz began solemnly. "In this unprecedented period of turmoil and uncertainty, I bring you *hope!* Please don't give up. Do not give in to your lesser impulses. Instead, I ask you to rise to your highest aspirations!"

On a monitor screen at the back of the Oval Office, Bill saw the feed narrowing from a wide shot to just the face of the President. She looked undeniably earnest and determined.

"*Rioting, hording,* and *taking revenge* for historical wrongs will not save us! Rather, that will drag us down and insure our eventual if not immediate demise. In light of the unfortunate failure of the Hermes mission, I'm here today to lay out to you a specific plan for how we are going to stop the Asteroid from hitting Earth."

Simple declarative sentences started her talk: masterfully written to grab the attention of any listener. Now she launched into a fuller explanation...

"It is a joint plan, developed between the United States of America, Japan, and India using brand new technology. After the bombing and destruction of the United Nations Building by radical religious zealots, our other allies and friends are understandably difficult to contact and engage. But as those other nations are able to restore their societal order, I assure you that they will join in this joint effort. As we speak, the following steps are being taken..."

Bill's attention wandered away from the President's speech which she was reading from the teleprompter. He'd already gone through it several times, in fact provided a few technical clarifications. He was pleased to see that she and her advisors had accepted his improvements.

On the viewscreen at the back he saw that the feed had cut to an orbital platform. There, a structure the size of a football field was being assembled. Its metallic segments glittered brightly in the unfiltered sunlight. Floating toward or away from it were conventional delivery space vehicles. A flock of spacesuited individuals were peppered across the surface of a massive, growing Dish. The spacewalkers were busily installing necessary equipment and guidance systems.

"...components being assembled in near Earth orbit, for further deployment. The final vehicle will launch in time to encounter and block the Asteroid," Swartz continued. "We expect to stop the Asteroid while it is still safely outside the moon's orbit, where..."

The feed on the monitors widened. Bill saw himself and the other societal Leaders again shown standing behind and to each side of the wooden desk. And behind them were three high windows looking out onto the green trees of the Rose Garden. Gold drapes were drawnback to each side. Two flags hung officially before the drapes, a red-white-blue American flag and the President's Flag. Framed paintings were regally displayed off to the extreme sides. It looked very official and reassuring.

But Bill King knew differently.

Outside on the streets of Washington D.C. there were ongoing riots. A solid ring of National Guard troops protected the White House. All segments of society were breaking down. As delivery services were curtailed, overstretched resources dwindled. People suddenly found themselves and their families starving. Local order shattered. Police were overwhelmed. National armies were stretched thin. Even worse, religious zealots happily used the *End of the World* as their immediate excuse for taking power and imposing their particular beliefs. Across the globe, long-stable governments were toppling. In their place increasingly rigid, intolerant theocracies were rising.

"...so why not just launch our nuclear missiles at the Asteroid and blow the damned thing up?" the President was bluntly explaining. "Well, our scientists assure me that this approach—although emotionally satisfying—is not feasible. The Asteroid is too big and moving too fast for even a swarm of our intercontinental missiles to put a dent in it, let alone destroy it or knock it off course. And that's assuming the nuclear missiles could reach that far out into space, which they can't. And, most discouraging, if we could deliver the missiles to the Asteroid, the energy of the blasts would mostly dissipate uselessly in the vacuum of space. Instead, at the Nevada Test Site, starting today we are..."

As she continued her explanation, another preset scene was inserted showing an arid wasteland upon which sat a huge *hexagonal geodesic dome!* Compared to the tiny jeeps and soldiers—who looked like ants creeping around its bottom—the structure was *massive:* a sphere rising up to over *a thousand feet* in height! It spread across the equivalent of *thirteen football fields.*

Gleaming metal pillars and struts held the sphere aloft, fixed in place, suspended above the hot sands.

Black, glistening panels were fitted inside each alternating hexagonal space. The structure gleamed in the bright sunlight like a partially assembled alien spaceship—or a giant insect eye!

It was Bill and Scott's next destination, along with most of the other dignitaries present. President Schwartz was remaining in the heavily fortified White House, watching the proceedings safely from afar.

If this didn't work, it was Bill's last day on earth.

His radioactive atoms would be spread out across the Nevada desert.

Even though the room temperature was comfortable in the Oval Office, Bill felt sweat trickling from his brow. He didn't like deserts. They were much too hot for him. He preferred an air conditioned office, typing away at a keyboard.

But Scott would be there with him, smoothing out everything. All Bill had to do was "smile."

Bill wished Susan was there with him. She was talented at dealing with other people and complexities. Despite his revulsion at the secret manipulations of Nashoba against his sister, things would have been much simpler if she'd just joined the Company at its onset. Plus she didn't tolerate bullies. She'd have protected him from Scott.

But now she was likely just a frozen corpse on a dead spacecraft. And Bill was alone, frightened and scared of everything, particularly this giant new project. "Star Shield" was too ambitious and complex. Bill was terrified there was no way they could get it to work in time to save Earth.

At best it was just window-dressing looking out on the Apocalypse: the end of everything.

Bill suddenly felt icy cold. The President's speech ended as everyone present broke out into applause. Bill tried to smile approvingly as he mechanically beat his hands together. The desert would probably warm up his shivering body. His soul was another matter entirely.

Chapter 21

ICE

Frozen rocks

Capable of making water

Elixir of life sitting dormant

Ready to spring to action

Flowing as rushing rivers

Suffusing vast, churning seas

Evaporating into the skies

Drifting as fluffy clouds

Plummeting as rain or snow

Wreaking havoc as hard hail

Hurtling down as cannon balls

Smashing and destroying

Melting once more

Coming out of faucets

Filling up your glass

Guzzled happily

Merging into YOU...

Ain't that a kick?

The Minstrel's Lark, 21:172-177

IMPACT MINUS TWO MONTHS, *SIDETRACKED...*
Susan awoke in a panic, trying to get up but failing.

Then she stopped struggling, realizing that she was strapped firmly in place.

She was shocked to realize that she was completely *naked!*

Someone was leaning over her. It was hard for her to see who it was. Her vision was blurred. All she could make out was a looming presence.

"Ben?" she gasped, her throat dry. Her eyes were glued together, difficult to open...

"He spaced himself," a small metallic voice replied. "He's gone."

Blinking her eyes she saw the fogged-up faceplate of a spacesuit above her. The voice was coming from an external small speaker on the side of the helmet.

"Kame, is that you? Where are we? Why am I naked?"

"We're sealed inside SAV-1. I got Adri into SAV-2. I just finished decontaminating the living and working areas."

"Decontamination?"

"Those small mushrooms that you found were..."

"—yes, the red ones!" Susan interrupted her. "I *ate* one of them, Kame! Did it *poisoned* me?"

"You and the entire ship's environment," the spacesuited figure finished the thought. "They released clouds of neurogenic spores that zipped throughout the ship. Apparently the little buggers each carry a concentrated dose of a powerful hallucinogen—an effective plant strategy to get crazed animals to spread the seeds far and wide."

"Hallucinogen?"

"Adri was immediately affected. She insisted that angels were descending from heaven to carry her up into the arms of God. Actually it was just me in my spacesuit. She always seemed agnostic to me. However, apparently she had a strong Catholic upbringing as a child. And before she got her life together she even joined a cult for a couple years. Go figure."

"Then I didn't really...?"

"What?"

"I thought I got captured by an army of red lobsters and transported to another dimension. Intelligent dinosaurs were there trying to stop us from reaching the Asteroid!" Susan shuddered, overcome with the vivid horror still fresh in her mind.

Kame laughed in a kindly but hysteric way.

"Ah...yes, the classic '*talking velociraptors are out to get me*' paranoid delusion," Kame's tinny voice drifted from her helmet's external speaker. "Lucky I was sealed up in my suit waiting for you to return with Ben's body for me to immediately take down into the vacuum to freeze. I wasn't affected by the spores. When I figured out what was happening I isolated and restrained Adriana first. Then I retrieved you from the jungle Hab. You were completely delirious, smeared with the juice and spores of those damn red mushrooms. You were mumbling incoherently about talking dinosaurs. It wasn't difficult to figure out what happened to you. I isolated you here in SAV-1 after cleaning you up with alcohol wipes. The air filters in the SAV did the rest."

Delirious...right...that definitely made much more sense than being snatched away to another Earth where some of the dinosaurs weren't wiped out by an asteroid strike, instead evolving into "dinosapiens"!

My childhood nightmares, lurking at the edge of my conscious mind, were "made-manifest" by the mushroom's hallucinogen. Amazing!

Such detailed visions from the mushroom toxin! But they distracted from the immediate problems. Her head was still spinning. She needed to get reoriented, fast!

"So what now?"

"Well, I had to initiate a complete decontamination sequence outside the locked-down SAVs and..."

"You mean...?"

"Yes," Kame's disembodied voice glumly stated. "Everything loose has been flushed out of opened airlocks. I had to do this several times to get all the loose spores out. Then I exposed the remaining surfaces to intense ultraviolet radiation—according to set protocol—killing anything remaining. So now we're free of the spores. But our soil got ejected. All the plants—living or dead—were likewise thrown into space. We've lost our cabin air plus backup volumes used to flush the ship, plus the ship's ambient humidity. What remains of our liquid water, I divided between SAV-1 and SAV-2."

"So your plan to make it to the Asteroid...?"

"—is toast. Ben and those damn red mushrooms destroyed it. Our only hope now is for you and Johansson to make it to those comets and bring back a fresh supply of H_2O. If you succeed, the still-abundant power from our nuclear reactor can quickly manufacture additional fuel and oxygen. Perhaps we can reconstitute our soil to regrow edible plants. We've still got George's body to supply calories during the interim. While you were recovering from your bout of delirium I provisioned the SAVs as best I could. Also I transferred the nano-cable coil into SAV-1, connecting it into the extrusion delivery system. So you and Adriana are ready to go."

"You're not coming?"

"There's insufficient remaining water and air for the three of us in the SAVs, Susan. I'm not needed on the comet expedition. I'll stay here. Someone's got to remain in command of Hermes."

The normally implacable Commander sounded like she was about to start sobbing. However, Susan was shocked to find that it was *her* eyes starting to drip tears.

Suddenly Kame's white-gloved hand *slapped* Susan sharply on the side of her face!

"What'd you do that for?" Susan gasped. Her cheek stung badly.

"Get it together, King. We're at the outer edge of the encounter window that you previously calculated. If you and Adri don't launch in the next few minutes then everything's lost, understand? You have to keep your mind focused on the mission. Above all else, you've *got* to make it to that *Asteroid!* And now your path there detours through a swarm of *comets*. Got it?"

As Kame pulled the restraining straps free—allowing Susan to drift up out of the SAV's command chair—Susan nodded.

There were no more tears in her eyes.

"Of course...that's our mission, above everything else. Where are my clothes?"

"Spaced with the rest of the spore-contaminated trash," Kame shrugged, floating backward away from Susan. "There's a fresh jumpsuit and undies for you in the locker. I've programmed into your SAV the updated, putative comet-swarm coordinates. Get dressed and ready to separate from Hermes in twelve minutes. Once you're free from Hermes, you're in command of the side-expedition to the comets. You won't be able to communicate back to Hermes through our mangled antennae array. You'll be too far away for your weak intra-HAV communications to reach me. But I'm sure you won't need me. Do what you think's best. You're in command and I've got full confidence in you."

Kame continued floating backward to the closed airlock, yanking it open to start exiting the small craft.

"Kame!"

The spacesuited figure paused, looking back...

"Thanks, Commander. We'll make it back—three days, top!"

Kame curtly nodded. They both knew the consequences should the side-expedition fail. They'd be dead, along with their precious planet.

But Susan couldn't be distracted by the global consequences. Immediate concerns demanded her attention.

She floated the short distance to the main locker and pulled out underwear and a folded jumpsuit. As she hastily slipped them on she recalled something strange...

Susan hadn't mentioned any "velociraptors"—so how had Kame known?

Floating back to the console and frantically starting through the prelaunch sequence, Susan shook her head ruefully. It was probably just a coincidence—or maybe Kame heard her mutter the phrase during her delirium.

This was no time to renew her paranoid suspicions of Kame—Ben had confessed to everything! But Susan couldn't help feeling something was very, very wrong. Maybe it was just the lingering effects of the red mushroom's toxic juice, but "reality" didn't seem so "real" anymore.

It was like she was in a VR simulation, playing a 3-dimensional, interactive "virtual reality" game. The overall view was completely believable, but little things were...off!

"*Susan...do you read me?*"

It was a tinny voice coming over SAV-1's communications speaker.

Shaking her head to clear her jumbled thoughts, Susan touched a pad to reply to Johansson.

"Yes, I'm here, Adri. And I'm so sorry about those mushroom spores. They caught me completely by surprise! Kame's already done most of the pre-launch setup here. Are you ready to launch?"

"Yes, I am."

"Then we'll fly in formation, keeping within visual line-of-sight of each other. Agreed?"

"Affirmative."

"On my mark then, let's do it together...*three...two...one...* separation!"

Susan felt a *shudder* as clamps snapped back away from SAV-1, allowing the craft to drift free of Hermes.

Looking out one of her two portholes Susan saw the long stack of Hermes slipping past. Above her she spotted the hexagonal shape of SAV-2, glittering silver in the sunlight. Once they were out of blast range of Hermes, so there was no risk of damaging the mother vehicle, they'd fire their main jets.

They'd still be proceeding up beyond the planetary disc along with Hermes, traveling at better than 60,000 mph—just at a slightly different angle. The swarm of possible comets was traveling roughly parallel to the Asteroid, but lagging behind and lower. Other clusters existed of accompanying comets, but they were too far away. To reach their intended target-cluster, Susan and Adriana fortunately weren't departing from Hermes' path, just inserting a temporary separation-distance.

"SAV-1 orientation is complete, main engine powering up—how are you doing, Adri?"

"I'm ready also."

"Then main engines firing in...*three...two...one...*now!"

Red flames flared outside the porthole.

But as Susan saw Hermes slip away and behind she had a sinking feeling in the pit of her stomach that they were *abandoning* the mother vessel. While on it, as awful as the conditions had become, Susan knew she had a home.

Now she was leaving it behind, stuck inside a small tin can.

The SAVs couldn't make it back to Earth. They were intended for ferrying crewmembers from Hermes down to the surface of Mars or its moons, not for long space journeys. If they didn't make it back to Hermes they'd be dead, lost in space.

The burn seemed to go on forever. But then it finally cut off, leaving Susan again floating free in zero-G.

"*ETA?*" Adri's voice crackled from the speakers on their ship-to-ship communication.

Susan checked her readouts and 3D chart of overlapping vectors.

"We're both right on course, Adri. That was a good burn. Estimated time of arrival at the comets is 17 hours, 28 minutes, and 14 seconds."

"*Good. Then there's time for a nap. I'm still zonked from being so sick, plus my time up in 'heaven' with angels. I was actually sad to wake up back on Hermes. Heaven was so beautiful!*"

"Yes, Kame told me what happened to you. You go back to your heavenly dream, Adri. I'll start working on designing the optimal net configuration. We'll want to start weaving it soonest. I sure *don't* want to go back to where *I* was!"

"*Those were darn good mushrooms, Susan—very vivid hallucinations!*"

"Well, I must agree with the 'vivid' part," Susan spoke into the microphone. "I had the same feeling of relief behind "escaped" from Hermes' hell-hole. But I'm surprised to hear that you've done drugs before?"

"*Oh, that was years ago—long before I came to NASA,*" the crackling reply thoughtfully added. "*I had a few youthful adventures back in Sweden. Our drug laws there are very strict, but mainly on the supply side. The penalties for users are minimal, mainly mandated treatment programs. Anyway, I did a bit of experimenting before I settled down and went to college.*"

"Kame mentioned you'd been in a cult."

Susan heard Adriana laugh. "*Yes, that was where I did the drugs. It wasn't entirely stupid of me. I was thrashing about trying to get my spiritual bearings. The small religious group did, however, have some serious teachings that helped me.*"

"Like what?"

"*Well, they were a branch of a primitive religion called 'Interactive Animists.' Animism teaches that all things possess spiritual Essence. The 'interactives' said that we can combine our essences to bring about collective spiritual intelligences outside of our actual minds.*"

"Fascinating!"

"*And the drugs were used to enhance this process...but, like all cults, it was mostly just an excuse to get high and have unfettered sex.*"

"And?"

"*Just like today, Susan, it all was way too intense and distracting! Dealing with Reality is tough enough without the temptation of slipping away into a make-believe world of consequence-free pleasure. After a few experiments I swore them off completely—that is, except for an occasional double-chocolate cake with vanilla ice cream on top!*"

"Good for you," Susan laughed. "When we get back to Earth it'll be my treat. We'll both 'pig-out' together. Is that allowed in your Animist religion?"

"*Oh, I'm long past that distraction, Susan. I'm more of an agnostic now than anything else.*"

"So milkshakes are ok?"

"*I'm absolutely looking forward to them when we get back to Earth. So give me a wake-up call in, say, four hours, ok?*"

"Sure. That gives us plenty of time to make any further course corrects before we reach the swarm."

"*And remember we'll need time to configure and string the net between our two spaceships. That's going to be a real trick.*"

"Well, you're the expert pilot Adri. That'll be mostly on you. But you're correct—we need to accomplish as much as possible before we encounter the comets. We've no time to waste getting back to Hermes. We left Kame with hardly any oxygen or water."

"*Can't she make more from the remaining hydrogen and CO_2 stores?*" Adri asked.

"Yes, she probably could. But then there'd be no fuel left for Hermes' upcoming course corrections. Remember, we were going to redirect the fuel from the SAVs for that critical purpose, which we're burning up right now! She didn't say it, but I think she'll leave Hermes' hydrogen fuel untouched for us to use for course corrects when we return—in case we don't find any additional water sources."

That was a depressing thought. Best not to dwell on it.

"*How much air does she have in her suit and the emergency canisters?*"

"As best I can figure, enough for three days."

"*So we've a day to get to the comets, a day to capture one, and then a day to get back?*"

"Roughly."

"*Kame's tough. She'll be alive and kicking when we return.*"

Susan hoped that was true, both parts: that they'd get back and that Kame would be there alive and well.

Kame was an irritating nag, but also brilliant. Without a flight engineer while out of communication with experts on Earth, Susan and Adriana by themselves would be in bad shape on Hermes. They needed Kame.

"Have a good nap, Adri. Give my best to God!"

Adriana snorted in reply: "*I just want a peaceful sleep, not Nirvana. You should rest also, Susan. I'm sure those mushrooms did a job on you as well.*"

"I'm too keyed up, Adri. I'll figure out the optimal net configuration for the nano-cable. You sleep!"

Susan cut off the communication, stifling an unexpected sob. She'd felt cut off from Earth on Hermes, but always had her crewmates. Now she was all by herself in a small tin can, floating in the vastness of outer space. If anything went wrong, she'd be lost forever in the icy void.

And she wouldn't last long in the small transport vehicle. The sophisticated air and water recycling equipment—plus the extensive farm of Hermes—was absent from the SAV. In the SAVs Susan and Adriana had to rely completely on stored water, air, and packaged food. Both SAVs were normally equipped to handle a crew of three for a week. But they'd had to appropriate the stored SAV stocks for Hermes once things went south in the main vehicle. In fact, Susan realized she should do a quick check of the supplies to make sure that she could even survive the three-day side trip.

"Alright, then," Susan sighed to herself. "Kame said she stocked us up, transferring in our remaining water. She must have split it between the two SAVs."

Yes, the water tank showed a gallon for her and probably the same for Adri. It still wasn't much. But with rationing it might last for three days.

"And what about air?" she asked herself.

Ah, yes. There was plenty of air. Ten canisters were stored below. But...those *weren't* the SAV canisters! No, they were the emergency canisters that should have been distributed throughout the living areas of Hermes!

Kame had given them all Hermes' air. After flushing the ship out several times, all the air the Commander had left on Hermes was what remained in her suit's tank. There was no way that Kame could survive until they returned.

Susan was shocked to realize whether or not they made it back to Hermes, Kame was as good as dead.

"How many are we setting off at once?"

"Just one—but it's a 100 megaton bomb. That'll test the system. It'll be the largest fusion explosion ever set off above ground. If it works as expected, we might choose subsequently to set off multiple bombs at once to increase the capture-yield even further."

"The largest above-ground test was the TSAR bomb, right?"

"Yes, that was 50 megatons, dropped as a test by the Soviets in 1961. It completely destroyed everything within a fifteen mile radius."

"And our bomb is *twice* as large?"

"That's right."

"And we're only *five* miles from the explosion site?"

"That's also correct."

"So...are we safe?"

"If the extraction system works as predicted then we're perfectly safe. There won't even be a detectable increase in radiation in the air outside our command bunker."

The small group of dignitaries inside the bunker looked none too reassured. Bill was nervous himself. What they were attempting was unprecedented. But the survival of the planet depended upon it. It *had* to work!

"Still, for an untested, proprietary technology...?" the speaker continued to complain.

"Half the world is now powered by SB technology," General Harclave patiently replied. "Although our friends in Nashoba Energy still insist upon retaining their proprietary secrecy on the methodology, there is no denying that vast amounts of energy can now be reliably stored and contained within comparatively tiny devices. In this manner we've harvested and mobilized many different energy sources previously unusable for heavy lift capacities."

"But nothing on this order of magnitude has...?"

"Or course we've conducted preliminary tests that..."

"—of nuclear explosions?"

"No, but our simulations..."

"I want *out* of here!" the questioner suddenly screamed, turning and running for the exit.

It was the Russian Ambassador. He'd been exiled in the United States when Russia sank into chaos due to the Chechen-Sunnis alliance. He hadn't wanted to be present today. The President had forced him to come as a show of global unity. Clearly, he was panicking.

A burly guard immobilized him, efficiently applying cuffs and a gag, then moving him into a corner.

Bill was impressed that none of the military or industrial technicians even looked up from their consoles during the brief commotion. Bill stood high on his tiptoes and looked out the narrow slit that directly revealed the actual desert outside. Although he was looking through three feet of tempered transparent glasteel, the distant *Sphere* was obvious and ominous—seeming to waver back and forth due to hot air rising up off the plateau.

"...so please make yourselves comfortable," the General concluded. "There are refreshments in the canteen. The detonation is in thirty seven minutes. If you'd like to sit in the gallery there are dark goggles at each chair, just in case the glare is more than predicted. You'll be looking out of the glasteel slit. Otherwise you're welcome to stand around and watch over the monitors."

She turned and walked away.

"This is very impressive, Dr. King. I congratulate you on this magnificent application of your invention."

Bill turned around to see the Ambassador from India holding out a hand to him. Tentatively, Bill took the man's hand, staring into the deep brown eyes of Ambassador Rahul Priyanka. He was an older gentleman wearing a traditional Nehru jacket that was white and ornate. It fell to his upper calves, buttoned, with ornate weave, and was embellished with a chain of hanging white pearls. On his head was a white straight cap, which blended with the short white hair to each side of his head. He was lean and trim, distinguished-looking.

"I don't believe we've met before?"

"Not formally, that's true. But I've been aware and impressed with the research of both you and your father. Indeed—in a modest way—I helped support Dave King's work over the years."

"Did you?"

"Yes, small anonymous donations. He never knew where they came from. Though I went into politics, I have a similar interest in accessing subspace depots."

"But...that was never a focus of his research. He and I were working on discredited cold fusion. It was Scott's innovations in high-temperature superconductivity that linked us into what's come to be known as 'trans-dimensional' energy storage: hording energy into a subspace 'pot.'"

"Yes, that's true," the Ambassador agreed. "It was a fortuitous congruence, common to the history of major scientific breakthroughs. And it may well save the world. At all costs, that damn Asteroid must be *disintegrated!* It must never be a threat to the world, *ever again!*"

Bill was wary. That was a peculiar way to state the obvious. And the Ambassador had that same look that Scott got from time-to-time: an unblinking, cold stare that seemed to look beyond the superficial to a deeper reality.

Actually, to Bill he looked like a predator eyeing his prey—targeted destruction driven by absolute hunger!

Jesus, what was happening to him? Bill felt like he was going crazy—mentally labelling an Ambassador as a soulless predator.

But, then again, everyone was on the edge. The whole future of the Earth hung in the balance.

"Well, I'm glad to have met you."

"It's too bad about Hermes, though."

Bill thought he saw a tear in the corner of the lean Ambassador's eye.

"Yes, my sister was..."

He paused, the Ambassador's name ringing a bell in his head. "But...wasn't another one of the crew from India?"

The Ambassador lowered his eyes, silent for a moment.

"He is my grandson, Benjamin Priyanka," he quietly replied. "I'm sure he did his duty on Hermes. But that was a longshot at best—attempting to rendezvous with a giant rock hurtling at us 60,000 mph to then nudge from its path. I tried to dissuade NASA from the attempt, to focus on the present project. But they insisted on making the effort. So my government wanted at least an Indian representative aboard, someone we trusted implicitly. My grandson, already at NASA, was the obvious choice. But, sadly, all that effort was for nothing. I only hope the Hermes expedition did not delay Star-Shield for too long. As it is, we're cutting it very short to..."

"But as I'm sure you know, Ambassador," Bill cut him off, trying not to sound impatient, "the Super-Batteries can't function too far beyond the moon's orbit. The energy depots they draw from—fixed as they are in Earth's gravity well—would be too distant. So we couldn't hope to impact the Asteroid any earlier than we're presently attempting to do so."

The Ambassador seemed ready to launch into an argument, his face starting to redden, when a *tall, elegant Japanese woman* suddenly intervened.

It was Atsuko Kiromura, the Japanese Ambassador.

She was a stern-faced woman with high-drawn eyebrows, red-slicked lips, and dyed black hair. With the heavy makeup from afar she seemed to be a young woman. But close up the sag lines under her eyes betrayed her true age. She was dressed in a smart purple jacket over a blue-brown blouse, wearing black pants.

"The Hermes expedition may still succeed. They have time."

"Ah...Madam Ambassador," Priyanka politely nodded. "I fear that my grandson and your niece are, sadly, dead. They made a noble effort, but too much stood in their path for..."

"Too much, indeed!" the Japanese Ambassador snapped angrily back at him.

Bill was getting confused. What was happening here? The lean, aristocratic Indian and the well-kept older Japanese woman obviously knew each other. That made sense because they were both Ambassadors to the U.S.A. But there was something more. Was it a deep *animosity?*

"Do you both, uhm, know something I don't?" Bill hesitantly asked. "Has there been word from Hermes?"

"No, none," Priyanka snapped, starting to turn away. "They're gone."

"Absence of proof is not proof of absence," Kiromura snarled right back at him.

"Well, I hope you are right, Madam Ambassador," Bill intervened. Emotions were too raw. They didn't need any further fights! "Regardless, the Star-Shield is a good failsafe plan for..."

"The gentleman is correct," Priyanka huffed, jumping back into the conversation. "If Hermes somehow gets to the Asteroid with crew intact then they'd only have several days left before entering the moon's orbit. And from there it'll be only a mere 7.7 hours until it slams into Earth. There will be no time for the Hermes crew to do anything significant, even if despite all appearances they survive the trip. Star-Shield *must* be in place!"

She hesitated, seeming to contain a great fury within her. Then her clenched fists relaxed.

"Of course...you're right, Ambassador," she mildly replied, turning away. "Star-Shield is absolutely necessary."

"WOULD EVERYONE PLEASE TAKE YOUR SEATS?" a loudspeaker suddenly broke through the various conversations. It was the General directing them from the control center. "THE DETONATION IS TWELVE MINUTES AWAY. ALL SYSTEMS ARE NOMINAL."

Bill followed Scott up into the back balcony from which they could directly look through the thick glass of the three-foot-high slit out onto the desert plateau. He started to put on the dark goggles hanging from the arm of the chair...

"You won't need those," Scott insisted. "A few photons will escape through the alternate opened panels in the hexagonal structure which allows concussive flexibility. But virtually all the energy will be absorbed into subspace via our panels. It's nothing to worry about. Plus we've got reporters watching and recording us, buddy—if we, the top officials in Nashoba, look scared, then they might get spooked as well."

Reluctantly, Bill lowered the goggles. He didn't have Scott's absolute faith, indeed wouldn't be surprised if in a few minutes they and their protective bunker were incinerated! But as always he gave-into Scott's demands, keeping the goggles in his trembling hands. Around him, most of the rest of the observers were putting the dark goggles on their heads. Bill hoped Scott was right. Otherwise—even if they somehow survived the massive nuclear explosion—he'd be blind!

"FIVE MINUTES TO DETONATION."

"God, I hate countdowns," Bill muttered under his breath.

This was it. In a handful of minutes they'd find out if *Star-Shield* was a viable idea or a terrible disaster. As if the enormity of the moment had also sunk into the rest of the observers, everyone stopped talking. They waited in silence, counting down the seconds...

Ambassador Kiromura settled into a seat right next to Bill. Apparently disdainful of the example of the others, she also left her goggles dangling from the chair's arm.

"I hear that your sister is a lovely woman," she whispered in Bill's ear. "I pray that she is fine on Hermes, nobly persisting onward."

"Thank you," he whispered back. "I hope the same for your countrywoman. NASA trains them well. I'm sure they are doing everything possible to survive and complete their mission."

Yep, he was getting very smooth as a diplomat. It took a lot out of him to deal with the complexities of human polite interactions. But he was getting quite good at lying.

In less than a minute I'll be joining you in death, Suzy—Bill fatalistically thought to himself. *That's not too long to wait to escape all these problems and headaches. I guess I can hang on until then...*

"ONE MINUTE AND COUNTING...60...59...58..."

Unexpectedly she grabbed Bill's hand and clung tightly to him. She was gripping his hand so tight it hurt! But he bit back a rebuke, just patted her thin hand with his other free one.

He wished he was back in Sulphur, Oklahoma, piddling away with his Dad looking for a few stray neutrons and gamma rays.

He feared that they were about to be *drenched* in an inferno of excess hard radiation!

"...10...9...8...7..."

To hell with the cameras—Bill thought as he tightly closed his eyes, turning his head away.

"...3...2...1..."

A bright FLASH penetrated his eyelids as he felt the entire command bunker *shudder* beneath him.

Opening his eyes, blinking, he saw five-miles-distant the immense geodesic sphere was *still standing* above the hot sands of the desert!

"Yes! It did it! It worked! It absorbed 100 megatons of energy!" Scott *whooped*, surging up out of his seat and dancing around in a circle.

"That...is good," Kiromura sighed as she released her death-grip on Bill's hand.

He gratefully pulled it away from her, unobtrusively flexing it. The knuckles of his mashed hand had turned white.

"—AND THAT IS ONLY THE START," General Harclave loudly continued over the loudspeaker. "WE'LL BE DOING A PROJECTED TEN DETONATIONS PER DAY, CONTINUALLY LOADING THE PANELS. SOON WE'LL BE DOING MULTIPLE DETONATIONS FIRED SIMULTANEOUSLY. HALF OF THE U.S. NUCLEAR ARSENAL WILL BE FED INTO THE PANELS. LIKEWISE, INDIA IS DONATING HALF OF THEIR ATOMIC BOMBS. INTACT PARTS OF THE NEW SOVIET FEDERATION HAVE ALSO PROMISED TO..."

Bill stopped listening, emotionally exhausted.

Well hell...I guess I have to keep on living, for a bit.

He dully watched Scott basking in the relieved congratulations and handshakes from the other dignitaries and guests. He had a wide smile that revealed his sparkling white teeth. His easy arrogance cast a confident, charismatic charm on those around him.

"We must save humanity!"

"What?"

Leaning close to him was the earnest face of Kiromura. She had a wild look in her eyes, almost hysterical!

"Uh...sure...of course."

"You *must* do what is necessary, Bill King," she whispered in his ear. "*Remember!*"

Bill watched in silence as she abruptly turned away and slid through the crowd. What the hell was she saying? Every word she'd just spoken was redundant!

But then again, she was the only one of these people willing to give Susan and Hermes even a hint of success. Yes, of course, Bill knew he had to do "what was necessary." But her warning was more than just doing the minimal. Somehow he felt reenergized. He viscerally felt a renewed need to *get to the bottom* of what was going on at Nashoba! The Japanese woman had rekindled his nagging curiosity. Even if Susan was already dead, this must be done for her—to honor her memory!

After all, she was *his* sister: *"The Girl Who Wrangled Asteroids!"*

At least that was what she'd told him her fellow graduate students at college labelled her. And, since her presumed death on the doomed Hermes expedition, her infamy had turned to grudging respect by the mass media, who publically labelled her with the same epitaph. Wow...she was something, alright. While others were out partying, going on dates, getting married and having children—she was searching the skies for asteroids and comets, *capturing* them in exquisite detail in her instruments. And then she actually went into space hunting them!

Susan King was either crazy or possessed—or both!

And Bill King desperately hoped that despite all evidence to the contrary, she was still alive.

Chapter 22

<u>GHOST ROCKS IN THE SKY</u>

A young gal went out soaring

High up into outer space

And in her spaceship she drifted

As she heard a mournful cry

It was herself a-howling

Reverberating her pain

As she looked to see the herd

Of ice balls zooming by

Remnants from primordial clouds

That formed the solar system

Ancient ghosts from eons past

5-billion years a-sleeping

Now at last fully awake

Leaping way up on high

Laughing, jeering, screaming

Wagging growing icy tails

Saying: "Catch me if you can!"

"Yippee-yi-ay, yippee-yi-o"...

Ghost Rocks in the sky!

The Minstrel's Lark, 22:31-35

IMPACT MINUS SEVEN WEEKS SIX DAYS, *HUNTING...*

"How many do you see, Adri?"

"*My radar scans pick up approximately twenty,*" her voice rang out through SAV-1's speakers.

"Yes, I've got nineteen on my scope that register larger than a small car. I also see a number of fainter blips that could be boulder-sized."

Through the small porthole of SAV-1 the comets were still too distant to be seen by the naked eye against the blackness of space. But the radar scans were definitely picking up a loose swarm just where they were supposed to be. Susan was hopeful.

"But what if they're just stray rocks?" Adriana asked over the speakers, sounding worried.

"I'm initiating a spectrographic analysis of their composition," Susan replied, running separate graphs for each of the larger blips. "I brought my own program that I developed back in my postdoc research days. The radar equipment on my SAV, of course, doesn't compare to what I used when analyzing the asteroid belt from Earth, but here we're close! We'll quickly know if there's any H_2O present—and approximately how much."

"Should we start stringing the net?"

"Start edging over to me, Adri. We'll get the nano-cable strung between us. We've still got four hours until we reach the swarm. I've got the optimal inter-ship weave sequences figured out, but the specific target will determine the final configuration. If our comet is bigger then we'll need a looser, larger web pattern. But if we're sweeping up random icy boulders then we'll have to make the net weave smaller and tighter."

"Roger that," Adriana answered. *"I'll be floating right next to you in five minutes."*

The spectral scans were accumulating data on each of the blips. Susan kept an eye on the growing data streams for each of the distant blips while also looking out the porthole to the side of her spaceship. Brief white bursts against the blackness of space indicated Adri was edging SAV-2 ever closer. Meanwhile, the graphs on the computer screen were detailing the spectroscopic analysis of each of the blips: with separate lines for percent-total methane, ammonia, carbon dioxide, hydrocarbons, and—most importantly—water ice.

One blip's graph in particular was showing a high percentage—nearly half of the reflective surface—of possible water ice.

"I'm closing in for grappling," Adriana's calm voice came from the speakers.

Startled, Susan realized she'd been focusing too intently on the graphs. SAV-2 was hanging just a dozen feet outside the porthole!

"Ready for grappling," Susan hastily replied, punching in the necessary commands for solid hooks to emerge from recesses on the exterior of SAV-1 along one of its eight flat sides.

She heard two solid "thunks" as grappling arms from SAV-2 grabbed tightly into the hooks. A soft "whirr" sounded as motors in both crafts pulled the latches inward, clamping the two crafts firmly side-to-side.

"Successful docking!" Adriana happily stated.

Susan looked out one of the two opposing portholes of SAV-1 to see Adri peering back from one of hers. Susan grinned, waving—as Adri waved back. Wow! Maybe they were still going to be lost in outer space forever, but this was a minor moment of triumph!

"How are our celestial 'water tanks' looking?"

"We'll know better when we're closer and can directly observe them, Adri," Susan replied into the ship's microphone, looking again at the accumulating data. "But one of them looks very interesting. It has a mass ten times that of one of Hermes' water tanks, roughly the volume of a medium-sized one-family house. So it may have sufficient water while not being too large for us to capture. The ultraviolet spectral-graph of the surface's reflectivity shows twenty percent frozen methane, ammonia, and carbon dioxide. Half of the rest of the surface is likely just rocks and dust."

"And the rest of the surface?"

"Thirty five percent of the total surface looks to be water ice! The rest is an assortment of other elements that..."

"So is that our target?"

"Yes, Ma'am, I do believe it is! So it's what we're going to weave a net to 'catch'—even though we'll not make the final decision until we arrive and can examine it visually."

"Your analysis sounds great, Susan."

"So far so good...but it's just surface reflectivity, Adri. It still might be a big solid rock with just a thin coating of ice and other frozen gases. That's not likely, though, from what we know of objects from the distant Oort Cloud—they should be mostly legitimate 'dirty-ice' comets. But prepare to be disappointed. We may have to search through the whole swarm, object by object."

"How will we know for sure?"

"I brought a unit for generating strong ground-penetrating radar. Kame was prescient enough to load it onto SAV-1. To get it to work, though, we'll need to be right on top of the comet. It is useless from this distance. It was intended for analyzing the Asteroid once we arrive there, but it will work just as well on these stray comets. It will give us confirmation if the water ice I'm reading is throughout the comet or only present as a superficial layer."

"Super! So when do we start weaving?"

"I'll thread the nano-cable to you across the linked conduit. Then I'll transmit the general instructions for our subsequent 'dance'! Once we're set to start the weave you can back off from the hooks."

"Am I leading or are you?"

"Are you kidding, Adri? I'm the stumble-footed student and you're the expert dance-instructor. My job is to keep one end of the cable firmly attached and spooling out to you while you zip in and out of the threads between us, anchoring it onto our protruded titanium hull hooks. I'll be counteracting the pulling-forces while keeping the growing net steady, while you do all the hard work."

"Sounds fun!"

"Then let's get to it."

Two hours later a glittering, woven net hung loosely in the gap between the two hexagonal-sided vehicles. The two SAVs were flying in formation two hundred feet from each other. Adriana's task was to stay close enough to keep the net loose such that the diamond-hard lines wouldn't slice through the non-titanium components, destroying their own ships, while far enough away to keep the net open and untangled. It was precision flying for sure, since they were now traveling in excess of 65,000 mph, fast-approaching the similarly speeding swarm of comets.

Indeed, Susan could now just make out the "dirty ice" rocks in the distance, glittering against the blackness of space. She'd expected them to be dispersed so widely that they'd have to search for a single specimen. Instead, they were clustered close together—perhaps remnants of a much larger body that the Asteroid had smashed through exiting from the Oort cloud.

Whatever, as the two crafts approached the sedately spinning objects Susan saw them rapidly growing. The largest hung in space before them like a giant boulder, fully the size of a large house!

"Careful, Adri," Susan cautioned, firing forward jets to slow their approach as she mirror her maneuvers.

They drifted up behind their target. It was twenty times as large as Susan's spacecraft. But it wasn't the snow-white ice ball she'd intuitively expected. Instead, it looked like a dirty giant rock hanging there in space. Around it Susan noticed a faint haze, its "coma" or atmosphere, composed of loose dust grains and gases. Susan could just make out the beginnings of two tails starting to stretch behind it, opposite to the still-distant sun below: a faint yellow dust tail and a distinctly whiter one made up of sublimated ions.

"I thought comets had big, long, thick tails?" Adriana asked from Susan's intercom, puzzled.

"It's not yet close enough to the sun for serious sublimation of the frozen gasses to occur," Susan answered. "We're still roughly parallel to Earth's orbit, far away from the sun. If this swarm swings on past Earth and inward, these rocks will become full blown comets as they approach the sun, with tails stretching out for miles. Big comets, the size of the Asteroid we're after—miles across—can have tails that are *millions* of miles long!"

"So does it have enough water ice for us?"

Yes, that was the key question. Susan needed to suppress her fascination with the space-object and focus on their immediate goal.

"Hold on a second…" Susan replied. "I just engaged the ground-penetrating radar."

Yes! Yes! Yes!

"Well? Do we snag it or look for another?"

"It's porous inside, Adri—much like the 2016 readings from the Rosetta Mission taken of comet 67P/Churyumov-Gerasimenko! But the differentials show that the rock here *is* riddled with ice flows, like frozen lava inside a dead volcano. Instead of being depleted of its frozen gases by continually swinging in past the sun—like the Rosetta Mission's comet back in 2016—this is likely a 'virgin' headed into the planetary disc for the first time. It's perfect for us, fully loaded with frozen, primordial gases!"

"So is there enough water here to fill Hermes' empty tanks?"

"There should be plenty, Adri—more than enough! Of course we'll have to 'mine it,' hacking out chunks to run through our liquid-recycling system to purify the H2O and get rid of the other frozen gases—but that shouldn't take long. Within a couple days of our return we should have water flowing into our dry storage tanks. We'll just have to do re-plumbing and expansion of the recycling system so that..."

"Then let's wrap it, snag it, and snatch it away!"

"Yes, you're right, Adri," Susan nodded in agreement, again trying to focus her drifting thoughts. She needed to keep sharp. Her mind, sleep-deprived and woozy to start with, was getting way too mushy! "We can figure out the details later."

"So how do you want to proceed?"

"I think similar to weaving the net. I'll stay stable on one side of the comet while you drag the net around to the other side. You encircle it completely with the net before grappling back with SAV-1. Then we cinch it tight and together pull it back to Hermes."

Well, that sounded straight forward. Of course, nothing's ever as simple as one imagines. They had to stay ready for unpleasant surprises...

"Aye, aye, Captain!"

Susan saw SAV-2 fire its steering jets, precisely slipping to the side and out-of-sight behind the looming wall of the comet, trailing the loosely glittering net behind it. Then Susan felt SAV-1 jerked to the side as the nano-cable net cut into the surface of the slowly spinning giant rock. Quickly she let out slack from the spool inside SAV-1. Fortunately they still had miles of the tiny thread to play with. It was going to work!

"Uh, oh..."

"What's wrong, Adri?"

"The net's caught on some jagged edges," Adriana replied. *"It looks like this big hunk got hit by something in the past that..."*

Her voice cut off.

"Adri?"

Nothing.

"Adri, what's happening? Answer me!"

"Sorry...the net's gotten tangled—I can't proceed further...I'm trying to back off, loosen it."

"Be careful! Those threads can slice through your SAV's skin like a knife through butter!"

"I am well aware of that fact, Susan, thank you very much. I am proceeding very gently..."

"Don't pull it tight!"

"I'm just brushing back against it. That should loosen the snags but not cause the lines to sink into anything delicate..."

"Be careful!"

"Oh, rats...I think I just made it worse...most of the net is snarled down into a deep ravine—we'll never get the comet surrounded and controlled now!"

"Then we'll cut the net loose and try again!"

"But that'll take too long! We've only a day to make it back! Kame's on tight rations as it is, and..."

"We've got no choice, Adri. We have to get this thing corralled. We can't pull the comet back to Hermes unless it's secured to the SAVs!"

"I really screwed this up."

"It wasn't your piloting, Adri," Susan sighed, trying to reassure Adriana while coming up with a realistic new plan. "I see now I was too enthusiastic. I made the net too complex, so that it easily snags. Seeing the rock here 'in person' I realize what we actually need is overlapping lines 'wrapped' around the comet, not a pre-woven net. But we've still got plenty of nano-cable on the spool. I'll cut the net loose at this end, pull free from it, and come around to help you."

"I'm stuck to the comet, Susan. When I pushed backward the net nudged up and wrapped around me. You'll have to do a spacewalk to free SAV-2. But we don't have enough air for an extended space-walk and still make it back to Hermes!"

"Yes, we do, Adri. Kame gave us a reserve supply."

"What?"

Susan gulped deeply before replying, trying to keep her voice from trembling as she drifted free from the pilot chair and over to the spacesuit locker.

"I didn't see them until after we departed. But she gave us all the emergency tanks from the Habs. They're split between our two SAVs, in our storage compartments."

"But that means...?"

"Yes, she's likely dead by now. She knew something like this might happen. She sacrificed herself for the good of the mission, Adri. We've got to honor her commitment and focus on the task at hand."

"Oh...oh, my...of course..."

Susan removed the molecular diamond cutter device from the spacesuit locker and floated over to the ejection tube. With a "snip" she cut the almost invisible thread. She carefully watched as the freed end pulled into the conduit and vanished into space. The tension at SAV-2 caused the thread to snake through the outer hooks as well. Satisfied that SAV-1 was loose from the nano-cable, she went back to the pilot's chair. On her navigation screen she saw the mountainous slope of the comet blocking out the stars. With tiny spurts of her maneuvering jets she nudged SAV-1 up to the side and over the top.

And there was SAV-2, on its side, mushed up against a deep gash in the side of the comet. A glittering web covered SAV-2.

"You weren't exaggerating, Adri—it's a mess!"

"There's an electrostatic charge out there," Adri's scared voice came over the speaker. *"The filaments are writhing! They're both repelled and attracted to each other along various planes. If you're doing a spacewalk you'll have to be careful not to touch anything. You've got the only spacesuit between the two of us. I won't be able to go out to rescue you!"*

Oh man, it should have been simple. But that was what real-world experiments do: show you the problems you couldn't or didn't anticipate.

"Ok, then, Adri. Don't move SAV-2. I'll cut you free."

Susan steadied SAV-1 with her jets, trying to position it motionless alongside the comet. But the comet was slowly spinning, which meant that intricate piloting was necessary. Even tethered to SAV-1,

Susan would be in imminent danger of being pulled away or pushed into the dangerously charged net. She only had small jets in her standard backpack. She couldn't go zipping around the comet!

"Adri, since we're this close can you link-into and pilot SAV-1 remotely while I'm outside?"

"That's an affirmative, Susan. We're certainly close enough now for tight, coupled transmission. You do the cutting. I'll keep everything else steady."

It was a plan. Theoretically they could accomplish it in an hour. But in reality it wound up taking a half day of delicate work. Susan had to suit up, exit the airlock, tether to SAV-1, float around SAV-2 delicately snipping the almost invisible webbing, finally free up SAV-2, and then go back inside and crawl out of her spacesuit.

Having finished her task, Susan was totally exhausted, barely able to keep her eyes open. She just managed to drink some of the remaining precious water, eat a couple of their last dry packaged energy wafers, and then curl up in the pilot's chair, strapping herself in place.

"Wake me in four hours, Adri," Susan muttered into the microphone. "I can't do anything else until I've rested."

"You and me both, Susan," Adriana replied from the intercom. *"I'm setting the automatic pilots to keep both of us roughly alongside the comet. I've got to get some sleep myself."*

"We'll finish this in a few hours..."

But it was longer than a few hours.

Both Susan and Adri—totally exhausted—slept through their set alarms for an uninterrupted ten hours. When they awoke they regrouped and figured out a new plan. Laying a fresh length of the nano-cable took yet another full day of work, slowly circling the comet to wrap it up in a progressively overlapping ball of the tiny thread.

Susan's job was the same as before, maintaining SAV-1 relatively motionless beside the comet—as Adriana expertly pulled the lengthening nano-cable around and around the big rock in a precise pattern designed to tie the comet snuggly to both SAVs.

Simultaneously, Adriana's SAV was conducting an exquisitely detailed multispectral penetrating scan of the comet to a few meters depth. Once they returned to Hermes they'd not have the time to do a leisurely study of each millimeter of the comet. They'd have to harvest the best sections for immediate processing inside Hermes.

Susan watched SAV-2 trailing its glittering thread around and around the comet. It was agonizingly slow, delicate work. Finally, though, SAV-1 and SAV-2 were back grappled firmly together. One side of both of the joined spacecraft was jammed flat upon the rough surface of the comet. Thus their small steering jets could work in unison, counteracting the spin of the comet to place it in optimal position for then firing the SAV main jets simultaneously.

The two airlocks were free of obstructions, situated at the forward ends of the SAVs. To the rear of the SAVs, the main rockets were likewise free. Fortunately the single main rockets were designed to "gimbal" so that the angle could counteract the momentum of the large rocky mass snuggly held by the nano-cable to the side of the combined spacecraft.

Adriana—using the small steering jets of both SAVs—carefully nudged the comet into the exact vector required. Then she fired the main rockets in unison, altering their forward path to tilt back downward toward Hermes.

And there—satisfyingly being dragged along with them—was their big house-sized ball of dirty ice!

Susan saw Adriana waving through the opposing porthole of SAV-2, then pumping her fist up in the air.

"Hey, we got it, Susan! Finally the Universe is cutting us a break! We wrangled a comet! Yippee!"

Susan wanly smiled back, too tired to wave.

"How soon until we rejoin Hermes?"

"Twenty-three hours, fourteen minutes, six seconds!"

"Right...a full day behind schedule..."

They both fell silent, sobered, realizing what they'd find on their return.

Susan couldn't celebrate. Sure, the Universe was giving them a comet—but in the same motion it had taken away their chief engineer. Kame was no doubt dead. There was no way that she could have survived on the depleted resources of the mothership.

The Universe was a cruel bitch!

Or—to put it into poor, dead Ben's Hindu religious terminology—both *Brahma* the Creator and *Vishnu* the Preserver were bowing together to *Shiva* the Destroyer.

Even the noblest effort inevitably ends in death and destruction...

Damn!

Susan suddenly felt more depressed then she'd ever been in her entire life.

Even the best success is built upon tragedy.

"Scott, you can't mean it! Please don't make me do it!"

"You have to go, Bill," Scott shrugged. "No one else is competent to oversee the optimal positioning for deploying the immense power we've socked away in the panels. You have to do your duty."

They were back in Oklahoma, at the skyscraper headquarters of Nashoba Energy—comfortably seated in the executive penthouse at its top floor. There'd been a total breakdown in transportation in Oklahoma similar to what was happening worldwide. By rights they and the locals should be starving, worldwide food distribution now at a standstill. Fortunately, nearby farms and ranches provided social stability and fresh food. While whole cities were starving to death, Sulphur Oklahoma still had plenty of homegrown beef, wild deer, and wheat. Bread, meat, and milk were plentiful. Grocery stores were just ravaged shells, with row after row of empty shelves. But the townspeople survived, especially since the Chickasaw Nation supplied a local militia to augment the overwhelmed city police force ensuring a fair distribution of local resources.

Bill felt safe in the towering building. It contained living quarters, corporate offices, worldwide communications, a dedicated electrical grid, research-manufacturing facilities, and a robust security force. In his laboratory in the basement he could hide away from the others, particularly Scott. Bill never wanted to leave there again, even to return to the White House!

And now Scott is telling me I have to go into outer space!

"But I can do what's needed from here, routed through Mission Control, on the ground, at my computer console!"

He got up from a comfortable, executive chair and went over to look through the ceiling-high windows. The small town of Sulphur was laid out below. Other than a few persistent commercial and house fires that were burning stubbornly, the place looked relatively normal.

"The fate of the world hangs in the balance, Bill," Scott firmly insisted. "The crew will likely have to make split-second decisions. We can't count on an acceptable time lag for distal communication. You don't have to command the mission, but you sure-as-hell have to be there directly controlling our proprietary technology!"

Bill angrily turned to the man sitting at the ornate central desk. Bill had the odd thought that the desk looked similar to the Resolute Desk in the Oval Office. He'd long suspected that Scott had political intentions. His tanned good looks would play well on the political stage, assuming anyone was left to vote after the next two months. And his predatory nature was perfect for excelling in "take-no-prisoners" politics.

"All they have to do is push the right button," Bill whined, shaking his head in frustration.

"I said it is *proprietary*, Bill, remember?" Scott snapped at him. "If there's sufficient time, you'll have backup support from the ground. But we can't give anyone the details for controlling and deploying the energy discharge sequences! It may have to be sculpted, focused, or timed exquisitely. The Tribe agrees we have to have someone onsite that we can totally trust!"

"Then why don't *you* go?"

"Well...I could..."

"Great!"

"But there's something we just discovered, which hasn't yet been leaked to the general public..."

"Well?"

"We just regained contact with HDST."

That was good! The *High Definition Space Telescope* could give them valuable information on the state of the Asteroid.

"Ah, so the riots are now under control in Greenbelt? They've been able to reopen the *Goddard Space Flight Center?* Is it still functioning?"

"Enough to access some of the latest pictures that were stored for transmission before communications were lost."

"Ok, so we have a better look at the Asteroid—so what? It's just a big hunk of rock, right? How does that change anything?"

Scott licked his lips, looking down at the desktop.

"Hermes just made a course correction," he quietly revealed.

Staggered, Bill slowly sank back down into his chair. He sucked in his breath, shocked. But that would mean...

"She's alive? Susan is still alive?"

"We don't know for sure," Bill hastily added, frowning. "But if so, we may need to coordinate our efforts with them when they come in range for low-quality communications. Remember, they managed to get two nuclear warheads onto Hermes. If Hermes prematurely blows the Asteroid into fragments we may not be able to incinerate them at the last second as they plummet into us! Even a few fragments of the comet getting past our energy barrier to hit Earth could cause immense damage."

"So just ask Hermes how they're doing! Maybe we won't need to deploy at all?"

"Goddard tried to contact them. But the *Deep Space Network* is still spotty, at best. Regardless, we've received no replies. There's dead silence from Hermes. So either the ship can't transmit or what the HDST saw was just an automatic, preprogrammed firing sequence. Remember, the last we heard from them they were being intensely bombarded with radiation from their nuclear reactor, had little food or water left, and were getting sicker and weaker by the day. I don't think we should get our hopes up that..."

"Ok, I'll go."

Bill stood up again, turning his back on Scott to stare out the high windows—this time not at the town but up at the beckoning blue sky.

"You will?"

"She's my sister," Bill firmly stated. "If she's alive then she's still a stubborn, tunnel-vision driven, science-obsessed *egghead!* The only person who could ever, in real time, talk her into changing her mind—assuming she gets off onto some bad tangent—is *me!*"

"That's what we thought also," Scott resignedly sighed. "There's only going to be a brief window to stop the Asteroid this close to Earth. The Star-Shield expedition will have to do *whatever* needs to be done! You understand that, right Bill?"

He suddenly moved next to Bill and gave him a sharp "thump" on his shoulder.

Cringing, Bill looked away, not wanting to meet Scott's intense gaze.

"I understand...I guess," he submissively whispered back.

What Scott was saying sounded ominous. But so was traveling back to the Nevada desert to the still-secured Area-51 military launch site. Bill was terrified of being fired up into orbit, even by their new, proprietary propulsion system! His few fantasies of being a heroic astronaut alongside Suzy were just that, childish dreams. The reality was horrifying! But Scott's stern admonition did make sense. Bill was one of the chief designers for Project Star-Shield. No one knew it better than he did. And it was nearing completion, ready for final testing and deployment. If his sister was brave enough to sacrifice herself to save mankind, how could he do any less?

But what if the two of them came to odds? On the unlikely chance that she was still alive, she didn't even know about Star-Shield, let alone have any faith in the radical new technology! She had maybe two functioning nuclear warheads. Bill and his team would have at their command the sum total of *tens of thousands* of warheads!

It was the largest accumulation of firepower ever concentrated in one place by the human race.

And if it were enough to incinerate the Asteroid, a tagging-along Hermes would likely be just a brief flicker in the overall explosion.

Will I have to kill my own sister?

"I'll...do whatever needs to be done," he sadly repeated, nursing his aching shoulder while totally buckling to the ever-persuasive Scott. Bill dejectedly turned to exit the penthouse office.

He had the paranoid thought that if there indeed was a conspiracy, this present wrinkle fitted perfectly. He had already discovered that stealthy meetings had indeed occurred between Nashoba Energy's top executives and unnamed secret parties—to which he was excluded. Something was going on that was "above his pay grade"—and had been underway for a long time. He was certainly *not* what the media perceived him as: "Founder" and "CEO." No, for a long time now, he was a mere *figurehead* with no real authority. It was humiliating but true. He'd given away his birthright for the temporary pleasures of the moment.

I'm a sniffling coward...

But even though he was under their thumb, Susan alive or dead was definitely still a pain in their side, for whatever reasons. And he was her brother.

Now both he and Susan were to be sent away into space...yet again!

Wait, what?

Bill had a strange feeling that things were *repeating...?*

But that was ridiculous. He'd never been to space. Certainly he and Susan had never faced down a giant Asteroid hurtling toward Earth!

Or had they?

Bill had a sudden vision of a looming, fierce-looking *dinosaur!*

Scott pulled him back, clamping a strong hand onto his shoulder muscles. Expecting a painful squeeze, Bill was surprised when Scott gave him a seemingly sincere hug before releasing him.

But rather than being reassured, Bill felt a chill creep down into his very bones, as if he were a mouse being "hugged" by a hungry snake.

"So let's get you to Area-51, buddy!"

Bill gulped, shoving the unsettling vision out of his head. For a moment there, Scott had a mouthful of long, pointed, carnivorous teeth—about to chomp on Bill!

Christ, I'm going crazy—Bill thought to himself. *Susan's silly childhood science fiction fantasies have infected me!*

He knew he should continue arguing with Scott. This whole venture wasn't right. Scott shouldn't be able to just order him around like a flunky. But then again, wasn't that what Bill had *always* been—just a weak-kneed lackey?

Then again, maybe at the assembly site he'd finally get away from Scott?

But he knew that he and the crew would still be employees of Nashoba Energy. He'd still be under Scott's heavy thumb.

"Right...and then up into orbit...why the hell not," he muttered, defeated.

Bill King did *not* want to go up into orbit. The very thought terrified him. Yet he realized he *must* do it. Somehow or other, he knew it was his destiny!

It had already happened. It couldn't be changed.

Like it or not, he and Susan *had* to face the Asteroid, together.

Chapter 23

<u>QUESTIONS</u>

A young girl stared at a rock.
She asked it: "Why am I not you?"
But the rock refused to reply
Making the little girl very angry
She lashed out, yelling and kicking
Stubbing a toe on it, causing her pain
She screamed at the terrible thing
"Why do you ignore me, you stupid lump?"
But an old man approached, proclaiming
"Don't just 'do' something, SIT there!"
Chastened, she sat down on the rock, musing
She nursed her toe, pondering on Identity
Now not so upset that the world was different
Apparently, her Assumptions incorrect
Requiring her to go back to the bare basics
"Then why am I ME?" she petulantly shouted back
"What is a 'me'?" he replied, grinning widely
And she laughed also, accepting Ignorance
Knowing the best thing in the world
Not the still silence of perfect Nirvana
But the confusing chaos of exciting Life!
So she made the rock her favorite pet...

The Minstrel's Lark, 23:17-22

IMPACT MINUS SEVEN WEEKS, THREE DAYS, *ABAN-DONED...*

"Jesus Christ, Adri—where the hell is *Hermes?*"

Susan was starting to panic. Her breath was coming in gasps and she was on the verge of screaming. She was frantically scanning the immediate region of space with her radar. Although the range of her SAV onboard unit was limited, she should have easily picked up the bulky structure of the long Hermes stack. Instead, there was absolutely nothing!

They were using their steering jets to rotate the captured comet so they could scan in all directions. They were still plastered onto the side of the small comet by the wrapped-around nano-cable. In this manner they accomplished a full 360° scan of nearby space.

"*I don't understand,*" Adriana replied over the intercom speaker. "*Even factoring in the extra day that our side trip took, these are the exact coordinates where Hermes should be. We should be literally right on top of it!*"

"It couldn't have vanished—could it?"

"*No...unless...*"

"Unless what?"

"*What if it prematurely accelerated?*"

"You mean...?"

"*If there were a catastrophic explosion—say the nuclear reactor blew up—there'd be debris. But there isn't any, right?*"

"The reactor can't explode, Adri. You know that. Besides, without coolant-flow Kame would have shut it off."

"*My point is that there wasn't an explosion.*"

"I agree—besides us, this region of space is completely empty."

"*Hermes wouldn't slow down—so it had to speed up! I think that Kame prematurely performed the next course correction, angling Hermes flatter above the solar plane, aligning it closer to the Asteroid's downward path!*"

"But that maneuver wasn't due for another week...?"

"*If she thought you and I weren't going to make it back, since we were delayed, then...?*"

"Yes, that's right, Adri," Susan agreed, starting to gain control of her inward panic. "And if she was desperate, knowing she was about to die..."

"—*then she'd set everything she could to automatic, program in the final course corrections, and use the last of her hydrogen fuel to send Hermes onward without a crew.*"

"But she'd do that to accomplish...what?"

"*The warheads are active, aren't they?*"

"Well, sure, but we won't know how to deploy them optimally until we catch up to and study the Asteroid. But the bombs *were* originally designed to be used on intercontinental ballistic missiles, so they have full programming capabilities for autonomous function. However..."

"*I think Kame set them to explode on impact, programming Hermes on a collision course.*"

The prospect chilled Susan.

"But that might merely fragment the Asteroid. There'd be no guarantee of destroying the threat. It might make things much worse for Earth!"

"*Yes, but as a final, desperate effort to stop the annihilation of mankind by the Asteroid, I'd do it also, especially if I knew I was about to die!*"

Susan closed her eyes, thinking hard.

"Ok, assuming that's what happened—can we catch up to Hermes? Do we have any idea where it is?"

"*It depends on when the course correction was implemented. Likely it was in the previous 24 hours—when we didn't arrive on schedule.*"

"Or—if Kame were dying at an earlier point, running out of air...?"

"*I think even if that happened she'd have given us the full three days to make it back. She'd have programmed Hermes' rocket engine to fire at the last possible moment to turn it into an unmanned guided missile, whether she were alive or not.*"

"Right—so we know when the course correction occurred, its possible magnitude, and the target. Theoretically we could perform another burn to put us on the new track?"

For a moment there was silence over the speakers.

"We're almost out of fuel, Susan," Adri quietly but calmly replied. *"We've got just one more good burn left in the main rockets. I can align us on whatever vector you choose. But you'll have to be the one making the calculations and final decision. You're the orbital genius here."*

"Yep, that *is* my job to accomplish...so I'll run the most-likely scenarios...determine the various probabilities..."

It took a few minutes, but Susan thought she knew where Hermes was: ten thousand kilometers off the previously projected course, traveling approximately 5,000 mph faster than anticipated.

She flipped back on her transmitter to talk with Adri next door in SAV-2.

"Alright, Adri, this is my best guess. Assuming I'm correct on the positioning, the ball's back in your expert pilot hands. Can we catch up to Hermes—and how long will it take us?"

Susan hit a link to transmit the graphs and charts to SAV-2. Then she waited, increasingly concerned as the minutes ticked past...

Finally an answer came from Adri: *"We can just make it if we jettison the comet. Its momentum is too great to overcome with the fuel we have left on your newly plotted course. Our two SAVs linked together can fire sequentially, performing a series of smaller course corrections to save on total fuel. It'll take us two more days to catch up to where we think Hermes will be. And by that time we'll be running out of air in our cabins."*

"We can't jettison the comet, Adri. That's not an option."

"We have limited fuel, Susan. We weren't supposed to do any more burns. Hermes was supposed to be here waiting for us!"

"So then...we need more fuel."

"Sure, of course we do. But how do we work that miracle? I don't see any spaceship gas stations nearby!"

Hmmm, not necessarily so...

"That's one of the main reasons we captured the comet, right?"

"Yes, but we don't have the recycling equipment to..."

"Let me worry about that. You figure out the optimal use of our remaining liquid fuel. Assume a sequential firing pattern to stretch what little we've left as long as possible. And start the first burns immediately, Adri. If we're ever to catch up with Hermes, we can't fall behind!"

"Alright, Susan—I'll trigger the first short burn in ten minutes, once I've aligned the comet using our steering jets. But still..."

"Shut up, Adri," Susan snapped. "I'm thinking!"

Obediently, Adriana's telecom went dead.

Alright, then—Susan furiously thought to herself. *I'm not an engineer, but I've got to figure out how to get fuel from frozen gases on a comet hurtling through space, using nothing but the equipment we've got on the SAVs!*

She was getting a splitting headache. She needed to take a drink of water. But there was only one single glassful left—which had to last her for two more days!

Kame, where are you, you bitch?—Susan silently lamented. *You left us in the lurch. And to get out of this predicament we need you onboard with us figuring out a brilliant engineering solution! I'm not an engineer, that's your job! Our minimal ship complement is a stellar charter, a pilot, and an engineer. But our engineer is dead! God, where's the JOY in this?*

She almost quit, giving-in to hopelessness.

But then her eyes narrowed. She got *angry!*

They'd come too far to just give up...

Wait—she calmed herself. *Take a deep breath and consider your assets. Sure you're not an engineer. But you know a lot related to engineering. You had to troubleshoot complex instruments in your career. And the biggest talent you have is in your being a tunnel-vision, focused, moderate introvert. Every manual ever written by NASA is stored in the memory banks of SAV-1's onboard computer. There must be something in those detailed manuals that could help you. And you've just the mindset and skills to find it!*

Nice affirmation...what?

Oh, right...

She felt the "whump" as the main engines of SAV-1 and SAV-2 lit up. Through the unobscured side porthole Susan saw the *red flare* of the last dregs of their fuel being consumed, thrusting them forward!

But she wasn't distracted. She was busily scanning through the extensive list of manuals stored in the central computer. There were many unknowns facing her—but the critical objective was clear: *find a way to extract fuel using present resources, usable by the SAVs to limp back to Hermes still firmly attached to their precious little comet!*

She should have been miserable but surprisingly was exhilarated.

Despite the pressure and stress, Susan now felt a heady "rush"—even though it was "life and death." Damn, this *was* fun!

And it was *much* better than being a rock...

Now why did that weird thought pop unbidden into her head? Oh yes, her old poetry book, beckoning her back to Hermes: *The Minstrel's Lark, chapter 23, verses 17-22,* the story about the curious little girl and her pet rock! It was one of her favorite passages.

Susan felt comforted that she'd brought the slim volume along with her, safely tucked into a large inner pocket of her flight suit. No other possession mattered as much to her. It was her inspiration, merging her intellect with her heart.

Indeed, that was what separated *Homo sapiens* from other animals. Give an ape a new tool and it'd be deadlier. Give it inspiration and it would be qualitatively different.

It would be human.

Area 51 was not just a supposed repository for secret alien artifacts. Now it was one of the last remaining sites on the planet where a large-scale space program could still be initiated and assembled.

Versus other sites overrun by hordes of desperate looters, Area 51 was secluded and well protected. Nestled safely inside the *Nellis Air Force Range* and the *Nevada Test Site*, Area 51 was off by itself in the dry Nevada desert, guarded by a substantial military force. Since Area 51 was close to where ongoing nuclear-absorption detonations were still occurring nonstop, it was the perfect place to assemble and then transport up into orbit the "loaded" panels.

Actually, that Area 51 "alien" stuff was just a silly government conspiracy theory. Bill was certain there'd never been any aliens who crashed on Earth, got captured by the government, and then were secretly exploited for their advanced technology by devious military agencies.

That was so ridiculous it was laughable.

But the gleaming, giant *Saucer* in front of Bill testified differently. It was stadium-sized, large enough to contain an entire football field. Plus it *hovered* in the dry desert air, *riding on a cushion of shimmering energy* that was projected from many black panels lining its underside. Its top surface was silvery, otherworldly looking. The top panels were unique, designed by Scott. They were transparent when looked through outward from within the saucer, but still capable of generating and shaping accumulated energy into intensely hot plasma discharges. In fact, the whole spaceship appeared to be one of the "flying saucers" Bill had seen in every B-rated "aliens attack" classic science fiction movie made since the 1950's.

"Impressive, right?"

It was General Cheryl S. Harclave. She was standing beside Bill as they witnessed the first test flight of the Saucer. Her cool blue eyes did not blink, even though a hot wind was blasting against them generated by the lift mechanism from the huge Saucer. Her brown dress uniform was crisp, the medals on her left upper chest perfectly aligned. The five stars on each of her shoulders were intimidating.

Her stern expression was that of a commander in complete control of her troops.

"Seeing it finally in action—the panels providing diffuse thrust—is...scary," Bill hesitantly answered, shielding his eyes with a trembling hand.

"Why? You designed the propulsion system, correct?"

He hesitated, unsure of how much to admit to the General, particularly in public. The truth was...he wasn't sure of anything anymore—neither how the "super-batteries" really worked nor how they'd been linked into this novel means of Saucer-lift. Scott and his mysterious collaborators provided the detailed designs, oversaw the installation, and personally trained the crew. Bill was increasingly afraid that he was included in the crew, again, only in his primary role as a figurehead. He was being *used!* His long documented association and experimentation with his father was a just a Nashoba Energy *smokescreen* that hid something...sinister.

"Uh...well...since the power of *two thousand* nuclear detonations are now stored inside those panels, I half-expected us to get lethally irradiated!" he tried to joke.

She did not look amused.

"So then, what is the radiation output?"

An array of technicians and equipment surrounded them, monitoring the hovering giant Saucer.

"But," Bill hurriedly continued on, "everything's fine. There's no radiation at all! The energy flow is exquisitely contained and tunable, twisted inward upon itself to provide a nice cushion rather than a blast. The propulsion system is ready to lift us gently right up into orbit whenever we wish. This is what you can do with virtually unlimited energy at your disposal!"

"And deployment of the Star-Shield?" she crisply asked, looking up into the deep blue desert sky.

"Well, we can't attempt that until we get into space. But we're ready to begin tests once we get everything to the main construction site. The Mirror Array being assembled there is almost complete."

"Why do we need an auxiliary structure? Can't the Saucer panels directly incinerate the Asteroid?"

Bill fully realized that the General already knew the answer. She was playing to a horde of reporters standing right behind her. She, Bill, the technicians, and the Saucer were being recorded for immediate world-wide propaganda and subsequent place in history.

"The Asteroid barrage can't be diffused, Ma'am, as it is in the Saucer drive," Bill politely replied. "The massive discharge will have to be focused and collated..."

"—like the sun's corona," Harclave thoughtfully nodded. "The huge gravitational and magnetic fields of the Sun manipulate the plasma to produce temperatures up to a few million degrees. So the Sun is much hotter outside than inside, right?"

"Yes, Ma'am," Bill dutifully replied. "Of course at the core of the sun the immense pressure there allows nuclear fusion to occur at even hotter temperatures, up to 27 million degrees. Except for a few transitory points—for only a few milliseconds—we can't duplicate the heart of the sun in the vacuum of space. As you correctly stated, though, what we're trying to produce, instead, is a stable 'corona' condition. Our plasma will have to endure for minutes to be effective, not just fleeting microseconds. And we want the delivery device—our

Saucer spaceship—to survive. An unfocused blast would melt our spaceship as surely as the rock of the hurtling Asteroid!"

The General nodded, now shielding her face with a hand from the continuing hot blasts.

"So focusing-mirrors external to the Saucer are necessary. How do they survive the plasma bursts?" Harclave continued her interrogation for the world audience and subsequent posterity. "According to your projections, the plasma will be dense and hot enough to destroy any known physical item."

"The 'mirrors' are more of our panels," Bill dutifully replied. "They're modified to produce a deflecting field rather than massive energy release. They're similar to the propulsion panels on the Saucer, but will only have to suffer minutes of plasma exposure rather than years."

"You're sure these...'panels'...will work as intended?"

"That's what we're going up into space now to test, Ma'am. Meanwhile, many more are being manufactured here on Earth, charged with incredible energy from further contained nuclear blasts, and lofted up by conventional means into orbit. In just seven weeks, when we meet the Asteroid safely outside the Moon's orbit, we'll hit it with a *series* of impenetrable plasma bursts!"

He tried to grin reassuringly. He only managed a weak grimace. He hoped the cameras weren't focused on him.

Harclave nodded approvingly. The hot wind barely touched her grey crewcut, while Bill felt his recently grown-out beard flipping around viciously. It was his minor act of defiance against Scott and Nashoba Energy. He no longer fit the perfect, clean-cut corporate image.

"Well, the people of Earth can certainly be reassured by what they see here today," she firmly stated for the videocams. "This is an unprecedented, global effort to stop that damn Asteroid dead in its tracks. Well done, Dr. King. The whole world is in your debt!"

Hah. "Dr." King, indeed—just an honorary Ph.D. hastily awarded to both him and Scott by surviving representatives of Bill's Dad's old alma mater, the *Department of Applied Physics* at Yale University. The venerable University's physical campus sites were closed and largely destroyed, of course. Higher institutions of learning didn't fare well against the worldwide meltdown: deep economic depression, new religious 'states' springing up like malignant mushrooms, massive refugee migrations, and vicious wars rocking the fragile framework of society. But well-protected U.S. White House officials had cobbled together enough of the on-the-run Yale Professors to confer the degree upon both him and Scott in a special, televised ceremony in the East Room. It made for a very impressive group photo: conferring a veneer of respectability and authority upon the immense project that was draining away much of the world's remaining scarce resources.

"It is my honor to be of service to my Nation and Planet," Bill stoically gave the expected reply, carefully "capitalizing" his spoken words. He firmly gripped General Harclave's extended hand. Her hand was surprisingly soft. He'd expected callouses and splinters!

He almost laughed, but just barely managed to keep his dead-serious expression intact.

They were selling "Project Star-Shield" as a *done deal:* a triumph of cooperation between Earth's remaining governments, scientific organizations, and industrial giants. The message was explicit: the rampaging people of the world should just *chill!* Maybe if it worked, society would gradually return to its normal "business-as-usual" model. But Bill knew that the uncertainties were immense. They had only one shot at stopping the deadly Asteroid.

And he'd be there right in the direct line of fire.

But that wasn't as bad as it sounded. If anything went wrong, it wouldn't matter if he was in space or on Earth. Except for a few lingering individuals starving in deep shelters—mankind would be gone.

Chapter 24

<u>RECOMBINATION</u>

We twist, rock-and-roll, and gyrate

Running far to return to the start

Pragmatically a huge waste of energy

Heroic struggle, heartache, and toil

Just to make it through another day

To face, yet again, the rising sun

Ending up where we'd earlier begun

Until Time crumbles our bodies

And we discover we're stuck

Old, weak, discouraged and tired

But, perhaps, subtly enriched

Changed by what we faced...

We're cast in a different light!

The Minstrel's Lark, 24:67-71

IMPACT MINUS SEVEN WEEKS, TWO DAYS, *PROSPECTING...*
Susan crept up the face of the frozen comet.

She was in her bulky white spacesuit, but the canisters that should have powered her steering jets were empty. If she slipped off the comet's surface into space she'd flounder. Fortunately she wouldn't drift away since a long tether leading back to SAV-1 would save her. But it would take time to pull herself in, hand-over-hand, before eventually getting herself back onto the face of the comet.

There was no time for such missteps.

But in the zero-G it was difficult to hang onto the surface. Even where dust and drifts existed, they were frozen solid in the near absolute-zero of space, slick and hard.

"Susan, do you see the vein?"

"Not yet."

She was running a cursory radar program from a handheld unit that showed up as a graph on the inside of her helmet's faceplate. It produced an "augmented reality" view of the surrounding stark surface. Readouts overlaid the concentration of various atoms onto the icy surface around her. Also, *stark-red lines* inside her helmet crisscrossed the surface: providing a stark warning of the near-invisible but deadly sharp nano-cables, across which Susan dare not drag an arm or leg!

She liked having her arms and legs attached to her body...

"*It should be there in that ravine, Susan.*"

"I know, I know!"

The multispectral, millimeter-by-millimeter, in-depth scan that Adriana had done—when spinning the "web" that succeeded in securing the comet to the SAVs—was proving its worth. Although not detected by Susan's initial long-distance spectral analysis, she was now zeroing-in on immediate, critically important deposits in the central ravine below the surface.

"*Is it there? Did you find it?*"

God, Adriana was annoying. Nag, nag, nag! But Susan knew they were both at the end of their endurance. Susan couldn't think straight. Her joints were stiff and leaden, the icy cold of space working its way into her thick spacesuit. Her lips were cracked and dry. She was so thirsty the only thing she could think of was "chugging" a big glass of pure, clear water! But she knew Adriana was just trying to help, to prod and guide her along.

The peaks and pits of the white/black comet surrounded Susan, calming her in an eerie sort of way. The shadows were deep black while the exposed surfaces *glared* hypnotically. She felt a sudden need to unlatch her helmet and surrender to the awesome stillness. But that was a crazy thought. There was *hope* if she could just persist!

But she was desperately weak, barely able to jam her makeshift climbing spike up into the surface with one hand as she held onto a slick protrusion with her other space-gloved hand. She was simultaneously starving and dehydrating inside her spacesuit.

"This is easy," she whispered to herself. "There's no gravity, Susan. Just keep anchored with the spike and creep along, slow and easy."

On a curved "stick" she'd torn out of SAV-1's inner plastic wall, she had rigidly affixed a long screwdriver. It substituted for an ice-climbing "pick." It gave her firm purchase when she slammed it into a frozen drift.

"What was that you said, Susan?"

"Nothing. Just keep the stove hot. I'll be in with some fresh meat presently."

"You're a good huntress, Susan. Keep at it!"

Hah. Adri was a good friend. No sense getting mad at her.

*Methane...ammonia...carbon dioxide...*and *water*—they were all there for the taking, exposed on the surface of the house-sized comet. Her general readouts displaying on the inside of her helmet confirmed that those precious commodities were all around her. So you'd think it was just a matter of figuring which was which in sufficient purity to warrant chipping off a bunch of chunks, storing them in an expandable bag at her waist, returning them to the SAVs, containing them properly, and using them to save her and Adri's lives!

Nope.

In reality, everything was covered with a layer of eons-old black-grey dust, composed of rock and simple organics, an uninformative sludge. The readings she'd gotten from her long range, powerful, spectrographic radar were from reflectivity beyond the visual range, penetrating several centimeters beyond the comet's surface. Just looking directly at the surface she couldn't tell where rock stopped and frozen gases began. And even if she could, the frozen gases weren't that much different from each other, with everything looking like dirty ice. And the gases weren't neatly separated into separate streams. Instead, they were jumbled together and mixed—down to the molecular level!

It seemed an impossible task to derive from this impossible frozen ancient mess a usable fuel for the SAVs—*unless...*

"You're there, Susan! If you can dig down I think you'll hit pay dirt!"

Susan knew that Adri was referring to the detailed spectral map derived from her own many close transits over the surface of the comet when she'd spun the web. Indeed, the key clues came when SAV-2 traversed right above the ravine. The brief slanted glimpses inside the deep gash were what prompted Susan to do her main prospecting there. She stuck her boots in small pits to each side of the split into the comet and swung her "pick" at the inward face.

Grey hunks floated off, revealing...

"My God, Adri! It *is* here!"

Yes, there it was—a *bluish* icy vein! Hallelujah! Praise the Lord! Yippee!

It was *molecular oxygen*, O2! When frozen near absolute zero, solid oxygen is a transparent substance with a light sky-blue color. But molecular oxygen is highly reactive. Indeed, oxygen was the second half of the SAV's fuel: liquid hydrogen gas combined with liquid oxygen gas. For many years frozen O2 wasn't expected to exist on comets. The existing models showed that primordial oxygen left over from the formation of the solar system which remained on comets would quickly react with hydrogen, producing water. But the researchers running the Rosetta space probe were astonished in 2016 to find molecular oxygen in Comet 67P's surrounding "atmosphere." It was theorized that the oxygen gas derived from solid frozen oxygen originally buried deep inside the growing cometary aggregation, which had survived untouched and unreacted for billions of years until sublimated by approaching the sun!

And here it was...

"*What else is in its immediate vicinity?*" Adriana asked, ever the pragmatist.

"Right...just a second, Adri..."

Susan's handheld, small spectrographic emission device was clipped to her workbelt. She fumbled it free and ran it back and forth around the blue vein, just a few inches off the ice. Numbers increased and decreased in the various categories on the inner surface of her faceplate.

"It's...the *motherlode*, Adri!" Susan gasped in delight.

Indeed, the whole face of the split into the comet's interior was— in addition to molecular oxygen—rich with nodules and streams of *methane hydrates, ammonia*, and *water*. In regards to their present crisis, methane was particularly interesting. Though it was not the first choice for rocket fuel, various experimental space vehicle engines had been designed that used liquid methane as their main fuel. After all, methane—CH_4—is the main component of natural gas, which is combusted together with atmospheric oxygen as a worldwide fuel. Ammonia was likewise proposed for use as a rocket engine fuel since it could also combust with oxygen. The famous X-15 hypersonic research aircraft's rocket engine was powered by liquid ammonia. But, for various reasons, ammonia never became a widely used fuel. Regardless, it could burn! So they had two potential fuels, plus the oxygen to ignite them.

"I see it here on my readouts, Susan. Can you carve out some chunks?"

"Yes, I do believe I can do that."

There was no way they were going to process out purified fuels or pressurized gasses from this raw jumble. But as to getting them into SAV-1 in their raw state...it was just a matter of powering up her suit's connected pencil-laser beam.

It wasn't near as powerful as the box-like laser they'd used near Earth that was powered by Nashoba Energy's super-batteries. And even this small pen-beam would quickly drain her remaining suit-batteries. But it should be sufficient for cutting into the frozen inner surface of the comet.

The red glare of her pen-laser was also helpful in seeing inside the blackness as she dropped into the man-sized ravine. She busily started carving out big frozen chunks: getting out as much of the blue ice as possible while also scooping out surrounding material.

Her net-bag at her side quickly filled up. Now it was equal in volume to her spacesuit.

"Coming back in," she said as she drifted up out of the ravine and pulled on her tether.

It took several trips, but eventually she filled up most of the free space inside SAV-1 with the frozen chunks. During this time, both the inner and outer hatches of the small airlock were kept wide open. Thusly, the temperature inside SAV-1 was near that of outside space, close to absolute zero. So the frozen chunks stayed nicely solid. It wouldn't do to let them start thawing out too soon.

"Company arriving, Adri!" Susan happily reported.

She carefully climbed over to the airlock of SAV-2, tightly gripping its outer handholds. Then she cycled-in and gratefully snapped off her helmet.

"God, it *smells* in here!" she gagged, grimacing.

The air in the cramped crew cabin was stale, thick, and musty.

"Well, you don't smell so good either!" Adri replied, grinning. "I'd offer you a drink, but unfortunately my water—like yours—ran out a day ago."

Yes, after hours in the spacesuit, sweating from the exertions, Susan was sure that she smelled rather "ripe" as well. And she'd dearly love a glass of iced-tea, lemonade, or even stale rainwater!

But that would have to wait.

"Wow, it's so nice to hear your real rich voice, Adri—not just the scratchy version over speakers."

"Same here, buddy."

"So how's our fuel?" Susan grinned wearily, quickly getting back to business. She floated over to the command-screens and into one of the chairs.

"Our liquid fuel is depleted," the red-haired woman curtly replied, now deadly serious. "We've still enough gaseous propellant for our steering jets. But without a further boost by our main engines we'll never catch up to Hermes."

"Then let's give it the 'boost' it needs!"

"—either that or blow ourselves to Kingdom Come," Adriana ominously replied, strapping herself in next to Susan.

"Let's hope that the manuals I found were accurate."

"I'll get us precisely oriented."

Susan felt a series of small "jars" as the steering jets fired, turning the two linked SAVs plus the attached comet into an exact alignment. It was the precise reversal of their previous orientation. Instead of the SAV rockets pointing to the rear and the airlocks forward, the airlocks were now pointed to the rear.

"Closing SAV-1's outer hatch door," Susan stated.

She heard a muffled "clang" as the outer airlock hatch of her former "home" slammed shut and its power-bar slid into place. The noise reverberated throughout the two side-to-side locked vehicles.

"Ok, warming up SAV-1's cabin."

As the interior of the other SAV gradually warmed from near absolute zero, Susan sat hunched forward, nervously watching several graphs on the screen.

"Susan, the interior pressure is building!" Adriana excitedly reported. "It's working! We've got gasification of methane, ammonia, hydrogen, and oxygen!"

"Great—but to make the reaction mixture burn optimally, we've got to get the excess, predominating water out. Are the drains ready?"

"Roger that—according to the manual you found, Susan, they're open and ready osmotically to suck away the free water."

"I can't wait to guzzle some of it!" Susan grinned, trying to relieve the tension. In the next few moments they were going to be either cheering deliriously or stone cold dead.

"It's going to taste awful without further purification."

"Who cares how it tastes?" Susan said anxiously, watching the cabin pressure of SAV-1 continue to build as the frozen gases thawed. The cabin had been built to hold 1-atmosphere pressure, not higher. If it cracked open prematurely then all this effort would be for nothing. She tried to wet her cracked lips but didn't have enough moisture on her swollen tongue. "I'd drink sulfuric acid if it were wet!"

"It's probably going to be basic rather than acidic," Adriana absently corrected her.

"Whatever!"

Massive amounts of gases frozen in the comet for eons were being liberated inside SAV-1's sealed crew cabin. Just one cubic meter of methane hydrate could produce 160 cubic meters of gaseous methane. The pressure inside of SAV-1 was nearing the point where it would soon explode the vehicle!

And that uncontrolled explosion would likely destroy the attached SAV-2 as well...

"I've got drainage!" Adri excitedly reported. "The grails are sucking out the water droplets. The fuel mixture is ready!"

"Then let's do it," Susan said, clenching her teeth together tightly.

She simultaneously released SAV-1's outer airlock hatch's cross-bar restraint while triggering a massive electrical short across the snapped-open gap...

KAWHOOSH-KABANG!

Susan felt rather than heard the huge explosion as the churning mass of highly pressurized compressed gases surged out the back of SAV-1, *igniting* as they burst out.

She and Adri were thrown back in their chairs, pressed down by a huge acceleration. After floating in zero-G for so long, it was a crushing blow to Susan. She was blacking out, finding it difficult to draw a breath...

And then the pressure lifted. They were back in zero-G.

"Are we still alive? Did it work?" Susan gasped, dazed.

"Maybe," Adriana replied, gulping. She reached forward shakily to examine her readouts. "Your manuals were indeed accurate—SAV-1 just barely withstood the various strains and stresses. It's still intact. It didn't blow up from the pressure inside or the combustion at its rear hatch. I think...we did it! We turned the whole vehicle into an auxiliary rocket!"

"So...transit time to Hermes?"

"If it shows up where we're guessing it's supposed to be at—we should reach it in four days!"

"Damn...that's good..."

"Want some water?"

"What?"

"While you were playing around outside the spacecraft, I connected some of the circulation conduits through our convergent ports. Our SAV-2 water tank is now filled to brimming!"

"Really? We've...got water?"

"Take a look!" Adriana triumphantly proclaimed.

Taking a squeezable bulb she attached its sucking nozzle to a tap. It filled up with a cloudy, grey fluid. Then she did the same with a second. She handed the first bulb to Susan.

"Bottoms up!"

Susan squirted a small spray into her open mouth. It was bitter like mouthwash, disgusting but drinkable! Susan shot another spurt into her mouth and swallowed lustily.

"Oh, God," Adriana grimaced from beside her, closing her eyes, "it's awful!"

"Sure is..." Susan agreed, continuing to squirt more into her mouth. "But it's the *best drink* I've ever tasted!"

"I guess it beats sewer water, but not by much," Adriana grinned. "If we filter it and adjust the PH, I'll bet it might actually be tolerable!"

"Sure, go ahead," Susan sighed, leaning back while continuing to squirt the nauseating H_2O-mix into her mouth. She was drinking water that'd circled the sun for five billion years. It had an excuse for tasting old and foul! But it didn't "dampen" her sudden jubilation.

Finally they were on their way back to Hermes, with everything they needed to restock and resupply the ship!

For the moment, life was good.

Bill *retched* pathetically, again throwing-up into his designated "barf bag."

It was getting to be an annoying, disgusting habit. His only consolation was that nothing much was left to eject from his intestines/stomach, up into his throat, and thence out his mouth in violent spurts. Floating past him along the long corridor, other crewmembers politely avoided his gaze. A cute young female airman patiently waited for his retching to calm as he feebly struggled to get his "space legs."

She'd been assigned as his personal assistant on the voyage. But in reality she'd spent most of her time being his nurse. She was the ship's medical laboratory technician, but since everyone else was healthy, she spent most of her time with him. She'd done a good job, though, keeping him well-supplied with barf bags and fluid nourishment for sipping, mainly squirt-bulbs filled with sugar-water.

He looked out the porthole beside his seat and once again felt the whirling vortex in his gut as his mind screamed-out in terror: *get me down from here!*

He longed to be back on Earth, in his nice safe office, typing on his computer keyboard, not facing a horde of strangers! But that comfortable hiding place was far, far away...

In the distance, set against the blackness of space, Bill saw Earth. It wasn't the subtle curve viewed when flying in a supersonic trans-oceanic jet at 40,000 feet. Neither was it the broad curve observed from the International Space Station flying in low Earth orbit at 250 miles above the Earth. Instead, Bill saw the *entire blue-white sphere* of the planet hanging in space 200,000 miles distant! Bill knew that if he traveled to the other side of the Saucer and looked out an opposite porthole he'd see, filling up the entire view, the white-cratered Moon.

They'd just arrived after 2.5 days of direct travel in zero-G at the so-called "L1" point located between Earth and the Moon. It was the "Lagrange" point where the gravitational pull of the earth balanced the gravitational pull of the moon. It provided a somewhat-stable platform to "park" big space projects near the Moon.

He should have been elated to arrive at their destination. Instead, he was miserable.

God, he *hated* space travel.

"You'll acclimate soon, Dr. King," the Airman assured him, taking his full barf bag and politely handing him another empty one. "Half of all astronauts experience some space sickness. But the symptoms rarely last longer than four days. You've just got to hang in there. It should subside soon."

Bill intellectually knew that his inner ear was trying to adapt to seemingly falling freely in every-which direction. His mind knew what was happening in zero-G but his gut refused to believe it!

"I think...I'm going...to die," he sputtered weakly, wiping vomit off of his lips with his sleeve.

"Well, the doc can still give you an anti-nausea patch if you want. It's not too late to accept one from him. Or, you can try dissolving some Dramamine in your sippy bottle?"

"Right...and then spend the entire trip lying in my bunk in my room, half-asleep. I know the side effects of those patches and pills. I've got to be sharp to stay up with events, in order to be helpful. Besides, I *hate* taking pills or any drugs!"

"Yes, that's all true," she nodded patiently at his outburst. "And your brother agrees you should remain fully cognizant, especially now that we've arrived at the Star-Shield launching array. Would you like to go for an initial inspection? Maybe that will distract you from your space-sickness."

"Sure...why the hell not?" Bill groaned, undoing his seat strap and floating up beside the pert Airman.

He'd already tried the magnetic boots that allowed crewmembers to "clomp" along the curved corridors. But they didn't do anything for his nausea, seemingly just making him sicker. Plus they slowed one's movement to a tentative shuffle.

He was already the crew's "weak-link" without seemingly crawling along on his belly!

And he had his duty to accomplish. He must get acclimated to zero-G as soon as possible. The world was depending on him, right? Wasn't he the inventor/genius behind this last ditch effort to save the planet? Or, more realistically, he was a figurehead manipulated by unseen forces. Well...whatever. He needed to stay on top of the construction progress, not sick in a hammock.

But his head was pounding so hard he could barely think. His gut was still twisting itself up into knots. He hadn't slept for two days straight. He couldn't keep down any solid food. Fortunately he could sip liquids and or they would have stuck an i.v. drip into him. Ugh! He hated needles. But every time he tried to eat something solid he up-chucked it! Was he doomed to spend his time in space sucking sugar-water?

Following his latest vomiting episode, however, he did feel better.

Perhaps going to see the growing Array would misdirect his rebellious gut?

"Alright then, let's go to the upper observation deck," he forced himself to "cheerfully" reply.

He closed his eyes tightly and went limp. She took his arm and pulled him patiently along, kicking expertly at the curved walls to propel them through the middle of the corridor.

Unfettered by the weight restrictions of liquid fuel-propelled spaceships, the Saucer's interior was almost luxurious. Several stories-high lounge corridors lined the inner hull of the giant ship, with large one-way portholes offering wide views of surrounding space. Personnel lingered in comfortable table areas, chatting or just looking out at the spectacular views. A canteen offered various drink-bulbs and packaged snacks. There was talk of designing future Saucers that could spin on their central axis, providing centripetal force to create an "artificial gravity" when people were steadily slung toward the exterior hull. Since the mission of this first Saucer, however, was so urgent, that hadn't been a consideration. So Bill resigned himself to being pulled along in zero-G by the young US. Air Force Airman.

He gingerly opened his eyes, hoping that wouldn't cause another bought of miserable retching.

"You know, Airman Rodriguez, you've been nicely helping me these last couple days...but I haven't even thought to ask your first name," Bill ventured, holding the empty barf bag at-ready but feeling progressively better. It helped that his last attempt at a solid meal had totally evacuated his stomach.

"Well, my first name is 'Maria,' Dr. King," she politely answered. "Though in front of my superiors—which are all the rest of the crew—please continue to call me Airman Rodriguez. Most of the crew is military except for a few civilian consultants such as you—and we maintain strict protocol, 'chain-of-command' behavior. You understand, right?"

"Oh, sure...and call me Bill when others aren't around and don't need to be 'impressed' by my honorary degree."

"Well, it's a pleasure to assist you.... *Bill*. And you *are* a true hero, saving the entire world!" she said, giving him a coy smile.

Bill should have been calmed by her friendly smile. Instead, he felt strangely abused—as if a prostitute on the street were beckoning him with a forced, false smile: *come and have great sex with me, big boy, while I give you a terrible venereal disease and steal all your money!*

God, he must be sicker than he'd thought to have such an uncharitable thought about such a nice, helpful crew member as Airman Rodriguez.

Pushing aside his misery, he focused on the young woman. Before, he'd been so absorbed in his continuing space sickness that he'd hardly even noticed people around him. Now, though, he forced himself to inspect her face. He saw a brown-skinned woman with a wide face, her dark hair straight and held tightly behind her head in a rubber-banded pigtail. She wore the standard blue flight suit of the Saucer's crew, with a prominent name-badge proclaiming "Rodriguez." And right above her name was the U.S. Air Force insignia for an Airman First Class: a white star on a blue circle sprouting two double "wings" to each side. That seemed to Bill a very low rank to justify her being on the first space-saucer crew going up to test a world-saving new technology. She couldn't have been in the Air Force for over a couple of years, at most. How could she have any in-depth technical expertise?

But, then again, he knew that she was a lab-tech in the infirmary. She was the lowest ranking crewmember, thusly stuck with the job of "babysitting" the embarrassingly up-chucking "dignitary."

They were drifting up toward the "top" of the three stories of observation decks: moving along the circular hull to its "highest" point located in the very center of the top of the Saucer.

"How'd you get recruited for this mission?" Bill asked, curious.

"I have connections," she grinned at him in a curiously "toothy" fashion. Now that she smiled at him, Bill was somewhat shocked by her oversized teeth. It was unsettling. Indeed, it was what he'd been scanning her face to find: something that was "off," justifying his unease.

When she grinned she looked predatory, like a *shark* circling in to snap-up its prey!

God, his depressive paranoia was really acting up today.

"Uh...ok..."

But then he forgot the young lady as they emerged onto the top, central command deck to look straight up through the one-way transparent canopy located at the top of the space vehicle.

Bill momentarily forgot his aching guts, stunned by what he saw. Spectacularly suspended in space above him was a *giant assembly array*. Tiny spacesuited figures were jetting along various parts of a huge, gleaming scaffold. Brief white spurts came from their jetpacks. Shuttle-type vessels were maneuvering big components into place. The entire framework looked to be the equivalent of a fifty-story high earth-bound skyscraper. And there being assembled within its open interior was a huge *concave dish* composed of a growing checker-board of glistening-black energy-panels. Each square panel was fully a hundred feet long on each side. Only a smaller ring at the bottom of the growing concave dish was left free of the panels. But that open ring was large enough for the entire Saucer eventually to slip easily into.

The initial framework had been assembled in near Earth orbit, and then pulled out to L1 to start receiving the loaded SB panels. The entire space operation was incredibly complicated and carefully sequenced. Now they were in the final stages.

Docked at the bottom of the assembly frame were conventional space transport vehicles from the space-capable nations of the world. It was truly an international effort. The world was finally pulling together to stave off utter destruction. From the conventional spacecraft docked at the assembly framework a steady stream of the flexibly tubed panels was being unloaded before allowed to unfold and flatten.

And to the side of everything hung *the huge white-black Moon*, with its many craters distinct and sharp. Bill could even see individual mountains jutting up below, located between the craters. Dark volcanic "seas" were flat and ominous. The white highlands glared with reflected sunlight, almost too bright to look at. The Moon was so close it obscured half of the black sky. It was a constant, fixed feature because the construction site did not orbit the heavenly body, merely hung before it at the "L1" site where the gravity of the Earth and the Moon balanced each other out.

"I'm told the pace will quicken as more of our Saucers come on-line and replace the volume-limited, liquid-fuel rockets," Airman Rodriguez volunteered. "The Dish should be ready for initial testing in just a few days. If it works as predicted it the final Star-Shield should be complete in just a few weeks, that is—if the panels are delivered on schedule."

Fascinated by the awe-inspiring sight, Bill forgot his normally cautious restraints and spoke freely.

"The 'initial testing' will be firing at what—I mean, what's the target?"

"I'm told it'll be one of the Moon's mountains, down below."

Bill gasped in shock. It wasn't just the audacious hubris to think they could use the Moon for target practice, but the fact that he was so out of the loop that a lowly Airman was informing him of the Dish's progress and target.

This was vivid confirmation that he was merely a figurehead. But even so, he could throw some weight around! Hah, that was funny. In zero-G he was weightless...

Regardless, he was going to have to "suck it up" and confront the true leaders of this project. There could be no more secrets. He had to get to the bottom of the Nashoba Energy conspiracy once and for all, reveal its true goals!

But the very thought of "sucking it up" sickened him and he again dry-retched into his barf bag, forgetting his momentary mental boldness.

Who was he kidding? Just like his Dad before him he was a failed tinkerer, but who'd lucked out to fall in with a high-powered organization. He wasn't smart like Suzy. He wasn't a young, handsome inventor like Scott. He was just a *fake*, trotted out by Nashoba Energy to give an air of respectability from a long research history to their nefarious plot—whatever *that* was!

"Want to try some more baby food?"

Bill nodded obediently, tears springing from his face as his dry heaves slowed. Rodriguez calmly captured the floating teardrops in a thin sponge she held in her hand. The young Airman was so kind, so pretty. She was his one and only true friend on this miserable voyage...wasn't she?

In fact—come to think of it—she was the only person he'd talked to so far on the Saucer. He'd been totally cut off from what was happening!

As her hand closed gently around his wrist and pulled him away from the spectacular view back toward his quarters which were located deeper inside the Saucer, he was suddenly and irrationally *afraid*.

What if this grand project didn't work? *Asteroid PHA-15384* was hurtling at them better than 60,000 mph. It was over six miles long! No matter what wall of fire they succeeded in placing in front of it, wouldn't the massive Asteroid just zip through—maybe getting toasted around its edges before plunging as a celestial dagger into the heart of humanity?

But it wasn't just the prospect of failure—heralding the impending destruction of Earth's surface and the doom of *Homo sapiens*—which filled Bill with dread. No, it was the sudden conviction that no matter what he tried to do, it wouldn't matter.

His fate was sealed. He was just a stupid patsy, a pawn to unseen superpowers, an abysmal failure. He might as well go find the nearest airlock and "space" himself!

It'd be less messy and disgusting than just sitting around puking himself to death.

"Here we are," the brown haired young woman said, opening the door to his cabin. "Do you want me to help you spoon up some baby food?"

Beside his hammock, small jars of various soft baby foods sat in a closed transparent cabinet. It also contained unused nausea patches and a vial of pills. To attempt eating semi-solid food he merely had to pop a top, stick a finger in, and scoop out the contents. He didn't need any help, or the prying eyes of his "escort."

"Thanks, Airman Rodriguez—I mean 'Maria.' I think I'll just get some rest in my hammock. Will you let me know if I'm needed on the bridge?"

"Of course, Bill," she smiled again, revealing those unsettlingly large teeth. "But first Major Green wants another blood test to track your progress. Is that ok?"

Major Green was the ship's physician, under whom Rodriguez worked.

"Alright...sure," he said as he floated to his hammock and curled into its fabrics. It wasn't a problem. He didn't even feel anything since the micro-needle in the diagnostic chip was so small, requiring only a tiny amount of blood. "Prick me!" he said, weakly extending a hand.

She opened the transparent cabinet and pulled out what looked like a sterilely wrapped tongue depressor. She snapped it opened, pressed the wide end up against his hand, and then floated to the computer terminal. She stuck the other end into a USB port. Immediately, pictures and data began scrolling across the screen.

"Am I still alive?" Bill croaked, watching the screen.

He wasn't a biologist, but knew enough of medical tests from his mother's long illness to understand Maria's reply.

"Your hematocrit is high, affirming that you're dehydrated..."

"Which we already know—ok, I'll get back to sipping my sugar-water..."

"WBC count is fine, no infections in progress. Your red blood cells look ok, neither shriveled nor inflated..."

Bill saw familiar red concave blood cells on the screen.

"—and your electrolytes are somewhat high, as expected," she continued, "but BUN and creatinine are normal. That's good news. In your last reading they were also elevated. So your kidneys are re-covering. I'll send these results to Major Green, but it doesn't look bad at all. I think you're over the worst of the space sickness, Dr. King...I mean, Bill."

"Well...good to know."

She pulled out the chip and pushed it into the wall recycler unit. Then she floated up from the computer station and over to the door leading out of the small cabin.

"Call me if you need anything—anything at all!"

It might have been his imagination, but he thought she *winked* at him as she exited, softly closing the door behind her.

He shuddered, suddenly feeling very isolated.

Yes, she was helpful...maybe *too* helpful. He was suspicious that her last offer seemed to be a sexual "come-on." If he weren't so sick, he might be tempted to accept her advances. Indeed, she was an at-tractive young lady. But he was forced by his nausea to back-off and think clearly.

Either he was in a dream fantasy—saving Earth with a sexy lady on his arm—or in a gilded prison, distracted from the bars by a toothi-ly grinning jailor! Which was it?

The accommodations on the Saucer were much like those on a submarine. The cabin was adequate but small, hardly more than an average earth-sized closet. Of course compared to the ISS or other older space vehicles it was incredibly luxurious for a single person even to have his own private cabin, cramped or not. He should be grateful. But Bill was too tired and weak to feel anything but abject misery.

Shaking off his deep funk, though, he resolutely flipped out of the hammock and floated down to the small desk. Looking again at the pictures of his stained white blood cells and concave RBCs he "clicked" off the clinical program then brought up key mission databases. He had top-secret clearance so he had access to just about anything he wanted. And the first thing he wanted was the service records of the entire crew complement of the Saucer, starting with the overly friendly Airman Rodriguez.

"Who are you really, Maria?" he muttered. "And why is such a low-ranking person on this mission?"

Yes, he was probably going conspiracy-crazy. But sometimes imagined conspiracies are real—and deadly!

And time was fast running out.

Chapter 25

<u>COMING HOME</u>

Yep, there it is!
After going up and down
Around the bend and back again
Over mountains, across seas
Through deserts and forests
The end is in sight
Just over that last hill
Finally, at last, your house
From whence you left so long ago
Going out young, spry, adventurous
You return old, stumbling, and busted
Grateful to just, at last, collapse
Into your favorite rocking chair
On your rickety, short porch
You close your eyes, sigh
And gratefully vegetate.

The Minstrel's Lark, 25:132-236

IMPACT MINUS SIX WEEKS, FIVE DAYS, *RETURNING HOME...*

Catching back up to Hermes was like coming home. It was an incredible relief to see it grow from a distant metallic dot into a long train of modules. But now Susan and Adriana must somehow dramatically *decrease* their speed in order to deliver the captured comet to their prior, thirsty habitat.

Fortunately, they now had an extra "rocket" to play with...

So they used the same trick to slow down they'd used to speed up. They mined more oxygen-rich veins to fill up the blasted-out shell of SAV-1. The water-drained hyper-pressurized mixture of gases was then again ignited at the released outer airlock door. The deceleration maneuver took precise positioning of the comet-SAV aggregation, but again Adriana was up to the task.

It was a crude way to decelerate, but it worked, slowing them enough to drift up next to the long stack of linked modules hanging lonely there in space before them. Using short burst of the steering jets Adri glided them into a fixed position beside Hermes.

"Hermes, do you read me? Kame, are you there?"

They were trying to get a reply from the Mars Transit Vehicle using their short ship-to-ship transmission equipment, hoping against hope that Kame had found a way to survive.

But, as expected, there was no reply. Hermes hung dead in space. No interior lights flashed through the portholes of the top, circular Observation Deck. And from monitored emitted radiation, even the nuclear reactor appeared to be offline.

"So how do we dock this baby?" Adriana asked.

They were both starving. They'd run out of food two days previous. Fortunately they now had plenty of water. As Adriana had predicted, once filtered and pH-adjusted, the ancient cometary $H2O$ proved remarkably drinkable. If they could link up with Hermes they could continue to mine the comet for the necessary water and liquid fuel to revive the mothership.

The problem now was just how to link with Hermes.

The comet was fully half as long as the entire Hermes-stack. It was much too large to just snuggle up to Hermes. But then maybe just as with the SAVs, *Hermes* could dock with the *comet?*

"Alright, Adri," Susan said as she floated over to the spacesuit and started laboriously putting it on. "I'll go outside and cut us free from the nano-cable. I'll pull the freed parts of the net over some of Hermes' struts to keep the comet temporarily secured. We can't have it drifting off after all the sacrifice it took to get it here! Then you dock SAV-2 on the Service Node. Expel the remaining air tanks of SAV-2 into the SN and OD to warm them up. Then go inside, get the reactor online, and fire up the robotic arm."

"There's likely no coolant for the reactor."

"We don't need much electricity, just enough to run the Arm plus minimal life support," Susan replied.

Adriana nodded as Susan suited herself up. Each movement was difficult. Susan's muscles were so weak she felt she was falling to pieces.

"Kame likely shut down the reactor to prevent it from overheating, melting to slag, and stopping permanently," Adriana mused. "We can start it at minimum, shutting it off if it starts to overheat, until we get enough cometary water into the tanks. From there we can split off coolant and bring the reactor up to full power."

Susan was almost into her spacesuit, doing the final checks.

"So once you get the Arm working you can grab onto the webbing and pull the comet tight to Hermes. I'll then use our remaining coiled nano-cable to lock the comet beneath the water tanks. Once it's firmly attached to Hermes I'll come on inside. When everything's stable we'll modify the recycling equipment, start mining the comet, and separate out more water and fuel-gases."

"Sounds like a plan."

Yes, it sounded simple, but it was greatly ambitious—tying the long Hermes-stack onto a small, house-sized comet? Hah! Susan didn't know if she could pull it off, especially in her starved, desperately weak state. But Adriana was determined and willing, an excellent crewmate. Together, they made a well-oiled team.

Getting the comet safely secured took them a whole day to accomplish, but finally Susan was inside the Service Node of Hermes, pulling off her helmet.

She was utterly exhausted. The air was thin but better than the stale atmosphere of her suit. Plus it was chilly inside.

Adriana handed her a filled bulb of water and Susan greedily drained it in one long slurp.

"Any...food?" Susan gasped, floating limp in the middle of the OD, not yet able to remove any of the rest of the spacesuit other than the helmet.

"Here..."

Adriana was holding out a congealed lump of what looked to be raw hamburger.

Without hesitation, Susan grabbed it and stuffed it in her mouth. Yes, it was meat. It was rubbery and foul-tasting, but still nutritious. A feeling of relief spread through her body as she greedily swallowed it. She hadn't realized how badly she needed calories. Both she and Adri had been literally starving to death!

"Oh...that was nasty-tasting, but still good," Susan gasped in relief, wiping her mouth. She absently noted that her hand came away bloody. "What was it? Did we miss some steaks at the back of our frozen food locker?"

Adriana looked strange. Her eyes were wide and not meeting Susan's gaze. She turned and floated up into the overhead Observation Deck. Over her shoulder she said in a small voice: "It's a gift from George."

"George?" Susan blankly replied, for a moment the word not registering in her exhausted brain.

"I started harvesting his meat while you were tying us to the comet," she explained. "It's all we have, except for..."

"*Kame!* Did you find her?"

Susan resolutely pushed aside the horrifying notion she'd just become a cannibal, choosing instead to focus on immediate, pressing tasks.

"She's in the Orion capsule," Adriana's voice faintly came to Susan from above. "You should go visit her before you completely collapse. In fact, I think we should both 'crash'—for as long as we need to recover. We've sufficient air, water, and 'food' for the moment. We can start reconfiguring and restocking Hermes from the ice of the captured comet once we've both gotten a good night's sleep. I'm getting into my hammock on the Observation Deck. As soon as you're ready, you should do the same. It's been a long day and..."

Her voice trailed off out of pure exhaustion in the O.D. as she settled into a constraining-hammock.

Afraid of what she was going to find Susan drifted to the closed airlock leading down into the Orion capsule. It seemed ages ago that they'd ridden the SLS up into orbit in their desperate attempt to link up with Hermes. Orion was now a relic from a distant past—a musty reminder of another world.

She lifted up the hatch, floating through the opened airlock down into the cramped capsule. There, strapped into one of the crew chairs, was the body of George. Adri had removed his cracked helmet. His white eyes stared out sightlessly at the blank screen in front of him. His blond, crewcut hair was covered with a thick layer of frost. A small icicle hung off the front his nose, dripping drops that floated out around him in a fog.

He was still in his flight suit, which was now slit along the left side of his body. The calf of his leg was exposed, which had been recently hacked-into. A big gouge showed where muscle-tissue had been removed, revealing white bone beneath.

Susan almost vomited but caught herself in time. George would have wanted his body's caloric value to be used in this manner, allowing the Mission to proceed.

"Hello, Susan."

Startled, Susan looked over to the other side of the crowded capsule. Sitting there still sealed in her spacesuit was Kame. Her helmet, unlike that of George, was still sealed, hiding her head behind a fogged-up faceplate.

"K-Kame?" Susan stammered, grabbing onto another seat and pulling herself into it to face the woman.

An internal battery-powered screen behind the spacesuited figure was activated, its laser-scanner flicking across Susan's body, recognizing her.

A blurry image of Kame's somber face filled the monitor. Her black eyes were resolute, set.

"Yes, as I'm sure you've realized, this is a preprogrammed message. I recorded another one, similar to this, specifically for Adriana. I hope you both hear these messages, meaning you made it back alive. If not, what the heck, hey? I've run out of air and I'm about to die. As I'm sure you've already figured out, I've set everything up so our remaining liquid fuel will send Hermes on a collision course with the Asteroid. The two hydrogen bombs onboard are set to detonate upon impact. The surface explosion probably won't do anything but dust off the surface of the Asteroid, but it's my last move. Might as well make the effort, right? It's likely futile. But if you're hearing this, then maybe you can come up with a better option. You can readily deactivate the bombs to utilize them more precisely. I've got faith in you both. You must get to that Asteroid, one way or another, no matter the cost! My life is a small price to pay. But I don't want to suffocate. So in a moment I'm going to inject myself with the syringe of synthetic curare that we were going to use on Ben, which I snagged away from you before sending you off to the comet. It's fitting, isn't it, that the poison I was willing to inflict on him I use instead on myself? The Universe is funny that way...but 'stuff happens,' right? Susan, I want you to have my ritual *seppuku* knife. You'll find it in my possessions. Keep it on you. I think you're going to need it. You can use a regular kitchen knife to harvest my flesh. The ritual knife is sacred, so please save it for a special occasion. I'm serious! It will defend you against something...against which I've also struggled but been unable to reject. Anyway, I brought up George's body from the sliced-open storage compartment below so it'll start thawing out. By the time you hopefully return it will be soft enough to start carving out chunks. Just in case the curare needs time to be deactivated in my tissues, I'd suggest eating George first. My last act of command is to power down the nuclear reactor, which is overheating dangerously—so it'll probably get cold here in Orion, preserving my flesh like in a refrigerator. You can transfer my body into the storage compartment below to freeze it solid if you wish, saving it until you are ready to eat it. Now don't waste anything. Don't be squeamish or prudish! Consume everything that's edible, including the bones. Remember, you've still got at least six weeks more to survive. Maybe you'll get another farm going, but that'll take a while. We have the genetically enhanced seeds to start a fresh ship's crop, but even the fast-growing varieties will take at least a month to produce edible fruit. You'll need a new batch of recycled 'soil' from your feces since the old soil got spaced. So calculate the caloric contents and do what you must to insure that you and Adri—if she's still alive also, God I hope so—make it alive to the Asteroid. But listen to me closely, Susan. If that's not possible then *you* must make it there, even if you have to kill and eat Adriana. She understands. She'll agree to this, if need be. The first message set to activate was to her, so she's prepared to do what needs to be done. Susan, you have a Mission that's grander than you even now imagine: to save not just the final remnants of humanity but the entire span of humanity's past, present, and future accomplishments. The *entire civilization* of humanity hangs in the balance! So, good luck, good eating, and goodbye—hope you like Japanese cuisine!"

The video snapped off.

*So now you finally get a sense of humor...*Susan sighed to herself.

Susan drifted over to Kame's still body and placed a hand on her cold helmet. Even though the faceplate was fogged over, Susan could vaguely make out Kame's closed eyelids. She just seemed asleep. But there was no sign of breathing or movement. She was clearly dead.

Regardless, Susan gave the hard helmet a quick *slap*—rocking the stiff head to the side.

"I'm *not* killing and eating Adri!" Susan snarled at the spacesuit. "If we lose our own humanity, what's the use in trying to save mankind? What is it with you wanting to kill and eat people? If we're just glorified cannibals, we might as well take our place alongside the extinct dinosaurs!"

She wanted to hear the message that Kame had left for Adriana, likely urging her to become the "sacrificial lamb" if necessary. But in trying to replay her own message, Susan discovered both files had self-erased themselves upon being first heard. Damn! Kame apparently didn't want them to hear each other's message, nor leave a record for any surviving future historian to mishandle. But that was probably for the best. There was no sense in dwelling on the gory details. The "take-home message" was clear: survive! They'd come all this distance, through many terrible problems, and now the end was in sight. Next stop, *Asteroid PHA-15384!*

There was still much work to accomplish between the "here" and the "there"—with many more things that could go wrong.

"Thanks, Commander," Susan muttered. She patted the helmet one more time—this time more gently—before drifting upward to the O.D. to have her first peaceful sleep in many a week.

She felt the poetry book pressing on her chest inside her spacesuit. As with her life, it leapt beyond accepted norms and boundaries, envisioning and planning for the unseen. It was immensely comforting.

"Damn!" Bill swore.

"What's wrong?" Maria asked, concerned.

She was floating to his side as he belted himself securely into his tilted crew chair. They were in a cramped Orion capsule, now twenty miles away in space from L1 where the test was set to occur in just a few minutes. Bill and his faithful assistant, along with others, were monitoring the test. A fleet of other vessels surrounded the Orion capsule. Everyone had evacuated from the assembly framework, which was now pointed directly at the surface of the Moon.

"I caught my thumb on the belt buckle!" Bill complained, holding up that hand.

A *bright red drop of blood* grew on his extended thumb, broke free, and floated away.

He watched it, fascinated...

Maria expertly snagged it with a tissue then pressed the fabric onto his thumb.

"Hold that in place for five minutes to coagulate the cut. It doesn't look bad, Bill. It's just a nick."

They were getting quite friendly. He reached over with his uninjured hand and gave her forearm a friendly squeeze. In lieu of Susan or Scott's steadying presence, she had become his lifeline. Despite his initial misgivings about her, Maria's comforting presence kept him from running screaming into his cabin, locking the door, and hiding from everything.

"What would I do without you?"

She smiled warmly at him before floating to another of the crew seats to buckle in next to him.

Bill happily focused his attention back on his readouts, descending into the pleasant world of bytes, graphs, and numbers. Through his terminal he could call up the exact orientation and power status of each of the many black panels that lined the giant concave Dish, plus the top of the convex Saucer located at the Dish's bottom. It was an "adaptive" array similar to what ground-based dispersed telescopes used to compensate for atmospheric distortion. Exquisitely orienting the exact angle, sequence, and duration of each discharge allowed Bill to simulate the magnetic plasma confinement of an earthbound nuclear fusion "torus" machine.

The best working example of that was ITER, the "International Thermonuclear Experimental Reactor," located in Cadarache, France. There, monstrous magnetic fields held plasma together for extended periods. Here in space, a complex mix of induced currents, resultant magnetic waves, and collision forces would "stabilize" the plasma. The local effect would only last for a fraction of a second. But in that split second the precisely generated plasma bursts would become self-confined, self-sustaining, and self-propelled. In essence the Dish would create "bullets" composed of plasma ripped straight from the interior of the sun: each the size of a stadium, initially burning at *27 million degrees!*

The plan was to get close enough to fire a whole series of them at Asteroid PHA-15384, each blast accelerating to nearly the speed of light and staying coherent long enough to reach and melt the six-mile-long rock. Nothing in the solar system could withstand such a sustained bombardment, no matter how fast it was traveling!

If it succeeded, they'd reduce the doomsday rock to a spreading cloud of harmless individual atoms.

At least that was the theory.

"Sixty seconds!"

It was the main mission commander, Colonel O'Keefe, there in the Orion capsule along with Bill, Maria, and other key technicians. Everyone had evacuated from the assembly array. The Saucer—an integral part of the entire "star-shield" apparatus—was now firmly secured at the bottom of the giant Dish. When they finally set out to meet the Asteroid, the Saucer would be fully manned. But now it was being operated distally from a safe distance, twenty miles away in space. If anything went wrong, it along with the entire assembly framework would be vaporized.

"...ten...nine...eight..."

"All panels are optimally configured, powering up," Bill reported.

"...five...four...three..."

Bill turned away from his readouts to look out of the port. In the distance, hanging against the blackness of space, was the small metallic dot that was the giant assembly array.

"...one...ignition!"

Brighter than the sun, a series of *brilliant pinpoints* burst from the metallic dot, leaping straight down toward the surface of the Moon...

"*Impact!* We have impact!" a technician cried-out.

Again looking at his computer screen, Bill saw an overhead telescopic view of a range of mountains far below. The mountains were set between large and small craters. Nothing seemed different, except...one of the craters was *smoking!*

Indeed, a *huge column of black soot* was steadily erupting up out of that crater, spreading as it towered up higher and higher.

Just a second ago, that crater had been an isolated, towering mountain.

A cheer went up inside the Orion capsule. Bill saw fists thrust triumphantly into the air.

"It's obliterated! It's completely gone!" someone gasped in disbelief.

Indeed, they'd expected the bombardment to explode the designated mountain of lunar rock, reducing it to rubble. But as the column of soot cleared he saw on the screen where there'd been the equivalent of a 5,000 foot high mountain was now just a smoldering caldron with bubbling red lava at its center. They'd scooped out a whole hunk of the moon, leaving it scarred forever!

"You did it! You did it!" Maria laughed, reaching over from her seat to grab his arm.

She unbuckled, kicked over, and slung her arms around his neck, hugging him tightly.

"Maria, not in public, please!" Bill laughed back.

He knew that shipboard romances were discouraged on military vessels, at least public expressions thereof. He didn't want to endanger her career by his growing romantic attraction to her. But he was nonetheless pleased by her warm embrace.

He was getting his strength back. The terrible, prolonged bout of space-sickness was now in the past. He was starting to eat solid food. Before, he'd been so sick and weak that his relationship with Maria was only the equivalent of good friends going on occasional dates. But now he knew it was time to take things to the next level.

"Meet me in my room when we get back to the Saucer?" he whispered to her.

"With pleasure!" she cooperatively replied, giving him a small kiss on his cheek above his thick beard before kicking back to her designation seat.

Wow! He was feeling a *lot* better! The test was an unqualified success. According to his readouts, none of the black panels were damaged by the discharges. Plus, the energy release to produce the plasma bullets had been minimal. The panels still had near their full charge of nuclear bomb-generated, subspace-stored energy. Once the final panels were delivered and installed, they'd be ready to leave L1 and proceed beyond the moon to encounter Asteroid PHA-15384 as far from Earth as possible. They couldn't go too far since the panels had to draw their stored energy from subspace depots locked into the Earth-Moon gravity-well. But now they could meet the Earth-killing "cosmic bullet" with bullets of their own! And he had an eager young girlfriend to accompany him on this world-saving adventure!

What could be better?

But his jubilant mood faded.

Well...certainly things would be better if he knew Susan was still alive on Hermes. There'd been no further news since the course correction was observed. The deep space communication arrays on Earth were now offline. They'd been severely damaged or destroyed during the escalating societal turmoil on Earth's surface as the Asteroid drew ever nearer. Plus, HDST could only confirm that Hermes was now set onto a collision course with the Asteroid, due to smash into it a day before it arrived at Earth.

By then, though, Hermes would be close enough that ship-to-ship transmission might be possible, assuming anyone was left alive. But Bill almost hoped that Susan and the other crewmembers were, indeed, dead. With just two fusion bombs onboard Hermes they had no hope of destroying the Asteroid. That task was now up to Bill and the Saucer crew. And just by virtue of being in the vicinity of the Asteroid, Hermes and any survivors would be only additional casualties. They'd be brief flickers as the entire area was repeatedly engulfed in the concentrated power of the sun.

Sobered, Bill sighed deeply. The sad reality was if Susan were somehow still alive, he'd have to kill her. There was no other option. For humanity to survive, she'd have to be sacrificed.

But it would be *so* good to hear his sister's voice, just one last time.

Chapter 26

<u>SPRINT TO THE FINISH</u>

You can see the finish line

After an eternity of running in circles

The flags are set to be waved

As you cross over, exhausted

But delirious with joy

To finally make it to the end

After such a huge effort

Gasping, lungs burning,

Running full-out ahead

Staggering, each step torture

You grimly steel yourself

For that last surge forward

While others thunder behind

Stomping up, heaving, at your side

Nose-to-nose you discover

You're not the jockey after all

Just the muscle, the beast, the animal

A long-legged horse stretching to full stride

A glorious, adrenalin-driven release...unless

Just a few steps from the goal you collapse!

Or find the strength for that one last surge.

The Minstrel's Lark, 26:39-45

IMPACT MINUS THREE WEEKS, *DETERIORATING...*

"I have to do it, Adri."

Susan floated in the middle of the OD, feeling very tired and cramped in her bulky MMU. She was going through the last system checks before donning her helmet.

"No, you don't, Susan," Adriana argued. "We've still got minimal life support. There's only three more weeks to go. We can hang on until then!"

Indeed, they had achieved a lot upon returning to Hermes. They mined half the small comet's various ice layers. They converted the recycling system into a water-and-gases separation mode: distilling, extracting, and storing. Now they had plenty of water in their tanks, compressed liquid fuels, and a calorie-producing hydroponic "farm." Though it was loathsome to eat the flesh of another human, George's body lasted until HAB-3 was completely filled with water and seeded with a fast-growing algae mix. George became the bridge that allowed them to cross the deadly divide from disaster to safety.

Their new safe "land" was their very own *ocean*, the quickest way to restart reprocessing their feces into food, though it was a bizarre setup never meant to be used on Hermes except in an extreme emergency. The abundance of water distilled from the comet was what allowed the desperate experiment. But all was not well. Although the algae grew rapidly in their artificial ocean, the high levels of radiation over the last part of their journey had mutated the seed mixture. The resultant complex of rapidly evolving organisms was...*different*. Fortunately, the bizarre mixture of single celled organisms still fulfilled its primary purpose. Siphoning off the complex mix of single-celled lifeforms provided Susan and Adriana with dried nutritious "flour" from which they could bake tasty bread. In addition, the watery "farm" performed the other main jobs of plant life: sucking up excess CO_2 from bubbled-through ship air and manufacturing breathable O_2. So things were looking up! But the seething mixture in HAB-3 was...ominous.

Yes, eating reprocessed feces as edible slime was yet another disgusting thing they had to endure. But Susan was beyond being disturbed by what their desperate situation forced upon them. Susan was glad they didn't have to eat Kame. Her intact body was nicely frozen away in the damaged cargo module, where George's body had

previously hung. Since it was open to space, it made a natural freezer.
Susan was glad that Kame would make it to the Asteroid intact. She
deserved that dignity. The algae's unexpectedly rapid growth in the
water-filled interior of HAB-3 saved Kame's body from being consumed. And even though the electrical output from the nuclear reactor was steadily decreasing, it still supplied sufficient energy via grow-
lights embedded in HAB-3's flexible walls to produce the equivalent
of a sun-drenched primordial ocean.

But as they stabilized Hermes, things perversely got worse, not
better. The nuclear reactor's electrical output was fast fading.

"If the lights go dark, Adri," Susan patiently explained for the official record they'd set the ship's computer to preserve for future gener-
ations (assuming humanity continued on and wasn't destroyed by the
rapidly approaching Asteroid), "—then our algae ocean will die. The
recycling systems will stop. The cryogenic tanks holding the stored
compressed gases will start heating up. We'll have explosions and
system-failures all across Hermes."

Susan slid her helmet over her head, absently noting how
scratched the faceplate was getting. Spending weeks slicing out
chunks of the comet had taken a grim toil on the spacesuit. The
MMU's exterior was stained, ripped, and clunky. Two of the steering
jets had stopped working, necessitating a tether most of the time in
order to retain the two remaining jets for emergencies. Susan felt
lucky that the MMU at least held its air pressure.

Jesus, everything is falling to pieces on Hermes!—she thought to
herself before resolutely "snapping" the vacuum seals in place for yet
one more time. *We brought it back from the brink of disaster and
now it's crumbling even faster!*

She tapped on the internal microphone with her tongue, hearing
loud "clicks" in the helmet speakers that told her it was working ac-
ceptably.

"It won't get that bad," Adriana desperately argued. Her voice
crackled over Susan's helmet speaker. "You don't have to do this!"

"We're at minimal power now and losing 10% more each day,"
Susan sharply replied over her microphone. "You can do the math as
well as me, Adri. We've got progressive coagulation of the reactor
tubes, stemming from the time it had insufficient coolant flowing

through its innards. The damn thing is progressively melting into slag, its electrical output dropping lower and lower each day! In a week we won't be able to run the computers. A week more and everything on Hermes will stop working. If we can't do a full repair of the reactor out here in the void, then we at least must stabilize it at its present low level of functionality. We've no choice in the matter."

"But we've still got battery storage," Adri pleaded, her voice sounding oddly artificial, picked up by the O.D. microphones and funneled through Susan's suit speakers. "We can do controlled burns of the liquid hydrogen and oxygen we've already accumulated from mining the comet ice. That will generate internal heat. Hell, Susan, we can try to adapt Orion's fuel cells to power Hermes, using the same purified gases in reverse electrolysis, producing electricity in that fashion. I know the fuel cells on Orion are spent, but maybe we can repair them and..."

Susan held up her spacesuit-gloved hand to silence her.

"Sure, Adri—if we had *months* then *maybe* we could get those adaptations to work," Susan interrupted, resolutely going through the exit checklist. "As it is, without our ship's engineer, we barely managed in an entire month just to get the recycler system reconfigured. Yes, we did succeed in processing half the comet's ice. That was a big achievement. But we're running out of time. In three weeks we'll arrive at the Asteroid where we require abundant electrical power to have a hope at accomplishing anything. What's the point of getting there if we're just two cavewomen huddled around a burning gas vent in an icy cave? And if there's any hope of stabilizing the reactor to stop the rampant degeneration, then it must be done *now!*"

Adriana scowled angrily.

"Then *I* should do it! If you go out there and open the casing you know that you'll likely receive a high radiation dosage!"

Susan shrugged dejectedly in her spacesuit.

"It no longer matters, Adri. We both acknowledged we're not making it back to Earth. This is a one-way trip—for both of us."

Adriana abruptly kicked over to the EVA airlock and physically blocked it, floating there right in front of it.

Susan drifted toward her, determined to push her aside if necessary.

"Susan, please be rational," Adriana said, "thumping" a closed fist petulantly onto Susan's spacesuit's breastplate. "You're the one who has to analyze the Asteroid. *You're* the expert on space rocks! I'm just a glorified jet jockey. I don't know anything about the structure of asteroids or comets or where best to place nuclear bombs!"

Susan gripped her with her big gloves and gently pushed her aside.

"By then you'll be close enough to contact Mission Control using Orion's screwed up antennae, Adri. And you *do* know about blowing things up. You were a fighter pilot, correct? Just pretend that the six-mile-long rock is an enemy battleship. Blast it out of the sky! Simple!"

"I still don't think..."

"That's just it!" Susan interrupted her, ready to exit Hermes. "*Don't* think, Adri. Do your job, ok? As soon as I'm out you can insert the damper rods as far as they'll go into the reactor's core. That'll drop the radiation considerably. Of course, it will simultaneously cut off electrical generation. You'll only have six hours of battery life. So I expect you to power up the reactor by four hours, top, whether I'm back inside the OD or not. Understand? If Hermes' remaining systems go down again, they might not be capable of rebooting."

Adriana narrowed her eyes. Susan knew the woman wasn't giving up without a fight.

"Look—at least let me go out there with you, to back you up. I can stay on this side of the final radiation shield. Give me a minute to put on one of our regular spacesuits and..."

"No!" Susan firmly stopped her. "You know full well that we don't have another MMU. I've used up the small nitrogen canisters from our regular EMUs harvesting the comet. You'd be useless to me outside, tethered behind the radiation shield. Besides, you're already sick as a dog, just like me. When you get to the Asteroid you have to be functional. I can't risk you getting exposed to any more radiation. And besides, you're needed at the controls, Adri. You're absolutely backing me up...but inside! If I...receive a lethal dose out there...then you can still continue onward. So it's settled. Now *get away from the airlock!* With Kame gone, *I'm* in command!"

Clearly unhappy, Adri sighed deeply but floated to the side.

"Actually, I'm the senior astronaut and should..." Adriana pointed out.

"Kame put me in command!" Susan stubbornly repeated.

"That was just the comet side-mission. Back on Hermes..."

"Take it up with Mission Control!"

They both knew that Mission Control was out of reach. But "for the record" would show that Adriana did her best to assert command.

Susan was satisfied that her friend was safe from a judgmental history, should that ever exist in the future.

"Well, I expect you to be back inside long before you get that lethal dose," Adriana petulantly snapped back at her. "And...I love you, buddy."

"Well, I love you too," Susan quietly replied, sliding the airlock bar to the side. She opened the hatch and floated into the cramped chamber. Then she paused and turned. "I mean, it's been a true pleasure serving with you. But don't write me off just yet, Adri. I'm coming back in as soon as possible. What are a few more 'rads' between friends, huh? We're both already way past our lifetime doses, right?"

"Right..."

"Then punch me out, Adri," Susan resolutely ordered, pulling the airlock door closed behind her.

Susan had gone through that airlock it seemed a thousand times before, what with mining half of the comet's volume of frozen ice to-date. But every time she waited for the air pressure to drop to zero in the OD airlock she felt a rush of anticipation. In a few seconds the outer airlock hatch would open and she'd be *one with the Universe*, in her own little spacesuit floating by herself in the vastness of outer space. It wasn't just an amazing experience, it was a *religious communion*. If God could at least be partially defined as the totality of the Laws of Nature, then on her spacewalks she truly appreciated the vast, unfathomable immensity of the Almighty.

The light above the exit turned green and Susan swung the hatch outward. Ever fresh and new, surrounding her were the *stars*— brilliant pinpoints glaring silently, the visible Universe. Many of the pinpoints were fellow suns of the Milky Way. Many others were distant galaxies, where one single point of light up there containing literally billions of suns of its own. It was beyond awesome. It was *transcendental!*

"I'm outside."

"Closing the outer airlock door behind you," Adriana replied.

But Susan didn't have time to admire the view. There was a job to do. She latched her tether and floated forward, one handhold at a time, moving over the top of the closest circular radiation shield. Then she floated across the twisted struts that still contained the three giant water tanks and saddle-backed square storage bins. At their end she distally unleashed the tether to reel it in. Then, securely attached locally, she took a deep breath and faced the last radiation shield.

"How's the reactor, Adri?"

Susan recalled—seemingly an eternity before—when she, Ben, and Vladimir welded the loose reactor module back into place. Surprisingly, they'd done quite a good job. The bolts they'd melted in place still held solidly. Through all the subsequent burns, Hermes' long stack had hung together. Good work!

But now she was on her own, going not just across the barrier but into the heart of the nuclear reactor. Vladimir was *killed* just by being exposed *outside* the reactor. She was going *into* it!

But she couldn't dwell on that thought. She had to work fast. She would likely start losing control of her irradiated nerves and muscles. She knew full-well the results of acute radiation poisoning from what had happened to Ben.

"I'm allowing the dampener rods to push in as far as they'll go," Adri's small voice came over the helmet speakers. "I'm switching Hermes to battery power. We may lose contact, Susan, when you go past the primary radiation shield. Good luck."

"Copy that, Adri," Susan answered, grasping the upper edge of the circular shield with her white-gloved hands. "I'm climbing over now."

Attached to her workbelt were a variety of tools. The two massive radiator wings of the module were already folded outward, so there was unimpeded access to the nuclear reactor module. Susan drifted onto its curved outer surface, knowing that even with the graphite rods inserted a steady concentrated stream of ionizing radiation was even now penetrating her suit and flesh. It would have been nice to have on Vladimir's lead-impregnated MMU, but that was lost in space when the dead commander drifted away. So she was totally exposed to the radiation. Her only defense was to get her work done as fast as possible.

She switched her spacesuit computer to audio mode. She was going to need help staying alert and focused. Normally when in contact with the crew or with Mission Control, readouts flashing upon the inner surface of their helmets were the best means of internal suit reporting. But the suit's computer could also respond audibly.

"Computer, I need you to record everything I say. Store it in your most protected inner memory chips. There's a wee bit of hard radiation out here."

"*...acknowledged...*" came the crisp, metallic reply.

"Super..." Susan said, her hands starting to shake. "Can you archive the video feed also?"

Who knows, future historians or visiting aliens might want to see what'd happened to the ill-fated Asteroid mission.

"*...video feed being archived...*"

"Starting on the first bolt of the primary cover plate," she reported into her microphone.

Likely no one would ever hear the words she recorded. But it was comforting to think that someone—maybe God—was listening and commiserating.

She half-expected Adri to reply, but there was nothing but incoming static. Susan was isolated, on her own, just her and the suit computer.

She lifted up her bolt-head adapter, clamping it onto a square head set-into the nearest edge of the large curved panel. The panel was thirty feet long, ten feet wide. A lot of compact hardware was hidden beneath it. She tightly held an extended handle, placing her magnetic boots to each side, then twisted with all her strength. For a moment she was afraid the bolt was too tight for her to loosen...but then she felt it give. With relief, she began screwing it out of its socket.

"*...radiation at dangerous levels...*"

"Tell me something I don't know."

"*...that data is unavailable...*"

"Get a sense of humor, computer."

"*...that data is unavailable...*"

Jesus, what she'd give to hear Adri's voice right now—her sly jokes could make everything so much better!

But the task at hand didn't merit humor. It was much too difficult and intense.

The nuclear reactor wasn't meant to be serviced by crewmembers. Once every ten years Hermes was put into a high orbit around Earth for a reconditioning that included swapping-out the reactor core. The reactor refurbishment wasn't done by humans, but by radiation-hardened, semi-autonomous space-robots. Human flesh wasn't designed for this job.

"The first bolt is out," she said, breathing heavily from the exertion. "I'm proceeding to the second bolt."

There were ten bolts that had to be unscrewed and left hanging on their own short tethers before she could lift up the main outer panel. The access panel was hinged to not drift away into space. Beneath the panel was the heart of Hermes, powering the entire space vehicle. It could be "put to sleep" but never entirely turned off.

It would have been simpler and easier if the nuclear reactor was constructed from discrete rods of radioactive material. Instead, it was a complex matrix of channeled materials. Tiny uranium particles coated with pyro-carbon were embedded in a graphite substrate that itself was coated with zirconium. Small channels ran throughout the matrix, through which superheated hydrogen gas streamed as a relative coolant, propellant, or both. Susan had no access to those channels. They were much too numerous and tiny. But since the reactor functioned both as an ionic rocket and a heat source driving an electrical turbine, it had a few larger inset tubes running out to the external fins. In that way the reactor in its superhot electrical-generating mode could dissipate excess heat. If the large channels became clogged, the rampant heat could not be dispersed and the matrix would be damaged. The reactor couldn't explode, but it could melt down into useless slag. This, in fact, was the problem Susan faced. She had to unclog those larger flow-channels.

"Jesus, it's getting hot," Susan muttered to herself as she continued to loosen and remove the stubborn outer bolts.

"...suit cooling is operating at maximum efficiency..."

"That's hard to believe."

"...suit cooling...maximum..."

Of Christ, was her suit computer dropping out? Something must be affecting the microelectronics!

Strangely, though sweat was running from her forehead into her eyes, the internal temperature display on the inside of her helmet showed a comfortable 70 degrees in her suit. What the hell?

Oh, right...extreme radiation poisoning...it's equally bad both for human cells and computer chips. Silly me!

Feeling hot and nauseous was ominous. She had to speed up the work!

Running crosswise through the reactor were additional large tubes into which graphite rods were pushed by preloaded springs. A mechanism actively kept each of the graphite rods normally extruded. In an emergency they were designed to automatically "snap" into place. The rods could "turn down" the activity of the nuclear matrix by absorbing neutrons that stoked the nuclear reactions. However, the rods could not "shut down" the reactor entirely, just slow it.

Thus Susan knew that this near the uranium matrix—even in a shut-down mode with the rods inserted—she was still exposed to a continuing stream of intense, penetrating radiation: *high energy x-rays*, *gamma rays*, and unabsorbed *neutrons*.

She didn't have long until she'd be unconscious or dead: maybe only a matter of minutes...

"Bolts are out. The panel is free for lifting outward."

She planted her boots against one of the side radiator fins, grasped two of the free bolts, and wriggled one side of the 30-foot-long panel upward.

Though on Earth it would have weighed half a ton, in the zero-G of space it easily swung upward. She saw revealed right below the outward-slanted, hinged panel the "guts" of the reactor module: a bewildering maze of gleaming metallic tubes and mechanisms. Intimately jammed together beneath her space-booted feet were the massive components of the reactor core itself plus associated propellant lines, control drums, internal shields, turbo-pumps, crankshafts, electrical generator, and modulating control mechanisms. She had to "operate" on the reactor core without disturbing any of the surrounding mechanisms.

"Alright, ok...access to the main coolant lines..."

Her vision was blurring disconcertingly as she squinted at her internal helmet display. What was going on? The reactor should be in minimal operational mode, taking hours to kill her, not mere minutes! To make things worse, she was getting mentally confused. What was she trying to do and where was she supposed to do it?

"Oh, right—I just said it. I've got to find the main coolant line access ports. Computer, please bring up the schematics of what I'm looking at."

"*...accessing...*"

After a flurry of flickering images, on the inside of her helmet a set of bewildering construction plans and equipment diagrams overlaid themselves one on top of another. She struggled to make sense of them, blinking some to the side and expanding others. *Damn! Kame would have known just what to do! Alright, Susan...concentrate!*

"Ok, then...the reactor core units, they're near the surface, in the center..."

Ah...right...through the gathering fog in front of her eyes she made out sinister-looking black units imbedded in the maze of tubes and cables. Each was a solid square, four feet long on each side. There were three of them, linearly aligned. And the one furthest from the rear rocket nozzles was *glowing red!*

"Oh, that's not good," Susan muttered, momentarily frozen in place. "Unit one is already melted down," she forced herself to continue reporting. "I can see the graphite rods still in the 'out' position. They can't even penetrate their channels."

Jesus, that unit wasn't put "asleep"! It's been pouring out lethal radiation at full blast all this time! No wonder the computer's been warning me!

As if to emphasize her conclusion, a loud *warning siren* began blaring in her ears. A *hazard sign* flashed on-and-off on the inside of her helmet: the international ionizing-radiation trefoil symbol.

"*...you must immediately...to a safer location...*"

"Christ, tell me something I don't know...all warnings *off!*" she verbally ordered.

With the distracting noise and symbols gone, she could focus on her immediate task. She knew she was being lethally irradiated. She didn't need to be reminded of it every second!

"Ok...what now?"

"*...please be...more specific...*"

"Oh, shut up computer. You're just distracting me—*audio off!*"

"*...are you sure you wish...terminated?*"

"No...sorry...I'm just confused...stay on."

She knew she needed any help possible. She wasn't an engineer. She didn't know this complicated system. If nothing more, the suit's computer might help her stay focused as her decision-making was progressively compromised by the intense radiation.

"So, what's this?" she murmured.

A whole series of "porcupine quails" extended out around that unit, protected by transparent sheaths. Susan saw that even though the active extrusion mechanism was no longer working, the sheaths were so melted the graphite spears couldn't enter the channels. But Susan forced herself to remember that, fortunately, the reactor core was modular. If one failed, then the coolant and propellant was re-routed on forward to the next in line.

"Unit Two...is hot but the rods have inserted," she stated, her lips growing increasingly cracked and painful. "Unit Three looks fine...for now."

Unit One was clearly beyond salvaging. It was red hot. The outer casing was actually bubbling. Susan could feel the blazing heat through her spacesuit. Even worse, the many mechanisms wrapped around and to the side of Unit One were also melting. This was likely the main cause of Adri getting intermittent readings from the nuclear reactor. The meltdown of Unit One was progressively damaging all the other equipment around it!

"Looking for the access ports to Unit Two and Three..."

Grabbing onto slick surfaces of various conduits she floated to the two still-working core modules. Vaguely, she noticed a *bright flare* off to her right.

"Oh...that's not good," she gasped, looking to the side.

Her tether line had drifted down across the melting Unit One and caught fire. Actually, since there was no oxygen in the vacuum of outer space, it wasn't burning. But the slender line was glowing *bright red* and separating!

"My tether's gone," she weakly reported, watching her cut end spiraling up around her spacesuit. She was breathing shallower and shallower, faster and faster. "If I lose my grip...then there's nothing to keep me from drifting away into the eternal night...it'll be goodbye Hermes."

Come on, Susan! You're almost there! Focus!—she mentally admonished herself.

"Ok, then, just got to keep a firm hold at all times," she verbally answered herself. "That's all—now where are those damn sewer cleanout lines?"

"*...the waste cycling lines are in the habitable modules...*"

"I know that!" she snapped back at the computer.

Her thoughts were getting confused. She wasn't cleaning out a sewer line, but a nuclear reactor's main coolant channels! That was a bad sign. The unexpectedly intense radiation was affecting her central nervous system: producing mental confusion. Susan knew from previous NASA training classes that "no recovery is expected" when her brain function started to go.

She recalled the Russian nuclear submarine K-19. It was a first-generation nuclear submarine. Trying to catch up to the United States in nuclear submarine technology, the Russian sub was hastily built. On its initial shakedown cruise in 1961 the nuclear reactor lost its coolant. Attempting repairs without proper lead-lined radiation suits, a number of sailors went into the engine room. They were able to avoid a nuclear meltdown and explosion, but everyone who went into the engine room died—either immediately or within two years—from acute radiation poisoning.

Susan was comforted in the thought that the Russian submariners were true heroes. Because of their sacrifice, a possible nuclear confrontation between the Soviet Union and the Western powers was averted. Indeed, a feature length movie was made about them: "*The Windowmaker*" in 2002. She'd watched it with Adriana and other NASA astronauts before they'd launched up into orbit. It had impressed her greatly.

Would a movie ever be made about her? Susan hoped so, not so much to have a brief moment of posthumous fame but because the human race survived to still make movies!

"Ah, *there* they are..."

It was funny. She almost laughed. The access ports *did* look like sewer line cleanout plugs! They were round, white, with a square bolt on top. Unscrewing them she'd have direct access to the main flow channels. There were three sets of them. She knew that it was a waste of time to try to clean out those leading into the first unit. But the next two units were repairable. That made a total of fourteen lines to clean out the aggregating gunk. She had a shot at slowing or stopping Unit Two and Unit Three's degeneration—saving them the fate of turning into the useless, deadly slag of Unit One.

"Just like...cleaning out...the sewer line...back home," she muttered, her skin now starting to itch all over her body. It felt like she was burning up! Her family home back in Sulphur, Oklahoma was decades old and had cracked sewer lines into which infiltrating tree roots loved to grow, blocking them up. So she often as a kid helped her dad use a large metallic "plumber's snake" to unclog them. It was just a matter of running the grinding teeth, at the tip of the steel cable, deep into the buried sewer lines. This was no different.

"Working on the caps..."

"*...radiation at lethal levels...*"

Oh, Christ, that was just what she needed—computer confirmation that she was dying!

She ignored her escalating radiation-poisoning symptoms and focused on the immediate job. Using another differently sized adaptor attached to her workbelt she loosened and methodically unscrewed each of the fourteen accessible cleanout plugs. Each hung on its own small tether so it wouldn't float out into space.

As each one opened up, a spray of immediately frozen gas spurted upward. The spray icily coated her faceplate and spacesuit. She used the back of her gloved hand to wipe the haze away. But it didn't help much. Everything was getting very blurry. But she suddenly realized it wasn't just the external haze. It was *cataracts* forming in her irradiated eyeballs.

"Caps are off...starting to do the cleanouts..."

She fumbled loose the small coiled line at her workbelt. Indeed, it was a miniaturized version of a standard plumber's snake. It operated off her suit's internal battery, into which it was plugged. She had to jam the diamond-tipped cutter end into an open channel and allow it to swirl, dragging itself to the extent of the line, a full three feet into the reactor unit. Then, she'd pull it back out and move to the next opened channel. Simple!

Her entire world shrank to the opened channel with its attached screw-out cap bobbing at its side.

"Sticking the snake in...activating..."

She felt the slender line spinning in her gloved hand, crawling its way into the radioactive guts of the nuclear reactor.

"Good thing...they stocked Hermes...for just about every conceivable...emergency...whether humans were supposed to do it or not," she grinned, struggling to keep hold of the vibrating "rotor-rooter" in her hand as she held onto a metallic cable with the other.

By the time she finished cleaning out all fourteen channels, she could barely see anything. White cataracts in both eyes were virtually blinding her. She was so weak she could barely screw in the caps, sealing the newly cleaned-out main coolant channels.

Then she paused, trying to remember what she was supposed to do next. She needed advice! She needed help! Oh, her suit's computer. Maybe it was still working?

"Uh...I'm...what's next?" she whispered into her helmet.

"*...restore...integrity...*"

Ah, yes, the looming panel had to be closed down and screwed back in place.

Panel? Where was it? She couldn't see even that huge object...

Fumbling upward she grabbed onto the closest edge of the big 30-foot-long protecting plate and managed to muscle it downward on its hinges. Then, working largely from feel, she slowly crept around its edges. She stopped at each of the ten holes to get the dangling attached bolt in her glove, jam it into its hole, screw it in, and tighten it in place with her belt tool.

"Job...finished."

"*...integrity of NTR module...restored...*"

"Thank you...computer...audio off."

This time there was no confirming query from her faithful suit's computer. Apparently it was nearly dead as well, its electronics as fried as her brain.

She could barely whisper. She noted that her lips were profusely bleeding, tasting sticky and salty on her swollen tongue. She was now completely blind. The skin of her face and arms felt burned completely off. Her gut ached terribly. She felt like throwing up. And she was uncontrollably trembling. She was now so weak she could barely hold onto the serrated panel behind her, let alone try to climb back to the OD without a tether. Her helmet display was sputtering on-and-off. But that was ok. She was totally spent, unable to hold on any longer.

She could barely hear anything as she let loose and drifted away from Hermes. Yes, there was a tearful buzzing that annoyingly babbled in her ear. Someone outside her suit was trying to communicate with her. She couldn't remember who that was. But it didn't matter because the babble was unintelligible to her in her present terminal condition. She was bound for glory, going to join Vladimir in the vastness of space!

Poor Adri... She was left alone. But she was tough. She'd make it to the Asteroid.

Susan tried to mumble something profound just in case her suit's recorder was still working after the intense radiation bombardment of the last hour. But she couldn't get any further sounds out of her swollen, constricted throat, not even a squeak.

But then Susan realized she'd already said it. Good last words: *Job finished!* Hah!

What could be more honorable?

She recalled one of her favorite passage from her old poetry book *The Minstrel's Lark*, which still nestled comfortably inside her shirt. It was from Chapter 26, verses 4-7...

> *"Past Time and Space*
> *And mundane concerns*
> *There is more than nothing*
> *And less than everything*
> *Neither Heaven nor Hell*

But the bottom of the clouds
Bespeaking a higher layer
Beyond our dim visions
Where we might rest
In sweet peace
At last..."

Susan knew it was time for her to enter that peaceful realm. The thought didn't frighten her. Actually, it was quite pleasant.

Preparing to depart lunar orbit, Bill was struck with a bout of regret. He remembered their triumphant return to the assembly framework following the initial test firing of the Dish, nearly a month ago.   So much had happened since then...

After the initial test firing, it didn't take long for the fleet of small spaceships to return to the evacuated assembly-array.   Correlating with Bill's readouts, they found the giant grid floating serenely in space.

Its outer edges were blackened where the plasma balls had shot past. But beside the scorch marks there was no damage from the passage of the vastly powerful energy spheres that'd been released from the center of the giant framework. Even the Saucer at the lower center of the half-finished Dish was untouched, gleaming pure white on top and deep black on its underside.

As the Orion capsule—its jets firing off brief bursts of white vapor—floated up to dock with the Saucer at the bottom of the Dish, Bill happily held hands with Maria. Bill was oblivious to the knowing glances and snickers from the other crewmembers. Damn it, Bill knew his shipboard romance wasn't professional, but he felt due for a bit of enjoyment! Here this pretty, young, intelligent lady seemed genuinely attracted toward him. He was due some human connection in the midst of the intense pressure of the world-saving mission there at L1.

Also, he consciously decided that he could finally "mellow out" and forget his suspicions and fears. If there was indeed a "conspiracy" in the Saucer, then it was just aiding in the defense of the planet: without which their precious planet Earth would be a sitting duck in a cosmic shooting gallery! Scott and his mysterious backers had come up with the "proprietary" additions that changed Bill's failed research hobby into a novel subspace energy *collector*, then a nuclear bomb *eater*, and finally a killer-Asteroid *stopper!*

If there was truly a conspiracy—not just his natural paranoia crippling his mind—then long live its success! Meanwhile, he got to hold hands with a delightful young girl, who seemed to like him as much as he liked her.

Maybe things weren't so dire?

"Be with you in a minute," Maria prettily said to him as they floated up through the airlock into the interior corridors of the Saucer. "I've got to get something from my quarters, plus change into more comfortable clothes."

"Hey, babe—I'll be waiting!"

"It'll just take a minute," she replied, kicking rapidly away as she blew him a kiss.

Ah, what a sweet moment that *had* been!

All this was fresh and sharp in his memory, as if it had happened yesterday. In reality, it happened four weeks ago: before everything took an *incredible turn for the worse...*

He recalled how he floated happily along toward his quarters, more relaxed than he'd been for years. He was content just to drift, luxuriating in the zero-G environment instead of suffering the misery of the puking-damned. Everything was so much better! He actually smiled at passing crewmembers, greeting them cheerfully. Indeed, they were all relieved to be back in the Saucer, still alive and kicking after the incredibly successful initial live-fire exercise.

Then Maria was back at his side. She'd discarded her standard blue crew uniform and now had on a silky black blouse and shorts. Her legs, arms, and feet were bare. Her brown hair, usually tied in a tight bun behind her head, was billowing free, floating around her head in the zero-G.

Wow. She'd looked just like a brown-skinned, long-haired angel!

He relished the memory...

"I brought wine with me," Maria had whispered in his ear as she kicked up next to him there in the inner corridor, holding up an unlabeled bottle. "Normally I don't drink during working hours, but we need to celebrate. Is it ok with you?"

He shrugged. "Well, I usually don't drink alcohol either, *anytime* actually. It's due to my fundamentalist-church upbringing—but what the heck? The asteroid-blaster works! We're both still alive. The Framework didn't disintegrate. And since we blew away an entire mountain on the moon, we may have a real chance at stopping that damn Asteroid! Hopefully we now have our whole lives ahead of us instead of just a few short weeks to live. So, ok, let's get drunk and crazy! Why not?"

"*Very* crazy," she said, snuggling closer and kissing him directly on his lips.

Ah...that was *four weeks ago*—how happy he'd been!

Bill remembered the sweet taste of those soft lips. Now, though, the thought brought a shudder of disgust.

But back then it'd been *wonderful...*

"Uhm...right," he'd mumbled as he unlocked the cabin door. Tightly entwined, they both slipped inside. Maria broke free and swam through the air into the hammock, laughing.

"We'll need sippy bulbs," she grinned, fiddling with the screw-top of the bottle. "Getting the wine into the bulbs will be a trick, since we don't want it spilling out and getting dispersed into the air throughout the cabin. If we first depress the bulbs, then the suction should safely yank in the fluid."

"Can do!" Bill cheerfully replied, turning his back and opening his small transparent cabinet. He had a couple bulbs in there. He reached for them.

Then he paused, still with his back to her. It would be a dirty thing to do. But it would finally put to rest his suspicions. His prior covert searches had turned up strange anomalies in the official crew records. Prior to their NASA careers there were parallel "blanks" in *all* of the crew members' official records. Seen in isolation, none of the gaps were suspicious. In fact, there was a reasonable explanation for each of the several-months-long "departures" where the person's activities weren't specifically documented: ascribed generally to extended vacations, family duties, religious activities, brief illnesses, or other things. But the gaps were clustered in the same time-frame

aniel Basil Lyle

right before Scott began collaborating with Bill on the room-temperature-superconductivity/cold-fusion joint research!

Maria, one of the youngest, had the suspicious gap situated in the middle of her eighth grade school year. It was labeled as a "home school" episode, but the four month lapse was obviously in line with all the others. Following it, she was back to her regular school program.

Maybe it was just coincidence, *but...*

"Here you go, Maria. How fast is your eye-hand coordination?"

He handed her a collapsed-in bulb, which she swiftly inserted into the mouth of the briefly opened wine bottle. Slowly releasing the pressure on the bulb, the red fluid "burbled" into it, sucked straight out of the bottle. Letting it float beside her in zero-G she used her thumb to cover the bottle's mouth before slapping the sippy-top onto it. Then she accepted the second mashed-in bulb from Bill.

In a few moments he was lying beside her in the gently embracing fabric of the zero-G hammock, feeling her warm body pressed against his, as they both held their sippy-bottles.

"Hey, let's see who can drink theirs the fastest!" Bill laughed, sticking the bulb to his lips and pushing hard onto the plastic.

She snickered and did the same, drinking deeply as she drained the entire contents in one long gulp. He pretended to do the same, but in actuality drank nothing. Instead, he pushed his bulb out of sight to the side, hidden mashed down into the fabric of the hammock.

She looked at him blearily as he smacked his lips together, pretending to be woozy.

"Wow, that's strong stuff!" he grinned at her as she tried to agree but then slumped to the side, her eyes closed tightly.

She began to *snore...*

It worked—faster than he'd anticipated. She was unconscious. Hastily he felt at her neck. Yes, her heartbeat was strong. She was steadily breathing, though noisily. She was fine, just knocked out. He felt a pang of guilt. He wasn't the type to "date-drug" a girl, certainly without her knowledge. But he'd earlier crushed all the pills of the entire bottle of unused Dramamine to a fine powder, planning just such a maneuver. He'd thought he'd have to deliver it in a bulb of plain water, but the wine was much better. Its color helped hide the haze of the dissolving pills.

"Sorry, Maria," he spoke to her unconscious body, "but you'll wake up in a few hours with me in the hammock apologizing for us both getting drunk and falling asleep, no worse for the wear. In the meantime, however..."

He took one of the remaining diagnostic clinical chips out of the cabinet that was left over from his ordeal with space sickness, ripped off its sterile packaging, and pressed the sampling end onto the back of Maria's small hand. A blinking light on the paddle's end went from red to green as it slurped up a tiny amount of her blood through a micro-needle. He floated across from the hammock to his computer terminal and snapped the other end of the paddle into the USB port.

Data immediately started scrolling up on his screen from the rapid clinical micro-tests.

"What the hell?" he gasped.

The stained red blood cells depicted on the screen were *nucleated*. In the middle of each red-tinted, oblong red blood cell was an unmistakably distinct, purple-stained nucleus! Matured, peripheral-blood RBCs in humans lose their nuclei to be more flexible and carry more oxygen. The matured stained red blood cells on the screen were unmistakably those of a *bird* or a *reptile!*

"This can't be," Bill gulped, typing in further commands. The clinical chip on the diagnostic stick was very sophisticated. On one micro-draw of circulating blood it could run a number of on-demand clinical tests in addition to the more routine ones. Bill ordered it to do one of the rarer, more sophisticated tests. As it proceeded, Bill brought up the general hematology and biochemistry results. Yes, they were distinctly different from those of any normal human. Either Maria was the strangest human he'd ever heard of...or she *wasn't human* at all!

DING!

"Oh, right."

It was the computer signaling to him that the result to his requested *chromosomal analysis* was ready. Bill gaped at the numbers popping up on the screen, the undeniable spread of greatly enlarged dark-stained X-shaped linked structures. There was absolutely no doubt. The "karyotype" analysis of the blood cells showed that Maria had a total of 17 pairs of chromosomes. Humans have a total of 23 pairs of chromosomes. Also, the total information contained within a human's 23 chromosomes is 3.2 billion bases. The gross estimate from the chip for the nucleated cells being surveyed was 5.4 billion bases. Maria's cells had fewer chromosomes containing significantly more total information than did human cells!

"Oh...Jesus Christ," he whispered to himself, looking at the softly snoring young lady in the hammock with equal parts regret and fear. "I guess that's the end of our romance."

It was a pity. He'd been happier than he'd ever remembered, just holding her hand and giving her a light kiss. Once they both "woke up" he'd have to claim resumed space-sickness nausea, get real busy in his work, and "sadly" have "no more time for extracurricular relationships." He couldn't let the rest of the crew know that he'd discovered that they were *aliens!* Though the purpose of the space adventure was still noble—saving Earth from the Asteroid—he was certain they had ulterior motives.

"My, but what big teeth you have," he hysterically giggled to himself.

He remembered the answer that the "big bad wolf" hiding beneath Little Red Riding Hood's grandmother's clothes gave: "—the better to *eat* you with!"

He shuddered, knowing without a doubt that he was on a spaceship filled with *nonhuman predators.*

And that was a month ago...

Since that chilling discovery he'd buried himself in his work, inspecting and overseeing the installation of each of the final, newly arrived nuclear bomb super-charged panels. Plus he'd written a completely new program to better control the plasma discharge boundaries, providing finer tuning of the size of the "bullets." If needed, they could now shoot out from the Dish a stream of small plasma spheres, much as a machine gun fires a devastating penetrating burst at short range—or a single more diffuse large blob lasting significantly longer before dissipating into space.

So he had an excuse to stay away from Maria. Despite her previous amorous overtures, though, she didn't seem to mind. Apparently her task had been to keep him occupied and distracted. Now that his work was seemingly consuming all his time, she didn't have to keep up her romantic act. What an "old fart" he'd been, thinking she was genuinely attracted to him! But he wasn't fooling himself anymore. He knew that an aging failure like him wasn't a chick magnet. But that was alright. He had a new quest to occupy his full attention, the one they'd tried to distract him from pursuing: *getting to the bottom* of their *true* intentions! When he installed his new plasma generation program, he also slipped cryptic monitors into the software of all the Saucer's computer terminals. Now, safely isolated in his locked cabin at night, he could monitor the intra-ship communications of everyone else on the ship, plus ingoing and outgoing messages.

Most of the traffic was routine. Some of it, however, was not just unusual, but startling. In fact, it was spoken in a completely different, foreign language—not just other-than-English, but something that didn't exist on Earth: a series of *complex clicks, whistles,* and *growls* that swept through and past the hearing range of human ears.

What they were saying to each other he had no idea. But images transmitted along with the audio tracks revealed a frightful preoccupation. They were covert views captured from classified security monitors from across the planet. Bill saw private shots of national leaders sobbing as they were hustled to underground bunkers or were summarily executed by firing squads. He saw rampaging mobs numbering in the millions leveling once-vibrant cities. He saw starving mothers cut open their own veins attempting to feed emaciated, dying babies. He saw once disciplined armies reduced to tattered marauding hordes under vicious warlords.

Horrified, Bill even saw his hometown of Sulphur, Oklahoma turned into an armed encampment. The large military force's obvious function was to protect the corporate headquarters of Nashoba Energy, which had absolute rule over the townsfolk. Protestors were rounded up and executed. Food was a reward handed out to the obedient. All else were left to starve. Dead, rotting corpses littered the empty streets. But there were plenty of recruits to repopulate the sleepy little town. Nashoba Energy was recruiting an extensive *corporate army.* He saw them being rigorously trained and lavishly equipped.

The aliens on the Saucer relished the images, passing them around excitedly to each other, like collectables. Of particular interest to them were the ever faster-deteriorating established national military installations and large cities. It was as if Earth were being softened up for an *invasion*.

But that was speculation. A more immediate explanation was stunningly obvious to Bill.

From the aggregate images, Bill clearly understood that mankind was finally falling prey to the Laws of Biology. He knew from his high school biology courses that any species will relentlessly expand until stopped by physical forces: depletion of food or other necessary resources, lack of additional territory to expand into, disease and illness, or effective predation. Humans were already the planet's top predator, had largely conquered most diseases, and thought they could control their environment. So mankind's numbers expanded in a few short centuries from a few million to billions. But it was a fragile balance, with the massive population poised upon a vast enabling network providing food, water, and energy. Bill had heard authoritative biologists describing how the "carrying capacity" of Earth for humans (where "sustainable" systems for humans could be balanced without destroying the rest of the ecosystem) was one billion humans. The present population of Earth was more than *ten times* that number! Now that the Asteroid had knocked the supports away from beneath society, everything was crumbling. Like a collapsing skyscraper, each successive story was being smashed harder by the accumulating descending weight from above!

Yes, the sudden Asteroid threat had knocked out the delicate supporting props beneath the blotted human society. But the cataclysmic collapse was being abated and encouraged by unseen forces— centered at *Nashoba Energy*, as viewed with delight by the alien denizens of the Saucer!

Bill knew he had to find a way to subvert the deceivers. He had to be prepared—at a moment's notice—to save not just Earth but Hermes as well.

If his sister was by some miracle still alive, he was determined to bring her back. He had the ability to take sole command of the Dish via covert controls seeded into his new software platform. Now he just needed a way to isolate the crew and take over the entire Saucer.

But first there was an unexpected arrival, a new addition to the outgoing crew. Despite prior denials, that person was now going to accompany them to face the onrushing Asteroid. And Bill wanted to give him a *very special present*.

Floating at the docking bay's airlock to greet the high-level newcomer was the Saucer's Captain, other top officers, and...Maria.

"Hi, Airman Rodriguez, how you doin'?" Bill jovially greeted her as he did a forward flip in the zero-G, expertly coming to rest alongside her.

She looked at him suspiciously. He'd tried to remain superficially friendly to her over the last month, always greeting her with a wide smile. But he knew she didn't believe one small bulb of wine had knocked her out. He'd been careful to flush her sippy bottle with water before putting uncontaminated wine back in. She'd sniffed it suspiciously after regaining consciousness but apparently detected nothing awry. He'd also pretended to be likewise knocked out, groggy and unable to continue their planed "hook-up." But she knew something was up. He just had to be a better actor than she, keeping up the pretense that nothing was wrong.

Both of their locked gazes were abruptly shifted as the airlock suddenly opened and a man floated through. His face was a delicate shade of *green*.

"Hi, Scott!" Bill cheerfully greeted him.

With deep satisfaction, Bill handed him a *fresh barf bag*. "Here's a present, buddy—just the thing for a rookie!"

Maria floated forward, solicitously taking the flailing arm of the Nashoba Energy's COO—one of the most powerful people in the world, who now looked poised to puke his guts out!

The Captain looked embarrassed by the weakly floundering man but said nothing.

"Oh, and Airman Rodriguez is an expert babysitter, Scott. She'll take real good care of you," Bill said as he turned his back to them and precisely kicked away.

Boy that felt good! He wasn't going to antagonize anyone needlessly, but it certainly wasn't "business as usual" anymore. Despite the Captain's status, everyone knew that Scott Nash was the unquestioned leader of this expedition. And Bill understood Scott in a way that nobody else did.

Yes, he hadn't escaped Scott. Even going to the moon didn't keep Scott from following and taking command. Bill was once again back under Scott's clenched fist. But things were no longer the same. Even "alpha dogs" had their weaknesses, best known and exploited by the oppressed male members of the pack!

If Bill could just keep his cool, watch for his chance, and resist Scott's overpowering domination—it's the whipped dog that bites the hardest.

Chapter 27

<u>OCEANS OF TIME</u>

Looking back over a lifetime
Say an unthinkably long hundred years
Viewed from youth as an eternity
Looking back reduced to a mere blink
A cascade of brief memories
Decades 1, 2, 3, 4, 5, 6, 7, 8, 9, 10
Gone in a flash, just that fast
Countdown to a sad ending
Of old age, illness, frailty
Where did the time go?
Was it even there at all?
A trillion-trillion-trillion years
Big Bangs, Expansions, and Big Rips
Entire Universes cycling up then down
Just the breathing of a sleeping giant?
Stretching out all-encompassing arms
And yawning himself awake...

The Minstrel's Lark, 27:61-66

IMPACT MINUS ELEVEN DAYS, *WAKING UP...*

Susan didn't want to wake up. She was having such a pleasant dream. She was back in the womb, submerged in a timeless warm saltwater bath, contained and protected by her loving, pregnant mother. But an irritating voice was calling to her, nagging and *threatening...*

—and *slapping* her in her face!

"Go away!" Susan yelled, bolting upright. "I don't want to get born...*what?*"

Immediately she began gagging and coughing, fluid spurting from her mouth and nose.

"Take it slow, Susan. You're ok. Breathe deeply! I just dragged you out. You've got to start breathing air again!"

It was Adri. She was holding Susan by the shoulders, gently shaking her. Between fits of coughing out gooey fluid from her lungs, Susan noticed that she was naked, shriveled up, wet—and *green!* Oh, Christ, it must be the radiation poisoning. Her flesh was decaying! Adri must have brought her back into Hermes to die in abject misery instead of peacefully floating away into space!

And then Adri tried to drown her? Say *what?*

But then again, as the gagging abated, Susan discovered she didn't feel all that terrible.

In fact, she felt better than she had for months!

"W-what h-happened?"

"You've been unconscious for ten days, Susan. I've been giving you...unconventional...therapy. But it seems to have worked. You're better now. And we're within viewing range of the Asteroid. I wanted to leave you in the tank for a while longer, at least until your skin condition cleared up, but you've got to see our latest telescopic pictures...that is, if you're up to it?"

"But...I was drifting away...you didn't have a spacesuit with jets to...?"

"I maneuvered the entire Hermes-stack. I had trouble with the steering jets but fortunately that didn't stop me from scooping you up. I just opened the outer EVA airlock door and Hermes swallowed you back inside."

"But...I was dying!"

"Yes, that's correct. But I got you out of your spacesuit and inserted you into Hab-3."

"The...the h-hydroponic algae t-tank?"

"It's much more than that now, Susan. It's more like a primordial ocean, like Earth experienced 500 million years ago, when single-celled life began combining and recombining, *evolving* into multi-cellular forms."

"But...how could that effect my...?"

"Hermes' seed crops were genetically engineered to be highly flexible and adaptable," Adriana interrupted her. "The seed stocks were continually irradiated during our progressive series of disasters. The genetically enhanced multi-genomes adapted to the extreme stresses. First they produced the mushroom forest. Then they became our superfast-growing, still-mutating algae ocean."

"S-so what...?"

"I stripped you of your clothes, attached a breather mask, and put you into the tank. The organisms infiltrated your flesh, Susan. They crawled through your entire tissue bed, adapting you to their environment and simultaneously repairing the radiation damage to your cells."

"That's...that's..."

"Right, it's totally unbelievable. It sounds like a science fiction novel. But it happened! It was the only way I could think of to keep you hydrated and fed throughout your entire tissue bed. I had no idea if it would work. But here you are!"

"Bright...*green?*"

"After a couple days you didn't need the breather mask anymore. You were absorbing oxygen directly through your skin. Chlorophyll molecules appeared in your surface squamous cells. You were directly absorbing light as an energy source. It was amazing! The protocells literally brought you back from the dead."

"B-by turning me into a p-plant?"

"I think that's a temporary condition, just symbiotic algae colonizing your outer skin layers. How do you feel?"

Susan floated naked in the zero-G, feeling suddenly exposed and violated.

"Adri, this is just too f-fantastic. I don't...see how what you're c-claiming is even p-possible."

"This is not a space-induced dream," Adri impatiently argued. "You didn't eat anything during the last ten days. You were absorbing energy directly from the grow-lights inside HAB-3. Oh, by the way, your 'plumbing' job on the reactor worked. I got the full report from your suit computer's shielded backup memory chips. The reactor module was still badly damaged, but cleaning out the cooling lines of

the two still-working units allowed self-diagnostic and repair mechanisms to kick in. Amazing job you did, Susan! Now we've got plenty
of electricity, though that may be not hold for too long."

Susan huddled herself up into a ball, grasping her folded green
legs with her green arms, squeezing her eyes tightly shut. She felt an
irrational desire to kick herself back over to the airlock into HAB-3
and reenter the warm, safe, womb-like environment. But then she
caught herself, steeled her mind, and accepted the new reality.

"Ok...so I'm a recovering v-vegetable," Susan said, straightening
out her legs and pushing away from Adri. "Do you have a towel for a
naked pseudo-mammal, maybe even f-fresh clothes?"

"They're right here. You've got to come up immediately to the
OD. I've got detailed photos of the Asteroid. You're not going to believe what's there!"

"Oh I think after this little experience I'll b-believe just about a-
anything, Adri," Susan sighed, toweling off her body.

It was indeed strange to see the green glow of her flesh. But then
again, her skin wasn't hanging in dry slabs, cooked by radiation. As
she floated away from Hermes in her battered spacesuit she was sure
she'd been fried like a potato chip. Now she felt bizarrely energetic,
even buoyant! The lights around her felt wonderful on her exposed
skin, like warm sun at a cool beach.

It was nice to be a plant.

"I had no idea it would work," Adri again said in a small, trembling voice. "I figured the tank would as likely absorb your flesh as
heal it. I was sure you'd rather contribute your calories to the tank
than just drift away into outer space so I..."

"So it was just a lucky accident that the critters in the tank repaired my body?"

Her voice was steadier. She was adapting rapidly to unexpectedly
still being alive.

"Actually, yes it was...unless, perhaps, there's some *greater force*
guarding us?"

"I thought you said you didn't believe in that Animism stuff anymore?"

"Before he went insane and spaced himself, Ben talked to me too, Susan. At the time I was just humoring him, but...a lot of the Hindu beliefs are in line with Animism."

Susan finished pulling on the dry underwear and overall jumpsuit, kicking with vigor against the device-covered wall of HAB-2 as she floated upward toward the OD.

Her head was now rapidly clearing. Her muscles were gaining strength. Her voice was strong.

"Well, whatever, Adri. Maybe God or whatever is looking out for us. If so, I could sure suggest some improvements over the plot to-date! Anyway, that *was* smart of you to try something so bizarre— and damn fine piloting I'm sure, bringing Hermes around to swallow me back up—especially if the steering jets were malfunctioning! But let's get back to it...you say you have photos of the Asteroid?"

They were both now kicking up through the Service Node, heading for the Observation Deck.

"We're rapidly catching up to the Asteroid. Remember how Kame put us on a collision course? In fact, she did it almost too well. We're traveling 2,000 mph too fast! We still have six days to figure out a breaking maneuver. But I'm not sure Hermes is up to it."

"Why not?"

"I think that Unit-1 of the reactor core has damaged the underlying mechanisms of the main liquid-fuel rocket. Also, the steering jets barely worked long enough to get you back into Hermes. I haven't dared to try them again, lest they fail entirely."

Susan nodded grimly.

"Yes, Unit-1 was melting-down when I did my 'plumbing' job on the other two units of the reactor, Adri. The heat it was generating certainly could have damaged large portions of the entire reactor module."

"And it's only gotten worse, Susan. I can't get any reliable readings out of the reactor module. The rest of Hermes is still receiving abundant electrical power, so the turbo-pumps must be working. But if we try to power up the main liquid-fuel rocket I'm afraid of a catastrophic explosion. It could destroy Hermes."

"But we have to slow down or we'll crash into that bloody Asteroid. Kame *did* do too good of a job of aiming us at that thing!"

"Yes, but there's a possibility we can go into orbit around it."

"Orbit? Are you kidding, Adri? It's much too small to have a significant gravitational field. We certainly won't have the time to maneuver into a tight orbit. And in a distant orbit we wouldn't be close enough to inspect its surface directly."

They were now in the OD. Susan was relieved to see that the eternal stars were still out there shining brightly through the portholes. And off in front of them Susan could just make out a *glimmering black spot...*

And beyond that was a tiny white-blue dot...

"Is that...?"

"It's the Asteroid and Earth, Susan. We've finally caught up to them as we're descending in-line with the Asteroid's path from above the planetary disc. But that's not what's so amazing. We're close enough now that I've gotten telescopic shots."

"What about communication with Earth?"

"Still nothing—just static. Either they're not transmitting or Ben's sabotage of our hardware/software was too effective. I'll keep trying. Maybe nearer we'll get back in contact. But so far..."

Susan was stunned.

"Wait! You know about Ben's sabotage? How's that possible? I kept it a secret after he confessed right before he spaced himself! I figured there was no point by then in bringing it up since the damage was done. And I still think there was a lot of good to him. I wanted to preserve his reputation if the Earth were somehow saved. But if he told you about his betrayal earlier, why didn't you tell me?"

Adriana paused, wetting her lips with her tongue as if considering what to say. Then she sighed deeply, as if resigned to the present situation: "At the end, Kame knew all about it. She told me in confidence. She'd figured it out. He was the only person with access to accomplish each of the sabotages. I agreed not to tell you. That was why she was so harsh with him, particularly about keeping him isolated."

"What? Why would she tell you and not me?"

"Well..."

"*Out* with it!"

"She thought you might be colluding with him."

"Me? That's ridiculous!"

"She...had her reasons...which made some sense, actually."

"What?"

"Well, all the well-publicized, strange things that happened to you before you came to NASA and..."

"So you thought I'd betray my country, my planet, my crewmates, and even *you?*"

She shrugged.

"I honestly didn't believe it, Susan...but..."

"But?"

"You never know for sure about anyone. People can do strange things for inexplicable reasons that..."

"And now?"

"After all we've been through, can you doubt me? I totally believe in you, Susan. We're more than comrades. We're *sisters!*"

"Yes, well..."

She was still hurt that Kame and Adri thought she might be a traitor. But, then again, she'd thought the same of Kame. And now that Adri revealed she had this inside knowledge...

Could she fully trust Adri?

"Alright then," Susan changed the topic, "show me what you've got new on the Asteroid."

Adriana slid into one of the flight deck chairs, strapping herself in and activating the computer screen.

Susan floated beside her, watching her tap a few keys on the keyboard. A video sprang up.

Susan sucked in her breath.

"That's the Asteroid? Are you sure?"

"Yes."

Susan saw a *black, undulating blob.* There were no details. It was a living fog, writhing and shooting out short tentacles.

"What the hell is that?" Susan gasped. "Is there something wrong with our telescopic array?"

"No, Susan. I think it's why JWST-2 couldn't get a clear shot of it. What we're seeing is a *thick atmosphere*, being agitated by the solar wind or, perhaps, internal magnetic flux."

"That's impossible, Adri! The Asteroid is only six miles long. It can't have any appreciable atmosphere. It only has a tiny gravitational field!"

Adri wearily put her head down on the keyboard, her red hair drifting lazily in the zero-G.

"That's what I kept telling myself, Susan," she sighed out of the side of her mouth. "I double and triple checked our equipment. This close, we're getting fairly good resolution. The Asteroid really does have a thick, black atmosphere."

Susan was stunned, staring at the writhing apparition on the screen.

"But you're correct also, Susan," Adri quickly continued, lifting her head back up. "I did the calculations and the Asteroid has the gravitation pull of a small planet. In fact, that's partly why we're in such a pickle. We're approaching it even faster than we predicted because it's *pulling* us in!"

"Oh, my God," Susan whispered, staring at the black blob. "Do you think it's maybe a hunk of a super-dense white dwarf or neutron star?"

"That was my first thought also—that it was a remnant from a dying star, somehow captured by our solar system's gravity field. So, I did a spectral analysis and found that I could get a fairly clear view of the Asteroid's surface scanning outside the visible spectrum."

"Ah, you did an infra-red interrogation of the object?"

"Right. It's only slightly above the near absolute zero of space itself, but enough to stand out in relief. So...I got *this!*"

A still photo replaced the frothing blob. In this view the atmosphere was only visible as a faint surrounding haze.

"Wow."

It wasn't anything like Susan imagined. She'd expected a rocky, crater-scared, rounded mountain. Instead, what she saw displayed on the computer screen was a dark *striated oblong.* It was deep black, sunlight glittering off many parallel layers that ran along its length. The layers looked melted, their edges smoothed over one upon the other.

"That's not just rocks...it looks like layered, forged *metal!*"

"Yes, that was my reaction as well."

Susan was shocked by the implications.

Damn! This whole expedition was getting more and more bizarre!

"How is this possible, Adri? This thing came from the Oort cloud. Star-remnant or not, it should look similar to the comet we found, a 'fossil' from 5 billion years in the past. How could it be made of forged metal?"

"There aren't metallic asteroids?"

"Well, sure there are, Adri. Many of the M-type asteroids are made out of nickel-iron. But they come from the inner asteroid belt. And this doesn't look like ore. This looks like a *formed* object!"

They were both silent for a moment, digesting the information.

"Well, then, what if it's already passed close to the sun—perhaps many times. That might explain the melted-over layers," Adri softly replied. "A much larger mass in the past might have gotten fused and melted-down into this hard lump over the eons. There are lots of examples on Earth where repeated physical natural forces produce supposed 'manufactured' features."

"Well, that makes more sense than a coherent hunk of a wandering star remnant," Susan agreed.

"Ok, but the main problem we have right now is not figuring out its composition or origin, but slowing Hermes down enough to rendezvous with it rather than crashing onto its surface!"

"Yes, you're absolutely right, Adri. We've got to find a way to slow Hermes—or at least swing around the Asteroid."

"I think we've got to attempt tentative test firings, both of our steering jets and the main liquid fuel rocket. If the jets are reliable we can swing Hermes around so that the liquid rocket faces forward and we can safely decelerate."

"Why not use the nuclear thermal rocket?" Susan frowned, her thoughts still somewhat chaotic. "The ionic thrust generated from just one of the three core reactor units should be enough to..."

"That was when we had plenty of lead time. That was when Kame hadn't accelerated us up to collision speed. That was when we weren't being pulled in by an impossibly large gravitational field!"

"Oh, right...so then...?"

"I'll start rechecking the circuitry and doing diagnostics on the control systems. Can you do more long range scans of the Asteroid, figuring out better what we're up against in terms of the gravity field? That could tell us if it's possible to swing into an orbit around the central mass. That's your expertise, Asteroid composition, right?"

"Right—and let's not forget the objective: to *shatter* the damn thing into dust!"

"Even if we succeed in not crashing onto it, but just swinging into a high orbit around it, we still won't have much time to figure out a viable plan," Adri sighed.

"How long?"

"At most we'll have upon arrival just a total of *four days* to figure out how best to divert or destroy it."

"But I thought we had only a day once we arrived...?"

"That was before our faster-than-planned acceleration, plus unexpected gravity assist."

"Jesus, this is confusing," Susan grimaced. "But if we can successfully put on the brakes, we'll have a longer period to find a solution!"

Adriana laughed. "At least we're finally almost there. That's good news, right?"

"Yes, but if it really has sufficient mass to generate a planetary-sized gravitational field, then we're sure not going to divert it," Susan grimly replied.

"And if it truly is made out of a sun-forged or star-remnant super-dense metal...?"

"—then our two nuclear bombs might not even dent it."

They looked at each other in horror. After all they'd gone through would the Asteroid still defeat them?

Not without a fight!

"Then let's get to work," Susan said, turning back to the screen. "We've got to narrow our options."

"Right."

Susan was still rocked by Adriana's revelation of knowing about Ben's treachery then keeping it from her. No wonder Kame had been cool toward her. The Commander thought she might be a coconspirator with Ben! But...it didn't make sense. Something about Adri's story didn't ring true. Even the timing was fuzzy.

Regardless, the final crisis was upon them. Susan had to put aside her unease and concentrate on her immediate tasks.

Adri began working on the various software programs that controlled access to the steering jets and to the rear liquid-fuel rocket. At the same time, Susan initiated a series of detailed scans of the distant space rock. What she saw further amazed her.

After a while she paused, overwhelmed by what she'd found.

"Adri, how are you doing?"

"I'm getting responses from the steering jets with a new algorithm, toggling them back and forth ok. I think we have limited guidance potential for jogging Hermes' path. But the thermal rocket still seems dead. That's probably just as well since I can't trust any of the controls to the hydrogen or oxygen tanks anymore. If I tried to trigger them to release their volatile gases through compromised red-hot fuel lines the tanks would likely explode. Fortunately we don't need them since the Ocean and its recycling system are working well, scrubbing our CO_2 and generating fresh oxygen. But that leaves us with no brakes, going full-speed at the Asteroid!"

"Ah, hell...we're zooming up on the Asteroid with no way to slow down," Susan grimaced.

"We'll figure something out. I've just got to concentrate, give it more thought."

"Can you take a brief break?" Susan asked her.

"Sure."

"Then come take a look at what I've found. It may change your flight calculations."

"Ok."

Adriana drifted through the air over to Susan's chair, floating in the cabin's air off to the side.

Susan brought up a detailed 3D representation of the Asteroid.

"What am I looking at?" Adriana asked.

"Halfway along its length, on top, inside that large depression..."

"Ah, yes. There's a narrow fissure. No telling how deep it goes. Are you thinking...?"

"Yes, that's our best bet to destroy the damn thing. If we can get our two fission bombs *inside* the Asteroid..."

"—then the blasts might not just dissipate uselessly into surrounding space!"

"Exactly!"

"Well, that's good news, Susan. Now we have a specific target. We can align our approach vector with the goal of getting our two nukes into that deep gash."

"But there's more bad news."

"How so?"

Susan displayed a series of spectral graphs.

"I can't be certain at this distance, but I've a preliminary analysis on the composition of the asteroid."

"And...?"

"First, the atmosphere isn't what we'd want to breathe."

"I suspected as much. It's black, like soot. What gases are in it?"

"It's composed mainly of hydrogen and helium, with iron contaminants that give it that black color."

"But...that sounds a lot like..."

"A *gas giant*—like the atmosphere of the planet Jupiter or Saturn..."

"Wow."

"Yes, 'wow' indeed, my friend—hardly a typical Asteroid."

"But if it has an atmosphere like Jupiter or Saturn, does that mean the gravity on the surface of the Asteroid will be massive? If we try to walk in our spacesuits, will we even be able to move?"

"I don't know yet, Adri. Saturn is much less dense than Earth so it only has 0.9 Earth's gravity. Jupiter, however, is massive with 2.5 G at its surface layers. But even if a high value exists on the Asteroid's surface we could still move, just with great difficulty. It'd be like carrying a two hundred fifty pound man on your shoulders."

"In our present condition?"

Susan shrugged. "Good question, Adri. We're both hardly in Olympian shape."

Indeed, they'd spent the last five months floating in zero-G, with no extra exercising most of that time. Overloaded with maintenance duties and bombarded with crises, time on exercise machines was a low priority. Their muscle tone and bone densities were abysmal, even before the severe consequences of radiation exposure and long periods of starvation.

"We may be crushed flat as pancakes. Who knows? This is unknown territory, Adri. I'm just trying to prepare us for what we may face down there."

"Understood, Susan," Adri kindly replied, squeezing Susan's shoulder with a weakly trembling hand.

The woman was very fragile, a shadow of her prior self.

But Susan appreciated the show of support. Somewhat invigorated, she continued: "And then there's the surface composition itself..."

"Is it metal?"

"Indeed it is—95% titanium!"

"Titanium...that's a very hard metal, right? It's common in Earth's crust. And if I remember correctly, it's also found in asteroids."

"Yes, it's not surprising to find titanium in asteroid ore—but hardly in such high concentration. And then there's something else."

"Oh?"

Susan paused before answering, reluctant to utter the dramatic, unbelievable words.

"It's hard to be sure from this distance, Adri—but it appears to be an *alloy*, with the titanium bonded mainly to zirconium and vanadium."

"So...did they melt together when the Asteroid swung close to the sun on previous orbits?"

"I suppose that's possible. But the alloy looks suspiciously like that which we use on earth in constructing armor plating, missiles, naval ships, and even aircraft."

"But...that would mean...?"

"—this thing isn't just a rock that got melted by the sun."

They were both silent for a moment, digesting the idea.

"So you're saying it's not just a wandering asteroid that by cosmic accident happened to zero-in on Earth?" Adri softly replied.

Susan laughed, somewhat hysterically.

Then she sobered up.

"There's even more, Adri. I did a rough map of the magnetic field."

"And?"

"You were right. There *is* a strong magnetic field that's roiling the iron-laden cloud that surrounds the Asteroid. And it's not a static field, like Earth's."

Adriana was silent for a moment, seemingly in shock.

"You mean it's *oscillating?*"

"Yes, which means the magnetic field can't be generated from just a molten metallic core that's spinning around inside the Asteroid, as one is on Earth, but..."

"You're...saying...it has to come from *oscillating* internal charge?" Adri gulped.

"That's what Maxwell's physics equations dictate. So it has to be things like..."

"—machinery, electrical circuits, power plants..."

"Yes, Adri...all of that possibly located inside a 5-billion year old *alien spacecraft!*"

Susan didn't know whether to laugh or just cry. But that was silly. They had too much work to do, in too little time.

"Well, we're still alive, that's something—and I have you to thank for that, Adri. We'll just do the best we can. What other choice do we have?"

Adriana narrowed her eyes, nodding. "Where there's life there's hope. That's one positive message I got from Ben, despite his betrayal. We'll stop that thing, Susan, whatever it is."

Susan smiled back at her friend, appreciating the encouragement. Other than withholding information at Kame's order, Adri had been nothing but helpful. But Susan had a cold feeling in the pit of her stomach: that she'd come this way *before*—and was totally defeated.

Sometimes the heroes don't win.

They were leaving L1, headed out beyond the moon. The initial tests were finished. Everything was working according to specs. Their payload was in place: the accumulated energy of thousands of nuclear detonations. Bill was relieved to be underway.

It'd been difficult maintaining the pretense on the spaceship that he was surrounded by regular humans, instead of cleverly disguised aliens! Now that they were underway, however, everyone in the crew was so busy they hardly paid him any attention to him. That is, except for Scott. Presently he was peering at Bill suspiciously.

Bill hid behind his naturally introverted withdrawal mechanism. He pretended his aversion to human contact kept him from meeting the eyes of others. But Scott knew him better than the rest. He knew that something was up.

"So how are you doing?" Scott casually asked from his flight chair.

They were in the upper control deck, gazing out through the one-way transparent top of the Saucer at the moon's cratered surface, which was receding off to the side.

"I'm just anxious," Bill carefully replied, trying to divert Scott's attention. "We're carrying with us the accumulated energy of nearly 20,000 detonated fusion bombs. If anything goes wrong, we're not even dust in the stellar wind."

The Dish was fully loaded with its entire complement of nuclear bomb-charged black panels. As long as they stayed within ten lunar distances from Earth, calculations suggested they would still have access to the massive subspace energy depots that'd been deposited into the Earth-Moon gravitational well. The larger the depot the further it radiated out into subspace. And the ones they'd made were *enormous...*

"—just scattered free atoms, is more like it," Scott laughed. "But don't worry, Bill. I designed this whole thing, remember? I'm a genius! And you did a great job installing it. You're quite...competent. We've got it all figured out. *Nashoba Energy* reigns triumphant! That stray Asteroid is toast. And we're the 'toasters'!"

"Right..."

Bill leaned back in his seat, wearily closing his eyes. Scott had to rub it in, didn't he? Bill had long ago accepted the fact that he was just a glorified technician. But he didn't like Scott advertising the fact. Then again, though, Bill secretly knew much more than they had any idea. For one thing, he knew from pirated JWST-2 views he'd secretly snagged that Hermes was still on course to collide with the Asteroid. Though there were still no detectable communications from Hermes, he hadn't given up hope that Susan might still be alive. Periodically he covertly swung the high-gain communication antennae of the Saucer at Hermes and tried to get a response. The others didn't know what he was doing, his covert computer programs well-hidden. He had full access to all the Saucer's systems from the privacy of his locked cabin.

But he feared that at any moment they might discover his secret operations and stop him dead in his tracks.

Should that happen, Bill regarded Scott as his "ace in the hand." It wasn't just his uneasy friendship with the man, but Bill's intimate knowledge of Scott's mindset. Bill knew that Scott was still sweet on Susan. If he could just convince Scott that Susan was alive on Hermes, then...

"Leaving lunar orbit," the Captain confidently reported, breaking Bill's train of thought. "President Swartz sends her best wishes for the success of the mission."

"That's nice," Bill wanly grinned to Scott. "At least the United States still has a government in place."

"The few surviving politicians are holed up in the Cheyenne Mountain Nuclear Bunker," Scott shrugged. "Washington D.C. is in chaos. The Washington Monument is down, blown apart by the 'People's Spiritual Liberation Front' fanatical gangs. It's a good thing that Project Star-Shield used up most of the nuclear bombs of the U.S. and collective world arsenal. Otherwise there'd be mushroom clouds going off all over the planet. It's incredible the number of atomic bombs mankind manufactured, enough to kill everyone many times over."

That was a curious thing for Scott to say. Of course the world was filled with nuclear bombs. Why wouldn't it be?

"So are you saying that even if we succeed in stopping the Asteroid, there won't be much left for us to return to?" Bill cautiously stated.

"Oh, Nashoba Energy will be fine. In fact, we and a few other multinational corporations will thrive. Billions of people will die, either from starvation, disease, or war. But that will just thin out the rampaging hordes to a livable level. The rest of us will rebuild. Eventually things will be even better than before."

"But rebuild *what?*" Bill angrily replied, trying to provoke a deeper response. "Do we just remake the same corrupt, self-destructive, short-sighted civilization as before? I'm not sure that humanity has it within itself to do any better than..."

"That's a good point you raise, Bill," Scott eagerly replied, rudely stopping him short. "They could certainly use wise leadership beyond their limited genetics to establish societal and species boundaries that make sense. Instead of being focused on individual pleasures of the moment, society could benefit from a longer, wider viewpoint."

"Like what?"

"Well, like accepting the need for overall tight population control, strict environmental impact laws, limited territorial domination, synergistic versus competitive outputs, competent lines of accepted authority, well-constrained talent utilization, and a strong world government."

"That sounds like a big curtailment of individual freedom."

"Yes, but if it prevented the worst expressions of human nature, it would be a minor sacrifice—don't you think?"

"True...but us humans won't accept such limitations."

"That's why the New World Order must be *imposed*, not developed 'hit-and-miss.'"

"And just who would do that 'imposing'?" Bill asked, trying to keep his voice neutral.

Bill was chilled by the penetrating gaze Scott shot back to him.

"Why, *we* will, of course."

"That's...just not possible," Bill softly replied.

"Why not, Bill? We'll return to Earth not just as its saviors, but as its absolute rulers. After all, we'll still have immense firepower left over inside the Dish. We can simply impose our will upon a defanged world that's depleted of its worst weapons. Society has already fragmented into weak warring clans. They'll be easily defeated by an organized army that's well funded and directed by the world's multinational corporations. Any significant resistance will be incinerated, by us, from high on orbit. With our overwhelming firepower, we can enforce reshaping national boundaries, herding humanity into sustainable enclaves. Even Cheyenne Mountain won't be able to stand against us. If need be, we'll melt it into a volcanic caldron. Remember what we did to that mountain on the moon? Believe me, Bill, this is the dawn of a peaceful, orderly, *renaissance* for all mankind!"

Bill just nodded, looking away.

Sure, a whole "new world order"—but *for* whom? It one way or the other, the Asteroid was bringing the end of *Homo sapiens* as the dominant species on the planet. According to Scott's cryptic words, "they" were destined to being "herded" into "enclaves." That sounded suspiciously like isolated reservations, or even *game preserves?*

Perversely, a picture of Airman Rodriguez' oversized teeth sprang to his mind.

Bill shuddered, steadfastly averting his gaze from the others.

He was convinced that something *else* was poised to take over—something that only he was in a position to stop.

Chapter 28

ASTEROID RENDEZVOUS

Anticipation of ecstasy
Fulfilling all your dreams
That thing you see in the future
Which will make everything alright
If only you can somehow reach it
Drawing nearer, agonizingly slowly
Taking weeks, months, even years
Of struggle, hardship, dedication
A goal that culminates your entire life
That you finally fight your way up to
Standing there on the peak of Everest
Seeing the entire world laid out below
A moment of pure triumph and relief
You discover to your shocked horror
That the only way forward is down
And you don't have the strength
To take even one more step...
Do you freeze or take a leap of faith?
The Minstrel's Lark, 28:13-17

IMPACT MINUS FOUR DAYS, *DECELERATING...*
"I wish there were some other way."
"This is our only choice, Adri, you know that."
"But it will destroy Hermes. And even if we survive the crash, there'll be no way for us to get back to Earth."

"We were never going to make it back to Earth, Adri," Susan quietly reminded Adriana. "We always knew this was a one-way trip. But it's our duty. We have to finish the job."

They were sitting side-by-side, strapped into the Orion capsule, shivering even inside their insulated flight suits. It was icy cold. Two days previous, yet *another* terrible catastrophe had almost destroyed Hermes!

They just couldn't get a break. The Universe hated them!

Actually, the present disaster was predictable. Slag from the melting Unit-1 reactor had finally permeated throughout the reactor module, triggering a chemical explosion. Shards of hot metal skewered the liquid fuel tanks, spilling out their precious contents into space. In one terrible moment they'd lost their electrical power generator plus their stored, pressurized liquid fuel—hydrogen, oxygen, and methane. The three water tanks, hiding behind the radiation shield, were fortunately undamaged. The fully charged ship batteries were still intact. But the two remaining reactor units were melting. Although they couldn't reach critical mass and trigger a nuclear explosion, the two surviving reactor units might yet combine with surrounding elements to produce yet another conventional explosion which might blow up what remained of Hermes.

So the situation was dire: Hermes was now a floating, uncontrollable *bomb* which might detonate at any moment!

Susan and Adri decided to save the ship's batteries for the final approach to the Asteroid. If Hermes could just hang together for 48 more hours, they'd arrive at their destination. Using the remaining batteries they could then activate the steering-jets to guide their final descent, using compressed air for propulsion. But in turning off the batteries for the last couple days, the two women had to endure icy conditions both inside Hermes and within the escape capsules. Fortunately, though, they'd been working too hard to notice.

They'd stocked the Orion capsule with their remaining supplies of dried algae, water, and everything else they could fit inside. It was almost impossible to move around in the crammed-full crew cabin. But it was their last refuge, likely their new "home" on the Asteroid.

Hermes, though, was doomed.

There was no way it could avoid crashing into the Asteroid. Indeed, the inexplicably large gravity was relentlessly pulling Hermes into the Asteroid's deadly embrace. Even if they achieved full deceleration with their weak steering jets, Hermes would still smash *hard* into the titanium surface of the mysterious celestial body.

This was a final "hail-Mary" maneuver to avoid disaster.

"I'm ready to rotate the stack, Susan. I'm bringing the batteries back online. Here's hoping the steering jets are working properly. Cross your fingers for luck!"

"First put your helmet on, Adri, with your faceplate locked down," Susan kindly reminded her. "Then make sure that your internal air supply is flowing. Let's be as safe as possible as we crash into pieces!"

"Right..." Adri grinned back, chuckling, "Safety first!"

They locked their helmets into place, snapped down their faceplates, and tested their internal microphones by thumping them with their tongues. Susan looked over to the *three other flight chairs*, half expecting their "occupants" to do the same.

But there were no "clicks" from them. In fact, there was zero movement.

What a bizarre "crew" they made...

Kame sat across from Susan—her suit helmet completely iced over from inside—the spacesuit stiff and bloated. They'd brought her in from the sliced-open transport compartment below the Orion capsule. She deserved a chance to get onto the surface in one piece. They owed her that much for her heroism in getting them there. But her previously frozen-solid body was starting to thaw, releasing decomposition gases inside the suit, causing the arms and legs to "balloon" outward. The two remaining flight chairs also had their own "occupants." Similarly strapped into each chair were the *two tactical nuclear bombs*. The pointed cylinders sat motionless, cold and deadly.

Susan felt the Orion capsule moving.

"Ok, we've rotated onto the top of the stack, Susan," Adri reported. "I'm jettisoning the cargo module."

Susan felt a violent jar as explosive bolts blew off the lower, already mutilated cargo container. Now Orion was free to move unimpeded once it separated from Hermes, guided in its own final descent by internal gas canisters spewing through small jets.

"We're set to attempt deceleration," Adri said, her voice sounding uncharacteristically strained.

Yep, no more chuckling...

Again, they were both speaking for history. Internal recorders were activated in each of their suits. Likely that would be yet another futile gesture, but it gave Susan a small sense of hope. Regardless, she felt oddly detached, as if observing herself and Adri from the distant future: watching and listening to a vivid virtual-reality playback.

Now they were mere minutes from crashing into the Asteroid. Attached or not to Hermes, at their present speed the Orion capsule would be crushed. They had to slow down! Outside the nearest porthole Susan saw the *black, roiling cloud* of the miles-long object that they were fast approaching.

"Ok, then, Adri. Once again, if we're both blown to Kingdom Come—it was a joy serving with you."

"Likewise..."

The Orion capsule was now rotated into the opposite configuration it'd taken for most of the six month mission. Before, it had hung on the underside of the Service Node, almost as an afterthought. But now it was poised on the "topside" of the Service Node, ready to take control. They'd chosen to use it as their escape vehicle and, hopefully, base of operations on the surface of the Asteroid. SAV-2 might have sufficed, but it was a much flimsier spacecraft than the sturdy Orion. At best they were about to endure a very rough landing. At worse they'd be squashed flat, a sad preview of what would soon happen to Earth.

What they were about to do would generate tremendous stress throughout the Hermes stack. It was not only a desperation maneuver, it was bizarrely foolish. They had no guarantee it would work. Indeed, it could catastrophically fail. If they could have used the liquid fuel engine and their stored fuel stocks, they might have had a reasonable chance of either getting into a high orbit around the Asteroid or landing intact. But that capability was gone, lost in the explosion triggered by reactor Unit-1. Instead, they were desperately attempting to accomplish a violent maneuver similar to what they'd previously jury-rigged with the comet. But now they were *not* using their single relatively sturdy SAV as an auxiliary "rocket." It was positioned wrong and couldn't hold enough "fuel" to slow sufficiently the large Hermes stack. Instead, their hopes rested on igniting their *three flimsy HABs.*

"Temperatures in the HABs are on schedule, as predicted," Susan said as the *roiling black cloud* grew ever larger outside the porthole, "We're ten minutes away from crashing."

"This is going to be close."

"That's for sure."

They both sat in silence, watching crawling graphs reporting on sensors located throughout the three HABs. Each graph showed the gradation of temperatures in each of the three chambers, plus the overlain evolving pressures of the sublimating oxygen, ammonia, and methane gasses. Tubes placed throughout the thawing ices were busily sucking away freshly liquefied water. The three HABs had to reach the optimal same internal conditions within microseconds of each other, staggered from outside to inside.

Susan looked away from her computer screen to glance at Adriana. The smaller woman looked very fragile in her pressure suit. Her red hair hung in tangles down across her wane face. Susan felt her prior suspicions evaporating. In times of extreme battle, when you had to depend on your comrades, minor questions were just static background noise.

Like it or not, they were bonded together forever.

"How are we doing?" Susan asked her.

It was less than a minute to smashing into the Asteroid. Perversely in the cold interior of Orion, Susan felt nervous sweat wetting her brow. It was irritating that she couldn't wipe the salty moisture away from her eyes. So she just blinked rapidly, trying to keep her vision sharp.

"Hermes' steering jets are keeping us precisely aligned," Adri reported. "We're still on target, HABs forward. This is it, Susan. I'll give us a countdown..."

"*Light up* them damn firecrackers!" Susan cheered.

Then she closed her eyes tightly, bracing in her seat. Their fate was now in Adriana's hands...

"*...ten...nine...eight...seven...*"

Susan was tired beyond exhaustion. Her bones ached. Her time in the "tank" unfortunately hadn't turned her into a superwoman. Yes, she was grateful to still be alive. She was happy the green tint of her skin had disappeared, the symbiotic algae dying once she left the watery environment. But she'd only been restored to her previously sick, weakened state. And the physical work they'd done—even in zero-G—over the last couple days was massive.

She opened her eyes again, resolved to face her final seconds on Hermes with a steely determination.

"*...six...five...four...*"

She'd chopped out most of the comet's remaining ice. Opening HAB-3's terminal airlock to space, they ejected their friendly salty ocean. It was sad to see it spew out, a pressurized, frothy green foam. Then, once the inner temperature plunged to near absolute zero, they filled most of the empty volume with selected chunks of the cometary ice. After first removing essential equipment up into the service Node, the process was repeated with HAB-2 then HAB-3. So the frozen ice chunks were moved ever deeper into Hermes while filling in behind.

All three HABs were set to blow by quickly raising the temperature of each module in exact sequence. The timing had to be precise, down to the split-second. The process had to allow for initial sublimation of the proper gasses, rapid draining of water residues, and buildup of internal pressure. But, unlike with SAV-1, the HABs were just inflatables with flimsy walls. They couldn't hold much pressure. Anything could go wrong. If a seam of a HAB split at the wrong moment, the desperation maneuver would come to nothing. Hermes would spin out of control and their mission would end as a "splat" on the titanium mountain seemingly rushing at them from below, rather than a controlled crash landing.

Well, they were about to find out if the improvised braking "rocket blasts" would work.

"*...three...two...one...*"

Time to toss the dice!

In that moment another favorite passage from The Minstrel's Lark sprang into Susan's mind, chapter 28 verses 1-3:

"Is 'free will' but an illusion?
Thinking we make our own Fate
Are we but pieces in a greater Game
Where others move us at will
And ours is but to stand upright
Thinking the step forward is ours
While our decisions are mute
Be we Kings, Queens, Knights,
Or just lowly, disposable pawns
But I think not, maybe...
We have more power than that
When we exercise our rights
And break all the Rules.
Isn't that fun?"

Oh sure, loads of fun...spinning around and around on a broken "merry-go-round," getting sicker and sicker with no way to dismount!

"Ignition..."

HAB-3 exploded in *a red ball of fire* that nearly blinded Susan as she stared forward out of a porthole. The Orion capsule was hit by high G's as she was slung forward against the backward-braking blast. Fortunately the wide straps of her seat held fast. But the near-simultaneous *second* blast from HAB-2 was not so gentle. It tore the seat loose from its moorings and flung Susan against one of the equipment-laden interior walls of the capsule. She felt her left arm *snap* under the crushing blow, but didn't have time to react to the pain as HAB-1—right beside the Service Node and immediately outside the Orion capsule—detonated in turn.

Glimpsed through the portholes, Susan saw that Orion was enveloped in a *cocoon* of fire!

"Releasing clamps!" Susan heard Adri's distant voice.

Susan saw the flaming remains of Hermes dropping away, headed straight for the *huge black object* right in front of them.

The Orion capsule was floating free.

"Guiding us in for landing..."

Fascinated, craning her neck to the side to keep the forward port-hole in view, ignoring the brutal pain in her broken left arm, Susan watched what remained of Hermes plummet *straight though* the *black fog* into a series of *high ridges*. The faithful spaceship bounced once before breaking up into large fragments. The three massive wa-ter tanks burst open, spreading a blanket of white snow upon the me-tallic mountain-sized ripples. Then what was left of the rear nuclear module *slammed* into an outcropping and spectacularly *exploded* in a ball of red-yellow flames.

As she bounced against one of the fusion bombs—both it and her still strapped into their torn-free flight chairs—Susan glimpsed out of all three portholes *massive black ridges* rising up to surround them.

Then there was jarring "thud" that flung Susan against another equipment laden wall, a sense of rolling, and a sudden, jarring *full-stop!*

"We're down," Adri gasped, her voice trembling.

"Uh...something's wrong," Susan managed to groan, the pain from her broken arm surpassed by yet a *new* and *even worse* misery!

She tried to move her good arm to unbuckle her seat straps, but couldn't. Something *very heavy* was pressing down upon her entire body, *squashing* her. Every nerve in her body was protesting loudly, filling her mind with flaming agony!

"It's...just...*gravity*," Adri said from her seat, also struggling to move.

"It...feels like...maybe 1.5 G?"

"More like...2.0 G, Susan," Adri grated, "God, it's awful!"

"Whatever, Adri—are we intact? Are we safe for the moment?"

The cabin was a jumble of containers and torn-off equipment. Plus it was dark inside. The internal lights had gone off when they crashed.

Ah, they flashed back on! At least they still had internal power.

"If you call being marooned on a giant Asteroid headed straight for Earth, traveling at 60,000 mph, with no way off, shepherding two fusion nuclear bombs being "safe"—then yes, Susan, we're in great shape!" Adriana hysterically laughed. Then she visibly caught herself and became deadly serious: "I don't know about the overall damage to

Orion, since everything bounced around so much, but we've still got atmospheric pressure here in the cabin. That's something..."

"Hah!" Susan croaked back at Adri, looking at the jumbled confusion within the capsule. Just about anything that could break free had done so. Looking down, she was glad to see that no bones were poking through the flesh of her throbbing left arm. That could have been even worse. "We're still alive, I guess."

"Are *you* ok, Susan?" Adriana asked, sounding very concerned.

Indeed, Susan was *not* ok. She was dazed and confused. Everything around her looked blurry. Her head was spinning. She could have easily gotten a concussion in the violent cabin movements, despite her protective helmet.

And Adri looked funny. She was upside down! No...it was Susan herself, having come to rest on her neck and side, feet stuck "up" in the air.

If not for the tight straps of her chair, she'd probably be crushed by her own weight, unconscious and dying. As it was, she was just in agony!

And it was so bizarre to have a real "up" and "down." To go from weightless zero-G to crushing 2G in a few seconds was horrendous!

"I need...a splint on my forearm...and maybe a new set of muscles...please?" she groaned.

"Ok, we'll do that," Adriana said, feeling gently at Susan's twisted left arm. "Our zero-G weakened muscles can't be replaced. But I'm sure we can get your arm in better shape. That looks serious, Susan. We'll get a splint in place right away. And then, once our situation is stabilized, we can get out onto the surface. We've got to set the nukes, Susan, as quickly as possible. Remember, we've limited air. And according to my readings, Orion's fuel cells are leaking. We'll lose power shortly. If we're going to accomplish anything, we've got to get going as soon as possible."

"Sure, of course," Susan replied, trying to power through the pain...

—when a sudden *crackling* startled them both!

"*...Hermes crew...copy...saw the crash landing...*"

"Jesus, Adri—that must be Mission Control!" Susan excitedly said. She pawed at the straps with her good arm as she tried to locate the communication console in the jumble inside the capsule. "The crash must have undone whatever Ben did to kill our Orion receivers!"

"Thank God for small blessings, huh?" Adri said, also fumbling through the wreckage.

"Where's the microphone?" Susan gasped. She tried to slip free of the straps to start painfully crawling through the cluttered debris...

"I've got it, relax," Adriana said, reaching beneath a tangle of cables to drag out a small microphone. She lifted it up to her now-opened faceplate. Then she spoke sharply into the microphone: "This is Hermes—what's left of us," she spoke excitedly into the microphone. "Johansson and King here, on the surface of the Asteroid. We're going to place our two nukes into a deep rift in its middle. The rest of the crew is dead and..."

"Susan! Are you really there?"

She flicked up her own faceplate and shouted in a strained voice, still fumbling at her seat straps: "I'm here! Who am I talking to?"

"It's Bill, Susan! I'm in space beyond the moon, inside a new vehicle that Nashoba Energy invented. It's extremely powerful and designed to shoot a stream of coherent plasma bursts using our super-battery technology! We're confident it will destroy the incoming Asteroid! I advise you to retreat from the Asteroid! Our experts say your two nukes will be worse than useless. Even if they fragment the Asteroid it could allow pieces to slip past our plasma bursts. Abort your mission, save yourselves and..."

The transmission abruptly cut out.

"Bill! Bill! Are you there?" Susan shouted.

But it was to no avail. There wasn't even static anymore. Their brief contact was gone. Whatever "repair" had happened to their communications systems, it was lost.

"Well, what do we do, Susan?"

Susan groaned, holding her throbbing left arm rigid against her side. "We can't count on new technology to stop this Asteroid, Adri. Bill and his crew don't have any idea what they're up against. Maybe their 'plasma' discharges might stop a loosely jumbled ice-mountain, but not a *solid titanium* cosmic bullet! We have to proceed as planned. Our only shot at stopping this thing is to blow it up from within!"

Susan saw Adri frown, then take off her helmet while painfully leaning back against piled containers.

Her red hair lay limp at the sides of her head, dragged down by the pervasive heavy gravity. Susan was shocked at how thin she looked once her hair wasn't floating about her head like it would have been doing in zero-G.

But they weren't in outer space anymore.

"We might still have enough air pressure left in our capsule canisters to power bursts from our steering jets, perhaps sufficient to slip off the surface and..."

"Forget it, Adri!" Susan stopped her. "Or you can try to escape if you want, I don't care! I only know that I'm taking our two nukes into the innards of this damn Asteroid-alien-spaceship, whatever-the-hell it is. I didn't come all this way, suffer everything we've gone through, just to slink away at the last minute!"

Adriana nodded.

"And neither did I," she gamely whispered.

Susan groaned from the crippling pain in her arm, angry at being handicapped so late in the game!

"Ok, then help me with my arm, Adri. I need a splint for my left forearm. We've got to lay out the spacesuits. It's going to be a job getting into them in this mess, in high gravity. And if that new spaceship from Earth fires its missiles or whatever before we get into that rift, then we'll be toast along with the surface rocks. We've got to get *out* of Orion!"

"Yes."

Susan wished more than anything that she could save her good friend Adri: see her safely float away to the side of the Asteroid inside the banged-up but still functional Orion capsule. With a broken arm, in crushing gravity, however, there was no way Susan could drag the two heavy nukes by her lonesome. That was clearly a two-woman job.

"So this is it, then...our last 'hurrah'!"

"We get the nukes into position and detonate them," Adriana nodded, looking at the two nose cones sticking up out of the wreckage in the cabin.

"I assume the crash didn't affect the codes?"

"I don't think the G-forces we suffered during our crash are any greater than an intercontinental ballistic missile would achieve. The bombs are already programmed with our biometric data. After uncovering the control pad we provide either of our thumbprints and punch in the code. The nukes will blow in sixty seconds, unless we input different commands."

"Then let's do it! Let's get this job done!"

"*Together!*" Adri likewise exclaimed, grinning widely.

"Together to the end," Susan gratefully replied.

She and Adri both gave a silent nod to *Kame*. The body of their martyred Commander was jammed into a corner under toppled heavy equipment. The thawing faceplate revealed a *smear of red* inside the spacesuit. What wasn't already rotted was now crushed to a bloody pulp. But she'd made it! She'd gotten to the Asteroid.

That warmed Susan's heart more than anything.

Bill jerked back from his computer screen as the flimsy door to his small cabin came crashing in, narrowly missing his head!

"*What* are you doing?"

It was an enraged Scott, followed closely by the Captain plus several burly security personnel.

Bill managed to type in a short command to his keyboard before he was tackled and plastered up against the wall.

"Scott...Susan's still alive!" Bill gasped, knowing his covert operation was busted but wanting to preempt anything worse from happening.

"We have to *stop* that Asteroid!" Scott *screamed* into Bill's ear.

"Of course we do!" Bill sputtered back, his face still jammed up against a wall. "But we've got to give Susan and Adriana a chance. They're both alive! They just landed on the Asteroid! If their nukes don't work we can still blast the damn thing with a train of plasma bursts and..."

"We're not waiting for them to try their little firecrackers," Scott said in a more normal voice. The burly guards pinned Bill's arms painfully behind his back then turned him around to face the others. "As you told them, it will likely only make our job more difficult. In just a day we'll be within range. We can't delay. As soon as we're close enough, we're firing the plasma bursts!"

"So you *knew* Susan was still alive?" Bill gasped again, incredulous.

"We weren't sure...we got weak RF signals, incoherent...but..."

"Why didn't you let me know?"

"Why did you go behind our backs and subvert the Saucer's controls? Are you one of those religious fanatics from home? Are you a covert agent, looking to destroy this mission?"

"What? No! That's preposterous, Scott. You've known me all your life. I'm not..."

"When I inspected the Saucer's programs upon arrival I saw your 'enhancements,' plus their hidden updates!" Scott glowered at Bill. He was clearly furious. "Tapping into your cabin's terminal we saw and heard what you were doing. That's why we stopped your attempt to contact Hermes. If news that some of the crew survived were to reach Earth, then there might be bureaucratic delays. President Swartz still has a few loyalists here aboard the Saucer."

That was news to Bill. He'd assumed the crew was completely alien. Apparently some of the suspicious gaps in the life histories of the crew were just that: coincidental. But Scott's extreme reaction told Bill that the alien threat inside the crew was both real and pervasive.

"I thought you'd be thrilled to learn she was still alive?"

Scott's fierce expression softened.

"Sure, I like Susan—but her presence...complicates...an already critical situation."

"Complicates?"

"To many, she's an *existential* threat."

"What the hell?"

"No matter, take him away!" Scott snapped at the two guards.

"I know what you *really* are!" Bill shouted as he was floated out of the room, the two security personnel holding him immobile between them.

"And what's that?" Scott said, floating out in front of him with his hands on his hips.

"You're *aliens* from outer space, looking to take over the Earth!"

Scott incongruously broke out laughing, his longish hair swirling around his tanned face. The Captain and others joined in the merriment.

Then they abruptly stopped laughing.

"Oh, it's far *worse* than that," Scott snarled at him, revealing sharply pointed teeth, "you little, *tasty* mammal!"

"What, you're going to *eat* me?"

But then Scott's teeth abruptly looked perfectly normal, white and rounded. His regular good-natured smile painted over his previously ferocious face.

"Just joking with you, Bill," he said as he floated alongside, grabbing Bill's arm to twist the biceps muscle painfully. "We're locking you away where you can't do any further damage. There's no need to 'make a stink' when we're this close to success, is there? As far as anyone else will know, you've just had another bout of space-sickness and are being treated by Maria in the infirmary. When we get back to Earth you can still be one of the conquering heroes. We'll need accepted authority figures to herd the surviving masses into their new 'safe' territories."

He released Bill's arm to kick against a wall of the tight corridor, starting to float disdainfully away.

"You need me outside the infirmary, Scott!" Bill called after him. "I *have* to be actively involved in the attack on the Asteroid!"

Something in Bill's voice stopped Scott, who grabbed a hanging cable to pull himself around in a half circle.

"What?"

"I put a 'dead man switch' in the software deviations which I previously constructed. If anything happens to me—my heart rate slows too much or stops entirely, or the nano-monitors I injected into my bloodstream are tampered with, or the programs themselves manipulated—then the computer programs in the Saucer will self-destruct, taking down the entire system. And I've put a hold on the firing sequence. Unless I personally unlock it with the proper keyword you can neither form nor fire-off any plasma bursts. So you *can't* kill me or isolate me. *I'm* the one making the demands here, not you!"

His claims were true except for one. That bit about "dead-man nano-switches" floating in his blood was a complete lie. But by the time they discovered the lie, it wouldn't matter. He'd have delayed them long enough from tampering with his computer codes, giving Susan the time she needed.

"Hold...him...tight!" Scott snarled, floating up and grabbing Bill by the throat.

The grip tightened. Bill couldn't breathe. He struggled uselessly as Scott efficiently suffocated him. Scott's fingernails dug into the flesh of his neck like talons!

"You'll have to kill me...and then you're...dead in space!" Bill managed to gasp out.

Then the grip relaxed and Bill raggedly sucked in air, suddenly more scared than he'd ever been before in his entire life!

"That's just a taste, Bill," Scott growled. "The fate of the world hangs in the balance. Whatever twisted scheme you've come up with to pretend that your pitiful failure of a life has any meaning *isn't* going to succeed. Either you give me that password *right now*, or you'll suffer torture far worse than anything you've ever imagined! It'll be tricky to accomplish it without altering your heartbeat too much, but I assure you I can do it!"

"Look...Scott," Bill croaked out of his damaged throat, "I just want to give Susan time to set her nukes and escape. If the Asteroid gets too close...whether Susan has succeeded or not...I'll give you the password and you can fire the plasma bursts. I promise!"

Scott's black eyes were piercing, unblinking. They seemed to peer deeply into Bill's soul.

"You're not lying," he grudgingly admitted. "Ok, then. We can wait twenty-four hours. That won't be cutting things too close. So she'll have a full day on the surface of the Asteroid to do whatever she's going to attempt. But then we incinerate that damn Asteroid, agreed?"

"Can we...inform her and Adriana about the time limitation?"

"No."

"But..."

"Take it or leave it, 'Doctor' King!" he growled contemptuously. "Overt contact with her at this stage will trigger...restrictions...that we can't risk being imposed upon us. You were right concluding that 'alien' things are in motion, reaching beyond our normal perceptions.

But if that Asteroid isn't stopped then I assure you an entire world *will* be destroyed! We absolutely share the imperative of stopping the Asteroid! Do I have your agreement?"

Bill frowned, his throat and arms hurting terribly. This ploy of his to bully the alien crew was taking a heavy toll on his introverted psyche. Now he *wanted* to retreat into a cozy jail cell, to just give up. Scott's overpowering presence was tying his guts into knots. He hated confrontations and this was the mother of all clashes!

But Bill knew he had to hang in there...for just a while longer.

"I want to be in the control room, watching the monitors. You don't have to give me access to a computer terminal, but I have to see what's happening."

"Sure."

"And you have to promise to tell me what's really going on!"

Scott exchanged a strange look with the Captain, as if they were telepathically communicating.

"We want your full cooperation, Bill. You won't like what we have to tell you, but you *can* have a prominent role in the fate of your species."

"The fate of...*my* species?"

Was Bill ready to admit that he and Maria were aliens in human form?

"Once you know the truth, everything will become clear. You can be the 'big man' you've always wanted to be. In fact, you could finally call yourself a *true* 'King' of the world, my dear Dr. *King!*"

Oh, this was getting too bizarre. These crew members were either real aliens from outer space or totally crazy power-maddened, mutated humans. Either way, getting them to tell their story might divert them from trying to decrypt his password, which was deceptively simple.

"I don't care about getting power. I'm doing this for my sister!" Bill spat at them. "In twenty-four hours you get the password. Now could you please get your goons off me?"

Scott gave them a brief gesture and they let loose of him.

He floated into the middle of the corridor, crumpled-up, clutching his throat, twisted with pain. Looking at their "predatory" stares, he knew that they'd happily resume the torture at a moment's notice.

Susan, do your thing!—Bill mentally pleaded. *You've got one day left! Then you, Adriana, the Orion capsule, and the Asteroid get incinerated! God help all of us.*

Chapter 29

<u>EXCAVATION</u>

So much is hidden below the surface

Under your skin a wealth of systems

Smooth-exterior concealing volumes

Libraries of knowledge informing

Organs, tissues, cells, networks

Biochemistry, hormones, genetics

In just one single microscopic cell

An incredible complexity swirling

All in dynamic balance, twirling

Keeping the trains running on time

While plotting world domination

A moment's careless mistake

Throwing everything awry

As you dig down gingerly

Layer by ever-deeper layer

Uncovering what was unknown

But now, at long last, is finally

Exposed to the light of the sun

Naked and shockingly revealed!

Don't think that you're done...

The Minstrel's Lark, 29:48-52

IMPACT MINUS THREE DAYS, *SLIPPING AND FALLING...*
"Unggghhh...I don't think I can go on," Adriana groaned.
They were in their spacesuits, struggling toward the distant ravine
on the surface of the Asteroid. Just standing in the 2X earth gravity

was difficult, especially after their months in weightlessness. So dragging a *heavy nuclear fusion bomb* behind each of them was sheer agony!

That which took only a finger to move in zero-G was now a *dead weight.*

"Let's...rest...for a minute," Susan spoke into her helmet microphone.

"Thank God," Adriana gasped back. "This is awful!"

It was hard for Susan to hear Adri. The other woman's voice was crackling in Susan's helmet speaker. The distortion wasn't just due to the damage to her battered spacesuit, but the fact that they were being constantly washed in large oscillating magnetic fields. The powerful fluxes were inducing random electrical currents within their suits, interfering with normal functions. Susan could barely get her suit helmet's inner display screen to light up, let alone provide the directions she was used to instantly calling up.

There was no hope of talking to her suit computer. That function was degraded beyond retrieval. She was just happy the spacesuit worked at all.

Adri collapsed onto the hard, smooth surface beneath them.

Susan likewise slumped next to her. She rested the back of her helmeted head on the other woman's splayed-out leg.

Off in the distance Susan saw the crashed cone of the Orion capsule. It'd been damaged far worse than they'd first thought, both by the exploding HAB modules and then by its final plunge onto the metallic surface of the Asteroid. One of its sloping sides was dented in. The other side was torn open, with cables and equipment dangling out. It was a miracle the inner shell maintained air pressurization for as long as it had. There was no possibility of riding it to safety away from the Asteroid. For better or worse, Susan knew that she and Adri were definitely there to stay.

"I'll be ok...in just a minute," Adri gasped, flattened out on the rocks.

The strap that led back to Adriana's trailing nuclear bomb was slack. They'd rigged up rough harnesses for each of the two bombs from the straps of Orion's flight chairs. The bombs were linked to each woman by more of the straps. By leaning forward and pushing hard with their upper bodies against a flat strip, they could drag the bombs along the slick surface. In normal earth gravity each hydrogen bomb weighed 200 lb. So in addition to twice their normal 1G body weight, each woman had to drag an equivalent 400-pound lump.

It was excruciating agony, especially for their six-month weakened, feeble muscles. The pain had subsided in Susan's broken arm but it was mostly useless, just dangling.

But Susan, surprisingly, wasn't overcome with discouragement. Instead, she felt oddly invigorated. She'd finally arrived at her unacknowledged lifetime goal: directly confronting the "heavenly body" of her nightmares...standing right there on the surface of a real Asteroid!

"This is...unique...isn't it, Adri?"

Around Susan were rippling, parallel ridges. Struggling to get her strength back, she paused to look around, fascinated. What she saw was breath-taking. The ridges were various shades of black, deep brown, and a faint white. And each ridge had its edges smoothed over, seemingly polished by the hands of an unseen giant.

Struggling to walk erect on the slick surface had triggered a long forgotten memory in Susan's mind. She recalled traveling to Athens Greece to attend an astrophysical conference while she was in graduate school. During free time, she'd gone to visit the famous, looming fortress/temple in the center of Athens, the Acropolis. The broken chunks of marble that covered the top of the hill were difficult to walk upon because they were so smooth and slick, polished by millions of feet from fellow sightseers over the millennia.

The slick surface of the Asteroid's rippling ridges imparted the same feeling to Susan: of her walking on a mammoth artifact deliberately constructed by intelligent beings eons ago in the far-distant past. Forgetting the fact of the impossibly large gravity and magnetic fields, Susan would have still been convinced that this wasn't just a space rock melted by passing too close too many times to the sun...but an *ancient spacecraft*.

And the swirling black fog around her made the scene the more unreal for Susan. It was similar to when she was inside the hydroponic tank on Hermes. The Asteroid's atmosphere was *thick!* Except for occasional clear areas, it did indeed feel like she was submerged in a watery, dark ocean.

The Asteroid was nothing like she'd ever imagined.

"I...think...I can go on," Adri muttered, breaking Susan's train of thought. The spacesuited woman pushed herself painfully back up to her knees.

"Yes, we'd best...get moving. There's no telling when...they'll fire that new weapon at us," Susan agreed. "If we're out here on the surface we'll surely be killed."

"How long...has it been?"

"Seems like days...but..."

Susan squinted at the flickering display of an old-fashioned hands-clock in the corner of her helmet display. Let's see, they'd landed at near noon on the ship's standard time and now it was...? Damn, the stupid clock was broken!

"Ah...much too long, Adri. It took most of a day to get the bombs ready and our gear together. And now we've been out here for at least two hours. That's making good time after surviving a crash onto an asteroid, I guess. But we're not progressing near as fast as we need. I can't imagine they'll let this damn thing get too near Earth before trying to vaporize it. As it is, we're just three days from impact and..."

"Susan," Adriana breathlessly interrupted her, "at this snail pace our rebreathers and small oxygen tanks will run out long before we ever get to that ravine. Either the energy blasts will kill us or we'll suffocate."

Oh, rats. There was no denying that logic.

"You're right, Adri. The way we're creeping along it could take another full day to reach the rift. We've got to change our game plan!"

"But what else can we do other than what we're doing now?"

Susan thought for a moment. Then it hit her...

"Did you ever see the movie 'Dr. Strangelove'?"

"Do you mean that old nuclear war spoof from the twentieth century?"

"Yes, that's the one..."

"—in school, I think. But I don't remember much from..."

"—'how I learned to stop worrying and love the bomb' was its subtitle, exemplified by Sam Pickens sitting astride a dropping nuclear bomb, whooping and yelling, waving his cowboy hat in the air as he plummeted downward, like he was riding a bucking horse!"

"Ah yes, I remember that. But...?"

"Let's do the same."

Adri shook her helmeted head in confusion. "Have you gone crazy, Susan? What would sitting here on our nuclear bombs accomplish?"

"We're going to let this huge gravity do the work for us, with a little help from our suits' steering jets. It's lucky we refurbished them before everything went south on Hermes, huh?"

"Ahhhh...did I ever tell you that you were a genius, Susan?" Adri grinned from behind her faceplate.

"Thanks, girl—let's do some reconfiguring!"

It took a full thirty minutes to accomplish, but at the end they'd combined the two bombs. The two large cylinders were now attached by rejiggered harnesses at their short fins. Astride both of the tied-together bombs—like kids on a bobsled—sat Susan and Adriana, Adriana in front. Their legs were drawn up beneath them. Susan clasped her friend around her waist with her functional right space-suited arm.

Ahead of them was a trough formed by two of the parallel ridges, which wound in a generally downward direction toward the distant deep ravine. It was hard to see if it was the best path forward because of the swirling black fog which obscured everything. But it was their best guess.

"Ready?" Adriana said from in front.

"Aye, aye, Captain!"

"Then let's shove off!"

Susan pushed out with her legs to each side, against the smooth metallic surface below. Nothing happened. She shoved harder...

They moved forward a few inches. She shoved again, even harder. Now they were moving slowly forward, gaining a little momentum.

"Fire the rockets!" Adriana happily ordered.

Susan saw Adri's spacesuit's small jets toggle outwards. She yanked up her legs as they both triggered their steering jets.

Trailing *four streams of white vapor*, the improvised toboggan began to pick up speed, bouncing down the rough gulley.

"Wahoo!" Adriana shouted as they began zipping along.

By yanking on the harness wrapped around the forward-pointed noses of the bombs, Adriana was able to keep them firmly centered inside the now rapidly descending trench. Susan clung onto her friend tightly, happy that the near frictionless surface allowed them to zip along like a toboggan on frozen snow.

"M-maybe we should think of s-slowing down?" Susan gulped, seeing the metallic walls growing taller to each side as they whipped past and the gulley deepened.

"C-can't, Susan," Adri replied as they bounced along, now traveling at a high rate of speed. "If you stick out a leg to try and slow us, you'll break it off at the hip! We're riding this baby to the end!"

Susan saw a *large black rift* rapidly approaching up ahead. It was the ravine. It had looked like a small slit when they were approaching the Asteroid. But now as they zoomed toward it Susan realized it was an ominously plunging canyon. They'd indeed chosen a good route to reach it—but in which they were now trapped!

"Hold on tight!" Adriana shouted as they *bounced high* over a lip and into the dark ravine...

The force of the fall tore Adriana away from Susan's grasp.

Susan saw Adri and the two bombs spinning away into the black fog to each side as she *bounced* painfully off a metallic cliff face. Her last thought before losing consciousness was the irony: here to destroy the damn thing, it had *swallowed* them both alive!

"Ok, Bill, your time's up. A deal's a deal. We allowed you an observational seat in the control room for twenty-four hours. Now give us the damn password!"

Bill's resolve was fast dwindling. Scott's words thundered in his head, echoing back and forth like commands from God!

"You haven't kept your side of the bargain," Bill whispered.

Bill stared up at the bright stars shining through the transparent canopy. The Asteroid was out there. It wasn't close enough yet to be visible by the naked eye. But it was approaching rapidly, at better than 60,000 mph. And on it was his sister.

"Of course I did!" Scott snarled back. "Whatever Johansson and Susan may have tried, it clearly failed," Scott relentlessly continued. "We're now in position, here at five times the distance of the moon from Earth. We're well within our energy retrieval limits while far enough from the planet to have time to launch several barrages. But if we don't fire soon, we won't get a second chance. The Asteroid will be here and past us. Earth will be helpless!"

"There's still time," Bill petulantly whispered.

Indeed, it was still three days until impact. That meant the Asteroid was 2.2 million miles from Earth, or one million miles from the present position of the Dish/Saucer combination. Since the plasma bursts from the Dish traveled close to that of coronal mass ejections from the sun, at a million miles per hour, it would take one hour for any discharges to reach the Asteroid. From the dispersal rates Bill had calculated during their test firings, he knew that the bursts started dissipating at just six minutes or 100,000 miles distant. At an hour's firing distance, the Asteroid was effectively still out of range.

That meant that Bill had "wiggle room" beyond the arbitrary deadline which Scott had set.

"*Give* us the password or we'll *beat* it out of you!" Scott sharply threatened, his voice deepening. "I don't want to hurt you Bill. Believe it or not, I've always liked you. But now's not the time to try and push me! Cooperate and you can return to being my side-kick. Don't, and I'll *kick the crap* out of you until you do!"

Looking into the cold black eyes of the man, Bill wondered how they'd ever been even casual friends.

"You *haven't* kept your side of the bargain!" Bill stubbornly repeated, cringing while still trying to maintain his resolve.

He saw Maria floating up through the air to his seat and taking his arm to smile gently at him. Ah yes, she was again in her role of the "good cop" to Scott's "bad cop."

"We're having trouble getting around the blocks you put into the software," she gently added. "Surely you want us to stop the Asteroid, don't you? Won't you please help us?"

"Keep your side of the bargain!" Bill shouted, fighting hard not to give in, playing for time.

Scott snarled, drawing back a hand which now sported actual claws! He was poised to lunge at Bill...

But Maria caught his hand, holding him back. Blinking, Bill no longer saw claws, just regular fingernails. Maria and Scott remained locked together for a moment, glaring at each other. Then Scott spat in disgust, turning away.

"You deal with him," he ordered her.

He kicked away from the chair in which Bill was tied, drifting back to the control consoles where crewmembers worked frantically.

"What more do we need do to in order to satisfy you?" Maria seemingly kindly asked. She snuggled enticingly up to Bill as he sat immobilized, tied onto the flight chair.

"That won't work on me. I know what you are."

She drew back, her eyes narrowing. "Do you? Just *what* do you think that I am?"

"You're an alien in the form of a human. And, even if I didn't know that fact, I know you want to *kill* my sister!"

She politely laughed.

"I take that as a bad joke, Dr. King," she softly replied. "I wish no harm to your sister. I don't even know her. But I *am* concerned for *your* health and welfare. Scott is getting impatient. The Captain's not happy with you either. If you don't cooperate, you certainly won't be welcomed as a returning hero back on Earth, set to take a key role in the next stage of *Homo sapiens'* history. In 'fact' you won't make it back at all. The others will just leave you out here. They'll eject you from an airlock without a spacesuit. I wouldn't want that to happen. I'd miss you, truly!"

"If you're interested in 'truth' then get Scott to talk to me," Bill pointedly replied. "He promised to *tell* me the truth, what's really going on!"

"Well, now," Maria smiled, stroking one of his arms, "technically he didn't actually agree to that, did he? He replied that you wouldn't like the truth, not that he'd reveal it to you."

"So what is it that you're so scared to tell me?"

"We want your full cooperation, Bill, but..."

"—which *isn't* possible if you insist on keeping me in the dark!" he shot back. Then, more softly, he glared into her beguilingly brown eyes and said: "I can handle it, Airman Rodriguez. I'm not an idealist like my sister. I'm very practical. I'd rather know the truth, no matter how unpleasant, than be coddled or misled."

She seemed to think about the matter. Her pretty eyes squinted. Then she patted his arm again: "I'll have a word with him. He'll be back shortly."

True to her word, in a couple minutes Scott was back at his side. Scott loosened the restraints on Bill's arm and handed him a sandwich and a bulb of water. Bill noted that Scott did not free his legs which were still tightly strapped to the chair.

"Thanks," Bill grudgingly said, taking the sandwich and gulping down a couple bites. It'd been a long time since he'd eaten. "I've got questions," he mumbled around his mouthful of food.

"I'll tell you what I can, no guarantees."

"Good enough. First, is the real Scott Yanash still alive?"

The bronze-skinned, handsome man looked shaken by the question. But he quickly recovered, glowering at Bill while quietly replying: "Yes, he is."

"So you replaced him right before you started feeding me your adaptations for my failed experiments. But the proprietary 'magic' that gave us super-batteries wasn't your 'genius,' just alien technology?"

"That's correct."

"And there are others who were replaced?"

"Yes, Scott's father, Losa, was taken, as were other key people who were in—or would wind up in—high positions in government, industry, even most of the people crewing this spacecraft."

"So where is the real Scott?"

"He's safely imprisoned on my home planet."

"Which is?

"Earth."

"Yes, I'm sure you also call your planet 'Earth,' but I meant its location—Alpha Centauri, or another other close star?"

"It's Earth, the same Earth we're both trying to save."

"That's impossible, unless...?"

"Unless?"

"—unless it's inside another, *separate* Dimension?"

Scott's expression didn't change. He wasn't surprised by the statement. Indeed, it was true!

"Now you're getting it, Bill," Scott shrugged. "Our Earths are one and the same, though separated by a thin barrier that is usually inviolable."

Oh, Christ. Suzy's science fiction stories of him and her out in the Park as kids! Were they true? Did those fanciful tales actually happen to him and her?

"So why do you hate Susan so much?" Bill angrily asked the stranger who was masquerading as his lifelong friend.

"Hate? Oh, no. We don't hate Susan King. In fact, we *revere* her! Without her, our entire civilization wouldn't even exist. She's our Mother, our Creator!"

"*My* Suzy, my *sister*, is your *Creator?*" Bill laughed. "Ok, let's set that absurdity aside. But even if it's true then why are you trying to kill her?"

Scott shook his head, his now tightly braided pigtail bouncing around at the back of his skull.

"No, not kill her—just to stop her from undoing what she allowed to happen 65 million years ago. If she dies, that's regrettable, but not the key objective. We're just trying to prevent her from changing a cosmic occurrence that allowed our people to come into existence."

"*What* the *bloody hell* are you talking about?"

"You were there also, Bill," Scott quietly replied, staring unblinkingly at him. "According to the legends passed to us from older friends from yet another Earth Dimension, 'Billy and Suzy' altered the history of the last great Cycle. An entire future civilization of *Homo sapiens* was obliterated. In its place on the parallel Earth arose the beginnings of a truly orderly, logical society. You'd call them *dinosa-piens.* They sprang from a distant ancestry of your 'velociraptors.' They had nimble hands and big brains. But they weren't as vulnerable to environmental upheaval as the massive dinosaurs, such as T-rex, which fell to the wayside while the velociraptors flourished and evolved."

"And…just *how*…did Suzy and *I* supposedly cause this to happen?"

"In the closest parallel Dimension to your Earth, you and she caused an asteroid to fragment that otherwise would have smashed intact into the Earth."

"An…*Asteroid*…you say?"

"Yes, very much like the Asteroid that's hurtling at us right now, Bill. She may not even consciously know it yet, but she intends to correct her mistake…"

"How?"

"—by inserting this Asteroid ahead of the other, but leaving it intact. In this way, she will restore the prior timeline. She feels guilty for those billions of humans in the other timeline that she prevented from existing, in essence killing them. Her 'crime' has haunted her for her entire life. It's what drove her to abandon her true interests to study asteroids then become a NASA astronaut."

Bill stared in disbelief at the man, weighing the matter-of-fact way he stated his incredible story. It was so farfetched might it actually be true? Who could make up such a tale?

"And…just how is it that you happen to know Susan's supposedly *un*conscious future Cosmic 'plans'?" Bill skeptically asked.

"We've been around a lot longer than you stupid little monkeys," Scott disdainfully growled. "We've developed sophisticated probability matrixes that can look into potential alternate timelines. We've become masters of our own destiny, you see. We know, within a margin of error, what's going to happen—and thus are able to modify the near future in our favor."

"There's a 'margin of error'?"

Scott looked at Bill shrewdly, nodding his head.

"Yes, there are certain…unwritten 'rules'…which prevent us from tampering too overtly. If we exert too heavy a hand then the opposite of our goals may gain on the probability matrix. It's sort of like expert weather prediction within a dynamic system. Time is surprisingly tweakable but fragile."

Ah. Ok—why not? Bill's head was spinning. Though it made a certain amount of weird sense, this story was still mind-blowing!

"So you're saying that if Susan somehow succeeds in altering the past timeline, then...?

"—my entire world, my people, my entire lineage will just cease to exist. My *entire race* will be *killed!*" he shouted. Then, getting his anger under control, he continued more calmly: "I wasn't lying to you, Bill, when I said an entire world and civilization hung in the balance. You assumed it was yours, but in reality it's mine!"

Bill noticed a flurry of activity around the main control console. At least a dozen crew members were floating back and forth through the air. One of them gestured urgently to Scott.

"I have to go," he said.

Bill caught him by the collar of his flight suit with a free hand and yanked him back: "One more question!"

"Make it fast."

"When you stop Susan and the Asteroid, what happens to the human race on my Earth?"

"We keep them from destroying their own planet, just as we discussed previously. By helping us you'll be saving them, just as much as my own people."

"You mean 'save' them by subjugating my world to alien invaders from another Dimension?"

"Oh, let's not be so melodramatic, Bill. It'll *not* be an 'alien invasion.' We'll just moderate their worst instincts. It's just as I've done with *you*—kindly directing, supporting, and empowering you, right?"

"By *controlling* me, *robbing* me of my own self-respect, and *humiliating* me!"

"Well yes, that's also true. You and the rest of your selfish, destructive species have a chronic need for *clear boundaries:* which, sadly, you're unwilling or unable to set for yourselves. So we'll do it for you. You should be grateful!"

"As you corral us into *game preserves?*"

"Why Bill, what a bloody imagination you have!" he snorted, revealing his now clearly overlarge teeth. "Our predatory animal selves are far in our past. No, we won't hunt or kill you weak, stupid little monkeys. But you *will* be required to stay in carefully controlled small communities that..."

"—opening up large areas to *colonization*, am I right?"

"Well, it *would* be a shame to waste the vast areas of your Earth that will return to their flourishing natural environmental states. And, yes, my people will enjoy coming here in their true forms: for vacationing, harvesting raw resources, and even homesteading."

"So you're still governed by your biology, just like us," Bill bitterly laughed.

"What?"

"Having filled up your own Earth you're reaching out to take another, then another, and yet another."

"Think what you will," Scott snapped, pulling away. "There's a crisis I need to handle, Bill. When I return, I expect you to give me that password!"

"I'll think about it."

As Scott floated away to the crowded central console, Maria drifted back up to Bill.

"Did you get the information you wanted?"

"You're a damn lizard, that's what!"

"I'm not a lizard and I'm not damned. I'm as real as any other human."

"That's a laugh."

"It took years of intricate surgery and tissue remodeling to attain this stunted, weak body. The resultant form and functions are not easily reversed. As a consequence I feel the same urges as any normal human. I truly am attracted to you, Bill. And I know you feel the same toward me, am I right?"

"Well..."

Bill winced as his arm was suddenly *savagely punched* by a returned, irate Scott!

"*Give* me the password!" Scott screamed.

"What?" Bill grimaced, the pain in his arm intense. "But we've got several hours before..."

"The Asteroid isn't just a rocky mountain! We just got long range scans back, showing its true nature: it's *a forged titanium structure!* We have to hit it with a prolonged series of bursts to destroy it, starting *right now!*"

"But they'll dissipate at that distance..."

"—softening it up, series-by-series: until the last plasma blasts finally vaporize it! But we have to start *right now!*"

Bill ground his teeth together, considering.

"But if the true Asteroid that you're so scared of is supposed to be in another Dimension, then how...?"

"But it isn't there! It's here! And this is where we're going to stop the threat—both to your Earth and to ours!" he again yelled.

The entire control room was silent as the crewmembers looked over at Scott and Bill. Bill was totally confused. He didn't understand what Scott was telling him. How could the Asteroid be mechanical? And, if so, how did that threaten the parallel lizard Dimension?

But Scott was now "thudding" his fist time and again into Bill's shoulder.

Enough! Enough! Enough!—Bill groaned to himself.

He was exhausted, battered to a pulp, both mentally and physically defeated.

"Billy and Suzy together," Bill muttered, hanging his head in defeat.

"*What?*"

"That's the password, you bastard. It's simple, typed as one word with no breaks or dashes: *billyandsuzytogether...*"

"Was that so hard!?" Scott shouted again, kicking angrily through the air back toward central command.

Clearly the tension was getting to everyone, alien-intelligent-disguised-dinosaurs and humans alike.

Maria wrapped her warm arms comfortingly around Bill's neck. For a lizard, she was surprisingly soft and friendly.

Outside and above him, through the transparent canopy, Bill saw the familiar sight of the gigantic inner surface of the Dish starting to glow with a red, pulsating, *wicked* light.

It was fixing to let loose the first barrage of *the fires of hell.*

Whatever Dimension-shattering fantasies that Susan held—whether or not what Scott claimed about her was true—her time was up.

She had *one hour* until the first of a series of devastating plasma bursts arrived at the Asteroid.

Bill shut his eyes tightly. He didn't want to give Scott or the other lizards the satisfaction of seeing him cry.

He'd made his choice. He'd given up.

Chapter 30

<u>CHOICES</u>

Don't "cry for me Argentina"
Because you never were
Just a societal construct
A brief expression of genetics
In turn merely Biological Laws
Rooted in the Foundations of Physics
Enshrined in Mathematical Theorems
A curious state of Determined Absolutism
Coupled with Quantum Uncertainty
Creating an illusion of Free Will
Wrapped up in Endless Cycles
A bundle of Marvelous Creativity
Heralding both Birth and Death
Countless, Struggling Species
All certain that they are Supreme
The center and intent of the Universe
Where from nothing comes something
And something always evolves
Into that which comes yet next
Even when Extinction looms
A merry-go-round of Context...
The Minstrel's Lark, 30:1-6

IMPACT MINUS THREE DAYS, *DESCENDING...*
Susan awoke floundering inside a *deep pink sea!*

Above her, she saw a greenish light and weakly kicked upward toward it.

She dragged herself out of the clinging fluid onto a sandy yellow beach.

Around her was a jumble of what looked like abstract art: *giant, flat-facetted crystals* looming far above her head and away to each side. It was a stunning spectacle, a huge *amethyst geode* cathedral, through which a pink bubbling river swept. A soft green light shone from somewhere behind the giant crystals. A recess at the back of the cavern led off into spooky darkness.

"Adri...?" Susan gasped, painfully levering herself with her one good arm onto her back. She frantically looked out of her scratched-up faceplate, trying to find her friend.

There she was!

Lying on her stomach in the yellow sand beside an up-thrust blue crystal was Adriana. Her spacesuited arms and legs lay sprawled limply to each side. She wasn't moving.

Susan crawled through the soft sand toward Adri, struggling against the incessant heavy gravity. She grabbed one of her motionless friend's shoulders and shook her hard.

"Adri! Are you alive? Come on, speak to me!"

Susan was glad to hear a groan over her helmet speaker.

"W-where...are...we?"

"I don't know...inside the Asteroid...we fell into the deep ravine and then..."

"Yes," Adriana replied weakly, still lying prone on her face. "We w-went through some s-sort of shimmering energy field. It drastically slowed our rate of descent. That's the last I remember."

"Are you hurt?"

"Every inch of me is bruised...but hopefully no broken bones. I think I fell onto something relatively soft."

"It's sand, Adri."

"Whatever...that energy field s-saved us, somehow lowering us to a soft l-landing."

"Can you move?"

"I think so...but...maybe I'll just rest here."

"What happened to our two nukes?" Susan urgently asked, remembering their mission.

"I...think they fell into...a pink liquid...right alongside you."

"They're in the water?"

"It's water?"

Susan looked back over to the bubbling pink river from which she'd so recently emerged. Adri was correct. It churned and flowed like water but was strangely "sticky"-looking. It reminded Susan of fluid strawberry jelly. She even saw coherent tendrils "flop" out onto the bank as if they were exploring, *searching* for Susan before withdrawing.

"We've got to get the nukes," Susan said, again grabbing Adri's arm and rotating her heavy spacesuited body over onto her back. "Get up, Adri. We're going to have to..."

Susan gasped in dismay.

"W-what's...w-wrong?" Adriana asked, looking up out of her faceplate in concern.

"It's your...your..."

"Oh, *hell!*" Adriana grimaced, her eyes focused on the faceplate just inches from her nose. It was shattered. Big open gaps let in the outside atmosphere. "I'm dead, Susan. My helmet must have hit something! I can't breathe..."

Susan just glared at her. Adriana was obviously breathing just fine. The air inside the Asteroid, outside their spacesuits, must contain sufficient oxygen.

Susan unsnapped her own helmet and started to lift it off her head.

"No, Susan. It might be poisonous! We haven't done any tests or taken any readings. Who knows what...?"

"You're alive, aren't you? That's the 'acid' test—whether it kills a human or not, right? Besides, how else are we going to get our bombs back?"

"What?"

Susan continued undoing and loosening the external overlays and rotating sockets of her spacesuit, wriggling out of it. Then she fit the pieces back together, snapping the helmet in place while activating the external control panel.

"I'm leaving it deflated so it will sink with me."

"Sink with you?"

"I'm going back into that 'river' where..."

"—but without your spacesuit's air supply you'll drown!"

"I think not," she said as she began dragging the heavy suit toward the edge of the flowing "river." Her voice, traveling through the thick air, sounded strangely muted even to her own ears. She now heard the muted "rumble" of the wide pink river's rapid flow. "Your suit's busted, but mine is intact. When I trigger it to inflate it should become a rubber life raft, lifting up whatever's attached."

"Wait!"

"No time, Adri. I don't know why, but I have a feeling I can do this. Wish me luck."

With that she stepped out of her thin flight suit, laying it to the side on the sandy bank. Then, clad only in her underwear, she waded back into the rushing pink fluid. It swept up and around her, cradling her body. It felt strangely warm and welcoming. And as her head submerged she felt no need to hold her breath. Indeed, her skin was doing a fine job of *absorbing oxygen directly* from the bubbling fluid surrounding her! *Super, my time in the algae ocean wasn't wasted!*—she thought to herself. There were advantages to having recently been "adapted" by a mutated ocean of single celled organisms.

Good old Hermes. Wow, she was sure going to miss that stinky old cramped spaceship.

This is totally crazy—she mused as she tightly clutched her collapsed spacesuit. She sank deeper and deeper into the bubbling fluid, away from the green light above. It seemed to take forever to descend. She'd have drowned for sure if she didn't have her brand new oxygen-absorbing skin.

But then she began to panic. Visibility was limited. She was losing track of where she'd entered the river, afraid of being swept away and lost...

Then a feeling of absolute peace swept over her mind. A gentle voice whispered in her head: "*Welcome, my child. You will not be harmed.*" Or perhaps she just imagined the voice, surrounded by soothing, lovely pink bubbles.

Her fear was gone. She felt right at home, floating lazily deeper and deeper. It would be so easy to just relax and allow the strong current to drag her away. But...she had a mission to accomplish!

She shook her head and tried to concentrate her mind, her hair flaring out around her head and into her eyes.

Now just where did you two little errant hydrogen bombs get off to? You're my babies! Come back to your loving Momma!"

Ah. Yes, there they were!

In the dim light a hundred feet or so below the surface Susan saw the two nukes sitting side-by-side, their pointed front ends stuck down into thick yellow mud at the bottom of the river. Their blunt, finned ends gleamed metallically, pointed upward. Fortunately, their harnesses hadn't torn free. The ends of the straps dangled out into the current, waving about lazily. It was easy for Susan to attach them onto her crumpled spacesuit's workbelt. Then, convinced they were as secure as possible, she triggered the gas canisters inside her empty spacesuit for *maximum suit inflation!*

Arms and legs popped out to each side. The inflated suit jerked upward toward the surface. Like a grotesque helium balloon molded in human form, it gently lifted the two hydrogen bombs tethered below.

Kicking with her legs, Susan cradled them in her arms like long-lost babies. It was surprisingly easy to guide them upward. Being underwater in the river was very much like being in the "neutral buoyancy tank" at the Johnson Space Center. The pink jelly flowing rapidly around her body was of the correct density to afford her a simulated weightless environment. In the strange "liquid" the bombs weren't heavy, maneuvering as easily as if they were in zero-G. Once the bombs got out of the "river" though, they'd again be enormous dead weights. But in the frothing fluid they were light as feathers!

Then Adriana's arms were reaching down from above, helping drag both Susan and the harnesses up out of the liquid onto the shoreline. As Susan's head rose out of the swirling river, she sputtered and coughed, reluctant to rejoin the land of the walking. It was difficult to breathe with lungs again, leaving behind her magically aquatic "womb."

Why did us stupid land animals have to crawl out of the wonderful water in the first place?—Susan sighed to herself as the relentlessly heavy gravity again drove her trembling body to its knees.

"That was incredible, Susan! You found them!"

"Yep, nothing to it," she coughed.

"What *is* that stuff, anyway?"

Susan watched droplets of pink fluid coalesce together as they fell from her body. Then they rolled as one big wet blob to rejoin the river.

"It's—'alive,' I think. It must serve a function inside the...the alien spaceship."

"Well, there's not much doubt of that now, that's for sure. Is your arm better? You're using it freely now."

"Huh, I guess so!" Susan smiled, feeling at her left arm with her right. "Maybe the bones weren't broken after all, just bruised. It feels a lot better."

"Or the 'repair' you experienced on Hermes is still working, giving you rapid healing?"

"Could be...I can still absorb oxygen directly through my skin. But I think I'm returning to normal."

"You're never normal, Susan. You're a superwoman!"

"Thanks, girlfriend."

As Susan laboriously put her flight suit back on, she noted that Adriana was also well recovered, her broken helmet dangling from its tether behind her neck. She was on her feet, unsteady, but still resolutely dragging the hydrogen bombs up onto the bank. Off to the side, still attached but in the water, flopped Susan's over-inflated spacesuit.

"What is this crystal cave, anyway?" Adriana mused. "It somehow seems...organic?"

"Maybe the entire thing is an ancient lifeform?" Susan replied. "Could the entire Asteroid be a 'space beetle'?"

"I don't think so," Adriana replied, now steadily pulling the flopping spacesuit by the still-attached straps to the shore. "So far it's too mechanical."

"Mechanical?" Susan asked as she crawled over to her suit and began deflating it in preparation for donning it yet again.

"What I glimpsed in the ravine as we fell was jagged and broken," Adri thoughtfully mused, looking around her at the crystalline cavern. "I'll bet something crashed into this spaceship eons ago, smashing a hole in its side. Then an automatic energy barrier sealed off the breach. This 'river' could be just an outer conduit, one of many. The 'smart-fluid' could deliver coolant, or provide shock absorption, or accomplish who knows how many other strange purposes."

Susan nodded thoughtfully.

"Yes," she nodded, "like our peripheral blood vessels—that makes a lot of sense, Adri. And we should remember that our own bodies are but biological machines. Seen up close by tiny intelligent invaders, we also might be mistaken for physical devices. In fact, this whole cavern could be a walled-off contusion from that ancient impact. Maybe the giant crystals around us are alien scar tissue! Wow, we could study this thing for centuries, Adri!"

Susan was painfully pulling the deflated spacesuit back onto her body, getting excited about the incredible secrets contained in this ancient artifact. But she had to focus on getting back into her rigid spacesuit. Though she was much more comfortable out of it, she had no idea what awaited them deeper in the Asteroid. The tough spacesuit offered additional protection on top of her flight suit.

"Too bad we have to destroy it," Adriana sighed.

"What?"

Adriana, breathing heavily, pointed to the two hydrogen bombs. They now lay side-by-side in the sand. The metallic cylinders were silent, impassive.

"Oh, right," Susan agreed, shaking her head rapidly from side-to-side. Her thoughts were wandering. She had to stay focused! Surely from the "soft underbelly" of the Asteroid—exploded from inside—the nuclear bombs might finally destroy the world-destroying projectile. They had less than three days to stop the Asteroid. How long had they been inside, anyway?

As if reading Susan's thoughts, Adriana pointed at her wrist. The outer surface of her digital clock was cracked, but unlike her helmet it was still intact. Unfortunately, the dials were whirling around chaotically. "Something's really screwed up in here, maybe the large magnetic fields we saw swirling the thick atmosphere on the surface. My watch is messed up. My best estimate is that we've been inside for an hour, Susan."

"That long?"

"Maybe longer...regardless, we're liable soon to start getting blasted by those 'plasma bursts' your brother mentioned. Maybe we won't need to complete the mission after all. Your brother and the new technology may be sufficient. Of course we'll both be dead, but Earth will be safe."

"I wouldn't count on them doing our job, Adri."

Susan pulled on her gloves, latching them in place. Then she made sure the now loosened helmet was hanging behind her head by its tether. Regardless of her new-found ability to absorb oxygen through her skin, that wouldn't help much if they hit a pocket of de-pressurization. She wanted to be able to snap her helmet into place at a moment's notice.

"Why not?" Adri asked. "We're getting close enough to Earth for their super-batteries to work. How they can deliver focused, coherent plasma bursts I have no idea, but if they can do that then..."

"There's *no* way they can stop this ancient titanium projectile!" Susan exclaimed fervently. "Remember, it's likely already passed through the *sun's corona* many times. It's still intact, isn't it?"

"But the sun's corona is only a few million degrees," Adriana re-plied. "If your brother can simulate the *interior* of the sun—at its very core—then that's *27 million degrees* Fahrenheit. Surely that would vaporize anything, titanium or not?"

"We've no guarantee they have such a cataclysmic weapon, Adri," Susan sighed, frowning at the heavy bombs, not eager to get back into her rigged pulling-harness. "To me that's highly unlikely. I know of no technology on Earth that could produce sustained unconfined plasma at that temperature. The *National Ignition Facility*, 'NIF,' in California can do so for only microseconds within a tiny volume. Shooting plasma bursts through space just isn't an option! We have to assume they'll just shoot off little fireballs that might blow off the dirty exterior atmosphere of the Asteroid. But I'm certain it'll leave the central mass intact."

"So we *do* need to set off our nukes," Adriana nodded. "We'll keep on dragging them as deep as possible into the interior. Then we'll detonate them."

"Yes, that's still the plan."

"And if somehow your brother and Nashoba Energy succeed?"

"Then good for them, Adri—vaporizing this rock would be far safer to Earth than us just blasting it into a hail of small fragments. Either way, we win!"

"And either way we're both dead," Adriana sighed.

"I guess everyone's got to die sometime, huh?" Susan shrugged.

"—and few as spectacular as us!" Adriana laughed back.

"So let's go see what else is in here!" Susan smiled, buoyed up by Adri's relentless good cheer.

"Ok," Adriana grinned widely. "Let's get to dragging!"

Steadfast to the end, Adri was a great companion. Her upbeat attitude in the face of certain death was in the true NASA tradition: "*Find a way.*" And if Bill and Scott succeeded—then that was even better. Instead of anticipating that last agonizing flash as they started the countdown on their two nukes, it'd be over before they even knew what happened.

Either way, Susan was satisfied. It'd been worth the effort. What an amazing adventure she'd had! In graduate school she earned the highest certification in astrophysics. Her Ph.D. allowed her to try to understand the incredible forces in play in the Universe. In her postgraduate research she was blessed to study at a distance the awesome structures of their very own solar system. And as an astronaut for NASA she traveled up into orbit then deep space. Now she was one of only two human beings ever to encounter and capture a comet. And finally she was inside an ancient alien spacecraft. If her life were snuffed out in the next minute she'd have no regrets. Truly, she *was* "The Girl Who Wrangled Asteroids!"

Hah. That was funny. She was certainly living up to the nickname from her postdoc days. Actually, someone should write a book with that title! Wouldn't that be something special?

Yeah, sure...probably no one would ever read it.

But it'd be great!

"Ten minutes until the first series reaches the Asteroid."

The stream of plasma bursts had been traveling for an hour. Bill didn't expect much from the first series. Each of the self-generated plasma containment fields had swollen to a hundred times their original diameters, the temperature of the plasma plummeting into the low millions of degrees. But the train of now-diffused bursts might soften the target up for tighter bursts following behind. As the Asteroid plummeted toward Earth it likewise drew nearer to each successive train of plasma "bullets," which on impact would be ever tighter, more focused, and hotter.

Oh, God, I'm cooking my own sister!

"You ok, Bill?"

It was Maria. She seemed genuinely worried about him. Bill didn't know whether it was an act or not. But it didn't matter. She was his "bodyguard," to put it diplomatically. Or, more truthfully, she was his jailor. Her job was clearly to make sure he didn't cause any further trouble. She stood there right beside him, shoulder-to-shoulder.

He was sure she could easily overpower him should he attempt to move from his designated spot. From what he'd discovered in the clinical tests he'd done on her cells when she was drugged, her muscle tissue was uncommonly dense. She could snap him in two like a dry twig.

"I'm killing my sister. How the hell do you think I feel?"

Bill stood dejectedly a few yards behind the main control console, letting his activated magnetic boots hold him firmly to the metallic floor. Maria was likewise rooted beside him. Most everyone else preferred to float free in zero-G than plod around on their own activated, cumbersome boots. But he didn't want to be in their way, while still in place to observe the data streams from the barrages they'd already fired off from the Dish.

They untied him after he gave them the password. Sure to his word, it had unlocked the covert blocks he'd put into the ship's complex computer codes. He supposed it was nice of them not to slit his throat and toss him out of an airlock. But he still knew far more than any of them about the coherence characteristics of the plasma bursts. They still needed him...for the moment. But if their efforts succeeded in stopping the massive, titanium Asteroid, they might yet give him the "space boot"!

But he was sure it would not come to that. If all else failed, he had a "doomsday" plan...

Scott startled him, floating down and "clomping" onto the deck beside Bill and Maria, his boots now activated.

Versus his previous rage, he now looked genuinely concerned.

"Come on, Bill. I know this has been rough on you. I wish there were a way to save Susan, I truly do. My people revere her as a Goddess! But she'd *want* for us to do this, don't you think? She went chasing after that Asteroid along with the rest of the NASA crew without any illusions. They were each prepared to give their lives to stop that abomination from impacting Earth."

"So where did it come from?" Bill absently asked. His eyes were glued to the large central display screen where a line of pinpoint lights were shown approaching a dark object. At the main computer console, a whole bevy of charts detailed their characteristics. "Surely your 'much more ancient' civilization with its 'advanced technology' and 'predictive probability' knows the Asteroid's origin, right?"

The main view on the central screen wasn't just a computer representation or radar scan. Bill knew it was an actual telescopic view taken from their communication platform deployed a mile to the side of the Saucer. In real time they were watching the fate of the entire Earth hanging in the balance.

Scott looked uncomfortable at the question, fidgeting as he stood on the deck.

"Well?" Bill prodded him, trying to keep the man-lizard's mind tied up with annoying questions. They thought that he was helpless. He couldn't let them suspect differently! If they knew what he had up his sleeve, they'd chop his arm off!

"We...don't know," Scott quietly replied. "We certainly didn't aim it toward your Earth, if that's what you're thinking. It really is a dark body in a very eccentric orbit that just happens to be on a course to smash into Earth. Apparently it's been orbiting the sun for eons. It's just cosmic bad luck."

"Not so bad for you lizard people, it seems."

"Well, it hasn't yet manifested itself on our side of the dimensional divide, or traveled back in time millions of years—that's true."

"Then why do you care about it?"

"I said 'yet'!" Scott snapped, snarling. "Now that we have its spectral content we've determined it is the *very same* Asteroid that killed off the dinosaurs in your Dimension while allowing the velociraptors to evolve in ours! We don't know how or why, just the *fact* of what I just said! I know it sounds crazy, Bill. It doesn't look like it could possibly fall into fragments. It's not a typical rocky asteroid. But we're *certain* it's *the very same object* that manifested 65 million years ago in both my and your Dimensions! Both of our civilizations hang in the balance! Somehow, Susan is going to try and use it to *change history*."

Bill sighed deeply, shaking his head slowly in denial. Not only was Scott's scenario crazy, it was preposterous.

"That's an awful lot of speculation, Scott," Bill quietly replied. "Maybe you're just getting paranoid. I still think you care little about my world and its people—other than to be your new hunting grounds!"

"There *is* a lot we don't know," Scott grudgingly admitted.

Maria suddenly *slapped* Bill hard on his face. It hurt!

"Hey, why'd you do that?" he said, cowering back, holding a hand to his smarting cheek.

"We're not heartless, Bill! We're saving your world, aren't we?"

"Sure, but saving it to turn it into *your* species' retirement home!"

Scott shook his head in apparent disgust, his eyes glued on the converging telescopic blips.

"They're almost together."

A bright *FLARE* showed on the screen as the first bright dot hit the dark object. Then there was a second, a third, a fourth, and yet a fifth.

The screen was now *solid white*. The pixels were maxed out from the glare of the powerful explosions. Gradually the camera adjusted and the blackness of deep space resumed.

"As expected, the object has *not* been destroyed," an officer at the command console reported. "It's still there. But the second series of plasma discharges is approaching the object. They're due to impact in twenty minutes."

"The plasma containment will be better," Bill muttered, wondering if Susan were still alive. Likely she was dead now, wiped off the surface of that big metallic rock. But she was resourceful, clever. If there were any possibility of finding a safe hiding place, she'd have done so.

"Let's go get a bulb of coffee, Bill," Maria said, tugging on his arm. "We've been standing here for two hours. You need to take a break."

"Maybe a short restroom break," he relented, feeling an uncomfortable pressure in his bladder.

"Maria will accompany you," Scott ordered, deactivating his magnetic boots and floating away in the air.

"I can pee by myself. I'm a big boy!" Bill scoffed.

"It's me or the guards," Maria kindly replied.

"Alright then," Bill said, stubbornly refusing to deactivate his magnetic boots, "clomping" toward the nearest bathroom. "You're a nurse. I'm sure you've seen people peeing before."

"I'm not a nurse. I'm a clinical laboratory technician."

"Whatever!"

She clomped along right beside him, apparently watchful and ready to stop him if he tried anything.

"You're funny, Bill. You make jokes even when you're being serious. I wish I could have met you under better circumstances."

He remained quiet, trying to ignore her. His mind was racing a million miles a minute. There had to be a way to get to a computer terminal and retake control of the ship! His superficial computer blocks weren't the only trick he had up his sleeve.

"I'll wait here as you use the cubicle."

"Fine."

He went into the small rectangle that was obscured from view. The suction device used for collecting urine was controlled by a computer program. Bill knew that if he pulled it out and accessed the fiber optics then maybe he could...

"Damn!" he muttered to himself, seeing that the computer line had been deliberately severed. The suction tube was left continually sucking, instead of only activating when it sensed human flesh. *Scott thinks he's so clever! He's always one damn step ahead of me!*—Bill growled to himself.

He finished his business and exited the cubicle, "clomping" along beside Maria to a nearby canteen. Various hot and cold dishes were displayed, each neatly packaged in plastic wrap. The drink-bulb dispensers were touch activated, offering no possibility of getting into the ship's computer.

"How about a nice gooey doughnut?" Maria urged him. "You've got to keep up your strength."

"Stop being so nice to me," he snapped at her, while still taking a couple of iced doughnuts to go with his hot coffee bulb. "I know it's just an act."

"But—I really do like you, Bill," she said, looking genuinely hurt.

They strapped into flimsy chairs to the side of the canteen, nursing their bulbs of hot coffee. Bill nibbled on the doughnuts. She was right. He was hungry. It was a long time since Scott brought him that sandwich.

"So what's your planet like?" he casually asked. Pointed questions might give him a chance to think, to plot, to do something she wouldn't notice.

"Oh...not as nice as your world."

"How so?"

"Well," she shrugged, "it's very crowded, for one thing. There aren't many natural environmental regions left. My species has been in control of the planet for the past ten million years, compared to your paltry few thousands. You are only just now completing the destruction of your biosphere—whereas we've mostly long-since finished the job. So I enjoy your wilderness areas, at least what I've seen in videos. In fact, I'd love to run free there for a time. Perhaps when we get back to your pacified world you could give me a tour?"

He ignored the "good cop" routine. She was trying to tantalize him into positive fantasies. Instead, he chose to probe yet deeper: "So were you a hospital lab tech back on your planet?"

She laughed, a disconcertingly deep bark: "Not likely. The present transplants into your Dimension come entirely from our Warrior Caste, including me. But that doesn't mean we can't also learn whatever other skills we need to achieve victory. I studied clinical technical work here and I liked it—healing rather than hurting. It's a nice change for me...as an adjunct to my primary abilities."

"*Castes*—you mean being born into a job category and doomed to remain there for the rest of your life, whether you want to or not?"

"No, Bill," she firmly stated. She looked very sincere. "It's a *genetic programming* that's as much about me being a warrior as you being a researcher like your Dad. Over the millennia my race has selectively bred and optimized our genetics for different roles. I was born to be a Warrior. That's who I am. In fact, I'm proud to be a certified *Master* Warrior."

"So you grew up that way?"

"Of course I did."

"And did you have a happy childhood?"

She paused, frowned, and then slowly replied: "From the time I was hatched I constantly trained, endured tough tests, going through combat trials. Being happy wasn't part of the equation. Joy for me and my kin was applying our skills in battle. Only a select few of my hatch-generation made it past childhood to become Master Warriors. Growing up for me was intensive training and tests."

"So what happened to the rest of your 'caste-mates'?"

She shrugged: "Most died. Our advanced combat trials are to the death. Those that survive go onward. Those that don't have their flesh sliced off, roasted, and consumed in celebratory feasts by their victors."

"Sounds lovely."

"That's the way of my caste. It's brutal, but not without its thrills. Refinement and advancement through lethal combat was the core purpose of my life."

A couple of crew members floated leisurely through the air, headed toward the main control console.

"Ah, so you should be deliriously happy now," Bill pressed her. "You're about to conquer a whole new world, right? What could be a greater victory than that?"

She thoughtfully nodded.

"Yes, it does satisfy a deep yearning within me, Bill. But still, I must confess that I'm conflicted by your soft monkey genetics that..."

"Oh, come off it, Maria," he snapped at her before sucking out the remainder of his coffee bulb and tossing it toward a trash-net. "I'm not a biologist, but even I know that's impossible. You can't combine the genomes from different species—let alone completely different animals—and have a viable hybrid."

She stared at her own coffee bulb. She'd hardly drunk any of it.

"It's not like that, Bill," she quietly answered. "I'm not a hybrid of my former self and you *Homo sapiens*. I'm a *blend* of your monkey cell tissues and mine. Your actual cells are necessary for best simulating your form and organs. They're placed around and on top of my own tissues. And to control the blended organs, portions of your neural structures had to be inserted into my brain. So I'm now part human. That causes me to experience strange...*urges*."

"Oh, like what?"

"Well, on my Earth, for our species to *reproduce* requires a highly regulated and formalized process. I guess it's similar to what I've learned of your reptilian lower lifeforms. They mate and reproduce seasonally. Females on my Earth are chemically stimulated to lay clutches of eggs which in state laboratories are incubated and fertilized with optimal sperm. Embryos are selected for the best traits and then further genetically enhanced. It's a clinical process."

"It sure doesn't sound romantic."

Her brown eyes widened, looking at him wistfully.

"That's correct," she quietly admitted. "So when I got strange tingles when we used to hold hands, even kissed, I..."

Starting to get intrigued by her words, Bill was perversely glad to see Scott drifting up to them, cutting off their conversation. Bill's hatred of the false-humans extinguished his momentary feelings of sympathy for Maria. He hated them both equally.

"The second wave is almost to the Asteroid," Scott broke into their conversation, floating up to them to while grabbing onto their fixed tabletop. "You'll want to study the effects, Bill. I'm told that the containment fields are now much tighter."

Bill held the gaze of Maria a moment longer. He hoped he was connecting with her mammalian female "neural structures." He could take advantage of her affections for him, assuming they were real and not just another lie. If he had a fleeting chance to sabotage the spaceship, he wanted her to hesitate just long enough to not stop him.

He tentatively smiled at her. She wasn't the only actor here. "We've got to go. Thanks for the doughnut and coffee."

She nodded, grabbing hold of his arm as they stood up from the table. "I'm here for you," she whispered in his ear. "Within the constraints of my orders, I want to help you. Please believe this!"

"Sure, Maria—and thanks," he replied, straining to hold a smile in place.

In actuality he found her alien touch *repulsive*.

As they clomped back over to the main control console, he had a conviction she didn't mean a word she was saying. She'd do whatever her "orders" required. To her, he was just a stupid pet "monkey" that needed to be restrained and controlled. But even with an intended prey, it's easy to get too attached, to hesitate a moment too long. Then the "victim" turns and instead of being on the defensive goes on the attack—sinking its *teeth* into you!

They were forcing him to kill his sister. Damn monsters! He *would* get his revenge!

"*One minute* to impact," the officer at the station intensely announced.

Bill looked up at the large display screen. The black object, already magnified many times, was larger this time. Indeed, it was 20,000 miles closer than before. Now it wasn't so indistinct. Instead of being a fuzzy blob, it was sharp and pointed. Bill saw that it wasn't a rounded, oblong mass. To his untrained eyes, it looked like a cosmic *bullet!*

"*Ten seconds.*"

Maria's clawed hand remained firmly on his arm, holding him in place next to her. He wished she'd relent, but she didn't. He had no hope of leaping forward to input commands.

A brilliant *FLARE* again momentarily whited-out the screen. Then as the white started to fade, there was another, another, and yet another!

The crewmembers stood, sat, or floated tensely in place.

The white overload on the screen slowly faded away.

"The object is *not* destroyed," the officer glumly stated. "But its infrared output is considerably greater. The surface layers have melted."

Indeed, Bill saw that the previously deep-black oblong was now glowing *red*. It was clearly being softened up. The next train of plasma bursts, set to hit the Asteroid in another twenty minutes, might do the job. They'd be even tighter and hotter, exposing the Asteroid to the interior of the sun!

If that series didn't do the job, they'd be out of time. The Asteroid would be on top of them and past.

But Bill was sure the object, no matter how tough it was, couldn't survive the next barrage.

"Goodbye, Susan," Bill whispered. "You were a good sister. I wish I'd not been so mean to you. I wish I'd listened to you better. You never trusted Scott or Nashoba Energy. I know you can't hear me, but I apologize. I was seduced by the money and fame. I gave in too easily to Scott's control. I should have trusted you."

"What's that?" Maria asked him.

"Nothing...nothing at all," he sighed, fighting back tears.

Chapter 31

<u>LOST</u>

Is that all there is?

Arriving at the Destination

Thinking you've "nailed" it

You discover your entire path

Was just another dead end

A tiny piece of a larger maze

Inside a yet more-complex puzzle

Wrapped in an unsolvable enigma

Floating in a vast shoreless ocean

"Infinity's Beach" a wonderful book

Containing and constraining words

Terrifying when lived out fully

Not as a diverting Sci-Fi story

But as stark reality

So cruel to be adrift

No horizon in sight

One's "safe harbor" a lie

"Tap-dance" finale...

Fade to black.

The Minstrel's Lark, 31:29-32

IMPACT MINUS THREE DAYS, *ENDURING HEAVY BOM-BARDMENT*...

"Are we deep enough?"

Susan grimaced as sweat continually poured off her brow into her eyes. She was exhausted, barely able to stand. Plus she hated the sweat smearing down in the double gravity, instead of "politely" beading up and drifting away in zero-G.

At the back of the crystalline cavern they'd found a fractured gap leading into a curiously rounded tunnel. Dragging the harnessed bombs behind them, they'd staggered into its beckoning darkness. Only dim glows from the helmets bobbing at their backs lighted their way forward. Around them were smooth black surfaces. The rounded "floor" at their feet was moist, making it easier to drag the heavy metallic bombs along. But the surface was also hard to stand upon, causing them to fall repeatedly, banging their bodies against the hard metal. The 2X earth-gravity was relentless, causing their weakened muscles incredible fatigue and pain.

"I don't know, Adri—I just don't know!"

They'd been staggering forward now for what seemed like hours, stumbling through tunnel after tunnel. At each turn there was a branch with three openings leading upward, down, or sideways. Susan tried to keep them on the "down" paths since those were easier to navigate dragging the nukes along behind them. But gravity perversely *tilted* in places, such that where Susan had felt they were going downward they suddenly had to struggle to drag the bombs up a steep incline! They could just as easily be still out in the outer regions of the Asteroid as approaching its center.

Suddenly the entire tunnel around them "wobbled," and then jerked again. The gravity abruptly *stopped*—causing them to float up into the center of the tunnel, floundering helplessly. Then the 2X gravity abruptly returned and they "thudded" hard down onto the smooth metal beneath them.

"Oh, Christ," Susan groaned, having landed directly on her bad arm. The renewed pain from the already damaged bones was awful. "Something must have hit the Asteroid," she gasped, the fierce pain making her head spin.

"It had to be the 'plasma bursts' your brother mentioned," Adriana faintly replied, likewise splayed out on the curved tunnel floor.

"But we're still three days away from impact with Earth..."

"They have to be distant from Earth but still within their firing sphere," Adriana groaned, "spitting out their 'bullets' at us! Maybe we should just stop here and detonate our two bombs, Susan. That might 'soften up' the Asteroid for their next bombardment. Perhaps then their little fireworks could do real damage? Beside, Susan, I don't think I can go much further."

Susan lay there waiting for the crippling pain in her arm to subside. It hurt so much she couldn't see straight. God, what she'd do for a shot of morphine! But then she'd be too zonked-out to be functional. This close to finally stopping the Asteroid, she had to keep her wits intact.

"No, Adri," Susan replied as she painfully used her good right arm to push herself up to her knees. "We're going on. If we keep to the 'down' tunnels they have to lead us to the center of the Asteroid. If we're near the outer surface when we trigger our nukes we might only blow another hole in its side. At the center, we've got a chance to destroy the entire armor-plated monstrosity."

"Ok, then," Adri faintly replied, slowly wobbling to her feet and resolutely leaning forward against the harness. "I think the tunnels are getting larger. Do you think that means we're getting somewhere?"

Yes, this present tunnel was definitely wider than the previous ones. Also, there was light now whereas the previous ones had been pitch black. The light wasn't much—just a green glow through cracks in the surfaces—but it was enough to let them turn off their suit helmets and save their dwindling suit batteries.

Around the next bend, Susan was astonished. The faint green glow intensified. The metallic rock to each side clarified. The walls changed into what looked like display cases! The wall substance was similar to prehistoric amber containing trapped insects. But in the walls to each side were not embedded bugs, but large, oval *eggs* in obvious clutches.

"Those...are awful big...eggs," Adri gulped as they lumbered past the amber "display cases."

Each egg was fully a foot long. Whatever eons ago incubated inside, after hatching would have grown into a large animal.

"Well, that was likely billions of years in the past. These have to be fossilized remains."

"Maybe they're the eggs of giant worms," Adri softly replied. Her eyes stretched wide as they lurched along a transparent wall loaded with thousands of the egg-clutches.

"Either giant worms or snakes," Susan agreed. "These rounded tunnels weren't made for us two-footed mammals. Since there are no flat surfaces, I think that big long creatures glided or slithered through these passageways. Whatever alien lifeforms this ship contained, though—they've been dead for a long, long time."

"Hopefully," Adri gasped, shoving her trembling legs forward.

"This ship is operating on some weak, innate power, Adri," Susan answered, concentrating on their task, fighting to put one foot forward then the other. "I think it lost its main power source eons ago."

"Maybe that was when it got hit and breached—at the ravine where we entered."

"Could be."

The entire rounded tunnel around them suddenly again *shivered*. The gravity switched off again and Susan found herself floundering in the air. This time, however, she managed to get her boots positioned "downward" pointed for when the gravity hopefully came on again. The two nuclear bombs floated between her and Adriana, still attached via their harnesses. Then a "bang" like a distant gong sounded. It reverberated through the air in the tunnel, making Susan slap her gloved hands to her ears. Suddenly the walls of the tunnel were *hot*, scorching their skin if they swung too close!

Then the gravity switched on again. But its orientation was different. Susan was horrified to no longer be plodding along a slanted horizontal tunnel but poised in a *hole* pointed straight down! The glowering heat from the walls suddenly vanished as if it'd been drained away. And then they were *helplessly falling* into what was now a deep well beneath them, sliding along its curved slanted wall, dodging the bouncing bombs, trying not to smash against each other, until...finally...reaching a slanted bottom and sliding-rolling out into a large cavern.

"Jesus Christ," Susan gasped, "that was one hell of a ride!"

"I think...we made it," Adri groaned, looking dazedly around. "We're there—at the center of the alien spacecraft!"

Susan followed her gaze. The cavern was at least *five hundred feet* high. Various oddly curved, interconnected giant devices sat precisely spaced out upon the cavern's curved floor. Around the periphery were many more of the "amber" chambers, within which various objects were fuzzily visible. And in the exact center of the chamber, looming up a full hundred feet into the air was...?

Susan couldn't believe her eyes.

"Oh my God, it's real!" Susan gasped, staring in amazement.

"What's real?" Adriana said, wobbling up to her feet.

"*That!*" Susan pointed.

Off in the distance at the center of the huge cavern was the red *Obelisk!* It was just as her father in her "fantasy hallucinations" had described it! It was twenty feet square, fully a hundred feet high. Yes, it was red. But it certainly wasn't glowing. Sitting upright there at the center of the alien spacecraft, it was likely a main controller or power source of the ship or both. But it was dead—just a looming slab of red rock.

"What's an Obelisk?" Adri asked, confused.

"It's something I thought I imagined when I was a young girl, but now it's our target. Let's get our nukes set up right against it, Adri. I think it's the key to taking out the entire Asteroid. Once it's destroyed, the threat to Earth is gone."

"I don't know about your fantasies, Susan—but we came here to blow this place to Kingdom Come. That's as good a place as any to get the job done. Let's do it!"

Susan hated not being able to explore the mysteries of the Obelisk and this ancient alien spaceship from five billion years in the past. But she knew there was no time. In a mere three days the Asteroid would slam into Earth, plunging the entire planet into a deadly "nuclear winter." To unravel or learn to control the alien technologies here could easily take decades or even centuries. It was a terrible thing to destroy such a wonderful space artifact, but it was unavoidable.

"Right," Susan grimaced, clutching her broken left arm to her side. She then resolutely leaned forward, putting her shoulder into dragging the heavy bombs.

Her head was down as she struggled forward, her eyes focused on the slick metal at her feet. She noticed *crumbling black fragments* on the surface. In the past there must have been a fire in the vast cavern, leaving behind charred remains. Here and there a long plastic-looking slab stuck up out of the crumbling ashes.

"Watch your feet, Adri—there's stuff down on the floor."

"I've...been noticing. What do you think it was—a forest made out of plastic trees?"

"Don't know...the surviving straight slabs could be construction-grade material. Whatever, there was certainly enough room down here for a weird ancient forest."

Indeed, off across the cavern, Susan saw that the going would get worse the closer they got to the central Obelisk. The ash layer became a confusing maze of long, straight-and-curved charred "timbers." The overlaid black remnants were hundreds of feet long. Struggling through that ancient debris might take hours. But setting up the nukes would only take minutes. And triggering them would take mere seconds.

It was a task, but the end was drawing near.

Susan felt relief that she was coming to the end of her journey—ending up where she'd begun as a child! She fell off her bike in the Park, bumped her head, and "remembered" a nightmare *centered* on the *Obelisk!* Now that mysterious object was her final goal. She felt her whole life circling back upon itself. Maybe Ben's Hindu philosophy was right: existence truly is a set of recurring cycles. If so, after being obliterated by the fusion bombs she might yet live again!

Hah, live again...but did she *want* to? If the Obelisk was here, then that meant her "fantasy" of being in the afterlife and having been given a second chance might also be real. So she might *already* be living out her second chance at "getting it right"!

And that triggered another strange thought in her head. There was something she'd repressed from her conscious memory, which was now trying to reassert itself: a terrible *guilt!* And was blowing up the Asteroid making things right? But it didn't *feel* right. It felt like—

yet again—she was about to make the same terrible world-shattering *mistake!*

Life was so confusing...

She recalled another of her favorite passages from her old poetry book. It was comforting to have it, here at the last, still safely tucked inside her inner flight suit pocket, right alongside Kame's flat cere-monial knife. The key passage was from The Minstrel's Lark, chapter 12, verses 16-21:

> *"Forged in the planet Mars*
> *The Hammer of a relentless God of War*
> *Holding the potential to save an entire race*
> *Or bring the world crashing down in ruins*
> *A Force unto itself, barely contained*
> *Configured to be directed and controlled*
> *Nevertheless so sophisticated it had its own thoughts*
> *Eager to jump out and direct its own destiny*
> *Or simply to explode in an orgy of destruction*
> *Proving once and for all its uniqueness*
> *That it was not a mere lump of soft stone*
> *But a living Entity self-directed*
> *Yet capable of being hijacked and stolen*
> *That thing which called itself 'Man'..."*

It was strange how an old poetry book could predict the future! It was clearly talking about the Obelisk. And here she was—"man"—about to destroy it.

But...the poem referred to "sophisticated thought" rather than heedless destruction.

What the hell did *that* mean?

Susan was saddened as she struggled alongside Adri, stubbornly dragging the seemingly increasingly heavy nukes toward the looming silent machine. Was mankind just a selfish predator, bent on de-stroying everything around it? Was that their role in the Universe, just to pillage and kill?

If so, then should she *not* set off the bombs? Could this be the final "death-knoll" that mankind richly deserved: to be hit by the giant titanium-clad Asteroid? If she and Adri deliberately *refused* to stop the Asteroid, would that rightly and *justly* doom Earth and mankind?

"It's up to us," she muttered to herself, straining forward, "or maybe not?"

Obviously, Scott and his confederates had utterly failed in their attempt to destroy the Asteroid. Their little fire-bombs had just heated up the surface, with some of that heat leaking through the metal of the alien spacecraft to the inner tunnels. So the final destruction of the Asteroid—or refusal to do so—now fell squarely upon her and Adriana.

Should they do it—or not?

It was chilling to have doubts here at the last minute. But Susan's inner debate was crucial...

Is humanity really worth saving?

Whatever, she had to decide quickly. In the crushing gravity, she and Adri didn't have the strength to keep on for much longer. It wasn't just their bodies deteriorating. Susan realized it was getting harder to think. The atmosphere in the Asteroid wasn't as innocuous as they'd hoped. Her mind was poisoned. She no longer trusted her senses. Everything around her was getting blurry and nightmarish.

"Adri...I'm sick, girlfriend," she gasped, blinking, desperate to clear her thoughts and vision.

She looked down, concentrating on the taunt strap of the harness that cut into her shoulder. It extended across her chest into her trembling right hand.

"Oh, Christ!" she gasped.

She saw *little black spiders* crawling on the strap and the back of her hand. "I'm hallucinating..."

"Suzy!" she heard a glad cry.

Jerking her head to the side she saw her mother, Sally King.

"*Launching* the third wave!"

After the second wave failed to destroy the Asteroid, they'd reconfigured the Dish to fire off their next round. Due to subspace dynamics, it took a while to "recharge their batteries" for the final volley. Also, Bill was finally put to work refining the plasma burst configuration. Instead of a series of "bullets" the Captain insisted on one huge ball of plasma to finally consume the Asteroid. The softened-up six mile long piece of metal would be zooming down their throats as they released the massive burst. Besides encompassing the entire Asteroid, the plasma ball would be incredibly dense and hot—only needing to travel a mere five minutes to smash into the Asteroid.

And now it was forming right above their heads.

"It's awesome!" Maria gasped, tightly clutching Bill's arm with both hands.

Indeed, the expanding plasma mass—glaring through the greatly darkened surface of the canopy above them—was the roiling heart of the sun!

And it grew larger and larger, "bubbling" out of the Dish just as a soap bubble is blown out of a giant loop. Its own internally generated magnetic fields contained it like a little sun, held back by its continuing link into subspace. But when that connection was cut it would leap away with incredible force!

"It's the biggest bomb that mankind has ever built," Bill sighed, horrified but transfixed by its majesty.

The telescopic view of the Asteroid was now much more detailed. The Asteroid was only six minutes out, hurtling through space toward Earth at a blistering 60,000 mph. Details of its surface stood out in stark relief. Bill was fascinated by the many smooth overlapping layers that ran the length of the pitch-black oblong. The obscuring dust cloud that'd been there had vanished—wiped away by the two previous series of plasma bursts. Sadly, there was no trace of either Hermes or the Orion capsule visible on the Asteroid's surface. It looked increasingly certain that Susan and her crewmate Johansson were dead...unless—had they managed to get into that small central ravine?

But the surface of the Asteroid was *roiling*. Bill could clearly see *waves* passing across its rippled surface. The metal making up its outer layers was clearly melted. One more trip into the Plasma Inferno and Bill was certain the Asteroid would evaporate!

The entire Saucer suddenly lurched to the side as the Dish released its artificial sun.

"Plasma burst is *away!*"

The sun-like sphere above them sped upward and outward. Bill tracked it on the main screen, hurtling toward the in-racing Asteroid.

"*Five minutes* to impact."

This time the Asteroid should finally meet its end, only seconds away from reaching the Saucer's position.

Bill tried to put Susan out of his mind for the moment. The Asteroid itself was a strange enough puzzle. It didn't look like any asteroid he'd ever seen a picture of—in fact, it looked like either a piece of petrified wood or...?

No, it couldn't be, could it? Was it really some sort of formed object, perhaps an *alien spacecraft?* No. That was crazy. He hadn't believed the earlier reports. The object wasn't maneuvering. It was just a strange looking cosmic rock.

"That monster will *melt!*"

It was Scott, scowling at the viewscreen. His normally piercing black eyes were especially fierce. He was practically foaming at the mouth, grinding his gleaming white teeth together in a snarl.

"It's only a threat to my Earth, Scott," Bill tiredly replied, trying to calm him. "There's no reason for you to get over-excited about..."

"Are you crazy?" Scott said, looking at him like he was truly a stupid monkey.

"If we fail, then it'll just destroy your 'retirement' homestead lands," Bill bitterly persisted. "You're safe whatever happens. Despite your claims to the contrary, I don't see how it could possibly threaten your Earth located off in another, parallel Dimension. It's just a big rock—well, maybe a strange looking one—but hardly something that could move between Dimensions or across time itself!"

"And just how do you think *we* got here?" Scott unexpectedly replied, staring at Bill with an unexpectedly haunted look. "Open your mind, 'Dr.' King—*anything* is possible! It's never a matter of supposed facts. It's always a matter of probabilities! And we *know* the probabilities!"

Several of the crewmembers turned from the compelling central viewing screen to stare at the shouting Scott.

"Well, then I think it's very *improbable* that a big space rock could threaten other planes of existence!" Bill snorted.

Actually, he wasn't thinking about his words. He was just releasing the incredible tension, babbling about whatever jumped into his mind. This was it. This was the final test. Either they'd destroy the Asteroid or it would flash past the Saucer to smash into Earth!

"It's not just a big rock," Scott growled petulantly. He kicked away to float over to the technicians surrounding the Captain as they stared intently at the screen.

"Scott, wait!" Bill said, switching off his magnetic boots to follow him...

But a strong hand grabbed onto his arm, holding him back. He hovered there in midair, rotating to face the solidly booted-down Maria.

"*You* must wait," she softly ordered him.

"But...?"

"It's too late to change anything, Bill," she sadly told him. "You have to accept your responsibilities."

"But...I...?"

"*Two minutes* to impact."

"I had a forbidden love affair on my planet, Bill."

Startled, he looked at her with wide-stretched brown eyes. She seemed completely sincere, staring past him at the two objects on the viewscreen—the *flaring artificial sun* racing toward the hurtling, black Asteroid.

"But, I thought you said you had clinical reproduction that was totally programmed and...?"

"Unofficially, totally forbidden, I struck up a relationship with a male member of the Religious Class. We met in secret, initially only for conversation. It was wonderful to stretch my mind beyond combat tactics and strategies."

"What, no sperm exchanges?"

Maria glared at him. "Don't be gross, Bill. I didn't know religion and he didn't know combat strategy. We exchanged viewpoints, initially to strengthen our individual skill sets...and, yes, after a while—we coupled."

"Ah...so you...?"

"Yes, we evaded our hormonal inhibitors and had unregulated, spontaneous sex! It was a long time ago, Bill. Don't be jealous."

He wasn't jealous. He was perplexed. Why was she telling him this, especially now?

"What does that have to do with my so-called 'responsibilities'?"

"We define *ourselves*. And then we carry that Divine Substance—for better or worse—into the future."

"What do you mean? Are you referring to 'karma'?"

"*One minute* to impact."

"Yes, sort of—I learned this from my lover. I guess that's why I'm not as tough as Scott anymore. But I'm convinced our individual responsibilities can be *refined* and *atoned-for* throughout the further cycling of the Universe."

"Cycling?"

"Yes, like 'eggs' and 'sperm'—do you see?"

"No!"

She laughed gently, hugging his arm against her warm side.

"Just don't beat yourself up, Bill. That's what I'm saying."

He frowned down at her.

"*Impact!*" the Captain shouted.

Bill's eyes snapped back up to the viewscreen. He saw the *artificial sun* and the *black Asteroid* merged as *one bright dot* which then *expanded...*

The viewscreen yet again turned *pure white!*

Everyone was holding their breath.

Bill's eyes went to the graphs on the central computer console screen. One by one they came back on line from being totally overloaded with data. One by one, they told the same story...

Nothing!

"The Asteroid is *obliterated!*" the captain yelled triumphantly.

The other crewmembers cheered, hugging each other and spinning around in the zero-G...except for Bill.

He pulled his arm away from Maria who was likewise cheering and clapping—and "clomped" his way out of the control room. He was headed back to his cabin to unbuckle his magnetic boots and float up into his hammock. He intended to sleep for as long as his exhausted body wished: for days if necessary!

"Goodbye, Susan," he mumbled to himself. Tears budded out from his eyes, floating away to each side of his face as he trudged along. He was a sad, zero-G, leaky water-fountain. "It all seemed so important, Susan," he sobbed quietly, "and now none of it matters."

He heard her voice once again in his head. He pictured a little girl with pigtails glaring at him indignantly after he'd said something incredibly dumb. She stood ready to skewer him with a blistering reply. Instead she just smiled at him and said: "You're a smart kid, Billy. I *like* having you for my brother, even if now and then you're really stupid."

Huh. *She* was dumb to say such a squishy thing!

But damned if he didn't feel the same way toward her...

And as Maria so inappropriately reminded him, there *is* something called "*atonement*."

And it would arrive soon enough.

Chapter 32

<u>REVENGE</u>

Ah, sweet retaliation

For the "knife in the back" a bomb

Blowing those sons-of-bitches to pieces

Sure, escalating the cycle of violence

But a slice of pie best served cold

Seemingly balancing the scales of Justice

While in reality a SCREAM of rage

Futilely flailing back against the Universe

That which ends up taking everything away

We want desperately to return something vile

As odious, cruel, uncaring, and brutal

Just to say that we didn't comply

But fought back in every way we could

When it came our time to expire...

Everybody shrieking in rhyme!

The Minstrel's Lark, 32:11-15

IMPACT MINUS TWO DAYS, *ENERGIZING...*

The entire cavern spun around in a circle—flinging Susan, Adri, and the two hydrogen bombs into the air.

They fell heavily. Susan knew all her bones should be broken. But she and Adri had crashed through a high pile of the brittle black scaffolds, which cushioned the blow. They were finally nearing the Obelisk, the remains of the ancient "forest" piled high around them. Susan saw the two bombs half buried to her side in the black rubble.

"What...was...that?" Adri gasped.

"It had to be...more plasma bursts—much more powerful than before."

Susan couldn't move. She was literally completely exhausted. Her muscles felt like they'd turned into jelly. Her head was spinning. Her mind was crumbling. She'd lost track of how long they'd been winding their way through the burnt black maze toward the Obelisk. It seemed like an eternity but it was probably no more than a day. And along most of the way she'd been happily chatting with her mother, *Sally King*.

She and Adriana had no food or water. They were both delirious, at the end of human endurance. Also, it was oppressively hot in the central cavern. Susan had loosened the connections of her spacesuit, allowing her breastplate to fall open. She desperately needed to drink water. But she'd long since drained the small water reservoir in the spacesuit. And in the dry, dusty cavern there was no fountain from which to drink.

So Susan mumbled incoherently, gesturing and growling as she staggered along, growing weaker and more delirious with each tortured step. It was nice to see and talk with her dead mother. But those pesky, ephemeral little *black spiders* kept crawling up and into her spacesuit. They tickled and itched. They were damn irritating!

She kept weakly swatting at them, trying to squash them. But they scampered away from her hand, seemingly laughing at her. Also, they were insubstantial. They turned into little black fogs only to re-materialize at another spot.

"I need some ghostly bug spray," Susan mumbled to herself, half-laughing.

Adriana didn't seem to notice, either the swarms of little "ghost" spiders or Sally Smith striding along beside Susan. Adriana just kept trudging stoically forward, her eyes half-closed, as if in a self-induced trance. But Susan vividly saw her mother, Sally King, walking beside the two of them as they dragged the two heavy bombs one torturous step after the next. And she wasn't the fat, old, tired, sick version of Susan's mother—but an invigorated, slim, spunky, young woman. So in Susan's fevered brain she had a long private conversation with the original *Girl with the Turtle Tattoo!*

Yes, Susan knew it wasn't her mother. It was probably just a hallucination induced by the toxins floating in the air, as were the itchy black spiders. But it was comforting to have this final talk with her sweet, gentle, smart mother. They talked of many things. Sally King told her daughter amazing stories which Susan had never heard before. But most importantly, Sally King reminded her daughter "Suzy" of the *Turtle Tattoos* which inked both of their left wrists. Susan had almost forgotten about that old tattoo. It hadn't flared up for a number of years. But now, at the end of her long journey, its presence signaled a silly cheerfulness. That coy smile on the bald baby turtle's cute head, hidden beneath the arm of Susan's spacesuit and the fabric of her flight suit, was a signal to not take everything so seriously!

It connected back to her poetry book: The Minstrel's *Lark*. A "minstrel" was a traveling entertainer, singer, and storyteller. And a "lark" was a bit of fun, a prank, a *game!* So was all this just a big game? Was she and Adri just pawns?

Suddenly she realized they *were!*

If it weren't so sad it'd be laughable.

Yes, Susan was now convinced that their "dire" mission to divert or destroy the Asteroid was really just a huge *Cosmic Comedy*—in which she, Adriana, Ben, Kame, George, Torey, and Vladimir played leading roles. It was also a *Cosmic Ballet*. They'd danced their hearts out. And it was also a *Cosmic Drama*, complete with tragedy, horror, suffering, and death. But Susan's apparitional dead mother convinced her that it wasn't the end of the play that mattered, but each individual's performance. After all, once having seen/heard the plot and music, why do audiences come back for repeat performances?

Well, it certainly wasn't for Susan's stunted talents. She'd given up her artistic yearnings long ago as a young child. To be in a Broadway play you'd have to be very talented, trained, and skilled.

In chatting with her dead mother, Susan realized that it is the power of *each individual's live performance* as an actor-artist-singer-musician-dancer-writer-whatever combined into an ever-changing kaleidoscope of colors, sounds, and emotions that continually fascinates an audience! And even though the overall plot repeats—going through the same overall sequence time and again—it's each individual's live-action part that makes everything fresh and new!

After all, even in the best scripted and practiced live plays, *anything* can happen! It's not just a set transcript, fixed book, musical recording, or a final movie: it's a *live* performance!

A curious peace descended upon her.

Susan was no longer obsessed by what would happen next, just joyfully observant of her own exquisite experience. She had, indeed—in the midst of all the failure and pain—achieved a measure of acceptance.

"Is this the end?" Adriana groaned. She lay motionless a few feet away from Susan, buried in the ubiquitous black fragments.

"I think...the curtain is coming down," Susan sighed in resignation.

Indeed, as the cavern shuddered and bounced, an actual *flaring curtain* of crackling *lightning bolts* filled the air around them. The blazing shafts descended from the high ceiling and smashed all around. The *thunder* was deafening. Only the insulation of the charred black materials beneath them saved Susan and Adri from instant electrocution. And the repeated walls of lightning *flowed* along the cavern's floor *into* the central red Obelisk—which greedily sucked them up like a dry sponge exposed to an ocean of water!

It began to *glow*...

And then, as fast as the final assault on the Asteroid started, it was over!

"Are we...still alive?" Adri gasped, floundering in the mass of black fragments around her, digging herself out.

"It...appears...that the plasma bursts outside didn't get us...but..."

"—but?" Adri asked as she raised her head and started to look around.

"I don't think we're alone anymore!"

Indeed, an alarming "RUSTLING" now echoed loudly around the high cavern. At first Susan thought it was just the electrically charged ancient burned scaffoldings shifting. But then she saw they weren't just vibrating, they were *merging* and *rising!*

All around her and Adri, *regenerating black shafts* were combining together, thrusting downward, and then pushing themselves upward.

"Adri, we've got to move! We've got to get to the Obelisk! Come on, girl—one last push! It isn't far from here! We're almost there!"

"What's...happening?" Adri groaned as she got her feet back under her and started to once again lean forward into her harness.

Susan saw the black "dust" around them was *aggregating*. It was forming into discrete shapes—thousands of rounded heads, glittering eyespots, bulging abdomens, and jointed sharp-pointed legs.

"These things must be the remains of what attacked the alien spaceship billions of years in the past. And now with the vast energy shot into the Asteroid by the plasma bursts, they're somehow *reanimating* themselves!"

"You mean they're *alive?*"

"Alive, angry, and missing a good meal for the last few *billions* of years!"

All around her and Adri, the fast-reassembled GIANT BLACK SPIDERS were rising up like the tentacle-sprouting robots of H.G. Well's "War of the Worlds." They seemed confused, disoriented: stumbling and crashing into each other. But Susan saw they were starting to act in concert, turning together toward the Obelisk!

Looking to the side in horror at the gathering threat, Susan ran *straight into* the solid flat side of the *Obelisk!* She groaned as she bounced off, falling to the ground. The two bombs slid up behind her, pinning her against the red rock. Mashed against the pulsating surface, Susan felt gentle warmth. Looking up, she saw that the semi-translucent material was now *pulsing* with a red, internal light!

Powered by the vast energy absorbed by the Asteroid, The Obelisk was likewise coming to life! It was beckoning her—to do what?

But that was irrelevant. Only one thing mattered: *arming* and simultaneously *detonating* their two hydrogen bombs!

Adriana swayed above her, a hand out to help her up.

Then Susan saw Adriana's mouth drop open, a strange look spreading through her eyes...

Above her glittered several *many-facetted red eyespots*, scattered along a *black carapace*. And a *long sharp talon* protruded from her chest, red blood dripping from its tip and shaft. Adriana was coughing up frothy red bubbles that stained her mouth and chin.

Other talons were stabbing down at the two bombs, starting to rip open their casings...

"*No!*" Susan screamed, leaping up and launching herself at the rounded carapace. She grabbed out the flat knife from inside her flight suit and jammed it repeatedly into the "head" of the Spider. It *SCREECHED* in apparent pain, releasing Adriana's body.

It scampered backward into a crowd of the still-assembling giant Spiders.

The lethally wounded woman slumped down, bleeding profusely.

"Adri..." Susan sobbed, cradling her head.

"I was...helping Ben sabotage the mission."

"*What?*"

"I'm sorry," she whispered. "But I locked you out of the controls. You can't activate the bombs. This must be...the final end...of both Earth and the Obelisk...mutually assured *obliteration*."

Her eyes closed for the last time.

Stunned, Susan paused for a moment. Adriana's dying confession made no sense. Ben went crazy because of radiation poisoning. But Adri wasn't insane. Why would she want to stop ADM-1 from getting to the Asteroid? Did it have something to do with that cult she'd been part of, maybe some misguided attempt to bring on the Apocalypse? But then why would she come all this way with Susan, helping her at every turn?

For a moment Susan considered sinking down beside Adri, resting her head against the soothing red Obelisk, and waiting her turn.

"No!" she shouted, surging to her feet and stumbling over to the two bombs. The *rustlings* and *cracklings* around her were getting ominously loud. She snapped back the two panels revealing the detonation controls. Good, they were still operational. The damage to the casings hadn't reached the inner mechanisms. She stripped off her glove, stuck her thumb onto the biometric plate, and then tried to punch in the activation code. Nothing!

"*Damn! Damn! Damn!*" she cursed, banging her fist down on the hard metal surface. All around her the forest of looming Spiders was inching closer...

"Well if I'm locked out, then I'll bet *you've* still got access," Susan growled as she grabbed one of Adri's space-gloved hands. Yanking off the glove she took a firm hold on her friend's thumb and with a jerk of her sharp knife *sliced* it off!

Ignoring spurting blood Susan slammed the digit down on the keypad. She was heartened that lights started flashing. Likewise she quickly activated the control panel of the other nuke, entered the codes into both, and set the bombs to their minimum countdowns. In sixty seconds they would simultaneously detonate.

Relieved she'd at last completed her task she stood up between the two cylinders, snapped her own glove back in place, and then brandished her bloody knife at the approaching Spiders. She was determined to protect the counting-down nukes to the last instant when...

WELCOME MY CHILD. YOU WILL NOT BE HARMED.

"What?" she gasped.

It was the same voice she'd thought she'd heard earlier. It wasn't verbal. Rather, it sprang from inside her head: a telepathic communication.

Spinning around she saw a panel hanging open, leading into the side of the Obelisk. A *noxious red fog* bellowed from the opening.

She coughed, the billions-year-old acrid mist searing her lungs.

Could the rebooting, ancient Obelisk protect her from the impending nuclear blast?

Might it even whisk me away, as Mom said it could?

"You're not tricking me like you fooled my mother. If you're really the heart of this ancient spaceship," she whispered, "then to stop the Asteroid for sure, I've got to stop you too!"

She slipped the knife back into her flight suit's inner pocket as she slapped the spacesuit's breastplate closed. In the same motion she jerked her dangling helmet onto her head and sealed her spacesuit. Then she grabbed one of the armed, ticking-down nuclear bombs, and with a super-human effort *dragged* it with her *into* the Obelisk!

"Hah!" she laughed, seeing the panel slam shut behind her. It was tight in the small compartment with the large, ticking nuke crammed in next to her. "Whether Ben or Adri would like it or not, I'm saving Earth while stopping *both* the Asteroid *and* the Obelisk!"

She wrapped her arms lovingly around the bomb, welcoming the sudden BLINDING FLASH and *searing heat*.

"We're almost home," Maria comforted Bill.

He refused to answer, just kept standing firmly attached to the metal deck by his magnetized boots. He was staring out a wide side porthole on the outer observation ring of the Saucer. Maria stood right there beside him, ever watchful. The masked dinosapiens wanted his cooperation in the coming full-scale invasion of Earth, but were still guarding him closely, distrustful of him.

"I'm sorry again about Susan," Scott said as he drifted out of the air to land with a "clomp" beside the both of them. He'd activated his boots to stand rigidly on the deck. "As far as the world will know, she died a hero. We're reporting that she succeeded in setting off her two nukes within a ravine in the rock, which together with our plasma bursts finally succeeded in destroying the Asteroid."

Bill still did not respond, absently studying the approaching L1 site where a "beehive" of activity swarmed. The big white moon filled most of the black sky. Backlit against its cratered surface, many conventional spacecraft from Earth came and went. They were docking then departing from the large framework which floated there suspended in space. The red/yellow tails of their firing chemical rocket engines was impressive.

Inside the construction framework a second, larger Dish was taking shape. It was half finished, its many black panels glittering in the unfiltered sunlight. Off to the side hung a second Saucer, this one even wider than the original in which Bill, Maria, and Scott stood. Bill was mildly amused to see the larger version rapidly spinning on its central axis. Clearly it was generating centripetal force as an artificial "gravity"—a marked improvement on their clunky magnetic boots.

"Why is there a second Dish?" Bill quietly asked.

"Well, there are three reasons for that," Scott happily grinned. "*First*, ours is nearly discharged. We've only 10% of our original capacity left. That's still immensely powerful, but not enough for our future purposes that..."

"So you're draining off the *entire nuclear warhead capacity of Earth* before launching your wholesale invasion?"

For a moment Scott was silent. Then he casually laughed.

"That's right, Bill," he smugly admitted. "They'll have no mean-ingful defense while we'll have total command from space. Any orga-nized resistance on the surface will be obliterated by us from orbit."

"And just why are they allowing you do this to them?"

Bill heard Scott lightly laugh, as if it were no big deal. Yes, the "stupid little monkeys" were complicit in their own destruction.

"We told the remaining governing bodies that a *swarm of comets* is following along behind the Asteroid. We're saying that the comets were sucked out of the Oort cloud by the first Asteroid's passage. We've convinced them we've still got a barrage of deadly projectiles aimed at us necessitating a continuing planetary defense. That's our story! And it *is* based on fact. Indeed, a swarm of comets did follow the path of the destroyed Asteroid, confirmed by the few working Earth-based telescopes. We 'slightly' exaggerated the threat, howev-er. None of their paths will come anywhere near to intersecting with Earth."

Bill nodded thoughtfully, now pointing out the porthole to a brand new structure hanging in space at L1: a *giant ring* big enough to encircle a small city. It floated off to the side of the main construc-tion framework, spinning. Its construction looked to be about two-thirds complete.

"So what's that?" Bill asked.

"Oh, that's a surprise," Scott grinned even wider, playfully punch-ing Bill on his shoulder.

Though it hurt, Bill didn't flinch. Yes, Scott liked to poke at him. Yes, Bill was the submissive male while Scott was the big, tough "al-pha" dog. But that *wouldn't last for long*. Bill just kept staring out at the busy space hub as it drew ever closer and larger.

In a few minutes they'd be part of it, returned to whence they'd begun.

"Let me guess," Bill replied. "It's a permanent space station."

"Bingo!" Scott chortled happily. "We convinced President Schwartz and her Cabinet—who are hidden away at the Cheyanne Mountain Nuclear Bunker—that it's their new totally secure site for a *world government!* That's our *second* 'rationale' for this marvelous activity! The Saucer fleet here at L1 will, supposedly, protect and em-power the new central world government."

"—which the President thinks she's going to be in charge of, up here in space...*really?*"

"Yes!" Scott gleefully chortled. "After the worldwide turmoil and destruction of society, the prospect of moving to a tranquil space sanctuary was eagerly accepted! So the remaining resources of the planet are focused on constructing the new Dish and Space Station. The Earth is collapsing under the weight of its own festering population and excesses, but 'space' is seemingly clean and limitless! It was an easy sell, especially when Nashoba Energy kindly volunteered to pick up half the tab."

"But that's not its real purpose, is it?"

"Ah, yes, you've a keen mind, my friend. The *third* reason for the new Dish is closely connected to the Ring, a supposed space station for the New World Government. You see, it takes enormous energy to pass from our Dimension into yours and..."

"—you'll use the plasma bursts from the new Saucer to open a Rift through which an *armada of lizard spacecraft* will erupt," Bill matter-of-factly concluded. "And you'll keep the opening to your Dimension stabilized and wide-open with the Ring. That's spectacular. So how soon will this momentous event occur?"

Scott was silent, his eyes narrowing, as if reassessing Bill.

"We've been moving across dimensions on a small scale for centuries," Maria jumped into the conversation. "But it's been powered from the other side, producing small transient portals only sufficient for individuals to cross over. But with your vast number of nuclear bombs to power it..."

"—the seminal achievement of our warlike species..." Bill ruefully sighed.

"—yes, well, we'll finally have the *permanent gateway* we need to transport large equipment and spacecraft," Maria concluded.

Her words sounded triumphant. But she didn't look happy. Indeed, she was looking down at her magnetic boots, not meeting Bill's eyes.

He was impressed. She seemed genuinely ashamed! Presumably, "overwhelming force" wasn't part of her "Warriors' Way" credo. Ah well, she'd just have to get used to blasting enemy armies into smithereens from afar, rather than bloodily and "nobly" fighting them hand-to-hand.

"Well, it seems you have everything figured out," Bill congratulated them. "I'm to take my place as your figurehead hero, for the moment, until you pull the rug out from under the human race."

"Now you're getting it!" Scott happily nodded.

They were sliding up to the giant framework. Spacesuited figures drifted past the porthole, above and below, with white spurts from their steering jets marking their passage. A bevy of accompanying spacecraft now surrounded Bill's returning Saucer. The spaceship was precisely drifting up to a *giant docking arm* which leisurely swung out in space to meet them. The old Dish that was still attached above the Saucer was coming to rest beside the new one, immediately outside the new Framework.

The big arm latched onto the Saucer and they slid to a stop with a slight jar.

"But you didn't answer my question, Scott," Bill quietly stated.

"Oh?"

"*When* will the Rift be in place—so that the many eager hordes of space-lizard-warrior-armies can come pouring through, such that the 'new world government' can be deposed, and I'm sent off to the 'old humans rest home'?"

He shrugged, "Soon enough."

"Ah—too *late*, then."

"What?"

A *shudder* ran through the Saucer, almost ripping the three of them from their magnetic perches on the metallic flooring. This was immediately following by an ominous "humming" so loud that it vibrated their teeth!

Something drastic was happening.

The Captain came floundering along the corridor, bouncing in the zero-G from one shuddering wall to the other.

"What's going on?" Scott yelled at him.

Maria was clutching Bill's arm so tightly he winced.

"The Dish is *firing up*—the remaining reserves *accumulating!*" the Captain yelled, being banged about from side to side. "You've got to bring up Dr. King to stop it! He knows how to manipulate the magnetic confinement fields better than any of us!"

Indeed, outside the window a *blood-red glare* was painting itself on the surrounding spacecraft and structures.

The ear-splitting RUMBLE was getting louder and louder.

"Can't you just shut the damn thing down?" Scott yelled back.

"We can't! It's out of control! It's a runaway chain reaction! The accumulating plasma cloud is getting denser and denser! It's not releasing and ejecting as it should!"

Scott twisted-about from looking at the Captain bouncing-about the shuddering, lurching corridor. He savagely grabbed Bill by the neck, simultaneously knocking Maria backward.

"*You* did this!"

Bill took hold of Scott's wrists and yanked them free of his neck, snarling back: "Yes, I did."

They were face-to-face.

"Then you've got to stop it!"

"Well, I'm afraid it's my 'fail safe' program, Scott," Bill calmly replied, speaking directly into the man's ear. "I hid it away beneath the obvious changes I made, so even if you got my password you'd still not notice the deeper instructions. If we got back to L1 it was set to trigger automatically—unless I stopped it in advance. But you didn't allow me access to the computers. Even if you would have, I had no incentive to turn it off. Now...well, there's just no time left, Scotty boy! Even I wanted to, I couldn't stop it."

"I'll *kill* you!"

The *glare* outside the porthole was blindingly bright. The VIBRATION was on the brink of tearing the Saucer to pieces. The *screeching* as the Dish tried to contain the uncontainable was deafening.

Long sharp CLAWS sprang from each of Scott's outstretched fingers as he grabbed for Bill's throat...

—Maria blocking Scott's lunge, knocking his arms to the side...

—as with a knotted fist, Bill *hit* Scott square in his face as hard as he could, *breaking* the man's nose, causing a *gush* of red blood to spray out and float in the zero-G around the man's head.

A bewildered expression appeared on Scott's bloodied face as he crumpled. Simultaneously, Maria slid an arm around Bill's waist and hugged him tightly.

He hugged her back, sad now that everything was ending.

Bill looked down in disdain at Scott, as the once-haughty man-lizard moaned pitifully and spat out broken teeth.

"Not bad...for a 'stupid little monkey,' huh?" Bill sneered.

"It won't stop us!" Scott sputtered from the floor.

"No...but it should slow you considerably, giving the remnants of humanity time to unite and fight back. Yes, we'll fight back—we always do."

The *NOVA-LIKE EXPLOSION* was seen the world over. It lit up the night sky of the Earth. It left a permanent black scorch-mark across the surface of the Moon. And it *utterly evaporated* everything parked at L1.

Chapter 33

LAST WILL AND TESTAMENT

Not another drab burial or wake

Where black-clad mourners huddle

But the wild raucous celebration

Of a New Orleans funeral-parade

Trumpets blaring, drums beating

The dead loved-one held up high

A coffin sailing on a sea of joy

"Passing on" to the other side...

The Minstrel's Lark, 33:6-8

IMPACT MINUS ONE DAY, *UNTETHERED...*

Stunned to still be alive, Susan opened her eyes in utter confusion. She was wobbly standing in her charred spacesuit *back on the rippled black surface* of the Asteroid! The 2X gravity was yet again smashing down on her, trying to force her to her knees.

And looking up in bewilderment through her scorched faceplate she saw the rapidly growing, blue-green globe of an onrushing Earth!

"How is this possible?" Susan gasped to herself.

She was in shock, barely able to stand upright. She noted that in the black star-studded sky the glaringly white moon was in front of her and somewhat off to the side. Beyond the moon was the Earth. From her present vantage spot, her home planet was the size of the moon seen from Earth's surface. Since Susan knew that from the moon Earth should look thirteen times the size of the moon in the sky, she did a rough calculation in her mind.

The distant, small blue-green marble in front of her—toward which she was hurtling—looked six times more distant than the orbit of the moon. It was thus 1.5 million miles away, just *one single day* until impact!

As far as Susan could tell, no spaceship was out in front of them tossing plasma bombs at the Asteroid. Did Bill's spaceship explode? Did it retreat?

"God...what happened?" she muttered, shaking her head inside her helmet to try and clear her thoughts.

The last thing she remembered she was being blasted to atoms inside the Obelisk. And now she was undeniably standing there on the surface of a still-intact Asteroid, with no memory of any intervening period.

"I *shouldn't* be standing here. I should be *vaporized!*"

The Obelisk! Somehow, despite her best efforts, it must have saved her, transporting her back to the surface—back to where she'd begun.

And the *Asteroid*, where...or *when* was it now?

That was a curious thought. She was plummeting toward Earth, right? There was no doubt that Earth hung in space a day's distance in front of her, right? But something felt very, very wrong.

Wow, this was so *confusing*...

"Adri?" Susan sobbed, turning her helmeted head, looking around to each side. She hoped that her friend would miraculously materialize, even though she'd been stabbed to her heart by that evil Spider.

But Susan was completely alone, surrounded by the stark black ripples and ridges of the massive Asteroid. The thick outer hull of the ancient spacecraft was obviously still intact, yet it looked...different?

It was no longer slick and metallic. Indeed, the ground beneath her feet was broken up and cracked.

She laboriously lifted a leg and dropped the heel of her tough spacesuit-boot onto the black surface. It dug into the ground a few inches, kicking up a cloud of black dust.

"Oh, Christ, it's *brittle*," she gasped to herself. "The hull's been degraded!"

Indeed, around her she now saw smoldering boulders and massive cracks. The Asteroid was badly damaged by the barrage it'd endured, both from the external plasma bursts and internal nuclear bombs. The surface looked fragile, ready to break it into pieces!

"Too bad I can't hit as hard as Scott liked to do to poor 'fraidy-cat Bill," Susan gasped into her helmet, staggering around in a circle. "I could break it apart with one big 'smack' to its arm!"

Looking in the direction of the ravine, Susan now saw *hot steam* spewing from it into space, a heavenly geyser starting to rain pink drops of congealing fluids down upon the black surface. Clearly, the two nukes did have an effect. The "circulatory fluid" inside the ravine was vaporized, now ejecting out of the ancient crack that was set-into the massive hull.

Hopefully the nuclear bombs had incinerated or driven the reanimated Black Spiders back into subspace. But now Susan was riding a *hollowed out bullet* aimed straight at the heart of the Earth! Talk about a lethal weapon! And she was witness to its final plunge, doomed to stand on its surface and watch the last hours of humanity play out!

Despairing, Susan was tempted to open her helmet and end it all right there—suffocated and flash-frozen on the spot. But then she spotted a *flat aluminum glint*. There, toward the ravine but beneath an overlapping slab of the titanium alloy, she saw something unnatural.

"Jesus Christ," she prayed, "let that be what I think it is!"

She staggered on leaden legs in the 2X gravity, stumbling toward the beckoning glint. Closer, she saw it was indeed light glancing off flat metal. Falling to her knees, she crawled the last bit of distance, beneath the overhang, and saw the crumpled remains of the *Orion capsule!*

"Oh...thank God," she gasped, reaching out a trembling hand. Her space-gloved hand tightly gripped the outer panel of the main airlock, which hung askew. She wrenched it fully open.

Then she managed to crawl inside, open the still-sealed inner door, push her body onward and slam the hatch shut behind her.

It was dark inside the crumpled capsule. There was no power and no air. Little if any starlight from outside trickled in through the portholes. Whatever titanic forces had bathed the surface of the Asteroid, they'd fortuitously spared the Orion capsule by smashing it up and beneath the protective overhanging ledge.

"E-emergency b-batteries...come on!" Susan grated to herself, fumbling through the wrecked interior to the manual control panel.

Normally the capsule was fully computerized. Now, though, since the computer terminals were dead, the final failsafe was a small panel set into the floor, beneath which were manually activated knobs and buttons. It wasn't ever supposed to be needed in spaceflight. But— thank God for the foresight of the NASA engineers—it was there for unforeseeable emergencies. It couldn't fly the capsule, but could re-activate rudimentary life support functions.

Susan lifted to the side the small panel, fumbled within, and felt a large handle. She yanked it over into its opposite configuration.

Coming from near absolute darkness, the dim light that sprang up inside the wrecked capsule momentarily blinded her. Then, as her eyesight returned, she jerked back in fear...

I'm not alone!

But she immediately recognized the motionless spacesuited figure that still sat strapped into one of the twisted flight chairs

It was Kame.

"Hey girl, you still here?" Susan hysterically snickered.

But no answer came from the bloated spacesuit. Its faceplate was frosted over, so that Susan—thankfully—didn't have to see the bloody, rotting interior.

Working more knobs, Susan was gratified to hear a "hissing" as the last of Orion's air reserves was discharged into the interior. Fortunately, the inner crew cabin shell was still intact and airtight. She saw lights coming on at the terminals. But they were haphazard and flickering. The central computer was powering up, but was clearly severely damaged. She doubted the terminals would help her much. She only hoped that the basic life support mechanisms would come online. Then she was relieved to see heaters in the walls glowing as they warmed the interior. She pushed debris to the side to access a terminal, punching shakily at a keypad. Readouts sprang up then flickered off. Yes, she'd seen enough to confirm the air pressure was holding, approaching Earth normal...

She ripped off her helmet and deeply sucked in the "fresh" air. In a fit of revulsion to the awful stink she'd been enduring inside her festering suit, she tore apart the seals of her spacesuit, throwing the sections off her body. She plugged the discarded life support backpack of her spacesuit into a terminal to recharge its internal batteries, air tanks, and water reserves. Hopefully automatic mechanisms would kick in and replenish her suit as much as possible.

"At least I'll be able to go out one more time, if I have to," she mumbled to herself.

First she found the still-intact water tank and greedily drank from a spigot until she was full to bursting.

"Yes!" she sighed, slumping back. That was the best water she'd ever drunk, even better than the comet-water she and Adri first harvested!

Then she crawled to a supply cabinet, managed to get its warped door open, and dragged out a pot of their harvested, dried algae. It was tasteless and unappetizing—in the dim light not more than a big dried sponge—but edible. She hungrily scarfed it down as she grabbed more water bulbs and sucked them empty. Wait...was that "sponge" from the HAB-3 algae ocean? In the dim light, the crumbs of what she'd eaten looked *red*. Oops, was the sponge not from the algae ocean but actually samples of the infamous red mushrooms, preserved for future analysis by the compulsively studious Kame?

"Hey, did *you* do this?" Susan snickered again at Kame's body, feeling very strange. Her head was spinning. Was she going on another mushroom-induced "trip"?

Whatever, it was "yummy for her tummy"! Satisfied she'd live until *Earth Impact* she leaned back against dead Kame's spacesuited, grotesquely bloated leg. It felt like an air-filled pillow. She contentedly closed her eyes, drifting off into an exhausted sleep.

Susan barely felt it as a *hand reached down* and slipped the knife out of her flight suit's inner pocket.

"You have to choose!"

Susan reluctantly opened her eyes, looking up at a bright blue sky. She was lying on something hard. Oh, right—the *sacrificial altar!*

Oh, Christ. That sponge *was* from the red mushrooms! She was back to her "other-worldly" hallucination. Damn! But...maybe it wasn't so bad to smash into Earth dreaming of a magical, beautiful alternative Dimension?

And, yes, now walking away from her Susan glimpsed an upright, human-sized *lizard,* its long green tail swinging merrily behind!

"W-what...?"

She felt gentle hands on her shoulders, holding her in place. Ben was smiling down at her, his wide brown eyes both sorrowful and understanding. A cool breeze was ruffling his white robe.

Yep, I'm right back there again—she sighed to herself. *This is either a dream or a nightmare. I'm still sleeping back in the Orion capsule, about to smash into Earth. I'm feverish and exhausted. Damn, I thought Kame spaced those red mushrooms! But maybe they just contaminated the brown mushrooms we stored away or the compartment within which the algae sponges were produced.*

Whatever, she had to wake up—to find a way to stop the Asteroid!

But...she knew that was now impossible. She'd tried everything within her power. She might as well just enjoy this fantasy, never wake up, and in a "peaceful" sleep drift away...joining humanity as it was *burnt to a crisp* in the resultant planet-wide firestorm.

"Well, hi there, Ben!" she sighed, compliantly swinging her legs over the edge of the altar and weakly standing up beside him. She put a hand on his thin shoulder to steady herself. At least this feverish dream let her be back in 1G for one last time. That was quite pleasant. "So where'd Freddy-boy go? But it's nice to see you again, dude. You look well. I thought you got blown away by those pterodactyl-jets?"

Sweet—she wryly grinned to herself, gingerly patting her body with the palm of her other hand. *I've dreamed myself out of my flight suit, underwear, and into a set of those spiffy robes Ben now wears. At least it's soft and warm. And I've been cleaned up, no longer coated with layers of stinking, itching sweat.*

Indeed, it was a glorious day back in her fantasized "religious-scientific retreat" of the velociraptor Dinosapiens. A few wispy white clouds floated by far above in a deep blue sky. Mists drifted past below the peak. A cool breeze wafted across her body, rustling her robe. She noted that the wrecked interdimensional observation dishes were back in place, suspended high above her. The same high peaks rose around the sanctuary, stark and majestic. Everything was peaceful.

"We'll see him soon," Ben calmly replied. "That previous attack was most regrettable. I almost died. But I'm better now."

"What happened?" she asked, enjoying her elaborate mushroom-induced fantasy.

"A radical military faction of the Warrior Caste attempted a coup of the world government. Normally the interests of society are delicately balanced, overseen by the Priestly Caste. But the present existential threat to our world's survival has thrown everything into chaos. Fortunately, other factions of the military came to our rescue. They backed the Priests in their plan to appeal to your sense of justice and family."

"Family? Justice?"

"Please come with me, Susan. There are people eagerly waiting to see you."

He smiled at her, wrinkles at the corners of his eyes crinkling. He certainly wasn't the young bushy-haired NASA astronaut Ben Priyanka anymore. Her overactive imagination must see him better as a bald headed, grey-mustached Gandhi clone. He turned and walked away, apparently assuming she'd follow.

She shrugged. Well, why the hell not? The gravity felt much more pleasant here, earth-normal versus the crushing 2X gravity of the Asteroid. It wasn't near as difficult to walk here. She was content to let the fantasy play itself out until she woke back up inside the crashed Orion capsule, or hit Earth.

"So where'd Fred go?"

"He and other world delegates are gathering in High Council. After you say hello to your friends, they await your presence."

"Uh, ok. Whatever, dude."

Around her were smooth white granite surfaces. The mountain retreat had the look of a vibrant scientific institution merged with an ancient, eons-old temple-complex. A few peculiarly large birds wheeled in the blue sky above her. They had long reptilian necks. Potted trees flourished in strategic spots, their canopies of green fronds waving in the breeze. High-domed structures stood elegantly in front of her. Only a few scorch marks were left to mark the failed coup's aerial attack.

Wow, what a great imagination I have—she congratulated her-self. *The details of this dream are fantastic!*

She followed Ben into a building, her eyes adjusting to the dim lighting.

"Suzy! It's so great to see you again! How are you, honey?"

Walking toward her out of the relative darkness was her mother. But it wasn't the young, lean woman of her previous fantasy, who'd kept her company on the brutal trek to the heart of the Asteroid. No, this was the woman Susan remembered: heavyset with grey stringy hair, clad in the ubiquitous white robe of the priests but with thick swollen ankles and a round, puffy face.

"Mom?"

The elderly woman shuffled up and hugged Susan tightly. It seemed so real! Susan could smell that familiar "old lady" aroma of her mother: musty and ammonia-hospital tinged. Yes, this version of her mother was definitely similar to the woman who'd been lost in Veterans Lake, sucked into the earthquake crevice.

"They said you were coming but I didn't believe them!" Sally King sighed happily. Susan noticed that this woman even had the *turtle tattoo* stretched out on her chubby left wrist.

What a great dream. That was a nice touch, very realistic!

"Is it really you, Mom?" Susan choked.

The heavy set woman pulled away, smiling. "What do I have to do, bake you some sugar cookies? Actually, I've moved away from my prior lifelong career of restaurant work. Here, they've let me..."

"—and just *how* did you get here?" Susan interrupted her. The story plot lines might as well get filled in.

"Oh...my 'rescuers' took me from that terminal care facility to an interdimensional 'portal' that was located near Veterans Lake. Unfor-tunately, their activation of the portal drained the lake. That was such a nice little lake! Anyway, dear, I'm their prisoner here. Oh, they haven't hurt me—in fact, they've cured my diabetes. But they won't let me return to our Earth. All of us are hostages here."

"All?"

Out of the shadows of the dimly lit room walked Scott and Bill. Bill had his arm around a young woman who Susan didn't know, of Hispanic appearance. She was pretty!

"Billy!" Susan exclaimed, running up to him, pushing past the young Hispanic woman. Susan hugged him closely. "I thought I'd never see you again."

"Same here, Suzy," he grinned, tears glittering in his eyes. "The Priests here snatched me off of the Saucer just as I caused both it and their L1 assembly station to explode. The Priests here are surprisingly humane. They intervene when they can, moderating the activities of the more brutal warrior caste. They're surprisingly adept, this other civilization of intelligent dinosaurs that..."

"Hello, Susan," Scott interrupted as he walked up to the two of them. "It's been years since I saw you last. We were just kids then. But I certainly recognize you. You look...*good*, very sexy in fact!"

Susan laughed, enjoying this final, vivid fantasy. Scott was much the same as she remembered him, tanned and handsome. But the hard edge that always made her suspicious of him was gone.

"Oh, Scott—I'm sorry I was so bitchy with you over joining Nashoba Energy," she confessed, realizing this final fantasy was a way to purge her inner turmoil. "My NASA career's been a total bust. It's come to nothing. Maybe I could have made a real difference joining your organization and..."

"That wasn't me," he interrupted her. "It was an imposter, a dinosapien genetically altered to look and behave like me. I've been a prisoner here all this time."

"Prisoner...but where are the guards?"

Sally King took Susan by the hand, leading her over to straight backed chairs. Susan was happy to sit, her exhausted legs trembling at having stood so long. Even one-G was too much for her zero-G weakened body.

"There's nowhere for us to go, honey," the older woman kindly explained, still holding her hand. "They let us move about freely here. In fact, they've encouraged us to explore our particular talents. I've gotten back to my mathematics-theory talents. I'm working right now on a new theorem of spatial dimensional convergence with their scientists that..."

Oh, sure—her mother who spent her whole lifetime waiting on tables and cooking hamburgers was a theoretical mathematician! That was a bit much, even for Susan's hyperactive imagination.

"I'm sorry, Susan," Ben interrupted. "There may be time for catching up later. But for now, time is short. We can't maintain our trans-dimensional lock on you much longer. There's a lot of interference. The Council wants to meet with you, right now!"

"But...?"

"It's worse than you think, Suzy," Bill sighed. "On the Saucer we thought that our last plasma burst dissolved the Asteroid, ending the threat to Earth. But it didn't, right?"

She frowned. This final fantasy was starting to get uncomfortable. She wanted to stay with her mother, to catch up for her many years of absence away at school. She wanted to hug her brother and never let him go, finding out more about his cute Hispanic girlfriend. And she particularly wanted to know more about this kinder, gentler Scott—perhaps as a real romantic interest for herself?

But Ben had her by the arm and was pulling her away.

"I'll see you later!" she called back to the trio.

They glumly waved goodbye.

And then she was out of the building, headed for a much larger one. Giant metallic statues guarded a marble-columned entrance. But the statues weren't of ancient human gods. No, they were of giant *T-rexes*, each glowering down from on high. Their long carnivorous teeth gleamed in the sunlight, set-into massive jaws.

Well, what better way was there to symbolize intellectual prowess than the giant "thunder-lizards" dominating the Raptor's evolutionary history?

She laughed from the absurdity. This dream was getting way too bizarre...

"I like the décor!" Susan grinned, deciding to roll with the fantasy.

"Those ancient monsters aren't emblems of the Intellectual Caste, but of the Warriors. This is a pluralistic, diverse civilization, Susan," Ben mildly answered as he led her up a series of wide marble steps.

It was tough going for Susan, climbing the steps. There must have been a hundred of them leading up to the Temple's entrance. Her weakened legs were trembling violently. She had to slow up, so she tried engaging Ben in a discussion.

"Just how many of these 'castes' exist?"

"There are four main ones: Warriors who *fight*, Intellectuals who *think*, Workers who *labor*, and Priests who *lead*."

"Shouldn't there be one for Artists?"

He wryly nodded as they slowly ascended the steps, apparently appreciating her question.

"I've observed amongst the population here that the artistic instinct-talent is inherent to excelling in each of the main Castes. It isn't a separate set of genetic characteristics, but central to overall success, no matter your job aptitude."

"What, no 'untouchables'?"

This stopped Ben at the top step. He apparently saw that Susan was breathing heavily and needed a short rest.

"In addition to the main four, there are many sub-castes and minor castes. Altogether there are thousands. A few do correspond to the 'untouchable' caste as seen on our Earth. It's sad but true. Every society needs a group to which they can relegate their rejects."

She started to breathe steadier, keenly appraising her phantom friend.

"Ben, just why are you a spokesperson for this planet of smart lizards?" she asked him. "Surely you with your Indian ancestry and obvious fondness for Gandhi can see how repulsive and illogical is institutionalized hereditary discrimination and repression?"

He frowned, dropping his head to stare at the marble at his feet.

"The inhabitants of this Earth are born into distinct genetic groups," he explained. "They are millions of years ahead of us in their evolutionary development, Susan. Castes here aren't an accident of random factors, tradition, societal intolerance, or inherited privilege. Rather, it is mainly a convenient expression of deliberately endowed specific genetic characteristics. It's the culmination of eons of genetic engineering, where babies are born adapted to and truly enjoying their explicitly diverse job categories."

"Huh...how about that," she laughed. "And yet it sounds so much like pre-Gandhian British India's 'orderly' society—which I just happened to write an extensive report on in one of my required general-education sociology classes in undergraduate college years!"

"Well, then you..."

"Yes, I know too well, as does my subconscious!"

Ben lifted up his head to stare straight at Susan. His expression hardened.

"This is no fevered dream you are experiencing, Dr. King," he firmly stated. "It is quite real, deadly serious!"

"Sure...whatever," she shrugged, turning toward the nearby high doorway. "Let's get this over with, ok? I'd like to go back to visiting with my *real* friends, not *traitors* to their own kind!"

She saw that she'd hurt the fantasy-Ben with her harsh rebuke. But despite his denial she knew this was merely a final fevered nightmare to be enjoyed or endured, not to be drawn into.

"I'm *not* a traitor!" he bitterly replied. "I'm a humanitarian, Susan—trying to save you from making a terrible mistake. No matter the outward form of people, *genocide* is always wrong! Gandhi *starved* himself to prevent religiously motivated slaughters!"

"Ok," she shrugged, turning away from him.

"Time is short!" Ben insisted. "Please just keep an open mind, Susan. That's all I ask."

"Fine," she sighed. She was tiring of this final dream.

As they entered the Temple she heard a distant rumble of deep *DRUMS* that grew louder and louder as they walked down a long marble hallway. To each side were glass exhibits that showed a progression of impressive Dinosapien cosmic accomplishments. It had the same feeling to Susan as being in the *Houston Space Center* or the *Smithsonian Air and Space Museum*. Strange craft were exhibited. Holographic vistas from other worlds sprang up as they walked past. Depicted were the surfaces of various moons from within the solar system, the red hills of Mars, and the roiling red spot of Jupiter seen up close in great detail. In each exhibition case, intelligent raptors were shown posing in form-fitted spacesuits along with their prizes. There was even an exhibit of an apparent starship in route, looking back on the entire solar system.

Susan was impressed. This was an industrious species that she'd dreamed up. Not only had they conquered their own planet, they were rapidly spreading out into space!

"*All rise!*" —a trumpeted command in English reverberated as she and Ben walked into a large amphitheater.

The drums of the orchestra abruptly stopped.

Seated around and above her were many of the raptor-appearing Dinosapiens. They were officially dressed in regal splendor. Susan saw robes of Priests, gleaming armor of Warriors, proud uniforms of Workers, and the fine silk of Intellectuals.

As one they stood up and started slapping their scaly palms together in a curious simulation of "clapping." Echoing from the hard stone surfaces of the temple, the clapping became a thunderous ovation! And there on a raised Dais in the center of the arena Susan recognized the Dinosapien she'd met in her previous dream, "Fred."

In a rigidly reptilian way, he was smiling at her, beckoning for her and Ben to join him on the platform.

Pained to have to do more climbing, Susan chose to stay below, turning in a circle to admire the gathered hundreds of world delegates.

"So this is the 'cream' of your society?" she yelled out, stopping their clapping. "I'm rather tired and out of sorts. Let's get to the point, shall we? Just what is it you want of me?"

Fred stared down at her, his large yellow eyes seeming to drill into her.

"They want what we want," Ben spoke into the stunned silence. Apparently the "lizard Council" was unused to being yelled at by an uppity mammal!

"And that is...?"

"They just want to live out their lives, be safe, care for their families, and have meaningful existences."

"Ok! That's fine with me! No problem! So can I leave now? And can someone please turn up the heat in here? It's getting quite *chilly!*"

Indeed, she found herself shivering, clutching her arms over her chest. The robe she had on was much too thin.

"Your Destiny is distinctive," Fred growled at her from the Dias, ignoring her request. "You are our Reverend Mother—and simultaneous our prophesized *Destroyer!* We plead with you to consider our merit, what our society has built up over the millennia. Please do not erase all of this! Have pity on us, Reverend Mother. To *create, build,* and *destroy* are not absolutes. They are *choices!*"

Man, it's freezing in here! How can these cold-blooded lizards stand it?

"They deserve your pity, Susan," Ben interjected. "They're not just scaly animals. They're people, just like us!"

Jesus Christ, what was wrong with these damn lizards? She wasn't going to "erase" them. And even if she wanted to, how could she possibly accomplish such a thing? The only thing in imminent peril was *her* Earth—where *humanity* hung in the balance, not a bunch of dinosaur rejects!

"They're correct, Susan," she heard a softer, higher voice from behind her loudly proclaim. "All sentient lifeforms with self-and-God awareness are equally precious!"

Turning around, she saw a petite woman walking through the doorway. Accompanying her was a squad of Raptor Warriors, clad in overlapping layers of gleaming armor—all to guard one small woman.

"Adri?" Susan gasped, not believing her eyes.

The short, red-haired Swede looked to be in good health. She wore the same white robe as did Susan. Her previously close-cropped hair was now down to her shoulders. Her skin, dried out and marred by the Hermes trip and their descent into the Asteroid, was now clean and soft-looking. Indeed, Adriana's blue eyes sparkled with vitality. She was very much the eager young astronaut trainee who'd helped Susan through her first year at NASA.

"Yes, it's me, Susan."

"Adri..." Susan sobbed, running over and embracing her. The looming, powerful guards moved off to the side as if respecting Susan's presence. "I'm so sorry I left you out there with the bomb, even though you were already dead and we were about to both be vaporized. I suppose your story is that the lizards 'rescued' you too with an inter-dimensional teleporter, right? And since 'time runs differently here' then now you're healed up and healthy? Wow, this is a great dream, just what I'd want to happen if..."

"There's little time," Adriana interrupted her. "The raptors think I'm on their side. That's why they snatched me here and healed me. But it's time for all this to stop."

"Stop?"

"I and my people put too much faith in you and your mother. The permutations you two produced were interesting. But ultimately they were futile. We always came back to the same set-point. Our 'play' has fulfilled its allotment of cycles."

"But...?"

Adriana sighed deeply. Her shoulders slumped in defeat as she continued to hug Susan, whispering softly...

"It would have been much simpler if the present Earth/time-continuum were *annihilated* by the Asteroid. Stopping the original Obelisk would have *reset* everything. But I suppose we can't fault you for exercising your heroic nature."

"Reset...?"

"Regardless of the limited wishes of our dinosapien hosts, it's time for this entire little pocket of the Universe to vanish."

"Just *who* are you?"

For a moment Adriana's face blurred...seeming to morph into a hippy-like, goateed young man. In an instant it was an older version of the same man, then a *snake* with a forked tongue...and then back into the sad-eyed, red-haired Swede.

Susan nodded, remembering the source of this new fantasy. Her mother had told her in the supposed "hallucination" Suzy had experience in the Park of how Sally King got her Turtle Tattoo: from a human-morphed member of a giant, telepathic race of observing *Snakes*. They were supposed to be from one of the alternate Earth Dimensions.

Susan held the "woman" off at arm's length.

"When I was a little girl...was it *you* that gave me my own Turtle Tattoo?"

"Yes. And I've been keeping an eye on you ever since. I did my best to protect you. But now things have moved beyond my or my race's ability to guide your path. You see, we're all of us but pawns in a greater game, Susan. And now we're finally going to be checkmated! I'm so sorry that..."

"Enough! Return to the Dais!"

Adriana drew Susan close, giving her a final hug, whispering: "Don't believe a word they tell you. Do what you have to do!"

"*You have to choose!*" Fred's amplified voice shouted from the Dias. A holographic image of the *black, oblong Asteroid* appeared, hanging ominously in the middle of the stadium. It was aimed straight at a vividly colored 3D image of the Earth.

"*Remember*, Susan," Ben said as he roughly pulled her away from Adriana. He *slapped* her in her face, startling her! "This is not just a world filled with intelligent beings that have created a magnificent civilization, but *your dearest friends* are here with us as well! Who do you value more than your brother, your childhood sweetheart Scott Yanash, your mother, and comrade-in-arms Adriana? They— and I, who still count you as a dear friend—are right *here!* And we're more than just hostages—we're *reminders* of the common thread that holds all intelligent species together that have evolved upon this precious planet: a shared sense of wonderment, of curiosity! We're not fundamentally different at our cores, just presented in different-looking bodies. Our Castes may vary, but our *hearts* are the same!"

"Ben...I don't understand...?"

She wanted to hear more, but couldn't. He was already fading away. Adriana was fading. The amphitheater was fading. And in their place a *new nightmare* was emerging.

Susan woke up shivering in the cramped Orion capsule. The temperature in the crew cabin was dropping precipitously. The wall heaters were barely putting out any warmth. The depleted batteries of the spaceship were failing. The air was stuffy, hardly circulating at all.

"Well...enough pleasant dreaming where all my dearest dead or missing friends are alive and healthy...gotta get back to the dreadful real world," Susan admonished herself, stiffly levering herself to her knees.

She heard a clatter and looked down. It was Kame's ceremonial knife. Had it fallen out of Susan's flight suit? She felt at her inner pocket. The flat small volume of *The Minstrel's Lark* was still safely tucked away there. The knife was missing. Yes, it must have slipped out...

"Ah, whatever—you can have it back, Kame. I don't think I need it anymore," Susan said. She placed the small blade into the motionless curled hand of the bloated spacesuit. "You stay and guard Orion. I'm going out for a walk."

She almost laughed, but stopped herself.

She'd just mirrored other *famous last words*. Susan vividly recalled again the ill-fated expedition of *Captain Robert Falcon Scott* who with his colleagues tried to be the first to reach the South Pole. They failed, beaten to the Pole by a Norwegian expedition. And on the way back they hit numerous problems, finally freezing to death while camped in tents during a snow storm. But not long before that sad ending, one of their number decided he was a burden on the rest. Stricken with frostbite and gangrene, holding them back—by Scott's written last testament—he announced to his comrades in their tent that night: *"I'm just going outside and may be some time."* With his final brave proclamation, *Captain Lawrence Oates* stumbled out of the tent without his boots, walking barefoot away into a raging blizzard.

He never returned and future retrieval teams never found his body.

It was a heroic last gesture by a proud explorer. Although he and his comrades had struggled mightily against terrible unforeseen problems, they died short of their goal—but still showing that "stiff upper lip" of a proud British military tradition!

"I doubt I'll be back, Kame," Susan sighed to the spacesuited rotting corpse, "but since my own spacesuit got nicely recharged and provisioned before Orion's power gave out, I might as well ride this Asteroid to the end of the line. A proud *Homo sapiens* should be there to take responsibility, or at least say goodbye to the Universe."

She methodically gathered the scattered parts to her spacesuit from the twisted tangle inside the crew capsule, sliding them carefully onto her body. She checked her backpack to make sure everything was working before reattaching it onto the suit.

She immediately felt warmth flowing back into her near-frozen limbs. Leaving her helmet off for the moment, she munched more of the algae sponges, carefully avoiding any red-looking areas. She felt her body gaining strength. Sucking dry the few remaining water bulbs she felt positively energized!

"Well, it's been fun!" she snickered to herself, knowing it had been totally the exact opposite. She slid her helmet into place, clamped down the faceplate, and made sure the air was flowing properly.

The chronometer in her suit was screwed up—the inner helmet displays flickering on/off or not on at all—so she didn't know how much time she had left. But it felt like she'd slept a long time. She felt rested. Plus it had taken a while to get her suit back on and eat her last meal. She was certain that this was the last time she'd be inside the Orion capsule.

"Goodbye, Kame," Susan solemnly saluted her fallen comrade. The spacesuited corpse sat motionless in the jumbled mess of the smashed crew cabin. "I wish you could have been in my dream so we could have chatted. I never had a chance to properly thank you for getting us to the Asteroid. You were a true friend to the end."

Then she hit the lever to discharge the crew cabin's remaining air, allowing the pressure to drop to near zero. Following that, she cranked open the inner airlock door.

Finally, she hit a switch to power-down Orion. Susan was leaving it in sleep mode, saving its dwindling batteries. Orion was a good ship. She'd served her crew well. Now the faithful vessel could rest in peace.

Looking through the wrenched-open outer hatch she saw the stark black ridges of the airless Asteroid. They *beckoned* to her: "Come to me!"

And so she did.

Chapter 34

COSMIC COLLISIONS

Even galaxies smash together
Spinning into each other
Twisting and tearing, over eons
Ripping apart billions of star systems
Black Holes at their centers merging
In cataclysmic crashes, gravity-wells flaring
Spitting off massive upheavals to space-time
Gravitational waves propagating unchecked
Splitting, shredding, reshaping, or destroying
Next to which consider a tiny little rock
Meteor, comet, or asteroid striking
Plummeting into a moon or planet
Hardly seems like anything...
Even the death of countless Species
Blasted, burned, and starved to death
The superficial debris of the blistering Impact
Hardly a matter of note on the Celestial Scale
But to the individual human trapped
Sitting astride that alien bullet
It means everything.

The Minstrel's Lark, 34:15-20

IMPACT MINUS ONE HOUR, *CONTEMPLATING...*
Susan stood outside the crumpled Orion capsule on the brittle surface of the decimated, brittle Asteroid. Her helmeted head was

bent back, intently peering upward into space. What she saw was fascinating and horrifying, both at the same time.

"It's so gorgeous," she whispered.

Earth was much larger—a brilliant blue-white globe hanging in the vastness of space—and moving perceptively closer with each minute. Susan could even start to make out continental boundaries beneath fluffy white cloud covers. She estimated she had just an hour left until she plunged into the planet's atmosphere. That meant the Asteroid had to be 60,000 miles distant from its target. It was that "magic" number again: the "$60,000 Question"!

Susan almost giggled at that odd thought, but *sobbed* instead.

She was home...

—but utterly helpless to keep that incredibly vibrant water-sphere from turning into a fiery hell!

"We almost saved you," she said, tears welling up in her eyes. "I'm so sorry."

She paused, glimpsing something strange from the corner of her eye. She laboriously turned, struggling in the high gravity. Something incongruous to the stark landscape of the Asteroid's surface was on the other side of the raised ledge that hid the crumpled Orion capsule.

"No...it can't be!" she gasped as she stomped around the small hill to the other side.

It lay there half-buried in the now loosened "soil" of the crumbling Asteroid. Smooth and metallic, the fins of the *second hydrogen bomb* stuck up out of the black rocks!

"What are you doing here?" she asked, amazed, bending to stroke the curved metal surface.

It had been with her in the Obelisk, ticking down to detonation. It should have been part of the explosion that blew out the interior of the Asteroid! But it was undeniably here. Was it deactivated and dead? A flashing red light caught her eye. The control panel was *not* dead, just dormant. It was patiently waiting to be triggered!

"Oh...m-my...G-God," Susan stammered in excitement, looking from the half-buried bomb to the ever-growing Earth in the sky. "How much time do I have left—less than an hour?"

Frantically she looked from the bomb to the Earth and back again.

She'd been given a *final chance* to stop the Asteroid! The Obelisk in its last moments must have somehow *chosen* to send both her and the bomb back to the surface! Perhaps it was deliberate, or just an accident of her cuddling up with the nuke at the last minute. Whatever, she'd stupidly dreamt away her remaining time, sleeping inside the Orion capsule! What could she do now, with just minutes remaining?

"I could trigger you right here, but to what purpose?" she mused, affectionately patting its smooth, curved surface. "You might blow off a few chunks of the Asteroid, since the outer surface is much looser now. But most of the blast would just dissipate harmlessly into space. And we're much too close for the explosion to blow you off course for impacting Earth...what's that?"

Off in the distance, the *pink plume* from the ravine caught her attention. It was almost depleted. But random spurts still shot up from the rift into space. It must still be open, a path to the interior!

"Ah...yes...I see," she nodded, understanding.

The other hydrogen bomb detonated deep in the interior hadn't destroyed the Asteroid. Neither did the plasma bursts fired at the Asteroid. But together they'd softened it up considerably. *One more* hydrogen fusion explosion inside the Asteroid but near to the surface, might splinter it into fragments! Indeed, Susan wouldn't be surprised if the crumbling Asteroid weren't blown into a cloud of small pebbles—which might burn up harmlessly in Earth's atmosphere!

"There's no time for me to drag you back to that ravine," she frowned, thinking harder and faster than she'd ever done. "What to do...what to do?"

Then she hit on a possible solution.

At best she had maybe half an hour. This was a "hail Mary" pass that might catastrophically fail. But it was her last shot!

She groaned as she pushed her heavy body back upward. Then she staggered around the hill to where Orion was jammed beneath the large overhanging ledge. Ripping open the outer hatch she lurched inside. She scrambled to the life support panel and cranked on the power, happily seeing lights spring up in the darkness. The crowded, jammed-packed interior was something she'd thought she'd never see again. But the jumbled clutter was a big problem. She had to clear out some space!

"Come on, Kame," she said to the bloated spacesuit. "You're the easiest and largest lump in here to move. You're with me!"

Frantically lurching as fast as she could in the crippling gravity she dragged the ballooned-out spacesuit through the open airlock. Then she grabbed chairs and cartons, containers and equipment, tossing them heedlessly out as well. She needed room!

Plus she needed someone to talk to...

"Suit computer, do you read me? Are you still working?"

God, she hoped it had rebooted when she plugged the suit into Orion for replenishment!

"*I...hear you,*" a faint mechanical voice sounded in her helmet. "*How...can I...be of...service?*"

Ah, it was working! It certainly was rudimentary, but maybe it might give her the edge she desperately needed.

"Can you communicate with Orion's computer?"

"*There...is interference...*"

"Interference—do you mean from Earth?"

"*Yes.*"

There was nothing Earth could do to help her. But if it was Bill's Saucer crew or Mission Control, they'd welcome the news that she was still attempting to save Earth! But she didn't have the time to try.

"Ok...for the moment, please tune them out. See if you can activate Orion's steering jets, assuming the nitrogen canisters are connected and working."

"*...attempting to communicate...*"

She staggered back through the open airlock and through the black dust kicked up by her prior passage. She grabbed the half-buried bomb by its fins and began dragging it toward Orion. It was incredibly difficult. She had to lever it back-and-forth, "snaking" it along.

"Anything?" she spoke into her helmet.

"*...yes...half the jets are inoperative...three are ready for firing...most of the canisters are still charged...*"

"Great! Will they be sufficient to jerk Orion out from under the ledge?"

"*Possibly...*"

"—and then scoot over the surface and fly into the Ravine?"

"*Possibly.*"

"Then program in the coordinates. There's no time for me to steer this mess along using Orion's manual controls. Adri might be able to do it, but she's dead. I'm going to hook the hydrogen bomb into Orion's circuitry. Once Orion takes the bomb as deep as possible into the Ravine, the nuke needs to explode on impact. Understand?"

"*Yes.*"

Gasping for breath, near collapsing, Susan just managed to "squirm" the hydrogen bomb back through the airlock and into Orion. She desperately yanked computer connections from the closest terminal and linked them into the bomb's control panel.

Shakily standing erect, she looked at her work. The connection looked solid.

"How's it going?" she asked her suit computer.

"*Connections...acquired. The programming is in progress. Now ready to fire the remaining steering jets...*"

"Super! How long do we have before Earth impact?"

"*Unknown...minutes, perhaps.*"

"Can you make course corrections from inside Orion?"

"*Negative...radar units not operational.*"

"So we'll have to guide it visually from outside?"

"*Affirmative...*"

Susan lurched out of the airlock, grabbed Kame's body in passing, and hauled it off with her to a safe distance.

"Fire the steering jets!" she ordered her suit computer.

Clouds of black dust sprang up, shooting out of the gap beneath the overhanging ledge. Susan saw gleaming metal as the crumpled Orion capsule began moving. Then it shot out of the gap, *bouncing wildly* on the broken surface of the Asteroid as three steering jets fired unevenly.

"To the left...five degrees to the right...straight ahead," Susan crisply spoke into her helmet, fiercely concentrating on the scampering capsule.

"*...adjusting...*"

The bouncing Orion capsule retreated into the distance toward the Ravine, white streams of frozen gases following it...

"Dive, dive, dive!" Susan shouted as the bouncing capsule skipped up above the Ravine.

The capsule disappeared into the interior of the Asteroid.

"Good! Is the bomb ticking?" she frantically asked the suit computer.

"*Losing...connection...but the program is in place.*"

"Then that's the best we can do," Susan sighed, slumping onto a big black bolder. Beside her lay the puffed-up spacesuit of dead Kame.

"So now we wait," she grinned at Kame's motionless body.

She looked up. Earth was huge in the sky. This close she was within radio range, perhaps even for her spacesuit's weak receptor.

"Can you patch me into any feeds, particularly from Mission Control?" she asked her suit's computer.

"*Negative.*"

"Why not—aren't you receiving any signals?"

"*Receiving strong signals.*"

"But?"

"*...contents...are not...any known human language.*"

"What?" Susan gasped in disbelief, looking up at her looming home planet. "How's that possible? Let me hear them!"

Static filled her helmet. And amongst the noise she heard distinct "clicks," "grunts," and "whistles." Say what?

"Oh...my...God," Susan frowned, a terrible realization coming over her...

—as a *brilliant flash* lit up the sky and landscape, a *terrible quake* tossed her up as if she were a toy doll, and a *cloud of black debris* descended upon her.

Susan was stunned, buried beneath a heavy layer of pebbles and dust. Yet again shocked to realize she was still alive, she dug upward frantically, emerging to find herself back on the still-intact surface of the Asteroid!

Frantically she swiped clinging black soot from off her outer face-plate.

Half-buried next to her was the bloated spacesuit of dead Kame. They should both be incinerated!

"Damnation, why didn't it work?" she shouted, now looking up at a *featureless black sky*.

So what was going on now?

Where was Earth? Where was the moon? Where were the stars?

Wait. The space above her wasn't featureless. She saw *patterns* glittering here and there—a *web of diamonds* in the sky!

And the diamond pattern was *rotating*. The whole sky was spinning! The still-intact Asteroid was *plunging* through some sort of *cosmic tunnel!*

Shocked, Susan realized what was happening.

"I saw this before...in the spaceship in my dreams. Billy and I—when we were traveling in a spaceship *back in time!*"

She realized that the *first* hydrogen bomb had powered the Obelisk to send her and the Asteroid into another Dimension. What she heard on her suit radio was a broadcast from Earth in an alien language on an Earth in a parallel Dimension. And then the *second* hydrogen bomb somehow sent them spinning into the past!

Where would they emerge?

"Computer, can you calculate our stellar coordinates?"

She knew she was asking a lot of her suit computer. But anything at all would be helpful!

There was no answer.

Her spacesuit's computer was broken or off-line. Susan was all by herself. She didn't even have the smashed Orion capsule to crawl inside. Her only companion now was the dead, squashed corpse of Kame.

Susan sat next to the puffed-out spacesuit, putting a shaking hand on its bloated knee.

"I guess it's just you and me, Commander."

Suddenly the sky cleared and the sparkling diamond pattern above vanished. They'd emerged from the time-tunnel!

"Jesus H. Christ..." she gasped.

Susan's helmeted head was bent back, intently peering upward into space. She sat motionless, frozen in place. She couldn't believe what she was seeing!

Yes, Earth was back and much larger than before. But that alone wasn't what left her stunned.

"How...can this...be?" she gasped to herself.

There wasn't just one Earth.

There were *two* Earths hanging out there, one beside the other. They appeared to be identical copies of each other. And behind each of the two Earths there were many others, fading away into the distance! And just on the edge of visibility, another translucent series were in *front* of the two Earths, extending to and *through* the Asteroid!

And that wasn't the worst of it.

"What *the hell* is going on here?" Susan angrily exclaimed, now standing up to stumble in a circle, her eyes focused on the black expanse above her.

Growing ever larger, seemingly plummeting toward her at the same rate the two Earths were approaching, she now made out *numerous celestial bodies*, including other planets and their moons!

And each of them had ghostly versions of themselves stretched out as long translucent "tails" behind them!

"That's Jupiter!" she gasped, recognizing a planet hanging in space seemingly right next to the Asteroid. It was ten times bigger than Earth. It had large brown wavy bands crossing its surface. And in its lower half was a big red "eye." Yes, it was definitely the largest planet in the solar system, hurtling ever closer in the black sky with each passing moment!

"And that's Mars," she noted, looking in another direction. Half the size of Earth, a *red sphere* hung in the sky, seemingly rushing at her!

"And the Moon, and Saturn, and Venus," she marveled, turning in a complete circle back to where she'd originally stood.

"But...that closest 'Earth'..." she mused to herself, focusing back on it. "I remember now, from when Billy and I were kicked backward in time! It's the *Cretaceous!*"

Once again, the recurring "nightmare" of her childhood was proving prescient. She saw that the continents weren't where they should be. They were misaligned! It was just as Billy had before described to her: the continents were positioned as they were *65 million years ago* in the past!

She could only conclude that she was now at the center of a *huge collapse* of both Space and Time!

"This...is...beyond incredible," she whispered, in awe of what was happening around her.

And as she stood there alone on the Asteroid, staring up into space, she tried to make sense of it all. Why was she here? Was it just a cosmic accident? Or was it some evil plot perpetuated by perversely laughing aliens? Or were the ancient Greeks and Romans correct in viewing life as a Game played by cruel gods? Or was this actually part of some incomprehensible Plan stemming from the true God of the Universe?

She felt overwhelmed, her senses over-stimulated into paralysis!

She closed her eyes, trying to steady her swirling thoughts.

"Jesus...I'm going bonkers...or something way beyond my comprehension is happening," she groaned. "I've got to get my mental bearings!"

In her mind she flipped through her favorite, "centering" passages from *The Minstrel's Lark*. The little book was still there in her inner flight suit pocket, warming her heart. It radiated a comforting intellectual/emotional heat. It reminded her of details and abstractions. And it helped her to put anything new into a fresh perspective.

As the seconds ticked past and the celestial objects plummeted ever nearer, she focused on one specific poetic passage. She whispered to herself from Chapter 34, verses 78-92:

> *"When it seems hopeless*
> *Everything you've done comes to nothing*
> *You've been squashed, trampled, and hurt*
> *Your little life just a brief flame*
> *So bright and playful, hot and dangerous*
> *A passing breeze blows it out*
> *And it's as if you never lived at all*

> *Don't forget that behind the fire*
> *Are Fundamental Laws of Nature*
> *Underlying and upholding a vast Reality*
> *Governing the seeming chance and chaos*
> *Bringing order and transcendent meaning*
> *Codified, clarified, and demonstrated*
> *Not by your eternal flame*
> *But in its flickering transience*
> *For that which is snuffed out*
> *Can re-appear a Universe away*
> *In a new form and place*
> *Made manifest in your Words..."*

"That's...correct," a dry, crackling voice spoke inside Susan's helmet.

Startled, Susan opened her eyes, now seeing the closest *two ancient Earths* in the black sky *touching and merging* as they came hurtling at her!

"Computer...is that you?" she asked, staring awestruck into the sky.

"No...it's someone else!"

"What do you want with me?" Susan grimaced.

"On both those Earths," the voice continued, stronger than before, "the *dinosaurs* are romping, killing, eating, and breeding—unaware of their impending doom."

The grim voice sounding her helmet seemed to come from behind her.

Spinning around, Susan took a short step backward in disbelief. There—standing wobbly upright, enveloped in black dust—was *Kame!*

And rigidly held in her tight spacesuited fist was her glittering, razor-sharp knife.

Oh, Christ! I guess giving back her seppuku knife was a big mistake!—Susan hysterically thought to herself.

"But...you're *dead!* In fact, you're *more* than dead! You're rotted and decomposed! You're just stinking *mush!*" Susan gasped out loud, stumbling backward a couple more steps in disbelief.

The still-bloated, bulging spacesuit stood on rubbery legs. The faceplate was obscured by a thick layer of black soot. What lurked inside the suit was unknown.

"Yes, that's true, Susan," the voice spoke with a controlled ferocity. "Kame *is* dead, but not as rotted as you think. I've taken control of her remnant tissues. The artificial curare she self-administered in her final moments helped preserve the key neural-muscular pathways for me to subsequently activate. They won't last long. But they'll serve well enough to *force* you to do that which you *must!*"

In the black sky above Susan, the onrushing celestial objects were collapsing Time down upon itself, compressing it into a tiny sphere. To Susan the entire Universe was crowding in on her. It was like the opposite of the "Big Bang." Everything was happening in slow motion. The chilling words from her dead Commander stretched out into long, slow phrases.

"So who are you really?" Susan gasped. She frantically looked around for a place to escape but saw none. She was trapped out on the surface of the Asteroid as surely as if she were sitting in a jail cell!

"You don't know me, but your mother did," the cackling, arrogant voice replied.

"What does that mean?" Susan said as she turned and started laboriously climbing up the ridge beneath which Orion had been protected. The ridge led upward to a "high" spot where she might be able to defend herself. It wasn't an escape, rather a "strategic retreat."

Behind her, the bulbous figure began slogging toward her, knife extended outward.

"I'm with the last of a group that operates beyond Time—of which Kame Yamamoto was a member."

"She was working against us all along?"

"She wanted the Asteroid blown up or diverted. Your and your friends' fate was a secondary concern, a means to an end. She cared nothing for you!"

Susan slogged upward, struggling. She heard the apparition's words but could not accept them.

"She *did* care for me—and Adri!" Susan protested. "Maybe she was part of some out-of-time conspiracy, but she was still our Commander! She *loved* Hermes and her fellow crewmembers! She sacrificed herself for us!"

"And now her animated body's tissues will finish her mission."

Susan could barely push her body up one step at a time. The 2X gravity was still pressing down on her. In addition, the surface was incredibly crumbly, offering hardly any purchase. At any moment she was in danger of slipping and falling—rolling back down to the pursuing zombie spacesuit!

"But now that you're here, with the Asteroid still intact, *you must choose!*"

"What?" Susan gasped, trying to grab onto a small crack above to pull her heavy body upward.

She felt a squishy pressure on her leg, looked down, and saw a bloated space glove latched onto her right ankle. Shuddering, she used her left boot to kick away the grasping hand, clambering ever higher!

"You've been appointed, Dr. King. It's your Destiny. You know this is true!"

Yes, Susan saw the unmistakable *green glow* of her Turtle Tattoo piercing even through the thick fabric of her spacesuit, shining from her left wrist. For whatever weird cosmic reason, she was unavoidably anointed as *The Girl with the Turtle Tattoo*—and thusly culpable. She realized that the fate of at least two worlds hung on her next words...

Then she was at the top of the ridge. A rocky protuberance thrust upward, resembling a cowboy's saddle. It was clearly the "highest" point on the Asteroid, from which she could view everything. Wearily, she sat astride it, lowering her helmeted head to rest on its "horn."

Thankfully, the dead Kame figure below was having an even harder time climbing up the steep slope.

"*Choose* the Earth on your right-hand side!" Susan heard the words shouted into her helmet, hurting her ears as she jerked her head back up.

"Why?"

"It's the Dinosapien's second Earth, closest to your Earth," Kame's voice insisted, now lower and slurred. The rotted tissues animating the spacesuit were clearly degrading. "They're just lizards. Let the Asteroid smash into it, 65 million years in their past!"

"*Why?*" Susan again yelled back in her helmet.

"Because then you'll *correct the damage* you previously did to their parallel Dimension," Kame's slurred voice tried to explain. "Before this present timeline began, you and your stupid little brother caused another asteroid to fragment, such that the Raptors survived and evolved. Instead of mammals, Dinosapiens evolved to take over the second Earth. This erased a whole parallel human civilization! Slamming this intact Asteroid into their planet right before the other duplicate Asteroid shows up will undue your prior perverted act! It will allow the magnificently ordered and peaceful human society of *Commissioner Sally* to reemerge in all its magnificent glory!"

"Are you talking about my mother, Sally King?" Susan gasped, looking upward. The Earths and other heavenly bodies now filled the sky, with hardly any blackness of outer space left between them!

Susan saw she had only moments until they converged from all sides upon the Asteroid.

"A version of your Mother from another Cycle caused that wonderful, orderly society to exist," Kame's fading voice continued. "You and your little brother destroyed an entire lineage of humans: *billions upon billions* of humans erased! You, Susan, who made that fateful decision, became the *biggest mass murderer* in human history! And now you have the chance to undo your infamous crime. Say these words, Susan! Say: '*I choose the second Earth!*'"

"This is nuts! One little asteroid can't be that important or..."

"You know I'm right! *Say* the words!"

Susan felt a deep stab of guilt. Yes, she knew in her soul that the haunting words from the reanimated Kame were true. This was what had fueled her lifelong nightmares. This was what drew her to science, cosmology, and becoming a NASA astronaut—the chance to correct her abysmal wrong, to put things right, to *atone* for her hideous sin!

She opened her mouth to utter the final, fatal words...

"*Don't* do it!" Sally heard yet another strident voice in her helmet. But this voice was softer and gentler than the harsh tones from Kame. She recognized the voice. It was Ben's.

Looking down, she saw him easily striding up the slippery slope. He looked just as he had in her supposedly red mushroom-generated "hallucination." He was smiling gently, gold glasses atilt on his brown face, white robe hanging to his sandaled feet.

"I know you *can't* be here," Susan squinted, suddenly unsure of what to do.

But then she saw a brief flicker as he momentarily blanked out, the stark rocks behind him revealed through his transparent body.

He was a projection! The Lizards from the other Earth weren't a dream after all. They were real and still trying to influence her!

"Susan, you know me—you trust me," his softer voice resonated in her helmet. "You must aim the Asteroid at *your* Earth, the one on your left. If you don't this, then humans will never evolve there! For them to exist, your direct ancestors, the Asteroid must strike *your* Earth 65 million years in your past, right now! Everyone you know— including your family members—will never exist if this Asteroid is diverted to the second Earth! This Asteroid is *the very one* that killed off the dinosaurs so that mammals could evolve into human beings!" he shouted at her, apparently desperate to make his point. "If you don't allow the historical Impact to occur, then *all* of humanity will be *erased*—not just from Earth but from the entire Universe! It will be as if *Homo sapiens*, your own species, never existed anywhere! You will *doom* your entire species!"

Then, more quietly, he held out his wrinkled, old-man hands in supplication: "Why should you care about bringing back a second human world? Isn't a single Earth for humans more than enough? You've got to protect your own evolutionary history, Susan. Aim the Asteroid at its *intended* target: your *own* planet 65 million years in the past! This will save *both* your world and my adopted world! Just say these words, Susan, and it will happen: '*I choose my own Earth!*'"

She laughed without humor, long and bitterly. She rested her aching helmeted head again on the "saddle horn" in front of her.

Time stood still.

All of human history was suspended before her.

"Ben...I thought you were all about Karma, cycles of death and rebirth—refining and improving our spirits. And now you're just trying to protect a world of upstart lizards? I don't think this is you speaking!"

His body flickered, shimmering brightly. His gentle, wide-stretched eyes were silently pleading with her. His mouth opened but no words emerged. Then, as Susan continued to stare at him in horror, the projection *morphed* into an armor-clad, weapon-welding ferocious Raptor!

"Do it *now!*" the raging lizard screamed inside her helmet.

But then it changed back into Ben, smiling at her in that disarmingly gentle way...

"Do *nothing!*" a third voice reverberated in her helmet.

Down on the rocky plain another white-clad figure was slowly walking toward Susan's perch. This was a red-haired, petite female. It was Adriana.

A blue-glowing energy shield enveloped her, protecting her.

"It that really you, Adri?"

"I'm what you knew as Adriana Johansson. I am her essence. I am your true friend."

"I'm not so sure about..."

"Don't be blinded by selfish personal desires. The Commissioner and the Holy Man only want to fulfill their own visions. Look beyond those stunted perspectives, Susan. Consider the Cosmic Consequences. Make *no statement* at all when Time resumes. Then when local space folds in upon itself, the Asteroid and its insidious, original Obelisk will be *obliterated* as if they never existed! Only then can the Universe resume its interrupted, predestined path."

"I trusted you once before, but..."

"—then trust me again!"

Time abruptly resumed its forward momentum.

The sky was now completely filled with overlapping onrushing planets and moons. Susan knew she only had seconds to decide before the Asteroid was overwhelmed by the celestial bodies. And, suddenly, she knew just the words she must distinctly articulate.

She opened her mouth...

But she had no chance to utter her fateful words. Apparently "The Commissioner" knew what she was going to say.

"I'll *kill* you!" Kame's animated corpse shrieked as it lunged the last few feet upward, straight through the flickering projection of Ben, attempting to knock Susan off her perch.

Flailing wildly, Susan teetered in the heavy gravity and rolled to the side...

Her helmeted head bounced face-first off the rocky surface. Her forehead smashed into the inner surface of the hard helmet. She felt warm blood running from her forehead down into her eyes. Blinking, she rolled over, staring through a curtain of red.

"If you will not restore my Timeline than all Earth's futures can likewise die! I hereby endorse the Snake's plea! *Say nothing* and allow the world to end!"

Susan floundered there at the top of the hill, lying on her back, desperately blinking, trying to regain her vision.

Both Adriana and Ben vanished. Simultaneously, the heavy, bloated spacesuit of Kame *smashed down* onto Susan's chest, momentarily knocking the air out of her lungs!

Gasping for air, she now saw two space-gloved, bloated fists wrapped together around the haft of Kame's glittering knife, plunging it straight toward Susan's faceplate!

"You...*bitch!*" Susan said as she batted the knife to the side, slipped out from under the bloated spacesuit, grabbed the bouncing blade, and *rammed it* straight into the top of Kame's helmeted head!

"*Noooooooooooooo!*" a long anguished scream rang inside Susan's helmet as Kame's helmeted head *exploded* in a cloud of red-and-white brain-gore.

But the arms and legs were still working.

The headless spacesuit flopped again upon Susan, attempting to pin her to the metallic surface, to crush her, preventing her from saying her last, fateful words.

"*Die, die,* and *die!*" Susan howled at Kame's spacesuit.

Again and again, Susan stabbed at the squirming blob on top of her, seeing yet more bloody decompression explosions as the fabric covering legs, arms, and torso of the decayed corpse was ruthlessly slashed.

"There," Susan gasped, going limp, "game over, Kame's puppet master, whoever you really are...and rest in peace, my old friend, wherever *you* are."

The slimy fabric of the hacked-apart spacesuit slid to the side.

Covered in congealing gore, Susan weakly sat up. Then she swiped clotted blood off the outside of her faceplate with the back of one gloved hand. Grimacing, she blinked away her own blood out of her eyes inside her helmet. Dropping the knife, she scrambled back to the "saddle" formation.

"Time...to take...my very last ride," she gasped.

Taking a firm grip on the rocky saddle's "horn" and locking her spacesuited legs tightly to the sides of the "seat," Susan tried to get her labored breathing under control. She needed to think clearly. Incredibly, she knew that her next words would seal the fate of humanity.

She was startled to feel a *strong hand* upon her spacesuited wrist and looked to the side.

Standing there smiling at her from the surface of the Asteroid was a *chubby, gray-bearded elderly man*. Susan recognized him as Yishai Hovah, "Jessie," from that restaurant years ago on Fisherman's Wharf in San Francisco. He still had on his same baggy pants and fisherman's vest. But he didn't look like a projection. Indeed, the grip from his big hand was firm and solid on her arm. But that was clearly impossible. He'd be freezing out there upon the surface of the airless Asteroid. He *couldn't* be there!

But he was...

And neither could the other figures standing serenely behind him: an *elderly smiling nun* wearing a black habit, a white-bearded wiry man cradling a rifle who looked like an aged version of the biblical *Jesus*, a fat ugly man in a dirty robe who reminded her of *Socrates*, a gaudily dressed man who looked like paintings she'd seen of *Galileo*, a smiling bald oriental man who was the spitting image of the 14th *Dalai Lama*, and Ben in his incarnation as a cloned *Ghandi*.

"I'm proud of you, Susan. We *all* are," Jessie's gravelly voice penetrated her helmet.

Then he and the others vanished.

Wow. That was quite an endorsement. And come to think of it, that bracing word of encouragement came from Jessie...Hova. *Jehovah?* Oh...my...God... Talk about a "cloud of witnesses"!

Celestial bodies filled up the black sky, hurtling down at her.

"Yes...taking a *Leap of Faith*," she smiled to herself, finally at peace with herself and the Universe.

Shaking her head, trying to clear her fevered brain, Susan knew she had only moments to decide her exact wording. Pushing aside all hallucinations and visions, demons and angels, she lifted up her helmeted head to the crowded sky, ready to speak her "official" proclamation. To whatever or whoever was controlling her final plunge she loudly yelled out:

"I choose...*everything!*"

With one gloved hand locked to the horn and her other waving wildly over her head, Susan *whooped* gleefully: *"Ride 'em cowgirl!"*— as she plunged into the atmosphere!

It was an incredibly exhilarating ride.

But she didn't see its end.

Before catastrophically smashing into the surface of the planet, the blazing heat of the passage turned her spacesuited body into ash.

Over 4.0 billion years in the past the trans-dimensional Asteroid joyfully ridden by Susan King plummeted straight into the forming gas giant *Jupiter*.

A massive detonation of the Asteroid's central power core caused Jupiter to veer out of its distant orbit and sweep in closer to the sun. As it careened across the protoplanetary disk it swept up many orbiting rocks while pushing others inward. Out of the inner accumulation, a proto-Earth began to take form.

Next, the exact same Asteroid impacted the forming planet Earth. As before, the alien spaceship's power core exploded, resulting in a liquid magma blob splitting off to become the Moon. Another impact by the trans-dimensional Asteroid hit Jupiter a second time. Jupiter spun off back into the outer regions of the solar system, eating up many more circling rocks. What was left behind formed the planet Mars.

Now just 3.6 billion years in the past, the same Asteroid plummeted into the wide oceans covering a third of the surface of the young planet Mars. In this case, the Asteroid didn't explode. But while knocking off a hefty hunk of the planet's crust and creating the giant mountain *Olympus Mons*, precious "seeds" were planted deep into the planet's molten interior.

Protected and nourished by the near-indestructible Obelisk, alien lifeforms hatched, developed, and flourished in deep underground caverns. But as the smaller planet's metallic core stopped spinning, its magnetic field dwindled. Unimpeded, solar radiation stripped away the young planet's atmosphere and water. Concomitant with Mars losing its liquid water, the flourishing subterranean alien civilization migrated to a wetter and more hospitable Earth located in a safer, nearby Dimension. From there they monitored and protected their legacy, overseeing the integrity and history of the entire solar system in its many incarnations and variations.

They watched with growing concern as their solar system was unable to produce similarly advanced lifeforms. Precious to them were the twin pillars of insatiable Curiosity and rampant Creativity. So the aliens plotted to cleanse a primary Earth of its larger land animals which were stifling the evolution of smaller, smarter lifeforms. The Martian Alien overlords knew that a proper "nudge" could allow simian forms to emerge and evolve upon Earth-prime. So the multidimensional Asteroid, again, accomplished this task. Again ridden by Susan King, it impacted Earth 65 million years in the past, killing off most of the dinosaurs. In a nearby Dimension, a similar event caused a second line of humans to emerge, a backup to the first. Other secondary, more-distant Dimensions were utilized as experimental variants, where various Dinosapiens evolved intelligence. The transplanted Martian Aliens—plus other, observing, Higher Powers—were pleased.

The mix was interesting.

This "cosmic balance," however, was greatly endangered as pesky Cycles repeatedly scrambled events. But once again the transdimensionally positioned Asteroid—the infinitely capable Aliens' "Mother Ship"—was sent to set matters right. Subservient to the Higher Powers, the translocated Martian Aliens nudged an anointed

Daniel Basil Lyle

young girl, in her own various incarnations, to accomplish their bidding. Her task was to fulfill her destiny of subverting the *Unholy Trinity* of Mother Nature, Lady Luck, and biological fragility. Locked into quantum-mechanical constraints of "free-will," her progress was touch-and-go, despite their tattooed prodding. But things turned out ok in the end.

So *Susan King* had many wild rides on her careening Asteroid, bravely and unselfishly sacrificing her own life each and every time while multiple Impacts resolved and coalesced.

Finally, the Martian Aliens were pleased with the results of their interventions—and immensely grateful.

Chapter 35

<u>TRUST</u>

Repetition engenders confidence
Confidence inspires poise
Poise allows peacefulness
Peacefulness empowers experimentation
And experimentation assures Trust.
Or, the illusion thereof... Hah!
Save the Last Waltz for me
I won't step on your toes
And if so, I sincerely apologize
I'm doing the best I can
While trying to learn and do better
But in the end I'm only human
Perhaps you can say the same
We're all bedeviled by the Unholy Trinity:
Mother Nature, Lady Luck, and Human Frailty,
Sent to wreak havoc and terror
Unless we choose to deny their power
Invoking our own triple antidote:
Awe, Adventure, and Advancement;
If not to gain the Ultimate Victory
Then at least to be able to claim:
"I made progress today."
The Minstrel's Lark, 35:19-21

IMPACT PLUS 65 MILLION YEARS, *REORIENTING...*
"You ok, Suzy?"
She opened her eyes, looking around in confusion.
She was flat on the ground. Her head hurt. And Billy was standing over her, looking down with concern. Tall trees and shrubs surrounded them. A bright blue sky stretched out above her. A few fluffy white clouds drifted past.
"Whu...what h-happened?" she stammered, reaching back with the flats of her hands to push herself to a sitting position.
"You fell off of your bike!" he said in alarm. "You smacked your head on a tree trunk! Should I go for help? I can be at the nursing home in a minute. They can bring a stretcher and doctors and..."
"No, no—I'm ok."
She was definitely woozy. She felt a growing lump on the side of her head beside one of her blond pigtails. Yep. She'd hit her head alright. But it wasn't bad. Her head was clearing. Visions of *giant naked rocks* and *empty black space* were rapidly fading away.
Huh?
She remembered something about *spacesuits, spaceships,* and *talking lizards*—what was going on with her?
"Help me to stand up," she said, reaching out a hand to Billy. He grasped it firmly, steadying her as she got her legs under her.
Back on her feet, she reached down for her bike and righted it. About to mount it and push off she paused, her head still spinning.
"Why'd you fall off, Suzy? You never fell off before!"
"I don't know. I think I got...distracted. I think I...saw something."
"What?"
"Something...spooky, scary—I don't remember."
It was Saturday in early springtime. Hardly anyone was out vacationing in the mostly empty campsites of the *Rock Creek Camping Grounds*. Everything around her looked placid and quiet.
She saw no lurking monsters, zombies, or man-sized lizards. Now why did those things pop into her head? Monsters, zombies, and giant lizards were the stuff of sci-fi movies, not real life!

"Suzy, there's nothing spooky out here—just trees and bushes. Are you sure you're ok?" Billy said, seemingly genuinely concerned about his big sister.

"I just need...to rest for a second."

As she stood there getting her bearings, Billy pulled out a harmonica and started playing a song, the *Battle Hymn of The Republic.*" It was mesmerizing. He was really good!

"So you ready to go back now?" he grinned at her, saliva dripping from the "juice harp" in his hand.

"I didn't know you played an instrument," she said, marveling at his expertise. "When did you pick that up? Did some old person at the Rest Home teach you?"

He looked amazingly spunky, full of energy. Wasn't he supposed to be withdrawn and moody? Wow, he must have chugged an energy drink or something!

"What? 'Course I do! I learned it at school. Your guitar would sound awful lame without it, don't you think?"

"My guitar? What are you talking about?"

"Man, you're banged up worse than you're admitting, Suzy! We're supposed to play in the band at church services tomorrow morning. Don't you remember?"

"Uh...I dunno...say what?" she mumbled, shaking her throbbing head. "Maybe we should just get on home."

She rode along beside him in silence through the graveled paths of the campgrounds. Her head hurt. She was greatly confused. The small, strictly fundamentalist congregation they attended didn't believe in instrumental music, only allowing "a-capella" harmony in their song-services. They certainly didn't have any band! What the heck was going on? But she was too confused to ask Billy any more questions.

When they got to the main road outside the camping grounds they stopped, looked carefully both ways, and then turned left headed toward the Park entrance. Exiting again to the left, they biked up 12th street toward their house.

Carrying their bikes up the front steps they entered their house. They propped the bikes up in the enclosed porch before entering the house proper.

"Suzy fell off her bike and hit her head!" Billy loudly announced as they entered the living room, before skipping happily on into the kitchen.

Suzy was again amazed at his pep and spunk. She heard him cheerfully singing away in the kitchen as he made himself a sandwich.

It was a church song. He sang it in a pure, strong, high-pitched little-kid voice. And it was the first time she ever remembered him singing!

"What? Are you alright? Where'd you hit yourself?"

It was Suzy's mother, Sally King. But her mother looked different than Suzy remembered. Suzy had an image in her mind of a heavyset woman with dull eyes and grey hair, dressed in a big floppy house-robe. *This* lady was lean, trim, and sported vibrant, dyed brown-red hair. She was dressed in a blue blouse and hiking shorts. And her bright green eyes twinkled with vitality!

"What's that I hear about someone hitting their head?"

David King came running into the room. Like Sally's mother he was also lean and fit, with strong hands feeling gingerly at Suzy's forehead. Suzy marveled at his bulging biceps. He was obviously in tip-top physical condition.

"Wow, you're strong, Dad!"

"Well, sure I am, Suzy—since I'm both the wrestling and tennis couch at school I've got to set an example, right? Now just be still while I feel your precious little noggin."

"I'm ok."

He frowned down at her, feeling again at the bump on the side of her head.

"Nope, you've got quite a lump there, kiddo. We're taking you to the hospital right now for a CAT scan. They'll probably want to hold you overnight for observation to make sure there's no subdural bleeding in your pretty little brain. Sally, would you please carry her out to the ORV? I'll call up the backup church band to cover for us at tomorrow morning's service in case we don't make it. Then I'll follow along behind in the van."

"I can walk," Suzy protested, but suddenly felt very unsteady on her feet. Those strange memories were sweeping over her, overwhelming her senses.

She recalled riding *bucking horses* that were made out of *rocks!* What the heck?

"We're not taking any risks, sweetie," her Mom firmly insisted. "You just relax."

She slumped into her mother's strong arms. Wow. How did her Mom get so buff?

"Do I really play the guitar?" Suzy mumbled as her mother lifted her up in strong arms, displacing her jumbled "cowgirl" thoughts.

"Sure, in our family band. Why you're a prodigy on the guitar—and sing like an angel!" Sally grinned. "Don't worry, honey. We'll just make sure you're alright at the emergency room. Then when the doctors confirm you're not in any danger, you can get back to making your wonderful music. There's plenty of time before church services tomorrow. And if you miss that, there'll be many other performances."

"Performances? Me?"

"Sure, Suzy. You still want to grow up to be a famous blues-pop, gospel-country, western-folk, rock-jazz-rapper songwriter and vocalist, right? Don't worry your banged up head. Everything's ok."

Say what? Vocalist? Song writer?

"Uhm, then I guess I can go sing at the restaurant for the customers?"

She had a sudden vision of her overweight mother in a big apron cooking burgers on a sizzling stove in the busy kitchen of a hometown diner.

"Restaurant?" Sally King asked, sounding puzzled. "Well, I suppose there are restaurants in town that might like some live entertainment. But don't you want to go to the *School of Music* at *Oklahoma University* before turning pro? That's where I went for my graduate degrees in mathematics, remember? Isn't that your plan? Or have you changed your mind?"

Yes, Suzy definitely felt that her mind had changed. But perhaps she shouldn't make too big a deal of it. Maybe she should just go with the flow.

"Oh, sure...I forgot."

Suzy settled back in her mother's comforting arms. She was certain the lump on her head would heal up. But—a career in music?

Really? Wow, that sounded...fun. It sounded...*right!* But for now she was content to be nestled in the collective arms of her loving family. Whatever they said or wanted was just fine with her.

"Then let's go get that CAT scan done," her mother said, gently sliding Suzy into the passenger side of their ORV.

As the sturdy Ranger sped off, headed for the local hospital, Suzy felt at peace. For the first time in a long while Susan King didn't worry about the future or the past.   She didn't fear horrific nightmares. And looking at her wrist she was doubly reassured, noting that her faithful *Turtle Tattoo* was faintly glowing. Perhaps she was still hallucinating, but she could swear it *winked* at her!

And that was "ok."

After all, it was in on the joke.

THE END

[continued in: *The Girl Who Rocked Stars*]

Thank you for reading!

Dear reader,

I hope you enjoyed **The Girl Who Wrangled Asteroids**. I had a great time researching the details of a near-future NASA mission for intersecting and deflecting an extinction-level Asteroid. Also, I found delving deeply into the Hindu beliefs a fitting climax to the theological subplots throughout the series to this point.

The sequel to this book, **The Girl Who Rocked Stars**, finds the "girl with the turtle tattoo" at the peak of her teenaged musical career: rich, famous, and adored by millions. But her forgotten past is about to catch up to her. I hope you are intrigued by the sequel's disturbing question: "What happens when you get to the top of the heap and your world is turned upside down?"

Finally, then, I need to ask you for a favor. If you enjoyed this book and would like to encourage others to read it, **a review written by you** on the Amazon page for this book would be greatly helpful. It's hard to get reviews nowadays and your support will be very important to both me and other readers. If you'd like to do this, I sincerely thank you in advance for your time and effort. It can be as long or short as you wish.

Thanks again for reading my **Girl with the Turtle Tattoo** books and traveling through space with me to a killer Asteroid. You are a good friend and companion on my epic journey.

Sincerely,

Dan Lyle

<u>About the Author</u>:

Daniel Basil Lyle holds a Ph.D. in Biology, is a lifelong amateur herpetologist, taught medical immunology at a University, completed a career in cell biology research, lectures on how to apply theological and psychological principles in practical ways, and has a strong interest in all aspects of cosmology and physics. From a small kid he was fascinated with dinosaurs. As such, he has always lived with exotic creatures, including harmless snakes, all housed in his own homemade habitats. Some of his tame pet pythons and anacondas ranged up to twelve feet in length. He is the author of over thirty books, many of which are religious in nature. His writings go beyond the ordinary, exposing deeper aspects of life. His books are meant to be fun, conversational, and helpful. His various works are available at LylePublishing.com and Amazon.com. The "Girl with the Turtle Tattoo" science fiction series was inspired by paintings done by his mother, movies adapting Stieg Larsson's crime novels, and various men and women sporting spectacular body-art tattoos. The story wasn't "plotted" in advance but flowed freely, with characters appearing on their own and taking charge of their own destinies. The author hopes that you, the reader, find his characters spontaneous, quirky, surprising, and even thought-provoking—just as did he!